PHILIPPA
GREGORY
ORDER OF DARKNESS

VOLUMES I-III

By the same author

History
The Women of the
Cousins' War:
The Duchess, The Queen
and the King's Mother

The Plantagenet and Tudor Novels
The Lady of the Rivers
The Red Queen
The White Queen
The Kingmaker's Daughter
The White Princess
The Constant Princess
The King's Curse
The Other Boleyn Girl
The Boleyn Inheritance
The Taming of the Queen
The Queen's Fool
The Virgin's Lover
The Other Queen

Order of Darkness Series
Changeling
Stormbringers
Fools' Gold

The Wideacre Trilogy
Wideacre
The Favoured Child
Meridon

The Tradescants
Earthly Joys
Virgin Earth

Modern Novels
Alice Hartley's Happiness
Perfectly Correct
The Little House
Zelda's Cut

Short Stories
Bread and Chocolate

Other Historical Novels
The Wise Woman
Fallen Skies
A Respectable Trade

PHILIPPA GREGORY

ORDER OF DARKNESS

VOLUMES I-III

SIMON & SCHUSTER

This bind-up edition first published in Great Britain in 2017
by Simon & Schuster UK Ltd
A CBS COMPANY

Changeling first published in Great Britain in 2012 by Simon & Schuster UK Ltd
Stormbringers first published in Great Britain in 2013 by Simon & Schuster UK Ltd
Fools' Gold first published in Great Britain in 2014 by Simon & Schuster UK Ltd

1 3 5 7 9 10 8 6 4 2

Simon & Schuster UK Ltd
1st Floor
222 Gray's Inn Road
London WC1X 8HB

www.simonandschuster.co.uk

Simon & Schuster Australia, Sydney
Simon & Schuster India, New Delhi

A CIP catalogue copy for this book
is available from the British Library.

PB ISBN: 978-1-4711-6425-5
E-BOOK ISBN: 978-1-4711-6426-2

Printed and bound by CPI Group (UK) Ltd, Croydon, CR0 4YY

MIX
Paper from
responsible sources
FSC® C020471

Simon & Schuster UK Ltd are committed to sourcing paper
that is made from wood grown in sustainable forests and support the Forest
Stewardship Council, the leading international forest certification organisation.
Our books displaying the FSC logo are printed on FSC certified paper.

CONTENTS

Changeling 1

Stormbringers 261

Fool's Gold 547

The story begins in . . .

CHANGELING

CASTLE SANT'ANGELO,
ROME, 1460

The hammering on the door shot him into wakefulness. The young man scrambled for the dagger under his pillow, stumbling to his bare feet on the icy floor of the stone cell. He had been dreaming of his parents, of his old home, and he gritted his teeth against the usual wrench of longing for everything he had lost: the farmhouse, his mother, the old life.

The thunderous banging sounded again, and he held the dagger behind his back as he unbolted the door and cautiously opened it a crack. A dark-hooded figure stood outside, flanked by two heavy-set men, each carrying a burning torch. One of them raised his torch so the light fell on the slight dark-haired youth, naked to the waist, wearing only breeches, his hazel eyes blinking under a fringe of dark hair. He was about seventeen, with a face as sweet as a boy, but with the body of a young man forged by hard work.

'Luca Vero?'

'Yes.'

'You are to come with me.'

They saw him hesitate. 'Don't be a fool. There are three of us and only one of you, and the dagger you're hiding behind your back won't stop us.'

'It's an order,' the other man said roughly. 'Not a request. And you are sworn to obedience.'

Luca had sworn obedience to his monastery, not to these strangers, but he had been expelled from there and now it seemed he must obey anyone who shouted a command. He turned to the bed, sat to pull on his boots, slipping the dagger into a scabbard hidden inside the soft leather, pulled on a linen shirt, and then threw his ragged woollen cape around his shoulders.

'Who are you?' he asked, coming unwillingly to the door. The man made no answer, but simply turned and led the way, as the two guards waited in the corridor for Luca to come out of his cell and follow.

'Where are you taking me?'

The two guards fell in behind him without answering. Luca wanted to ask if he was under arrest, if he was being marched to a summary execution, but he did not dare. He was fearful of the very question, he acknowledged to himself that he was terrified of the answer. He could feel himself sweating with fear under his woollen cape, though the air was icy and the stone walls were cold and damp. He knew that he was in the most serious trouble of his young life. Only yesterday four dark-hooded men had taken him from his monastery and brought him here, to this prison, without a word of explanation. He did not know where he was, or who was holding him. He did not know what charge he might face. He did not know what the punishment might be. He did not know if he was going to be beaten, tortured or killed.

'I insist on seeing a priest, I wish to confess ...' he said.

They paid no attention to him at all, but pressed him on, down the narrow stone-flagged gallery. It was silent, with the closed doors of cells on either side. He could not tell if it was a prison or a monastery, it was so cold and quiet. It was just after midnight and the place was in darkness and utterly still. Luca's guides made no noise as they walked along the gallery, down the stone steps, through a great hall, and then down a little spiral staircase, into a darkness that grew more and more black as the air grew more and more cold.

'I demand to know where you are taking me,' Luca insisted, but his voice shook with fear.

No-one answered him; but the guard behind him closed up a little.

At the bottom of the steps, Luca could just see a small arched doorway and a heavy wooden door. The leading man opened it with a key from his pocket and gestured that Luca should go through. When he hesitated, the guard behind him simply moved closer until the menacing bulk of his body pressed Luca onwards.

'I insist ...' Luca breathed.

A hard shove thrust him through the doorway and he gasped as he found himself flung to the very edge of a high narrow quay, a boat rocking in the river a long way below, the far bank a dark blur in the distance. Luca flinched back from the brink. He had a sudden dizzying sense that they would be as willing to throw him over, onto the rocks below, as to take him down the steep stairs to the boat.

The first man went light-footed down the wet steps, stepped into the boat and said one word to the boatman who stood in the stern, holding the vessel against the current with the deft movements of a single oar. Then he looked back up to the handsome white-faced young man.

'Come,' he ordered.

Luca could do nothing else. He followed the man down the greasy steps, clambered into the boat and seated himself in the prow. The boatman did not wait for the guards but turned his craft into the middle of the river and let the current sweep them around the city wall. Luca glanced down into the dark water. If he were to fling himself over the side of the boat he would be swept downstream – he might be able to swim with the current and make it to the other side and get away. But the water was flowing so fast he thought he was more likely to drown, if they did not come after him in the boat and knock him senseless with the oar.

'My lord,' he said, trying for dignity, 'May I ask you now where we are going?'

'You'll know soon enough,' came the terse reply. The river ran like a wide moat around the tall walls of the city of Rome. The boatman kept the little craft close to the lee of the walls, hidden from the sentries above, then Luca saw ahead of them the looming shape of a stone bridge and, just before it, a grille set in an arched stone doorway of the wall. As the boat nosed inwards, the grille slipped noiselessly up and, with one practised push of the oar, they shot inside, into a torch-lit cellar.

With a deep lurch of fear Luca wished that he had taken his chance with the river. There were half a dozen grim-faced men waiting for him and, as the boatman held a well-worn ring on the wall to steady the craft, they reached down and hauled Luca out of the boat, to push him down a narrow corridor. Luca felt, rather than saw, thick stone walls on either side, smooth wooden floorboards underfoot, heard his own breathing, ragged with fear, then they paused before a heavy wooden door, struck it with a single knock and waited.

A voice from inside the room said 'Come!' and the guard swung the door open and thrust Luca inside. Luca stood, heart pounding, blinking at the sudden brightness of dozens of wax candles, and heard the door close silently behind him.

A solitary man was sitting at a table, papers before him. He wore a robe of rich velvet in so dark a blue that it appeared almost black, the hood completely concealing his face from Luca, who stood before the table and swallowed down his fear. Whatever happened, he decided, he was not going to beg for his life. Somehow, he would find the courage to face whatever was coming. He would not shame himself, nor his tough stoical father, by whimpering like a girl.

'You will be wondering why you are here, where you are, and who I am,' the man said. 'I will tell you these things. But, first, you must answer me everything that I ask. Do you understand?'

Luca nodded.

'You must not lie to me. Your life hangs in the balance here, and you cannot guess what answers I would prefer. Be sure to tell the truth: you would be a fool to die for a lie.'

Luca tried to nod but found he was shaking.

'You are Luca Vero, a novice priest at the monastery of St Xavier, having joined the monastery when you were a boy of eleven? You have been an orphan for the last three years, since your parents died when you were fourteen?'

'My parents disappeared,' Luca said. He cleared his tight throat. 'They may not be dead. They were captured by an Ottoman raid but nobody saw them killed. Nobody knows where they are now; but they may very well be alive.'

The Inquisitor made a minute note on a piece of paper before him. Luca watched the tip of the black feather as the quill moved across the page. 'You hope,' the man said briefly. 'You hope that they are alive and will come back to you.' He spoke as if hope was the greatest folly.

'I do.'

'Raised by the brothers, sworn to join their holy order, yet you went to your confessor, and then to the abbot, and told them that the relic that they keep at the monastery, a nail from the true cross, was a fake?'

The monotone voice was accusation enough. Luca knew this was a citation of his heresy. He knew also, that the only punishment for heresy was death.

'I didn't mean . . .'

'Why did you say the relic was a fake?'

Luca looked down at his boots, at the dark wooden floor, at the heavy table, at the lime washed walls – anywhere but at the shadowy face of the softly spoken questioner. 'I will beg the abbot's pardon and do penance,' he said. 'I didn't mean heresy. Before God, I am no heretic. I meant no wrong.'

'I shall be the judge if you are a heretic, and I have seen younger men than you, who have done and said less than you, crying on the rack for mercy, as their joints pop from their sockets. I have heard better men than you begging for the stake, longing for death as their only release from pain.'

Luca shook his head at the thought of the Inquisition, which could order this fate for him and see it done, and think it to the glory of God. He dared to say nothing more.

'Why did you say the relic was a fake?'

'I did not mean ...'

'Why?'

'It is a piece of a nail about three inches long, and a quarter of an inch wide,' Luca said unwillingly. 'You can see it, though it is now mounted in gold and covered with jewels. But you can still see the size of it.'

The Inquisitor nodded. 'So?'

'The abbey of St Peter has a nail from the true cross. So does the abbey of St Joseph. I looked in the monastery library to see if there were any others, and there are about four hundred nails in Italy alone, more in France, more in Spain, more in England.'

The man waited in unsympathetic silence.

'I calculated the likely size of the nails,' Luca said miserably. 'I calculated the number of pieces that they might have been broken into. It didn't add up. There are far too many relics for them all to come from one crucifixion. The Bible says a nail in each palm and one through the feet. That's only three nails.' Luca glanced at the dark face of his interrogator. 'It's not blasphemy to say this, I don't think. The Bible itself says it clearly. Then, in addition, if you count the nails used in building the cross, there would be four at the central joint to hold the cross bar. That makes seven original nails. Only seven. Say each nail is about five inches long. That's about thirty-five inches of nails used in the true cross. But there are thousands of relics. That's not to say whether any nail or any fragment is genuine or not. It's not for me to judge. But I can't help but see that there are just too many nails for them all to come from one cross.'

Still the man said nothing.

'It's numbers,' Luca said helplessly. 'It's how I think. I think about numbers – they interest me.'

'You took it upon yourself to study this? And you took it upon yourself to decide that there are too many nails in churches around the world for them all to be true, for them all to come from the sacred cross?'

Luca dropped to his knees, knowing himself to be guilty. 'I meant no wrong,' he whispered upwards at the shadowy figure. 'I just started wondering, and then I made the calculations, and then the abbot found my paper where I had written the calculations and—' He broke off.

'The abbot, quite rightly, accused you of heresy and forbidden studies, misquoting the Bible for your own purposes, reading without guidance, showing independence of thought, studying without permission, at the wrong time, studying forbidden books ...' the man continued, reading from the list. He looked at Luca: 'Thinking for yourself. That's the worst of it, isn't it? You were sworn into an order with certain established beliefs and then you started thinking for yourself.'

Luca nodded. 'I am sorry.'

'The priesthood does not need men who think for themselves.'

'I know,' Luca said, very low.

'You made a vow of obedience – that is a vow not to think for yourself.'

Luca bowed his head, waiting to hear his sentence.

The flame of the candles bobbed as somewhere outside a door opened and a cold draught blew through the rooms.

'Always thought like this? With numbers?'

Luca nodded.

'Any friends in the monastery? Have you discussed this with anyone?'

He shook his head. 'I didn't discuss this.'

The man looked at his notes. 'You have a companion called Freize?'

Luca smiled for the first time. 'He's just the kitchen boy at the monastery,' he said. 'He took a liking to me as soon as I arrived, when I was just eleven. He was only twelve or thirteen himself. He made up his mind that I was too thin, he said I wouldn't last the winter. He kept bringing me extra food. He's just the spit lad really.'

'You have no brother or sister?'

'I am alone in the world.'

'You miss your parents?'

'I do.'

'You are lonely?' The way he said it sounded like yet another accusation.

'I suppose so. I feel very alone, if that is the same thing.'

The man rested the black feather of the quill against his lips in thought. 'Your parents ...' He returned to the first question of the interrogation. 'They were quite old when you were born?'

'Yes,' Luca said, surprised. 'Yes.'

'People talked at the time, I understand. That such an old couple should suddenly give birth to a son, and such a handsome son, who grew to be such an exceptionally clever boy?'

'It's a small village,' Luca said defensively. 'People have nothing to do but gossip.'

'But clearly, you are handsome. Clearly, you are clever. And yet they did not brag about you, or show you off. They kept you quietly at home.'

'We were close,' Luca replied. 'We were a close small family. We troubled nobody else, we lived quietly, the three of us.'

'Then why did they give you to the Church? Was it that they thought you would be safer inside the Church? That you were specially gifted? That you needed the Church's protection?'

Luca, still on his knees, shuffled in discomfort. 'I don't know. I was a child: I was only eleven. I don't know what they were thinking.'

The Inquisitor waited.

'They wanted me to have the education of a priest,' he said eventually. 'My father—' He paused at the thought of his beloved father, of his grey hair and his hard grip, of his tenderness to his funny quirky little son. 'My father was very proud that I learned to read, that I taught myself about numbers. He couldn't write or read himself, he thought it was a great talent. Then, when some gypsies came through the village, I learned their language.'

The man made a note. 'You can speak languages?'

'People remarked that I learned to speak Romany in a day. My father thought that I had a gift, a God-given gift. It's not so uncommon,' he tried to explain. 'Freize, the spit boy, is good with animals, he can do anything with horses, he can ride anything. My father thought that I had a gift like that, only for studying. He wanted me to be more than a farmer. He wanted me to do better.'

The Inquisitor sat back in his chair as if he was weary of listening, as if he had heard more than enough. 'You can get up.'

He looked at the paper with its few black ink notes as Luca scrambled to his feet. 'Now I will answer the questions that will be in your mind. I am the spiritual commander of an Order appointed by the Holy Father, the Pope himself, and I answer to him for our work. You need not know my name nor the name of the Order. We have been commanded by Pope Nicholas V to explore the mysteries, the heresies and the sins, to explain them where possible, and defeat them where we can. We are making a map of the fears of the world, travelling outwards from Rome to the very ends of Christendom to discover what people are saying, what they are fearing, what they are fighting. We have to know where the Devil is walking through the world. The Holy Father knows that we are approaching the end of days.'

'The end of days?'

'When Christ comes again to judge the living, the dead, and the undead. You will have heard that the Ottomans have taken Constantinople, the heart of the Byzantine empire, the centre of the Church in the east?'

Luca crossed himself. The fall of the eastern capital of

the Church to an unbeatable army of heretics and infidels was the most terrible thing that could have happened, an unimaginable disaster.

'Next, the forces of darkness will come against Rome, and if Rome falls it will be the end of days – the end of the world. Our task is to defend Christendom, to defend Rome – in this world, and in the unseen world beyond.'

'The unseen world?'

'It is all around us,' the man said flatly. 'I see it, perhaps as clearly as you see numbers. And every year, every day, it presses more closely. People come to me with stories of showers of blood, of a dog that can smell out the plague, of witchcraft, of lights in the sky, of water that is wine. The end of days approaches and there are hundreds of manifestations of good and evil, miracles and heresies. A young man like you can perhaps tell me which of these are true, and which are false, which are the work of God and which of the Devil.' He rose from his great wooden chair and pushed a fresh sheet of paper across the table to Luca. 'See this?'

Luca looked at the marks on the paper. It was the writing of heretics, the Moors' way of numbering. Luca had been taught as a child that one stroke of the pen meant one: I, two strokes meant two: II, and so on. But these were strange rounded shapes. He had seen them before, but the merchants in his village and the almoner at the monastery stubbornly refused to use them, clinging to the old ways.

'This means one: 1, this two: 2, and this three: 3,' the man said, the black feather tip of his quill pointing to the marks. 'Put the 1 here, in this column, it means one, but put it here and this blank beside it and it means ten, or put it here and two blanks beside it, it means one hundred.'

Luca gaped. 'The position of the number shows its value?'

'Just so.' The man pointed the plume of the black feather to the shape of the blank, like an elongated O, which filled the columns. His arm stretched from the sleeve of his robe and Luca looked from the O to the white skin of the man's inner wrist. Tattooed on the inside of his arm, so that it almost appeared engraved on skin, Luca could just make out the head and twisted tail of a dragon, a design in red ink of a dragon coiled around on itself.

'This is not just a blank, it is not just an O, it is what they call a zero. Look at the position of it – that means some-thing. What if it meant something of itself?'

'Does it mean a space?' Luca said, looking at the paper again. 'Does it mean: nothing?'

'It is a number like any other,' the man told him. 'They have made a number from nothing. So they can calculate to nothing, and beyond.'

'Beyond? Beyond nothing?'

The man pointed to another number: -10. 'That is beyond nothing. That is ten places beyond nothing, that is the numbering of absence,' he said.

Luca, with his mind whirling, reached out for the paper. But the man quietly drew it back towards him and placed his broad hand over it, keeping it from Luca like a prize he would have to win. The sleeve fell down over his wrist again, hiding the tattoo. 'You know how they got to that sign, the number zero?' he asked.

Luca shook his head. 'Who got to it?'

'Arabs, Moors, Ottomans, call them what you will. Mussulmen, Muslim-men, infidels, our enemies, our new conquerors. Do you know how they got that sign?'

'No,'

'It is the shape left by a counter in the sand when you have taken the counter away. It is the symbol for nothing, it looks like a nothing. It is what it symbolises. That is how they think. That is what we have to learn from them.'

'I don't understand. What do we have to learn?'

'To look, and look, and look. That is what they do. They look at everything, they think about everything, that is why they have seen stars in the sky that we have never seen. That is why they make physic from plants that we have never noticed. They are a most scholarly, most brilliant people. A fearful enemy. My fearful enemy.'

'You know them?' Luca asked.

'Like a brother,' the man replied drily. He pulled his hood closer, so that his face was completely shadowed. 'They will defeat us unless we learn to see like they see, to think like they think, to count like they count. Perhaps a young man like you can learn their language too.'

Luca could not take his eyes from the paper where the man had marked out ten spaces of counting, down to zero and then beyond.

'So, what do you think?' the Inquisitor asked him. 'Do you think ten nothings are beings of the unseen world? Like ten invisible things? Ten ghosts? Ten angels?'

'If you could calculate beyond nothing,' Luca started, 'you could show what you had lost. Say someone was a merchant, and his debt in one country, or on one voyage, was greater than his fortune, you could show exactly how much his debt was. You could show his loss. You could show how much less than nothing he had, how much he would have to earn before he had something again.'

'Yes,' the man said. 'With zero you can measure what is not there. The Ottomans took Constantinople and our empire in the east not only because they had the strongest armies and the best commanders, but because they had a weapon that we did not have: a cannon so massive that it took sixty oxen to pull it into place. We would not think of such a thing; we could not make it. They have knowledge of things that we don't understand. The reason that I sent for you, the reason that you were expelled from your monastery but not punished there for disobedience or tortured for heresy, is that I want you to learn these mysteries; I want you to explore them, so that we can know them, and arm ourselves against them.'

'Is zero one of the things I must study? Will I go to the Ottomans and learn from them? Will I learn about their studies?'

The man laughed and pushed the piece of paper with the Arabic numerals towards the novice priest, holding it with one finger on the page. 'I will let you have this,' he promised. 'It can be your reward when you have worked to my satisfaction and set out on your mission. And yes, perhaps you will go to the infidel and live among them and learn their ways. But for now, you have to swear obedience to me and to our Order. I will send you out to be my ears and eyes. I will send you to hunt for mysteries, to find knowledge. I will send you to map fears, to seek darkness in all its shapes and forms. I will send you out to understand things, to be part of our Order that seeks to understand everything.'

He could see Luca's face light up at the thought of a life devoted to inquiry. But then the young man hesitated. 'I won't know what to do,' Luca confessed. 'I wouldn't know where to begin. I understand nothing! How will I know where to go or what to do?'

'I am going to send you to be trained. I will send you to study with masters. They will teach you the law, and what powers you have to convene a court or an inquiry. You will learn what to look for and how to question someone. You will understand when someone must be released to earthly powers – the mayors of towns or the lords of the manor; or when they can be punished by the Church. You will learn when to forgive and when to punish. When you are ready, when you have been trained, I will send you on your first mission?'

Luca nodded.

'You will be trained for some months and then I shall send you out into the world with my orders,' the man said. 'You will go where I command and study what you find there. You will report to me. You may judge and punish where you find wrong-doing. You may exorcise devils and unclean spirits. You may learn. You may question every-thing, all the time. But you will serve God and me, as I tell you. You will be obedient to me and to the Order. And you will walk in the unseen world and look at unseen things, and question them.'

There was a silence. 'You can go,' the man said, as if he had given the simplest of instructions. Luca started from his silent attention and went to the door. As his hand was on the bronze handle the man said: 'One thing more . . .'

Luca turned.

'They said you were a changeling, didn't they?' The accusation dropped into the room like a sudden shower of ice. 'The people of the village? When they gossiped about you being born, so handsome and so clever, to a woman who had been barren all her life, to a man who could neither read nor write. They said you were a changeling, left on her doorstep by the faeries, didn't they?'

There was a cold silence. Luca's stern young face revealed nothing. 'I have never answered such a question, and I hope that I never do. I don't know what they said about us,' he said harshly. 'They were ignorant fearful country people. My mother said to pay no attention to the things they said. She said that she was my mother and that she loved me above all else. That's all that mattered, not stories about faerie children.'

The man laughed shortly and waved Luca to go, and watched as the door closed behind him. 'Perhaps I am sending out a changeling to map fear itself,' he said to himself, as he tidied the papers together and pushed back his chair. 'What a joke for the worlds seen and unseen! A faerie child in the Order. A faerie child to map fear.'

THE CASTLE OF LUCRETILI

At about the time that Luca was being questioned, a young woman was seated in a rich chair in the chapel of her family home, the Castle of Lucretili, about twenty miles north-east of Rome, her dark blue eyes fixed on the rich crucifix, her fair hair twisted in a careless plait under a black veil, her face strained and pale. A candle in a rose crystal bowl flickered on the altar as the priest moved in the shadows. She knelt, her hands clasped tightly together, praying fervently for her father, who was fighting for his life in his bed-chamber, refusing to see her.

The door at the back of the chapel opened and her brother came in quietly, saw her bowed head and went to kneel beside her. She looked sideways at him, a handsome young man, dark-haired, dark-browed, his face stern with grief. 'He's gone, Isolde, he's gone. May he rest in peace.'

Her white face crumpled and she put her hands over her eyes. 'He didn't ask for me? Not even at the end?'

'He didn't want you to see him in pain. He wanted you to remember him as he had been, strong and healthy. But his last words were to send you his blessing, and his last thoughts were of your future.'

She shook her head. 'I can't believe he would not give me his blessing.'

Giorgio turned from her and spoke to the priest, who hurried at once to the back of the chapel. Isolde heard the big bell start to toll; everyone would know that the great crusader, the Lord of Lucretili, was dead.

'I must pray for him,' she said quietly. 'You'll bring his body here?'

He nodded.

'I will share the vigil tonight,' she decided. 'I will sit beside him now that he is dead though he didn't allow it while he lived.' She paused. 'He didn't leave me a letter? Nothing?'

'His will,' her brother said softly. 'He planned for you. At the very end of his life he was thinking of you.'

She nodded, her dark blue eyes filling with tears, then she clasped her hands together, and prayed for her father's soul.

~

Isolde spent the first long night of her father's death in a silent vigil beside his coffin, which lay in the family chapel. Four of his men-at-arms stood, one at each point of the compass, their heads bowed over their broadswords, the light from the tall wax candles glittering on the holy water that had been sprinkled on the coffin lid. On top of the coffin lay a broadsword locked into an ornate scabbard – a crusader sword.

Isolde, dressed in white, knelt before the coffin all night long until dawn when the priest came to say Prime, the first office of prayers of the day. Only then did she rise up and let her ladies-in-waiting help her to her room to sleep, until a message from her brother told her that she must get up and show herself, it was time for dinner and the household would want to see their lady.

She did not hesitate. She had been raised to do her duty to the great household and she had a sense of obligation to the people who lived on the lands of Lucretili. Her father, she knew, had left the castle and the lands to her; these people were in her charge. They would want to see her at the head of the table, they would want to see her enter the great hall. Even if her eyes were red from crying over the loss of a very beloved father, they would expect her to dine with them. Her father himself would have expected it. She would not fail them or him.

~

There was a sudden hush as she entered the great hall where the servants were sitting at trestle tables, talking quietly, waiting for dinner to be served. More than two hundred men-at-arms, servants and grooms filled the hall, where the smoke from the central fire coiled up to the dark-ened beams of the high ceiling.

As soon as the men saw Isolde followed by the three women of her household, they rose to their feet and pulled their hats from their heads, and bowed low to honour the daughter of the late Lord of Lucretili, and the heiress to the castle.

Isolde was wearing the deep blue of mourning: a high conical hat draped in indigo lace hiding her fair hair, a priceless belt of Arabic gold worn tightly at the high waist of her gown, the keys to the castle on a gold chain at her side. Behind her came her women companions, firstly Ishraq, her childhood friend, wearing Moorish dress, a long tunic over loose pantaloons with a long veil over her head held lightly across her face so that only her dark eyes were visible as she looked around the hall.

Two other women followed behind her and as the household whispered their blessings on Isolde, the women took their seats at the ladies' table to the side of the raised dais. Isolde went up the shallow stairs to the great table, and recoiled at the sight of her brother in the wooden chair, as grand as a throne, that had been their father's seat. She knew that she should have anticipated he would be there, just as he knew that she would inherit this castle and would take the great chair as soon as the will was read. But she was dull with grief, and she had not thought that from now on she would always see her brother where her father ought to be. She was so new to grief that she had not yet fully realised that she would never see her father again.

Giorgio smiled blandly at her, and gestured that she should take her seat at his right hand, where she used to sit beside her father.

'And you will remember Prince Roberto.' Giorgio indicated a fleshy man with a round sweating face on his left, who rose and came around the table to bow to her. Isolde gave her hand to the prince and looked questioningly at her brother. 'He has come to sympathise with us for our loss.'

The prince kissed her hand and Isolde tried not to flinch from the damp touch of his lips. He looked at her as if he wanted to whisper something, as if they might share a secret. Isolde took back her hand, and bent towards her brother's ear. 'I am surprised you have a guest at dinner when my father died only yesterday.'

'It was good of him to come at once,' Giorgio said, beckoning the servers who came down the hall, their trays held at shoulder height loaded with game, meat, and fish dishes, great loaves of bread and flagons of wine and jugs of ale.

The castle priest sang grace and then the servers banged down the trays of food, the men drew their daggers from their belts and their boots to carve their portions of meat, and heaped slices of thick brown bread with poached fish, and stewed venison.

It was hard for Isolde to eat dinner in the great hall as if nothing had changed, when her dead father lay in the chapel, guarded in the vigil by his men-at-arms, and would be buried the next day. She found that tears kept blurring the sight of the servants coming in, carrying more food for each table, banging down jugs of small ale, and bringing the best dishes and flagons of best red wine to the top table where Giorgio and his guest the prince picked the best and sent the rest down the hall to those men who had served them well during the day. The prince and her brother ate a good dinner and called for more wine. Isolde picked at her food and glanced down to the women's table where Ishraq met her gaze with silent sympathy.

When they had finished, and the sugared fruits and marchpane had been offered to the top table, and taken away, Giorgio touched her hand. 'Don't go to your rooms just yet,' he said. 'I want to talk to you.'

Isolde nodded to dismiss Ishraq and her ladies from their dining table and send them back to the ladies' rooms, then she went through the little door behind the dais to the private room where the Lucretili family sat after dinner. A fire was burning against the wall and there were three chairs drawn up around it. A flagon of wine was set ready for the men, a glass of small ale for Isolde. As she took her seat the two men came in together.

'I want to talk to you about our father's will,' Giorgio said, once they were seated.

Isolde glanced towards Prince Roberto.

'Roberto is concerned in this,' Giorgio explained. 'When Father was dying he said that his greatest hope was to know that you would be safe and happy. He loved you very dearly.'

Isolde pressed her fingers to her cold lips and blinked the tears from her eyes.

'I know,' her brother said gently. 'I know you are grieving. But you have to know that Father made plans for you and gave to me the sacred trust of carrying them out.'

'Why didn't he tell me so himself?' she asked. 'Why would he not talk to me? We always talked of everything together. I know what he planned for me; he said if I chose not to marry then I was to live here, I would inherit this castle and you would have his castle and lands in France. We agreed this. We all three agreed this.'

'We agreed it when he was well,' Giorgio said patiently. 'But when he became sick and fearful, he changed his mind. And then he could not bear for you to see him so very ill and in so much pain. When he thought about you then, with the very jaws of death opening before him, he thought better of his first plan. He wanted to be certain that you would be safe. Then, he planned well for you – he suggested that you marry Prince Roberto here, and agreed that we should take a thousand crowns from the treasury as your dowry.'

It was a tiny payment for a woman who had been raised to think of herself as heiress to this castle, the fertile pastures, the thick woods, the high mountains. Isolde gaped at him. 'Why so little?'

'Because the prince here has done us the honour of indicating that he will accept you just as you are – with no more than a thousand crowns in your pocket.'

'And you shall keep it all,' the man assured her, pressing her hand as it rested on the arm of her chair. 'You shall have it to spend on whatever you want. Pretty things for a pretty princess.'

Isolde looked at her brother, her dark blue eyes narrowing as she understood what this meant. 'A dowry as small as this will mean that no-one else will offer for me,' she said. 'You know that. And yet you did not ask for more? You did not warn Father that this would leave me without any prospects at all? And Father? Did he want to force me to marry the prince?'

The prince put his hand on his fleshy chest and cast his eyes modestly down. 'Most ladies would not require forcing,' he pointed out.

'I know of no better husband that you might have,' Giorgio said smoothly. His friend smiled and nodded at her. 'And Father thought so too. We agreed this dowry with Prince Roberto and he was so pleased to marry you that he did not specify that you should bring a greater fortune than this. There is no need to accuse anyone of failing to guard your interests. What could be better for you than marriage to a family friend, a prince, and a wealthy man?'

It took her only a moment to decide. 'I cannot think of marriage,' Isolde said flatly. 'Forgive me, Prince Roberto. But it is too soon after my father's death. I cannot bear even to think of it, let alone talk of it.'

'We have to talk of it,' Giorgio insisted. 'The terms of our father's will are that we have to get you settled. He would not allow any delay. Either immediate marriage to my friend here, or . . .' He paused.

'Or what?' Isolde asked, suddenly afraid.

'The abbey,' he said simply. 'Father said that if you would not marry, I was to appoint you as abbess and that you should go there to live.'

'Never!' Isolde exclaimed. 'My father would never have done this to me?'

Giorgio nodded. 'I too was surprised, but he said that it was the future he had planned for you all along. That was why he did not fill the post when the last abbess died. He was thinking even then, a year ago, that you must be kept safe. You can't be exposed to the dangers of the world, left here alone at Lucretili. If you don't want to marry, you must be kept safe in the abbey.'

Prince Roberto smiled slyly at her. 'A nun or a princess, my princess,' he suggested. 'I would think you would find it easy to choose.'

Isolde jumped to her feet. 'I cannot believe Father planned this for me,' she said. 'He never suggested anything like this. He was clear he would divide the lands between us. He knew how much I love it here; how I love these lands and know these people. He said he would will this castle and the lands to me, and give you our lands in France.'

Giorgio shook his head as if in gentle regret. 'No, he changed his mind. As the oldest child, the only son, the only true heir, I will have everything, both in France and here, and you, as a woman, will have to leave.'

'Giorgio, my brother, you cannot send me from my home?'

He spread his hands. 'There is nothing I can do. It is our father's last wish and I have it in writing, signed by him. You will either marry – and no-one will have you but Prince Roberto – or you will go to the abbey. It was good of him to give you this choice. Many fathers would simply have left orders.'

'Excuse me,' Isolde said, her voice shaking as she fought to control her anger, 'I shall leave you and go to my rooms and think about this.'

'Don't take too long!' Prince Roberto said with an intimate smile. 'I won't wait too long.'

'I shall give you my answer tomorrow.' She paused in the doorway, and looked back at her brother. 'May I see my father's letter?'

Giorgio nodded and drew it from inside his jacket. 'You can keep this. It is a copy. I have the other in safe-keeping; there is no doubt as to his wishes. You will have to consider not whether you will obey him, but only how you obey him. He knew that you would obey him.'

'I know,' she said. 'I am his daughter. Of course I will obey him.' She went from the room without looking at the prince, though he rose to his feet and made her a flourishing bow, and then winked at Giorgio as if he thought the matter settled.

~

Isolde woke in the night to hear a quiet tap on her door. Her pillow was damp beneath her cheek; she had been crying in her sleep. For a moment she wondered why she felt such a pain, as if she were heartbroken – and then she remembered the coffin in the chapel and the silent knights keeping watch. She crossed herself: 'God bless him, and save his soul,' she whispered. 'God comfort me in this sorrow. I don't know that I can bear it.'

The little tap came again, and she put back the richly embroidered covers of her bed and went to the door, the key in her hand. 'Who is it?'

'It is Prince Roberto. I have to speak with you.'

'I can't open the door, I will speak with you tomorrow.'

'I need to speak to you tonight. It is about the will, your father's wishes.'

She hesitated. 'Tomorrow ...'

'I think I can see a way out for you. I understand how you feel, I think I can help.'

'What way out?'

'I can't shout it through the door. Just open the door a crack so that I can whisper.'

'Just a crack,' she said, and turned the key, keeping her foot pressed against the bottom of the door to ensure that it opened only a little.

As soon as he heard the key turn, the prince banged the door open with such force that it hit Isolde's head and sent her reeling back into the room. He slammed the door behind him and turned the key, locking them in together.

'You thought you would reject me?' he demanded furiously, as she scrambled to her feet. 'You thought you – practically penniless – would reject me? You thought I would beg to speak to you through a closed door?'

'How dare you force your way in here?' Isolde demanded, white-faced and furious. 'My brother would kill you—'

'Your brother allowed it,' he laughed. 'Your brother approves me as your husband. He himself suggested that I come to you. Now get on the bed.'

'My brother?' She could feel her shock turning into horror as she realised that she had been betrayed by her own brother, and that now this stranger was coming towards her, his fat face creased in a confident smile.

'He said I might as well take you now as later,' he said. 'You can fight me if you like. It makes no difference to me. I like a fight. I like a woman of spirit, they are more obedient in the end.'

'You are mad,' she said with certainty.

'Whatever you like. But I consider you my betrothed wife, and we are going to consummate our betrothal right now, so you don't make any mistake tomorrow.'

'You're drunk,' she said, smelling the sour stink of wine on his breath.

'Yes, thank God, and you can get used to that too.'

He came towards her, shrugging his jacket off his fleshy shoulders. She shrank back until she felt the tall wooden pole of the four-poster bed behind her, blocking her retreat. She put her hands behind her back so that he could not grab them, and felt the velvet of the counterpane, and beneath it the handle of the brass warming pan filled with hot embers that had been pushed between the cold sheets.

'Please,' she said. 'This is ridiculous. It is an offence against hospitality. You are our guest, my father's body lies in the chapel. I am without defence, and you are drunk on our wine. Please go to your room and I will speak kindly to you in the morning.'

'No,' he leered. 'I don't think so. I think I shall spend the night here in your bed and I am very sure you will speak kindly to me in the morning.'

Behind her back, Isolde's fingers closed on the handle of the warming pan. As Roberto paused to untie the laces on the front of his breeches, she got a sickening glimpse of grey linen poking out. He reached for her arm. 'This need not hurt you,' he said. 'You might even enjoy it . . .'

With a great swing she brought the warming pan round to clap him on the side of his head. Glowing embers and ash dashed against his face and tumbled to the floor. He let out of a howl of pain as she drew back and hit him once again, hard, and he dropped down like a fat stunned ox before the slaughter.

She picked up a jug and flung water over the coals smouldering on the rug beneath him and then, cautiously, she kicked him gently. He did not stir, he was knocked out cold. Isolde went to an inner room and unlocked the door, whispering 'Ishraq!' When the girl came, rubbing sleep from her eyes, Isolde showed her the man crumpled on the ground.

'Is he dead?' the girl asked calmly.

'No. I don't think so. Help me get him out of here.'

The two young women pulled the rug and the limp body

of Prince Roberto slid along the floor, leaving a slimy trail of water and ashes. They got him into the gallery outside her room and paused.

'I take it your brother allowed him to come to you?'

Isolde nodded, and Ishraq turned her head and spat contemptuously on the prince's white face. 'Why ever did you open the door?'

'I thought he would help me. He said he had an idea to help me then he pushed his way in.'

'Did he hurt you?' The girl's dark eyes scanned her friend's face. 'Your forehead?'

'He knocked me when he pushed the door.'

'Was he going to rape you?'

Isolde nodded.

'Then let's leave him here,' Ishraq decided. 'He can come to on the floor like the dog that he is, and crawl to his room. If he's still here in the morning then the servants can find him and make him a laughing-stock.' She bent down and felt for his pulses at his throat, his wrists and under the bulging waistband of his breeches. 'He'll live,' she said certainly. 'Though he wouldn't be missed if we quietly cut his throat.'

'Of course we can't do that,' Isolde said shakily.

They left him there, laid out like a beached whale on his back, with his breeches still unlaced.

'Wait here,' Ishraq said and went back to her room.

She returned swiftly, with a small box in her hand. Delicately, using the tips of her fingers and scowling with distaste, she pulled at the prince's breeches so that they were gaping wide open. She lifted his linen shirt so that his limp nakedness was clearly visible. She took the lid from the box and shook the spice onto his bare skin.

'What are you doing?' Isolde whispered.

'It's a dried pepper, very strong. He is going to itch like he has the pox, and his skin is going to blister like he has a rash. He is going to regret this night's work very much. He is going to be itching and scratching and bleeding for a month, and he won't trouble another woman for a while.'

Isolde laughed and put out her hand, as her father would have done, and the two young women clasped forearms, hand to elbow, like knights. Ishraq grinned, and they turned and went back into the bedroom, closing the door on the humbled prince and locking it firmly against him.

~

In the morning, when Isolde went to chapel, her father's coffin was closed and ready for burial in the deep family vault – and the prince was gone.

'He has withdrawn his offer for your hand,' her brother said coldly as he took his place, kneeling beside her on the chancel steps. 'I take it that something passed between the two of you?'

'He's a villain,' Isolde said simply. 'And if you sent him to my door, as he claimed, then you are a traitor to me.'

He bowed his head. 'Of course I did no such thing. I am sorry, I got drunk like a fool and said that he could plead his case with you. Why ever did you open your door?'

'Because I believed your friend was an honourable man, as you did.'

'You were very wrong to unlock your door,' her brother reproached her. 'Opening your bedroom door to a man, to a drunk man! You don't know how to take care of yourself. Father was right, we have to place you somewhere safe.'

'I was safe! I was in my own room, in my own castle, speaking to my brother's friend. I should not have been at risk,' she said angrily. 'You should not have brought such a man to our dinner table. Father should never have been advised that he would make a good husband for me.'

She rose to her feet and went down the aisle, her brother following after her. 'Well anyway, what did you say to upset him?'

Isolde hid a smile at the thought of the warming pan crashing against the prince's fat head. 'I made my feelings clear. And I will never meet with him again.'

'Well, that's easily achieved,' Giorgio said bluntly. 'Because you will never be able to meet with any man again. If you will not marry Prince Roberto, then you will have to go to the abbey. Our father's will leaves you with no other choice.'

Isolde paused as his words sank in, and put a hesitant hand on his arm, wondering how she could persuade him to let her go free.

'There's no need to look like that,' he said roughly. 'The terms of the will are clear, I told you last night. It was the prince or the nunnery. Now it is just the nunnery.'

'I will go on a pilgrimage,' she offered. 'Away from here.'

'You will not. How would you survive for one moment? You can't keep yourself safe even at home.'

'I will go and stay with some friends of Father's – anyone. I could go to my godfather's son, the Count of Wallachia, I could go to the Duke of Bradour ...'

His face was grim. 'You can't. You know you can't. You have to do as Father commanded you. I have no choice, Isolde. God knows I would do anything for you, but his will is clear, and I have to obey my father – just as you do.'

35

'Brother – don't force me to do this.'

He turned to the arched wall of the chapel doorway, and put his forehead to the cold stone, as if she was making his head ache. 'Sister, I can do nothing. Prince Roberto was your only chance to escape the abbey. It is our father's will. I am sworn on his sword, on his broadsword, to see that his will is done. My sister – I am powerless, as you are.'

'He promised he would leave the broadsword to me.'

'It is mine now. As is everything else.'

Gently she put her hand on his shoulder. 'If I take an oath of celibacy, may I not stay here with you? I will marry no-one. The castle is yours, I see that. In the end he did what every man does and favoured his son over his daughter. In the end he did what all great men do and kept a woman from wealth and power. But if I will live here, poor and powerless, never seeing a man, obedient to you, can I not stay here?'

He shook his head. 'It is not my will, but his. And it is – as you admit – the way of the world. He brought you up almost as if you had been born a boy, with too much wealth and freedom. But now you must live the life of a noblewoman. You should be glad at least that the abbey is nearby, and so you don't have to go far from these lands that I know you love. You've not been sent into exile – he could have ordered that you go anywhere. But instead you will be in our own property: the abbey. I will come and see you now and then. I will bring you news. Perhaps later you will be able to ride out with me.'

'Can Ishraq come with me?'

'You can take Ishraq, you can take all your ladies if you wish, and if they are willing to go. But they are expecting you at the abbey tomorrow. You will have to go, Isolde.

You will have to take your vows as a nun and become their abbess. You have no choice.'

He turned back to her and saw she was trembling like a young mare will tremble when she is being forced into harness for the first time. 'It is like being imprisoned,' she whispered. 'And I have done nothing wrong.'

He had tears in his own eyes. 'It is like losing a sister,' he said. 'I am burying a father and losing a sister. I don't know how I will live without you here.'

THE ABBEY OF LUCRETILI

A few months later, Luca was on the road from Rome, riding east, wearing a plain working robe and cape of ruddy brown, and newly equipped with a horse of his own.

He was accompanied by his servant Freize, a broad-shouldered, square-faced youth, just out of his teens, who had plucked up his courage when Luca left their monastery, and volunteered to work for the young man, and follow him wherever the quest might take him. The abbot had been doubtful, but Freize had convinced him that his skills as a kitchen lad were so poor, and his love of adventure so strong, that he would serve God better by following a remarkable master on a secret quest ordained by the Pope himself, than by burning the bacon for the long-suffering monks. The abbot, secretly glad to lose the challenging young novice priest, thought the loss of an accident-prone spit lad was a small price to pay.

Freize rode a strong cob and led a donkey laden with their belongings. At the rear of the little procession was a surprise addition to their partnership: a clerk, Brother Peter, who had been ordered to travel with them at the last moment, to keep a record of their work.

'A spy,' Freize muttered out of the side of his mouth to his new master. 'A spy if ever I saw one. Pale-faced, soft hands, trusting brown eyes: the shaved head of a monk and yet the clothes of a gentleman. A spy without a doubt.

'Is he spying on me? No, for I don't do anything and know nothing. Who is he spying on, then? Must be the young master, my little sparrow. For there is no-one else but the horses and they're not heretics, nor pagans. They are the only honest beasts here.'

'He is here to serve as my clerk,' Luca replied irritably. 'And I have to have him whether I need a clerk or no. So hold your tongue.'

'Do I need a clerk?' Freize asked himself as he reined in his horse. 'No. For I do nothing and know nothing and, if I did, I wouldn't write it down – not trusting words on a page. Also, not being able to read or write would likely prevent me.'

'Fool,' the clerk Peter said as he rode by.

'"Fool," he says,' Freize remarked to his horse's ears and to the gently climbing road before them. 'Easy to say: hard to prove. And anyway, I have been called worse.'

They had been riding all day on a track little more than a narrow path for goats, which wound upwards out of the fertile valley, alongside little terraced slopes growing olives

40

and vines, and then higher into the woodland where the huge beech trees were turning gold and bronze. At sunset, when the arching skies above them went rosy pink, the clerk drew a paper from the inner pocket of his jacket. 'I was ordered to give you this at sunset,' he said. 'Forgive me if it is bad news. I don't know what it says.'

'Who gave it you?' Luca asked. The seal on the back of the folded letter was shiny and smooth, unmarked with any crest.

'The lord who hired me, the same lord who commands you,' Peter said. 'This is how your orders will come. He tells me a day and a time, or sometimes a destination, and I give you your orders then and there.'

'Got them tucked away in your pocket all the time?' Freize inquired.

Grandly, the clerk nodded.

'Could always turn him upside down and shake him,' Freize remarked quietly to his master.

'We'll do this as we are ordered to do it,' Luca replied, looping the reins of his horse casually around his shoulder to leave his hands free to break the seal to open the folded paper. 'It's an instruction to go to the abbey of Lucretili,' he said. 'The abbey is set between two houses, a nunnery and a monastery. I am to investigate the nunnery. They are expecting us.' He folded the letter and gave it back to Peter.

'Does it say how to find them?' Freize asked gloomily. 'For otherwise it's bed under the trees and nothing but cold bread for supper. Beechnuts, I suppose. All you could eat of beechnuts. You could go mad with gluttony on them. I suppose I might get lucky and find us a mushroom.'

'The road is just up ahead,' Peter interrupted. 'The abbey

is near to the castle. I should think we can claim hospitality at either monastery or nunnery.'

'We'll go to the convent,' Luca ruled. 'It says that they are expecting us.'

~

It did not look as if the convent was expecting anyone. It was growing dark, but there were no warm welcoming lights showing and no open doors. The shutters were closed at all the windows in the outer wall, and only narrow beams of flickering candlelight shone through the slats. In the darkness they could not tell how big it was; they just had a sense of great walls marching off either side of the wide-arched entrance gateway. A dim horn lantern was hung by the small door set in the great wooden gate, throwing a thin yellow light downward, and when Freize dismounted and hammered on the wooden gate with the handle of his dagger they could hear someone inside protesting at the noise and then opening a little spy hole in the door, to peer out at them.

'I am Luca Vero, with my two servants,' Luca shouted. 'I am expected. Let us in.'

The spy hole slammed shut, then they could hear the slow unbolting of the gate and the lifting of wooden bars and, finally, one side of the gate creaked reluctantly open. Freize led his horse and the donkey, Luca and Peter rode into the cobbled yard as a sturdy woman-servant pushed the gate shut behind them. The men dismounted and looked around as a wizened old lady in a habit of grey wool, with a tabard of grey tied at her waist by a plain rope, held up the torch she was carrying, to inspect the three of them.

'Are you the man they sent to make inquiry? For if you are not, and it is hospitality that you want, you had better go on to the monastery, our brother house,' she said to Peter, looking at him and his fine horse. 'This house is in troubled times, we don't want guests.'

'No, I am to write the report. I am the clerk to the inquiry. This is Luca Vero, he is here to inquire.'

'A boy!' she exclaimed scornfully. 'A beardless boy?'

Luca flushed in irritation, then swung his leg over the neck of his horse, and jumped down to the ground, throwing the reins to Freize. 'It doesn't matter how many years I have, or if I have a beard or not. I am appointed to make inquiry here, and I will do so tomorrow. In the meantime we are tired and hungry and you should show me to the refectory and to the guest rooms. Please inform the Lady Abbess that I am here and will see her after Prime tomorrow.'

'Rich in nothing,' the old woman remarked, holding up her torch to take another look at Luca's handsome young face, flushed under his dark fringe, his hazel eyes bright with anger.

'Rich in nothing, is it?' Freize questioned the horse as he led him to the stables ahead. 'A virgin so old that she is like a pickled walnut and she calls the little lord a beardless boy? And him a genius and perhaps a changeling?'

'You, take the horses to the stables and the lay sister there will take you to the kitchen,' she snapped with sudden energy at Freize. 'You can eat and sleep in the barn. You—' She took in the measure of Peter the clerk and judged him superior to Freize but still wanting. 'You can dine in the kitchen gallery. You'll find it through that doorway.

43

They'll show you where to sleep in the guesthouse. You—'
She turned to Luca. 'You, the Inquirer, I will show to the
refectory and to your own bedroom. They said you were a
priest?'

'I have not yet said my vows,' he said. 'I am in the service
of the Church, but I am not ordained.'

'Too handsome by far for the priesthood, and with his
tonsure grown out already,' she said to herself. To Luca
she said: 'You can sleep in the rooms for the visiting priest,
anyway. And in the morning I will tell my Lady Abbess that
you are here.'

She was leading the way to the refectory when a lady
came through the archway from the inner cloister. Her
habit was made of soft bleached wool, the wimple on her
head pushed back to show a pale lovely face with smiling
grey eyes. The girdle at her waist was of the finest leather
and she had leather slippers, not the rough wooden pattens
that working women wore to keep their shoes out of the
mud.

'I came to greet the Inquirer,' she said, holding up the set
of wax candles in her hand.

Luca stepped forwards. 'I am the Inquirer,' he said.

She smiled, taking in his height, his good looks and his
youth in one swift gaze. 'Let me take you to your dinner,
you must be weary. Sister Anna here will see that your
horses are stabled and your men comfortable.'

He bowed and she turned ahead of him, leaving him
to follow her through the stone archway, along a flagged
gallery that opened into the arching refectory room. At
the far end, near the fire that was banked in for the night,
a place had been laid for one person; there was wine in

the glass, bread on the plate, a knife and spoon either side of a bowl. Luca sighed with pleasure and sat down in the chair as a maidservant came in with a ewer and bowl to wash his hands, good linen to dry them, and behind her came a kitchen maid with a bowl of stewed chicken and vegetables.

'You have everything that you need?' the lady asked.

'Thank you,' he said awkwardly. He was uncomfortable in her presence; he had not spoken to a woman other than his mother since he had been sworn into the monastery at the age of eleven. 'And you are?'

She smiled at him and he realised in the glow of her smile that she was beautiful. 'I am Sister Ursula, the Lady Almoner, responsible for the management of the abbey. I am glad you have come. I have been very anxious. I hope you can tell us what is happening and save us . . .'

'Save you?'

'This is a long-established and beautiful nunnery,' Sister Ursula said earnestly. 'I joined it when I was just a little girl. I have served God and my sisters here for all my life, I have been here for more than twenty years. I cannot bear the thought that Satan has entered in.'

Luca dipped his bread in the rich thick gravy, and concentrated on the food to hide his consternation. 'Satan?'

She crossed herself, a quick unthinking gesture of devotion. 'Some days I think it really is that bad, other days I think I am like a foolish girl, frightening myself with shadows.' She gave him a shy, apologetic smile. 'You will be able to judge. You will discover the truth of it all. But if we cannot rid ourselves of the gossip we will be ruined: no family will send their daughters to us, and now the farmers are starting to refuse to trade with us. It is my duty to make sure that the abbey earns its own living, that we sell our goods and farm produce in order to buy what we need. I can't do that if the farmers' wives refuse to speak with us when I send my lay sisters with our goods to market. We can't trade if the people will neither sell to us nor buy from us.' She shook her head. 'Anyway, I will leave you to eat. The kitchen maid will show you to your bedroom in the guesthouse when you have finished eating. Bless you, my brother.'

Luca suddenly realised he had quite forgotten to say grace: she would think he was an ignorant mannerless hedge friar. He had stared at her like a fool and stammered when he spoke to her. He had behaved like a young man who had never seen a beautiful woman before and not at all like a man of some importance, come to head a papal inquiry. What must she think of him? 'Bless you, Lady Almoner,' he said awkwardly.

She bowed, hiding a little smile at his confusion, and walked slowly from the room, and he watched the sway of the hem of her gown as she left.

~

On the east side of the enclosed abbey, the shutter of the ground-floor window was slightly open so that two pairs of eyes could watch the Lady Almoner's candle illuminate her pale silhouette as she walked gracefully across the yard and then vanished into her house.

'She's greeted him, but she won't have told him anything,' Isolde whispered.

'He will find nothing unless someone helps him,' Ishraq agreed.

The two drew back from the window and noiselessly closed the shutter. 'I wish I could see my way clear,' Isolde said. 'I wish I knew what to do. I wish I had someone who could advise me.'

'What would your father have done?'

Isolde laughed shortly. 'My father would never have let himself be forced in here. He would have laid down his life before he allowed someone to imprison him. Or, if captured, he would have died attempting to escape. He wouldn't just have sat here, like a doll, like a cowardly girl, crying, missing him, and not knowing what to do.'

She turned away and roughly rubbed her eyes. Ishraq put a gentle hand on her shoulder. 'Don't blame yourself,' she said. 'There was nothing we could do when we first came here. And now that the whole abbey is falling apart around us, we can still do nothing until we understand what is going on. But everything is changing even while we wait, powerless. Even if we do nothing; something is going to happen. This is our chance. Perhaps this is the moment when the door swings open. We're going to be ready for our chance.'

Isolde took the hand from her shoulder and held it against her cheek. 'At least I have you.'

'Always.'

~

Luca slept heavily; not even the church bell tolling the hour in the tower above his head could wake him. But, just when the night was darkest, before three in the morning, a sharp scream cut through his sleep and then he heard the sound of running feet.

Luca was up and out of his bed in a moment, his hand snatching for the dagger under his pillow, peering out of his window at the dark yard. A glint of moonlight shining on the cobblestones showed him a woman in white, racing across the yard to scrabble at the beams barring the heavy wooden gate. Three women pursued her, and the old porteress came running out of the gatehouse and grabbed the woman's hands as she clawed like a cat at the timbers.

The other women were quick to catch the girl from behind and Luca heard her sharp wail of despair as they grabbed hold of her, and saw her knees buckle as she went down under their weight. He pulled on his breeches and boots, threw a cape over his naked shoulders, then sprinted from his room, out into the yard, tucking the dagger out of sight in the scabbard in his boot. He stepped back into the shadow of the building, certain they had not noticed him, determined to see their faces in the shadowy light of the moon, so that he would know them, when he saw them again.

The porteress held up her torch as they lifted the girl, two women holding her shoulders, the third supporting her legs. As they carried her past him, Luca shrank back into the concealing darkness of the doorway. They were so close that he could hear their panting breaths.

It was the strangest sight. The girl's hand had swung down as they lifted her; now she was quite unconscious. It seemed that she had fainted when they had pulled her from the barred gate. Her head was rolled back, the little laces from her nightcap brushing the ground as they carried her, her long nightgown trailing in the dust. But it was no normal fainting fit. She was as limp as a corpse, her eyes closed, her young face serene. Then Luca gave a little hiss of horror. The girl's swinging hand was pierced in the palm, the wound oozing blood. They had folded her other hand across her slight body and Luca could see a smudge of blood on her nightgown. She had the hands of a girl crucified. Luca froze where he stood, forcing himself to stay hidden in the shadows, unable to look away from the strange terrible wounds. And then he saw something that seemed even worse.

All three women carrying the sleeping girl wore her expression of rapt serenity. As they shuffled along, carrying their limp bleeding burden, all three were slightly smiling, all three were radiant as if with an inner secret joy.

And their eyes were closed like hers.

Luca waited till they had sleepwalked past him, steady as pall-bearers, then he went back into the guesthouse room and knelt at the side of his bed, praying fervently for guidance to somehow find the wisdom, despite his self-doubt, to discover what was so very wrong in this holy place, and put it right.

~

He was still on his knees in prayer when Freize banged open the door with a jug of hot water for washing, just before dawn. 'Thought you'd want to go to Prime.'

'Yes.' Luca rose stiffly, crossed himself, and kissed the cross that always hung around his neck, a gift from his mother on his fourteenth birthday, the last time he had seen her.

'Bad things are happening here,' Freize said portentously, splashing the water into a bowl and putting a clean strip of linen beside it.

49

Luca sluiced his face and hands with water. 'I know it. God knows, I have seen some of it. What do you hear?'

'Sleepwalking, visions, the nuns fasting on feast days, starving themselves and fainting in the chapel. Some of them are seeing lights in the sky, like the star before the Magi, and then some wanted to set off for Bethlehem and had to be restrained. The people of the village and the servants from the castle say they're all going mad. They say the whole abbey is touched with madness and the women are losing their wits.'

Luca shook his head. 'The saints alone know what is happening. Did you hear the screams in the night?'

'Lord save us, no. I slept in the kitchen and all I could hear was snoring. But all the cooks say that the Pope should send a bishop to inquire. They say that Satan is walking here. The Pope should set up an inquiry.'

'He has done! That's me,' Luca snapped. 'I shall hold an inquiry. I shall be the judge.'

'Course you will,' Freize encouraged him. 'Doesn't matter how old you are.'

'Actually, it *doesn't* matter how old I am. What matters is that I am appointed to inquire.'

'You'd better start with the new Lady Abbess, then.'

'Why?'

'Because it all started as soon as she got here.'

'I won't listen to kitchen gossip,' Luca declared haughtily, rubbing his face. He tossed the cloth to Freize. 'I shall have a proper inquiry with witnesses and people giving evidence under oath. For I am the Inquirer, appointed by the Pope, and it would be better if everyone remembered it. Especially those people who are supposed to be in service to me, who should be supporting my reputation.'

'Course I do! Course you are! Course you will! You're the lord and I never forget it, though still only a little one.' Freize shook out Luca's linen shirt and then handed him his novice's robe, which he wore belted high, out of the way of his long stride. Luca strapped his short sword on his belt and notched it round his waist, dropping the robe over the sword to hide it.

'You speak to me like I was a child,' Luca said irritably. 'And you're no great age yourself.'

'It's affection,' Freize said firmly. 'It's how I show affection. And respect. To me, you'll always be "Sparrow", the skinny novice.'

'"Goose", the kitchen boy,' Luca replied with a grin.

'Got your dagger?' Freize checked.

Luca tapped the cuff of his boot where the dagger was safe in the scabbard.

'They all say that the new Lady Abbess had no vocation, and was not raised to the life,' Freize volunteered, ignoring Luca's ban on gossip. 'Her father's will sent her in here and she took her vows and she'll never get out again. It's the only inheritance her father left her, everything else went to the brother. Bad as being walled up. And, ever since she came, the nuns have started to see things and cry out. Half the village says that Satan came in with the new abbess. Cause she was unwilling.'

'And what do they say the brother is like?' Luca asked, tempted to gossip despite his resolution.

'Nothing but good of him. Good landlord, generous with the abbey. His grandfather built the abbey with a nunnery on one side and a brother house for the monks nearby. His father endowed both houses and handed the woods and the high pasture over to the nuns, and gave some farms and fields to the monastery. They run themselves as independent houses, working together for the glory of God, and helping the poor. Now the new lord in his turn supports it. His father was a crusader, famously brave, very hot on religion. The new lord sounds quieter, stays at home, wants a bit of peace. Very keen that this is kept quiet, that you make your inquiry, take your decision, report the guilty, exorcise whatever is going on, and everything gets back to normal.'

Above their heads the bell tolled for Prime, the dawn prayer.

'Come on,' Luca said, and led the way from the visiting priest's rooms towards the cloisters and the beautiful church.

They could hear the music as they crossed the yard, their way lit by a procession of white-gowned nuns, carrying torches and singing as they went like a choir of angels gliding through the pearly light of the morning. Luca stepped back, and even Freize fell silent at the beauty of the voices rising faultlessly into the dawn sky. Then the two men, joined by Brother Peter, followed the choir into the church and took their seats in an alcove at the back. Two hundred nuns, veiled with white wimples, filled the stalls of the choir either side of the screened altar, and stood in rows facing it.

The service was a sung Mass; the voice of the serving priest at the altar rang out the sacred Latin words in a steady baritone, and the sweet high voices of the women answered. Luca gazed at the vaulting ceiling, the beautiful columns carved with stone fruit and flowers, and above them, stars and moons of silver-painted stone, all the while listening to the purity of the responses and wondering what could be tormenting such holy women every night, and how they could wake every dawn and sing like this to God.

At the end of the service, the three visiting men remained seated on the stone bench at the back of the chapel as the nuns filed out past them, their eyes modestly down. Luca scanned their faces, looking for the young woman he had seen in such a frenzy last night, but one pale young face veiled in white was identical to another. He tried to see their palms, for the telltale sign of scabs, but all the women kept their hands clasped together, hidden in their long sleeves. As they filed out, their sandals pattering quietly on the stone floor, the priest followed them, and stopped before the young men to say pleasantly, 'I'll break my fast with you and then I have to go back to my side of the abbey.'

'Are you not a resident priest?' Luca asked, first shaking the man's hand and then kneeling for his blessing.

'We have a monastery just the other side of the great house,' the priest explained. 'The first Lord of Lucretili chose to found two religious houses: one for men and one for women. We priests come over daily to take the services. Alas, this house is of the order of Augustine nuns. We men are of the Dominican order.' He leaned towards Luca. 'As you'd understand, I think it would be better for everyone if the nunnery were put under the discipline of the Dominican order. They could be supervised from our monastery and enjoy the discipline of our order. Under the Augustinian order these women have been allowed to simply do as they please. And now you see what happens.'

'They observe the services,' Luca protested. 'They're not running wild.'

'Only because they choose to do so. If they wanted to stop or to change, then they could. They have no rule, unlike us Dominicans, for whom everything is set down. Under the Augustinian order every house can live as they please. They serve God as they think best and as a result—'

He broke off as the Lady Almoner came up, treading quietly on the beautiful marble floor of the church. 'Well, here is my Lady Almoner come to bid us to breakfast, I am sure.'

'You can take breakfast in my private chamber,' she said. 'There is a fire lit there. Please, Father, show our guests the way.'

'I will, I will,' he said pleasantly and, as she left them, he turned to Luca. 'She holds this place together,' he said. 'A remarkable woman. Manages the farmlands, maintains the buildings, buys the goods, sells the produce. She could have been the lady of any castle in Italy, a natural Magistra: a teacher, a leader, a natural lady of any great house.' He beamed. 'And, I have to say, her rooms are the most comfortable in this place and her cook second to none.'

He led the way out of the church across the cloister through the entrance yard to the house that formed the eastern side of the courtyard. The wooden front door stood open, and they went in, where a table was already laid for the three of them. Luca and Peter took their seats. Freize stood at the doorway to serve the men as one of the lay-woman cooks passed him dishes to set on the table. They had three sorts of roasted meats: ham, lamb and beef; and two types of bread: white manchet and dark rye. There were local cheeses, and jams, a basket of hard-boiled eggs, and a bowl of plums with a taste so strong that Luca sliced them on a slice of wheat bread to eat like sweet jam.

'Does the Lady Almoner always eat privately and not dine with her sisters in the refectory?' Luca asked curiously.

'Wouldn't you, if you had a cook like this?' the priest asked. 'High days and holy days, I don't doubt that she sits with her sisters. But she likes things done just so; and one of the privileges of her office is that she has things as she likes them, in her own house. She doesn't sleep in a dormitory nor eat in the refectory. The Lady Abbess is the same in her own house next door.

'Now,' he said with a broad smile. 'I have a drop of brandy in my saddlebag. I'll pour us a measure. It settles the belly after a good breakfast.' He went out of the room and Peter got to his feet and looked out of the window at the entry courtyard where the priest's mule was waiting.

Idly, Luca glanced round the room as Freize cleared their plates. The chimney breast was a beautifully carved wall of polished wood. When Luca had been a little boy his grandfather, a carpenter, had made just such a carved chimney breast for the hall of their farmhouse. Then, it had been an innovation and the envy of the village. Behind one of the carvings had been a secret cupboard where his father had kept sugared plums, which he gave to Luca on a Sunday, if he had been good all the week. On a whim, Luca turned the five bosses along the front of the carved chimney breast one after the other. One yielded under his hand and, to his surprise, a hidden door swung open, just like the one he'd known as a child. Behind it was a glass jar holding not sugared plums but some sort of spice: dried black seeds. Beside it was a cobbler's awl – a little tool for piercing lace holes in leather.

Luca shut the cupboard door. 'My father always used to hide sugared plums in the chimney cupboard,' he remarked.

'We didn't have anything like this,' Peter the clerk replied. 'We all lived in the kitchen, and my mother turned her roast meats on the spit in the fireplace and smoked all her hams in the chimney. When it was morning and the fire was out and we children were really hungry, we'd put our heads up into the soot and nibble at the fatty edges of the hams. She used to tell my father it was mice, God bless her.'

'How did you get your learning in such a poor house?' Luca asked.

Peter shrugged. 'The priest saw that I was a bright boy, so my parents sent me to the monastery.'

'And then?'

'Milord asked me if I would serve him, serve the order. Of course I said yes.'

The door opened and the priest returned, a small bottle discreetly tucked into the sleeve of his robe. 'Just a drop helps me on my way,' he said. Luca took a splash of the strong liquor in his earthenware cup, Peter refused, and the priest took a hearty swig from the mouth of the bottle. Freize looked longingly from the doorway, but decided against saying anything.

'Now I'll take you to the Lady Abbess,' the priest said, carefully stoppering the cork. 'And you'll bear in mind, if she asks you for advice, that she could put this nunnery under the care of her brother monastery, we would run it for her, and all her troubles would be over.'

'I'll remember,' Luca said, without committing himself to one view or the other.

The abbess's house was next door, built on the outer wall of the nunnery, facing inwards onto the cloister and outwards to the forest and the high mountains beyond. The windows that looked to the outer world were heavily leaded, and shielded with thick metal grilles.

'This place is built like a square within a square,' the priest told them. 'The inner square is made up of the church, with the cloister and the nuns' cells around it. This house extends from the cloister to the outer courtyard. The Lady Almoner's half of the house faces the courtyard and the main gate, so she can see all the comings and goings, and the south wall is the hospital for the poor.'

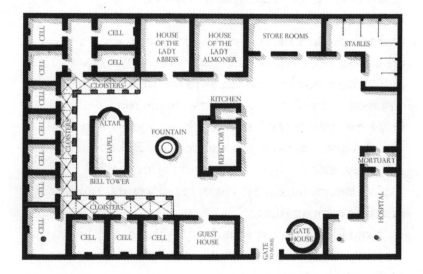

The priest gestured towards the door. 'The Lady Abbess said for you to go in.' He stood back, and Luca and Peter went in, Freize behind them. They found themselves in a small room furnished with two wooden benches and two very plain chairs. A strong wrought-iron grille in the wall on the far side blocked the opening into the next room, veiled by a curtain of white wool. As they stood waiting, the curtain was silently drawn back and on the other side they could just make out a white robe, a wimple headdress, and a pale face through the obscuring mesh of the metal.

'God bless you and keep you,' a clear voice said. 'I welcome you to this abbey. I am the Lady Abbess here.'

'I am Luca Vero.' Luca stepped up to the grille, but he could see only the silhouette of a woman through the richly wrought ironwork of grapes, fruit, leaves and flowers. There was a faint light perfume, like rosewater. Behind the lady, he could just make out the shadowy outline of another woman in a dark robe.

'This is my clerk Brother Peter, and my servant Freize. And I have been sent here to make an inquiry into your abbey.'

'I know,' she said quietly.

'I did not know that you were enclosed,' Luca said, careful not to offend.

'It is the tradition that visitors speak to the ladies of our order through a grille.'

'But I shall need to speak with them for my inquiry. I shall need them to come to report to me.'

He could sense her reluctance through the bars.

'Very well,' she said. 'Since we have agreed to your inquiry.'

Luca knew perfectly well, that this cool Lady Abbess had not agreed to the inquiry: she had been offered no choice in the matter. His inquiry had been sent to her house by the lord of the Order, and he would interrogate her sisters with or without her consent.

'I shall need a room for my private use, and the nuns will have to come and report to me, under oath, what has been happening here,' Luca said more confidently. At his side the priest nodded his approval.

'I have ordered them to prepare a room for you next door to this one,' she said. 'I think it better that you should hear evidence in my house, in the house of the Lady Abbess. They will know then that I am co-operating with your inquiry, that they come here to speak to you under my blessing.'

'It would be better somewhere else altogether,' the priest said quietly to Luca. 'You should come to the monastery and order them to attend in our house, under our supervision. The rule of men, you know … the logic of men … always a powerful thing to invoke. This needs a man's mind on it, not a woman's fleeting whimsy.'

'Thank you, but I will meet them here,' Luca said to the priest. To the Lady Abbess he said, 'I thank you for your assistance. I am happy to meet with the nuns in your house.'

'But I do wonder why,' Freize prompted under his breath to a fat bee bumbling against the small leaded window pane.

'But I do wonder why,' Luca repeated out loud.

Freize opened the little window and released the bee out into the sunshine.

'There has been much scandal, and some of it directed against me,' the Lady Abbess said frankly. 'I have been accused personally. It is better that the house sees that the inquiry is under my control, is under my blessing. I hope that you will clear my name, as well as discovering any wrong-doing and rooting it out.'

'We will have to interview you, as well as all the members of the order,' Luca pointed out.

He could see through the grille that the white figure had moved, and realised she had bowed her head as if he had shamed her.

'I am ordered from Rome to help you to discover the truth,' he insisted.

She did not reply but merely turned her head and spoke to someone out of his sight and then the door to the room opened and the elderly nun, the porteress Sister Anna who had greeted them on their first night, said abruptly, 'The Lady Abbess says I am to show you the room for your inquiry.'

It appeared that their interview with the Lady Abbess was over, and they had not even seen her face.

~

It was a plain room, looking out over the woods behind the abbey, in the back of the house so that they could not see the cloister, the nuns' cells, or the comings and goings of the courtyard before the church. But, equally, the community could not see who came to give evidence.

'Discreet,' Peter the clerk remarked.

'Secretive,' Freize said cheerfully. 'Am I to stand outside and make sure no-one interrupts or eavesdrops?'

'Yes.' Luca pulled up a chair to the empty table and waited while Brother Peter produced papers, a black quill pen and a pot of ink, then seated himself at the end of the table, and looked at Luca expectantly. The three young men paused. Luca, overwhelmed with the task that lay before him, looked blankly back at the other two. Freize grinned at him, and made an encouraging gesture like someone waving a flag. 'Onward!' he said. 'Things are so bad here, that we can't make them worse.'

Luca choked on a boyish laugh. 'I suppose so,' he said, taking his seat, and turned to Brother Peter. 'We'll start with the Lady Almoner,' he said, trying to speak decisively. 'At least we know her name.'

Freize nodded and went to the door. 'Fetch the Lady Almoner,' he said to Sister Anna.

She came straight away, and took a seat opposite Luca. He tried not to look at the serene beauty of her face, her grey knowing eyes that seemed to smile at him with some private knowledge.

Formally, he took her name, her age – twenty-four – the name of her parents, and the duration of her stay in the abbey. She had been behind the abbey walls for twenty years, since her earliest childhood.

'What do you think is happening here?' Luca asked her, emboldened by his position as the Inquirer, by his sense of his own self-importance, and by the trappings of his work: Freize at the door, and Brother Peter with his black quill pen.

She looked down at the plain wooden table. 'I don't know. There are strange occurrences, and my sisters are very troubled.'

'What sort of occurrences?'

'Some of my sisters have started to have visions, and two of them have been rising up in their sleep – getting out of their beds and walking though their eyes are still closed. One cannot eat the food that is served in the refectory, she is starving herself and cannot be persuaded to eat. And there are other things. Other manifestations.'

'When did it start?' Luca asked her.

She nodded wearily, as if she expected such a question. 'It was about three months ago.'

'Was that when the new Lady Abbess came?'

A breath of a sigh. 'Yes. But I am convinced that she has nothing to do with it. I would not want to give evidence to an inquiry that was used against her. Our troubles started then – but you must remember she has no authority with the nuns, being so new, so inexperienced, having declared herself unwilling. A nunnery needs strong leadership, supervision, a woman who loves the life here. The new Lady Abbess lived a very sheltered life before she came to us, she was the favoured child of a great lord, the indulged daughter of a great house; she is not accustomed to command a religious house. She was not raised here. It is not surprising that she does not know how to command.'

'Could the nuns be commanded to stop seeing visions? Is it within their choice? Has she failed them through her inability to command?'

Peter the clerk made a note of the question.

The Lady Almoner smiled. 'Not if they are true visions from God,' she said easily. 'If they are true visions, then nothing would stop them. But if they are errors and folly, if they are women frightening themselves and allowing their fears to rule them ... If they are women dreaming and making up stories ... Forgive me for being so blunt, Brother Luca, but I have lived in this community for twenty years and I know that two hundred women living together can whip up a storm over nothing if they are allowed to do so.'

Luca raised his eyebrows. 'They can invoke sleep-walking? They can invoke running out at night and trying to get out of the gates?'

She sighed. 'You saw?'

'Last night,' he confirmed.

'I am sure that there are one or two who are truly sleep-walkers. I am sure that one, perhaps two, have truly seen visions. But now I have dozens of young women who are hearing angels, and seeing the movement of stars, who are waking in the night and are shrieking out in pain. You must understand, Brother, not all of our novices are here because they have a calling. Very many are sent here by families who have too many children at home, or because the girl is too scholarly, or because she has lost her betrothed or cannot be married for some other reason. Sometimes they send us girls who are disobedient. Of course, they bring their troubles here, at first. Not everyone has a vocation, not everyone wants to be here. And once one young woman leaves her cell at night, against the rules, and runs around the cloisters, there is always someone who is going to join her.' She paused. 'And then another, and another.'

'And the stigmata? The sign of the cross on her palms?'

He could see the shock in her face. 'Who told you about that?'

'I saw the girl myself, last night, and the other women who ran after her.'

She bowed her head and clasped her hands together; he thought for a moment that she was praying for guidance as to what she should say next. 'Perhaps it is a miracle,' she said quietly. 'The stigmata. We cannot know for sure. Perhaps not. Perhaps – Our Lady defend us from evil – it is something worse.'

Luca leaned across the table to hear her. 'Worse? What d'you mean?'

'Sometimes a devout young woman will mark herself with the five wounds of Christ. Mark herself as an act of devotion. Sometimes young women will go too far.' She took a nervous shuddering breath. 'That is why we need strong discipline in the house. The nuns need to feel that they can be cared for, as a daughter is cared for by her father. They need to know that there are strict limits to their behaviour. They need to be carefully ruled.'

'You fear that the women are harming themselves?' Luca asked, shocked.

'They are young women,' the Lady Almoner repeated. 'And they have no leadership. They become passionate, stirred up. It is not unknown for them to cut themselves, or each other.'

Brother Peter and Luca exchanged a horrified glance, Brother Peter ducked down his head and made a note.

'The abbey is wealthy,' Luca observed, speaking at random, to divert himself from his shock.

She shook her head. 'No, we have a vow of poverty, each and every one of us. Poverty, obedience and chastity. We can own nothing, we cannot follow our own will, and we cannot love a man. We have all taken these vows; there is no escaping them. We have all taken them. We have all willingly consented.'

'Except the Lady Abbess,' Luca suggested. 'I understand

that she protested. She did not want to come. She was ordered to enter the abbey. She did not choose to be obedient, poor, and without the love of a man.'

'You would have to ask her,' the Lady Almoner said with quiet dignity. 'She went through the service. She gave up her rich gowns from the great chests of clothes that she brought in with her. Out of respect for her position in the world she was allowed to change her gown in private. Her own servant shaved her head and helped her dress in coarse linen, and a wool robe of our order, with a wimple around her head and a veil on top of that. When she was ready she came into the chapel and lay alone on the stone floor before the altar, her arms spread out, her face to the cold floor, and she gave herself to God. Only she can know if she took the vows in her heart. Her mind is hidden from us, her sisters.'

She hesitated. 'But her servant, of course, did not take the vows. She lives among us as an outsider. Her servant, as far as I know, follows no rules at all. I don't know if she even obeys the Lady Abbess, or if their relationship is more . . .'

'More what?' Luca asked, horrified.

'More unusual,' she said.

'Her servant? Is she a lay sister?'

'I don't know quite what you would call her. She was the Lady Abbess's personal servant from childhood, and when the Lady Abbess joined us, the slave came too; she just accompanied her when she came, like a dog follows his master. She lives in the house of the Lady Abbess. She used to sleep in the storeroom next door to the Lady Abbess's room, she wouldn't sleep in the nun's cells, then she started to sleep on the threshold of her room, like a slave. Recently she has taken to sleeping in the bed with her.' She paused.

'Like a bedmate.' She hesitated. 'I am not suggesting any-thing else,' she said.

Brother Peter's pen was suspended, his mouth open; but he said nothing.

'She attends the church, following the Lady Abbess like her shadow; but she doesn't say the prayers, nor confess, nor take Mass. I assume she is an infidel. I really don't know. She is an exception to our rule. We don't call her Sister, we call her Ishraq.'

'Ishraq?' Luca repeated the strange name.

'She was born an Ottoman,' the Lady Almoner said, her voice carefully controlled. 'You will notice her around the abbey. She wears a dark robe like a Moorish woman, some-times she holds a veil across her face. Her skin is the colour of caramel sugar, it is the same colour: all over. Naked, she is golden, like a woman made of toffee. The last lord brought her back with him as a baby from Jerusalem when he returned from the crusades. Perhaps he owned her as a trophy, perhaps as a pet. He did not change her name nor did he have her baptised; but had her brought up with his daughter as her personal slave.'

'Do you think she could have had anything to do with the disturbances? Since they started when she came into the abbey? Since she came in with the Lady Abbess, at the same time?'

She shrugged. 'Some of the nuns were afraid of her when they first saw her. She is a heretic, of course, and fierce-looking. She is always in the shadow of the Lady Abbess. They found her ...' She paused. 'Disturbing,' she said, then nodded at the word she had chosen. 'She is dis-turbing. We would all say that: disturbing.'

'What does she do?'

'She does nothing for God,' the Lady Almoner said with sudden passion. 'For sure, she does nothing for the abbey. Wherever the Lady Abbess goes, she goes too. She never leaves her side.'

'Surely she goes out? She is not enclosed?'

'She never leaves the Lady Abbess's side,' she contradicted him. 'And the Lady Abbess never goes out. The slave haunts the place. She walks in shadows, she stands in dark corners, she watches everything, and she speaks to none of us. It is as if we have trapped a strange animal. I feel as if I am keeping a tawny lioness, encaged.'

'Are you afraid of her, yourself?' Luca asked bluntly.

She raised her head and looked at him with her clear grey gaze. 'I trust that God will protect me from all evil,' she said. 'But if I were not certain sure that I am under the hand of God she would be an utter terror to me.'

There was silence in the little room, as if a whisper of evil had passed among them. Luca felt the hairs on his neck prickle, while beneath the table Brother Peter felt for the crucifix that he wore at his belt.

'Which of the nuns should I speak to first?' Luca asked, breaking the silence. 'Write down for me the names of those who have been walking in their sleep, showing stigmata, seeing visions, fasting.'

He pushed the paper and the quill before her and, without haste or hesitation, she wrote six names clearly, and returned the paper to him.

'And you?' he asked. 'Have you seen visions, or walked in your sleep?'

Her smile at the younger man was almost alluring. 'I wake

in the night for the church services, and I go to my prayers,' she said. 'You won't find me anywhere but warm in my bed.'

As Luca blinked that vision from his mind, she rose from the table and left the room.

'Impressive woman,' Peter said quietly, as the door shut behind her. 'Think of her being in a nunnery from the age of four! If she'd been in the outside world, what might she have done?'

'Silk petticoats,' Freize remarked, inserting his broad head around the door from the hall outside. 'Unusual.'

'What? What?' Luca demanded, furious for no reason, feeling his heart pound at the thought of the Lady Almoner sleeping in her chaste bed.

'Unusual to find a nun in silk petticoats. Hair shirt, yes – that's extreme perhaps, but traditional. Silk petticoats, no.'

'How the Devil do you know that she wears silk petticoats?' Peter demanded irritably. 'And how dare you speak so, and of such a lady?'

'Saw them drying in the laundry, wondered who they belonged to. Seemed an odd sort of garment for a nunnery vowed to poverty. Started to listen. I may be a fool but I can listen. Heard them whisper as she walked by me. She didn't know I was listening, she walked by me as if I was a stone, a tree. Silk gives a little *hss hss hss* sound.' He nodded smugly at Peter. 'More than one way to make inquiry. Don't have to be able to write to be able to think. Sometimes it helps to just listen.'

Brother Peter ignored him completely. 'Who next?' he asked Luca.

'The Lady Abbess,' Luca ruled. 'Then her servant, Ishraq.'

'Why not see Ishraq first, and then we can hold her next door while the Lady Abbess speaks,' Peter suggested. 'That way we can make sure they don't collude.'

'Collude in what?' Luca demanded, impatiently.

'That's the whole thing,' Peter said. 'We don't know what they're doing.'

'Collude.' Freize carefully repeated the strange word. 'Col-lude. Funny how some words just sound guilty.'

'Just fetch the slave,' Luca commanded. 'You're not the Inquirer, you are supposed to be serving me as your lord. And make sure she doesn't talk to anyone as she comes to us.'

Freize walked round to the Lady Abbess's kitchen door and asked for the servant, Ishraq. She came veiled like a desert-dweller, dressed in a tunic and pantaloons of black, a shawl over her head pinned across her face, hiding her mouth. All he could see of her were her bare brown feet – a silver ring on one toe – and her dark inscrutable eyes above her veil. Freize smiled reassuringly at her; but she responded not at all, and they walked in silence to the room. She seated herself before Luca and Brother Peter without uttering one word.

'Your name is Ishraq?' Luca asked her.

'I don't speak Italian,' she said in perfect Italian.

'You are speaking it now.'

She shook her head and said again: 'I don't speak Italian.'

'Your name is Ishraq.' He tried again in French.

'I don't speak French,' she replied in perfectly accented French.

'Your name is Ishraq,' he said in Latin.

'It is,' she conceded in Latin. 'But I don't speak Latin.'

'What language do you speak?'

'I don't speak.'

Luca recognised a stalemate and leaned forwards, drawing on as much authority as he could. 'Listen, woman: I am commanded by the Holy Father himself to make inquiry into the events in this nunnery and to send him my report. You had better answer me, or face not just my displeasure, but his.'

She shrugged. 'I am dumb,' she said simply, in Latin. 'And of course, he may be your Holy Father, but he is not mine.'

'Clearly you can speak,' Brother Peter intervened. 'Clearly you can speak several languages.'

She turned her insolent eyes to him, and shook her head.

'You speak to the Lady Abbess.'

Silence.

'We have powers to make you speak,' Brother Peter warned her.

At once she looked down, her dark eyelashes veiling her gaze. When she looked up Luca saw that her dark brown eyes were crinkled at the edges, and she was fighting her desire to laugh out loud at Brother Peter. 'I don't speak,' was all she said. 'And I don't think you have any powers over me.'

Luca flushed scarlet with the quick temper of a young man who has been mocked by a woman. 'Just go,' Luca said shortly.

To Freize, who put his long face around the door, he snapped: 'Send for the Lady Abbess. And hold this dumb woman next door, alone.'

Isolde stood in the inner doorway, her hood pulled so far forwards that it cast a deep shadow over her face, her hands hidden in her deep sleeves, only her lithe white feet showing below her robe, in their plain sandals. Irrelevantly Luca noticed that her toes were rosy with cold and her insteps arched high. 'Come in,' Luca said, trying to recover his temper. 'Please take a seat.'

She sat; but she did not put back her hood, so Luca found he was forced to bend his head to peer under it to try to see her. In the shadow of the hood he could make out only a heart-shaped jaw line with a determined mouth. The rest of her remained a mystery.

'Will you put back your hood, Lady Abbess?'

'I would rather not.'

'The Lady Almoner faced us without a hood.'

'I was made to swear to avoid the company of men,' she said coldly. 'I was commanded to swear to remain inside this order and not meet or speak with men except for the fewest words and the briefest meeting. I am obeying the vows I was forced to take. It was not my choice, it was laid upon me by the Church. You, from the Church, should be pleased at my obedience.'

Brother Peter tucked his papers together and waited, pen poised.

'Would you tell us of the circumstances of your coming to the nunnery?' Luca asked.

'They are well-enough known,' she said. 'My father died three and a half months ago and left his castle and his lands entirely to my brother, the new lord, as is right and proper. My mother was dead, and to me he left nothing but the choice of a suitor in marriage or a place in the abbey. My brother, the new Lord Lucretili, accepted my decision not to marry and did me the great favour of putting me in charge of this nunnery, and I came in, took my vows, and started my service as their Lady Abbess.'

'How old are you?'

'I am seventeen,' she told him.

'Isn't that very young to be a Lady Abbess?'

The half-hidden mouth showed a wry smile. 'Not if your grandfather founded the abbey and your brother is its only patron, of course. The Lord of Lucretili can appoint who he chooses.'

'You had a vocation?'

'Alas, I did not. I came here in obedience to my brother's wish and my father's will. Not because I feel I have a calling.'

'Did you not want to rebel against your brother's wish and your father's will?'

There was a moment of silence. She raised her head and from the depth of her hood he saw her regard him thoughtfully, as if she were considering him as a man who might understand her.

'Of course, I was tempted by the sin of disobedience,' she said levelly. 'I did not understand why my father would treat me so. He had never spoken to me of the abbey nor suggested that he wanted a life of holiness for me. On the contrary, he spoke to me of the outside world, of being a woman of honour and power in the world, of managing my lands and supporting the Church as it comes under attack both here and in the Holy Land. But my brother was with my father on his deathbed, heard his last words, and afterwards he showed me his will. It was clearly my father's last wish that I come here. I loved my father, I love him still. I obey him in death as I obeyed him in life.' Her voice shook slightly as she spoke of her father. 'I am a good daughter to him; now as then.'

'They say that you brought your slave with you, a Moorish girl named Ishraq, and that she is neither a lay sister nor has she taken her vows.'

'She is not my slave; she is a free woman. She may do as she pleases.'

'So what is she doing here?'

'Whatever she wishes.'

Luca was sure that he saw in her shadowed eyes the same gleam of defiance that the slave had shown. 'Lady Abbess,' he said sternly. 'You should have no companions but the sisters of your order.'

She looked at him with an untameable confidence. 'I don't think so,' she said. 'I don't think you have the authority to tell me so. And I don't think that I would listen to you, even if you said that you had the authority. As far as I know there is no law that says a woman, an infidel, may not enter a nunnery and serve alongside the nuns. There is no tradition that excludes her. We are of the Augustine order, and as Lady Abbess I can manage this house as I see fit. Nobody can tell me how to do it. If you make me Lady Abbess then you give me the right to decide how this house shall be run. Having forced me to take the power, you can be sure that I shall rule.' The words were defiant, but her voice was very calm.

'They say she has not left your side since you came to the abbey?'

73

'This is true.'

'She has never gone out of the gates?'

'Neither have I.'

'She is with you night and day?'

'Yes.'

'They say that she sleeps in your bed?' Luca said boldly.

'Who says?' the Lady Abbess asked him evenly.

Luca looked down at his notes, and Brother Peter shuffled the papers.

She shrugged, as if she were filled with disdain for them and for their gossipy inquiry. 'I suppose you have to ask everybody, everything that they imagine,' she said dismissively. 'You will have to chatter like a clattering of choughs. You will hear the wildest of talk from the most fearful and imaginative people. You will ask silly girls to tell you tales.'

'Where does she sleep?' Luca persisted, feeling a fool.

'Since the abbey became so disturbed she has chosen to sleep in my bed, as she did when we were children. This way she can protect me.'

'Against what?'

She sighed as if she were weary of his curiosity. 'Of course, I don't know. I don't know what she fears for me. I don't know what I fear for myself. In truth, I think no-one knows what is happening here. Isn't this what you are here to find out?'

'Things seem to have gone very badly wrong since you came here.'

She bowed her head in silence for a moment. 'Now that is true,' she conceded. 'But it is nothing that I have deliberately done. I don't know what is happening here. I regret

74

it very much. It causes me, me personally, great pain. I am puzzled. I am ... lost.'

'Lost?' Luca repeated the word that seemed freighted with loneliness.

'Lost,' she confirmed.

'You don't know how to rule the abbey?'

Her head bowed down as if she were praying again. Then a small silent nod of her head admitted the truth of it: that she did not know how to command the abbey. 'Not like this,' she whispered. 'Not when they say they are possessed, not when they behave like madwomen.'

'You have no vocation,' Luca said very quietly to her. 'Do you wish yourself on the outside of these walls, even now?'

She breathed out a tiny sigh of longing. Luca could almost feel her desire to be free, her sense that she should be free. Absurdly, he thought of the bee that Freize had released to fly out into the sunshine, he thought that every form of life, even the smallest bee, longs to be free.

'How can this abbey hope to thrive with a Lady Abbess who wishes herself free?' he asked her sternly. 'You know that we have to serve where we have sworn to be.'

'You don't.' She rounded on him almost as if she were angry. 'For you were sworn to be a priest in a small country monastery; but here you are – free as a bird. Riding around the country on the best horses that the Church can give you, followed by a squire and a clerk. Going where you want and questioning anyone. Free to question me – even authorised to question me, who lives here and serves here and prays here, and does nothing but sometimes secretly wish ...'

'It is not for you to pass comment on us,' Brother Peter

intervened. 'The Pope himself has authorised us. It is not for you to ask questions.'

Luca let it go, secretly relieved that he did not have to admit to the Lady Abbess his joy at being released from his monastery, his delight in his horse, his unending insatiable curiosity.

She tossed her head at Brother Peter's ruling. 'I would expect you to defend him,' she remarked dismissively. 'I would expect you to stick together, as men do, as men always do.'

She turned to Luca. 'Of course, I have thought that I am utterly unsuited to be a Lady Abbess. But what am I to do? My father's wishes were clear, my brother orders everything now. My father wished me to be Lady Abbess and my brother has ordered that I am. So here I am. It may be against my wishes, it may be against the wishes of the community. But it is the command of my brother and my father. I will do what I can. I have taken my vows. I am bound here till death.'

'You swore fully?'

'I did.'

'You shaved your head and renounced your wealth?'

A tiny gesture of the veiled head warned him that he had caught her in some small deception. 'I cut my hair, and I put away my mother's jewels,' she said cautiously. 'I will never be bare-headed again, I will never wear her sapphires.'

'Do you think that these manifestations of distress and trouble are caused by you?' he asked bluntly.

Her little gasp revealed her distress at the charge. Almost, she recoiled from what he was saying, then gathered her courage and leaned towards him. He caught a glimpse of intense dark blue eyes. 'Perhaps. It is possible. You would be the one to discover such a thing. You have been appointed to discover such things, after all. Certainly I don't wish things as they are. I don't understand them, and they hurt me too. It is not just the sisters, I too am—'

'You are?'

'Touched,' she said quietly.

Luca, his head spinning, looked to Brother Peter, whose pen was suspended in midair over the page, his mouth agape.

'Touched?' Luca repeated wondering wildly if she meant that she was going insane.

'Wounded,' she amended.

'In what way?'

She shook her head as if she would not fully reply. 'Deeply,' was all she said.

There was a long silence in the sunlit room. Freize outside, hearing the voices cease their conversation, opened the door, looked in, and received such a black scowl from Luca that he quickly withdrew. 'Sorry,' he said as the door shut.

'Should not the nunnery be put into the charge of your brother house, the Dominicans?' Peter asked bluntly. 'You could be released from your vows and the head of the monastery could rule both communities. The nuns could come under the discipline of the Lord Abbot, the business affairs of the nunnery could be passed to the castle. You would be free to leave.'

'Put men to rule women?' She looked up as if she would laugh at him. 'Is that all you can suggest – the three of you? Going to the trouble to come all the way from Rome on your fine horses, a clerk, an Inquirer and a servant, and

77

the best idea you have is that a nunnery shall give up its independence and be ruled by men? You would break up our old and traditional order, you would destroy us who are made in the image of Our Lady Mary, and put us under the rule of men?'

'God gave men the rule over everything,' Luca pointed out. 'At the creation of the world.'

Her flash of laughing defiance deserted her as soon as it had come. 'Oh, perhaps,' she said, suddenly weary. 'If you say so. I don't know. I wasn't raised to think so. But I know that is what some of the sisters want, I know it is what the brothers say should happen. I don't know if it is the will of God. I don't know that God particularly wants men to rule over women. My father never suggested such a thing to me and he was a crusader who had gone to the Holy Land himself and prayed at the very birthplace of Jesus. He raised me to think of myself as a child of God and a woman of the world. He never told me that God had set men over women. He said God had created them together, to be helpers and lovers to each other. But I don't know. Certainly God – if He ever stoops to speak to a woman – does not speak to me.'

'And what is your own will?' Luca asked her. 'You, who are here, though you say you don't want to be here? With a servant who speaks three languages but claims to be dumb? Praying to a God who does not speak to you? You, who say you are hurt? You, who say you are touched? What is your will?'

'I have no will,' she said simply. 'It's too soon for me. My father died only fourteen weeks ago. Can you imagine what that is like for his daughter? I loved him deeply, he was my only parent, the hero of my childhood. He commanded everything, he was the very sun of my world. I wake every morning and have to remind myself that he is dead. I came into the nunnery only days after his death, in the first week of mourning. Can you imagine that? The troubles started to happen almost at once. My father is dead and everyone around me is either feigning madness, or they are going mad.

'So if you ask me what I want, I will tell you. All I want to do is to cry and sleep. All I want to do is to wish that none of this had ever happened. In my worse moments, I want to tie the rope of the bell in the bell tower around my throat and let it sweep me off my feet and break my neck as it tolls.'

The violence of her words clanged like a tolling bell itself into the quiet room. 'Self-harm is blasphemy,' Luca said quickly. 'Even thinking of it is a sin. You will have to confess such a wish to a priest, accept the penance he sets you, and never think of it again.'

'I know,' she replied. 'I know. And that is why I only wish it, and don't do it.'

'You are a troubled woman.' He had no idea what he should say to comfort her. 'A troubled girl.'

She raised her head and, from the darkness of her hood, he thought he saw the ghost of a smile. 'I don't need an Inquirer to come all the way from Rome to tell me that. But would you help me?'

'If I could,' he said. 'If I can, I will.'

They were silent. Luca felt that he had somehow pledged himself to her. Slowly, she pushed back her hood, just a little, so that he could see the blaze of her honest blue eyes. Then Brother Peter noisily dipped his pen in the bottle of ink, and Luca recollected himself.

'I saw a nun last night run across the courtyard, chased

by three others,' he said. 'This woman got to the outer gate and hammered on it with her fists, screaming like a vixen, a terrible sound, the cry of the damned. They caught her and carried her back to the cloister. I assume they put her back in her cell?'

'They did,' she said coldly.

'I saw her hands,' he told her; and now he felt as if he were not making an inquiry, but an accusation. He felt as if he were accusing her. 'She was marked on the palms of her hand, with the sign of the crucifixion, as if she was showing, or faking, the stigmata.'

'She is no fake,' the Lady Abbess told him with quiet dignity. 'This is a pain to her, not a source of pride.'

'You know this?'

'I know it for certain.'

'Then I will see her this afternoon. You will send her to me.'

'I will not.'

Her calm refusal threw Luca. 'You have to!'

'I will not send her this afternoon. The whole community is watching the door to my house. You have arrived with enough fanfare, the whole abbey, brothers and sisters, know that you are here and that you are taking evidence. I will not have her further shamed. It is bad enough for her with everyone knowing that she is showing these signs and dreaming these dreams. You can meet her; but at a time of my choosing, when no-one is watching.'

'I have an order from the Pope himself to interview the wrong-doers.'

'Is that what you think of me? That I am a wrong-doer?' she suddenly asked.

'No. I should have said I have an order from the Pope to hold an inquiry.'

'Then do so,' she said impertinently. 'But you will not see that young woman until it is safe for her to come to you.'

'When will that be?'

'Soon. When I judge it is right.'

Luca realised he would get no further with the Lady Abbess. To his surprise, he was not angry. He found that he admired her; he liked her bright sense of honour, and he shared her bewilderment at what was happening in the nunnery. But more than anything else, he pitied her loss. Luca knew what it was to miss a parent, to be without someone who would care for you, love you and protect you. He knew what it was to face the world alone and feel yourself to be an orphan.

He found he was smiling at her, though he could not see if she was smiling back. 'Lady Abbess, you are not an easy woman to interrogate.'

'Brother Luca, you are not an easy man to refuse,' she replied, and she rose from the table without permission, and left the room.

~

For the rest of the day Luca and Brother Peter interviewed one nun after another, taking each one's history, and her hopes, and fears. They ate alone in the Lady Almoner's chamber, served by Freize. In the afternoon, Luca remarked that he could not stand another white-faced girl telling him that she had bad dreams and that she was troubled by her conscience, and swore that he had to take a break from the worries and fears of women.

They saddled their horses and the three men rode out into the great beech forest where the massive trees arched high above them, shedding copper-coloured leaves and beech mast in a constant whisper. The horses were almost silent as their hooves were muffled by the thickness of the forest floor and Luca rode ahead, on his own, weary of the many plaintive voices of the day, wondering if he would be able to make any sense of all he had heard, fearful that all he was doing was listening to meaningless dreams and being frightened by fantasies.

The track led them higher and higher until they emerged above the woodland, looking down the way they had come. Above them, the track went on, narrower and more stony, up to the high mountains that stood, bleak and lovely, all around them.

'This is better.' Freize patted his horse's neck as they paused for a moment. Down below them they could see the little village of Lucretili, the grey slate roof of the abbey, the two religious houses placed on either side of it, and the dominating castle where the new lord's standard fluttered in the wind over the round gatehouse tower.

The air was cold. Above them a solitary eagle wheeled away. Brother Peter tightened his cloak around his shoulders and looked at Luca, to remind him that they must not stay out too long.

Together they turned the horses and rode along the crest of the hill, keeping the woodland to their right, and then, at the first woodcutter's trail, dropped down towards the valley again, falling silent as the trees closed around them.

The trail wound through the forest. Once they heard the trickle of water, and then the drilling noise of a woodpecker.

Just when they thought they had overshot the village they came out into a clearing and saw a wide track heading to the castle of Lucretili which stood, like a grey stone guard post, dominating the road.

'He does all right for himself,' Freize observed, looking at the high castle walls, the drawbridge and the rippling standards. From the lord's stables they could hear the howling of his pack of deerhounds. 'Not a bad life. The wealth to enjoy it all, hunting your own deer, living off your own game, enough money to take a ride into Rome to see the sights when you feel like it, and a cellar full of your own wine.'

'Saints save her, how she must miss her home,' Luca remarked, looking at the tall towers of the beautiful castle, the rides which led deep into the forest and beyond to lakes, hills, and streams. 'From all this wealth and freedom to four square walls and a life enclosed till death! How could a father who loved his daughter bring her up to be free here, and then have her locked up on his death?'

'Better that than a bad husband who would beat her as soon as her brother's back was turned, better that than die in childbirth,' Brother Peter pointed out. 'Better that than being swept off her feet by some fortune-hunter, and all the family wealth and good name destroyed in a year.'

'Depends on the fortune-hunter,' Freize volunteered. 'A lusty man with a bit of charm about him might have brought a flush to her cheek, given her something pleasant to dream about.'

'Enough,' Luca ruled. 'You may not talk about her like that.'

'Seems we mustn't think of her like a pretty lass,' Freize remarked to his horse.

'Enough,' Luca repeated. 'And you don't know what she looks like, any more than I do.'

'Ha, but I can tell by her walk,' Freize said quietly to his horse. 'You can always tell a pretty girl by the way she walks. A pretty girl walks like she owns the world.'

～

Isolde and Ishraq were at the window as the young men came back through the gate. 'Can't you just smell the open air on their clothes?' the first one whispered. 'When he leaned forwards I could just smell the forest, and the fresh air, and the wind that comes off the mountain.'

'We could go out, Isolde.'

'You know I cannot.'

'We could go out in secret,' the other replied. 'At night, through the little postern gate. We could just walk in the woods in the starlight. If you long for the outside, we don't have to be prisoners here.'

'You know that I took vows that I would never leave here ...'

'When so many vows are being broken?' the other urged. 'When we have turned the abbey upside down and brought hell in here with us? What would one more sin matter? How does it matter what we do now?'

The gaze that Isolde turned on her friend was dark with guilt. 'I can't give up,' she whispered. 'Whatever people think I have done or say I have done, whatever I have done – I won't give up on myself. I'll keep my word.'

～

The three men attended Compline, the last service before the nuns went to bed for the night. Freize looked longingly at the Lady Almoner's stores as the three men walked out of the cloister and separated to go to their rooms. 'What I wouldn't give for a glass of sweet wine as a nightcap,' he said. 'Or two. Or three.'

'You really are a hopeless servant for a religious man,' Peter remarked. 'Wouldn't you have done better in an ale house?'

'And how would the little lord manage without me?' Freize demanded indignantly. 'Who watched over him in the monastery and kept him safe? Who fed him when he was nothing more than a long-legged sparrow? Who follows him now wherever he goes? Who keeps the door for him?'

'Did he watch over you in the monastery?' Peter asked, turning in surprise to Luca.

Luca laughed. 'He watched over my dinner and ate everything I left,' he said. 'He drank my wine allowance. In that sense he watched me very closely.'

At Freize's protest, Luca thumped him on the shoulder. 'Ah, all right! All right!' To Peter he said: 'When I first entered the monastery he watched out for me so that I wasn't beaten by the older boys. When I was charged with heresy he gave witness for me, though he couldn't make head nor tail of what they said I had done. He has been loyal to me, always, from the moment of our first meeting when I was a scared novice and he was a lazy kitchen boy. And when I was given this mission he asked to be released to go with me.'

'There you are!' Freize said triumphantly.

'But why does he call you "little lord"?' Peter pursued.

Luca shook his head. 'Who knows? I don't.'

'Because he was no ordinary boy,' Freize explained eagerly. 'So clever and, when he was a child, quite beautiful like an angel. And then everyone said he was not of earthly making …'

'Enough of that!' Luca said shortly. 'He calls me "little lord" to serve his own vanity. He would pretend he was in service to a prince if he thought he could get away with it.'

'You'll see,' Freize said, nodding solemnly to Brother Peter. 'He's not an ordinary young man.'

'I look forward to witnessing exceptional abilities,' Brother Peter said drily. 'Sooner rather than later, if possible. Now, I'm for my bed.'

Luca raised his hand in goodnight to the two of them and turned into the priest house. He closed the door behind him and pulled off his boots, putting his concealed dagger carefully under the pillow. He laid out the paper about the number zero on one side of the table, and the statements that Peter had written down on the other. He planned to study the statements and then reward himself with looking at the manuscript about zero, working through the night. Then he would attend the service of Lauds.

At about two in the morning, a tiny knock at the door made him move swiftly from the table to take up the dagger from under his pillow. 'Who's there?'

'A sister.'

Luca tucked the knife into his belt, at his back, and opened the door a crack. A woman, a veil of thick lace completely obscuring her face, stood silently in his doorway. He glanced

86

quickly up and down the deserted gallery and stepped back to indicate that she could come inside. In the back of his mind he thought he was taking a risk letting her come to him without witnesses, without Brother Peter to take a note of all that was said. But she too was taking a risk, and breaking her vows, to be alone with a man. She must be driven by something very powerful to step into a man's bedroom, alone.

He saw that she held her hands cupped, as if she were hiding something small in her palms.

'You wanted to see me,' she spoke so softly he could hardly hear her. 'You wanted to see this.'

She held out her hands to him. Luca flinched in horror as he saw that in the centre of both was a neat shallow hole, and each palm was filled with blood. 'Jesu save us!'

'Amen,' she said instantly.

Luca reached for the linen washcloth and tore a strip roughly off the side. He splashed water onto it from the ewer, and gently patted each wound. She flinched a little as he touched her. 'I am sorry, I am sorry.'

'They don't hurt much, they're not deep.'

Luca dabbed away the blood and saw that both wounds had stopped bleeding and were beginning to form small scabs. 'When did this happen?'

'I woke just now, and they were like this, newly marked. It has happened before. Sometimes I have woken in the morning and found them wounded but they have already stopped bleeding, as if they came earlier in the night, without even waking me. They are not deep, you see, they heal within days. I have been sleeping with my friend to protect me. I shall keep her by my side.'

'Do you have a vision?'

'A vision of horror!' she suddenly broke out. 'I cannot believe it is the work of God to wake me with bleeding hands. I have no sense of holiness, I feel nothing but terror. This cannot be God stabbing me. These must be blasphemous wounds.'

'God might be working through you, mysteriously ...' Luca tried.

She shook her head. 'It feels more like punishment. For being here, for following the services, and yet being cursed with a rebellious heart.'

'How many of you are here unwillingly?'

'Who knows? Who knows what people think when they go through each day in silence, praying as they are commanded to do, singing as they are ordered? We are not allowed to speak to one another during the day except to repeat our orders or say our prayers. Who knows what anyone is thinking? Who knows what we are all privately thinking?'

She spoke so powerfully to Luca's own sense that the nunnery was full of secrets that he could not bring himself to ask her anything more, but chose to act instead. He took a sheet of clean paper. 'Put your palms down on this,' he commanded. 'First the right and then the left.'

She looked as if she would like to refuse but did as he ordered, and they both looked, in horror, at the two neat triangular prints that her blood left on the whiteness of the manuscript and the haze of her bloody palm print around them.

'Brother Peter has to see your hands,' Luca decided. 'You will have to make a statement.'

He expected her to protest; but she did not. She bowed her head in obedience to him.

'Come to my inquiry room tomorrow, first thing,' he said. 'Straight after Prime.'

'Very well,' she said easily. She opened the door and slipped through.

'And what is your name, Sister?' Luca asked, but she was already gone. It was only then that he realised that she would not come to the inquiry room and testify, and that he did not know her name.

~

Luca waited impatiently after Prime, but the nun did not come. He was too irritated with himself to explain to Freize and Brother Peter why he would see no-one else, but sat in the room, the door open, the papers on the table before them.

In the end, he declared that he had to ride out to clear his head, and went to the stables. One of the lay sisters was hauling muck out of the stable yard, and she brought his horse and saddled it for him. It was odd to Luca, who had lived for so long in a world without women, to see all the hard labouring work done by women, all the religious services observed by women, living completely self-sufficiently, in a world without men except for the visiting priest. It added to his sense of unease and displacement. These women lived in a community as if men did not exist, as if God had not created men to be their masters. They were complete to themselves and ruled by a girl. It was against everything he had observed and everything he had been taught and it seemed to him no wonder at all that everything had gone wrong.

As Luca was waiting for his horse to be led out, he saw Freize appear in the archway with his skewbald cob tacked up, and watched him haul himself into the saddle.

'I ride alone,' Luca said sharply.

'You can. I'll ride alone too,' Freize said equably.

'I don't want you with me.'

'I won't be with you.'

'Ride in the other direction then.'

'Just as you say.'

Freize paused, tightened his girth, and went through the gate, bowing with elaborate courtesy to the old porteress who scowled at him, and then he waited outside the gate for Luca to come trotting through.

'I told you, I don't want you riding with me.'

'Which is why I waited,' Freize explained patiently. 'To see what direction you were going in, so that I could make sure I took the opposite one. But of course, there may be wolves, or thieves, highwaymen or brigands, so I don't mind your company for the first hour or so.'

'Just shut up and let me think,' Luca said ungraciously.

'Not a word,' Freize remarked to his horse, who flickered a brown ear at him. 'Silent as the grave.'

He actually managed to keep his silence for several hours as they rode north, at a hard pace away from the abbey, from Castle Lucretili, and the little village that sheltered beneath its walls. They took a broad smooth track with matted grass growing down the middle and Luca put his horse in a canter, hardly seeing the odd farmhouse, the scattering flock of sheep, the carefully tended vines. But then, as it grew hotter towards midday, Luca drew up his horse, suddenly realising that they were some way from the abbey, and said, 'I suppose we should be heading back.'

'Maybe you'd like a drop of small ale and a speck of bread and ham first?' Freize offered invitingly.

'Do you have that?'

'In my pack. Just in case we got to this very point and thought we might like a drop of small ale and a bite to eat.'

Luca grinned. 'Thank you,' he said. 'Thank you for bringing food, and thank you for coming with me.'

Freize nodded smugly, and led the way off the road into a small copse where they would be sheltered from the sun. He dismounted from his cob and slung the reins loosely over the saddle. The horse immediately dropped its head and started to graze the thin grass of the forest floor. Freize spread his cape for Luca to sit, and unpacked a stone jug of small ale, and two loaves of bread. The two men ate in silence, then Freize produced, with a flourish, a half bottle of exquisitely good red wine.

'This is excellent,' Luca observed.

'Best in the house,' Freize answered, draining the very dregs.

Luca rose, brushed off the crumbs, and took up the reins of his horse, which he had looped over a bush.

'Horses could do with watering before we go back,' Freize remarked.

The two young men led the horses back along the track, and then mounted up to head for home. They rode for some time until they heard the noise of a stream, off to their left, deeper in the forest. They broke off from the track and, guided by the noise of running water, first found their way to a broad stream, and then followed it downhill to where it formed a wide deep pool. The bank was muddy and well-trodden, as if many people came here for water, an odd sight in the deserted forest. Luca could see the marks in the mud of the wooden pattens that the nuns wore over their shoes when they were working in the abbey gardens and fields.

Freize slipped, nearly losing his footing, and exclaimed as he saw that he had stepped in a dark green puddle of goose-shit. 'Look at that! Damned bird. I would snare and eat him, I would.'

Luca took both horses' reins and let them drink from the water as Freize bent to wipe his boot with a dock leaf.

'Well, I'll be . . . !'

'What is it?'

Wordlessly, Freize held out the leaf with the dirt on it.

'What?' asked Luca, leaning away from the offering.

'Look closer. People always say that there's money where muck is – and here it is. Look closer, for I think I have made my fortune!'

Luca looked closer. Speckled among the dark green of the goose-shit were tiny grains of sand, shining brightly. 'What is it?'

'It's gold, little lord!' Freize was bubbling with delight. 'See it? Goose feeds on the reeds in the river, the river water is carrying tiny grains of gold washed out of a seam some-where in the mountain, probably nobody knows where. Goose eats it up, passes it out, I find it on my boot. All I need to do now is to find out who owns the lands around the stream, buy it off them for pennies, pan for gold, and I am a lord myself and shall ride a handsome horse and own my own hounds!'

'If the landlord will sell,' Luca cautioned him. 'And I

think we are still on the lands of the Lord of Lucretili. Perhaps he would like to pan for his own gold.'

'I'll buy it from him without telling him,' Freize exulted. 'I'll tell him I want to live by the stream. I'll tell him I have a vocation, like that poor lass, his sister. I'll tell him I have a calling, I want to be a holy hermit and live by the pool and pray all day.'

Luca laughed aloud at the thought of Freize's vocation for solitary prayer but suddenly Freize held up his hand. 'Someone's coming,' he warned. 'Hush, let's get ourselves out of the way.'

'Why should we hide? We're doing no harm.'

'You never know,' Freize whispered. 'And I'd rather not be found by a gold-bearing stream.'

The two of them backed their horses deeper into the forest, off the path, and waited. Luca threw his cape over his horse's head so that it would make no noise, and Freize reached up to his cob's ear and whispered one word to it. The horse bent his head and stood quietly. The two men watched through the trees as half a dozen nuns wearing their dark brown working robes wound their way along the path, their wooden pattens squelching in the mud. Freize gently gripped the nose of his horse so that it did not whinny.

The last two nuns were leading a little donkey, its back piled high with dirty fleeces from the nunnery flock. As Freize and Luca watched through the sheltering bushes, the women pegged the fleeces down in the stream, for the waters to rinse them clean, and then turned the donkey round and went back the way they had come. Obedient to their vows, they worked in silence, but as they led the little donkey away they struck up a psalm and the two young men could hear them singing:

'The Lord is my Shepherd, I'll not want . . .'

'I'll not want,' Freize muttered, as the two emerged from hiding. 'Damn. Damn "I'll not want" indeed! Because I will want. I do want. And I will go on wanting, wanting and dreaming and always disappointed.'

'Why?' Luca asked. 'They're just washing the fleeces. You can still buy your stream and pan for gold.'

'Not them,' Freize said. 'Not them, the cunning little vixens. They're not washing the fleeces. Why come all this way just to wash fleeces, when there are half a dozen streams between here and the abbey? No, they're panning for gold in the old way. They put the fleeces in the stream – see how they've pegged them out all across the stream so the water flows through? The staple of the wool catches the grains of gold, catches even the smallest dust. In a week or so, they'll come back and pull out their harvest: wet fleeces, heavy with gold. They'll take them back to the abbey, dry them, brush out the gold dust and there they are with a fortune on the floor! Little thieves!'

'How much would it be worth?' Luca demanded. 'How much gold would a fleece of wool hold?'

'And why has no-one mentioned this little business of theirs?' Freize demanded. 'I wonder if the Lord of Lucretili knows? It'd be a good joke on him if he put his sister in the nunnery only for her to steal his fortune from under his nose, using the very nuns he gave her to rule.'

Luca looked blankly at Freize. 'What?'

'I was jesting . . .'

'No, it might not be a joke. What if she came here

and found the gold, just like you did, and set the nuns to work. And then thought that she would make out that the nunnery had fallen into sin, so that no-one came to visit any more, so that no-one would trust the word of the nuns . . .'

'Then she wouldn't be caught in her little enterprise and, though she'd still be a Lady Abbess, she could live like a lady once more,' Freize finished. 'Happy all the day long, rolling in gold dust.'

'I'll be damned,' Luca said heavily. He and Freize stood in silence for a long moment, and then Luca turned without another word, mounted his horse and kicked it into a canter. He realised as he rode that he was not just shocked by the massive crime that the whole nunnery was undertaking, but personally offended by the Lady Abbess – as if he thought he could have done anything to help her! As if his promise to help her had meant anything to her! As if she had wanted anything from him but his naïve trust, and his faith in her story. 'Damn!' he said again.

They rode in silence, Freize shaking his head over the loss of his imaginary fortune, Luca raging at being played as a fool. As they drew near to the nunnery, Luca tightened his reins and pulled his horse up until Freize drew level. 'You truly think it is her? Because she struck me as a most unhappy woman, a grieving daughter – she was sincere in her grief for her father, I am sure of that. And yet to face me and lie to me about everything else . . . do you think she is capable of such dishonesty? I can't see it.'

'They might be doing it behind her back,' Freize conceded. 'Though the madness in the nunnery is a good way of keeping strangers away. But I suppose she might be in ignorance of it all. We'd have to know who takes the gold to be sold. That's how you'd know who was taking the fortune. And we'd have to know if it was going on before she got here.'

Luca nodded. 'Say nothing to Brother Peter.'

'The spy,' supplemented Freize cheerfully.

'But tonight we will break into the storeroom and see if we can find any evidence: any drying fleeces, any gold.'

'No need to break in, I have the key.'

'How did you get that?'

'How did you think you got such superb wine after dinner?'

Luca shook his head at his servant, and then said quietly, 'We'll meet at two of the clock.'

The two young men rode on together and, behind them, making no more sound than the trees that sighed in the wind, Ishraq watched them go.

~

Isolde was in her bed, tied like a prisoner to the four posts, her feet strapped at the bottom, her two hands lashed to the two upper posts of the headboard. Ishraq pulled the covers up under her chin and smoothed them flat. 'I hate to see you like this. It is beyond bearing. For your own God's sake tell me that we can leave this place. I cannot tie you to your bed like some madwoman.'

'I know,' Isolde replied, 'but I can't risk walking in my sleep. I can't bear it. I will not have this madness descend on me. Ishraq, I won't walk in the night, scream out in dreams. If I go mad, if I really go mad, you will have to kill me. I cannot bear it.'

Ishraq leaned down and put her brown cheek to the other girl's pale face. 'I never would. I never could. We will fight this, and we will defeat them.'

'What about the Inquirer?'

'He is talking to all of the sisters, he is learning far too much. His report will destroy this abbey, will ruin your good name. Everything they tell him blames us, names you, dates the start of the troubles to the time when we arrived. We have to get hold of him. We have to stop him.'

'Stop him?' she asked.

Ishraq nodded, her face grim. 'We have to stop him, one way or another. We have to do whatever it takes to stop him.'

~

The moon was up, but it was a half moon hidden behind scudding clouds and shedding little light as Luca went quietly across the cobbled yard. He saw a shadowy figure step out of the darkness: Freize. In his hand he had the key ready, oiled to make no sound, and slid it quietly in the lock. The door creaked as Luca pushed it open and both men froze at the sound, but no-one stirred. All the narrow windows that faced over the courtyard were dark, apart from the window of the Lady Abbess's house, where a candle burned, but other than that flickering light, there was no sign that she was awake.

The two young men slipped into the storeroom and closed the door quietly behind them. Freize struck a spark from a flint, blew a flame, lit a tallow candle taken from his pocket, and they looked around.

'Wine is over there.' Freize gestured to a sturdy grille. 'Key's hidden up high on the wall, any fool could find it – practically an invitation. They make their own wine. Small ale over there, home-brewed too. Foods are over there.' He pointed to the sacks of wheat, rye and rice. Smoked hams in their linen sleeves hung above them, and on the cold inner wall were racks of round cheeses.

Luca was looking around; there was no sign of the fleeces. They ducked through an archway to a room at the back. Here there were piles of cloth of all different sorts of quality, all in the unbleached cream colour that the nuns wore. A pile of brown hessian cloth for their working robes was heaped in another corner. Leather for making their own shoes, satchels, and even saddlery, was sorted in tidy piles according to the grade. A rickety wooden ladder led up to the half-floor above.

'Nothing down here,' Freize observed.

'Next we'll search the Lady Abbess's house,' Luca ruled. 'But first, I'll check upstairs.' He took the candle and started up the ladder. 'You wait down here.'

'Not without a light,' pleaded Freize.

'Just stand still.'

Freize watched the wavering flame go upwards and then stood, nervously, in pitch darkness. From above he heard a sudden strangled exclamation. 'What is it?' he hissed into the darkness. 'Are you all right?'

Just then a cloth was flung over his head, blinding him, and as he ducked down he heard the whistle of a heavy blow in the air above him. He flung himself to the ground and rolled sideways, shouting a muffled warning as something thudded against the side of his head. He heard Luca coming quickly down the ladder and then a splintering sound as the ladder was heaved away from the wall. Freize struggled against the pain and the darkness, took a wickedly placed kick in the belly, heard Luca's whooping shout as he fell, and then the terrible thud as he hit the stone floor. Freize, gasping for breath, called out for his master, but there was nothing but silence.

~

Both young men lay still for long frightening moments in the darkness, then Freize sat up, pulled the hood from his head, and patted himself all over. His hand came away wet from his face; he was bleeding from forehead to chin. 'Are you there, Sparrow?' he asked hoarsely.

He was answered by silence. 'Dearest saints, don't say she has killed him,' he moaned. 'Not the little lord, not the changeling boy!'

He got to his hands and knees and crawled his way around, feeling across the floor, bumping into the heaped piles of cloth, as he quartered the room. It took him painful stumbling minutes to be sure: Luca was not in the store-room at all.

'Fool that I am, why did I not lock the door behind me?' Freize muttered remorsefully to himself. He staggered to his feet and felt his way round the wall, past the broken stair, to the opening. There was a little light in the front storeroom, for the door was wide open and the waning moon shone in. As Freize stumbled towards it, he saw the iron grille to the wine and ale cellar stood wide open. He rubbed his bleeding head, leaned for a moment on the trestle table, and went on towards the light. As he reached the doorway, the abbey bell rang for Lauds and he realised he had been unconscious for perhaps half an hour.

He was setting out for the chapel to raise the alarm for Luca when he saw a light at the hospital window. He turned towards it, just as the Lady Almoner came hastily out into the yard. 'Freize! Is that you?'

He stumbled towards her, and saw her recoil as she saw his bloodstained face. 'Saints save us! What has happened to you?'

'Somebody hit me,' Freize said shortly. 'I have lost the little lord! Raise the alarm, he can't be far.'

'I have him! I have him! He is in a stupor,' she said. 'What happened to him?'

'Praise God you have him. Where was he?'

'I found him staggering in the yard just now on my way to Lauds. When I got him into the infirmary he fainted. I was coming to wake you and Brother Peter.'

'Take me to him.'

She turned, and Freize staggered after her into the long low room. There were about ten beds arranged on both sides of the room, poor pallet beds of straw with unbleached sacking thrown over them. Only one was occupied. It was Luca – deathly pale, eyes shut, breathing lightly.

'Dearest saints!' Freize murmured, in an agony of anxiety. 'Little lord, speak to me!'

Slowly Luca opened his hazel eyes. 'Is that you?'

'Praise God, it is. Thank Our Lady that it is, as ever it was.'

'I heard you shout and then I fell down the stairs,' he said, his speech muffled by the bruise on his mouth.

'I heard you come down like a sack of kindling,' confirmed Freize. 'Dearest saints, when I heard you hit the floor! And someone hit me ...'

'I feel like the damned in hell.'

'Me too.'

'Sleep then, we'll talk in the morning.'

Luca closed his eyes. The Lady Almoner approached. 'Let me bathe your wounds.' She was holding a bowl with a white linen cloth, and there was a scent of lavender and crushed leaves of arnica. Freize allowed himself to be persuaded onto another bed.

'Were you attacked in your beds?' she asked him. 'How did this happen?'

'I don't know,' Freize said, too stunned by the blow to make anything up. Besides, she could see the open door to the storeroom as well as he, and she had found Luca in the yard. 'I can't remember anything,' he said lamely and, as she dabbed and exclaimed at the bruises and scratches on his face, he stretched out under the luxury of a woman's care, and fell fast asleep.

~

Freize woke to a very grey cold dawn. Luca was snoring slightly on the opposite bed, a little snuffle followed by a long relaxed whistle. Freize lay listening to the penetrating noise for some time before he opened his eyes, and then he blinked and raised himself up onto his arm. He could not believe what he saw. The bed next to him was now occupied by a nun, laid on her back, her face as white as her hood, which was pushed back exposing her clammy shaven head. Her fingers, enfolded in a position of prayer on her completely still breast, were blue, the fingernails rimmed as if with ink. But worst of all were her eyes, which were horribly open, the pupils dilated black in black. She was completely still. She was clearly – even to Freize's inexperienced frightened stare – dead.

A praying nun knelt at her feet, endlessly murmuring the rosary. Another knelt by her head, muttering the same prayers. The narrow bed was ringed with candles, which illuminated the scene like a tableau of martyrdom. Freize sat up, certain that he was dreaming, hoping that he was dreaming, pinched himself in the hope of waking, and put his feet on the floor, silently cursing the thudding in his head, not daring to stand yet. 'Sister, God bless you. What happened to the poor girl?'

The nun at the head of the bed did not speak until she finished the prayer but looked at him with eyes that were dark with unshed tears. 'She died in her sleep,' she said eventually. 'We don't know why.'

'Who is she?' Freize crossed himself with a sudden superstitious fear that it was one of the nuns who had come to give evidence to their inquiry. 'Bless her soul and keep her.'

'Sister Augusta,' she said, a name he did not know.

He stole a quick glance at the white cold face and recoiled from the blackness of her dead gaze.

'Saint's sake! Why have you not closed her eyes and weighted them?'

'They won't close,' the nun at the foot of the bed said, trembling. 'We have tried and tried. They won't close.'

'They must do! Why would they not?'

She spoke in a low monotone: 'Her eyes are black because she was dreaming of Death again. She was always dreaming of Death. And now He has come for her. Her dark eyes are filled with that last vision, of Him coming for her. That's why they won't close, that's why they are as black as jet. If you look deeply into her terrible black eyes you will see Death himself reflected in them like a mirror. You will see the face of Death looking out at you.'

The first nun let out a little wail, a cold keening noise. 'He will come for us all,' she whispered.

They both crossed themselves and returned to their muttered prayers as Freize shuddered and bowed his head in a prayer for the dead. Gingerly, he got up and, gritting his teeth against his swimming head, walked cautiously around the nuns to the bed where Luca still snored. He shook his shoulder: 'Little lord, wake up.'

'I wish you wouldn't call me that,' said Luca groggily.

'Wake up, wake up. One of the nuns is dead.'

Luca sat up abruptly then held his head and swayed. 'Was she attacked?'

Freize nodded at the praying nuns. 'They say she died in her sleep.'

'Can you see?' Luca whispered.

Freize shook his head. 'She has no head wound, I can't see anything else.'

'What do they say?' Luca's nod indicated the praying nuns who had returned to their devotions. To his surprise, he saw Freize shiver as if a cold wind had touched him.

'They don't make any sense,' Freize said, denying the thought that Death was coming for them all.

Just then, the door opened and the Lady Almoner came

in, leading four lay sisters. The nuns at the head and foot of the corpse rose up and stood aside as the women in brown robes carefully lifted the lifeless body onto a rough stretcher, and took it through an arched stone doorway into the neighbouring room.

'That is our mortuary. They will dress her and prepare her for burial tomorrow,' the Lady Almoner said in reply to Luca's questioning glance. She was white with strain and fatigue. The nuns took their candles and went to keep their vigil in the cold outer room. Luca saw their shadows jump huge on the stone walls, big as black monsters, as they set down their lights and knelt to pray, then someone closed the door on them.

'What happened to her?' he asked quietly.

'She died in her sleep,' the Lady Almoner said. 'God alone knows what is happening here. When they went to wake her early, for she was to serve at Prime, she was gone. She was cold and stiff and her eyes were fixed open. Who knows what she saw or dreamed, or what came to torment her?' Quickly she crossed herself and put her hand to the small gold cross that hung from a gold chain on her belt.

She came closer to Luca and looked into his eyes. 'And you? Are you dizzy? Or faint?'

'I'll live,' he said wryly.

'I'm faint,' Freize volunteered hopefully.

'I'll get you some small ale,' she said, and poured some from a pitcher. She handed them both a cup. 'Did you see the assassin?'

'Assassin.' Freize repeated the word, strange to him, which usually meant a hired Arab killer.

'Whoever it was who tried to kill you,' she amended.

'And anyway, what were you doing in the storeroom?'

'I was searching for something,' Luca said evasively. 'Will you take me there now?'

'We should wait for sunrise,' she replied.

'You have the keys?'

'I don't know . . .'

'Then Freize will let us in with his key.'

The look she gave Freize was very cold. 'You have a key to my storeroom?'

Freize nodded, his face a picture of guilt. 'Just for essential supplies. So as not to be a nuisance.'

'I don't think you are well enough to walk over there,' she said to Luca.

'Yes I am,' he said. 'We have to go.'

'The stair is broken.'

'Then we'll get a ladder.'

She realised that he would insist. 'I'm afraid. To be honest, I am afraid to go.'

'I understand,' Luca said with a quick smile. 'Of course you are. Terrible things happened last night. But you have to be brave. You will be with us and we won't be caught like fools again. Take courage, come on.'

'Can we not go after sunrise, when it is fully light?'

'No,' he said gently. 'It has to be now.'

She bit her lip. 'Very well,' she said. 'Very well.'

She lifted a torch from the sconce in the wall and led the way across the courtyard to the storerooms. Someone had closed the door and she opened it, and stood back to let them go in. The wooden ladder was still on the floor, where it had been thrown down. Freize lifted it back into place, and shook it to make sure that it was firm. 'This time, I'll lock the door behind us,' he remarked, and turned the key and locked them in.

'Oh, she can get through a locked door,' the Lady Almoner said with a frightened little laugh. 'I think she can go through walls. I think she can go anywhere she wishes.'

'Who can?' Luca demanded.

She shrugged. 'Go on up, I will tell you everything. I will keep no more secrets. A nun has died under this roof, in our care. The time has come for you to know everything that has been done here. And you must stop it. You must stop her. I have been driven far beyond defending this nunnery, far beyond defending this Lady Abbess. I will tell you everything now. But first you shall see what she has done.'

Luca went carefully up the steps, the Lady Almoner following, holding her robe out of the way as she climbed. Freize stood at the bottom with the torch, lighting their way.

It was dark in the loft, but the Lady Almoner crossed to the far wall and threw open the half-door, for the dawn light. The beams from the rising sun poured into the loft through the opening and shone on glistening fleeces of gold, hanging up to dry, as the gold dust sifted through the wool to fall onto the linen sheets spread on the floor below. The room was like a treasure chamber, with gold dust underfoot and golden fleeces hanging like priceless washing on the bowed lines.

'Good God,' Luca whispered. 'It is so. The gold ...' He looked around as if he could not believe what he was seeing. 'So much! So bright!'

She sighed. 'It is. Have you seen enough?'

He bent and took a pinch of the dust. Here and there

were little nuggets of gold, like grit. 'How much? How much is this worth?'

'She harvests a couple of fleeces a month,' the Lady Almoner said. 'If she is allowed to continue it will add up to a fortune.'

'How long has this been going on?'

She closed the half-door to shut out the sunlight, and barred it. 'Ever since the Lady Abbess came. She knows the land, being brought up here; she knows it better than her brother, for he was sent away for his education while she stayed at home with their father. The stream belongs to our abbey, it is in our woods. Her slave, being a Moor, knew how her people pan for gold and she taught the sisters to soak the fleeces in the stream, telling them it would clean the wool. They have no idea what they are doing, she plays them for fools – she told them that the stream has special purifying qualities for the wool, and they know no better. They peg out the fleeces in the stream and bring them back here to dry; they never see them drying out and the gold pattering down on the linen sheets. The slave comes in secretly to sweep up the gold dust, takes it to sell, and the sisters come in when the gold is gone and the loft is empty, and take the fleeces away to card and spin.' She laughed bitterly. 'Sometimes they remark how soft the wool is. They are fools for her. She has made fools of us all.'

'The slave brings the money to you? For the abbey?'

The Lady Almoner turned to go down the ladder. 'What do you think? Does this look like an abbey that is rich in its own gold? Have you seen my infirmary? Have you seen any costly medicines? You have seen my storeroom, I know. Do we seem wealthy to you?'

'Where does she sell it? How does she sell the gold?'

The Lady Almoner shrugged. 'I don't know. Rome, I suppose. I know nothing about it. She sends the slave in secret.'

Luca hesitated, briefly, as if there were something more he would ask, but then he turned and went down after her, ignoring the bruise on his shoulder and the pain in his neck. 'You are saying that the Lady Abbess uses the nuns to pan for gold and keeps the money for herself?'

She nodded. 'You have seen it for yourself now. And I think she hopes to close the nunnery altogether. I believe that she plans to open a gold mine here, on our fields. I think she is deliberately leading the nunnery into disgrace so that you recommend it should be closed down. When it is abolished as a nunnery she will say she is free from her father's will. She will renounce her vows, she will claim it as her inheritance from her father, she will continue to live here, and she and the slave will be left here alone.'

'Why didn't you tell me this before?' Luca demanded. 'When I opened the inquiry? Why keep this back?'

'Because this place is my life,' she said fiercely. 'It has been a beacon on the hill, a refuge for women and a place to serve God. I hoped that the Lady Abbess would learn to live here in peace. I thought God would call her, that her vocation would grow. Then I hoped that she would be satisfied with making a fortune here. I thought she might be an evil woman, but that we might contain her. But since a nun has died – in our care—' She choked on a sob. 'Sister Augusta, one of the most innocent and simple women who has been here for years—' She broke off.

'Well, now it is all over,' she said with dignity. 'I can't hide what she is doing. She is using this place of God to hide her fortune-hunting, and I believe that her slave is practising witchcraft on the nuns. They dream, they sleep-walk, they show strange signs, and now one has died in her sleep. Before God, I believe that the Lady Abbess and her slave are driving us all mad so that they can get at the gold.'

Her hand sought the cross at her waist and Luca saw her hold it tightly, as if it were a talisman.

'I understand,' he said, as calmly as he could, though his own throat was dry with superstitious fear. 'I have been sent here to end these heresies, these sins. I am authorised by the Pope himself to inquire and judge. There is nothing that I will not see with my own eyes. There is nothing I will not question. Later this morning I will speak to the Lady Abbess again and, if she cannot explain herself, I will see that she is dismissed from her post.'

'Sent away from here?'

He nodded.

'And the gold? You will let the abbey keep the gold so that we can feed the poor and establish a library? Be a beacon on the hill for the benighted?'

'Yes,' he said. 'The abbey should have its fortune.'

He saw her face light up with joy. 'Nothing matters more than the abbey,' she assured him. 'You will let my sisters stay here and live their former lives, their holy lives? You will put them under the discipline of a good woman, a new Lady Abbess who can command them and guide them?'

'I will put it under the charge of the Dominican broth-ers,' Luca decided. 'And they will harvest the gold from the stream and endow the abbey. This is no longer a house in the service of God, as it has been suborned. I will put it under the control of men, there will be no Lady Abbess. The gold shall be restored to God, the abbey to the brothers.'

She gave a shuddering sigh and hid her face in her hands. Luca stretched his hand towards her to comfort her and only a warning glance from Freize reminded him that he was still in holy orders and he should not touch her.

'What will you do?' Luca asked quietly.

'I don't know. My whole life has been here. I will serve as Lady Almoner until we come under the command of the Brothers. They will need me for the first months, no-one but me knows how this place is run. Then perhaps I will ask if I may go to another order. I would like an order that was more enclosed, more at peace. These have been terrible days. I want to go to an order where the vows are kept more strictly.'

'Poverty?' Freize asked at random. 'You want to be poor?'

She nodded. 'An order that respects the commands, an order with more simplicity. Knowing that we were storing a fortune of gold in our own loft . . . not knowing what the Lady Abbess was doing or what she intended, fearing she was serving the Devil himself . . . it has been heavy on my conscience.'

The bell tolled the call to chapel, echoing in the morning air. 'Prime,' she said. 'I have to go to church. The sisters need to see me there.'

'We'll come too,' Luca said.

They closed the door to the storeroom and locked it behind them. While Luca watched, she turned to Freize and held out her hand for his key. Luca smiled at her simple dignity as she stood still while Freize patted his pockets in a pantomime of searching, and then, reluctantly, handed over the key. 'Thank you,' she said. 'If you want anything from the abbey stores you may come to me.'

Freize gave a funny little mock bow, as if to recognise her authority. She turned to Luca. 'I could be the new Lady Abbess,' she said quietly. 'You could recommend me for the post. The abbey would be safe in my keeping.'

Before he could answer she looked beyond him at the windows of the hospital, suddenly paused, and put her hand on Luca's sleeve. At once he froze, acutely aware of her touch. Freize behind him stopped still. She held her finger to her lips for silence and then slowly pointed ahead. She was indicating the mortuary beside the hospital, where a little light gleamed from the slatted shutters, and they could see someone moving.

'What is it?' Luca whispered. 'Who is in there?'

'The lights should be shielded, and the nuns should be still and silent in their vigil,' she breathed. 'But someone is moving in there.'

'The sisters, washing her?' Luca asked.

'They should have finished their work.'

Quietly, the three of them moved across the yard and looked in the open door to the hospital. The door leading from the hospital ward through to the mortuary was firmly closed. The Lady Almoner stepped back, as if she were too afraid to go further.

'Is there another way in?'

'They take the pauper coffins out through a back door, to the stables,' she whispered. 'That door may be unbolted.'

Quickly, they crossed the stable yard to the double door to the mortuary, big enough for a cart and a horse, barred by a thick beam of wood. The two young men silently lifted the beam from its sockets and the door stood closed, held shut only by its own weight. Freize lifted a pitchfork from the nearby wall, and Luca bent and took his dagger from the scabbard in his boot.

'When I give the word, open it quickly,' he said to the Lady Almoner. She nodded, her face as white as her veil.

'Now!'

The Lady Almoner flung the door open, the two young men rushed into the room, weapons at the ready – then fell back in horror.

Before them was a nightmare scene, like a butcher's shop, with the butcher and his lad working over a fresh carcass. But it was worse by far than that. It was not a butcher, and it was no animal on the slab. The Lady Abbess was in a brown working gown, her head tied in a scarf, and Ishraq was in her usual black robe covered with a white apron. The two girls had their sleeves rolled up, and were blood-stained to the elbows, standing over the dead body of Sister Augusta, Ishraq wielding a bloodied knife in her hand, disembowelling the dead girl. The nuns keeping vigil were nowhere to be seen. As the men burst in, the two young women looked up and froze, the knife poised above the open belly of the dead nun, blood on their aprons, blood on the bed, blood on their hands.

'Step back,' Luca ordered, his voice ice-cold with shock. He pointed his dagger at Ishraq, who looked to the Lady Abbess for her command. Freize raised his pitchfork as if he would spear her on the tines.

'Step back from that body, I command you,' Luca said. 'Leave this – whatever it is that you are doing.' He could not bear to look, he could not find the words to name it. 'Leave it, and step against the wall.'

He heard the Lady Almoner come in behind him and her gasp of horror at the butchery before them. 'Merciful God!' She staggered and he heard her lean against the wall, then retch.

'Get a rope,' Freize said, without turning his head to her. 'Get two ropes. And fetch Brother Peter.'

She choked back her nausea. 'What in the name of God are you doing? Lady Abbess, answer me! What are you doing to her?'

'Go,' said Luca. 'Go at once.'

They heard her running feet cross the cobbles of the stable yard as the Lady Abbess raised her eyes to Luca. 'I can explain this,' she said.

He nodded, gripping the dagger. Clearly, nothing could explain this scene: her sleeves rolled to her elbows, her hands stained red with the blood of a dead nun.

'I believe that this woman has been poisoned,' she said. 'My friend is a physician—'

'Can't be,' Freize said quietly.

'She is,' the Lady Abbess insisted. 'We ... we decided to cut open her belly and see what she had been fed.'

'They were eating her.' The Lady Almoner's voice trembled from the doorway. She came back into the room, Brother Peter white-faced behind her. 'They are witches, as I thought and the two of them were eating her in a Satanic Mass. They were eating the body of Sister Augusta. Look at the blood on their hands. They were drinking her blood.

113

The Lady Abbess has gone over to Satan and she and her heretic slave are holding a Devil's Mass on this, our sanctified ground.'

Luca shuddered and crossed himself. Brother Peter stepped towards the slave with a rope held out before him. 'Put down the knife and put out your hands,' he said. 'Give yourself up. In the name of God, I command you, demon or woman or fallen angel, to surrender.'

Holding Freize's gaze, Ishraq put down the knife on the bed beside the dead nun, then suddenly darted for the doorway that led into the empty hospital. She flung it open and was through it, followed in a moment by the Lady Abbess. As Luca and Freize raced after the two young women, she led the way, running across the yard to the main gate.

Luca bellowed to the porteress, 'Bar the gate! Stop thief!' and flung himself on the Lady Abbess as she sprinted ahead of him, bringing her down to the ground in a heavy tackle and knocking the air out of her. As they went down, her veil fell from her head and a tumble of blonde hair swept over his face with the haunting scent of rosewater.

The Moorish girl was half way up the outer gate now, springing from hinge to beam like a lithe animal, as Freize grabbed at her bare feet and missed, and then leaped up and snatched a handful of her robe and tore her off the gate, bringing her tumbling down to fall backwards on the stone cobbles with a cry of pain.

Freize gripped her arms to her sides so tightly that she could barely breathe, while Brother Peter tied her hands behind her back, roped her feet together, and then turned to the Lady Abbess, still pinned down by Luca. As Luca dragged her to her feet, holding her wrists, her thick golden-blonde hair tumbled down over her shoulders, hiding her face.

'Shame!' the Lady Almoner exclaimed. 'Her hair!'

Luca could not drag his eyes from this girl who had veiled her face from him, and hooded her hair so that he should never know what she looked like. In the golden light of the rising sun he stared at her, seeing her for the first time, her dark blue eyes under brown up-swinging brows, a straight perfect nose, and a warm tempting mouth. Then Brother Peter came towards them and he saw her blood-stained hands as the clerk bound them with rope, and Luca realised that she was a thing of horror, a beautiful thing of horror, the worst thing between heaven and hell: a fallen angel, a satan.

'The lay sisters will be coming into the yards to work, the nuns will be coming from church, we must tidy up,' the Lady Almoner ruled. 'They cannot see this. It will distress them beyond anything . . . it will break their hearts. I must shield them from this evil. They cannot see Sister Augusta so abused. They cannot see these . . . these . . .' She could not find the words for the Lady Abbess and her slave. 'These devils. These pilgrims from hell.'

'Do you have a secure room for them?' Brother Peter asked. 'They will have to stand trial. We'll have to send for Lord Lucretili. He is the lord of these lands. This is outside our jurisdiction now. This is a criminal matter, this is a hanging offence, a burning offence; he will have to judge.'

'The cellar of the gatehouse,' the Lady Almoner replied promptly. 'The only way in or out is a hatch in the floor.'

Freize had the Moorish girl slung like a sack over his shoulder. Brother Peter took the tied hands of the Lady

Abbess and led her to the gatehouse. Luca was left alone with the Lady Almoner.

'What will you do with the body?'

'I will ask the village midwives to put her into her coffin. Poor child, I cannot let her sisters see her. And I will send for the priest to bless what is left of her poor body. She can lie in the church for now and then I will ask Lord Lucretili if she can lie in his chapel. As soon as they have cleaned her up and dressed her again she shall go to sanctified ground away from here.'

She shuddered and swayed, almost as if she might faint. Luca put his hand around her waist to support her and she leaned towards him for a moment, resting her head on his shoulder.

'You were very brave,' he said to her. 'This has been a terrible ordeal.'

She looked up at him, and then, as if she had suddenly realised that his arm was around her, and that she was leaning against him, he felt her heart flutter like a captured bird and she stepped away. 'Forgive me,' she said. 'I am not allowed . . .'

'I know,' he said quickly. 'It is for you to forgive me. I should not have touched you.'

'It has been so terrible . . .' There was a tremble in her voice that she could not conceal.

Luca put his hands behind his back so that he would not reach for her again. 'You must rest,' he said helplessly. 'This has been too much for any woman.'

'I can't rest,' she said brokenly. 'I must put things to rights here. I cannot let my sisters see this terrible sight, or find out what has been done here. I will fetch the women to clean up. I must make everything right again. I will command them, I will lead them, out of error into the ways of righteousness; out of darkness into light.' She smoothed her robe and shook it out. Luca heard the seductive whisper of her silk shift, and then she turned away from him to go to her work.

At the door of the hospital she paused and glanced back. She saw that he was looking after her. 'Thank you,' she said, with a tiny smile. 'No man has ever held me, not in all my life before. I am glad to know a man's kindness. I will live here all my life, I will live here inside this order, perhaps as the Lady Abbess, and yet I will always remember you and your tenderness.'

He almost stepped towards her as she held his gaze for just a moment and then was gone.

Freize and Brother Peter joined Luca in the cobbled yard. 'Are they secure?' Luca asked.

'Regular gaol they have there,' Freize remarked. 'There were chains fixed on the wall, handcuffs, manacles. He insisted that we put everything on them, and I hammered them on as if they were both slaves.'

'Just till the Lord Lucretili gets here,' Brother Peter replied defensively. 'And if we had left them in ropes and they had got themselves free, what would we have done?'

'Caught them again when we opened the hatch?' Freize suggested. To Luca he said, 'They're in a round cave, no way in or out except a hatch in the roof and they can't reach that until it is opened and a wooden ladder lowered in. They aren't even stone walls, the cellar is dug down into solid rock. They're secure as a pair of mice in a trap. But he had to put them in irons as if they were pirates.'

Luca looked at his new clerk and saw that the man was deeply afraid of the mystery and the terrible nature of the two women. 'You were right to be cautious,' he said, reassuringly. 'We don't know what powers they have.'

'Good God, when I saw them with blood up to the elbows, and they looked at us, their faces as innocent as scholars at a desk! What were they doing? What Satan's work were they doing? Was it a Mass? Were they really eating her flesh and drinking her blood in a Satanic Mass?'

'I don't know,' Luca said. He put his hand to his head. 'I can't think ...'

'Now look at you!' Freize exclaimed. 'You should still be in bed, and the Lord knows I feel badly myself. I'll take you back to the hospital and you can rest.'

Luca recoiled. 'Not there,' he said. 'I'm not going back in there. Take me to my room and I will sleep till Lord Lucretili gets here. Wake me as soon as he comes.'

~

In the cellar, the two young women were shrouded in darkness as if they were already in their grave. It was like being buried alive. They blinked and strained their eyes but they were blind.

'I can't see you,' Isolde said, her voice catching on a sob.

'I can see you.' The reply came steadily out of the pitch blackness. 'And anyway, I always know when you are near.'

'We have to get word to the Inquirer. We have to find some way to speak with him.'

'I know.'

'They will be fetching my brother. He will put us on trial.'

There was a silence from Ishraq.

'Ishraq, I should be certain that my brother will hear me, that he will believe what I say, that he will free me – but more and more I think that he has betrayed me. He encouraged the prince to come to my room, he left me no choice but to come here as Lady Abbess. What if he has been trying to drive me away from my home all along? What if he has been trying to destroy me?'

'I think so,' the other girl said steadily. 'I do think so.'

There was a silence while Isolde absorbed the thought. 'How could he be so false? How could he be so wicked?'

The chains clinked as Ishraq shrugged.

'What shall we do?' Isolde asked hopelessly.

'Hush.'

'Hush? Why? What are you doing?'

'I am wishing . . .'

'Ishraq – we need a plan, wishing won't save us.'

'Let me wish. This is deep wishing. And it might save us.'

～

Luca had thought he would toss and turn with the pain in his neck and shoulder, but as soon as his boots were off and his head was on the pillow he slipped into a deep sleep. Almost at once he started to dream.

He dreamed that he was running after the Lady Abbess again, and she was outpacing him easily. The ground beneath his feet changed from the cobbles of the yard to the floor of the forest, and all the leaves were crisp like autumn, and then he saw they had been dipped in gold and he was running through a forest of gold. Still she kept ahead of him, weaving in and out of golden tree trunks, passing bushes crusted with gold, until he managed a sudden burst of speed, far faster than before, and he leaped towards her, like a mountain lion will leap on a deer, and caught her around the waist to bring her down. But as she fell, she turned in his arms and he saw her smiling as if with desire, as if she had all along wanted him to catch her, to hold her, to lie foot to foot, leg against leg, his hard young body against her lithe slimness, looking into her eyes, their faces close enough to kiss. Her thick mane of blonde hair swirled around him and he smelt the heady scent of rosewater again. Her eyes were dark, so dark; he had thought they were blue so he looked again, but the blue of her eyes was only a tiny rim around the darkness of the pupil. Her eyes were so dilated they were not blue but black. In his head he heard the words 'beautiful lady' and he thought, 'Yes, she is a beautiful lady.'

'*Bella donna.*' He heard the words in Latin and it was the voice of the slave to the Lady Abbess with her odd foreign accent as she repeated, with a strange urgency: '*Bella donna! Luca, listen! Bella donna!*'

The door to the guest room opened, as Luca lurched out of his dream and held his aching head.

'Only me,' Freize said, slopping warmed small ale out of a jug as he banged into the room with a tray of bread, meat, cheese and a mug.

'Saints, Freize, I am glad that you waked me. I have had the strangest of dreams.'

'Me too,' Freize said. 'All night long I dreamed that I was gathering berries in the hedgerow, like a gipsy.'

'I dreamed of a beautiful woman, and the words *bella donna.*'

At once Freize burst into song:
'Bella donna, give me your love –
Bella donna, bright stars above ...'
'What?' Luca sat himself at the table and let his servant put the food before him.

'It's a song, a popular song. Did you never hear it in the monastery?'

'We only ever sang hymns and psalms in the church,' Luca reminded him. 'Not love songs in the kitchen like you.'

'Anyway, everyone was singing it last summer. Bella donna: beautiful lady.'

Luca cut himself a slice of meat from the joint, chewed thoughtfully, and drank three deep gulps of small ale. 'There's another meaning of the words *bella donna*,' he said. 'It doesn't just mean beautiful lady. It's a plant, a hedgerow plant.'

Freize slapped his head. 'It's the plant in my dream! I dreamed I was in the hedgerow, looking for berries, black berries; but though I wanted blackberries or sloe berries or even elderberries, all I could find was deadly nightshade ... the black berries of deadly nightshade.'

Luca got to his feet, taking a hunk of the bread in his hand. 'It's a poison,' he said. 'The Lady Abbess said that they believed the nun was poisoned. She said they were cutting her open to see what she had eaten, what she had in her belly.'

'It's a drug,' Freize said. 'They use it in the torture rooms, to make people speak out, to drive them mad. It gives the wildest dreams, it could make—' He broke off. 'A woman go mad. It could make a whole nunnery of women go mad,' Luca finished for him. 'It could make them have visions, and sleepwalk – it could make them dream and imagine things. And, if one was given too much . . . it would kill her.'

Without another word the two young men went to the guesthouse door and walked quickly to the hospital. In the centre of the entrance yard the lay sisters were making two massive piles of wood, as if they were preparing for a bonfire. Freize paused there, but Luca went past them without a second glance, completely focused on the hospital where he could see through the open windows, the nursing nuns moving about setting things to rights. Luca went through the open doors, and looked around him in surprise.

It was all as clean and as tidy as if there had never been anything wrong. The door to the mortuary was open and the body of the dead nun was gone, the candles and censers taken away. Half a dozen beds were made ready with clean plain sheets, a cross hung centrally on the lime washed walls. As Luca stood there, baffled, a nun came in with a jug of water in her hand from the pump outside, poured it into a bowl and went down on her knees to scrub the floor.

'Where is the body of the sister who died?' Luca asked. His voice sounded too loud in the empty silent room. The nun sat back on her heels and answered him. 'She is lying in the chapel. The Lady Almoner closed the coffin herself, nailed it down and ordered a vigil to be kept in the chapel. Shall I take you to pray?'

He nodded. There was something uncanny about the complete restoration of the room. He could hardly believe that he had burst through that door, chased the Lady Abbess and her slave, knocked her to the ground and sent them chained into a windowless cellar; that he had seen them, bloodstained to their elbows, hacking into the body of the dead nun.

'The Lady Almoner said that she is to lie on sacred ground in the Lucretili chapel,' the nun remarked, leading the way out of the hospital. 'Both for her vigil and her burial. The Lord Lucretili is to bring a wagon for the coffin and take her to lie for a night in the castle chapel. Then she'll be buried in our graveyard. God bless her soul.'

As they went past the piles of wood, Freize fell into step beside Luca. 'Pyres,' he said out of the corner of his mouth. 'Two pyres for two witches. Lord Lucretili is on his way to sit in judgement, but it looks like they have already decided what the verdict will be and are preparing for the sentence already. These are the stakes and firewood for burning the witches.'

Luca halted, in shock. 'No!'

Freize nodded, his face grim. 'Why not? We saw ourselves what they were doing. There's no doubt they were engaged in witchcraft, a Satanic Mass, or cutting up the body. Either way it's a crime punishable by death. But I will say that your Lady Almoner doesn't waste much time in preparation. Here she is with two bonfires ready before the trial has even started.'

The waiting nun tapped her foot. Luca turned back to her. 'What are these wood piles for?'

'I think we are selling the firewood,' she said. 'The Lady Almoner ordered the lay sisters to make two piles like this. May I show you to the chapel now? I have to get back to the hospital and wash the floor.'

'Yes, I am sorry to have delayed you.'

123

Luca and Freize followed her past the refectory, through the cloisters to the chapel. As soon as the nun pushed open the heavy wooden door they could hear the low musical chanting of nuns keeping vigil over the body. Blinking, as their eyes were blinded by the darkness, they went slowly up the aisle until they could see that the space before the altar was covered with a snowy white cloth, and on the cloth lay a newly made simple wooden coffin with the lid nailed firmly shut.

Luca grimaced at the sight. 'We have to see the body,' he whispered. 'It's the only way we can know if she was poisoned.'

'Rather you than me,' Freize said bluntly. 'I wouldn't want to tell the Lady Almoner that I'm opening a sanctified coffin because I had a funny dream.'

'We have to know.'

'She won't want anyone seeing the body,' Freize whispered to Luca. 'She was horribly cut up. And if those witches ate her flesh, then the poor girl will bleed when she is resurrected, God help her. The Lady Almoner won't want the nuns to know that.'

'We'll have to get permission from the priest,' Luca decided. 'We'd better ask him, not the Lady Almoner – we'll give him a request in writing. Peter can write it.'

They stepped back and watched the priest. He was swinging a heavy silver censer leaving a misty layer of incense smoke all around the coffin. When the air was chokingly thick with the heavy perfume, he handed it to one of the nuns and then took the holy water from another and doused the coffin. Then he went to the altar and, turning his back on them all, he lifted his hands in prayer for their departed sister.

The two men bowed to the altar, crossed themselves, and went quietly out of the church. At once they could hear a commotion from the stable yard, the sound of many horses arriving, and the great gates being thrown open.

'Lord Lucretili,' Luca guessed, and strode back to the yard.

The lord, and patron of the abbey, was mounted on a big black warhorse, which pawed the ground, its iron horseshoes throwing sparks from the cobbles. As Luca watched the lord threw his red leather reins to his pageboy and jumped easily from the saddle. The Lady Almoner went up to him, curtseyed, and then stood quietly, her hands hidden inside her long sleeves, her head bowed, her hood modestly shielding her face.

Following Lord Lucretili into the courtyard came half a dozen men wearing the lord's livery of an olive bough overlaid with a sword, signifying the peaceful descendant of a crusader knight. Three or four grave-looking clerks came in on horseback, then the Lord Abbot of Lucretili with his own retinue of priests.

As the men dismounted, Luca stepped forwards.

'You must be Luca Vero. I am glad you are here,' Lord Lucretili said pleasantly. 'I am Giorgio, Lord Lucretili. This is the Lord Abbot. He will sit in judgement with me. I understand you are in the middle of your investigation here?'

'I am,' Luca said. 'Forgive me, but I have to go to the visitors' house. I am looking for my clerk.'

The Lord Lucretili intervened. 'Fetch the Inquirer's clerk,' he said to his pageboy, who set off to the visitors' house at a run. The lord turned back to Luca. 'They tell me that it was you who arrested the Lady Abbess, and her slave?'

'His own sister,' Freize breathed from behind. 'Doesn't seem very upset.'

'Myself, my clerk Brother Peter, and my servant Freize, together with the Lady Almoner,' Luca confirmed. 'Brother Peter and my servant put the two women in the cellar below the gatehouse.'

'We'll hold our trial in the gatehouse,' Lord Lucretili decided. 'That way they can be brought up the ladder, and we'll keep it all out of the way of the nunnery.'

'I would prefer that,' the Lady Almoner said. 'The fewer people who see them, and know of this, the better.'

The lord nodded. 'It shames us all,' he said. 'God alone knows what my father would have made of it. So let's get it over and done with.'

Two horses with black trappings pulled a cart into the yard, and stood waiting. 'For the coffin,' the lord explained to Luca. To the Lady Almoner he said: 'You'll see it's loaded up and my men will take it to my chapel?'

The Lady Almoner nodded, then turned from the men and led the way to the gatehouse room, where she watched the clerks set a long table and chairs for the Lord Lucretili, the Lord Abbot, Luca and Brother Peter. The lord's squire brought in the crusader broadsword and set it in a stone so it stood upright in the centre of the room.

'What's that?' Luca asked.

'My sister will recognise it at once,' the lord said. 'It's a crusader sword. My father swapped his sword with that of his dearest friend. They engraved a sentence of great power on their blades and bolted the sword in the scabbard. My father would have the sword before him when he was going to pass a death sentence. She knows that.'

'You can bring yourself to do this?' Luca asked curiously. 'To your sister?'

'It is my duty,' the lord replied.

Luca nodded and drew him to one side. 'There's something else,' he said. 'I think we need to have the coffin opened before Sister Augusta is buried,' he said quietly. 'I am sorry to say that I suspect the sister was poisoned.'

'Poisoned?'

Luca nodded.

The lord shook his head in shock. 'God save her soul and forgive my sister her sins. But anyway, we can't open the coffin here. The nuns would be far too distressed. It would cause a riot. Come to my castle this evening and we'll do it privately at my chapel. In the meantime, we'll question the Lady Abbess and her slave.'

'They won't answer,' Luca said certainly. 'The slave swore she was dumb in three languages when I questioned her before.'

The lord laughed shortly. 'I think they can be made to answer. You are an Inquirer for the Church, you have the right to use the rack, the press, you can bleed them. They are only young women, vain and frail as all women are. You will see that they will answer your questions rather than have their joints pulled from the sockets. They will speak rather than have boulders placed on their chests. I can promise you that my sister will say anything rather than have leeches on her face.'

Luca went white. 'That's not how I make an inquiry. I have never . . .' he started. 'I would never . . .'

The older man put a gentle hand on his shoulder. 'I will do it for you,' he said. 'You shall wrestle with them for their souls until their evil pride has been broken and they are crying to confess. I will prepare them. I have seen it done, it is easily done. You can trust me to make them ready for their confession.'

'I could not allow . . .' Luca choked.

'The room is ready for your lordship.' The Lady Almoner came out from the gatehouse and stood aside as the lord went in without another word. He seated himself behind the table where the great chair, like a throne, was placed ready for him, the Lord Abbot to his left. Luca was on his right, with a clerk at one end of the table and Brother Peter at the other. When everyone was seated, the lord ordered the door to the yard closed, and Luca saw Freize's anxious face peering in, as Lord Lucretili said, 'My Lord Abbot, will you bless the work that we are doing today?'

The abbot half-closed his eyes and folded his hands over his curved stomach. 'Heavenly Father, bless the work that is done here today. May this abbey be purified and cleansed of sin and returned to the discipline of God and man. May these women understand their sins and cleanse their hearts with penitence, and may we, their judges, be just and right-eous in our wrath. May we offer you a willing brand for the burning, Lord, always remembering that vengeance is not ours; but only yours. Amen.'

'Amen,' Lord Lucretili confirmed. He gestured to the two priests who were standing guard at the outer door. 'Get them up.'

Brother Peter rose to his feet. 'Freize has the key to the chains,' he said. He opened the door to get the ring of keys from Freize, who was hovering on the threshold. The men inside the courtroom could see the stable yard filled with curious faces. Brother Peter closed the door on the crowd outside, stepped forwards and opened the trap-door set in the wooden floorboards. Everyone went silent as Brother Peter looked down into the dark cellar. Leaning against the wall of the gatehouse room was a rough wooden ladder. One of the priests lifted it and lowered it into the darkness of the hole. Everyone hesitated. There was something very forbidding about the deep blackness below, almost as if it were a well, and the women far below had been drowned in the inky waters. Brother Peter handed the keys to Luca, and everyone looked at him. Clearly they were all expecting him to go down into the darkness and fetch the women up.

Luca found that he was chilled, perhaps by a blast of cold air from the windowless deep room below. He thought of the two young women down there, chained to the damp walls, waiting for judgement, their eyes wide and glassy in the darkness. He remembered the black glazed look of the dead nun and thought that perhaps the Lady Abbess and her Moorish slave would be drugged into hallucinations too. At the thought of their dark eyes, shining in the darkness like waiting rats, he got to his feet, determined to delay. 'I'll get a torch,' he said and went out into the entrance yard.

Outside, in the clean air, he sent one of the lord's servants running for a light. The man returned with one of the sconces from the refectory, burning brightly. Luca took it in his hand and went back into the gatehouse, feeling as if he were about to go deep into an ancient cave to face a monster.

He held the torch up high as he stepped on the first rung

of the ladder. He had to go backwards, and he could not help looking over his shoulder and down between his feet, trying to see what was there waiting for him in the darkness.

'Take care!' Brother Peter said, his voice sharp with warning.

'What of?' Luca asked impatiently, hiding his own fear. 'Are they not chained?' Two more rungs of the ladder and he could see the walls were black and shiny with damp. The women would be chilled, weighted with iron fetters, down here in the darkness. Two steps more and he could see a little pool of light at the foot of the ladder and his own leaping shadow on the wall and the shadow of the ladder like a black hatched line going downwards into nothingness. He was at the bottom rung now. He kept one hand on the rough wood for safety, as he turned and looked around.

Nothing.

There was nothing there.

There was nobody there.

He swung the pool of light ahead of him; the stone floor was empty of anything, and the dark wall just six paces away from him on all sides was blank stone, black stone. The cellar was empty. They were not there.

Luca exclaimed and held the torch higher, looking all around. For a moment he had a terror of them making a sudden rush at him out of the darkness, the two women freed and dashing at him like dark devils in hell; but there was no-one there. His eye caught a glint of metal on the floor.

'What is it?' Brother Peter peered down from the floor above. 'What's the matter?'

Luca raised the torch high, so that the beams of light

raked the darkness of the circular room all around him. Now, he could see the handcuffs and leg-cuffs lying on the ground, still safely locked, still firmly chained to the wall, intact and undamaged. But of the Lady Abbess and the Moorish girl there was no sign at all.

'Witchcraft!' Lord Lucretili hissed, his face as white as a sheet, looking down at Luca from the floor above. 'God save us from them.' He crossed himself, kissed his thumbnail, and crossed himself again. 'The manacles are not broken?'

'No.' Luca gave them a kick and they rattled but did not spring open.

'I saw them myself, I made no mistake,' Brother Peter said, scrambling down the ladder and shaking as he tested the chains on the wall.

Luca thrust the torch at Peter and swarmed his way up the ladder to the light, obeying a panic-stricken sense that he did not want to be trapped in the dark cellar from which the women had, so mysteriously, disappeared. Lord Lucretili took his hand and heaved him up the last steps and then stayed hand clasped with him. Luca, feeling his own hands were icy in the lord's warm grip, had a sense of relief at a human touch.

'Be of good heart, Inquirer,' the lord said. 'For these are dark and terrible days. It must be witchcraft. It must be so. My sister is a witch. I have lost her to Satan.'

'Where could they have gone?' Luca asked the older man. 'How?'

'Anywhere they choose, since they got out of locked chains and a closed cellar. They could be anywhere in this world or the next.'

Brother Peter came up from the darkness, carrying the torch. It was as if he came out of a well and the dark water closed behind him. He shut the door of the hatch, and stamped the bolt into place as if he were afraid of the very blackness beneath their feet. 'What shall we do now?' he asked Luca.

Luca hesitated, unsure. He glanced towards Lord Lucretili who smoothly took command. 'We'll set a hue and cry for them, naming them as witches, but I don't expect them to be found,' the lord ruled. 'In her absence I shall declare my sister dead.' He turned his head, to hide his grief. 'I can't even have Masses said for her soul ... A sainted father and a cursed sister both gone within four months. He will never even meet her in heaven.'

Luca gave him a moment to recover. 'Admit the Lady Almoner,' he said to Brother Peter.

She was waiting outside the door. Luca caught a glimpse of Freize's grimace of curiosity as she came quietly in and closed the door behind her. She observed the closed hatch, and looked to Luca for an explanation. Carefully, she did not address the Lord Lucretili. Luca assumed that her vows forbade anything but the briefest of contact with men who were not already ordained in the priesthood. 'What has happened, my brother?' she asked him quietly.

'The accused women are missing.'

Her head jolted up to exchange one swift glance with Lord Lucretili. 'How is it possible?' she demanded.

'These are mysteries,' Luca said shortly. 'My question, though, is this: now that we have no suspects, now their guilt is strongly shown by their disappearance, and the way they have got away – what is to be done? Should I continue

132

my inquiry? Or is it closed? You are the Lady Almoner, and in the absence of the Lady Abbess you are the senior lady of the abbey. What is your opinion?'

He could see her flush with pleasure that he had consulted her, that he had named her as the most senior woman of the abbey. 'I think you have completed your inquiry,' she said quietly to him. 'I think you have done everything that anyone could ask of you. You found the very cause of the troubles here, you proved what she was doing, you arrested her and her heretic slave and named them as witches, and they are now gone. Their escape proves their guilt. Your inquiry is closed and – if God is merciful – this abbey is cleansed of their presence. We can get back to normal here.'

Luca nodded. 'You will appoint a new Lady Abbess?' he asked Lord Lucretili.

The Lady Almoner folded her hands inside her sleeves and looked down, modestly, at the floor.

'I would.' He paused, still very shaken. 'If there was anyone I could trust to take the place of such a false sister! When I think of the damage that she might have done!'

'What she did!' the Lady Almoner reminded him. 'The house destroyed and distracted, one nun dead—'

'Is that all she has done?' Luca inquired limpidly.

'All?' the lord exclaimed. 'Escaping her chains and practising witchcraft, keeping a Moorish slave, heretical practices and murder?'

'Give me a moment,' Luca said thoughtfully. He went to the door and said a quiet word to Freize, then came back to them. 'I am sorry. I knew he would wait there all day until he had a word from me. I have told him to pack our things, so we can leave this afternoon. You are ready to send your report, Brother Peter?'

Luca looked towards Brother Peter but sensed, out of the corner of his eye, a second quick exchange of glances between the Lord Lucretili and the Lady Almoner.

'Oh, of course.' Luca turned to her. 'Lady Almoner, you will be wondering what I recommend for the future of the abbey?'

'It is a great concern to me,' she said, her eyes lowered once more. 'It is my life here, you understand. I am in your hands. We are, all of us, in your hands.'

Luca paused for a moment. 'I can think of no-one who would make a better Lady Abbess. If the nunnery were not handed over to the monastery but were to remain a sister house, an independent sister house for women, would you undertake the duty of being the Lady Abbess?'

She bowed. 'I am very sure that our holy brothers could run this order very well, but if I were called to serve ...'

'But if I were to recommend that it remain under the rule of women?' For a moment only he remembered the bright pride of the Lady Abbess when she told him that she had never learned that women should be under the rule of men. Almost, he smiled at the thought of her.

'I could only be appointed by the lord himself,' the Lady Almoner said deferentially, recalling him to the present.

'What do you think?' Luca said, turning to the lord.

'If the place were to be thoroughly exorcised by the priests, if my Lady Almoner were to accept the duty, if you recommend it, I can think of no-one better to guide the souls of these poor young women.'

'I agree,' said Luca. He paused as if a thought had

suddenly struck him. 'But doesn't this overset your father's will? Was the abbey not left entirely to your sister? The abbey and the lands around it? The woods and the streams? Were they not to be in your sister's keeping and she to be Lady Abbess till death?'

'As a murderer and a witch, then she is a dead woman in law,' the lord said. 'She is disinherited by her sins; it will be as if she had never been born. She will be an outlaw, with no home anywhere in Christendom. The declaration of her guilt will mean that no-one can offer her shelter, she will have nowhere to lay her false head. She will be dead to the law, a ghost to the people. The Lady Almoner can become the new Lady Abbess and command the lands and the abbey and all.' He put his hand up to shield his eyes. 'Forgive me, I can't help but grieve for my sister!'

'Very well,' Luca said.

'I'll draw up the finding of guilt and the writ for her arrest,' Brother Peter said, unfurling his papers. 'You can sign it at once.'

'And then you will leave, and we will never meet again,' the Lady Almoner said quietly to Luca. Her voice was filled with regret.

'I have to,' he said for her ears alone. 'I have my duty and my vows too.'

'And I have to stay here,' she replied. 'To serve my sisters as well as I can. Our paths will never cross again – but I won't forget you. I won't ever forget you.'

He stepped close so that his mouth was almost against her veil. He could smell a hint of perfume on the linen. 'What of the gold?'

She shook her head. 'I shall leave it where it lies in the waters of the stream,' she promised him. 'It has cost us too dear. I shall lead my sisters to renew their vows of poverty. I won't even tell Lord Lucretili about it. It shall be our secret: yours and mine. Will you keep the secret with me? Shall it be the last thing that we share together?'

Luca bowed his head so that she could not see the bitter twist of his mouth. 'So at the end of my inquiry, you are Lady Abbess, the gold runs quietly in the stream, and the Lady Isolde is as a dead woman.'

Something in his tone alerted her keen senses. 'This is justice!' she said quickly. 'This is how it should be. This is your decision.'

'Certainly, I am beginning to see that this is how some people think it should be,' Luca said drily.

'Here is the writ of arrest and the finding of guilt for the Lady Isolde, formerly known as Lady Abbess of the abbey of Lucretili,' Brother Peter said, pushing the document across the table, the ink still wet. 'And here is the letter approving the Lady Almoner as the new Lady Abbess.'

'Very efficient,' Luca remarked. 'Quick.'

Brother Peter looked startled at the coldness of his tone. 'I thought we had all agreed?'

'There is just one thing remaining,' Luca said. He opened the door and Freize was standing there, holding a leather sack. Luca took it without a word, and put it on the table, then untied the string. He unpacked the objects in order. 'A shoemaker's awl, from the Lady Almoner's secret cupboard in the carved chimney breast of her parlour ...' He heard her sharp gasp and whisper of denial. He reached into his jacket pocket and took out the piece of paper. Slowly, in the silently attentive room, he unfolded it and showed them the print of the bloodstained palm of the nun who had come to him in the night and shown him the stigmata. He put the sharp triangular point of the shoemaker's awl over the bloodstained print: it fitted exactly.

Luca gritted his teeth, facing the fact that his suspicions were true, though he had hoped so much that this hunch, this late awareness, would prove false. He felt like a man gambling with blank-faced dice; now he did not even know what he was betting on. 'There is only one thing that I think certain,' he said tightly. 'There is only one thing that I can be sure of. I think it most unlikely that Our Lord's sacred wounds would be exactly the shape and size of a common shoemaker's awl. These wounds, which I saw and recorded on the palm of a nun of this abbey, were made by human hands, with a cobbler's tools, with this tool in particular.'

'They were hurting themselves,' the Lady Almoner said quickly. 'Hysterical women will do that. I warned you of it.'

'Using the awl from your cupboard?' He took out the little glass jar of seeds, and showed them to the Lady Almoner. 'I take it that these are belladonna seeds?'

Lord Lucretili interrupted. 'I don't know what you are suggesting?'

'Don't you?' Luca asked, as if he were interested. 'Does anyone? Do *you* know what I am suggesting, my Lady Almoner?'

Her face was as white as the wimple that framed it. She shook her head, her grey eyes wordlessly begging him to say nothing more. Luca looked at her, his young face grim. 'I have to go on,' he said, as if in answer to her unspoken question. 'I was sent here to inquire and I have to go on. Besides, I have to know. I always have to know.'

'There is no need ...' she whispered. 'The wicked Lady Abbess is gone, whatever she did with the awl, with belladonna ...'

'I need to know,' he repeated. The last object he brought out was the book of the abbey's accounts that Freize had taken from her room.

'There's nothing wrong with the list of work,' she said, suddenly confident. 'You cannot say that there is anything missing from the goods listed and the market takings. I have been a good steward to this abbey. I have cared for it as if it were my own house. I have worked for it as if I were the lady of the house, I have been the Magistra, I have been in command here.'

'There is no doubt that you have been a good steward,' Luca assured her. 'But there is one thing missing.' He turned to the clerk. 'Brother Peter, look at these and tell me, do you see a fortune in gold mentioned anywhere?'

Peter took the leather-bound book and flipped the pages quickly. 'Eggs,' he volunteered. 'Vegetables, some sewing work, some laundry work, some copying work – no fortune. Certainly no fortune in gold. Brother Luca? What are you saying?'

'You know I didn't take the gold,' the Lady Almoner said, turning to Luca, putting a pleading hand on his arm. 'I stole nothing. It was all the Lady Abbess, she that is a witch. She set the nuns to soak the fleeces in the river, she stole the gold dust and sent it out for sale to the gold merchants. As I told you, as you saw for yourself. It was not me. Nobody will say it was me. It was done by her.'

'Gold?' Lord Lucretili demanded. 'What gold?'

'The Lady Abbess and her slave have been panning for gold in the abbey stream, and selling it,' the Lady Almoner told him quickly. 'I learned of it by chance when they first came here. The Inquirer discovered this only yesterday.'

'And where is the gold now?' Luca asked.

'Sold to the merchants on Via Portico d'Ottavia, I suppose,' she flared at him. 'And the profit taken by the witches. We will never get it back. We will never know for sure.'

'But who sold it?' Luca asked, as if genuinely curious.

'The slave, the heretic slave, she must have gone to the Jews, to the gold merchants,' she said quickly. 'She would know what to do, she would trade with them. She would speak their language, she would know how to haggle with them. She is a heretic like them, greedy like them, allowed to profiteer like they are. As bad as them ... worse.'

Luca shook his head at her, almost as if he was sorry as his trap closed on her. 'You told me yourself that she never left the nunnery,' he reminded her. He nodded at Brother Peter. 'You took a note of what the Lady Almoner said, that first day, when she was so charming and so helpful.'

Brother Peter turned to the page in his collection of papers, riffling the manuscript pages. 'She said: "She never leaves the Lady Abbess's side. And the Lady Abbess never goes out. The slave haunts the place."'

Luca turned back to the Lady Almoner whose grey eyes flicked – just once – to the lord, as if asking for his help, and then back to Luca.

139

'You told me yourself she was the Lady Abbess's shadow,' Luca said steadily. 'She never left the nunnery: the gold has never left the nunnery. You have it hidden here.'

Her white face blanched yet more pale but she seemed to draw courage from somewhere. 'Search for it!' she defied him. 'You can tear my storeroom apart and you will not find it. Search my room, search my house, I have no hidden gold here! You can prove nothing against me!'

'Enough of this. My damned sister was a sinner, a heretic, a witch, and now a thief,' Lord Lucretili suddenly intervened. He signed the contract for her arrest without hesitation, and handed it back to Brother Peter. 'Get this published at once. Announce a hue and cry for her. If we take her and her heretic familiar, I shall burn them without further trial. I shall burn them without allowing them to open their mouths.' He reached towards Luca. 'Give me your hand,' he said. 'I thank you, for all you have done here. You have pursued an inquiry and completed it. It's over, thank God. It's done. Let's make an end to it now, like men. Let's finish it here.'

'No, it's not quite over,' Luca said, detaching himself from the lord's grip. He opened the gatehouse door and led all of them out to the yard where they were loading the coffin of the dead nun onto the black-draped cart.

'What's this?' the lord said irritably, following Luca outside. 'You can't interfere with the coffin. We agreed. I am taking it to a vigil in my chapel. You cannot touch it. You must show respect. Hasn't she suffered enough?'

The lay sisters heaved at the coffin, sweating with effort. There were eight of them hauling it onto the low cart. Luca observed, grimly, that it was a heavy load.

The lord took Luca firmly by the arm. 'Come tonight to the castle,' he whispered. 'We can open it there if you insist. I will help you, as I promised I would. Spare the women this.'

Luca was watching Freize, who had gone to help the lay sisters slide the coffin onto the cart. First he shouldered the coffin with them, and then nimbly climbed up into the cart, standing alongside the coffin, a crowbar in his hand.

'Don't you dare touch it!' The Lady Almoner was on the cart, beside him, in a moment, her hands on his forearm. 'This coffin is sanctified, blessed by the priest himself. Don't you dare touch her coffin, she has been censed and blessed with sanctified water, let her rest in peace!'

There was a murmur from the lay sisters and one of them, seeing Freize's determined face as he gently put the Lady Almoner aside, slipped away to the chapel where the nuns were praying for their departed sister's soul.

'Get down,' the Lady Almoner commanded Freize, holding on to his arm. 'I order it. You shall not abuse her in death! You shall not see her poor sainted face! This is sacrilege!'

'Tell your man to get down,' Lord Lucretili said quietly to Luca, as one man to another. 'Whatever you suspect, it won't help if there is a scandal now, and these women have borne too much already. We have all gone through too much today. We can sort this out later in my chapel. Let the nuns say farewell to their sister and get the coffin away.'

The nuns were pouring out of the chapel towards the yard, their faces white and furious. When they saw Freize on the cart, they started to run.

'Freize!' Luca shouted a warning, as the women fell onto the cart like a sea of white, keening high notes, like a mad choir turning on an enemy. 'Freize, leave it!'

He was too late. With the Lady Almoner clawing at his shoulder Freize had got his crowbar beneath the lid and heaved it up as the first nuns reached the cart and started to grab at him. With a terrible creak the nails yielded on one side and the lid lifted up. Dourly triumphant, Freize fended off the women, and nodded down at Luca. 'As you thought,' he said.

The first of the nuns recoiled at the sight of the open coffin and whispered to the others what they had seen. The others, running up, checked and stopped, as someone at the back let out a bewildered sob. 'What is it now? What in the name of Our Lady is it now?'

Luca climbed up beside Freize and the Lady Almoner, and the sight of the coffin blazed at him. He saw that the dead nun had been packed in bags of gold and one of them had split, showering her with treasure so that she appeared like a glorious pharaoh. Gold dust filled her coffin, gilded her face, enamelled the coins on her staring eyes, glittered in her wimple and turned her gown to treasure. She was a golden icon, a Byzantine glory, not a corpse.

'The witches did this! It's their work,' the Lady Almoner shouted. 'They put their stolen treasure in with their victim.'

Luca shook his head at this, his young face grave. 'I charge you, Lady Almoner, with the murder of this young woman, Sister Augusta, by feeding her belladonna to cause dreams and hallucinations to disturb the peace and serenity of this nunnery, to shame the Lady Abbess and drive her from her place. I charge you, Lord Lucretili, of conspiring with the Lady Almoner to drive the Lady Abbess from her home, which was her inheritance under the terms of her father's will, and setting the Lady Almoner to steal the gold from the abbey. I charge you both with attempting to smuggle this gold, the Lady Abbess's property, from the abbey in this coffin, and of falsely accusing the Lady Abbess and her slave of witchcraft and conspiring to cause their deaths.'

The lord tried to laugh. 'You're dreaming too. They've driven you mad too!' he started. 'You're wandering in your wits!'

Luca shook his head. 'No, I am not.'

'But the evidence?' Brother Peter came to the side of the wagon and urgently muttered to him. 'Evidence?'

'The slave never sold the gold, she never left the abbey – the Lady Almoner told us so. So neither she nor the Lady Abbess ever profited from the gold-panning. But the Lady Almoner accused them, she even knows the street in Rome where the gold merchants trade. The only people who tried to get this month's gold out of the abbey were the Lady Almoner and the Lord Lucretili – right now in this coffin. The only woman who showed any signs of wealth was the Lady Almoner, in her silk petticoats and her fine leather slippers. She plotted with the lord to drive his sister from the abbey so that she could become Lady Abbess and they would share the gold together.'

Lord Lucretili looked at Brother Peter, Freize and Luca, and then at his own men-at-arms, the clerks and priests. Then he turned to the blank-faced nuns who were swaying like a field of white lilies and whispering, 'What is he saying? What is the stranger saying? Is he saying bad things? Is he accusing us? Who is he? I don't like him. Did he kill Sister Augusta? Is he the figure of Death that she saw?'

'Whatever you believe, whatever you say, I think you are outnumbered,' Lord Lucretili said in quiet triumph. He smiled. 'You can leave now safely, or you can face these madwomen. Just as you like. But I warn you, I think they are so crazed that they will tear you apart.'

The crowd of young women, more than two hundred of them, gathered closer to the coffin cart, one after the other, to see the icon that had been made of their innocent sister, and their sibilant whispers were like a thousand hissing snakes as they saw her lying there in her opened coffin, bathed in gold, and Freize standing above her like an abusing man – an emblem of all the wickedness of the world – with a crowbar in his hands.

'This man is our enemy,' the Lady Almoner told them. 'He is defending the false Lady Abbess, who killed our sister. He has broken into our sister's consecrated coffin.'

The nuns' faces turned towards her, their expressions blank. 'Our enemy,' they repeated. 'Our enemy, our enemies. They should be crucified like the Lord.'

'They will do what is right,' Luca claimed. He turned to the white-faced women, and tried to capture their attention.

'Sisters, listen to me. Your Lady Abbess has been driven from her home and you have been driven half-mad by belladonna fed to you in bread from this woman's table. Are you still so sick with the drug that you will be obedient to her? Or will you find your own way? Will you think for yourselves? Can you think for yourselves?'

There was a terrible silence broken only by the whispered word 'enemy!'. Luca could see the haunted faces of all the women staring blankly up at him and for a moment he thought that they were indeed so sick from the drug that they would take him and Freize and Brother Peter and tear them to pieces. He took hold of the side of the cart with one hand, so that no-one could see he was shaking, and he pointed his other hand at the Lady Almoner. 'Get down from the cart. I am taking you to Rome to answer for your crimes against your sisters, against the Lady Abbess, and against God.'

She stayed where she was, surrounded by the nuns, whose faces turned obediently towards her. Then she said three short terrible words. 'Sisters! Kill him!'

Luca whirled around, pulling his dagger from his boot, and Freize jumped down to stand alongside him. Brother Peter moved towards them, but in a second the three men were surrounded. The nuns, pale and dull-faced, formed themselves into an unbreakable circle, like a wall of coldness, took one step towards the three men, and then took another step closer.

'St James the Greater protect me,' Freize swore. He raised his crowbar, but the nuns neither flinched nor stopped their steady onward pace.

The first nun put her hand to her head, took hold of her wimple, and threw it down on the ground. Horridly, her shaven head above her pale gown made her look like neither man nor woman, but a strange being, some kind of hairless animal. Beside her the next nun did the same, then they all threw their wimples down showing their heads, some cropped, some shaven quite bald.

'God help us!' Luca whispered to his comrades on either side of him. 'What are they doing?'

'I think—' Brother Peter began.

'Traitor!' the nuns whispered together, like a choir.

Luca looked desperately around, but there was no way to break out of the circle of women.

'Traitor!' they said again, more loudly. But now they were not looking at the men, they were looking over the men's heads, upwards, to the Lady Almoner high on the hearse.

'Traitor!' they breathed again.

'Not me!' she said, her voice cracked with sudden fear. 'These men are your enemies, and the witches who are fled.'

They shook their bald heads in one terrible movement, and now they closed on the cart and their grasping hands reached past the men, as if they were nothing, reached up to pull the Lady Almoner down. She looked from one sister to another, then at the locked gate and the porteress who stood before it, arms folded. 'Traitor!' they said and now they had hold of her robe, of her silk petticoats beneath her robe, and were pawing at her, shaking her gown, pulling at her, grasping hold of the fine leather belt of her rosary, gripping the gold chain of keys, bringing her to her knees.

She tore herself from their grip and jumped over the side of the cart to Luca, clinging to his arm. 'Arrest me!' she said with sudden urgency. 'Arrest me and take me now. I confess. I am your prisoner. Protect me!'

'I have this woman under arrest!' Luca said clearly to the nuns. 'She is my prisoner, in my charge. I will see that justice is done.'

'Traitor!' They were closing in steadily and fast; nothing could stop them.

146

'Save me!' she screamed in his ear.

Luca put his arm in front of her but the nuns were pressing forwards. 'Freize! Get her out of here!'

Freize was pinned to the cart by a solid wall of women.

'Giorgio!' she called to Lord Lucretili. 'Giorgio! Save me!'

He shook his head convulsively, like a man in a fit, flinching back from the mob of nuns.

'I did it for you!' she cried to him. 'I did it all for you!'

He turned a hard face to Luca. 'I don't know what she's saying, I don't know what she means.'

The blank-faced women came closer, pressing against the men. Luca tried to gently push them away but it was like pushing against an avalanche of snow. They reached for the Lady Almoner with pinching hands.

'No!' Luca shouted. 'I forbid it! She is under arrest. Let justice be done!'

The lord suddenly tore himself away from the scene, strode past them all to the stables, and came out at once on his red-leather caparisoned horse with his men-at-arms closed up around him. 'Open the gate,' he ordered the porteress. 'Open the gate or I will ride you down.'

Mutely she swung it open. The nuns did not even turn their heads as his cavalcade flung themselves through the gate and away down the road to his castle.

Luca could feel the weight of the women pressing against him. 'I command ...' he started again, but they were like a wall bearing down on him, and he was being suffocated by their robes, by their remorseless thrusting against him as if they would stifle him with their numbers. He tried to push himself away from the side of the cart; but then he lost his footing and went down. He kicked and rolled in a spasm of terror at the thought that they would trample him, unknowingly, that he would die beneath their sandalled feet. The Lady Almoner would have clung to him but they dragged her off him. Half a dozen women held Luca down as others forced the Lady Almoner to the pyre that she herself had ordered them to build. Freize was shouting now, thrashing about as a dozen women pinned him to the floor. Brother Peter was frozen in shock, white-robed nuns crushing him into silence, against the side of the cart.

She had ordered them to make two high pyres of dry wood, each built around a central pole, set strongly in the ground. They carried her to the nearest, though she kicked and struggled and screamed for help, and they lashed her to the pole, wrapping the ropes tight around her writhing body.

'Save me!' she screamed to Luca. 'For the love of God, save me!'

He had a wimple over his face so he could not see, he was suffocating on the ground under the fabric, but he shouted to them to stop, even as they took the torch from the gatehouse porteress, who gave it silently to them, even as they held it to the tarred wood at the foot of the pile, even as she disappeared from view in a cloud of dark smoke, even as he heard her piercing scream of agony as her expensive silk petticoats and her fine woollen gown blazed up in a plume of yellow flames.

~

The three men rode away from the abbey in silence, sickened by the violence, glad to escape without a lynching themselves. Every now and then Luca would shudder and violently brush smuts from the sleeves of his jacket, and Freize would pass his broad hand over his bewildered face and say, 'Sweet saints ...'

They rode all the day on the high land above the forest, the autumn sun hard in their eyes, the stony ground hard underfoot, and when they saw the swinging bough of holly outside a house that marked it as an inn they turned their horses into the stable yard in silence. 'Does Lord Lucretili own this land?' Freize asked the stable lad, before they had even dismounted.

'He does not, you are out of his lordship's lands now. This inn belongs to Lord Piccante.'

'Then we'll stay,' Luca decided. His voice was hoarse; he hawked and spat out the smell of the smoke. 'Saints alive, I can hardly believe we are away from it all.'

Brother Peter shook his head, still lost for words.

Freize took the horses to the stables as the other two went into the taproom, shouting for the rough red wine of the region to take the taste of wood smoke and tallow from their mouths. They ordered their food in silence and prayed over it when it came.

'I need to go to confession,' Luca said, after they had eaten. 'Our Lady intercede for me, I feel filthy with sin.'

'I need to write the report,' Brother Peter said.

They looked at one another, sharing their sense of horror. 'Who would ever believe what we have seen?' Luca wondered. 'You can write what you like: who would ever believe it?'

'He will,' Brother Peter said. 'He will understand. The lord of the Order. He has seen all this, and worse. He is studying the end of days. Nothing surprises him. He will read it, and understand it, and keep it under his hand, and wait for our next report.'

'Our next report? We have to go on?' Luca asked disbelievingly.

'I have our next destination under his own seal,' the clerk said.

'Surely this inquiry was such a failure that we will be recalled?'

'Oh no, he will see this as a success,' Brother Peter said grimly. 'You were sent to inquire after madness and manifestations of evil at the abbey and you have done so. You know how it was caused: the Lady Almoner giving the nuns belladonna so that they would run mad. You know why she did it: her desire to win the place of the Lady Abbess for herself and grow rich. You know that Lord Lucretili encouraged her to do it so that he could murder his sister under the pretence that she was a witch and so gain her inheritance of the abbey and the gold. It was your first investigation, and – though I may have had my doubts as to your methods – I will tell my lord that you have completed it successfully.'

'An innocent woman died, a guilty woman was burned by a mob of madwomen, and two women who may be innocent of theft but who are undoubtedly guilty of witchcraft have disappeared into thin air, and you call that a success?' Luca demanded angrily.

Brother Peter allowed himself a thin smile. 'I have seen worse investigations with worse outcomes.'

'You must have been to the jaws of hell itself, then!'

He nodded, utterly serious. 'I have.'

Luca paused. 'With other investigators?'

'There are many of you.'

'Young men like me?'

'Some like you, with gifts and a curiosity like you. Some quite unlike you. I don't think I have ever met one with faerie blood before.'

Luca made a quick gesture of denial. 'That's nonsense.'

'The master of the Order picks out the Inquirers himself, sends them out, sees what they discover. You are his private army against sin and the coming of the end of days. He has been preparing for this, for years.'

'Why? How?'

The older man shrugged. 'I don't know,' he said. 'I know that he was born to a great position and he and his twin brother were sent as hostages to the Ottomans.'

'He was enslaved?' Luca asked, thinking of his mother and father.

'He was raised as a Muslim,' Brother Peter replied. 'He came home determined to fight against them; against all heresy and evil. His twin brother stayed.'

'He must have seen horrors,' Luca observed.

'He has,' Brother Peter agreed.

Luca pushed back his chair from the table. 'I'm going to bed. I hope to heaven that I don't dream.'

'You won't dream,' Brother Peter assured him. 'He chose well with you. You have the nerves to bear it, and the courage to undertake it. Soon you will learn the wisdom to judge more carefully.'

'And then?'

'And then he will send you to the frontier of Christendom, where the heretics and the devils muster to wage war against us and there are no good people at all.'

151

The women rode side by side, with their horses shoulder to shoulder. Now and then Isolde would give a shuddering sob, and Ishraq would put out a hand to touch her fists, clenched tightly on the reins.

'What do you think will become of the abbey?' Isolde asked. 'I have abandoned them. I have betrayed them.'

The other girl shrugged her shoulders. 'We had no choice. Your brother was determined to get it back into his keeping, the Lady Almoner was determined to take your place. Either she would have poisoned us, or he would have had us burned as witches.'

'How could she do such a thing – the poisoning, and driving us all mad?'

Ishraq shrugged. 'She wanted the abbey for herself. She had worked her way up, she was determined to be Lady Abbess. She was always against you, for all that she seemed so pleasant and so kind when we first got there. And only she knows how long she was plotting with your brother. Perhaps he promised her the abbey long ago.'

'And the Inquirer – she misled him completely. The man is a fool.'

'She talked to him, she confided in him when you would not. Of course he learned her side of the story. But where shall we go now?'

Isolde turned a pale face to her friend. 'I don't know. Now we are truly lost. I have lost my inheritance and my place in the world, and we have both been named as witches. I am so sorry, Ishraq. I should never have brought you into the abbey, I should have let you return to your homeland. You should go now.'

'I go with you,' the girl said simply. 'We go together, wherever that is.'

'I should order you to leave me,' Isolde said with a wry smile. 'But I can't.'

'Your father, my beloved lord, raised us together and said that we should be together always. Let us obey him in that, since we have failed him in so much else.'

Isolde nodded. 'And anyway, I can't imagine living without you.'

The girl smiled at her friend. 'So where to? We can't stay on Lucretili lands.'

Isolde thought for a moment. 'We should go to my father's friends. Anyone who served with him on crusade would be a friend to us. We should go to them, and tell them of this attack on me, we should tell them about my brother, and what he has done to the abbey. We should clear my name. Perhaps one of them will restore me to my home. Perhaps one will help me accuse my brother and win the castle back from him.'

Ishraq nodded. 'Count Wladislaw was your father's dearest friend. His son would owe you friendship. But I don't see how we'd get to him, he lives miles away, in Wallachia, at the very frontier of Christendom.'

'But he'd help me,' Isolde said. 'His father and mine swore eternal brotherhood. He'd help me.'

'We'll have to get money from somewhere,' Ishraq warned. 'If we're going to attempt such a journey we'll have to hire guards, we can't travel alone. The roads are too dangerous.'

'You still have my mother's jewels safe?'

'I never take off the purse. They're in my hidden belt. I'll sell one at the next town.' Ishraq glanced at Lady Isolde's downturned face, her plain brown gown, the poor horse she was riding and her shabby boots. 'This is not what your father wanted for you.'

The young woman bowed her head and rubbed her eyes with the back of her hand. 'I know it,' she said. 'But who knows what he wanted for me? Why would he send me into the abbey if he wanted me to be the woman that he raised me to be? But somewhere, perhaps in heaven, he will be watching over me and praying that I find my way in this hard world without him.'

Ishraq was about to reply when she suddenly pulled up her horse. 'Isolde!' she cried warningly, but she was too late. A rope that had been tied across the road to a strong tree was suddenly snatched tight by someone hidden in the bushes, catching the front legs of Isolde's horse. At once the animal reared up and, tangled in the rope, staggered and went down on its front knees, so that Isolde was flung heavily to the ground.

Ishraq did not hesitate for a moment. Holding her own reins tightly she jumped from the horse and hauled her friend to her feet. 'Ambush!' she cried. 'Get on my horse!'

Four men came tumbling out of the woods on either side of the road, two holding daggers, two holding cudgels. One grabbed Isolde's horse, and threw the reins over a bush, while the other three came on.

'Now, little ladies, put your hands in the air and then throw down your purses and nobody will get hurt,' the first man said. 'Travelling on your own? That was foolish, my little ladies.'

Ishraq was holding a long thin dagger out before her, her other hand clenched in a fist, standing like a fighter, well-balanced on both feet, swaying slightly as she eyed the three men, wondering which would come first. 'Come any closer and you are a dead man,' she said briefly.

He lunged towards them and Ishraq feinted with the knife and spun round, slashed at the arm of another man, and turned back, her fist flying out to crunch against the first man's face. But she was outnumbered. The third man raised the cudgel and smashed it against the side of her head, she went down with a groan, and Isolde at once stepped over her to protect her, and faced the three men. 'You can have my purse,' she said. 'But leave us alone.'

The wounded man clapped his hand over his arm and cursed as the blood flowed between his fingers. 'She-dog,' he said shortly.

The other man gingerly touched his bruised face. 'Give us the purse,' he said angrily.

Isolde untied the purse that hung at her belt and tossed it to him. There was nothing in it but a few pennies. She knew that Ishraq had her mother's sapphires safe in a belt tied inside the bodice of her tunic. 'That's all we have,' she said. 'We're poor girls. That's all we have in the world.'

'Show me your hands,' said the man with the cudgel.

Isolde held out her hands.

'Palms up,' he said.

She turned her hands upwards and at once he stepped forwards, twisted her arms behind her back, and she felt the other man rope her tightly.

'Lady's hands,' he jeered. 'Soft white hands. You've never done a stroke of work in your life. You'll have a wealthy family or friends somewhere who will pay a ransom for you, won't you?'

'I swear to you that no-one will pay for me.' Isolde tried to turn but the ropes bit tight into her arms. 'I swear it. I am alone in the world, my father just dead. My friend is alone too. Let me . . .'

'Well, we'll see,' the man said.

On the ground Ishraq stirred and tried to get to her feet. 'Let me help her,' Isolde said. 'She's hurt.'

'Tie them up together,' the man said to his fellows. 'In the morning we'll see if anyone is missing two pretty girls. If they aren't, then we'll see if anyone wants two pretty girls. If they don't, we'll sell them to the Turks.' The men laughed and the one with the bruised face patted Isolde's cheek.

The chief hit his hand away. 'No spoiling the goods,' he said. 'Not till we know who they are.' He heaved Ishraq to her feet and held her as she too was roped. 'I'm sorry,' she mumbled to Isolde.

'Give me water for her,' Isolde commanded the man. 'And let me bathe her head.'

'Come on,' was all he said to the others and he led the way off the track to their hidden camp.

~

Luca and his two companions were quiet the following morning when they started at dawn. Freize was nursing a headache from what he said was the worst ale in Christendom, Brother Peter seemed thoughtful, and Luca was reviewing all that had been said and done at the abbey, certain that he could have done better, sure that he had

156

failed, and – more than anything else – puzzling over the disappearance of the Lady Abbess and her strange companion, out of chains, out of a stone cellar, into thin air.

They left the inn just as the sky was turning from darkness to grey, hours before sunrise, and they wrapped their cloaks tightly around them against the morning chill. Brother Peter said that they were to ride north, until he opened their next orders.

'Because we like nothing more than when he breaks that seal, unfolds that paper, and tells us that some danger is opening up under our feet and we are to ride straight into it.' Freize addressed the attentive ears of his horse. 'Mad nuns one day, what's for today? We don't even know.'

'Hush,' Luca said quietly. 'We don't know, nobody knows; that's the very point of it.'

'We know it won't be kindly,' Freize's horse rolled an ear back towards him and seemed to sympathise.

They went on in silence for a little while, following a dusty track that climbed higher and higher between bare rocks. The trees were fewer here, an odd twisted olive tree, a desiccated pine tree. Above they could see an eagle soaring and the sun was bright in their faces though the wind from the north was cold. As they reached the top of the plateau there was a little forested area, to the right of the road. The horses dropped their heads and plodded, the riders slumped in their saddles, when Luca's eye was caught by something that looked like a long black snake lying in the dust of the road before them. He raised his hand for a halt and, when Freize started to speak, he turned in the saddle and scowled at him, so the young man was silent.

'What is it?' Brother Peter mouthed at him.

Luca pointed in reply. In the road in front of them, scuffed over with dust and hidden with carefully placed leaves, was a rope, tied to a tree on one side, disappearing into the woods on the right.

'Ambush,' Freize said quietly. 'You wait here; act like I've gone for a piss. … Saints save us! That damned ale!' he said more clearly. He hitched his trousers, slid off his horse and went, cursing the ale, to the side of the road. A swift glance in each direction and he was stepping delicately and quietly into the trees, circling the likely destination of the rope into the bushes. There was a brief silence and then a low whistle like a bird call told the others that they could come. They pushed their way through the little trees and scrubby bushes to find Freize seated like a boulder on the chest of a man frozen with fear. Freize's big hand was over his mouth, his large horn-handled dagger blade at the man's throat. The captive's eyes rolled towards Luca and Brother Peter as they came through the bushes, but he lay quite still.

'Sentry,' Freize said quietly. 'Fast asleep. So a pretty poor sentry. But there'll be some band of brigands within ear-shot.' He leaned forwards to the man, who was gulping for air underneath his weight. 'Where is everyone else?'

The man rolled his eyes to the woods on their right.

'And how many are you?' Freize asked. 'Blink when I say. Ten? No? Eight? No? Five, then?' He looked towards Luca. 'Five men. Why don't we just leave them to do their business? No point looking for trouble. We could just ride on by?'

'What is their business?' Luca asked.

'Robbery,' Brother Peter said quietly. 'And sometimes they kidnap people and sell them to the Ottomans for the galleys.'

'Not necessarily,' Freize interrupted quickly. He scowled at Brother Peter to warn him to say no more. 'Might just be poaching a bit of game. Poachers and thieves. Not doing a great deal of harm. No need for us to get involved.'

'Kidnap?' Luca repeated icily.

'Not necessarily so . . .' Freize repeated. 'Probably nothing more than poachers.'

It was too late. Luca was determined to save anyone from the galleys of the Ottoman pirates. 'Gag him, and tie him up,' he ordered. 'We'll see if they're holding anyone.' He looked around the clearing; a little path, scarcely more than a goat's track, led deeper into the woods. He waited till the man was gagged and bound to a tree, and then led the way, sword in one hand, dagger in the other, Freize behind him and Brother Peter bringing up the rear.

'Or we could just ride on,' Freize suggested in an urgent whisper.

'Why are we doing this?' Brother Peter breathed.

'His parents.' Freize nodded towards Luca's back. 'Kidnapped and enslaved into the Ottoman galleys. Probably dead. It's personal for him. I hoped for a moment, that you might have taken my hint, and kept your mouth shut – but no . . .'

The slight scent of a damped-down fire warned them that they were near a camp and Luca halted and peered through the trees. Four men lay sleeping around a doused fire, snoring heavily. A couple of empty wineskins and the charred bones of a stolen sheep showed that they had eaten and drunk well before falling asleep. To the side of them, tied back to back, were two figures, hooded and cloaked.

Gambling that the roaring snores would cover any noise

that they made, Luca whispered to Freize and sent him towards the horses. Quiet as a cat, Freize moved along the line of tied animals, picked out the two very best and took their reins, and untied the rest. 'Gently,' he said softly to them. 'Wait for my word.'

Brother Peter tiptoed his way back to the road. Their own three horses and the donkey were tied to a tree. He mounted his horse and held the reins of the others, ready for a quick escape. The brightness of the morning sun threw the shadows darkly on the road. Brother Peter prayed briefly but fervently that Luca would save the captives – or whatever he was planning to do – and come away. Bandits were a constant menace on these country roads and it was not their mission to challenge each and every one. The lord of the Order would not thank him if Luca was killed in a brawl when he was showing such early talent as an Inquirer for the Order.

Back in the clearing, Luca watched Freize take control of the horses, then slid his sword into the scabbard and wormed his way through the bushes to where the captives were tied to each other, and roped to a tree. He cut the rope to the tree and both hooded heads came up at once. Luca put his finger to his lips to warn them to be quiet. Quickly, in silence, they squirmed towards him, bending away from their bonds so that he could cut the rope around their wrists. They rubbed their wrists and their hands, without saying a word, as Luca bent to their boots and cut the ropes around their feet. He leaned to the nearest captive and whispered, 'Can you stand? Can you walk?'

There was something that snagged his memory, as sharp as a tap on the shoulder, the minute he leaned towards the captive, and then he realised that this was no stranger. There was a scent of rosewater as she put back her hood and the sea of golden hair tumbled over her shoulders and the former Lady Abbess smiled up at him and whispered, 'Yes, Brother, I can; but please help Ishraq, she's hurt.'

He recoiled from her at once, clenching his fist in the country sign against witchcraft.

'Don't be a fool,' she briefly recommended. 'I can explain. Help us get away from these men.'

He could not argue with her in whispers. 'You are my prisoner,' he said stiffly and was rewarded with her merry smile.

'Help me with Ishraq,' she said.

He pulled Isolde to her feet, and then bent to help the other woman. At once he could see that she had taken a blow to the side of her head. There was blood on her face, her beautiful dark skin was bruised like a plum, and her legs buckled beneath her when he tried to get her up.

'You go to the horses,' he whispered to Isolde. 'Quiet as you can. I'll bring her.'

She nodded and went silent as a doe through the trees skirting the clearing to reach Freize, who helped her up into the saddle of the best horse. Luca came behind her carrying Ishraq and bundled her onto a second horse. Tapping the horses' chests, urging them with whispers to back away from where they had been tethered, the two men led the animals with the girls on their backs down a little track to where Brother Peter waited on the road.

'Oh no,' Brother Peter said flatly when he saw the white face and the thick blonde hair of the Lady Abbess. At once she pulled her brown hood up over her hair to hide her face, and lowered her eyes. Peter turned to Freize. 'You let him risk his life for this? You let him risk us? His sacred mission?'

Freize shrugged. 'Better go,' was all he said. 'And maybe we'll get away with it.'

Freize mounted his own cob, and then cocked an ear to the woods behind them. In the clearing, one of the sleeping men grunted, and turned over in his sleep, and another one cursed and raised himself onto one elbow. The horses left untethered turned their heads and whinnied for their companions, and one started to move after them.

'Go!' Luca ordered.

Freize kicked his cob into a canter, leading Ishraq's horse, with her clinging, half-conscious, to the horse's mane. Isolde snatched up her reins and urged her horse alongside them. Luca vaulted into his saddle as they heard the men shouting from behind. The first loose horse came out of the woods, trotting to catch up with him, and then all the others followed, their reins trailing. Freize yelled an incomprehensible word of warning to the horses as they clattered from the woods and came towards him. The gang of thieves scrambled after their runaway horses, then saw the little group on the road, and realised they had been robbed.

'Full gallop!' Luca yelled, and ducked as the first arrow whistled overhead. 'Go!' he shouted. 'Go! Go!'

They all hunched low over their horses' necks, thundering down the road as the men spilled out of the wood, cursing and swearing, sending a shower of misdirected arrows after them. One of the stray horses bucked and screamed as it took an arrow in the rump, and raced ahead. The others weaved around them, making aim even more difficult. Luca held the pace as fast as he dared on the stony road, finally pulling up his frightened horse so it slowed to a canter and then a walk and then halted, panting, when they were well out of range.

The stray horses collected around Freize. 'Gently, my loves,' he said. 'We're safe if we are all together.' He got down from his cob and went to the wounded horse. 'Just a scratch, little girl,' he said tenderly. 'Just a scratch.' She bowed her head to him and he pulled gently at her ears. 'I'll bathe it when we get to wherever in God's earth we are going, sweetheart.'

Ishraq was clinging on to the neck of her horse, exhausted and sick with her injury. Freize looked up at her. 'She's doing poorly. I'll take her up before me.'

'No,' Isolde said. 'Lift her up onto my horse. We can ride together.'

'She can barely stay on!'

'I'll hold her,' she said with firm dignity. 'She would not want to be held by a man, it is against her tradition. And I would not like it for her.'

Freize glanced at Luca for permission and, when the young man shrugged, he got down from his own horse and walked over to where the slave swayed in the saddle.

'I'll lift you over to your mistress,' he said to her, speaking loudly.

'She's not deaf! She's just faint!' Luca said irritably.

'Both as stubborn as each other,' Freize confided to the slave girl's horse as her rider tumbled into his arms. 'Both as stubborn as the little donkey, God bless him.' Gently, he carried Ishraq over to Isolde's horse and softly set her in the saddle and made sure that she was steady. 'Are you sure you can hold her?' he asked Isolde.

'I can,' she said.

'Well, tell me if it is too much for you. She's no light-weight, and you're only a weakly little thing.' He turned to Luca. 'I'll lead her horse. The others will follow us.'

'They'll stray,' Luca predicted.

'I'll whistle them on,' Freize said. 'Never hurts to have a few spare horses, and maybe we can sell them if we need.'

He mounted his own steady cob, took the reins of Ishraq's horse, and gave a low encouraging whistle to the other four horses who at once clustered around him, and the little cavalcade set off steadily down the road.

'How far to the nearest town?' Luca asked Brother Peter.

'About eight miles, I think,' he said. 'I suppose she'll make it; but she looks very sick.'

Luca looked back at Ishraq, who was leaning back against Isolde, grimacing in pain, her face pale. 'She does. And then we'll have to turn her over to the local lord for burning when we get there. We've rescued her from bandits and saved her from the Ottoman galleys to see her burned as a witch. I doubt she will think we have done her a kindness.'

'She should have been burned as a witch yesterday,' Brother Peter said unsympathetically. 'Every hour is a gift to her. She should use the time for penitence'

Luca reined back to bring his horse up alongside Isolde. 'How was she injured?'

'She took a blow from a cudgel while she was trying to defend us. She's a clever fighter, but there were four of them. They jumped us on the road trying to steal from us and when they saw we were women without guards they thought to take us for ransom.' She shook her head as if to rid herself of the memory. 'Or for the galleys.'

'They didn't –' he tried to find the words '– er, hurt you?'

'You mean, did they rape us?' she asked, matter-of-factly. 'No, they were keeping us for ransom and then they got drunk. But we were lucky.' She pressed her lips together. 'I was a fool to ride out without a guard. I put Ishraq in danger. We'll have to find someone to travel with.'

'You won't be able to travel at all,' Luca said bluntly. 'You are my prisoners. I am arresting you under charges of witchcraft.'

'Because of poor Sister Augusta?'

He blinked away the picture of the two young women, bloodied to their elbows like butchers. 'Yes. And your escape from a locked room.'

'When we get to the next town and the doctor sees Ishraq, will you listen to me, before you hand us over? I will explain everything to you, I will confess everything that we have done and what we have not done, and you can be the judge as to whether we should be sent back to my brother for burning. For that is what you will be doing, you know. If you send me back to him, you will sign my death warrant. I will have no trial worth the writing, I will have no hearing worth the listening. You will send me to my death. Won't that sit badly on your conscience?'

Brother Peter brought his horse alongside. 'The report has gone already,' he said with dour finality. 'And you are listed as a witch. There is nothing that we can do but release you to the civil law.'

'I can hear her,' Luca said irritably. 'I can hear her out. And I will.'

She looked at him. 'The woman you admire so much is a liar and an apostate,' she said bluntly. 'The Lady Almoner is my brother's lover, his dupe, and his accomplice. I would swear to it. He persuaded her to drive the nuns mad and blame it on me so that you would come and destroy my rule at the abbey. She was his fool and I think you were hers.'

Luca felt his temper flare at being called a fool by this girl, but gritted his teeth. 'I listened to her when you would not deign to speak to me. I liked her when you would not even show me your face. She swore she would tell the truth when you were – who knows what you were doing? At any rate, I had nothing to compare her with. But even so I listened out for her lies, and I understood that she was putting the blame on you when you did not even defend yourself to me. You may call me a fool – though I see you were glad enough for my help back there with the bandits – but I was not fooled by her – whatever you say.'

She bowed her head, as if to silence her own hasty words. 'I don't think you are a fool, Inquirer,' she said. 'I am grateful to you for saving us. I shall be glad to explain my side of this to you. And I hope you will spare us.'

~

The physician called to the Moorish slave as they rested in the little inn in the small town pronounced her bloodied and bruised but no bones broken. Luca paid for the best bed for her and Isolde, and paid extra for them not to have to share the room with other travellers.

'How am I to report that we are now paying for two women to travel with us?' Brother Peter protested. 'Known criminals?'

'You could say that I need servants, and you have provided me with two bonny ones,' Freize suggested, earning him a sour look from the clerk.

'No need to report anything at all. This is not an inquiry,' Luca ruled. 'This is just the life of the road, not part of our work.'

~

Isolde put Ishraq into the big bed, as if she were an equal, spooned soup into her mouth as if she were her sister, cared for her like her child and sat with her as she slept.

'How is the pain?'

'No better,' Ishraq grimaced. 'But at least I don't think I am doomed any more. That ride was like a nightmare, the pain went on and on. I thought I was going to die.'

'I couldn't protect you from the roughness of the road nor the stumbles of the horse. It jolted me, it must have been horrible for you.'

'It was hard to bear.'

'Ishraq, I have failed you. You could have been killed or murdered or enslaved. And now we are captured again. I have to let you go. You can go now, while I talk to them. Please – save yourself. Go south, get away to your homeland and pray to your god we will meet again one day.'

The girl opened her bruised eyes and gleamed at Isolde. 'We stay together,' she ruled. 'Didn't your father raise us as sisters of the heart, as companions who were never parted?'

'He may have done so, but my mother didn't give it her blessing, she fought against us being together every day of her life,' Isolde shrewdly reminded her. 'And we have had nothing but heartache since we lost my father.'

'Well, my mother blessed our friendship,' Ishraq replied. 'She told me: "Isolde is the sister of your heart". She was happy that I was with you all the day long, that we did our lessons together and played together, and she loved your father.'

'They taught you languages,' Isolde reminded her with pretended resentment. 'And medicine. And fighting skills. While I had nothing to learn but music and embroidery.'

'They prepared me to be your servant and companion,' Ishraq said. 'To serve and protect you. And so I am. I know the things I need to know to serve you. You should be glad of it.'

A quick tap of a finger on her cheek told her that Isolde was glad of it.

'Well, then,' Ishraq said. 'I need to sleep. You go to dinner. See if you can get him to release us. And if he will, see if you can make him give us some money.'

'You think very highly of my powers of persuasion,' Isolde said ruefully.

'Actually, I do.' Ishraq nodded as her eyes closed. 'Especially with him.'

~

Luca sent for Isolde at dinnertime, planning to question her privately as they ate together, but then he found that both Brother Peter and Freize intended to be in the room with them.

'I shall serve the food,' Freize said. 'Better me than some wench from the inn, listening to everything you say, interrupting as like as not.'

'While you are notably reticent.'

'Reticent,' Freize repeated, committing the word to memory. 'Reticent. D'you know? I imagine that I am.'

'And I shall take a note. This is still an inquiry for murder and witchcraft,' Brother Peter said severely. 'Just because we found them in yet more trouble, does not prove their innocence. Quite the opposite. Good women stay at home and mind their manners.'

'We can hardly blame them for being homeless when their abbey was going to burn them for witches,' Luca said irritably. 'Or blame her for being expelled by her brother.'

'Whatever the reason, she and her servant are homeless and uncontrolled,' Brother Peter insisted. 'No man rules them and no man protects them. They are certain to get into trouble and to cause trouble.'

'We know they were innocent of stealing the gold. But what of the rest?' Luca said, looking from one determined face to the other.

'We were satisfied as to the drugging, the poisoning and the murder,' Peter said. 'Satisfied that the great crimes were performed by the Lady Almoner. But what were the two of them doing in the mortuary that night? Tampering with the corpse, and the Lady Almoner saying they were having a Satanic Mass on the nun's body?'

Freize nodded. 'He's right. They have to explain.'

'I'll ask,' Luca said. 'I'll ask about everything. But if you remember her brother coming in, secretly hand in glove with that woman, and his readiness to see his sister burn before him – you can't help but pity her. And, anyway, if her answers are not satisfactory we can hand them over to the Lord Piccante who is the master here, and he can burn the two of them as the Lord Lucretili would have done. Is that your wish?' He looked at their glum faces. 'You want to see them dead? Those two young women?'

'My wish is to see justice done,' said Brother Peter. 'Forgiveness is for God.'

'Or I suppose we could just turn a blind eye and let them get away in the morning,' Freize suggested, as he headed out of the room.

'Oh, for goodness' sake!' Luca exclaimed.

Just then, Isolde came down the stairs for dinner, wearing a gown she had borrowed from the innkeeper's wife. It was made of some coarse material, dyed a dark blue, and on her head she had a cap like countrywomen wore. It showed the golden fold of her hair where she had it twisted back into a plait. Luca remembered the tumble of gold when he had tackled her in the stable yard and the scent of rosewater when he had held her down. In the simple outfit her beauty was suddenly radiant and Luca and even Brother Peter were tongue-tied.

'I hope you are recovered,' Luca muttered as he set a chair for her.

Her eyes were downcast, her smile directed to her feet. 'I was not injured, I was only frightened. Ishraq is resting and recovering. She will be better in the morning, I am sure.'

Freize entered, banging the door, and started to slap down dishes onto the table. 'Fricassée of chicken – they killed an old rooster specially. Stew of beef with turnip, a pâté of pork – I wouldn't touch it myself. Some sausage which looks quite good and a few slices of ham.' He went back out and came in again with more dishes. 'Some march-pane from the local market which tastes almost like the real thing, but I wouldn't swear to its youth; some pastries which the goodwife made herself, I saw them come out of the oven and I tasted them for your safety and approve them. They have no fruit here at all but some apples which are so green that they are certain to half-kill you, and some sugared chestnuts which they have saved for visiting gentry for a good year. So I would not answer for them.'

'I am sorry,' Luca said to Isolde.

'No,' she said with a smile. 'He is very engaging and probably truthful, which matters more.'

'Some very good wine, that I took the liberty of tasting for you in the cellar, which would do my lady no harm at all.' Freize was encouraged by Isolde's praise into pouring the wine with a flourish. 'Some small ale to quench your thirst that they brew here from the mountain water, and is actually rather good. You wouldn't drink the water in any case, but you probably could here. And if you fancy a couple of eggs I can get them boiled or scrambled up as you wish.'

'He likes to think he is devoted to my service, and really he is very good to me,' Luca said in an undertone.

'And moreover,' Freize said, bearing down upon Isolde, 'there is a nice sweet wine for your voider course, and some good bread coming out of the oven now. They don't have wheat, of course, but the rye bread is sweet and light, being made with some kind of honey – which I established by a long conversation with the cook who is no other than the goodwife, and a very good wife, I would think. She says that the gown becomes you better than her, and so it does.'

'But sometimes, of course, he is quite unendurable,' Luca finished. 'Freize, please serve the meal in silence.'

'Silence, he says.' Freize nodded at Isolde with a

conspiratorial smile. 'And silent I am. See me: utterly silent. I am reticent, you know. Reticent.'

She could not help but laugh as Freize folded lip over lip, put all the remaining dishes on the table, bowed low, and stood with his back to the door, facing the room like a perfect servant. Brother Peter sat down and started to help himself to the dishes, with his manuscript beside him and his ink pot adjacent to his wine glass.

'I see that you are questioning me, as well as feeding me,' she said to Luca.

'As the sacred Mass,' Brother Peter answered for him. 'Where you have to answer for your soul and your faith before you partake. Can you answer for your soul, my lady?'

'I have done nothing that I am ashamed of,' she said steadily.

'The attack on the dead woman?'

Luca shot a quelling look at Brother Peter but Isolde answered without fear. 'It was no attack. We had to know what she had been given to eat. And by discovering that she had been poisoned we saved the others. I knew Sister Augusta, and you did not. I tell you: she would have been glad that we did that to her – after death – so that we could save her sisters pain in their lives. We found the specks of belladonna in her belly, which proved that the nuns were being poisoned, that they were not possessed or going mad as we all feared. I hoped we could have given you the berries as evidence and saved the abbey from my brother and the Lady Almoner.'

Luca spooned the fricassée of chicken onto a big slice of rye bread and passed it to her. Daintily, she produced a little fork from the sleeve of her gown and ate the meat from the top of the bread. None of them had seen such table manners before. Luca quite forgot his questions. Freize at the doorway was transfixed.

'I've never seen such a thing,' Luca remarked.

'It's called a fork,' Isolde said, as if it were quite ordinary. 'They use them in the court of France. For eating. My father gave me this one. I always keep it in a pocket of my sleeve.'

'Never eaten anything that couldn't be speared on the tip of a dagger,' Freize offered from the doorway.

'Enough,' Luca advised this most interfering servant.

'Or sucked it up,' Freize said. He paused for a moment, to explain more clearly. 'If soup.'

'"If soup!"' Luca turned on him wrathfully. '"If soup!" For God's sake, be silent. No, better still, wait in the kitchen.'

'Keeping the door,' Freize said, motioning that his work was essential. 'Keeping the door from intruders.'

'God knows, I would rather have an intruder, I would rather have a band of brigands burst in, than have you commenting on everything that takes place.'

Freize shook his head in remorse and once again folded lower lip over upper lip to indicate his future silence. 'Like the grave,' he said to Luca. 'You go on. Doing well: probing but respectful. Don't mind me.'

Luca turned back to Isolde. 'You don't need an interrogation,' he said. 'But you must understand that we cannot release you unless we are convinced of your innocence. Eat your dinner and tell me honestly what happened at the abbey and what you plan for your future.'

'May I ask you what happened at the abbey? Have you closed it down?'

'No,' he said. 'I will tell you more later, but we left the abbey with the nuns in prayer and a new Lady Abbess will be appointed.'

'The Lady Almoner?'

'Dead,' was all he told her. 'Now you tell me all that you know.'

Isolde ate a little more and then put the slice of bread to one side. Brother Peter served the ragout onto her slice of bread, and dipped his pen in the ink.

'When I came to the abbey, I was grieving for my father and opposed to his wishes,' she said honestly. 'Ishraq came with me – we have never been parted since my father brought her and her mother home from the Holy Land.'

'She is your slave?' Brother Peter asked.

Vehemently, Isolde shook her head. 'She is free. Just because she is of Moorish descent everyone always thinks she is enslaved. My father honoured and respected her mother and gave her a Christian burial when she died when Ishraq was seven years old. Ishraq is a free woman, as her mother was free.'

'Freer than you?' Luca asked.

He saw her flush. 'Yes, as it turns out. For I was bound by the terms of my father's will to join the abbey, and now that I have lost my place I am a wanted criminal.'

'What were you doing with the body of Sister Augusta?'

She leaned forwards, fixing her dark blue gaze on him. Luca would have sworn she was speaking the truth. 'Ishraq trained with the Moorish physicians in Spain. My father took us both to the Spanish court when he was advising them about a new crusade. Ishraq studied with one of the greatest doctors: she studied herbs, drugs and poisons.

We suspected that the nuns were being drugged, and we knew that I was having the most extraordinary dreams and waking with wounds in my hands.'

'You had the stigmata on your own hands?' Luca interrupted her.

'I believed that I did,' she said, suddenly downcast at the memory. 'At first I was so confused that I thought the marks were true: painful miracles.'

'Was it you that came to my room and showed me your hands?'

Silently, she nodded.

'There is no shame in it,' Luca said gently to her.

'It feels like a sin,' she said quietly. 'To show the wounds of Our Lord and to wake so troubled, after dreams of running and screaming . . .'

'You thought it was the drug belladonna that made you dream?'

'Ishraq thought it so. She thought that many of the nuns were taking the drug. Ishraq never ate in the refectory, she ate with the servants, and she never had the dreams. None of the servants were having dreams. Only the sisters who ate the refectory bread were affected. When Sister Augusta died so suddenly Ishraq thought that her heart had ceased to beat under the influence of the drug; she knew that if you have too much it kills you. We decided to open her belly to look for the berries.'

Brother Peter shaded his eyes with his hands, as if he could still see the two of them, bloodied to the elbow, about their terrible work.

'It was a very great sin to touch the body,' Luca prompted her. 'It is a crime as well as a sin to touch a corpse.'

'Not to Ishraq.' She defended her friend. 'She is not of our faith, she does not believe in the resurrection of the body. To her it was no greater sin than examining an animal. You can accuse her of nothing but of practising the craft of Moorish medicine.'

'It was a great sin for you,' he persisted. 'And surely unbearable? How could you – a young lady – do such a thing?'

She bowed her head. 'For me it was a sin. But I thought it had to be done, and I would not leave Ishraq to do it alone. I thought I should be . . .' She paused. 'I thought I should be courageous. I am the Lady Lucretili. I thought I should be as brave as the name I bear. And at least we saw the berries in her belly, dark specks of the ground-up dried berries.' She put her hand into the pocket of her gown and brought out a couple of flecks of dark hard berries like pepper. 'We found these. This is proof of what we were doing, and what we found.'

Luca hesitated. 'You took these from the dead woman's belly?' he asked.

She nodded. 'It had to be done,' she said. 'How else could we prove to you that the nuns were being fed belladonna berries?'

Gingerly, Luca took the little seeds, and quickly passed them over to Brother Peter. 'Did you know the Lady Almoner was working with your brother?'

She nodded, sadly. 'I knew there was something between them, but I never asked. I should have demanded the truth – I always felt that she . . .' She broke off. 'I didn't know, I saw nothing for sure. But I sensed that they were . . .'

'Were what?'

176

'Could they possibly have been lovers?' she asked, very low. 'Is it possible? Or is it my jealous imagining? And my envy of her beauty?'

'Why would you say such a thing? Of the Lady Almoner?'

She shrugged. 'I sometimes think things, or see things, or almost smell things, that are not very clear, or not apparent to others . . . in this case it was as if she belonged to him, as if she was . . . his shirt.'

'His shirt?' Luca repeated.

Again she shook her head as if to shake away a vision. 'As if his scent was upon her. I can't explain better than that.'

'Do you have the Sight?' Brother Peter interrupted, staring at her over the top of his quill.

'No.' She shook her head in rapid denial. 'No, nothing like that. Nothing so certain, nothing so clear. I would not attend to it if I did have, I don't set myself up as some kind of seer. I have a sense of things, that is all.'

'But you sensed that she was his woman?'

She nodded. 'But I had no evidence, nothing I could accuse her of. It was just like a whisper, like the silk of her petticoat.'

A rumbling cough from the doorway reminded the men that it was Freize who had first noted the silk petticoat.

'It's hardly a crime to wear a silk petticoat,' Brother Peter said irritably.

'It was a suggestion,' she said thoughtfully. 'That she was not what she seemed, that the abbey under her command was not as it seemed. Not as it should be. But . . .' She shrugged. 'I was new to the life, and she seemed in charge of everything. I did not question her

177

and I did not challenge her rule of the abbey at first. I should have done so. I should have sent for an Inquirer at once.'

'How did you get out of the cellar beneath the gate-house?' Brother Peter suddenly changed the course of questioning, hoping to throw her. 'How did you get out and escape when there were handcuffs and leg-cuffs and the cellar was dug into solid stone?'

Luca frowned at the harshness of his tone, but Brother Peter just waited for the answer, his pen poised. 'It's the major charge,' he remarked quietly to Luca. 'It's the only evidence of witchcraft. The work of the slave is the work of a heretic, she is not under the command of the Church. The attack on the body is the other woman's work also – we might think of it as evil but the heretic is not under our jurisdiction. The Lady Abbess has committed no crime, but her escape is suspicious. Her escape looks like witchcraft. She has to explain it.'

'How did you get out?' Luca asked her. 'Think carefully before you reply.'

She hesitated. 'You make me afraid,' she said. 'Afraid to speak.'

'You should be afraid,' Luca warned her. 'If you got out of the handcuffs and the cellar by magical means or with the assistance of the Devil then you will face a charge of witchcraft for that alone. I can acquit you of tampering with the dead woman, but I would have to charge you with invoking the Devil to aid your escape.'

She drew a breath. 'I can't tell you,' she started. 'I can't tell you anything that makes sense.'

Brother Peter's pen was poised over the page. 'You had better think of something; this is the one remaining charge against you. Getting out of the manacles and through the walls is witchcraft. Only witches can walk through walls.'

There was a terrible silence as Isolde looked down at her hands and the men waited for her answer.

'What did you do?' Luca said quietly.

She shook her head. 'Truly, I don't know.'

'What happened?'

'It was a mystery.'

'Was it witchcraft?' Brother Peter asked.

There was a long painful silence.

'I let her out,' Freize suddenly volunteered, stepping into the room from his post at the door.

Brother Peter rounded on him. 'You! Why?'

'Mercy,' Freize said shortly. 'Justice. It was obvious they had done nothing. It wasn't them panning for gold and swishing around in silk petticoats. That brother of hers would have burned her the moment he got his hands on her, the Lady Almoner had the pyres built ready. I waited till you were all busy in the yard, deciding what should be done, then I slipped down to the cell, released them, helped them up the ladder, got them into the stable yard on horses, and sent them on their way.'

'You freed my suspects?' Luca asked him, disbelievingly.

'Little lord.' Freize spread his hands apologetically. 'You were going to burn two innocent women, caught up in the excitement of the moment. Would you have listened to me? No. For I am well-known as a fool. Would you have listened to them? No. For the Lady Almoner had turned your head and this lady's brother was quick and ready with a torch. I knew you would thank me in the end, and here we are, with you thanking me.'

'I don't thank you!' Luca exclaimed, angry beyond measure. 'I should dismiss you from my service and charge you with interfering with a papal inquiry!'

'Then the lady will thank me,' Freize said cheerfully. 'And if she doesn't, maybe the pretty slave will.'

'She's not my slave,' Isolde said, quite at a loss. 'And you will find that she never thanks anyone. Especially a man.'

'Perhaps she will come to value me,' Freize said with dignity. 'When she knows me better.'

'She will never know you better for you are about to be dismissed,' Luca said furiously.

'Seems harsh,' Freize said, glancing at Brother Peter. 'Wouldn't you say? Given that it was me that stopped us from burning two innocent women, and then saved all five of us from the brigands. Not to mention gaining some valuable horses?'

'You interfered with the course of my inquiry and released my prisoners,' Luca insisted. 'What can I do but dismiss you and send you back to the monastery in disgrace?'

'For your own good,' Freize explained. 'And theirs. Saving you all from yourselves.'

Luca turned to Brother Peter.

'But why did you fasten up the handcuffs after you had released them?' Brother Peter asked.

Freize paused. 'For confusion,' he said gravely. 'To cause more confusion.'

Isolde, despite her anxiety, choked back a laugh. 'You

have certainly done that,' she said. A small smile exchanged between them made Luca suddenly frown.

'And do you swear you did this?' he asked tightly. 'However ridiculous you are?'

'I do,' Freize said solemnly. 'However ridiculous I am.'

Luca turned to Brother Peter. 'This vindicates them from the charge of witchcraft.'

'The report has gone,' Brother Peter ruled thoughtfully. 'We said that the captives were missing, accused of witchcraft, but that their accusers were definitely guilty. The matter is closed unless you want to reopen it. We don't have to report that we met them again. It is not our job to arrest them if we have no evidence of witchcraft. We're not holding an inquiry now. Our inquiry is closed.'

'Sleeping dogs,' Freize volunteered.

Luca rounded on him. 'What in hell do you mean now?'

'Better let them lie. That's what people say. Let sleeping dogs lie. Your inquiry is completed, everyone is happy. We're off on some other damn fool mission. And the two women who were wrongly accused are free as little birds of the air. Why make trouble?'

Luca was about to argue, but then he paused. He turned towards Isolde. After one powerful blue gaze that she had shot at Freize when he had confessed to releasing them, she had returned to studying her hands held in her lap.

'Is it true that Freize released you? He let you go? As he says?'

She nodded.

'Why did you not say so at once?'

'I didn't want to get him into trouble.'

Luca sighed. It was unlikely, but if Freize was holding to his confession and Isolde would offer no other explanation, then he could not see what more he should do. 'Who is going to believe this?'

'Better this, than you trying to tell everyone that we melted through leg-cuffs and handcuffs,' she pointed out. 'Who would believe that?'

Luca glanced at Brother Peter. 'Will you write that we are satisfied that our servant released them, exceeding his duties but believing that he was doing the right thing? And that now we are clear that there was no witchcraft? And they are free to go?'

Brother Peter was wearing his most dour look. 'If you instruct me so to do,' he said pedantically. 'I think there is more to it than your servant stepping out of his place. But since he always steps out of his place and since you always allow it, and since you seem determined that these women shall go free, I can write this.'

'You will clear my name?' Isolde pressed.

'I will not accuse you of escaping by witchcraft,' Brother Peter specified. 'That's all I am prepared to do. I don't know that you are innocent of everything; but as no woman is innocent since the sin of Eve, I am prepared to agree that there is no evidence and no charge to set against you for now.'

'It's good enough,' Luca ruled.

'So she's innocent,' Freize confirmed.

Luca nodded. 'Certainly there are no charges that we would bring against her.'

'Then I have something for you,' Freize told her with a

bow. 'In the confusion of leaving, I thought I should take it.'

Brother Peter looked at Luca. 'Has he stolen something?' he asked. 'From the Abbey? Do you allow him to steal now?'

Luca spread his hands to show his complete ignorance of what Freize had done, or might do, as Freize went to his room and returned, carrying something long and thin wrapped in a saddle-cloth.

'It's your own goods,' he said cheerfully to Isolde. 'So not stealing. Your brother brought it for you, and then left it behind in his hurry. I took it that he didn't want it any more, and I thought that you might like it. If we had not met up with you I would have kept it for the little lord, as a young man who should have a great sword.'

As they watched him, he unwrapped the crusader broadsword and laid it gently on the table. They could see the engraved scabbard and the sparkle of embedded jewels. They could see the beautiful metalwork of the cross-guard where a bolt had been made to forge the sword into the scabbard. The sword could not be drawn unless someone struck off the metal guard.

'It is my father's crusader sword,' Isolde said quietly. She put her hand on the hilt, and she looked at Freize. 'You have given me a great gift, the greatest thing anyone has given me,' she said. 'My father's friend's sword.'

'It's not your father's sword?' Luca asked.

She shook her head. 'When he came back from the crusade with his dearest friend, my godfather, they both had their swords engraved with a great secret. Each of them had a secret to put on their sword. They sheathed their swords and hid their secrets and had their swords bolted into their scabbards. They gave their swords to each other, and they said that if ever they were in need, or if they needed the secret to be told, they would meet again and draw their swords.'

'What's the secret?' Freize asked,

She smiled. 'Of course, I don't know. No-one knows. And anyway, this sword does not hold my father's secret, it's the secret my godfather gave him to keep. This is my godfather's sword. But my father kept it with him, took it with him everywhere. It was a reminder of their friendship, and a reminder of when he fought for God. He promised to give it to me, so that I could be a lord and a crusader like him. But then he changed his mind and left everything to my brother.'

She fell silent.

'Perhaps he did not,' Luca suggested. 'We have seen that your brother would not hesitate to cheat you. I think he was planning to murder you. Perhaps he changed your father's will to force you into the abbey so that he could discredit you and all the nuns.'

Her hand closed on the handle of the sword. 'Yes,' she said. 'I think he did. I think he was planning to destroy me, and then kill me. But I have this now, and I will turn on him. I will meet him and I will know what was my father's will. I will know the truth of this, and I will not rest until I do.'

Brother Peter looked gravely at her. 'But committing no crime,' he recalled her to the present.

She smiled at him. 'No,' she said. 'I might declare war on him, but I won't trick him or cheat him as he cheated me.'

'And remembering womanly virtues of modesty,

obedience and peace-making,' Brother Peter urged on her.

A little giggle escaped her. 'I don't think I can promise that,' she said.

'Where will you go?' Luca asked.

'I have been puzzled as to what I should do. But this gift, this very great gift shows me the way. I will go to the son of my father's friend, my godfather's son. I can trust him and he has a reputation for being a tenacious fighter. I will ask him to clear my name, and to ride with me against my brother. It seems my brother did all of this to steal my inheritance from me, to kill me. So I will take his inheritance from him. I shall take back what is mine.'

'There is more than you know,' Luca told her. 'It is worse than you know. He had commanded the Lady Almoner to set the nuns to pan for gold in the stream in your woods.'

She looked puzzled. 'Gold?'

'It's probably why your brother was determined to drive you out of the abbey. There may be a fortune in gold in the hills, draining out into the stream in dust.'

'They were panning for gold?'

He nodded. 'He was using the Lady Almoner to steal gold from your abbey lands. Now she is dead and you have run away, the abbey and the lands and the gold are all his.'

He saw her jaw harden. 'He has won my home, my inheritance, and a fortune as well?'

Luca nodded. 'He left the Lady Almoner to her death and rode away.'

She turned on Brother Peter. 'But you didn't charge him!

You didn't pursue *him* for all the sins since Adam! Though I am responsible for everything done by Eve?'

He shrugged his shoulders. 'He committed no crime that we saw at the time. Now he pans for his own gold on his own land.'

'It is not his own land. It is mine. I will hold him to account. I will return and take back my lands. I am no longer bound by obedience to my father's will when my brother is such a bad guardian of our family honour. I will drive him out as he drove me away. I will go to my god-father's son and get help.'

'Was your godfather a man of substance? Your brother has his own castle and a small army to command.'

'He was Count Wladislaw of Wallachia,' she said proudly. 'His son is the new count. I will go to him.'

Brother Peter's head jerked up. 'You are the god-daughter of Count Wladislaw?' he asked curiously.

'Yes, my father always said to go to him in time of trouble.'

Brother Peter lowered his eyes and shook his head in wonderment. 'She has a powerful friend in him,' he said quietly to Luca. 'He could crush her brother in a moment.'

'Where does he live?'

'It's a long journey,' she admitted. 'To the east. He is in exile at the court of Hungary.'

'That would be beyond Bosnia?' Freize asked.

'Yes.'

'Further east than that?'

She nodded.

'How are two pretty girls like you and the slave going to make that journey without someone stealing from you ...

or worse?' Freize asked bluntly. 'They will skin you alive.'

She looked at Freize and smiled at him. 'Do you not think that God will protect us?'

'No,' he said flatly. 'My experience is that He rarely attends to the obvious.'

'Then we will travel with companions, with their guards, wherever we can. And take our chances when we cannot. Because I have to go. I have no-one else to turn to. And I will have my revenge on my brother, I will regain my inheritance.'

Freize nodded cheerfully at Luca. 'Might as well have burned them when you got the chance,' he observed. 'For you are sending them out to die anyway.'

'Oh, don't be ridiculous,' Luca said impatiently. 'We will protect them.'

'We have our mission!' Brother Peter objected.

Luca turned to Isolde. 'You may travel with us under our protection until our ways diverge. We are on a mission of inquiry, appointed by the Holy Father himself. We don't yet know our route but you may travel with us until our ways part.'

'Very important,' Freize supplemented, with a nod to the young woman. 'We are very important.'

'You can accompany us and when you find safe and reputable travellers on the road you can transfer to them, and travel with them.'

She bowed her head. 'I thank you. I thank you for myself and for Ishraq. And we will not delay nor distract you.'

'It is absolutely certain that they will do both,' Brother Peter remarked sourly.

'We can help them on their way at least,' Luca ruled.

'I should give you my name,' the young woman said. 'I am Lady Abbess no longer.'

'Of course,' Luca said.

'I am Lady Isolde of Lucretili.'

Luca bowed his head to her, but Freize stepped forwards, bowed low, his head almost to his knees, straightened up and thumped his clenched fist against his heart. 'Lady Isolde, you may command me,' he said grandly.

She was surprised, and giggled for a moment. Freize looked at her reproachfully. 'I would have thought you would have been brought up to understand a knight's service when it is offered?'

'He is a knight now?' Brother Peter asked Luca.

'Seems so,' came the amused response.

'Say a squire then,' Freize amended. 'I will be your squire.'

Lady Isolde rose to her feet and extended her hand to Freize. 'You do right to remind me to respond graciously to an honourable offer of service. I accept your service and I am glad of it, Freize. Thank you.'

With a triumphant glance at Luca, Freize bowed and touched her fingers with his lips. 'I am yours to command,' he said.

'I take it you will house and clothe and feed him?' Luca demanded. 'He eats like ten horses.'

'My service, as the lady well understood, is that of the heart,' Freize said with dignity. 'I am hers to command if there is a knightly quest or a bold venture. The rest of the time I carry on as your manservant, of course.'

'I am very grateful,' Isolde murmured. 'And as soon as I have a bold venture or knightly quest I will let you know.'

When Isolde entered the bedroom, Ishraq was sleeping, but as soon as she heard the soft footsteps, she opened her eyes and said, 'How was dinner? Are we arrested?'

'We're free,' Isolde said. 'Freize suddenly told his master that it was he who released us from the cellar under the gatehouse.'

Ishraq raised herself up onto one elbow. 'Did he say that? Why? And did they believe him?'

'He was convincing. He insisted. I don't think they wholly believed him but at any rate, they accepted it.'

'Did he say why he confessed to such a thing?'

'No. I think it was to be of service to us. And better than that, they have said that we can travel with them while our roads lie together.'

'Where are they going?'

'They follow orders. They go where they are told. But there is only one way out of the village so we will all go east for the time being. We can travel with them and we will be safer on the road than with strangers or alone.'

'I don't like Brother Peter much.'

'He's all right. Freize swore to be my knight errant. He gave me the crusader broadsword.'

'He stole it?'

'For me. He has a good heart. You might be glad of him one day. He certainly served us tonight.'

Isolde stripped off the blue gown, and came in her chemise to the side of the bed. 'Is there anything you want? A small ale? Shall I sponge your bruises?'

'No, I am ready to sleep again.'

The bed creaked gently as Isolde got in beside her. 'Goodnight, my sister,' she said, as she had said almost every night of her life.

'Goodnight, dearest.'

VITTORITO, ITALY,
OCTOBER 1453

The little party lingered for two more days in the village while Ishraq's bruises faded and she grew strong again. Isolde and Ishraq bought light rust-coloured gowns for travelling, and thick woollen capes for the cold nights, and on the third day they were ready to set out at sunrise.

Freize had pillion saddles on two of the horses. 'I thought you would ride behind the lord,' he said to Isolde. 'And the servant would come up behind me.'

'No,' Ishraq said flatly. 'We ride our own horses.'

'It's tiring,' Freize warned her, 'and the roads are rough. Most ladies like to ride behind a man. You can sit sideways, on the pillion saddle you don't have to go astride. You'll be more comfortable.'

'We ride alone,' Isolde confirmed. 'On our own horses.'

Freize made a face and winked at Ishraq. 'Another time, then.'

'I don't think there will be any time when I will want to ride behind you,' she said coolly.

He unfastened the girth on the pillion saddle and swept it from the horse's back. 'Ah, you say that now,' he said confidently, 'but that's because you hardly know me. Many a lass has been indifferent at first meeting but after a while . . .' He snapped his fingers.

'After a while what?' Isolde asked him, smiling.

'They can't help themselves,' Freize said confidentially. 'Don't ask me why. It's a gift I have. Women and horses, they both love me. Women and horses – most animals really – just like to be close to me. They just like me.'

Luca came out to the stable yard, carrying his saddle pack. 'Are you not tacked up yet?'

'Just changing the saddles. The ladies want to ride on their own, though I have been to the trouble of buying two pillion saddles for them. They are ungrateful.'

'Well, of course they would ride alone!' Luca said impatiently. He nodded a bow to the young women, and when Freize led the first horse to the mounting block he went to Isolde and took her hand to help her up as she stepped to the top of the mounting block, put her foot in the broad stirrup and swung herself into the saddle.

Soon, the five of them were mounted and, with the other four horses and the donkey in a string behind them, they rode out onto the little track that they would follow through the forest.

Luca went first, with Isolde and Ishraq side by side just

behind him. Behind them came Brother Peter and then Freize, a stout cudgel in a loop at the side of his saddle and the spare horses beside him.

It was a pleasant ride through the beech woods. The trees were still holding their copper-brown leaves and sheltered the travellers from the bright autumn sun. As the path climbed higher they came out of the woods and took the stony track through the upper pastures. It was very quiet; sometimes they heard the tinkle of a few bells from a distant herd of goats, but mostly there was nothing but the whisper of the wind.

Luca reined back to ride with the two girls and asked Ishraq about her time in Spain.

'The Lord Lucretili must have been a most unusual man, to allow a young woman in his household to study with Moorish physicians,' he observed.

'He was,' Ishraq said. 'He had a great respect for the learning of my people, he wanted me to study. If he had lived I think he would have sent me back to Spanish universities, where the scholars of my people study everything from the stars in the sky to the movement of the waters of the sea. Some people say that they are all governed by the same laws. We have to discover what those laws might be.'

'Were you the only woman there?'

She shook her head. 'No, in my country women learn and teach too.'

'And did you learn the numbers?' Luca asked her curiously. 'And the meaning of zero?'

She nodded. 'I did not study; but of course I know the numbers,' she said.

'My father believed that a woman could understand as well as a man,' Isolde remarked. 'He let Ishraq study whatever she wanted.'

'And you?' Luca turned to her. 'Did you attend the university in Spain?'

She shook her head. 'My father intended me to be a lady to command Lucretili,' she said. 'He taught me how to calculate the profits from the land, how to command the loyalty of people, how to manage land and choose the crops, how to command the guard of a castle under attack.' She made a funny little face. 'And he had me taught the skills a lady should have – love of fine clothes, dancing, music, speaking languages, writing, reading, singing, poetry.'

'She envies me the skills he taught me,' Ishraq said with a hidden smile. 'He taught her to be a lady and me to be a power in the world.'

'What woman would not want to be a lady of a great castle?' Luca wondered.

'I would want it,' Isolde said. 'I do want it. But I wish I had been taught to fight as well.'

At sunset on the first evening, they pulled up their horses before an isolated monastery. Ishraq and Isolde exchanged an anxious glance. 'The hue and cry?' she muttered to Luca.

'It won't have reached here. I doubt your brother sent out any messages once he was away from the abbey. I would guess he signed the writ only to demonstrate his own innocence.'

She nodded. 'Just enough to keep me away,' she said. 'Naming me as a witch and declaring me dead, leaves him with the castle and the abbey under his control, giving him the abbey lands and the gold. He wins everything.'

Freize dismounted and went to pull the great ring outside the closed door. The bell in the gatehouse rang loudly, and the porter heaved the double gates open. 'Welcome, travellers, in the name of God,' he said cheerfully. 'How many are you?'

'One young lord, one clerk, one servant, one lady and her companion,' Freize replied. 'And nine horses and one donkey. They can go in the meadow or in the stables as suits you.'

'We can put them out on good grass,' the lay brother said, smiling. 'Come in.'

He welcomed them into a big yard and Brother Peter and Luca swung down from their saddles. Luca turned to Isolde's horse and held up his arms to lift her down. She smiled briefly and gestured that she could get down on her own, then swung her leg and, lithe as a boy, jumped to the ground.

Freize went to Ishraq's horse and held out his arm. 'Don't jump,' he said. 'You'll faint the moment you touch the ground. You've been near to fainting any time this last five miles.'

She gathered her dark veil across her mouth and looked at him over the top of it.

'And don't look daggers at me either,' Freize said cheerfully. 'You'd have done better behind me with your arms around my waist and my back to lean on, but you're as stubborn as the donkey. Come on down, girl, and let me help you.'

Surprisingly, she did as he suggested and leaned towards

him and let herself fall into his arms. He took her gently and set her on her feet with his arm around her to keep her steady. Isolde went to her and supported her. 'I didn't realise . . .'

'Just tired.'

The porter gave them a light to the guesthouse, indicated the women's rooms on one side of the high wall and the entry to the men's rooms on the other. He showed them the refectory and told them that they might get their dinner with the monks after Vespers, while the ladies would be served in the guesthouse. Then he left them with lit candles and a blessing.

'Goodnight,' Isolde said to Luca, bowing her head to Brother Peter.

'I'll see you in the morning,' Luca said to both women. 'We should leave straight after Prime.'

Isolde nodded. 'We'll be ready.'

Ishraq curtseyed to the two men and nodded at Freize.

'Pillion saddle tomorrow?' he asked her.

'Yes,' she said.

'Because you were overtired with the ride today?' Freize said, driving the point home.

She showed him a warm frank smile before she tucked her veil across her face. 'Don't gloat,' she said. 'I'm tired to my very bones. You were right, I was wrong, and foolishly proud. I'll ride pillion tomorrow and be glad of it; but if you mock me I will pinch you every step of the way.'

Freize ducked his head. 'Not a word,' he promised her. 'You will find me reticent to a fault.'

'Reticent?'

He nodded. 'It is my new ambition. It's my new word: reticent.'

~

They left immediately after Prime and breakfast, and the sun was up on their right-hand side as they headed north. 'Thing is,' Freize remarked to Ishraq quietly as she rode behind him, seated sideways, her feet resting on the pillion support, one hand around his waist, tucked into his belt, 'thing is, we never know where we are going. We just go along, steady as the donkey, who knows no more than us but plods along, and then that pompous jackal suddenly brings out a piece of paper and tells us we are to go somewhere else entirely and get into God knows what trouble.'

'But of course,' she said. 'Because you are travelling as an inquiry. You have to go and inquire into things.'

'I don't see why we can't know where we are going,' Freize said. 'And then a man might have a chance of making sure we stopped at a good inn.'

'Ah, it is a matter of dinner,' she said, smiling behind her veil. 'I understand now.'

Freize patted the hand that was holding his belt. 'There are very few things more important than dinner to a hard-working man,' he said firmly. Then, 'Hulloah? What's this?'

Ahead of them in the road were half a dozen men, struggling with pitchforks and flails to hold down an animal which was netted and roped and twisting about in the dirt. Freize halted and Isolde, Luca and Peter pulled up behind him.

'What have you got there?' Luca called to the men.

One of the men broke from the struggle and came towards them. 'We'd be glad of your help,' he said. 'If we could rope the creature to two of your horses we'd be able to get it along the road. We can't get forwards or backwards at the moment.'

'What is it?' Luca asked.

The man crossed himself. 'The Lord save us, it is a were-wolf,' he said. 'It has been plaguing our village and forests every full moon for a year but last night my brother and I, and our friends, and cousin, went out and trapped it.'

Brother Peter crossed himself, and Isolde copied him. 'How did you trap it?'

'We planned it for months, truly months. We didn't dare to go out at night – we were afraid his power would be too strong under the moon. We waited till it was a waning moon when we knew that his power would be weakened and shrunken. Then we dug a deep pit on the track to the village and we staked out a haunch of mutton on the far side. We thought he would come to the village as he always does and smell the meat. We hoped he would follow the track to the meat and he did. We covered the pit with light branches and leaves, and he didn't see it. It collapsed beneath him and he fell in. We kept him there for days, with nothing to eat so he weakened. Then we dropped the nets on him and pulled them tight and hauled him out of the pit. Now we have him.'

'And what are you going to do with him?' Isolde looked fearfully at the writhing animal, laden with nets, struggling on the road.

'We are going to cage it in the village till we can make a silver arrow, as only a silver arrow can kill it, and then we are going to shoot it in the heart and bury it at the cross-roads. Then it will lie quiet and we will be safe in our beds again.'

'Pretty small for a wolf,' Freize observed, peering at the thrashing net. 'More like a dog.'

'It grows bigger with the moon,' the man said. 'When the moon is full it waxes too – as big as the biggest wolf. And then, though we bolt our doors and shutter our windows, we can hear it round the village, trying the doors, sniffing at the locks, trying to get in.'

Isolde shuddered.

'Will you help us get it to the village? We're going to put it in the bear pit, where we bait the bears at the inn, but it's a good mile away. We didn't think it would struggle so, and we're afraid to get too close for fear of being bitten.'

'If it bites you, you turn into a werewolf too,' a man said from the back. 'I promised my wife that I wouldn't go too close.'

Freize looked across their heads at Luca, and at a nod from his master, got down from his cob and went to the bundle in the road. Under the pile of nets and tangles of rope he could just see an animal crouched down and curled up. A dark angry eye looked back at him; he saw small yellow teeth bared in a snarl. Two or three of the men held their ropes out and Freize took one from one side and then one from the other side and tied them to two of the spare horses. 'Here,' he said to one of the men. 'Lead the horse gently. Did you say two miles to the village?'

'Perhaps one and a half,' the man said. The horse snorted in fear and sidled as the bundle on the road let out a howl. Then the ropes were tightened and they set off, dragging the helpless bundle along behind them. Sometimes the creature convulsed and rolled over, which caused the horses to jib in fear and the men leading them had to tighten their reins and soothe them.

'A bad business,' Freize said to Luca as they entered the village behind the men, and saw the other villagers gather around with spades and axes and flails.

'This is the very thing that we were sent out to understand,' Brother Peter said to Luca. 'I shall open a report, and you can hold an inquiry. We can do it here, before continuing with our journey and our mission. You can find what evidence there is that this is a werewolf, half-beast, half-man, and then you can decide if it should be put to death with a silver arrow or not.'

'I?' Luca hesitated.

'You are the Inquirer,' Brother Peter reminded him. 'Here is a place to understand the fears and map the rise of the Devil. Set up your inquiry.'

Freize looked at him; Isolde waited. Luca cleared his throat. 'I am an Inquirer sent out by the Holy Father himself to discover wrong-doing and error in Christendom,' he called to the villagers. There was a murmur of interest and respect. 'I will hold an inquiry about this beast and decide what is to be done with it,' he said. 'Anyone who has been wronged by the beast or is fearful of it, or knows anything about it, is to come to my room in the inn and give evidence before me. In a day or two I shall tell you my decision, which will be binding and final.'

Freize nodded. 'Where's the bear pit?' he asked one of the farmers, who was leading a horse.

'In the yard of the inn,' the man said. He nodded to the

big double doors of the stable yard at the side of the inn. As the horses came close, the villagers ran ahead and threw the doors open. Inside the courtyard, under the windows of the inn, there was a big circular arena.

Once a year, a visiting bear leader would bring his chained animal to the village on a feast day and everyone would bet on how many dogs would be killed, and how close the bravest would get to the throat of the bear, until the bear leader declared it over, and the excitement was done for another year.

A stake in the centre showed where the bears were chained by the leg when the dogs were set on them. The arena had been reinforced and made higher by lashed beams and planks so that the inner wall was nearly as high as the first-floor windows of the inn. 'They can jump,' the farmer said. 'Werewolves can jump, everyone knows that. We built it too high for the Devil himself.'

The villagers untied the ropes from the horses and pulled the bundle in the net towards the bear pit. It seemed to struggle more vigorously and to resist. A couple of the farmers took their pitchforks and pricked it onwards which made it howl in pain and snarl and lash out in its net.

'And how are you going to release it into the bear pit?' Freize wondered aloud.

There was a silence. Clearly this had not been foreseen. 'We'll just lock it in and leave it to get its own self free,' someone suggested.

'I'm not going near it,' another man said.

'If it bites you once, you become a werewolf too,' a woman warned.

'You die from the poison of its breath,' another disagreed.

'If it gets the taste of your blood it hunts you till it has you,' someone volunteered.

Brother Peter and Luca and the two women went into the front door of the inn and took rooms for themselves and stables for the horses. Luca also hired a dining room that overlooked the bear pit in the yard and went to the window to see his servant, Freize, standing in the bear pit with the beast squirming in its net beside him. As he expected, Freize was not able to leave even a monster such as this netted and alone.

'Get a bucket of water for it to drink, and a haunch of meat for it to eat when it gets itself free,' Freize said to the groom of the inn. 'And maybe a loaf of bread in case it fancies it.'

'This is a beast from hell,' the groom protested. 'I'm not waiting on it. I'm not stepping into the pit with it. What if it breathes on me?'

Freize looked for a moment as if he would argue, but then he nodded his head. 'So be it,' he said. 'Anyone here have any compassion for the beast? No? Brave enough to catch it and torment it but not brave enough to feed it, eh? Well, I myself will get it some dinner, then, and when it has untied itself from these knots, and recovered from being dragged over the road for a mile and a half, it can have a sup of water and a bite of meat.'

'Mind it doesn't bite you!' someone said and everyone laughed.

'It won't bite me,' Freize rejoined stolidly. 'On account of nobody touches me without my word, and on account of I wouldn't be so stupid as to be in here when it gets loose. Unlike some, who have lived alongside it and complained that they heard it sniffing at their door and yet took months to capture the poor beast.'

A chorus of irritated argument arose at this, which Freize simply ignored. 'Anyone going to help me?' he asked again. 'Well, in that case I will ask you all to leave, on account of the fact that I am not a travelling show.'

Most of them left, but some of the younger men stayed in their places, on the platform built outside the arena so that a spectator could stand and look over the barrier. Freize did not speak again but merely stood, waiting patiently until they shuffled their feet, cursed him for interfering, and went.

When the courtyard was empty of people, Freize fetched a bucket of water from the pump, went to the kitchen for a haunch of raw meat and a loaf of bread, then set them down inside the arena, glancing up at the window where Luca and the two women were looking down.

'And what the little lord makes of you, we will know in time,' Freize remarked to the humped net, which shuffled and whimpered a little. 'But God will guide him to deal fairly with you even if you are from Satan and must die with a silver arrow through your heart. And I will keep you fed and watered for you are one of God's creatures even if you are one of the Fallen, which I doubt was a matter of your own choosing.'

∼

Luca started his inquiry into the werewolf as soon as they had dined. The two women went to their bedroom, while the two men, Brother Peter and Luca, called in one witness after another to say how the werewolf had plagued their village.

All afternoon they listened to stories of noises in the night, the handles of locked doors being gently tried, and losses from the herds of sheep which roamed the pastures under the guidance of the boys of the village. The boys reported a great wolf, a single wolf running alone, which would come out of the forest and snatch away a lamb that had strayed too far from its mother. They said that the wolf sometimes ran on all four legs, sometimes stood up like a man. They were in terror of it, and would no longer take the sheep to the upper pastures but insisted on staying near the village. One lad, a six-year-old shepherd boy, told them that his older brother had been eaten by the werewolf.

'When was that?' Luca asked.

'Seven years ago, at least,' the boy replied. 'For I never knew him – he was taken the year before I was born, and my mother has never stopped mourning for him.'

'What happened?' Luca asked.

'These villagers have all sorts of tales,' Brother Peter said quietly to him. 'Ten to one the boy is lying, or his brother died of some disgusting disease that they don't want to admit.'

'She was looking for a lamb, and he was walking with her as he always did,' the boy said. 'She told me that she sat down just for a moment and he sat on her lap. He fell asleep in her arms and she was so tired that she closed her eyes for only a moment, and when she woke he was gone. She thought he had strayed a little way from her and she called for him and looked all round for him but she never found him.'

'Absolute stupidity,' Brother Peter remarked.

'But why did she think the werewolf had taken him?' Luca asked.

'She could see the marks of a wolf in the wet ground round the stream,' the boy said. 'She ran about and called and called, and when she could not find him she came running home for my father and he went out for days, tracking down the pack, but even he, who is the best hunter in the village, could not find them. That was when they knew it was a werewolf who had taken my brother. Taken him and disappeared, as they do.'

'I'll see your mother,' Luca decided. 'Will you ask her to come to me?'

The boy hesitated. 'She won't come,' he said. 'She grieves for him still. She doesn't like to talk about it. She won't want to talk about it.'

Brother Peter leaned towards Luca and spoke quietly to him. 'I've heard a tale like this a dozen times,' he said. 'Likely the child had something wrong with him and she quietly drowned him in the stream and then came back with a cock-and-bull story to tell the husband. She won't want to have us asking about it, and there's no benefit in forcing the truth out of her. What's done is done.'

Luca turned to his clerk and raised his papers so that his face was hidden from the boy. 'Brother Peter, I am conducting an inquiry here into a werewolf. I will speak to everyone who has any knowledge of such a satanic visitor. You know that's my duty. If along the way I discover a village where baby-killing has been allowed then I will inquire after that too. It is my task to inquire into all the fears of Christendom: everything – great sins and small. It is my task to know what is happening and if it foretells the end of days. The death of a baby, the arrival of a werewolf, these are all evidence.'

'Do you have to know everything?' Brother Peter demanded sceptically. 'Can we let nothing go? This is an inquiry for Milord not the exploration of the world.'

'No, I must know everything,' Luca nodded. 'And that is my curse that I carry just like the werewolf. He has to rage and savage. I have to know. But I am in the service of God and he is in the service of the Devil and is doomed to death.'

He turned back to the boy. 'I'll come to your mother.'

He got up from the table and the two men with the boy – still faintly protesting and crimson to his ears – led the way down the stairs and out of the inn. As they were going out of the front door, Isolde and Ishraq were coming down the stairs.

'Where are you going?' Isolde asked.

'To visit a farmer's wife, this young man's mother,' Luca said.

The girls looked at Brother Peter, whose face was impassive but clearly disapproving.

'Can we come too?' Isolde asked. 'We were just going out to walk around.'

'It's an inquiry, not a visit,' Brother Peter said.

But Luca said, 'Oh, why not?' and Isolde walked beside him, while the little shepherd boy, torn between embarrassment and pride at all the attention, went ahead. His sheepdog, which had been lying in the shadow of a cart outside the inn, pricked up its ears at the sight of him, and trotted at his heels.

He led them out of the dusty market square, up a small rough-cut flight of steps to a track that wound up the side of the mountain, following the course of a fast-flowing stream, and then stopped abruptly at a little farm, a pretty duck pond before the yard, a waterfall from the small cliff behind it. A ramshackle roof of ruddy tiles topped a rough wall of wattle and daub which had been lime-washed many years ago and was now a gentle buff colour. There was no glass in the windows but the shutters stood wide open to the afternoon sun. There were chickens in the yard and a pig with piglets in the walled orchard to the side. In the field beyond there were two precious cows, one with a calf, and as they walked up the cobbled track the front door opened and a middle-aged woman came out, her hair tied up in a scarf, a hessian apron over her homespun gown. She stopped in surprise at the sight of the wealthy strangers.

'Good day to you,' she said, looking from one to another. 'What are you doing, Tomas, bringing such fine folks here? I hope he has been no trouble, sir? Can I offer you some refreshment?'

'This is the man from the inn who brought the werewolf in,' Tomas said breathlessly. 'He would come to see you, though I told him not to.'

'You shouldn't have told him anything at all,' she observed. 'It's not for small boys, small dirty boys, to speak with their betters. Go and fetch a jug of the best ale from the still room, and don't say another word. Sirs, ladies – will you sit?'

She gestured to a bench set into the low stone wall before the house. Isolde and Ishraq took a seat and smiled up at her. 'We rarely have company here,' she said. 'And never ladies.'

Tomas came out of the house carrying two roughly carved three-legged stools and put them down for Brother Peter and Luca, then dashed in again for the jug of small ale, one glass and three mugs. Bashfully, he offered the glass to Isolde and then poured ale for everyone else into mugs.

Luca and Brother Peter took their seats and the woman stood before them, one hand twisting her apron corner. 'He is a good boy,' she said again. 'He wouldn't mean to talk out of turn. I apologise if he offended you.'

'No, no, he was polite and helpful,' Luca said.

'He's a credit to you,' Isolde assured her.

'And growing very big and strong,' Ishraq remarked.

The mother's pride beamed out of her face. 'He is,' she said. 'I thank the Lord for him every day of his life.'

'But you had a previous boy.' Luca put down his mug and spoke gently to her. 'He told us that he had an older brother.'

A shadow came across the woman's broad handsome face and she looked suddenly weary. 'I did. God forgive me for taking my eye off him for a moment.' At the thought of him she could not speak; she turned her head away.

'What happened?' Isolde asked.

'Alas, alas, I lost him. I lost him in a moment. God forgive me for that moment. But I was a young mother and so weary that I fell asleep and in that moment he was gone.'

'In the forest?' Luca prompted.

A silent nod confirmed the fact.

Gently, Isolde rose to her feet and pressed the woman

down onto the bench so that she could sit. 'Was he taken by wolves?' she asked quietly.

'I believe he was,' the woman said. 'There were rumours of wolves in the woods even then, that was why I was looking for the lamb, hoping to find it before nightfall.' She gestured at the sheep in the field. 'We don't have a big flock. Every beast counts for us. I sat down for a moment. My boy was tired so we sat to rest. He was not yet four years old, God bless him. I lay down with him for a moment and fell asleep. When I woke he was gone.'

Isolde put a comforting hand on her shoulder.

'We found his little shirt,' the woman continued, her voice trembling with unspoken tears. 'But that was some months later. One of the lads found it when he was bird's-nesting in the forest. Found it under a bush.'

'Was there any blood on it?' Luca asked.

She shook her head. 'It was washed through by rain,' she said. 'But I took it to the priest and we held a service for his innocent soul. The priest said I should bury my love for him and have another child – and then God gave me Tomas.'

'The villagers have captured a beast that they say is a werewolf,' Brother Peter remarked. 'Would you accuse the beast of murdering your child?'

He expected her to flare out, to make an accusation at once; but she looked wearily at him as if she had worried and thought about this for too long already. 'Of course when I heard there was a werewolf I thought it might have taken my boy Stefan – but I don't know. I can't even say that it was a wolf that took him. He might have wandered far and fallen in the stream and drowned, or in a ravine, or just been lost in the woods. I saw the tracks of the wolves but I didn't see my son's footprints. I have thought about it every day of my life; and still I don't know.'

Brother Peter nodded and pursed his lips. He looked at Luca. 'Do you want me to write down her statement and have her put her mark on it?'

Luca shook his head. 'Later we can, if we think there is need,' he said. He bowed to the woman. 'Thank you for your hospitality, goodwife. What name shall I call you?'

She rubbed her face with the corner of her apron. 'I am Sara Rossi,' she said. 'Wife of Raul Rossi. We have a good name in the village, anyone can tell you who I am.'

'Would you bear witness against the werewolf?'

She gave him a faint smile with a world of sorrow behind it. 'I don't like to talk of it,' she said simply. 'I try not to think of it. I tried to do what the priest told me and bury my sorrow with the little shirt, and thank God for my second boy.'

Brother Peter hesitated. 'We will certainly put it on trial and if it is proven to be a werewolf it will die.'

She nodded. 'That won't bring back my boy,' she said quietly. 'But I should be glad to know that my son and all the other children are safe in the pasture.'

They rose up and left her. Brother Peter gave his arm to Isolde as they walked down the stony path, Luca was beside Ishraq.

'Why does Brother Peter not believe her?' Ishraq asked him when she was close enough to speak softly. 'Why is he always so suspicious?'

'This is not his first inquiry; he has travelled before and seen much. I think he is suspicious of everyone. Your lady, Isolde, was very tender to her.'

'She has a tender heart,' Ishraq said. 'Children, women, beggars, her purse is always open and her heart is always going out to them. The castle kitchen gave away two dozen dinners a day to the poor. She has always been this way.'

'And has she ever loved anyone in particular?' Luca asked casually. There was a big rock in the pathway and he stepped over it and turned to help Ishraq.

She laughed. 'Nothing to do with you,' she said abruptly. When she saw him flush she said, 'Ah, Inquirer! Do you really have to know everything?'

'I was just interested . . .'

'No-one. She was supposed to marry a fat indulgent sinful man and she would never have considered him. She would never have stooped to him. She took her vows of celibacy with ease. That was not the problem for her. She loves her lands, and her people. No man has taken her fancy.' She paused as if to tease him. 'So far,' she conceded.

Luca looked away. 'Such a beautiful young woman is bound to . . .'

'Quite,' Ishraq said. 'But tell me about Brother Peter. Is he always so miserable?'

'He was suspicious of the mother here,' Luca explained. 'He thinks she may have killed the child herself, and tried to blame it on a wolf attack. I don't think so myself; but of course, in these out-of-the-way villages, such things happen.'

Decisively, she shook her head. 'Not her. That is a woman with a horror of wolves,' she said. 'It's no accident she was not down in the village, though everyone else was there to see them bring it in.'

'How do you know that?' Luca said.

Ishraq looked at him as if he were blind. 'Did you not see the garden?'

Luca had a vague memory of a well-tilled garden, filled with flowers and herbs. There had been a bed of vegetables and herbs near to the door to the kitchen, and flowers and lavender had billowed over the path. There were some autumn pumpkins growing fat in one bed, and plump grapes on the vine which twisted around the door. It was a typical cottage garden: planted partly for medicine and partly for colour. 'Of course I saw it, but I don't remember anything special.'

She smiled. 'She was growing a dozen different species of aconite, in half a dozen colours, and her boy had a fresh spray of the flower in his hat. She was growing it at every window and every doorway – I've never seen such a collection, and in every colour that can bloom, from pink to white to purple.'

'And so?' Luca asked.

'Do you not know your herbs?' Ishraq asked teasingly. 'A great Inquirer like yourself?'

'Not like you do. What is aconite?'

'The common name for aconite is wolfsbane,' she said. 'People have been using it against wolves and werewolves for hundreds of years. Dried and made into a powder it can poison a wolf. Fed to a werewolf it can turn him into a human again. In a lethal dose it can kill a werewolf outright, it all depends on the distillation of the herb and the amount that the wolf can be forced to eat. For sure, no wolf will touch it; no wolf will go near it. They won't let their coats so much as brush against it. No wolf could get into that house – she has built a fortress of aconite.'

'You think it proves that her story is true and that she fears the wolf? That she planted it to guard herself against the wolf, in case it came back for her?'

Ishraq nodded at the boy who was skipping ahead of them like a little lamb himself, leading the way back to the village, a sprig of fresh aconite tucked into his hatband. 'I should think she is guarding him.'

~

A small crowd had gathered around the gate to the stable yard when Luca, Brother Peter and the girls arrived back at the inn.

'What's this?' Luca asked, and pushed his way to the front of the crowd. Freize had the gate half-open and was admitting one person at a time on payment of a half-groat, chinking the coins in his hand.

'What are you doing?' Luca asked tersely.

'Letting people see the beast,' Freize replied. 'Since there was such an interest, I thought we might allow it. I thought it was for the public good. I thought I might demonstrate the majesty of God by showing the people this poor sinner.'

'And what made you think it right to charge for it?'

'Brother Peter is always so anxious about the expenses,' Freize explained agreeably, nodding at the clerk. 'I thought it would be good if the beast made a contribution to the costs of his trial.'

'This is ridiculous,' Luca said. 'Close the gate. People can't come in and stare at it. This is supposed to be an inquiry, not a travelling show.'

'People are bound to want to see it,' Isolde observed. 'If

they think it has been threatening their flocks and themselves for years. They are bound to want to know it has been captured.'

'Well, let them see it, but you can't charge for it,' Luca said irritably. 'You didn't even catch it, why should you set yourself up as its keeper?'

'Because I loosed its bonds and fed it,' Freize said reasonably.

'It is free?' Luca asked, and Isolde echoed nervously: 'Have you freed it?'

'I cut the ropes and got myself out of the pit at speed. Then it rolled about and crawled out of the nets,' Freize said. 'It had a drink, had a bite to eat, now it's lying down again, resting. Not much of a show really, but they are simple people and not much happens here. And I charge half price for children and idiots.'

'There is only one idiot here,' Luca said severely. 'And he came in with us. Let me in, I shall see it.' He went through the gate and the others followed him. Freize quietly took coins off the remaining villagers and opened the gate wide for them. 'I'd wager it's no wolf,' he said quietly to Luca.

'What do you mean?'

'When it got itself out of the net I could see. It's curled up now in the shadowy end, so it's harder to make out, but it's no beast that I have ever seen before. It has long claws and a mane, but it goes up and down from its back legs to all fours, not like a wolf at all.'

'What kind of beast *is* it?' Luca asked him.

'I'm not sure,' Freize conceded. 'But it is not much like a wolf.'

Luca nodded and went towards the bear pit. There was

a set of rough wooden steps and a ring of trestles laid on staging, so that spectators to the bear baiting could stand all around the outside of the pit and see over the wooden walls.

Luca climbed the ladder and moved along the trestle so that Brother Peter and the two girls and the little shepherd boy could get up too.

The beast was huddled against the furthest wall, its legs tucked under its body. It had a thick long mane, and a hide tanned dark brown from all weathers, discoloured by mud and scars. On its throat were two new rope burns; now and then it licked a bleeding paw. Two dark eyes looked out through the matted mane and, as Luca watched, the beast bared its teeth in a snarl.

'We should tie it down and cut into the skin,' Brother Peter suggested. 'If it is a werewolf we will cut the skin and beneath it there will be fur. That will be evidence.'

'You should kill it with a silver arrow,' one of the villagers remarked. 'At once, before the moon gets any bigger. It will be stronger then, they wax with the moon. Better kill it now while we have it and it is not in its full power.'

'When is the moon full?' Luca asked.

'Tomorrow night,' Ishraq answered. The little boy beside her took the aconite from his hat and threw it towards the curled animal. It flinched away.

'There!' someone said from the crowd. 'See that? It fears wolfsbane. It's a werewolf. We should kill it right now. We shouldn't delay. We should kill it while it is weak.'

Someone picked up a stone and threw it. It caught the beast on its back and it flinched and snarled and shrank away as if it would burrow its way through the high wall of the bear pit.

One of the men turned to Luca. 'Your honour, we don't have enough silver to make an arrow. Would you have some silver in your possession that we might buy from you, and have forged into an arrowhead? We'd be very grateful. Otherwise we'll have to send to Pescara, to the money-lender there, and it will take days.'

Luca glanced at Brother Peter. 'We have some silver,' he said cautiously. 'Property of the Church.'

'We can sell it to you,' Luca ruled. 'But we'll wait for the full moon before we kill the beast. I want to see the transformation with my own eyes. When I see it become a full wolf then we will know that it is the beast you report, and we can kill it when it is in its wolf form.'

The man nodded. 'We'll make the silver arrow now, so as to be ready.' He went into the inn with Brother Peter, discussing a fair price for the silver, and Luca turned to Isolde and took a breath. He knew himself to be nervous as a boy.

'I was going to ask you, I meant to mention it earlier, there is only one dining room here ... in fact, will you dine with us tonight?' he asked.

She looked a little surprised. 'I had thought Ishraq and I would eat in our room.'

'You could both eat with us at the large table in the dining room,' Luca said. 'It's closer to the kitchen, the food would be hotter, fresher from the oven. There could be no objection.'

She glanced away, her colour rising. 'I would like to ...'

'Please do,' Luca said. 'I would like your advice on ...' He trailed off, unable to think of anything.

She saw at once his hesitation. 'My advice on what?' she asked, her eyes dancing with laughter. 'You have decided what to do with the werewolf, you will soon have orders as to your next mission. What can you possibly want with my opinion?'

He grinned ruefully. 'I don't know. I have nothing to say. I just wanted your company. We are travelling together, you and I, Brother Peter and Ishraq, Freize who has sworn himself to be your man – I just thought you might dine with us.'

She smiled at his frankness. 'I shall be glad to spend this evening with you,' she said honestly. She was conscious of wanting to touch him, to put her hand on his shoulder, or to step closer to him. She did not think it was desire that she felt; it was more like a yearning just to be close to him, to have his hand upon her waist, to have his dark head near to hers, to see his hazel eyes smile.

She knew that she was being foolish, that to be close to him, a novice for the priesthood, was a sin, that she herself was already in breach of the vows she had made when she had joined the abbey; and she stepped back. 'Ishraq and I will come sweet-smelling to dinner,' she remarked at random. 'She has got the innkeeper to bring the bathtub to our room. They think we are madly reckless to bathe when it's not even Good Friday – that's when they all take their annual bath – but we have insisted that it won't make us ill.'

'I will expect you at dinner, then,' he said. 'As clean as if it was Easter.' He jumped down from the platform and put out his hands to help her. She let him lift her down and as he put her on her feet he held her for a moment longer than was needed to make sure she was steady. He felt her lean slightly towards him, he could not have been mistaken; but then she stepped away and he was sure that he had been mistaken. He could not read her movements, he could not imagine what she was thinking, and he was bound by vows of celibacy to take no step towards her. But at any rate, she had said that she would come to dinner and she had said that she would like to dine with him. That at least he was sure of, as she and Ishraq went into the dark doorway of the inn.

Luca glanced up, self-consciously, but Freize had not observed the little exchange. He was intent on the werewolf as it turned around and around, as dogs do before they lie down. When it settled and did not move, Freize announced to the little audience, 'There now, it's gone to sleep. Show's over. You can come back tomorrow.'

'And tomorrow we'll see it for free,' someone claimed. 'It's our werewolf, we caught it, there's no reason that you should charge us to see it.'

'Ay, but I feed him,' Freize said. 'And my lord pays for his keep. And he will examine the creature and execute it with our silver arrow. So that makes him ours.'

They grumbled about the cost of seeing the beast as Freize shooed them out of the yard and closed the doors on them. Luca went into the inn and Freize to the back door of the kitchen.

'D'you have anything sweet?' he asked the cook, a plump dark-haired woman who had already experienced Freize's most blatant flattery. 'Or at any rate, d'you have anything half as sweet as your smile?' he amended.

'Get away with you,' she said. 'What are you wanting?'

'A slice of fresh bread with a spoonful of jam would be very welcome,' Freize said. 'Or some sugared plums, perhaps?'

'The plums are for the lady's dinner,' she said firmly. 'But I can give you a slice of bread.'

'Or two,' Freize suggested.

She shook her head at him in mock disapproval but then cut two slices off a thick rye loaf, slapped on two spoonfuls of jam and stuck them face to face together. 'There, and don't be coming back for more. I'm cooking dinner now and I can't be feeding you at the kitchen door at the same time. I've never had so many gentry in the house at one time before, and one of them appointed by the Holy Father! I have enough to do without you at the door night and day.'

'You are a princess,' Freize assured her. 'A princess in disguise. I shouldn't be surprised if someone didn't come by one day and snatch you up to be a princess in a castle.'

She laughed delightedly and pushed him out of the kitchen, slamming the door after him, and Freize climbed up on the viewing platform again and looked down into the bear pit where the werewolf had stretched out and was lying still.

'Here.' Freize waved the slice of bread and jam. 'Here – do you like bread and jam? I do.'

The beast raised its head and looked warily at Freize. It lifted its lips in a quiet snarl. Freize took a bite from the two slices, and then broke off a small piece and tossed it towards the animal.

The beast flinched back from the bread as it fell, but then caught the scent of it and leaned forwards. 'Go on,' Freize whispered encouragingly. 'Eat up. Give it a try. You might like it.'

The beast sniffed cautiously at the bread and then slunk forwards, first its big front paws, one at a time, and then its whole body, towards the food. It sniffed, and then licked it, and then gobbled it down in one quick hungry movement. Then it sat like a sphinx and looked at Freize.

'Nice,' Freize said encouragingly. 'Like some more?'

The animal watched him as Freize took a small bite, ate it with relish, and then once again broke off a morsel and threw it towards the beast. This time it did not flinch but it keenly followed the arc of the throw, and went at once to where the bread landed, in the middle of the arena, coming closer all the time to Freize, leaning over the wall.

It gobbled up the bread without hesitation and then sat on its haunches, looking at Freize, clearly waiting for more.

'That's good,' Freize said, using the same gentle voice. 'Now come a little bit closer.' He dropped the last piece of bread very near to his own position, but the werewolf did not dare come so close. It yearned towards the sweet-smelling bread and jam, but it shrank back from Freize, though he stood very still and whispered encouraging words.

'Very well,' he said softly. 'You'll come closer for your dinner later, I don't doubt,' and he stepped down from the platform and found Ishraq had been watching him from the doorway of the inn.

'Why are you feeding him like that?' she asked.

Freize shrugged. 'Wanted to see him properly,' he said. 'I suppose I just thought I'd see if he liked bread and jam.'

'Everyone else hates him,' she observed. 'They are planning his execution in two nights' time. Yet you feed him bread and jam.'

'Poor beast,' he said. 'I doubt he wanted to be a werewolf. It must have just come over him. And now he's to die for it. It doesn't seem fair.'

He was rewarded with a quick smile. 'It isn't fair,' she

said. 'And you are right – perhaps it is just his nature. He may be just a different sort of beast from any other that we have seen. Like a changeling: one who does not belong where he happens to be.'

'And we don't live in a world that likes difference,' Freize observed.

'Now that's true,' said the girl who had been different from all the others from birth with her dark skin and her dark slanting eyes.

'Now then,' said Freize, sliding his arm around Ishraq's waist. 'You're a kind-hearted girl. What about a kiss?'

She stood quite still, neither yielding to his gentle pressure nor pulling away. Her stillness was more off-putting than if she had jumped and squealed. She stood like a statue and Freize stood still beside her, making no progress and rather feeling that he wanted to take his arm away, but that he could not now do so.

'You had better let me go at once,' she said in a very quiet even voice. 'Freize, I am warning you fairly enough. Let me go; or it will be the worse for you.'

He attempted a confident laugh. It didn't come out very confident. 'What would you do?' he asked. 'Beat me? I'd take having my ears boxed from a lass like you with pleasure. I will make you an offer: box my ears and then kiss me better!'

'I will throw you to the ground,' she said with a quiet determination. 'And it will hurt, and you will feel like a fool.'

He tightened his grip at once, rising to the challenge. 'Ah, pretty maid, you should never threaten what you can't do,' he chuckled, and put his other hand under her chin to turn up her face for a kiss.

It all happened so fast that he did not know how it had been done. One moment he had his arm around her waist and was bending to kiss her, the next she had used that arm to spin him around, grabbed him, and he was tipped flat on his back on the hard cobbles of the muddy yard, his head ringing from the fall, and she was at the open doorway of the inn.

'Actually, I never threaten what I can't do,' she said, hardly out of breath. 'And you had better remember never to touch me without my consent.'

Freize sat up, got to his feet, brushed down his coat and his breeches, shook his dizzy head. When he looked up again, she was gone.

~

The kitchen lad toiled up the stairs carrying buckets of hot water, to be met at the door of the women's room by either Ishraq or Isolde who took the buckets and poured them into the bath that they had set before the fire in their bedroom. It was a big wooden tub, half of a wine barrel, and Ishraq had lined it with a sheet and poured in some scented oil. They closed and bolted the door on the boy, undressed, and got into the steaming water. Gently, Isolde sponged Ishraq's bruised shoulder and forehead, and then turned her around, tipped back her head and washed her black hair.

The firelight glowed on their wet gleaming skin and the girls talked quietly together, revelling in the steaming hot water, and the flickering warmth of the fire. Isolde combed Ishraq's thick dark hair with oils, and then pinned it on top of her head. 'Will you wash mine?' she asked. Ishraq soaped her back and shoulders and washed her tangled golden hair.

'I feel as if all the dirt of the road is in my skin,' she said, as she took a handful of salt from the dish beside the bath, and rubbed it with oil in her hands and then spread it along her arms.

'You certainly have a small forest in your hair,' Ishraq said, pulling out little twigs and leaves.

'Oh, take it out!' Isolde exclaimed. 'Comb it through, I want it completely clean. I was going to wear my hair down tonight.'

'Curled on your shoulders?' Ishraq asked, and pulled a ringlet.

'I suppose I can wear my hair as I please,' Isolde said, flicking her head. 'I suppose it is nobody's business but mine, how I wear my hair.'

'Oh, for sure,' Ishraq agreed with her. 'And surely the Inquirer has no interest in whether your hair is curled and clean and spread over your shoulders or pinned up under your veil.'

'He is sworn to the Church, as am I,' Isolde said.

'Your oaths were forced at the time, and are as nothing now; and for all I know his oaths are the same,' Ishraq said roundly.

Isolde turned and looked at her, soapsuds running down her naked back. 'He is sworn to the Church,' she repeated hesitantly.

'He was put into the Church when he was a child, before he knew what was being promised. But now he is a man, and he looks at you as if he would be a free man.'

Isolde's colour rose from the level of the water, slowly to her damp forehead. 'He looks at me?'

'You know he does.'

'He looks at me ...'

'With desire.'

'You can't say that,' she said, in instant denial.

'I do say it ...' Ishraq insisted.

'Well, don't ...'

~

In the yard outside, Luca had gone out to take one last look at the werewolf before dinner. Standing on the platform with his back to the inn, he suddenly realised he could see the girls in their bathtub as a reflection in the window opposite. At once he knew he should look away, more than that, he should go immediately into the inn without glancing upwards again. He knew that the image of the two beautiful girls, naked together in their bath, would burn into his mind like a brand, and that he would never be able to forget the sight of them: Ishraq twisting one of Isolde's blonde ringlets in her brown fingers, stroking a salve into each curl and pinning it up then gently sponging soap onto her pearly back. Luca froze, quite unable to look away, knowing he was committing an unforgivable trespass in spying on them, knowing that he was committing a terrible insult to them and worse, a venal sin, and, finally, as he jumped down from the platform and blundered into the inn, knowing that he had fallen far beyond liking, respect and interest for Isolde – he was burning up with desire for her.

~

Dinner was unbearably awkward. The girls came downstairs in high spirits, their hair in damp plaits, clean linen and clean clothes making them feel festive, as if for a party. They were met by two subdued men. Brother Peter disapproved of the four of them dining together at all, and Luca could think of nothing but the stolen glimpse of the two girls in the firelight, with their wet hair around their shoulders like mermaids.

He choked out a greeting to Isolde and bowed in silence to Ishraq, then rounded on Freize at the door, who was fetching ale and pouring wine. 'Glasses! The ladies should have glasses.'

'They're on the table as any fool can see,' Freize replied stolidly. He did not look at Ishraq but he rubbed his shoulder as if feeling a painful bruise.

Ishraq smiled at him without a moment's embarrassment. 'Have you hurt yourself, Freize?' she asked sweetly.

The look he shot at her would have filled any other girl with remorse. 'I was kicked by a donkey,' he said. 'Stubborn and stupid is the donkey, and it does not know what is best for it.'

'Better leave it alone then,' she suggested.

'I shall do so,' Freize said heavily. 'Nobody tells Freize anything a second time. Especially if it comes with violence.'

'You were warned,' she said flatly.

'I thought it might be shy,' he said. 'This stupid donkey. I thought it might resist at first. I wouldn't have been surprised by a coy little nip by way of rebuke and encouragement, all at once. What I didn't expect was for it to kick out like a damn mule.'

'Well, you know now,' replied Ishraq calmly.

He bowed, the very picture of offended dignity. 'I know now,' he agreed.

'What is this all about?' Isolde suddenly asked.

'You would have to ask the lady,' Freize said, with much emphasis on the noun.

Isolde raised an eyebrow at Ishraq, who simply slid her eyes away, indicating silence, and no more was said between the two girls.

'Are we to wait all night for dinner?' Luca demanded, and then suddenly thought he had spoken too loudly and, in any case, sounded like a spoiled brat. 'I mean: is it ready, Freize?'

'Bringing it in at once, my lord,' Freize said with injured dignity, and went to the top of the stairs and ordered that dinner be served, by the simple technique of hollering for the cook.

The two girls did most of the talking at dinner, speaking of the shepherd boy, his mother, and the prettiness of their little farm. Brother Peter said little, silent in his disapproval, and Luca tried to make casual and nonchalant remarks but kept tripping himself up as he thought of the dark gold of Isolde's wet hair, and the warm gleam of her wet skin.

'Forgive me,' he suddenly said. 'I am quite distracted this evening.'

'Has something happened?' Isolde asked. Brother Peter fixed him with a long slow stare.

'No. I had a dream, that was all, and it left my mind filled with pictures, you know how it does? When you can't stop thinking about something.'

'What was the dream?' Ishraq asked.

At once Luca flushed red. 'I can hardly remember it. I can only see the pictures.'

'Of what?'

'I can't remember them, either,' Luca stammered. He glanced at Isolde. 'You will think me a fool.'

She smiled politely and shook her head.

'Sugared plums,' Freize remarked, bringing them suddenly to the table. 'Great deal of fuss about these in the kitchen. And every child in the village waiting at the back door for any that you leave.'

'I'm afraid we cause a great deal of trouble,' Isolde remarked.

'Normally a party with ladies would go on to a bigger town,' Brother Peter pointed out. 'That's why you should be with a larger group of travellers who have ladies with them already.'

'As soon as we meet up with such a group we'll join them,' Isolde promised. 'I know we are trespassing on your kindness by travelling with you.'

'And how would you manage for money?' Brother Peter asked unkindly.

'Actually, I have some jewels to sell,' Isolde said.

'And they have the horses,' Freize volunteered from the door. 'Four good horses to sell whenever they need them.'

'They hardly own them,' Brother Peter objected.

'Well, I'm sure *you* didn't steal them from the brigands, and the little lord would never steal, and I don't touch stolen horseflesh, so they must be the property of the ladies and theirs to sell,' Freize said stoutly.

Both girls laughed. 'That's kind of you,' Isolde said. 'But perhaps we should share them with you.'

'Brother Peter can't take stolen goods,' Freize said. 'And

he can't take the fee for showing the werewolf, either, as it's against his conscience.'

'Oh, for heaven's sake!' Peter exclaimed impatiently and Luca looked up, as if hearing the conversation for the first time.

'Freize, you can keep the money for showing the werewolf but don't charge the people any more. It will only cause bad feeling in the village and we have to have their consent and good will for the inquiry. And of course the ladies should have the horses.'

'Then we are well provided for,' Isolde said with a smile to Brother Peter and a warm glance to Luca. 'And I thank you all.'

'Thank you, Freize,' Ishraq said quietly. 'For the horses came to your whistle and followed you.'

Freize rubbed his shoulder as if he was in severe pain, and turned his head away from her, and said nothing.

～

They all went to bed early. The inn had only a few candles and the girls took one to light themselves to bed. When they had banked in the fire in their bedroom and blown out the light, Ishraq swung open the shutter and looked down into the bear pit below the window.

In the warm glow of the yellow near-full moon she could make out the shape of Freize, sitting on the bear-pit wall, his legs dangling inside the arena, a fistful of chop bones from dinner in his hand.

'Come on,' she heard him whisper. 'You know you like chop bones, you must like them even more than bread and jam. I saved a little of the fat for you, it's still warm and crispy. Come on now.'

Like a shadow, the beast wormed its way towards him and halted in the centre of the arena, sitting on its back legs like a dog, facing him, its chest pale in the moonlight, its mane falling back from its face. It waited, its eyes on Freize, watching the chops in his hand, but not daring to come any closer.

Freize dropped one just below his feet, then tossed one a little further away, and then one further than that, and sat rock-still as the beast squirmed to the farthest bone. Ishraq could hear it lick, and then the crunching of the bone as it ate. It paused, licked its lips and then looked longingly at the next bone on the earthen floor of the bear pit.

Unable to resist the scent, it came a little closer, and took up the second bone. 'There you go,' Freize said reassuringly. 'No harm done and you get your dinner. Now, what about this last one?'

The last one was almost under his dangling bare feet. 'Come on,' Freize said, urging the beast to trust him. 'Come on now, what d'you say? What d'you say?'

The beast crept the last few feet to the last bone, gobbled it down and retreated, but only a little way. It looked at Freize, and the man, unafraid, looked back at the beast. 'What d'you say?' Freize asked again. 'D'you like a lamb chop? What d'you say, little beast?'

'Good,' the beast said, in the light piping voice of a child. 'Good.'

~

Ishraq clapped her hand over her mouth to stifle her gasp of surprise. She expected Freize to fling himself off the arena wall and come running into the inn with the amazing news that the beast had spoken a word, but he did not move at all. He was frozen on the bear-pit wall. He neither moved nor spoke, and for a moment she wondered if he had not heard, or if she had misheard or deceived herself in some way. Still Freize sat there like a statue of a man, and the beast sat there like a statue of a beast, watching him; and there was a long silence in the moonlight.

'Good, eh?' Freize said, his voice as quiet and level as before. 'Well, you're a good beast. More tomorrow. Maybe some bread and cheese for breakfast. We'll see what I can get you. Goodnight, beast – or what shall I call you? What name do you go by, little beast?'

He waited, but the beast did not reply. 'You can call me Freize,' the man said gently to the animal. 'And perhaps I can be your friend.'

Freize swung his legs over to the safe side of the wall and jumped down, and the beast stood four-legged, listening for a moment, then went to the shelter of the furthest wall, turned around three times like a dog, and curled up for sleep.

Ishraq looked up at the moon. Tomorrow it would be full and the villagers thought that the beast would wax to its power. If it could speak now, with the skill of a devil, what might the creature do then?

～

A delegation from the village arrived the next morning saying respectfully but firmly that they did not want the inquiry to delay justice against the werewolf. They did not see the point of the Inquirer speaking to people, and writing things down. Instead, all the village wanted to come to

230

the inn at moonrise, moonrise tonight, to see the changes in the werewolf, and to kill it.

Luca met them in the yard, Isolde and Ishraq with him, while Freize, unseen in the stable, was brushing down the horses, listening intently. Brother Peter was upstairs completing the report.

Three men came from the village: the shepherd boy's father, Raul Rossi; the village headman, Guglielmo Mugnaio; and his brother. They were very sure they wanted to see the wolf in its wolf form, kill it, and make an end to the inquiry. The blacksmith was hammering away in the village forge making the silver arrow even as they spoke, they said.

'Also, we are preparing its grave,' Guglielmo Mugnaio told them. He was a round red-faced man of about forty, as pompous and self-important as any man of great consequence in a small village. 'I am reliably informed that a werewolf has to be buried with certain precautions so that it does not rise again. So to make certain sure that the beast will lie down when it is dead and not stir from its grave, I have given orders to the men to dig a pit at the crossroads outside the village. We'll bury it with a stake through its heart. We'll pack the grave with wolfsbane. One of the women of the village, a good woman, has been growing wolfsbane for years.' He nodded at Luca as if to reassure him. 'The silver arrow and the stake through its heart. The grave of wolfsbane. That's the way to do it.'

'I thought that was the undead?' Luca said irritably. 'I thought it was the undead who were buried at crossroads?'

'No point not taking care,' Mugnaio said, glowingly confident in his own judgement. 'No point not doing it right, now that we have finally caught it and we can kill it at our leisure. I thought we would kill it at midnight, with our silver arrow. I thought we would make a bit of an event of it. I myself will be here. I thought I might make a short speech.'

'This isn't a bear baiting,' Luca said. 'It's a proper inquiry, and I am commissioned by His Holiness as an Inquirer. I can't have the whole village here, the death sentence agreed before I have prepared my report, and rogues selling seats for a penny.'

'There was only one rogue doing that,' Mugnaio pointed out with dignity. The noise of Freize grooming the horse and whistling through his teeth suddenly loudly increased. 'But the whole village has to see the beast and see its death. Perhaps you don't understand, coming from Rome as you do. But we've lived in fear of it for too long. We're a small community, we want to know that we are safe now. We need to see that the werewolf is dead and that we can sleep in peace again.'

'I beg your pardon, sir, but it's thought that my first son was taken by the beast. I'd like to see an end to it. I'd like to be able to tell my wife that the beast is dead,' Raul Rossi, the shepherd boy's father, volunteered to Luca. 'If Sara knew that the beast was dead then she might feel that our son Tomas can take the sheep out to pasture without fear. She might sleep through the night again. Seven years she has wakened with nightmares. I want her to be at peace. If the werewolf was dead, she might forgive herself.'

'You can come at midnight,' Luca decided. 'If it is going to change into a wolf then it will do so then. And if we see a change, then I shall be the judge of whether it has become a wolf. Only I shall make that judgement, and only I will rule on its execution.'

'Should I advise?' Mugnaio asked hopefully. 'As a man of experience, of position in the community? Should I consult with you? Help you come to your decision?'

'No.' Luca crushed him. 'This is not going to be a matter of the village turning against a suspect and killing him out of their fear and rage. This is going to be a weighing of the evidence and justice. I am the Inquirer. I shall decide.'

'But who is going to fire the arrow?' Mugnaio asked. 'We have an old bow which Mrs Louisa found in her loft, and we have restrung it, but there's nobody in the village who is trained to use a longbow. When we're called up to war we go as infantry with billhooks. We haven't had an archer in this village for ten years.'

There was a brief silence as they considered the difficulty. Then: 'I can shoot a bow,' Ishraq volunteered.

Luca hesitated. 'It's a powerful weapon,' he said. He leaned towards her. 'Very heavy to bend,' he said. 'It's not like a lady's bow. You might be skilled in archery, ladies' sports, but I doubt you could bend a longbow. It's a very different thing from shooting at the butts.'

Freize's head appeared over the stable door to listen, but he said nothing.

In answer, she extended her left hand to Luca. On the knuckle of the middle finger was the hard callous, the scar of an archer that identified him like a tattoo. It was an old blister, worn by drawing the arrow shaft across the guiding finger. Only someone who had shot arrow after arrow would have his hand marked by it.

'I can shoot,' she said. 'A longbow. Not a lady's bow.'

'However did you learn?' Luca asked, his hand with-drawing from her warm fingers. 'And why do you practise all the time?'

'Isolde's father wanted me to have the skills of the women of my people, even though I was raised far from them,' she said. 'We are a fighting people – the women can fight as well as the men. We are a hard people, living in the desert, travelling all the time. We can ride all day. We can find water by smell. We can find game by the turn of the wind. We live by hunting, falconry and archery. You will learn that if I say I can shoot, I can shoot.'

'If she says she can, she probably can,' Freize commented from inside the stable. 'I, for one, can attest that she can fight like a barbarian. She could well be a time-served archer. Certainly, she is no lady.'

Luca glanced from Freize's offended face, looming over the stable door, to Ishraq. 'If you can do it, then I shall appoint you executioner and give you the silver arrow. It's not a skill that I have. There was no call for it in the monastery. And I understand that no-one else here can do it.'

She nodded. 'I could hit the beast, though it is only a little beast, from the wall of the arena, shooting across to where it cowers, at the far side.'

'You're sure?'

She nodded with quiet confidence. 'Without fail.'

Luca turned to the headman and the two others. 'I will watch the beast through the day and as the moon rises,' he said. 'If I see it transform into a full wolf I will call you, and in any case you can come at midnight. If I judge that it is a wolf in shape as well as nature then this young woman here will serve as executioner. You will bring the silver arrow and we will kill it at midnight, and you can bury it as you see fit.'

'Agreed,' the headman said. He turned to go and then he suddenly paused. 'But what happens if it does not turn? If it does not become wolf? What if it remains as it is now, wolfish but small and savage?'

'Then we will have to judge what sort of beast it is and what might be done with it,' Luca said. 'If it is a natural beast, an innocent animal ordained by God to run free, then I may order it to be released in the wild.'

'We should try it with tortures,' someone volunteered.

'I will try it with the Word,' Luca said. 'That is my inquiry, that I am appointed to do. I will take evidence and study the scriptures and decide what it is. Besides, I want to know for my own satisfaction what sort of beast it is. But you can be assured: I will not leave you with a werewolf at your doors. Justice will be done; your children will be safe.'

Ishraq glanced to the stable, expecting Freize to say that it was a speaking beast, but the look he showed her over the stable door was that of the dumbest servant who knows nothing and never speaks out of turn.

~

At midday the bishop of the region arrived after a day's journey from the cathedral town of Pescara, accompanied by four attending priests, five scholars, and some servants. Luca greeted him on the doorstep of the inn and welcomed him with as good a grace as he could muster. He could not help but feel that he was completely outclassed by a fully-fledged bishop, dressed all in purple and riding a white mule. He could not help but feel diminished by a man of fifty who had with him nine advisors and what seemed like endless servants.

Freize tried to cheer the cook by explaining that it would all be over one way or another by tonight and that she would have to provide only one great dinner for this unique assembly of great men.

'Never have I had so many lords in the house at any one time,' she fretted. 'I will have to send out for chickens and Jonas will have to let me have the pig that he killed last night.'

'I'll serve the dinner, and help you in the kitchen too,' Freize promised her. 'I'll take the dishes up and put them before the gentry. I'll announce each course and make it sound tremendous.'

'The Lord knows that all you do is eat, and steal food for that animal in the yard. It's causing more trouble to me out there than ever it did in the forest.'

'Should we let it go, d'you think?' Freize asked playfully.

She crossed herself. 'Saints save us, no! Not after it took poor Mrs Rossi's own child and she never recovered from the grief. And last week a lamb, and the week before that a hen right out of the yard. No, the sooner it's dead the better. And your master had better order it killed or there will be a riot here. You can tell him that, from me. There are men coming into the village, shepherds from the highest farms, who won't take kindly to a stranger who comes here and says that our werewolf should be spared. Your master should know that there can only be one ending here: the beast must die.'

'Can I take that ham bone for it?' Freize asked.

'Isn't that the very thing that was going to make soup for the bishop's dinner?'

'There's nothing on it,' Freize urged her. 'Give it to me for the beast. You'll get another bone anyway when Jonas butchers the pig.'

'Take it, take it,' she said impatiently. 'And leave me to get on.'

'I shall come and help as soon as I have fed the beast,' Freize promised her.

She waved him out of the kitchen door into the yard and Freize climbed the platform and looked over the arena wall. The beast was lying down, but when it saw Freize it raised its head and watched him.

Freize vaulted to the top of the wall, swung his long legs over, and sat in comfort there, his legs dangling into the bear pit. 'Now then,' he said gently. 'Good morning to you, beast. I hope you are well this morning?'

The beast came a little closer, to the very centre of the pit, and looked up at Freize. Freize leaned into the pit, holding tightly on to the wall with one hand, leaned down so far that the ham bone was dangling just below his feet. 'Come,' he said gently. 'Come and get this. You have no idea what trouble it cost me to get it for you, but I saw the ham carved off it last night and I set my heart on it for you.'

The beast turned its head a little one way and then the other, as if trying to understand the string of words. Clearly, it understood the gentle tone of voice, as it yearned upwards to the silhouette of Freize, on the wall of the bear pit. 'Come on,' said Freize. 'It's good.'

Cautious as a cat, the beast approached on all fours. It came to the wall of the arena and sat directly under Freize's feet. Freize stretched down to it and slowly the beast uncurled, put its front paws on the walls of the

237

arena and reached up. It stood tall, perhaps more than four feet. Freize fought the temptation to shrink back from it, imagining it would sense his fear; but also he was driven on to see if he could feed this animal by hand, to see if he could bridge the divide between this beast and man, driven by his love of the dumb, the vulnerable, the hurt. He stretched down a little lower and the beast stretched up its shaggy head and gently took the ham bone in its mouth, as if it had been fed by a loving hand, all its life.

The moment it had the meat in its strong jaws, it sprang back from Freize, dropped to all fours and scuttled to the other side of the bear pit. Freize straightened up – and found Ishraq's dark eyes on him.

'Why feed it if I am to shoot it tonight?' she asked quietly. 'Why be kind to it, if it is nothing but a dead beast waiting for the arrow?'

'Perhaps you won't have to shoot it tonight,' Freize answered. 'Perhaps the little lord will find that it's a beast we don't know, or some poor creature that was lost from a fair. Perhaps he will rule that it's an oddity, but not a limb of Satan. Perhaps he will say it is a changeling, put among us by strange people. Surely it is more like an ape than a wolf? What sort of a beast is it? Have you, in all your travels, in all your study, seen such a beast before?'

She looked uncertain. 'No, never. The bishop is talking with your lord now. They are going through all sorts of books and papers to judge what should be done, how it should be tried and tested, how it should be killed, and how it should be buried. The bishop has brought in all sorts of scholars with him who say they know what should be done.'

She paused. 'If it can speak like a Christian, then that alters everything. Your lord, Luca Vero, should be told.'

Freize's glance never wavered. 'Why would you think it could speak?' he said.

She met his gaze without coquetry. 'You're not the only one who takes an interest in it,' she said.

~

All afternoon Luca was closeted with the bishop, his priests, and his scholars, the dining table spread with papers which recorded judgements against werewolves and the histories of wolves going back to the very earliest times: records from the Greek philosophers' accounts, translated by the Arabs into Arabic and then translated back again into Latin. 'So God knows what they were saying in the first place,' Luca confided in Brother Peter. 'There are a dozen prejudices that the words have to get through, there are half a dozen scholars for every single account, and they all have a different opinion.'

'We have to have a clear ruling for our inquiry,' Brother Peter said, worried. 'It's not enough to have a history of anything that anyone thinks they have seen, going back hundreds of years. We are supposed to examine the facts here, and you are supposed to establish the truth. We don't want antique gossip – we want evidence, and then a judgement.'

They cleared the table for the midday meal and the bishop recited a long grace. Ishraq and Isolde were banned from the councils of men and ate dinner in their own room, looking out over the yard. They watched Freize sit on the wall of the bear pit, a wooden platter balanced on his knee,

239

sharing his food with the beast that sat beneath him, glancing up from time to time, watching for scraps, as loyal and as uncomplaining as a dog, but somehow unlike a dog – it had a strange presence, a sort of independence.

'It's a monkey for sure,' Isolde said. 'I have seen a picture of one in a book my father had at home.'

'Can they speak?' Ishraq asked. 'Monkeys? Can they speak?'

'The picture looked as if it could speak, it had lips and teeth like us, and eyes that looked as if it had thoughts and wanted to tell them.'

'I don't think this beast is a monkey,' Ishraq said, carefully. 'I think this beast can speak.'

'Like a parrot?' Isolde asked.

They both watched Freize lean down and the beast reach up. They saw Freize pass a scrap of bread and apple down to the beast and the beast take it in his paw, not in his mouth – take it in his paw and then sit on his haunches and eat it, holding it to his mouth like a big squirrel.

'Not like a parrot,' Ishraq said. 'I think it can speak like a Christian. We cannot kill it, we cannot stand by and see it killed until we know what it is. Clearly it is not a wolf, but what is it?'

'It's not for us to judge.'

'It is,' Ishraq said. 'Not because we are Christians – for I am not. Not because we are men – for we are not. But because we are like the beast: outsiders that other people dread. People don't understand women who are neither wives nor mothers, daughters nor confined. People fear women of passion, women of education. I am a young woman of education, of colour, of unknown religion and my own faith, and I am as strange to the people of this little village as the beast. Should I stand by and see them kill it because they don't understand what it is? If I let them kill it without a word of protest, what would stop them coming for me?'

Ishraq laughed awkwardly. 'You might be strange to them; but nobody would think you are a beast.'

'At the first moment that something went wrong, something that frightened them, something that they could not understand. At that moment, believe me, they would look around for something that was strange to them and they would see me. And in the next moment they would call me a beast. So that they could kill me like a beast.'

'Will you tell Luca this?'

Ishraq shrugged. 'What's the use? He's listening to the bishop, he's not going to listen to me.'

~

At about two in the afternoon the men agreed on what was to be done and the bishop stepped out to the doorstep of the inn to announce their decision. 'If the beast transforms into a full wolf at midnight then the heretic woman will shoot it with a silver arrow,' he ruled. 'The villagers will bury it in a crate packed with wolfsbane at the crossroads and the blacksmith will hammer a stake through its heart.'

'My wife will bring the wolfsbane,' Raul Rossi volunteered. 'God knows she grows enough of it.'

'If the beast does not transform . . .' The bishop raised his hand, and raised his voice, against the murmur of disbelief. 'I know, good people, that you are certain that it will . . . but just suppose that it does not . . . then we will release it to the authorities of this village, the lord and yourself, Master Mugnaio, and you may do with it what you will. Man has dominion over the animals, given to him by God. God Himself has decreed that you can do what you want with this beast. It was a beast running wild near your village, you caught it and held it, God has given you all the beasts into your dominion – you may do with it what you wish.'

Mugnaio nodded grimly. There was little doubt in anyone's mind that the beast would not last long after it was handed over to the village.

'They will hack it to pieces,' Ishraq muttered to Isolde.

'Can we stop them?' she whispered back.

'I don't know.'

'And now,' the bishop ruled, 'I advise you to go about your business until midnight when we will all see the beast. I myself am going to the church where I will say Vespers and Compline and I suggest that you all make your confessions and make an offering to the church before coming to see this great sight which has been wished upon your village.' He paused. 'God will smile on those who donate to the church tonight,' he said. 'The angel of the Lord has passed among you, it is meet to offer him thanks and praise.'

'What does that mean?' Ishraq asked Isolde.

'It means: "pay up for the privilege of a visit from a bishop",' Isolde translated.

'You know, I thought it did.'

～

There was nothing to do but to wait until midnight. Freize fed the beast after dinner and it came and sat at his feet and looked up at him, as if it would speak with him, but it could find no words. In turn Freize wanted to warn the beast, but with its trusting brown eyes peering at him through its matted mane he found he could not explain what was to happen. As the moon rose, man and beast kept a vigil with each other, just as the bishop was keeping vigil in the church. The beast's leonine head turned up to Freize as he sat, darkly profiled against the starlit sky, murmuring quietly to it, hoping that it would speak again; but it said nothing.

'It would be a good time now for you to say your name, my darling,' he said quietly. 'One "God bless" would save your life. Or just "good" again. Speak, beast, before midnight. Or speak at midnight. Speak when everyone is looking at you. But speak. Make sure you speak.'

The animal looked at him, its eyebrows raised, its head on one side, its eyes bright brown through the tangled hair. 'Speak, beast,' Freize urged him again. 'No point being dumb if you can speak. If you could say "God bless" they would account it a miracle. Can you say it? After me? "God bless"?'

~

At eleven o'clock the people started to gather outside the stable door, some carrying billhooks and others scythes and axes. It was clear that if the bishop did not order the animal shot with the silver arrow then the men would take the law into their own hands, cleave it apart with their tools or tear it apart with their bare hands. Freize glanced through the door and saw some men at the back of the crowd levering up the cobbles with an axe head, and tucking the stones into their pockets.

Ishraq came out of the inn to find Freize, reaching down into the bear pit to give the beast a morsel of bread and cheese.

'They are certain to kill it,' she said. 'They have not come for a trial; they have come to see it die.'

'I know,' he nodded.

'Whatever sort of beast it is, I doubt that it is a werewolf.'

He shrugged. 'Not having seen one before, I couldn't say. But this is an animal which seeks contact with humans, it's not a killer like a wolf, it's more companionable than that. Like a dog in its willingness to come close, like a horse in its shy pride, like a cat in its indifference. I don't know what sort of beast it is. But I would put my year's wages on it being an endearing beast, a loving beast, a loyal beast. It's a beast that can learn, it's a beast that can change its ways.'

'They're not going to spare it on my word or yours,' she said.

He shook his head. 'Not on any word from either of us. Nobody listens to the unimportant. But the little lord might save it.'

'He's got the bishop against him, and the bishop's scholars.'

'Would your lady speak up for it?'

She shrugged. 'Who ever listens to a woman?'

'No man of any sense,' he replied instantly and was pleased to see the gleam of her smile, at the joke.

She looked down at the beast. It looked up at her and its ugly truncated face seemed almost human. 'Poor beast,' she said.

'If it was a fairytale you could kiss it,' Freize volunteered. 'You could bend down and kiss it and it would become a prince. Love can make miracles with beasts, so they say. But no! Forgive me, I remember now, that you don't kiss. Indeed, you throw a good man down in the mud for even thinking that you might.'

She did not respond to his teasing, but for a moment she looked very thoughtful. 'You know, you're right. Only love can save it,' she said. 'That is what you have been showing from the moment you first saw it. Love.'

'I wouldn't say that I...' Freize started, but in that moment she was gone.

~

In a very little while, the head of the village, Guglielmo Mugnaio, hammered at the gate of the inn and Freize and the inn servant opened the great double doors to the stable yard. The villagers flooded in and took their places on the tables that surrounded the outer wall of the arena, just as they would for a bear baiting. The men brought strong ale with them, and their wives sipped from their cups, laughing and smiling. The young men of the village came with their sweethearts, and the cook in the kitchen sold little cakes and pies out of the kitchen door, while the maids ran around the stable yard selling mulled ale and wine. It was an execution and a party: both at once.

Ishraq saw Sara Rossi arrive, a great basket of wolfsbane in her arms, and her husband followed behind, leading their donkey loaded with the herb. They tied the donkey in the archway and came into the yard, their boy with his usual sprig of wolfsbane in his hat.

'You came,' Isolde said warmly, stepping forwards. 'I am glad that you are here. I am glad that you felt you could come.'

'My husband thought that we should,' Sara replied, her face very pale. 'He thought it would satisfy me to see the beast dead at last. And everyone else is here. I could not let the village gather without me, they shared my sorrow. They want to see the end of the story.'

'I am glad you came,' Isolde repeated. The woman clambered up on the trestle table beside Ishraq, and Isolde followed her.

'You have the arrowhead?' the woman asked Ishraq. 'You are going to shoot it?'

Without a word, the young woman nodded and showed her the longbow and the silver-tipped arrow.

'You can hit it from here?'

'Without fail,' Ishraq said grimly. 'If he turns into a wolf, then the Inquirer will see him turn, he will tell me to kill him, and I will do so. But I think he is not a wolf, nor anything like a wolf, not a werewolf nor any animal that we know.'

'If we don't know what it is, and can't tell what it is, it's better dead,' the man said firmly, but Sara Rossi looked from the beast to the silver arrowhead and gave a little shiver. Ishraq gazed steadily at her and Isolde put her hand over the woman's trembling fingers. 'Don't you want the beast dead?' Isolde asked her.

She shook her head. 'I don't know. I don't know for sure if it took my child, I don't know for sure if it is the monster that everyone says. And there is something about it that moves me to pity.' She looked at the two young women. 'You will think me very weak; but I am sorry for it,' she said.

She was still speaking as the doors of the inn opened and

Luca, Brother Peter and the bishop, the scholars, and the priests came out. Isolde and Ishraq exchanged one urgent glance. 'I'll tell him,' Isolde said swiftly and jumped down from the stand and made her way to the door of the inn, pushing through the crowd to get to Luca.

'Is it near to midnight?' the bishop asked.

'I have ordered the church bell to be tolled on the hour,' one of the priests replied.

The bishop inclined his head to Luca. 'How are you going to examine the supposed werewolf?' he asked.

'I thought I would wait till midnight, and watch it,' Luca said. 'If it changes into a wolf we will clearly be able to see it. Perhaps we should douse the torches so that the beast can feel the full effect of the moon.'

'I agree. Put out the torches!' the bishop ordered.

As soon as the darkness drowned the yard, everyone was silent, as if fearful of what they were doing. The women murmured and crossed themselves, and the younger children clung to their mothers' skirts. One of them whimpered quietly.

'I can't even see it,' someone complained.

'No, there it is!'

The beast had shrunk back into its usual spot as the yard had filled with noisy people; now, in the darkness it was hard to see, its dark mane against the dark wood of the bear-pit wall, its dark skin concealed against the mud of the earth floor. People blinked and rubbed their eyes, waiting for the dazzle of the torches to wear off, and then Guglielmo Mugnaio said, 'He's moving!'

The beast had risen to its four feet and was looking around, swinging his head as if fearful that danger was coming but not knowing what was about to happen. There was a whisper like a cursing wind that ran around the arena as everyone saw him move, and most men swore that he should be killed at once. Freize saw people feeling for the cobbles they had tucked into their pockets, and knew that they would stone the beast to death.

Isolde got to Luca's side and touched his arm; he leaned his head to listen. 'Don't kill the beast,' she whispered to him.

At the side of the arena, Freize exchanged one apprehensive look with Ishraq, saw the gleam of the silver arrowhead and her steady hand on the bow, and then turned his gaze back to the beast. 'Now gently,' he said, but it could not hear his voice above the low curses that rumbled around it, and it pulled back its head and hunched its shoulders as if it was afraid.

Slowly, ominously, as if announcing a death, the church bell started to toll. The beast flinched at the noise, shaking its mane as if the sonorous clang was echoing in its head. Someone laughed abruptly, but the voice was sharp with fear. Someone said: 'See? He hates the sacred bell. That's proof!' Everyone was watching as the final notes of the midnight bell died on the air and the full moon, bright as a cold sun, rose slowly over the roof of the inn and shone down on the beast as it stood at bay, not moving, sweating in its terror.

There was no sign of hair growing, there was no sign of the beast getting bigger. Its teeth did not grow, nor did it sprout a tail. It stayed on four legs, but the watchers, looking intently, could see that it was shivering, like a little deer will shiver when chilled by frost.

'Is it changing?' the bishop asked Luca. 'I can't see anything. I can't see that it is doing anything.'

'It's just standing, and looking round,' Luca replied. 'I can't see any hair growing, and yet the moon is full on it.'

Somebody in the crowd cruelly howled in a joking impression of a wolf, and the beast turned its head sharply towards the sound as if it hoped it were real, but then shrank back as it realised that it was a harsh jest.

'Is it changing now?' the bishop asked again, urgently.

'I can't see,' Luca said. 'I don't think so.' He looked up. A cloud, no bigger than a clenched fist, was coming up over the full moon, wisps of it already darkening the arena. 'Maybe we should get the torches lit again,' Luca said anxiously. 'We're losing the light.'

'Is the beast changing to wolf?' the bishop demanded even more urgently. 'We will have to tell the people our decision. Can you order the girl to shoot it?'

'I can't,' Luca said bluntly. 'In justice, I cannot. It's not turning to wolf. It's in full moon, it's washed in moonlight, and it's not turning.'

'Don't shoot,' Isolde said urgently to him.

It was getting swiftly darker as the cloud came over the moon. The crowd groaned, a deep, fearful sound. 'Shoot it! Shoot it quickly!' someone called.

It was pitch black now. 'Torches!' Luca shouted. 'Get some torches lit!'

Suddenly there was a piercing terrible scream, and the sound of someone falling: a thud as she hit the ground and then a desperate scrabbling noise as she struggled to her feet.

'What is it?' Luca fought to the front of the crowd

and strained his eyes, peering down into the darkness of the arena. 'Light the torches! In God's name what has happened?'

'Save me!' Sara Rossi cried out in panic. 'Dear God, save me!' She had fallen from the wall into the bear pit and was alone in the arena, her back pressed against the wooden wall, her eyes straining into the darkness as she looked for the beast. The animal was on its feet now, peering towards her with its amber eyes. It could see well in the darkness, though everyone else was blind. It could see the woman, her hands held out before her, as if she thought she could fend off fangs and pouncing claws.

'Ishraq! Shoot!' Luca shouted at her.

He could not see her dark hood, her dark eyes, but he could see the glint of the silver of the arrow, he could see the arrow on the string pointed steadily towards the dark shadow, which was the beast scenting the air, taking one hesitant step forwards. And then he heard her voice; but she was not calling to him, she was shouting down to Sara Rossi as she froze in terror, pinned against the wall of the arena.

'Call him!' Ishraq shouted to Sara. 'Call the beast.'

The white blur of Sara's frightened face turned up to Ishraq. 'What?' She was deaf with terror: too afraid to understand anything. 'What?'

'Don't you know his name?' Ishraq demanded gently, the silver arrow pointing unwaveringly at the beast slowly creeping closer.

'How should I know the name of the beast?' she whispered up. 'Get me out! Get me up. For the love of God! Save me!'

'Look at him. Look at him with your love. Who have you missed for all this time? What was his name?'

Sara stared at Ishraq as if she were speaking Arabic, and then she turned to the beast. It was closer still, head bowed, moving its weight from one side to the other, as if readying for a pounce. It was coming, without a doubt. It snarled, showing yellow teeth. Its head raised up, smelling fear; it was ready to attack. It took three stiff-legged steps forwards; now it would duck its head and run and lunge for her throat.

'Ishraq! Shoot the beast!' Luca yelled. 'That's an order!'

'Call him,' Ishraq urged the woman desperately. 'Call him by the name you love most in the world.'

Outside the arena, Raul Rossi dashed to the stables shouting for a ladder, leaving his son frozen with horror on the bear-pit fence, watching his mother face the beast.

Everyone was silent. They could just see the beast in the flickering light of the two torches, could see it slowly coming towards the woman, in the classic stalk of a wolf, its head down, level with its hunched shoulders, its eyes on the prey, sinuously moving forwards.

Freize thrust one torch into Luca's hand and readied himself to jump down into the bear pit with another flaming in his grip as Sara spoke: 'Stefan?' she asked in a hushed whisper. 'Stefan? Is that you?'

The beast stopped, putting its head on one side.

'Stefan?' she whispered. 'Stefan, my son? Stefan – my son?'

Freize froze on the side of the arena, silently watching as the beast rose from his four legs to his hind legs, as if he was remembering how to walk, as if he was remembering the woman who had held his hands for every step that he took. Sara pushed herself off the arena wall and moved towards him, her legs weak beneath her, hands outstretched.

'It's you,' she said wonderingly, but with absolute certainty. 'It's you . . . Stefan. My Stefan, come to me.'

He took a step towards her, then another, and then in a rush which made the watching people gasp with fear but which made his mother cry out with joy, he dashed at her and flung himself into her arms. 'My boy! My boy!' she cried out, wrapping her arms around his scarred body, pulling his matted head to her shoulder: 'My son!'

He looked up at her, his dark eyes bright through his matted mane of hair. 'Mama,' he said in his little boy's voice. 'Mama.'

~

The bishop got hold of Luca for a whispered angry consultation. 'You knew of this?'

'Not I.'

'It was your heretic servant who had an arrow on the bow and didn't shoot. It was your fool of a servant who has been feeding the beast and coaxing it. He must have known, but he led us into this trap.'

'She was ready with the arrow, you saw her yourself. And my servant was about to jump into the arena and get between the woman and the beast himself.'

'Why didn't she shoot? She said that she could shoot. Why didn't she do so?'

'How would I know? She is no servant of mine. I will ask her what she thought she was doing and I will write it up in my report.'

'The report is the last of our worries!'

'Forgive me, Your Eminence, it is my principal concern.'

'But the beast! The beast! We came to kill it and show a triumph for the Church over sin. There can be no killing of the beast now.'

'Of course not,' Luca said. 'As my report will show. He is no beast. His mother has claimed him back. She will take him and bathe him and cut his hair and nails and teach him to wear clothes again and to speak.'

'And what do you think you will say in your report?' the bishop said acidly. 'You had a werewolf in your keeping and behold now you have nothing but a dirty wild boy. You don't come out of this very well, any more than we do.'

'I shall say that your scholarship revealed to us what happened here,' Luca said smoothly. 'Among the other accounts that your scholars prepared, you brought us the classical story of Romulus and Remus, who were raised by a wolf and founded the City of Rome, our rock. You told us of other stories of children who had been lost in the forest and were raised by wolves and then by God's grace found again. Your library held these stories, your scholarship recognised them, your authority warned us what might have happened here.'

The bishop paused, mollified, his rounded belly swelling with his vanity. 'The people were waiting for an execution,' he warned. 'They won't understand the miracle that has happened here. They wanted a death, you are offering them a restoration.'

'That is the power of your authority,' Luca said quickly. 'Only you can explain to them what happened. Only you have the scholarship and the skill to tell them. Only you can

253

proclaim a miracle. Will you preach now? It is the theme of the Prodigal Son, I think: the return of the lost one whose father sees him afar off and runs to greet him, loving him dearly.'

The bishop looked thoughtful. 'They will need guidance,' he considered, one plump finger to his lips. 'They were expecting a trial to the death. They will want a death. They are a savage unlearned people. They were expecting an execution and they will want a death. The Church shows its power by putting evil-doers to death. We have to be seen to conquer over sin. There is nothing that brings more people to the church than a witch-burning or an execution.'

'Your Grace, they are lost in the darkness of their own confusion. They are your sheep; lead them to the light. Tell them that a miracle has taken place here. A little child was lost in the wood, he was raised by wolves, he became like a wolf. But as Your Eminence watched, he recognised his mother. Who can doubt that the presence of a bishop made all the difference? These are an ignorant and fearful people but you can preach a sermon here that people will remember forever. They will always remember the day that the great bishop came to their village and a miracle took place.'

The bishop rose up and straightened his cape. 'I will preach to them from the open window of the dining room,' he said. 'I will preach now, while they are gathered before me. I shall preach a midnight sermon, extempore. Get torches to shine on me. And take notes.'

'At once,' Luca said. He hurried from the room and gave the order to Freize. The balcony glowed with torchlight, the people, abuzz with speculation and fear, turned their faces upwards. As their attention went to the bishop, glorious in his purple cope and mitre at the window, Freize and Ishraq, Raul Rossi and his younger son, unbarred the single entrance door into the arena, and went in to fetch Sara Rossi, her eldest son held tightly in her arms.

'I want to take him home,' she said simply to her husband. 'This is our son Stefan, returned to us by a miracle.'

'I know it,' Raul replied. His wind-burned cheeks were wet with tears. 'I knew him too. As soon as he said "Mama", I knew it. I recognised his voice.'

Stefan could barely walk; he stumbled and leaned on his mother, his dirty head on her shoulder.

'Can we put him on the donkey?' Freize suggested.

They lifted the panniers of wolfsbane from the donkey's back but the herb was still in its mane and clinging to the animal's back. Sara helped him up, and he did not flinch either at the touch of the herb or the smell of the flowers. Ishraq, watching quietly in the darkness, gave a quick affirmative nod.

Freize led the donkey away from the village, up the twisting little steps, as Sara walked beside her son cooing soothingly to him. 'Soon we will be home,' she said. 'You will remember your home. Your bed is just as it was, the sheets on the bed, the pillow waiting for you. Your little poppet Roos – do you remember your toy? – still on your pillow. In all these years I have never changed your room. It has always been waiting for you. I have always been waiting for you.'

On the other side of the donkey, Raul Rossi held his son steady, one hand on his little tanned leg, one hand on his scarred back. Ishraq and Isolde came behind with his little brother Tomas, his dog at his heels.

The farmhouse was shuttered for the night, but they brought the wolf-boy into the hall and he looked around, his eyes squinting against the firelight, without fear, as if he could just remember, as in a dream, when this had been his home.

'We can care for him now,' Raul Rossi said to the girls and Freize. 'My wife and I thank you from our hearts for all you have done.'

Sara went with them to the door. 'You have given me my son,' she said to Ishraq. 'You have done for me what I prayed the Virgin Mary would do. I owe you a debt for all my life.'

Ishraq made a strange gesture: she put her hands together in the gesture of prayer and then with her fingertips she touched her own forehead, her lips, and her breast, and then bowed to the farmer's wife. '*Salaam*. It was you who did a great thing. It was you who had the courage to love him for so long,' she said. 'It was you who lived with grief and tried to bury your sorrow and yet kept his room for him, and your heart open to him. It was you that did not accuse the beast – when the whole village howled for vengeance. It was you who had pity for him. And then it was you who had the courage to say his name when you thought you faced a wolf. All I did was throw you down into the pit.'

'Wait a moment,' Freize said. 'You threw her down into the bear pit to face a beast?'

Isolde pursed her lips in disapproval, but clearly she was not at all surprised.

Ishraq faced Freize. 'I'm afraid I did.'

Raul Rossi, one arm around his wife, one around Tomas's shoulders, looked at Ishraq. 'Why did you do it?' he asked simply. 'You took a great risk, both with my wife's life and with your own. For if you had been wrong, and she had been hurt, the village would have mobbed you. If she had died there, attacked by the beast, they would have killed you and thrown your body down for the wolf to eat.'

Ishraq nodded. 'I know,' she said. 'But in the moment – when I was sure it was your son, and I was certain they would order me to shoot him – it was the only thing I could think of doing.'

Isolde laughed out loud, put her arm around her friend's shoulders and hugged her close. 'Only you!' she exclaimed. 'Only you would think that there was nothing to do but throw a good woman into a bear pit to face a beast!'

'Love,' Ishraq said. 'I knew that he needed love. I knew that she loved her son.' She turned to Freize. 'You knew it too. You knew that love would see through the worst of appearances.'

Freize shook his head, and stepped outside into the moonlight. 'I'll be damned,' he said to the changing sky. 'I will be damned and double damned if I ever understand how women think.'

~

The next morning they saw the bishop leave in his pomp, his priests before him on their white mules, his scholars carrying the records, his clerks already writing up and copying his sermon on 'The Prodigal Son', which they said was a model of its kind.

'It was very moving,' Luca told him on the doorstep. 'I have mentioned it in my report. I have quoted many of the passages. It was inspirational, and all about authority.'

As soon as he was gone, they ate their own midday dinner and ordered their horses brought out into the stable yard. Freize showed Ishraq her horse, saddled and bridled. 'No pillion saddle,' he said. 'I know you like to ride alone. And the Lord knows, you can handle yourself and, I daresay, a horse as well.'

'But I'll ride alongside you, if I may,' she said.

Freize narrowed his eyes and scrutinised her for sarcasm. 'No,' he said after a moment's thought. 'I'm just a servant, you are a lady. I ride behind.'

His smile gleamed at the consternation on her face.

'Freize – I never meant to offend you . . .'

'Now you see,' he crowed triumphantly. 'Now you see what happens when you throw a good man down on his back on the cobbles – when you go tipping good women into bear pits. Too strong by half, is what I would say. Too opinionated by half, is what I would propose. Too proud of your opinion to make any man a good sweetheart or wife. Bound to end in a cold grave as a spinster, I would think. If not burned as a witch, as has already been suggested.'

She raised her hands as if in surrender. 'Clearly I have offended you—' she began.

'You have,' Freize said grandly. 'And so I shall ride behind, like a servant, and you may ride ahead, like an opinionated overly powerful lady, like a woman who does not know her place in the world, nor anyone else's. Like a woman who goes chucking men onto their backs, and women into bear pits, and causing all sorts of upset. You shall ride ahead, in your pomp, as vain as the bishop, and we know which of us will be the happier.'

Ishraq bowed her head under his storm of words, and mounted her horse without replying. Clearly, there was no dealing with Freize in his state of outrage.

Isolde came out of the inn and Freize helped her into the saddle and then Luca came out followed by Brother Peter.

'Where to?' Ishraq asked Luca.

He mounted his horse and brought it alongside hers. 'Due east, I think,' he said. He looked to Brother Peter. 'Isn't that right?'

Brother Peter touched the letter in his jacket pocket. 'North-east it says on the outside of the letter, and at breakfast tomorrow, at Pescara, if we get there, God willing, I am to open our orders.'

'We will have another mission?' Luca asked.

'We will,' Brother Peter said. 'All I have is the directions to Pescara, but I don't know what the instructions will say nor where they will take us.' He looked at Isolde and Ishraq. 'I take it that the ladies will be travelling with us to Pescara?'

Luca nodded.

'And leaving us there?' Brother Peter prompted.

'Can't go soon enough for me,' Freize said from the mounting block as he tightened his girth and got on his horse. 'In case she takes it into her head to throw me into a river – or into the sea when we get there, which clearly she might do if she takes it into her own wilful head.'

'They will leave us when they find safe companions,' Luca ruled. 'As we agreed.' But he brought his horse alongside Isolde and reached out to put his hand on hers, as she

259

held her reins. 'You will stay with us?' he asked quietly. 'While our roads go together?'

The smile that she gave him told him that she would. 'I will stay with you,' she promised. 'While our roads lie together.'

The little cavalcade of Luca and Isolde, Brother Peter and Ishraq, with Freize behind them, surrounded by his beloved extra horses, clattered out of the gateway of the inn, not yet knowing where they were going, nor what they had to do, and headed north-east for Pescara – and for whatever lay beyond.

*Find out what happens as the group
continue their journey in . . .*

STORMBRINGERS

THE ROAD FROM ROME TO PESCARA, ITALY, NOVEMBER 1460

The five travellers on horseback on the rutted track to Pescara made everyone turn and stare: the woman who brought them weak ale in a roadside inn; the peasant stacking the hewn stones for a wall by the side of the road; the boy trailing home from school to work in his father's vineyard. Everyone smiled at the radiance of the couple at the front of the little cavalcade, for they were beautiful, young, and – as anyone could see – falling in love.

'But where's it all going to end, d'you think?' Freize asked Ishraq, nodding ahead to Luca and Isolde as they rode along the ruler-straight track that ran due east towards the Adriatic coast.

It was golden autumn weather and, though the deeply scored ruts in the dirt road would be impassable in winter-time, the going was good for now, the horses were strong and they were setting a fair pace to the coast.

Freize, a square-faced young man with a ready smile, only a few years older than his master Luca, didn't wait for Ishraq's response. 'He's head over heels in love with her,' he continued, 'and if he had lived in the world and ever met a girl before, he would know to be on his guard. But he was in the monastery as a skinny child, and so he thinks her an angel descended from heaven. She's as golden-haired and beautiful as any fresco in the monastery. It'll end in tears, she'll break his heart.'

Ishraq hesitated to reply. Her dark eyes were fixed on the two figures ahead of them. 'Why assume it will be him who gets hurt? What if he breaks *her* heart?' she asked. 'For I have never seen Isolde like this with any other boy. And he will be her first love too. For all that she was raised as a lady in the castle, there were no passing knights allowed, and no troubadours came to visit singing of love. Don't think it was like a ballad, with ladies and chevaliers and roses thrown down from a barred window; she was very strictly brought up. Her father trained her up to be the lady of the castle and he expected her to rule his lands. But her brother stole everything and she was bundled into a nunnery. These days on the road are her first chance to be free in the real world – mine too. No wonder she is happy.

'And anyway, I think that it's wonderful that the first man she meets should be Luca. He's about our age, the most handsome man we've – I mean – *she's* ever met; he's kind, he's really charming, and he can't take his eyes off her. What girl *wouldn't* fall in love with him on sight?'

'There is another handsome young man she sees daily,'

Freize suggested. 'Practical, kind, good with animals, strong, willing, useful ... and handsome. Most people would say handsome, I think. Some would probably say irresistible.'

Ishraq delighted in misunderstanding him, looking into his broad smiling face and taking in his blue honest eyes. 'You mean Brother Peter?' she glanced behind them at the older clerk who followed leading the donkey. 'Oh no, he's much too serious for her, and besides he doesn't even like her. He thinks the two of us will distract you from your mission.'

'Well, you do!' Freize gave up teasing Ishraq and returned to his main concern. 'Luca is commissioned by the Pope himself to understand the last days of the world. His mission is to understand the end of days. If it's to be the terrible day of judgement tomorrow or the day after – as they all seem to think – he shouldn't be spending his last moments on earth courting with an ex-nun.'

'I think he could do nothing better,' Ishraq said stoutly. 'He's a handsome young man, finding his way in the world, and Isolde is a beautiful girl just escaped from the rule of her family and the command of men. What better way could they spend the last days of the world, than falling in love?'

'Well, you only think that because you're not a Christian, but some sort of pagan,' Freize returned roundly, pointing to her pantaloons under her sweeping cape and the sandals on her bare feet. 'And you lack all sense of how important we are. He has to report to the Pope for all the signs that the world is about to end, for all the manifestations of evil in the world. He's young, but he is a member of a most important order. A secret order, a secret papal order.'

She nods. 'I do, so often, lack a sense of how very important men are. You do right to reproach me.'

He heard, at once, the ripple of laughter in her voice,
and he could not help but delight in her staunch sense of
independence. 'We *are* important,' he insisted. 'We men
rule the world, and you should have more respect for me.'

'Aren't you a mere servant?' she teased.

'And you are – a what?' he demanded. 'An Arab slave?
A scholar? A heretic? A servant? Nobody seems to know
quite what you are. An animal like a unicorn, said to be
very strange and marvellous but actually rarely seen and
probably good for nothing.'

'Oh, I don't know,' she said comfortably. 'I was raised
by my dark-skinned beautiful mother in a strange land to
always be sure who I was – even if nobody else knew.'

'A unicorn indeed,' he said.

She smiled. 'Perhaps.'

'You certainly have the air of a young woman who knows
her own mind. It's very unmaidenly.'

'But of course, I do wonder what will become of us both,'
she conceded more seriously. 'We have to find Isolde's
godfather's son, Count Wladislaw, and then we have to
convince him to order her brother to give back her castle
and lands. What if he refuses to help us? What shall we do
then? However will she get home? Really, whether she's in
love with Luca or not is the least of our worries.'

Ahead of them, Isolde threw back her head and laughed
aloud at something Luca had whispered to her.

'Aye, she looks worried sick,' Freize remarked.

'We are happy, *inshallah*,' she said. 'She is easier in her
mind than she has been in months, ever since the death of

her father. And if, as your Pope thinks, the world is going to end, then we might as well be happy today, and not worry about the future.'

The fifth member of their party, Brother Peter, brought his horse up alongside them. 'We'll be coming into the village of Piccolo as the sun sets,' he said. 'Brother Luca should not be riding with the woman. It looks ...' He paused, searching for the right reproof ...

'Normal?' Ishraq offered impertinently.

'Happy,' Freize agreed.

'Improper,' Brother Peter corrected them. 'At best it looks careless, and as if he were not a young man promised to the Church.' He turned to Ishraq. 'Your lady should ride alongside you, both of you with your heads down and your eyes on the ground like maidens with pure minds, and you should speak only to each other, and that seldom and very quietly. Brother Luca should ride alone in prayer, or with me in thoughtful conversation. And anyway, I have our orders.'

At once, Freize slapped his hand to his forehead. 'The sealed orders!' he exclaimed wrathfully. 'Any time we are minding our own business and going quietly to somewhere, a pleasant inn ahead of us, perhaps a couple of days with nothing to do but feed up the horses and rest ourselves, out come the sealed orders and we are sent off to inquire into God knows what!'

'We are on a mission of inquiry,' Brother Peter said quietly. 'Of course we have sealed orders which I am commanded to open and read at certain times. Of course we are sent to inquire. The very point of this journey is not – whatever some people may think – to ride from one pleasant inn to another, meeting women; but to discover what signs there are of the end of days, of the end of the world. And I have to open these orders at sunset today, and discover where we are to go next and what we are to inspect.'

Freize put two fingers in his mouth and made an ear-piercing whistle. At once the two lead horses, obedient to his signal, stopped in their tracks. Luca and Isolde turned round and rode the few paces back to where the others were halted under the shade of some thick pine trees. The scent of the resin was as powerful as perfume in the warm evening air. The horses' hooves crunched on the fallen pine cones and their shadows were long on the pale sandy soil.

'New orders,' Freize said to his master Luca, nodding at Brother Peter, who took a cream manuscript, heavily sealed with red wax and ribbons, from the inside pocket of his jacket. To Brother Peter he turned and said curiously, 'How many more of them have you got tucked away in there?'

The older man did not trouble to answer the servant. With the little group watching he broke the seals in silence and unfolded the stiff paper. He read, and they saw him give a little sigh of disappointment.

'Not back to Rome!' Freize begged him, unable to bear the suspense for a moment longer. 'Tell me we don't have to turn round and go back to the old life!' He caught Ishraq's gleam of amusement. 'The inquiry is an arduous duty,' he corrected himself quickly. 'But I don't want to leave it incomplete. I have a sense of duty, of obligation.'

'You'd do anything rather than return to the monastery and be a kitchen lad again,' she said accurately. 'Just as I would rather be here than serving as a lady companion in an isolated castle. At least we are free, and every day we wake up and know that anything could happen.'

'I remind you, we don't travel for our own pleasure,' Brother Peter said sternly. 'We are commanded to go to the fishing village of Piccolo, take a ship across the sea to Split and travel onwards to Zagreb. We are to take the pilgrim road to the chapels of St. George and St. Martin at Our Lady's church outside Zagreb.'

There was a muffled gasp from Isolde. 'Zagreb!' A quick gesture from Luca as he reached out for her – and then snatched back his hand, remembering that he might not touch her – betrayed him too.

'We travel on your road,' he said, the joy in his voice audible to everyone. 'We can stay together.'

The flash of assent from her dark blue eyes was ignored by Brother Peter who was deep in the new orders. 'We are to inquire on the way as to anything we see that is out of the ordinary,' he read. 'We are to stop and set up an inquiry if we encounter anything that indicates the work of Satan, the rise of unknown fears, the evidence of the wickedness of man, or the end of days.' He stopped reading and refolded the letter, looking at the four young people. 'And so, it seems, that since Zagreb is on the way to Buda-Pest, and since the ladies insist that they must go there to seek Count Wladislaw, that God Himself wills that we must travel the same road as these young ladies.'

Isolde had herself well under control by the time Brother Peter raised his eyes to her. She kept her gaze down, careful not to look at Luca. 'Of course we would be grateful for your company,' she said demurely. 'But this is a famous pilgrims' road. There will be other people who will be going the same way. We can join them. We don't need to burden you.'

The bright look on Luca's face told her that she was no burden; but Brother Peter answered before anyone else could speak. 'Certainly, I would advise that as soon as you meet a party with ladies travelling to Buda-Pest you should join them. We cannot be guides and guardians for you. We have to serve a great mission; and you are young women – however much you try to behave with modesty you cannot help but be distracting and misleading.'

'Saved our bacon at Vittorito,' Freize observed quietly. He nodded towards Ishraq. 'She can fight and shoot an arrow, and knows medicine too. Hard to find anyone more useful as a travelling companion. Hard to find a better comrade on a dangerous journey.'

'Clearly distracting,' Peter sternly repeated.

'As they say, they will leave us when they find a suitable party to join,' Luca ruled. His delight that he was to be with Isolde for another night, and another after that, even if it was only a few more nights, was clear to everyone, especially to her. Her dark blue eyes met his hazel ones in a long silent look.

'You don't even ask what we are to do at the sacred site?' Brother Peter demanded reproachfully. 'At the chapels? You don't even want to know that there are reports of heresy that we are to discover?'

'Yes, of course,' Luca said quickly. 'You must tell me what we are to see. I will study. I will need to think about it. I will create a full inquiry and you shall write the report and send it to the lord of our order, for the Pope to see. We shall do our work, as commanded by our lord, by the Pope, and by God Himself.'

'And best of all, we can get a good dinner in Piccolo,' Freize remarked cheerfully, looking at the setting sun. 'And tomorrow morning will be time enough to worry about hiring a boat to sail across to Croatia.'

PICCOLO, ITALY, NOVEMBER 1460

The little fishing village was ringed on the landward side by high walls pierced by a single gate that was officially closed at sunset. Freize shouted up for the porter, who opened the shutter to stick his head out of the window and argue that travellers should show respect for the rules, and might not enter the village after the curfew bell had tolled and the village gates closed for the night.

'The sun's barely down!' Freize complained. 'The sky is still bright!'

'It's down,' the gatekeeper replied. 'How do I know who you are?'

'Because, since it's not darkest night, you can perfectly well see who we are,' Freize replied. 'Now let us in, or it will be the worse for you. My master is an Inquirer for the Holy

Father himself, we couldn't be more important if we were all cardinals.'

Grumbling, the porter slammed the shutter on his window and came down to the gate. As the travellers waited outside, in the last golden light of the day, they could hear him, complaining bitterly as he heaved the creaking gate open, and they clattered in under the arch.

The village was no more than a few streets running down the hill to the quay. They dismounted once they were inside the walls and led the horses down the narrow way to the quayside, going carefully on the well-worn cobble-stones. They had entered by the west gate of the perimeter wall which ran all round the village, pierced by a little bolted doorway on the high north side and a matching door to the south. As they picked their way down to the harbour they saw, facing the darkening sea, the only inn of the village with a welcoming door standing wide open, and bright windows twinkling with candlelight.

The five travellers led their horses to the stable yard, handed them over to the lad, and went into the hallway of the inn. They could hear, through the half-open windows, the slap of the waves against the walls of the quay, and could smell the haunting scent of salt water and the marshy stink of fishing nets. Piccolo was a busy port with nearly a dozen ships in the little harbour, either bobbing at anchor in the bay or tied up to rings set in the harbour wall. The village was noisy even though the autumn darkness was falling. The fishermen were making their way home to their cottages, and the last travellers were disembarking from the boats that plied their trade crossing and recrossing the darkening sea. Croatia was less than a hundred miles due east and people coming into the inn, blowing on their cold fingers, complained of a contrary wind which had prolonged their journey for nearly two days, and had chilled them to the bone. Soon it would be winter, and too late in the year for sea voyages for all but the most fearless.

Ishraq and Isolde took the last private bedroom in the house, a little room under the slanting roof. They could hear the occasional scuffling from mice and probably rats under the tiles, but this did not disturb them. They laid their riding cloaks on the bed and washed their hands and faces in the earthenware bowl.

Freize, Luca and Brother Peter would bed down in the attic room opposite with half a dozen other men, as was usual when there were many travellers on the road and the inn was crowded. Brother Peter and Luca tossed a coin for the last place in the big shared bed and when Luca lost he had to make do with a straw mattress on the floor. The landlady of the inn apologised to Luca whose good looks and good manners earned him attention everywhere they went, but she said that the inn was busy tonight, and tomorrow it would be even worse as there was a rumour that a mighty pilgrimage was coming into town.

'How we'll feed them all I don't know,' she said. 'They'll have to take fish soup and bread and like it.'

'Where are they all going?' Luca asked, ashamed to find that he was hoping that they were not taking the road to Zagreb. He was anxious to be alone with Isolde, and determined that she should not join another party.

'Jerusalem, they say,' she replied.

'What a journey! What a challenge!' he exclaimed.

She smiled at him. 'Not for me,' she said. 'It's challenge

enough making gallons of soup. What will the ladies want for their dinner?'

Freize, who sometimes served their dinner and sometimes ate with them, depending on the size of the inn and whether they needed help in the kitchen, was sent into the private dining room by the landlady and took his place with his friends at the table.

He was greeted with little smiles from both girls. He bowed to Lady Isolde and noticed that her blonde hair was coiled demurely under a plain headdress, and her dark blue eyes were carefully turned away from Luca, who could not stop himself glancing towards her. Brother Peter, ignoring everyone, composed a lengthy grace and Isolde and Luca prayed with him.

Ishraq kept her dark eyes open and sat in quiet thought while the prayer went on. She never recited the Christian prayers, but as Freize noted – peeking through his fingers – she seemed to use the time of Grace for her own silent thoughts. She did not seem to pray to her god either; as far as he knew, she carried no prayer mat with her few clothes and he had never seen her turn to the east. She was in this, as in so much else, a mystery, Freize thought, and a law to herself.

'Amen!' he said loudly, as he realised that Brother Peter had finally finished and that dinner might be served.

The innkeeper's wife had excelled herself, and brought five dishes to the table: two sorts of fish, some stewed mutton, a rather tough roast pheasant, and a local delicacy, pitadine, which was a pancake wrapped around a rich savoury filling. Freize tried it in the spirit of adventure and pronounced it truly excellent. She smiled and told him he could have pitadine for breakfast, dinner and supper, if he liked it so much. The filling changed according to the time of day, but the pancake remained the same. There was coarse brown bread baked hot from the oven with local butter, and some honey cakes for pudding.

The travellers dined well, hungry from their long ride, and easy and companionable together. Even Brother Peter was so warmed by good food and the friendliness of the inn that he poured a glass of wine for the two young women and wished them, '*Salute.*'

After dinner the ladies rose and said goodnight, and Ishraq went up to the little bedroom while Isolde lingered on the stairs. Luca rose casually from the dining table, and, heading for the inn's front door, happened to arrive at the foot of the stairs in time to say goodnight to her. She was hesitating on the first two steps, holding her lit candle, and he laid his hand over hers on the stair rail.

'And so it seems we travel together for a little longer,' he said tentatively, looking up at her.

She nodded. 'Though I will have to keep my word to Brother Peter, and go with another party if we meet one,' she reminded him.

'Only a suitable one,' he reminded her.

She dimpled. 'It would have to be very suitable,' she agreed.

'Promise me, you will be very careful who you choose?'

'I shall be extremely careful,' she said, her eyes dancing, and then she lowered her voice and added more seriously, 'I shall not readily leave you, Luca Vero.'

'I can't imagine parting from you,' he exclaimed. 'I really can't imagine not seeing you first thing in the morning, and talking to you through the day. I can't imagine making this journey without you now. I know it is foolish – it's been only a few weeks, but I find you more and more . . .'

He broke off, and she came down one step of the stair, so that her head was only a little higher than his. 'More and more?' she whispered.

'Essential,' he said simply, and he stepped up on the bottom step so they were level at last. Tantalisingly, they were so close that they could have kissed if he had leaned only a little more, or if she had turned her face towards him.

Slowly, he leaned a little more; slowly, she turned . . .

'Shall we plan our journey before we go to bed?' Brother Peter asked drily from the doorway of the dining room. 'Brother Luca? So that we can make an early start tomorrow?'

Luca turned from Isolde with a quiet exclamation. 'Yes,' he said, 'of course.' He stepped back down to Brother Peter. 'Yes, we should. Goodnight, Isolde.'

'Goodnight,' she said sweetly and watched him as he went back into the little dining room and shut the door. Only when he was gone did she put her hand to her mouth as if she had been longing for the kiss that could not happen on this night, and should never happen at all.

In the morning the quayside was alive with noise and bustle. The boats that had been out at sea since dawn were jostling for position in the port. The earliest arrival was tied up alongside the harbour wall, the others tied to it and the farthest ones throwing ropes at bow and stern and the fishermen walking on planks laid across one boat to another with huge round woven baskets of fish dripping on their broad shoulders till they reached the shore and stacked them in their usual place for the buyers to come and see what they had landed.

The air above the boats was filled with seagulls, circling and swooping for offcuts of fish, their cries and screams a constant babel, the flash of their white wings bright in the morning sunshine.

A little auction of the catch was taking place at the harbour wall, a man yelling prices to the crowd, who raised their hands or shouted their names when he reached a price that they could meet, with the winner going forward, paying up, and hefting the basket to their cart to take inland, or carrying it up the stone steps into the town, higher up the hill, to the central market.

Basket after basket heaped with shoals of sardines came ashore, the fish brilliantly shining and stippled black like tarnished silver, and the landlady of the inn walked along the quay with two baskets and had the lad from the stables carry them home for her. The other women of the town hung back and waited for the buyers to drive down the prices before they approached and offered their money for a single fish. Wives and daughters went to their boats and took the pick of their catches for a good dinner that night. Fishermen had sets of scales on the quayside and leaned from their boats to sling iridescent-scaled fish into the tray, holding up the balance to show to the waiting women, who then hooked the fish and dropped them into the bottom of their baskets.

Sleek cats wound their way around the legs of the buyers and sellers alike, waiting for the fish to be gutted and cleaned and scraps dropped down to them. In the sky above, the seagulls still wheeled and cried, the cold sunlight of the early morning shining on them as brightly as on the dazzling scales of the fish, as if the air, the land and the sea, were all celebrating the

284

richness of the ocean, the courage of the fishermen and the profitable trade of Piccolo.

Freize was strolling through the bustle of the quayside, sniffing the pungent scent of fish, marsh and salt, pulling off his cap to the prettier of the fish wives, stepping around the boxes of fish and the lobster pots, relishing the noise and the joy and the vitality of the port. He revelled in being far from the quiet solitude of the monastery as he made his way through the crowd to find a ship that would take them due east, to the port of Split. He had spoken to one master already and wanted to find another to compare the price. 'Though I don't doubt they'll have seen me coming and fixed the price already,' he grumbled to himself. 'A party on the road from Rome, two beautiful ladies and an Inquirer of the Church – bound to put the price up. Not to mention Brother Peter's long face. I myself would charge double for him, for the sheer misery of his company.'

As he paused, looking around him, a ginger kitten came and wound herself around his ankles. Freize looked down. 'Hungry?' he asked. The little face came up, the tiny pink mouth opened in a mew. Without thinking twice, Freize bent down and lifted the little animal in one hand. He could feel the little ribs through the soft fur. It was so small its body fitted in his broad palm. It started to purr, its whole body resonating with the deep, happy sound. 'Come on then,' Freize said. 'Let's see what we can find for you.'

In a corner of the harbour, seated on a stone seat and sheltered from the cold morning wind by a roughly built wall, a woman was gutting her fish and throwing the entrails down on the floor where they were snatched at once by bigger cats. 'Too big for you,' Freize remarked to the kitten. 'You'll have to grow before you can fight for your dinner there.' To the woman he said, 'Bless you, Sister, can I have a morsel for this kitten here?'

Without raising her head she cut a little piece off the tail and handed it up to him. 'You'd better have deep pockets if you're going to feed stray cats,' she said disapprovingly.

'No, for see, you are kind to me, and I am kind to her,' Freize pointed out, and sat beside her, put the little cat on his knee, and let her eat the tail of the fish, working from plump flesh to scaly end with remarkable speed.

'Are you planning to sit around all day looking at a kitten? Do you have no work to do?' she asked, as the kitten sat on Freize's knee and started to wash her paws with her little pink tongue.

'There I am! Forgetting myself!' Freize jumped to his feet, snatching up the kitten. 'I have work to do and important work it is too! So thank you, and God bless you, Sister, and I must go.'

She looked up, her face criss-crossed with deep wrinkles. 'And what urgent work do you do, that you have the time and the money to stop and feed stray kittens?'

He laughed. 'I work for the Church, Sister. I serve a young master who is an Inquirer for the Pope himself. A brilliant young man, chosen above all the others from his monastery for his ability to study and understand everything – unknown things. He is an Inquirer,

286

and I am his friend and servant. I am in the service of God.'

'Not a very jealous God,' she said, showing her black teeth in a smile. 'Not a God who demands good time-keeping.'

'A God who would not see a sparrow fall,' Freize said. 'Praise Him and all the little beings of His creation. Good day.'

He tucked the kitten in his pocket where she curled around and put her paws on the top seam so that her little head was just poking out and she could see her way as they went through the crowd to where the fishermen were spreading out their nets for mending, taking down sails and coiling ropes on the ships.

At last Freize found a master who was prepared to take them across the sea to the town of Split for a reasonable fee. But he would not go until midday. 'I have been fishing half the night, I want my breakfast and dry clothes and then I'll take you,' he said. 'Sail at noon. You'll hear the church bells for Sext.'

They shook hands on the agreement and Freize went back to the inn, pausing at the stables to order the grooms to have the horses ready for sailing at midday. It seemed to him that the crowds at the quayside had grown busier, even though the market had finished trading. At the inn, there were many young people at the front door, peering into the hallway, and in the stable yard about a dozen children were sitting on the mounting block and the wall of the well. One or two of them had hauled up the dripping bucket from the well and were drinking from their cupped hands.

'What are you doing here?' he asked a group of about six

boys, none of them more than twelve years old. 'Where are your parents?'

They did not answer him immediately, but solemnly crossed themselves. 'My Father is in heaven,' one of them said.

'Well, God bless you,' Freize said, assuming that they were a party of begging orphans, travelling together for safety. He crossed the yard and went into the inn through the kitchen door, where the landlady was lifting half a dozen good-sized loaves of rough rye bread from the oven.

'Smells good,' Freize said appreciatively.

'Get out of the way,' she returned. 'There is nothing for you until breakfast.'

He laughed and went on to the small stone hall at the entrance of the inn and found Luca and Brother Peter talking with the innkeeper.

Luca turned as he heard Freize's step. 'Oh, there you are. Are there many people outside?' he asked.

'It's getting crowded,' Freize replied. 'Is it a fair or something?'

'It's a crusade,' the innkeeper explained. 'And we're going to have to feed them somehow and get them on their way.'

'Is that what it is? Your wife said yesterday that she was expecting some pilgrims,' Freize volunteered.

'Pilgrims!' the man exclaimed. 'Aye, for that was all that someone told us. But now they are starting to come into town and they say there are hundreds of them, perhaps thousands. It's no ordinary pilgrimage, for they travel all together as an army will march. It's a crusade.'

'Where are they going?' Brother Peter asked.

The innkeeper shook his head. 'I don't know. Their leader walks with them. He must have some idea. I have to go and fetch the priest; he will have to see that they are housed and fed. I'll have to tell the lord of the manor; he'll want to see them moved on. They can't come here, and besides, half of them have no money at all; they're begging their way along the road.'

'If they are in the service of God then He will guide them,' Brother Peter said devoutly. 'I'll come with you to the priest and make sure that he understands that he must offer them hospitality.'

Luca said to Freize, 'Let's take a look outside. I heard they are going to Jerusalem.'

The two young men stepped out of the front door of the inn and found the quayside now crowded with boys and girls, some of them barefoot, some of them dressed in little more than rags, all of them travel-stained and weary. Most were seated, exhausted, on the cobblestones; some of them stood looking out to sea. None were older than sixteen, some as young as six or seven, and more of them were coming in through the town gate all the time, as the gatekeeper watched in bewilderment, racking his brains for an excuse to close the gate and shut them out.

'God save us!' Freize exclaimed. 'What's going on here? They're all children.'

'There's more coming,' Isolde called from the open window above them. She pointed north, over the roofs of the little town where the road wound down the hill. 'I can see them on the road. There must be several hundred of them.'

'Anyone leading them? Any adult in charge?' Luca called up to her, completely distracted by the sight of her tumbled hair and the half-open collar of her shirt.

Isolde shaded her eyes with her hand. 'I can't see anyone. No-one on horseback, just a lot of children walking slowly.'

Almost under their feet a girl of about nine years old sat down abruptly and started to sob quietly. 'I can't walk,' she said. 'I can't go on. I just can't.'

Freize knelt down beside her, saw that her feet were bleeding from blisters and cuts. 'Of course you can't,' he said. 'And I don't know what your father was doing letting you out. Where d'you live?'

Her face was illuminated at once, sore feet forgotten. 'I live with Johann the Good,' she said.

Luca bent down. 'Johann the Good?'

She nodded. 'He has led us here. He will lead us to the Promised Land.'

The two young men exchanged an anxious glance.

'This Johann,' Luca started, 'where does he come from?'

She frowned. 'Switzerland, I think. God sent him to lead us.'

'Switzerland?' exclaimed Freize. 'And where did he find you?'

'I was working on a farm outside Verona.' She reached for her little feet and chafed them as she spoke. At once her hands were stained red with her blood but she paid no attention. 'Johann the Good and his followers came to the farm to ask for food and to be allowed to sleep in a barn for the night, but my master was a hard man and drove them away. I waited till he was asleep and then my brother and I ran away after them.'

'Your brother's here?' Freize asked, looking round. 'You have an older brother? Someone to look after you?'

She shook her head. 'No, for he's dead now. He took a fever and he died one night and we had to leave him in a village; they said they would bury him in the churchyard.'

Freize put a firm hand on Luca's collar and pulled him back from the child. 'What sort of fever?' he asked suspiciously.

'I don't know, it was weeks ago.'

'Where were you? What was the village?'

'I don't know. It doesn't matter, I am not to grieve for I will see my brother again, when he rises from the dead. Johann said that he will meet us in the Promised Land where the dead live again and the wicked burn.'

'Johann said that the dead will rise?' Luca asked. 'Rise from their graves and we will see them?'

Freize had his own question. 'So who takes care of you, now that your brother is dead?'

She shrugged her thin shoulders, as if the answer must be obvious. 'God takes care of me,' she said. 'He called me and He guides me. He guides all of us and Johann tells us what He wants.'

Luca straightened up. 'I'd like to speak with this Johann,' he said.

The girl rose to her feet, wincing with the pain. 'There he is,' she said simply, and pointed to a circle of young boys who had come through the town gate all together and were leaning their sticks against the harbour wall and dropping their knapsacks down on the cobbles.

'Get Brother Peter,' Luca said shortly to Freize. 'I'm

going to need him to take notes of what this lad says. We should understand what is happening here. It may be a true calling.'

Freize nodded, and put a gentle hand on the little girl's shoulder. 'You stay here,' he said. 'I'll wash your feet when I get back and find you some shoes. What's your name?'

'Rosa,' she said. 'But my feet are all right. God will heal them.'

'I'll help Him,' Freize said firmly. 'He likes a bit of help.'

She laughed, a childish giggle at his impertinence. 'He is all powerful,' she corrected him gravely.

'Then He must get extra help all the time,' Freize said with a warm smile to her.

Luca stood watching the child pilgrims as Freize jogged up the narrow street from the quayside to the market square, where the church stood, raised above the square by a flight of broad steps. As Freize went upwards, two at a time, the door of the church above him opened, and Brother Peter came out.

'Luca needs you,' Freize said shortly. 'He wants you to take notes as he speaks to the youth who leads the pilgrims. They call him Johann the Good.'

'An inquiry?' Brother Peter asked eagerly.

'For sure, something strange is going on.'

Brother Peter followed Freize back to the quayside to find it even more crowded. Every moment brought new arrivals through the main gate of the town and through the little gate from the north. Some of them were children of nine or ten, some of them were young men, apprentices who had run from their masters, or farm boys who had left the plough. A group of little girls trailed in last, holding hands in pairs as if they were on their way to school. Luca guessed that at every halt the smaller, weaker children caught up with the others; and sometimes some of them never caught up at all.

Brother Peter spoke to Luca. 'The priest is a good man and has money to buy food for them, and the monastery is baking bread and the brothers will bring it down to the market to give to them.'

'It seems to be a pilgrimage of children led by a young man,' Luca said. 'I thought we should question him.'

Brother Peter nodded. 'He might have a calling,' he said cautiously. 'Or he might have been tempted by Satan himself to steal these children from their parents. Either way, the Lord of our Order needs to know. This is something we should understand. We should inquire into it.'

'He says that the dead will rise,' Luca told Peter.

The rising of the dead was a key sign of the end of days: when the graves would give up their dead and everyone would be judged.

Brother Peter looked startled. 'He is preaching of the end of days?'

'Exactly,' Luca said grimly.

'Which one is he?'

'That one, called Johann,' Luca said, and started to make his way through the weary crowd to the boy who stood alone, his head bowed in prayer. 'The girl called him Johann the Good.'

There were so many children coming through the gate and down to the quayside now, that Luca could only wait and watch as they passed. He thought there were seven hundred of them in all, most of them exhausted and hungry, but all of them looking hopeful, some of them even inspired, as though driven by a holy determination to press on. Luca saw Freize take Rosa to the inn kitchen to bathe her feet, and thought that there must be many girls like her on the march, barely able to keep up, with no-one looking after them, driven by an unchildlike conviction that they were called by God.

'It could be a miracle,' Brother Peter said uncertainly, struggling through the sea of young people to get to Luca's side. 'I have seen such a thing only once before. When God calls for a pilgrimage and His people answer, it is a miracle. But we have to know how many there are, where they are going, and what they hope to achieve. They may be healers, they may have the Sight, they may have the gift of tongues. Or they might be terribly misguided. Milord will want to know about their leader, and what he preaches.'

'Johann the Good,' Luca repeated. 'From Switzerland, she said. That's him there.'

As if he felt their gaze upon him, the youth waiting at the gate as his followers went past, raised his head and gave them a brilliant smile. He was about fifteen years old, with long blond hair that fell in untidy ringlets down to his shoulders. He had piercing blue eyes and was dressed like a Swiss goatherd, with a short robe over thick leggings laced criss-cross, and strong sandals on his feet. In his hand he had a stick, like a shepherd's crook, carved with a series of crucifixes. As they watched, he kissed a cross, whispered a prayer, and then turned to them.

'God bless and keep you, Masters,' he said.

Brother Peter, who was more accustomed to dispensing blessings than receiving them, said stiffly, 'And God bless you too. What brings you here?'

'God brings me here,' the youth answered. 'And you?'

Luca choked on a little laugh at Brother Peter's surprise at being questioned by a boy. 'We too are engaged on the work of God,' he said. 'Brother Peter and I are inquiring into the well-being of Christendom. We are commissioned by the Holy Father himself to inquire and report to him.'

'The end of days is upon us,' the boy said simply. 'Christendom is over, the end of the world has begun. I have seen the signs. Does the Holy Father know that?'

'What signs have you seen?' Luca asked.

'Enough to be sure,' the lad replied. 'That's why we are on our journey.'

'What have you seen?' Luca repeated. 'Exactly what?'

Johann sighed, as if he were weary of miracles. 'Many, many things. But now I must eat and rest and then pray with my family. These are all my brothers and sisters in the sight of God. We have come far, and we have further still to go.'

'We would like to talk with you,' Brother Peter said. 'It is our mission to know what things you have seen. The Holy Father himself will want to know what you have seen. We have to judge if your visions are true.'

The boy nodded his head as if he were indifferent to their opinion. 'Perhaps later. You must forgive me. But many people want to know what I have seen and what I know. And I have no interest in the judgements of this world. I will preach later. I will stand on the steps of the church and preach to the village people. You can come and listen if you want.'

'Have you taken Holy Orders? Are you a servant of the Church?' Brother Peter asked.

The boy smiled and gestured to his poor clothes, his shepherd's crook. 'I am called by God, I have not been taught by His Church. I am a simple goatherd, I don't claim to be more than that. He honoured me with His call as He honoured the fishermen and other poor men. He speaks to me Himself,' the boy said simply. 'I need no other teacher.'

He turned and made the sign of the cross over some children who came through the gate singing a psalm and gathered around him to sit on the stone cobbles of the quay as comfortably as if they were in their own fields.

'Wouldn't you like to come into the inn and break your fast with us?' Luca tempted him. 'Then you can eat, and rest, and tell us of your journey.'

The boy considered them both for a moment. 'I will do that,' he said. He turned and spoke a quick word with one of the children nearest to him and at once they settled down on the quayside and unpacked their knapsacks and started to eat what little they were carrying – a small bread roll and some cheese. The other children, who had nothing, sat dully where they were, as if they were too tired for hunger.

'And your followers?' Luca asked him.

'God will provide for them,' the youth said confidently.

Luca glanced towards Brother Peter. 'Actually, the priest is bringing food for them, the abbey is baking bread,'

Brother Peter told him, rather stiffly. 'I see you are not fasting with them.'

'Because I knew that God would provide,' Johann confirmed. 'And now you tell me He has done so. You invite me to breakfast and so God provides for me. Why should I not trust Him and praise His holy name?'

'Why not indeed?' Brother Peter said glacially, and led the way to the dining room of the inn.

~

Ishraq and Isolde did not join the men for breakfast. They peeped through the open door to see the boy Johann, and then carried their plates upstairs to their bedroom and ate, sitting at the window, watching the scene on the quayside as children continued to pour into the town, the smallest and the frailest coming last as if they could hardly keep up. Their ragged clothes showed that they were from many different areas. There were children from fishing villages further north up the coast who wore the rough smocks of the region, and there were children who had come from farms and wore the capes and leggings of shepherds and goatherds. There were many girls, some of them dressed as if they had been in service, in worsted gowns with goatskin aprons. Isolde nudged Ishraq as three girls in the robes of novices of a convent came through the gate of the town, their rosaries in their hands, their veiled heads bowed, and passed under the overhanging window.

'They must have run away from a nunnery,' she said.

'Like us,' Ishraq agreed. 'But where do they think they're going?'

In the dining room the youth prayed in silence over the food, blessed the bread, and then ate a substantial breakfast that Freize brought up from the kitchen. After the boy had finished, he gave thanks in a lengthy prayer to God and a short word of appreciation to Luca. Brother Peter took out his papers from his travelling writing-box and dipped his pen in ink.

'I have to report to my lord who, in turn, reports to the Holy Father,' he explained as the boy looked at his preparations. 'If your journey is blessed by God then the Holy Father will want to know the proofs. If he thinks you have a calling he will support you. If not, he will want to know about you.'

'It is blessed,' the boy said. 'D'you think we could have come all this way if God had not guided us?'

'Why, how far have you come?' Luca asked cautiously.

'I was a goat herder in the canton of Zurich when I heard God's voice,' the boy said simply. 'He told me that a terrible thing had happened in the east. A worse thing than the great flood itself. A greater wrong than the flood that drowned everyone but Noah. He said that the Ottomans had come against Christendom in a mighty wave of men, and had taken Constantinople, our holy city, the heart of the Church in the east, and destroyed it. Did I hear right or no?'

'You did,' Luca said. 'But any passing pedlar could have told you so.'

'But it was not a passing pedlar who told me so, for I was up in the hills with my goats. Every dawn I left the village and took the goats up the paths to the higher fields where the grass grows fresh and sweet. Every day I sat in the fields with them, and watched over them. Sometimes I played my pipe, sometimes I lay on my back and watched the clouds. When the sun sat in the top branches of the silver birch tree I ate the bread and cheeses that my mother had tied into a cloth for me. Every evening as the sun started to go down, I brought my flock safe home again and saw them into my neighbours' fields and stables. I saw no-one, I talked to no-one. I had no companion but an angel. Then one day, God spoke to me and He told me that the infidels had taken the holy church of Constantinople. He said that the sea had risen so high that they had rowed their galleys right over the land, over the harbour wall, over the city walls, and into the harbour. He said that the greatest church in the whole world was once called Hagia Sophia and that now it is in the hands of the infidels and they will make it into a mosque, take down the altar and defile its sacred aisles, and that this is a true sign of the end of days. Did I hear right or no?'

'They took the cathedral,' Luca confirmed uneasily. 'They took the city.'

'Did the priests pray at the altar as the infidels came in the door and cut them down?' Johann asked.

Luca glanced to Brother Peter. 'They served the Mass until the last moment,' Brother Peter confirmed.

'Did they row their galleys over the land?'

'It can't be true,' Luca interrupted.

'It wasn't exactly true,' Brother Peter explained. 'It was a trick of war. They mounted the galleys on great rollers and pushed them across the land into the inner harbour. The Devil himself guided them to put the rowers to the oars and the drummers to the beat so they looked as if they were rowing through the air. Everyone said it looked like a fleet of galleys sailing along the road.'

'Why would they do such a thing?' Luca demanded.

'To spread terror,' Brother Peter replied. 'See? A goatherd in Switzerland dreams of it seven years later.'

The boy nodded, as if he had seen the terrifying sight and then the sacrilege himself. 'God told me that the infidels would come and bring terror to every village in the world, and that just as they have come through Greece they will come on and on, and nothing can stop them. He said they would come into my own canton, they will come to every village in Switzerland. He said that they are led by a young man only a little older than me. Is that right?'

Luca looked at Brother Peter. 'Sultan Mehmet was nineteen years old when he took Constantinople.'

'God told me that this is a war for young people and for children. The infidels are led by a young man; I heard my calling. I knew that I must leave my home.'

The two men waited.

'I took my crook and my knapsack and I said farewell to my father and mother. The whole village came out to see me leave. They knew that I was inspired by God Himself.'

'Did anyone leave with you?'

He shook his head and stared at the window as if he could see on the dim pieces of the horn panes the poverty of the dirty village street, the dreary lives of the people who scratched a living from the thin mountain soil, who were hungry and cold every winter and knew, even in the warmth of summer, that the cold and hunger of winter would come again. People who confidently expected that nothing would ever change, that life would go on in the same cycle of hard winters and bright summers in a remorseless unchanging round – until the day that they heard that the Turks were coming and understood that everything had suddenly got worse and would get worse still.

'Children joined me as I walked,' Johann said. 'They heard my voice, they understood. We all know that the end of days is coming. We all want to be in Jerusalem for judgement day.'

'You think you're going to Jerusalem?' Freize demanded incredulously from the doorway. 'You're leading these children to Jerusalem?'

The boy smiled at him. 'God is leading them to Jerusalem,' he said patiently. 'I am only walking with them. I am walking beside them.'

'Then God has chosen an odd route,' Freize said rudely. 'Why would He send you to the east of Italy? Why not go to Rome and get help? Why not take a ship from there? Why walk these children such a long way?'

The boy looked a little shaken at Freize's loud scepticism. 'I don't lead them, I don't choose the route, I go where God tells me,' he said quietly. He looked at Brother Peter. 'The way is revealed to me, as I walk. Who is this man questioning me?'

'This is Brother Luca's servant,' Brother Peter said irritably. 'You need not answer his questions. He has no part in our inquiry.'

'Oh, beg pardon for interrupting, I'm sure,' Freize said,

not sounding at all sorry. 'But am I to give your leavings out at the door? Your followers seem to be hungry. And there are broken meats from your breakfast, and the untouched bread. You dined quite well.'

The boy passed his plate and the bread in the basket without giving it another glance. 'God provides for us,' he said. 'Give it all to them with my blessing.'

'And see that the food is shared fairly when it comes from the monastery,' Brother Peter ordered Freize, who nodded and went out. They could hear him stamping to the kitchen and the back door. Brother Peter turned his attention back to the boy. 'And your name is?'

'Johann Johannson.'

'And your age?'

'I think I am almost sixteen years old. I don't know for sure.'

'Had you seen any miracles or heard anything before this year?'

He smiled. 'I used to hear a singing in the church bells of my village,' he confided. 'When they rang for Mass I used to hear them calling my name, as if God himself wanted me to come to His table. Then sometimes, when I was with the goats in the high pasture in summer, I would hear voices, beautiful voices, calling my name. It was an angel who used to meet me in the highest meadows. I knew that there would be a task for me. But I did not know it would be this.'

'And how do you plan to get to Jerusalem, from here?' Luca asked.

'God has told me that the sea will dry up before us,' the boy said simply. 'As it did before the children of Israel.

We will walk to the southernmost point of Italy and then I know that the waves will part and we will walk to the Holy Land.'

Luca and Brother Peter exchanged a wondering look at his confidence. 'It's a long, long way,' Luca suggested gently. 'Do you know the way? Do you know how far?'

'It doesn't matter to me what the road is called, nor how far it is,' the boy said confidently. 'God guides me, not signposts or worldly maps. I walk in faith, I am not the toy of men who draw maps and try to measure the world. I don't follow their vision but that of God.'

'And what will you do, when you get there?' Brother Peter asked.

'This is not a crusade of weapons,' the boy replied. 'It is a children's crusade. When we get there the children of Israel will come to us. The Turk children will come to us. Ottoman children will come. Arab children will come to us and we will all serve the one God. If there are any Christian children left alive in those lands, then they will come to us too. They will all explain to their fathers and their mothers and there will be peace. The children of all the enemies will bring peace to the world. It is a children's crusade and every child will answer the call. Then Jesus will come to Jerusalem and the world will end.'

'You have seen all this in a vision?' Brother Peter confirmed. 'You are certain?'

His face shining with conviction, the boy nodded. 'It is a certainty,' he said. 'How else would all these children have joined me already? They come from the villages and from the little farms. They come from dirty workshops and the backstreets of evil cities. They come with their brothers and sisters. They come with their friends. They come from different countries, they come even if they cannot understand my language, for God speaks to them. The Arab children, the Jewish children will come too.' He wiped his mouth on his sleeve, like the simple peasant boy he was. 'I see you are amazed, my masters, but this is how it is. It is a children's crusade and it is going to change the world.

'And now I must pray with my brothers and sisters,' he said. 'You may join us if you want.' He rose up, picked up his crook, and went to the doorway.

'How will the waters part?' Luca asked him curiously.

Johann made a gesture with his hands, pushing the air away before him. 'As it did before,' he said. 'For Moses. However that was. The waves will part on one side and the other. We will see the sea bed beneath our feet. We will see the wrecks of ships that lie on the bed of the sea and we can pick up their treasure as we walk. We can gather pearls as if they were flowers. We will go dry-shod all the way to Palestine.' He paused. 'Angels will sing,' he said, pleased. He went from the room, leaving Luca and Brother Peter alone.

'What an extraordinary boy!' Luca exclaimed, pushing back his chair from the table. 'He has a gift, it can't be denied.' He brushed his forearm and ran his hand up the nape of his neck. 'My hairs are standing on end. I believe him. I am truly persuaded. I wish I could follow him. If I had heard him when I was a child I would have left a plough in the field and gone after him.'

'A natural leader,' Brother Peter decided. 'But whether

he is a dreamer or whether he is a prophet, or even a false prophet, I can't tell. We must hear him preach and perhaps question him some more. I'll have to get news of this to Milord at once. This is urgent.'

'He will want to know of such a boy?'

'Of such a boy, and of such a crusade. This could be another sign of the end of days. He will want to know everything. Why, if they get to Palestine and do half of what they promise, then the Ottoman Empire will sink beneath them. It will be their worst nightmare knocking at their front door, a faith to confront their heresy. With such a large band of children they'll either have to arrest them, or let them enter into the holiest places. Either way these children could upset everything. This may turn out to be the greatest weapon we could have devised against our enemies. We would never have thought of such a device but they could be far more powerful than any Christian army of grown men. If Johann can appeal to Ottoman children and Turk children and they join him in a Christian crusade, then the world would be turned upside down.'

'Do you really think they can get all that way to Jerusalem?'

'Who would have thought they could have got here? And yet they have, in their thousands.'

'Certainly hundreds,' Luca said cautiously.

'There are hundreds of children following that boy already. How many more can he recruit as he marches south?'

'You can't think that the sea will part before them?' Luca asked. 'How could such a thing happen?'

'Do you believe that the Red Sea parted for the children of Israel?' the older man put to him.

'I have to believe it. The Bible is clear that it did. To question it would be heresy.'

'Then why should such a miracle not happen again?'

Luca shook his head. 'I suppose it could. I just—' He broke off. 'I just can't understand how such a thing could be. How it could happen. Don't question my faith, I believe the Bible as I am bound to do. I am not denying one word of it. But this sea rushing back from the sea bed? And these children walking dry-shod to Palestine? Can such a thing be possible?'

'We have to see if it can be done. But if the sea does not part for them it may be that Milord will get them ships.'

'Why would he take the trouble?' Luca hesitated, noticing the excitement in the older man's face. 'Is our work about the end of days, or is the Order more interested in defeating the Ottomans? Are we seeking the truth or forging a weapon?'

'Both, of course, both,' Brother Peter replied roundly. 'Both, always. It is one and the same thing. The world will end when the Ottomans enter the gates of Rome, and at that moment the dead will rise from their graves for judgement. You and I have to travel throughout Christendom to watch for the signs of the dead rising, of Satan emerging, and the Ottoman armies coming ever closer. The infidels in Jerusalem and Jesus descending from heaven is one and the same thing, both signs of the end. What we have to know is when it takes place. These children may be a sign, I really believe that they are a sign. We must write to Milord, and we have to know more.'

~

Luca tapped on the door of Isolde's room and she opened it wide when she saw him. 'I can't stay,' he said. 'But I wanted to warn Ishraq.'

The dark girl appeared behind Isolde. 'Me?'

'Yes. You've seen the children, coming into town. They're a crusade, hundreds of children, perhaps more. They're heading south, on their way to Jerusalem to defeat the Ottomans.'

'We've seen them from the window. They look exhausted.'

'Yes, but they are very sure that they are on their way to Palestine, a mighty crusade and a sign of the end of days. They know of the sack of Constantinople by the Ottomans. If you go down into the streets at all, you must not wear your Arab dress. They might turn on you. I don't know what they would think.'

'I should not wear Arab dress? I am not to wear my own clothes? I am to deny my heritage?'

'Not while so many children are here. Wear what Lady Isolde wears for now.'

Ishraq gave him a steady look from her dark eyes. 'And what shall I do about my skin? Is it too Arab also?'

Luca flushed. 'You are a beautiful colour, God knows there are few women to match your looks, the colour of heather honey and eyes as dark as midnight,' he said fervently. 'But you cannot wear your pantaloons and your robe and veil until the crusade leaves the town, or until we get the ship out of here. You must dress like Isolde, like a Christian woman, for your own safety.'

'She will,' Isolde ruled, cutting short the argument. 'Will we still sail at noon?'

'No. We have to speak more with these children and we have to send a report to Rome. Brother Peter believes they are inspired by God, but certainly if they can get to Jerusalem with or without His guidance, they will pose a huge challenge to the Ottomans.'

'Are they walking onwards?'

'I expect they'll go on this afternoon. People are giving them food and money to send them on their way. The church here is feeding them. And they are determined to go on. It's a remarkable pilgrimage; I am glad to have seen it. When you talk with the boy, Johann, it's inspiring. You know, I would go too if I were free.'

'D'you think they can possibly get to Jerusalem?' Ishraq wondered.

'Who would have thought they could come this far? Children led by a youth who doesn't even know where Jerusalem is? Brother Peter thinks they are part of the signs that we have been sent out to observe. I'm not sure, but I have to see that it is a sort of miracle. He is an ignorant country lad from Switzerland, and here he is in Italy, on his way to Jerusalem. I have to think it is almost a miracle.'

'But you're not sure,' Ishraq observed.

He shrugged. 'He says the waters will part for them – I can't imagine how. It would be a miracle in this place and time and I can't see how it would happen. But perhaps they will be able to walk south to Messina and someone will give them ships. There are many ways that they could get to Jerusalem dry-shod. There are other miracles as great as parting the waters.'

'You believe that this boy can find his way to Messina?' Ishraq asked him sceptically.

Luca frowned. 'It's not your faith,' he said defensively. 'I see that you would not believe these pilgrims. You would think them fools, led by a charlatan. But this boy Johann has great power. He knows things that he could only have learned by revelation. He claims that God speaks to him and I have to believe that He does. And he has already come so far!'

'Can we come and listen to him?' Isolde asked.

Luca nodded. 'He is preaching this afternoon. If you cover your heads and wear your capes, you can join us. I should think half the village will be there to listen to him.'

~

Isolde and Ishraq, wearing grey gowns with their brown cloaks, came out of the front door of the inn and walked along the stone quayside. Most of the fishing ships were moored in the harbour, bobbing on the quiet waves, the men ashore mending their nets or coiling ropes and patching worn sails. The two girls ignored the whistles and catcalls as the men noted the slim, caped figures and guessed that there were pretty faces under the concealing hoods. Isolde blushed and smiled at a shouted compliment but Ishraq turned her head in disdain.

'You need not be so proud, it's not an insult,' Isolde remarked to her.

'It is to me,' Ishraq said. 'Why should they think they can comment on me?'

They turned up one of the narrow alleyways which led up the hill to the market square and walked below criss-cross lines of washing strung from one overhanging balcony to another. A few old ladies sat on their doorsteps, their hands busy with mending or lace-making, and nodded at the girls as they went by, but most of the people were already in the market square to hear Johann preach.

Isolde and Ishraq passed the bakery, as the baker came out and closed up shop for the day, his face and hair dusted white with flour. The cobbler next door sat cross-legged in his window, a half-made shoe on his last, looking out at the gathering crowds. The next shop was a ships' chandlers, the dark interior a jumble of goods from fishing nets to cork floats, fish knives and rowlocks, screws by the handful, nails in jars, blocks of salt and barrels. Next door to him was a hatter and milliner, doing poor trade in a poor town; next to her a saddler.

The girls went past the shops with barely a glance into the shadowy interiors, their eyes drawn to the steps of the church and to the shining fair head of the boy who waited, cheek against his simple crook, as if he were listening for something.

Before him, the crowd gathered, murmuring quietly, attentively. Behind him, in the darkened doorway of the church, stood Brother Peter, Luca and Freize beside the village priest. Many of the fishermen and almost all the women and children of the village had come but Isolde noticed that some of the older children were absent. She guessed they had been sent to sea with their fathers, or ordered to stay at home – not every family wanted to risk its children hearing Johann preach. Many mothers regarded him as a sort of dangerous piper who might dance their children out of town, never to be seen again. Some of them called him a child-stealer who should be feared, especially by mothers who had only one child.

The children of the crusade had been fed on a mean breakfast of bread and fish. The priest had collected food from his parishioners and the people of the market had handed out the leftovers. The monks in the abbey had sent down baskets of fresh-baked bread and honey scones. Clearly some of the children were still hungry, and many of them would have been hungry for days. But they still showed the same bright faces as when they had first walked into the village of Piccolo.

Ishraq, sensitive to the mood of a crowd, could almost feel the passionate conviction of the young crusaders: the children wanted to believe that Johann had been called by God, and had convinced themselves that he was leading them to Jerusalem.

'This is not faith,' she whispered to Isolde. 'This is longing: a very different thing.'

'You ask me why we should walk all the way to the Holy Land?' Johann started suddenly, without introduction, without telling them to listen, without a bidding prayer or calling for their attention. He did not even raise his voice, he did not raise his eyes from the ground nor his cheek which was still resting thoughtfully against his shepherd's crook, yet the hundreds of people were immediately silent and attentive. The round-faced priest in the grey unbleached robes of the Cistercian order, who had never in all his life seen a congregation of this size, lowered his gaze to the doorstep of his little church. Brother Peter stepped slightly forwards, as if he did not want to miss a word.

'I will tell you why we must go so far,' Johann said quietly. 'Because we want to. That's all! Because we choose to do so. We want to play our part in the end of days. The infidels have taken all the holy places into their keeping, the infidels have taken the greatest church in Constantinople and the Mass is celebrated no more at the most important altar in the world. We have to go to where Jesus Christ was a child and we have to walk in His footsteps. We have to be as children who enter the kingdom of heaven. He promised that those who come to him as little children will not be forbidden. We, His children, will go to Him and He will come again, as He promised, to judge the living and the dead, the old and the young, and we will be there, in Jerusalem, we will be the children who will enter the kingdom of heaven. D'you see?'

'Yes,' the crowd breathed. The children responded readily, at once, but even the older people, even the villagers who had never heard this message before were persuaded by Johann's quiet authority. 'Yes,' they said.

Johann tossed his head so his blond ringlets fell away from his face. He looked around at them all. Luca had a sudden disconcerting sense that Johann was looking at him with his piercing blue eyes, as if the young preacher knew something of him, had something to say especially to him. 'You are missing your father,' the

312

boy said simply to the crowd. Luca, whose father had disappeared after an Ottoman raid on his village, when Luca was only fourteen, gave a sudden start and looked over the heads of the children to Isolde, whose father had died only five months ago. She was very pale, looking intently at Johann.

'I can feel your sorrow,' he said tenderly. Again his blue gaze swept across Luca and then rested on Isolde. 'He did not say goodbye to you,' Johann observed gently. Isolde bit her lip at that deep, constant sorrow and there was a soft moan from the crowd, from the many people who had lost fathers – at sea or to illness, or in the many accidents of daily life. Ishraq, standing beside Isolde, took her hand and found that she was trembling. 'I can see a man laid cold and pale in his chapel and his son stealing his place,' Johann said. Isolde's face blanched white as he told her story to the world. 'I can see a girl longing for her father and him crying her name on his deathbed but they kept her from him, and now, she can't hear him and he will never speak again.'

Luca gave a muffled exclamation and turned to Brother Peter. 'I didn't tell him anything about her.'

'Nor I.'

'Then how does he know this?'

'I can see a bier in a chapel alone,' Johann went on. 'But nobody mourns for the man who has gone.' There was a sob from a woman in the crowd who fell to her knees. Isolde stood like a statue, listening to the young man describing the loss of her father. 'I can see a daughter driven from her home and longing to return.'

Isolde turned to Ishraq. 'He is speaking of me.'

313

'It seems so,' Ishraq cautiously responded. 'But this could be true of many people.'

'I see a girl whose father died without her at his side, whose brother stole her inheritance, who longs, even now, to be back in her home, to see her father again,' Johann said his voice low and persuasive. 'And I have good news for you. Good news. I see this young woman, her heart broken by her loss, and I can tell you that she will return. She will return and take her place again.'

Isolde clutched at Ishraq's steady hand. 'He says I will return!'

'And I see more,' Johann went on. 'I can see a young man, a boy. A young boy, and his father lost at sea. Oh! I can see that boy waiting and waiting on the quayside and looking for the sails of a boat that never comes home.'

A muffled sob from one youth in the huge crowd was repeated all around the people. Clearly, Johann saw truly. Many people recognised themselves in his vision. Someone cried out for the blessing of God on a fatherless family, and one woman was comforted, softly weeping for her father who would never come back from the sea.

'This is an easy guess in a port,' Ishraq muttered to Isolde and got a look of burning reproach in reply.

'I see a boy, a youth, learning that his father has been taken by the infidels themselves. They came at night in their terrible galleys and stole away his father, his mother, and everything they owned, and that boy wants to know why. That boy wants to know how. That boy will spend the rest of his life asking questions.'

Freize, who had been with Luca in the monastery when the abbot had called him out of chapel to tell him that there had been an Ottoman slaving raid and his mother and father were missing, exchanged one level look with Luca. 'Odd,' was all he said.

'A youth who has lost his father without explanation will ask questions for all his life,' Johann stated.

Luca could not take his eyes from the young preacher; it was as if the boy was describing him, as if he knew Luca at the deepest level.

'I can answer his questions,' the boy reassured the crowd, his voice sweet as if he were quite entranced. 'I can answer that boy who asks, "where is my father?", "Where is my mother?" God will tell me the answers. I can tell you now, that you will hear your father, I can tell you how to hear his voice.'

He looked over towards Isolde who was hidden among the village women, all dressed alike, with her hood completely covering her shining blonde hair. 'I can tell you how to claim your inheritance and sit in your father's chair where he wants you to be. I can tell you how to return home. Do you have his crusader sword?'

A little cry broke from Isolde, and Luca checked himself from moving towards her.

'Come with us,' the boy said quietly. 'Come to Jerusalem where the dead will rise and your fathers will meet you. Come with me, come with all of us and we will go to Jerusalem and the world will have no end and your father will put his hand on your head with a blessing once more, and you will feel his love and know you are his child.'

Isolde was openly weeping, as was half the crowd. Luca gulped down his emotion, even Freize knuckled his eyes. Johann turned to the priest. 'Now we will pray,' he said. 'Father Benito will hear confession and pray with us. May I confess, Father?'

The priest, deeply moved, nodded, and led the way into the darkness of the church. Most of the crowd knelt where they stood and closed their eyes in prayer. Isolde dropped to her knees on the dirty cobblestones of the market and Ishraq stood beside her, almost as if she would guard her from this revelation, from grief itself. Freize, looking over, met Ishraq's steady dark gaze and knew himself to be shaken and puzzled by what they had heard.

'He knows things that we didn't tell him,' Luca said in a rapid undertone to Brother Peter. 'He knows things that are impossible that he should know other than by revelation. He spoke of me, and of my childhood, and I had said nothing of either to him. He spoke of the Lady Isolde and he hasn't even seen her. Nobody in this village knows anything about any of us.'

'Would Freize . . .' Brother Peter asked doubtfully.

Freize shook his head. 'I'm not the one who gives breakfast to boys begging on the harbour wall,' he said loftily. 'And I don't gossip. I haven't said one word to him that you have not heard. If you ask me, he made a few lucky guesses and saw the response he got.'

'You wept,' Luca said bluntly.

'He said things that would make a stone weep!' Freize returned. 'Just because it makes you cry, doesn't mean that it's true.'

'To speak of an Ottoman raid to me?' Luca challenged him. 'That's not a guess. To speak of Isolde driven from her castle? That's no wild guess, there is no way that he would think of it, no way that he could know such things. He knew nothing of her, she kept out of his way. And yet he spoke of her father laid on a cold bier and her brother stealing her inheritance.'

'I believe he is inspired,' Brother Peter agreed, overruling Freize's scepticism. 'But I shall ask the priest for his opinion. I shall ask him what Johann tells him.' He glanced into the shadowy interior of the church where the priest was kneeling on one side of a carved wooden screen and Johann was kneeling on the other side, reverently whispering his confession with his fair head bowed.

'Johann's confession must be secret,' Luca remarked. 'Between him, the priest and God.'

Brother Peter nodded. 'Of course. But Father Benito is allowed to give me an impression. And as soon as I have spoken with him I shall send our report to Rome. Whether the boy is a visionary or a fraud I should think that Milord will want to know all about this. It could be very important. It is a crusade of its own making, a rising up of the people, much more powerful than the lords ordering their tenants to war. It is the very thing that the Pope has been calling for and getting no response. It could change everything. As Johann goes through Italy he could gather thousands of followers. Now I have seen him preach I understand what he might do. He might make an army of faith – unstoppable. Milord will want to see that they are fed and shipped to the Holy Land. He will want to see that they are

317

guarded and have arms. He will want to make sure they do not fall into heresy. A movement as poweful as this must be harnessed by the Church.'

'And he spoke of fathers,' Luca went on, indifferent to Brother Peter's plan for a new great crusade. 'He spoke of me, and my father. He spoke of Isolde and her father. It was not general, it was not ordinary preaching. He spoke of Isolde, he spoke of me. He knew things he could not know except by a genuine revelation.'

'He is inspiring,' Brother Peter conceded. 'Perhaps a visionary indeed. Certainly he has the gift of tongues – did you see how they listened to him?'

Luca made his way through the praying crowd to Isolde and found her on her knees with Ishraq standing over her. When she crossed herself, and looked up, he gave her his hand and helped her to her feet.

'I thought he was speaking of me,' he said tersely. 'And of the loss of my father.'

'I am sure he was speaking of me,' she agreed. 'Speaking to me. He said things that only one who had been at the castle, or who had been advised by God, could know. He was inspired.'

'You believe him?'

She nodded. 'I do. I have to believe him. He could not have guessed at the things he said. He was too specific, it was too vivid a vision.'

He offered her his arm, and she put her hand in the crook of his elbow and they walked together down the narrow steps to the quayside inn. Freize and Ishraq followed them in sceptical silence; the little ginger kitten rushing behind them, following Freize.

'I don't see you weeping?' Freize remarked to the young woman at his side.

'I don't cry easily,' she said.

'I cry like a baby,' Freize confessed. 'But not today. He was inspiring. But I don't know what to think.'

'He could have said that stuff anywhere,' Ishraq said roundly. 'Every port on the coast will have women who have lost a father. Most villages will have someone cheated of their inheritance.'

'You don't believe he is inspired by God?'

She gave a short laugh and risked the confession: 'I'm not even sure about God.'

He smiled. 'Are you a pagan indeed?'

'I was raised by my mother as a Muslim, in a Christian household,' she explained. 'I was educated by Isolde's father the Lord of Lucretili to be a scholar and to question everything. I don't know what I believe for sure.'

Ahead of them Luca and Isolde were talking quietly together.

'I have missed my father more than I would have believed,' Luca confided. 'And my mother . . .' He broke off. 'It was not knowing that has been so dreadful. I didn't know what happened when they were kidnapped and I still don't know if they are alive or dead.'

'They sent you to the monastery?' she asked.

'They were convinced that I was a boy of extraordinary abilities and that I had to be given a chance to be something more than a farmer. They had their own farm, and it gave us a good living, but if I had inherited it after them and stayed there, then I would have known nothing more than the hills around my home and the weather. I would

319

have done nothing but keep the farm after their death and handed it on to my son. They wanted me to be able to study. They wanted me to rise in the Church. My mother was convinced that I was gifted by God. My father just saw that I could understand numbers quicker than the merchants, speak languages almost at the first hearing. He said that I must be educated. He said that they owed it to themselves to give me a chance.'

'But could you see them again? After they put you into your novitiate?'

'Yes. Bless them, they came to the abbey church most mornings, twice on Sundays. I would see them standing at the back and looking for me, when I was a choir boy too small to see over the choir stall. I had to stand on a kneeler so that I could see them in the congregation every week and twice on Sundays. My mother came to visit me every month and always brought me something from home, a sprig of lavender or a couple of eggs. I know how much she missed me. I was her only child. God Himself only knows how much I missed her.'

'Did she not want to keep you at home, despite your father's ambition?' Isolde asked, thinking of the delightful boy that Luca must have been.

He hesitated. 'There was something else,' he admitted. 'Another reason for them to send me away. You see – they were quite old when they had me. They had prayed for a son for years and God had not given them a child, so there were many people in the village who were surprised when I was born.'

'Surprised?' she queried. The cobblestones were slippery;

she skidded for a moment and he caught her. The two of them paused as if struck by the other's touch, then they walked together, in step, their long stride matching easily together.

'To tell you the truth, it was worse than that,' Luca said honestly. 'I don't like to speak of it. There was gossip – insulting gossip. The village said that I was a changeling, a child given to my parents, not made by them. People said that they had found me on their doorstep, or perhaps in the woods. People called me a f . . .' He could not bring himself to say the word. 'A f . . .'

'A faerie child?' she asked, her voice very low, conscious of his painful embarrassment.

He nodded as if he were confessing to a crime.

'There's no shame in that,' she said stoutly. 'People say the most ridiculous things, and ignorant people long to believe in magic rather than an ordinary explanation.'

'We were shamed,' he admitted. 'There was a wood near to our house, on our own land, that they called a faerie wood. They said that my mother had gone there, desperate to have a child, and that she had lain with a faerie lord. They said that she gave birth to me and passed me off to my father as a mortal boy. Then, when I grew up and could learn languages, and understand numbers in the blink of an eye, they all said that it proved that I had wisdom beyond the making of mortals.'

Isolde's face was filled with pity as she turned to the handsome young man. 'People can be so cruel. They thought you the child of a faerie lord?'

He turned his head away and nodded in silence.

'And so your parents sent you away? Just because you

were such a clever boy? Because you were gifted? Because you were so good-looking?'

'I thought then that it was a curse and not a gift,' he admitted. 'I used to stand beside my father when he was seated by the fire and he would put his arm around me, and take coins from his pocket and ask me to calculate the value if he spent half of them, if he spent a third, if he put half out at interest and earned fifteen per cent but lost the other half. And always I was right – I could just see the answers as if written on the air, I could see the numbers as if they were shining with colours, and he would kiss my forehead and say "my boy, my clever boy", and my mother would say "he *is* your boy" as if it should be repeated, and he should be reassured.

'And then, one summer, strangers came to the village, a travelling troupe of Egyptians, and I went down to see them with the other village children and I heard them speaking amongst themselves. The children laughed at them, and someone threw a stone; but one of the gypsies saw me watching them and said something aside to me, and I answered him – I had their language in a moment, the very moment that I heard it. That was the end of it really. Next morning we found a thick ring of salt, all around the farmhouse, and a horseshoe at north, south, east and west.'

'Salt?'

'A faerie can't cross iron and salt. They thought that they would imprison me. That decided it. My parents were afraid that they would trap me inside the house and then burn the house down.' He shrugged. 'It happens. People are afraid of what they cannot understand. It was not that they did not respect my father. But I did not have playmates among the village children, I was never quite like them, I could never talk easily with them. I could not fit with them. I was different and we couldn't deny it any more. My mother and father agreed that it was too dangerous for me to be in the outside world and they sent me to the monastery for safety.'

'Did you fit there?' she asked, thinking of her own experience in the nunnery where she had been isolated and alone except for Ishraq, another outsider.

'Freize took a liking to me,' he smiled. 'He was the only one. He was the kitchen boy and he used to steal food to feed me up. And as soon as they taught me to read and calculate I started to ask questions.'

'Questions?'

He shrugged. 'I couldn't help it. I just wanted to know more. But it turned out that most questions are heresies.'

'And then the Ottoman slaving galleys took your mother and father?' Isolde prompted him quietly.

Luca sighed, as if he still could not bear to think of it. 'You know, it's been four years now, but I think of them every day ... I have to know if they survived the raid. If they are alive I should save them. They did everything for me. I must see them again. And if I am too late and they are dead, then I should honour their deaths and see them properly buried. If Johann is right and they will rise again in Jerusalem then I feel as if I have to go with him. It's like a calling; a sacred duty.'

Isolde flushed a warm rose colour. 'You're not thinking of going to Jerusalem?'

Reluctantly, Luca nodded. 'Part of me feels that I should go on with my quest. I have been commanded by Milord and licensed by the Pope, I have only just started ... but if I can get permission from the lord of our order, I feel that I should go. I feel as if Johann spoke to me and promised me that I would meet my parents in Jerusalem. What calling could be greater than to see them again, before the end of all the world? At the very moment of the end of the world?'

They arrived at the quayside and turned towards the inn, dawdling to prolong their time together.

'I'm going to go too,' Isolde said fervently. 'I won't go to Hungary, not now that I have heard this. I carry the death of my father like a wound. It is terrible to me. Every day I wake up and I think I am in my old bedroom at Lucretili and he is alive, and every day I have to remember that he is dead, and I have lost my home and I am half-lost myself. If I could only see him again! Just once. I would go anywhere for that chance.'

'You really think you will see him again in Jerusalem? You believe Johann?'

'While he was speaking I was certain of it – but now – when you ask me like that, of course I'm not so sure.'

She paused, and they stood together: her hand on his arm, the seagulls crying over their heads, and the boats beside them, bobbing at anchor. A pale moon started to lift in the twilight of the winter afternoon and lay a silver path across the sea.

'I know it sounds so incredible. And yet – you are here, commanded by the Pope because he believes that the end of days is coming. The Pope himself thinks it could be any day now. We know it must come now that the infidel are in Constantinople. We all know that the dead will rise on judgement day ...' She puzzled over it, then put her hand to the neck of the plain gown as if to feel the pace of her heart. It was as if the steady beat reassured her: 'Why should it not be true? I believe Johann has a vision. This must be a sign. It has to be a sign. I'm going to Jerusalem and I pray that I will meet my father there, among the risen dead, and that he will forgive me for failing him. And he will tell me how I can win back my home.'

Moved by her grief, Luca reached out his hand and touched her shoulder, and then, more daringly, put the back of his hand against the smooth line of her cheek. As soon as she felt his gentle touch on her skin, he felt her tremble. For a moment she stood quite still and then, with an inarticulate murmur, she moved aside.

'Why do you say that you failed him?' he asked very quietly.

'When my father was dying my brother told me that he didn't want me to see him in pain and despair. I believed my brother, and I prayed in the chapel while my father died alone. When I discovered that my brother had lied to me and stolen my inheritance, I feared that he had lied to my father about me too. What if my father died asking for me, but my brother told him that I would not come? I cannot bear to think of that.'

Her voice was choked with tears. She cleared her throat.

'Why did you trust your brother?' Luca asked Isolde gently. 'Why did you not defy him at once?'

Her beautiful mouth twisted. 'I was raised to be a lady,' she said bitterly. 'A lady should be above lies and deceit, she is honourable and trustworthy. A lady plays her part in the world with honour, and trusts a man to play his. I believed my brother to be an honourable man, the son of a great lord, raised to be as good a man as my father. Not even in the nunnery, with the evidence before me could I see him as a thief. It has taken me weeks to understand that I have to choose my own life, find my own road. I could not trust his honour. I could not wait to be rescued.'

They resumed their slow walk towards the inn, Isolde's hand tucked in the crook of Luca's arm, their steps matched. 'D'you really think your father will rise from the grave?' he asked her, curiously.

'I don't know how such a thing could be; but now I can't help but think it. How could Johann look at me, and describe my father? How could he speak of a cold bier in a chapel if he was not seeing, with the eyes of God, my own father's bier in our cold chapel? He must know the unknown things, see things that we are blind to.'

They paused before the open door of the inn, unable to prolong their walk any longer, and Luca took both of her hands in his. 'Odd that we should both be orphans,' he said.

Isolde looked up at him, her face warm. 'It makes me want to comfort you,' she whispered.

He took a breath. 'And I, you.'

They stood handclasped. Ishraq and Freize hesitated on the quayside behind them, watching the young couple.

'Would you think of me as your friend?' Luca said very quietly to Isolde.

She did not hesitate for a moment. 'We're both alone in the world,' she said. 'I would like to have a friend who could be constant as my father was, patient as he was, faithful as he was.'

'I'd want a friend that I could be proud of,' Luca said quietly. 'Perhaps I'll never be able to take you to meet my mother. Perhaps my mother has been dead for many years. But I would like to think that I could have taken you to meet my mother and she would have liked you ...'

He broke off, suddenly remembering his vows. She felt him almost snatch his hands away from their warm mutual hold.

'Of course, I cannot think of anything more than a friendship. I am in the early stages of the priesthood, I am going to be a priest, a celibate priest.'

'Only the early stages,' Isolde whispered. 'Not yet sworn.'

Luca looked at her as if she was tempting him. 'I am not yet sworn,' he confirmed. 'I am not bound by my word. It was my intention to join the priesthood ... before ...' He broke off before he could be tempted to say, 'before you.'

⌒'

While the crowd before the church slowly dispersed, wondering at what they had heard and what it might mean, Brother Peter waited patiently for Johann to finish his whispered confession to Father Benito. After a little while the young man stood up, crossed himself, nodded respectfully to the priest and then walked across the church to kneel in silent prayer on the chancel steps, his head resting against the thickly carved rood screen which protected the mystery of the Mass from the congregation. No-one but an ordained priest was allowed near to the altar.

Behind him, in the silent church, Brother Peter glanced around, and seeing that he was unobserved, crossed the church to kneel in confession. On the other side of the screen the parish priest waited in silence.

'Father Benito, I need your advice on this matter,' Brother Peter confided, folding his hands together but clearly not preparing to confess his sins.

The priest was bowed over his rosary, saying his prayers. His hands were shaking. He hardly lifted his head. 'I can tell you nothing.'

'This could not be more important.'

'I agree. This is the most important thing. I have never known anything of greater importance in this world.'

'I have to ask . . .'

The priest collected himself and sat back. 'Ah, you will want to know if he has a true vision,' he guessed.

'I must know. This is not a matter of curiosity about a herdboy with a following of half a dozen. This is becoming a mighty crusade. If they get to the Holy Land it could change everything. I have to advise the Lord of my Order who advises the Holy Father whether this is a true crusade. If this young man is a charlatan, I have to know at once, we have to be prepared. If he is a saint, it is even more important: we need to know all about him. He just confessed to you. Your opinion is most important.'

The parish priest looked through the carved wooden screen at the great man from Rome. 'My son, truly, I cannot help you.'

'It is a matter of the good of the Church itself. I command you to speak.'

Again the priest refused. 'I cannot help you.'

'Father Benito, I don't need details, you need not break the seal of the confessional. Just give me an idea. Just tell me: does he sin like a mortal boy? For if he confesses like a foolish ill-educated boy who has the knack of talking to a crowd, but nothing else, then he is a fraudster on a great mission, and we can treat him as such. We have dozens like him popping up every year and we manage them for the good of the Church and the glory of God. Help me to know what we must do with this lad.'

The priest thought for a moment. 'No, you misunderstand me. I am not refusing to help you. I mean that I cannot tell you anything. He confessed nothing.'

'He refused to confess?' Brother Peter was surprised at the defiance.

'No! No! He confessed nothing.' The priest looked up and met Brother Peter's amazed face. 'Exactly. I am breaking no confessional secrets for there was no confession. I have nothing to hint at, nothing that I have to hold in silence, as a sinful secret. Johann came to me and made a full confession: and there was nothing. He lives a life without sin. I set him no penance for he had no sins to atone.'

'No man is without sin,' Brother Peter said flatly.

The priest shrugged. 'I questioned him, and there was nothing.'

'Pride,' Brother Peter said, thinking of Johann's sermon and the hundreds of people listening, and how he himself would feel if he could preach like that and call people out of their homes to walk across Christendom. 'He sees himself

329

as a vehicle of God,' he said, thinking that would be how the boy felt.

'He takes no pride in himself,' replied the priest. 'I tested him, and this is true. He takes no credit for himself. He has no pride, though he is a leader of hundreds. He says God leads them and he walks alongside.'

'Greed.' Brother Peter thought of the young man who ate a good breakfast.

'He fasts or eats as God commands him, it depends on whether God sends them food or not. Frequently he fasts because he believes that God wants him to hunger as the poor. Mostly he just goes hungry because there is little food to be had, and all that there is, they share. I am not surprised if he ate well at your table. He would believe that God had brought the food to him, and it was his duty to eat. Did he say grace?'

'Yes.'

'Did he thank you for your hospitality?'

'He did,' Brother Peter grudgingly allowed.

'Then what more do you ask of him?'

Brother Peter shrugged.

'If God commands him to eat, he does so. If God commands him to thirst, he does so. Then God releases him and he is free to do His work.'

'Does he take the children? Does he call them away from their parents when they should stay at home? Could we call him a thief? Does he covet followers?'

'He says he does the will of God. I asked him about the children. He says that since he was called by God his sins have emptied out of him so he is a vessel, not a man. He holds only God's will, not the sins of man. I asked him specifically, and he answered with conviction. I asked him if he felt desire especially for the older girls and he said no. He convinced me. I think that he may be a saint in the making. In all my years of hearing confessions I have never spoken to a young man who opened his life to me and it was a clean page. I never would have expected this. It is beyond the dreams of a priest.'

'Lust?' Brother Peter said. 'In the past? In his village?'

'He says he is a virgin and I believe him.'

Brother Peter's head was spinning. 'Can this be true? A pure young man? An innocent?'

'Brother – I believe in him. If he will allow me, if the bishop will give me leave, I am going with him.'

'You?'

'I know. I must seem ridiculous. I am a comfortable parish priest, grown plump and lazy in a good living. But this boy knows that the end of days is coming. He told me some of the signs. They are all as the Bible predicts them. He has not been taught what to say, it has been revealed to him. He says we must be in Jerusalem if we hope to be saved. I believe God has truly warned Johann of the end of days. I will close up my house and go with the children's crusade to Jerusalem, if I am allowed. I want to go more than anything in this world.'

Brother Peter rose to his feet, his head whirling. 'I must send my report,' he said.

'Tell them,' the priest urged him. 'Tell them in Rome that a miracle is happening right here and now. A miracle in this little town, before us, worldly fools. God be praised that I am here to see it. God be praised that into this sinful house should come Johann the Good to lead me to Jerusalem.'

331

Brother Peter and Luca wrote the report together, while Freize found a stable lad willing to undertake the long ride to Avezzano.

'You'll take the old Roman road,' Freize explained to the lad who had been summoned into the dining room to take the precious letter. 'It's clear enough, you can't miss your way.'

'When you get there, you must go to the church of St Paul and ask for the parish priest,' Brother Peter told him. 'He will tell you his name is Father Josef. You can give him this letter. He will send it on.'

Luca watched Brother Peter double-fold the letter, and light a taper at the dining room fire. From his little writing box, Brother Peter took a stick of sealing wax and held it to the flame, dripping the scarlet wax in three separate pools on the fold. While the wax was still warm and soft he took a sealing ring from a cord around his neck and pressed it into the hardening wax. It left the image that Luca had seen, tattooed on the arm of the man who had recruited him into the secret order. It was a drawing of a dragon eating its tail.

'You will wait,' Brother Peter told the round-eyed lad who looked at these preparations as a man might watch an alchemist make gold. 'You will wait that night, and the next day. You will stay in the church house and they will give you food and a bed. In the evening you will go to the church again, see Father Josef and he will give you a letter to bring to me. You will take it, keep it safely, bring it to me without reading it. Do you understand?'

'The boy can't read,' Freize said. 'So you're safe enough in that. Us servants know nothing. He won't read your secrets, he would not dream of breaking your seal. But he understands what you're saying. He's a bright enough boy.'

Reluctantly, Brother Peter handed the letter to Luca, who paused for only a moment to study the seals and then passed it to the boy, who knuckled his forehead in a sort of rough salute and went out.

'What does it mean?' Luca asked. 'That seal? I saw it on the arm of the man who recruited me to the order.'

'It is the symbol of the order that you know as the Order of Darkness,' Brother Peter replied quietly. He waited till the door had closed behind Freize and then he rolled up the sleeve of his robe to his shoulder and showed a faded version of the design, tattooed over his upper arm. He looked at Luca's shocked face.

'It's pale, because I have worn it for so long,' he said. 'I entered the Order when I was younger than you. I swore to it heart and soul.'

'No-one has asked me to take the symbol on my body.' Luca said uneasily. 'I don't know if I would.'

'You're an apprentice,' Brother Peter replied. 'When you have held enough inquiries, and learned enough, when you are wise enough and thoughtful enough: then they may invite you to join the Order.'

'Who? Who will invite me?'

Brother Peter smiled. 'It's a secret order. Not even I know who serves in it. I report to Milord, and he reports to the Holy Father. I know you. I know two other Inquirers that I have served with. I know no more than them. We look for the signs of God and Satan in the world and we warn of the end of days.'

'And do we only defend?' Luca asked shrewdly. 'Or do we also attack?'

'We do as we are commanded,' Brother Peter said smoothly. 'In defence or attack we are obedient to the Order.'

'And the one that you call Milord – it was him who took me from my monastery to Castle Sant'Angelo, who spoke to me, who gave me this mission and sent me to be trained?'

'Yes.'

'Is he the commander of the Order?'

'Yes.'

'Do you know his name?'

In reply Brother Peter showed Luca the blank reports in his writing box that were already addressed, ready for dispatch. They all read only:

Urgent

'No name?'

'No name.'

'He has no name but your letter will get to him? Just that? Just the seal of the dragon? It needs no name nor direction?'

'It will get to him, if the boy gets it to Father Josef in Avezzano.'

'This Father Josef – the parish priest of the church of St Paul, Avezzano – he is of our Order?'

'He's not called Josef. And he's not the parish priest of Avezzano. But yes, if the boy gets the letter to him, he will open it, see the sign of the Order, and he will get it to Milord. Without fail. None of us would fail to pass on a report. We never know how important a report might be. It could be news of the end itself.'

'So if there is a man in a small town like Avezzano, whose name is not Josef, who knows the seal and knows where to take the letter, there may be many men, other men serving like him, all over Italy?'

'Yes,' Brother Peter admitted. 'There are.'

'All over France? All over Spain? All over Christendom?'

'I don't know how many,' Brother Peter said cautiously. 'I know of those I need to know, to get my reports to Milord, and to receive my orders from him. Every time I leave Rome on a new inquiry he tells me who I can rely on – in any direction. He tells me who to ask for at each church along the way.'

There was a tap on the door and Freize put his head inside. 'He's gone. I have sent him on my horse Rufino, who is a good horse, and he has promised to ride, take your letter, and wait for a reply, and then come back. It wasn't easy to persuade him to go. Half the town swears that they will go on this crusade and he wanted to go too.'

Brother Peter rose. 'He is sure of the church and who to ask for?'

'Yes, and he will wait there for the reply from Rome.'

'You have told him he must not fail?'

'He's a good lad. He'll do his best. And Rufino is a good horse and can be trusted to find the way.'

'Very well, you can go.' Brother Peter released him; but Freize leaned on the door to look in at Luca.

'In deep,' was all he observed. 'In very deep.' And then he picked up the kitten and went from the room.

Inspired by Johann the Good, the people who had come into the little town for the market went back to their villages and farms and spoke of him to their friends and neighbours. Next day, hundreds more people came into Piccolo bringing food and wine and money for the children's crusade, and to hear Johann preach. Once again he stood on the doorstep of the church and promised them all that if they would come with him to Jerusalem they would walk again with the people that they had loved and lost. These were people who had been orphaned young, who had lost their first-born children: when Johann spoke to them of the rising of the dead they wept as if for the first time. Isolde and Ishraq went to hear him preach, standing in the hot sun of the market square with the common people. Luca and Brother Peter stood inside the shadow of the door of the church with the priest and listened intently.

'Come home,' Johann said surprisingly to the crowd, who were all born and bred within about ten miles and whose homes were mostly unwelcoming hovels. 'Come home to your real home. Come home to Jerusalem. Come home to Bethlehem.' He seemed to look towards Ishraq who was dressed as modestly as a lady on a pilgrimage, her cape shielding her face, a gown down to her ankles, and strong riding boots hiding her brown feet with the silver rings on her toes. 'Come home to Acre, those of you who were born with the taste of milk and honey. Come back to where your mother first opened her eyes. Come to your motherland.'

Ishraq swallowed and turned to look at Isolde. 'Can he mean me?' she whispered. 'Does he really mean that Acre, the beautiful Arab city, is my true home?'

'I can hear your mother calling you,' he said simply. 'I can hear her calling you from across the sea.'

A woman from the crowd called out: 'I can hear her! I can hear Mama!'

'When we get to Jerusalem and the Lord puts out his hand for us, that will be the end of sorrow, that will be the end of grieving. Then shall the orphan find his mother and the girl know her father.' He glanced towards Ishraq. 'Then shall the girl who has lived all her life among strangers be with her people again. You will be warmed by the sun that you saw first, when your eyes first opened. You will taste the fruits of your homeland.'

'How can he know?' Ishraq whispered to Isolde. 'How can he know that I was born in Acre? How can he know that my mother promised me that one day we would go home? He must hear the voice of God. I have doubted him; but this must be a true revelation.'

338

Around the two young women, people were crying and pressing forward, asking the young man about their families; one woman begged him to tell her that her son, her lost son, was in heaven and she would see him again. He put out his hand so that they did not jostle him, and the people at the front of the crowd fell to their knees and linked arms before him as if he were an icon, to be carried through the crowd at shoulder height on a saint's day.

'Come with us,' he said simply. 'Come and see for yourself on that wonderful day of judgement when your children, your father and' – his bright blue gaze went to Ishraq – 'your mother takes your hand and welcomes you to your home.'

Ishraq stepped forwards as if she could not help herself, as if she were in a dream. 'My father?' she asked. 'My mother?'

'They are waiting for you,' Johann said, speaking only to her with a quiet certainty which was far more convincing than if he had shouted, as most preachers did. 'The ones that you loved and lost are waiting for you. The father whose name you don't know, the mother who died without telling you. She will be there, she will tell you then. You will see them together and they will smile at you, their daughter. We will all rise up together.'

'Now,' he said quietly. 'I am going to confess and pray. God bless you.'

Without another word, he turned into the doorway of the church and Brother Peter and Luca stepped back for him, and the priest Father Benito went inside to kneel with this most surprising prophet. The priest unlocked the rood screen and took him inside, up to the very steps of the altar, where only those ordained by God might go, and they knelt down side by side, the village priest and the boy that he thought was a saint.

~

The girls found their way to Luca in the private dining room talking with Brother Peter. 'We've decided, for sure,' Isolde told him. 'Ishraq is as convinced as I am. The prophet Johann has spoken to her too. We're not going to Croatia. We're not going to Hungary.'

Luca was not even surprised. 'You're going to Jerusalem? You're certain? Both of you? You want to go with Johann?' He looked at Ishraq. 'You, of all people, want to join a Christian crusade?'

'I have to,' she said almost unwillingly. 'I am convinced. At first I thought it was some kind of trick. I thought he might talk to people, to work out what to say to convince them, take a bit of gossip and twist it into a prediction so that it sounds like a foretelling. I've seen fortune-tellers and palmists and all sorts of saltimbancos work a crowd like that. It's easy enough to do: you make a guess and when you strike lucky and someone cries, then you know that you're on to something and you say more. But this is something different. I believe he has a vision. I believe he knows. He has said things to Isolde, and today he said things to me that no-one in this town knows. He spoke of me in a way that I don't even acknowledge to myself. It's not possible that it could be a lucky guess. I think he must have a vision. I think he sees true.' She looked down, not meeting his questioning eyes, and cleared her throat.

'He spoke of my mother,' she said quietly. 'She died

without telling me the name of my father. She died speaking of Acre, her home, my birthplace. He knew that too.'

'We believe he has a true vision,' Luca confirmed. 'Brother Peter and I have reported it to Rome. We're waiting for the reply. And I have asked if we may go with him.'

'You have?' Isolde breathed.

'He spoke to me too,' Luca reminded her. 'He spoke of my father, of his kidnap by the Ottoman slavers. Nobody knows about that but the people I have told: Freize and yourself, but no one else. Freize spoke of it once to Brother Peter, but no-one in this village knows anything about us but that we are travelling together on a pilgrimage, and that I am authorised by the Holy Father. He can have learned nothing else from kitchen-door gossip. So he must have some way of knowing about us that is not of this world. I have to assume that it is as he says – that he is guided by God.'

'No questions?' Ishraq asked him with a little smile. 'Inquirer, I thought you always had questions. I thought you were a young man who could not help but question?'

'I have many,' Luca gave a little laugh. 'Dozens. But from all I have seen, for the moment, I believe Johann. I take him on trust.'

'I too,' Brother Peter said. 'The answer should come from Rome, the day after tomorrow. I think they will command us to go with the children's crusade, and help them on their way.'

Ishraq's eyes were shining. 'He said that I should go home,' she said. 'I have never thought of the Holy Land as my home. I was taught to call Lucretili my home; but now, suddenly, everything looks different.'

341

'You won't be different?' Isolde asked her, speaking almost shyly. 'You won't change with me? Even if you find your family in Acre?'

'Never,' Ishraq said simply. 'But to be in my mother's country and to hear her language! To feel the heat of the sun that she told me about! To look around and see people with skin the colour of mine wearing clothes like mine, to know that somewhere there is my family, my mother's family. Perhaps even my father is there.'

'He spoke to you as if you were a Christian and would see the Last Day like the rest of us,' Brother Peter observed.

'My mother would have said that we were all People of the Book,' she replied. 'We all worship the same God: Jews, Christians and Muslims. We all have the one God and we only have different prophets.'

'Your mother would be very wrong,' Brother Peter told her gently. 'And what you say is heresy.'

She smiled at him. 'My mother was a woman from Acre in a country where Jesus is honoured as a prophet but where they are certain he is not a god. She was with me in Granada, in a country of Christian, Jew and Muslim. I saw with my own eyes the synagogue next to the church next to the mosque, and the people working and reading and praying alongside each other. They called it the *Convivencia* – living alongside each other in harmony, whatever their beliefs. For the enemy is not another person who believes in a god, the enemy is ignorance and people who believe in nothing and care for nothing. You should know that by now, Brother Peter.'

'Three days after they had sent the message to Rome, Freize, waiting outside the little church, saw his horse, Rufino, coming down the hill and through the main town gates. He called his name, and the horse put his head up and his ears forward at Freize's voice, whinnying with pleasure, and went towards him.

Freize took the reins and led the horse down the steep steps to the quayside inn. In the stable yard he helped the weary lad from the saddle, took the sealed letter from him and tucked it inside his jerkin. 'You've done well,' he said to the lad. 'And you've missed nothing here. There's been a lot of praying and promising and some planning, but the children's crusade is still in town and if your Ma will let you – and I would have thought she would forbid you – you can still march out with them. So go and get your dinner now, you've been a good boy.' He dismissed the lad and turned to the horse.

'Now, let's settle you,' he said tenderly to his horse, taking the reins and leading the tired animal into the stall. He took off the saddle and the bridle and rubbed the horse all over with a handful of straw, talking to him all the time, congratulating him on a long journey and promising a good rest. Gently, he slapped the horse's tired muscles, and then brushed the patterned white, black and brown coat till it shone. When he had made sure that the animal had a small feed, with hay and water for the night, he lifted the ginger kitten from where she was sleeping in the manger, and went to the inn.

'Here's your reply,' he said, handing the sealed letter to Luca, who was sitting in the dining room with Brother Peter. The two men had been studying prophecies together, from the manuscripts that they had brought with them in carefully rolled scrolls and a bound Bible spread out on the dining room table before them. In the seat by the window, catching the last of the evening light, the two girls were bent over their sewing, working in silence.

Luca broke the seals and spread out the letter on the table so that he and Brother Peter could read it together. Freize and the girls waited.

'He says we can go,' Luca announced breathlessly. 'Milord says that we can go to Jerusalem with Johann.'

The two girls gripped each other's hands.

'He says that I must observe Johann's preaching, and . . .' He broke off, the excitement draining from his face. 'He says I must watch him for heresy or crime, examine everything he says, and report it to the bishop, wherever we are, if I think he says something which is outside the Church's teachings. I must question him for signs that he has made a pact with the Devil, and watch him for any ungodly acts. If I see anything suspicious, I must report him at once to the Church authorities and they will arrest him.' He turned to Brother Peter. 'That's not an inquiry, that's spying.'

'No, see what Milord says.' Brother Peter pointed to the letter. 'It is part of our usual inquiry. We are to travel with him and look for the light of God in all that he does, ensure that his mission is a true one, watch him for any signs that he is a true prophet of the end of days. If we see any trickery or falsehood we are to observe it, and report it; but if we think he is hearing the voice of God and doing His bidding, we are to help him and guide him.

'The Holy Father himself will send money and arms to help the children get to the Holy Land. He says that we are to guide them to Bari where he himself will see that there will be enough ships to take us to Rhodes. The Hospitallers will guide and guard us from there. It is their duty to guide pilgrims to the Holy Land. The Holy Father will warn them that greater numbers than they have ever seen before are coming – and then – who knows what the Hospitallers will do to guard this army of children?'

'Does your lord not expect the sea to part for the children?' Freize asked. 'Surely that's the plan? Why would you need ships? Why would you need the Hospitallers? Isn't God going to part the oceans?'

Brother Peter looked up, irritated by the interruption and by Freize's sarcastic tone. 'God is providing for the children,' he said. 'If a miracle takes place we are to report it, of course.'

'I won't spy on him and I won't entrap him,' Luca stipulated.

Brother Peter shrugged. 'You are to inquire,' he said simply. 'Look for God, look for Satan. What else have you been appointed to do?'

It was true that Luca had agreed to inquire into anything and everything. 'Very well,' he said. 'We will look clear-sighted at whatever happens. I won't entrap him, but I will watch him closely. I'll tell Johann we will travel with him and pay for the ships.'

'Does your lord send money for feeding the children?' Freize asked dulcetly.

'A letter for the priest, and for other religious houses along the way,' Brother Peter answered, showing him the messages. 'To tell them to prepare food and distribute it. His Holiness will see that they are reimbursed.'

'I'll take that to the church then,' Freize said. 'That's probably more important than the protection of the Hospitallers, who are, if I hear truly, an odd bunch of men.'

'They are knights devoted to the service of God and the guarding of pilgrims on their way to Jerusalem,' Brother Peter said firmly. 'Whatever they do, they do it for the great cause of Christian victory in the Holy Land.'

'Murderers, who have found a good excuse to wage war in the name of God,' Freize said quietly, as he went out and closed the door to silence his own insubordination.

~

Luca found Johann sitting on a wooden mooring post on the quayside looking out to sea. 'May I speak with you?' he asked.

'Of course.' Johann smiled his sweet smile. 'I was listening to the waves and wondering if I could hear God. But He will speak to me in His own time, not mine.'

'I have written of you to Milord, the commander of our order, and he has spoken of you to the Holy Father.'

Johann nodded but did not seem particularly excited by the attention of the great men.

'The Holy Father says that I am to guide you to Bari, further down the coast, where he will arrange for ships to take you and the children to Rhodes. From there, the Hospitallers will help you to Jerusalem.'

'The Hospitallers? Who are they?'

Luca smiled at the boy's ignorance. 'Perhaps you won't have heard of them in Switzerland? They're an order of knights who help pilgrims to and from the Holy Land. They nurse people who fall sick, and support people on their way. They are soldiers too, they guard pilgrims against attack from the infidels. They are a powerful and mighty order and if you are under their protection you will be safe. They can protect you from attack, and can help you with food and medicine if it is needed. The Holy Land has been conquered by the infidels and sometimes they attack pilgrims. It can be a fearfully dangerous road. You will need a friend on the way. The Hospitallers will be your guardians.'

The boy took in the information but did not seem very impressed. 'God will provide for us,' he said. 'He always has done. We need no help but His. And He is our friend. He is the only guardian we need.'

'Yes,' Luca agreed. 'And perhaps this is His way to help you, with His Holy Order of Hospitallers. Will you let me

347

guide you to Bari and we can all go on the ships that the Holy Father will send for us? It's a long way to the Holy Land, and better for us all if there are good ships waiting for us and the Hospitallers to guard us.'

Johann looked surprised. 'We are not to walk all the way? We are not to wait for the seas to part?'

'Milord says that the Holy Father suggests this way. And he has sent me letters that we can show at holy houses, abbeys and monasteries all along the way, and at pilgrims' houses, and they will feed the children.'

'And so God provides,' Johann observed. 'As He promised He would. Are you coming with us all the way to Jerusalem, Luca Vero?'

'I would like to do so, if you will allow it. I am travelling with a lady and her servant, and they would like to come too. I will bring my servant Freize and my clerk Brother Peter.'

'Of course you can all come,' Johann said. 'If God has called you, you have to obey. Do you think He has called you? Or are you following the commands of man?'

'I felt sure that you were speaking of me when you spoke of a fatherless boy,' Luca said. He was shy, telling this youth of his deepest sorrow. 'I am a man who lost both his father and mother when he was only a boy and I have never known where they are, nor even if they are alive or dead. I believed you when you said that I should see them in Jerusalem. Do you really think it is so?'

'I know it is so,' the boy said with quiet conviction.

'Then I hope I can help you on the journey, for I am certain that it is my duty as their son that I should come with you.'

'As you wish, Brother.'

'And if you have any doubts about your calling,' Luca said, feeling like a Judas, tempting the boy to betray himself. 'Then you can tell me. I am not yet a priest – I was a novice when I was called from the monastery to serve in this way – but I can talk with you and advise you.'

'I have no doubts,' Johann said, gently smiling at him. 'The doubts are all yours, Brother Luca. You doubted your calling to the monastery, and now you doubt your mission. You doubt your instructions, you doubt the lord of your order, and you doubt even the words you speak to me now. Don't you think I can hear the lies on your tongue and see the doubts in your mind?'

Luca flushed at the boy's insight. 'I had no doubts when I heard you speak. I had no doubts then. My father was taken by the slavers when I was only fourteen. I long to see him again. My mother was taken too. Sometimes I dream of them and the childhood that I had with them. Sometimes even now I cannot bear that they are lost to me, cannot bear to think that they may be suffering. I was helpless to save them then, I am helpless now.'

Johann was silent for a moment, his brilliant blue eyes searching Luca's face. 'You will see them,' he said gently. 'You will see them again. I know it.'

Luca put his hand on his heart, as if to hold down his grief. 'I pray for it,' he said.

'And I will pray for you,' Johann said. 'And tomorrow morning at dawn, we will walk on.'

'To Bari?' Luca confirmed. 'You will allow me to guide you and help you to Bari?'

'As God wills,' Johann said cheerfully.

349

~

In the top bedroom of the inn Ishraq and Isolde were packing their few clothes in a saddlebag, for the journey on the next day. Isolde twisted back her plait of fair hair. 'D'you think the landlady would send up a bath and hot water?'

Ishraq shook her head. 'I already asked. She is boiling our linen in her washday copper and she was displeased at having to get that out for us. She washes her own things once a month. They bathe only once a year, and that on Good Friday. She was scandalised when I said we wanted more than a jug of water for washing.'

Isolde laughed out loud. 'No! So what are we to do?'

'There's a little lake in the woods outside the west gate – the stable boy told me that the lads go there to swim in summer. Could you bear to wash in cold water?'

'Better than nothing,' Isolde agreed. 'Shall we go now?'

'Before the sun goes down,' Ishraq agreed with a shiver. 'And whether she likes it or not I shall have some linen towels from the landlady to dry us off, and our clean clothes to wear.'

~

Discreetly, the two girls watched Luca talking to Johann on the quayside, checked that Freize was helping in the kitchen and Brother Peter studying in the dining room and then went up the cobbled steps to the market square, and out through the west gate. The porter watched them go. 'Gate closes at dusk!' he shouted.

'We'll be back before then,' Ishraq called back. 'We're just going for a walk.'

He shook his head at the peculiarities of ladies and let them go, distracted by the stable boy from the inn. 'Shouldn't you be at work?' the gatekeeper demanded.

'Afternoon off,' the lad replied.

'Well the gate closes . . .'

'At sunset!' the boy finished cheekily. 'I know. We all know.'

~

The swimming lake was as round as the bowl of a fountain, tucked in the deep green of the forest, completely secluded with a guarding circle of trees, grass down to the soft sand edge, and clean clear water down to twenty feet.

'It's beautiful,' Isolde said.

'It'll be cold,' Ishraq predicted, looking at the darker depths.

'Better jump in then!' Isolde laughed, and shed her gown and her linen petticoat and, wearing only a little linen chemise, took a bare-legged run and a great joyful leap into the water. She screamed as she went under and then came up laughing, her golden hair floating around her shoulders. 'Come on! Come on! It's lovely!'

Ishraq was naked in a moment and waded into the water, shivering and hugging herself. Isolde swam up to her and then turned on her back and kicked a little spray into Ishraq's protesting face.

'Oh! Cold! Cold!'

'It's fine when you're in,' Isolde insisted. 'Come on.' She took her friend's hands and pulled her in deeper. Ishraq gave a little scream at the cold and then plunged in, swimming swiftly after Isolde who turned and splashed away as fast as she could.

They played like a pair of dolphins, twisting and turning in the water until they were breathless and laughing, and then Ishraq went to the side of the pool where they had left their clothes and gave Isolde a bar of coarse lye soap.

'I know,' she said at Isolde's little disappointed sniff. 'But it's all they had. And I have some oil for our hair.'

Isolde stood knee deep in the water and lathered herself all over, and then, passing the soap to Ishraq, lowered herself into the clean water, and stepped out of the pool. She stripped off her wet chemise and wrapped herself in the linen towel, then held a towel for Ishraq who, washed and rinsed, came out too, teeth chattering.

Warmly wrapped, they combed their wet hair and smoothed the rose-perfumed oil from scalp to tip, and then Isolde turned her back to Ishraq, who twisted her golden locks into a plait and then turned her own back as Isolde plaited Ishraq's dark hair into a coil at the nape of her neck.

'Elegant,' Isolde said with pleasure in her own handiwork.

'Wasted,' Ishraq pointed out as she threw on her dress and pulled the hood of her cape over her head. 'Who ever sees me?'

'Yes, but at least we know we are clean and our hair plaited,' Isolde said. 'And we are making a long journey tomorrow, and who knows when we will be able to wash again?'

'I hope it's hot water next time,' Ishraq remarked as they took up their little bundles and set off down the road. 'Do you remember in Granada, the Moorish baths with hot steam and hot water and heated towels?

Isolde sighed. 'And in the women's bathhouses the old lady who scrubs you with soap, and rinses you with rose-water, and then washes your hair and oils it and combs it out?'

Ishraq smiled. 'Now that is civilised.'

'Perhaps in Acre?' Isolde asked.

'In Acre for sure.' Ishraq smiled. 'Perhaps our next bath will be a proper Moorish bath in the Acre bathhouse!'

~

The girls got back to the inn unnoticed, and were on time for dinner that evening, ready to plan for their departure with the pilgrimage on the next day. Luca was clear that he could not ride while children walked. He could not bring himself to be mounted high on an expensive horse while Johann led everyone else on foot. He was going to walk alongside them to Bari. Ishraq and Isolde said that he was right, and they would walk also; Brother Peter agreed. Only Freize pointed out that it was too far for the young women to walk without exhaustion and discomfort, that if they travelled alongside the pilgrimage they would have to stop and eat where the children ate, and that would mean that food would be scarce and poor. Were they to eat nothing but rye bread and drink water from streams? Were the ladies to sleep in barns and in fields? he demanded irritably. And how were they to carry the tools of the Inquirer's trade: Brother Peter's little writing desk, the manuscripts for reference, the Bible, the money bag? How were they to carry their luggage: the broadsword, the ladies' clothes and shoes, their combs, their hand mirrors, their little pots of scented oils? Would it satisfy their desire to appear more humble if they walked like poor people, but Freize followed behind them riding one horse, leading four others, and the donkey with the baggage tied at the end of the string? Would they not be play-acting a pilgrimage and pretending to poverty? And how was that more holy?

'Surely we can walk with them during the day, and stay in pilgrim houses or inns for the night?' Isolde asked.

'Walk away and leave them sleeping in a bare field?' Freize suggested. 'Join them in the morning after you've had a good sleep and a hearty breakfast? And then there's illness. One of you is almost certain to take a fever from a sickly child, and then either you'll be left behind or we'll all have to stay with you, and nobody going anywhere.'

'He's right. This is ridiculous. And you can't walk all that way,' Luca said to Isolde.

'I could not allow it,' Freize said pompously.

'I can walk!' Isolde said indignantly. 'I can walk with the children. I'm not afraid of discomfort.'

'You'll get headlice,' Freize warned her. 'And fleas. It's not a beautiful mortification of the flesh that you'll look back on with secret pride: it's dirt and bites and rats and disease. And long tedious days of trudging along while your boots rub your feet raw and you hobble like an old lady with aching bones.'

'Freize,' she said. 'I am determined to go to the Holy Land.'

'You'll get corns on your feet,' he warned her. 'And you'll never be able to wear a pretty shoe again.'

It was inarguable, and he knew it. Despite her serious intentions she was silenced.

'You'll smell,' he said, clinching the argument with a mighty blow. 'And you'll get spots.'

'Freize,' she said. 'This is not a whim, it is a vision. I am sure that my father would want me to go. Ishraq is determined to go. We are going. Nothing will stop us.'

'What about a nice boat to Bari?' Freize suggested.

'What?'

'Go by boat,' Freize repeated. 'We can ship the horses and the baggage and the ladies by boat, we three men can walk with the children and help as we are required to do. The ladies can get there without walking, get there before us, find themselves an inn and wait in comfort till we arrive.'

He looked at Isolde's mutinous face. 'My lady, dearest lady, you will have to travel in heat and dirt when you get to the Holy Land. Don't think you are taking the easy way. Discomfort will come. If you want to trudge along in burning heat and miserable dirt, attacked half the time by madmen in turbans, scratching yourself raw with fleabites, sleeping in sand with cobras under your pillow, your ambition will be satisfied. But do it when you get to the Holy Land. There's no particular merit in walking on rough ground in Italy.'

'Actually,' Brother Peter intervened. 'If the ladies were to be at Bari first then they could make sure that the ships were waiting for us. We'll be – what? – five days on the road? Perhaps more?' He turned to the two of them. 'If you were willing to go ahead, I could give you the papal letters of authorisation, and you could get the food ready for the children, and make sure there were enough ships. It would be very helpful.'

'You would be helping the pilgrimage, not escaping the walk,' Luca said to Isolde. 'This is important.'

'I don't know ...' She hesitated.

'Perhaps they can't do it alone,' Freize said. 'I could go too. Perhaps I had better accompany them.'

Luca gave him a long narrow gaze from his hazel eyes. 'You go by boat as well?'

'Just to help,' Freize said. 'And guard them.'

'And so you go by comfort in the ship and escape a long and uncomfortable walk,' Luca accused.

'Why not?' Freize asked him. 'If my faithless heart is not in it? If I would only blunt your resolve with my sinful doubts? Better keep me out of it. Better by far that only those who have the vision should take the walk.'

'Oh very well,' Luca ruled. 'Isolde, you and Ishraq and Freize will go by boat to Bari, take all the horses, and we will join you there. Freize, you will keep the girls safe, and you will find ships that will take the children to Rhodes, agree a price, and take the papal letter of credit to the priest and to the moneylenders.'

'I want to walk,' Isolde insisted.

'I don't,' Ishraq said frankly. 'Freize is right, we'll walk enough when we get there.'

'So we are agreed,' Brother Peter said. He opened his little writing desk and took out the papal letters. 'These will draw on credit with the goldsmiths of Bari,' he said. 'They will no doubt be Jews, but they will recognise the authority; do the best you can to get a good price. They are a wicked people. They have a guilt of blood on their heads and will carry it forever.'

Ishraq took the paper and tucked it in her sleeve. 'And yet you are depending on their honesty and their trustworthiness,' she observed tartly. 'You are sending them a letter and expecting them to give you credit on that alone. You know that they will understand the authorisation and they will lend you money. That's hardly wicked. I would have thought it was very obliging. The Pope himself is trusting them, they are doing the work that you allow them to do, they are doing it with care and good stewardship. I don't see why you would call them wicked.'

'They are heathens and infidels,' Brother Peter said firmly.

'Like me,' she reminded him.

'You are in service to a Christian lady,' Peter avoided her challenge. 'And anyway, I have seen that you are a good and loyal companion.'

'Like the women of my race,' she pressed. 'Like the other infidels.'

'Perhaps,' he said. 'We'll know more when we have landed in the Holy Land.'

Isolde gave a little shiver of joy. 'I can't imagine it.'

Ishraq smiled at her. 'Me neither.'

In the morning, after breakfast, the two girls, with the
hoods of their capes pulled forward for modesty, came out
of the inn door and walked along the quayside to the ship
that would take them south, down the coast to Bari. Luca
and Brother Peter went with them, Brother Peter carrying
the precious manuscripts stitched into packages of oiled
sheepskin against the damp, his writing box strapped on
his back. On the quayside, amid the ships returning from
their dawn fishing voyages, Freize was loading the donkey
and the five horses.

The gangplank was wide and strong from the quayside onto the deck of the boat, and the first three horses
went easily across the little bridge and into their stalls

359

for the journey. Ishraq watched as the last horse, Brother Peter's mount, jibbed at the gangplank and tried to back away. Freize put a hand on its neck and whispered to it, a few quiet words, and then unclipped the halter so the horse was quite free. Brother Peter exclaimed and looked around, ready to summon help to catch a loose horse, but Luca shook his head. 'Wait,' he said. 'He knows what he's doing.'

For a moment the horse stood still, realising that it had been loosed, and then Freize touched its neck once more and turned his back on it, walking across the gangplank on his own. The horse pricked its ears forwards as it watched him, and then delicately followed, its hooves echoing on the wooden bridge. When it came freely onto the deck, Freize patted it with a few words of quiet praise, and then clipped the rope on again and led it into the stalls in the ship.

'They love him,' Luca remarked, coming beside the two young women. 'They really do. All animals trust him. It's a gift. It's like St Francis of Assisi.'

'Does he have a kitten in his pocket?' Ishraq asked, making Luca laugh.

'I don't know. I wouldn't be surprised.'

'I think he has been feeding a stray kitten and carrying it around,' she said. 'I moved his jacket from the dining room chair last night, and it squeaked.'

Isolde laughed. 'It's a ginger kitten – he found it days ago. I didn't know he still had it.'

Freize came back off the boat. 'There's a little cabin and a cooking brazier,' he told the girls. 'You should be comfortable enough. And the weather is supposed to be good, and we will be there in a few hours. We should get into port at about dinner time.'

'Shall we go aboard?' Isolde asked Luca. The master was on the ship, shouting orders, the sailors ready to let go the ropes. The children of the crusade idly watched the preparations.

'God bless them,' Isolde said earnestly, one foot on the gangplank, her hand in Luca's grasp. 'And God bless you too, Luca. I will see you in Bari.'

'In just a few days' time,' he said quietly to her. 'It's better that you travel like this, although I will miss you on the road. I won't fail you. I shall see you there soon.'

'Cast off!' the master shouted. 'All aboard!'

Brother Peter handed his box of manuscripts and his precious writing case to Freize to take into the little cabin. Isolde, holding the broadsword, turned to go up the gangplank when she felt the quayside suddenly shake beneath her feet. For a moment she thought that a ship had knocked against the quay and shaken the great slabs of stone, and she put out her hand and grasped the gangplank's end beam. But then the shake came again and a deep low rumble, a noise so massive and yet hushed that she snatched Ishraq's hand for fear and looked around. At once there was an anxious slapping on the side of the quay as a thousand little waves rippled in, as if blown by a sudden gale, though the sea was flat calm.

The children on the quayside jumped to their feet, as the ground shook beneath them, the younger ones cried out in fear. 'Help me! Help me!'

'What was that?' Isolde asked. 'Did you hear it? That terrible noise?'

361

Ishraq shook her head. 'I don't know. Something strange.'

'I know that my Redeemer lives!' Johann called out. Everyone turned to look at him. He was quite undisturbed. He spread his arms and smiled. 'Do you hear the voice of God? Do you feel the touch of His holy hand?'

Luca stepped forwards to the girls. 'Better go back to the inn ...' he started. 'Something is wrong ...'

The great noise came again, like a groan, so deep and so close that they looked up at the clear sky though there were no thunderclouds, and down again to the sea which was stirred with quick little waves.

'God is speaking to us!' Johann called to his followers, his voice clear over their questions. 'Can you hear Him? Can you hear Him speaking through earthquake, wind and fire? Blessed be His Name. He is calling us to His service! I can hear Him. I can hear Him!'

'Hear Him!' the children repeated, the volume of their voices swelling like a chorus. 'Hear Him!'

'Earthquake?' Isolde asked. 'He said: earthquake, wind and fire?'

'We'd better wait at the inn,' Ishraq said uneasily. 'We'd better not get on the boat. We'd better get under cover. If a storm is coming ...'

Isolde turned with her, to go to the inn, when one of the children shouted, 'Look! Look at that!'

Everyone looked where the child was pointing, to the steps of the quay where the water was splashing over the lower steps in an anxious rapid rhythm. As they watched, they saw an extraordinary thing. The tide was going out, ebbing at extraordinary speed, rushing like a river in spate, faster than any tide could go. The wet step dried in the bright sunshine as the next step was laid bare. Then, as the water receded, the green weed of the step beneath came into view, and the step below that, all the way down to the floor of the harbour. Water was pouring off the steps like a sudden waterfall, steps that no-one had seen since they were built in ancient times were now suddenly dry and in the open air, and in the harbour bed the sea was flowing backwards, running away from the land, falling away from the walls so that the depths were revealing all the secrets and becoming dry land once more.

It was a strange and hypnotic sight. Brother Peter joined the others as they crowded to the edge of the quay and gazed down as the water seeped away. The sea revealed more and more land as it crept further and further out. The horses on the deck neighed in terror as their boat grounded heavily on the harbour floor, other boats nearby hung on their ropes at the quayside wall or, further out in what had been deeper water, dropped and then rolled sideways as the sea fled away from them, leaving them abandoned and their anchors helplessly exposed, thrust naked into the silt – huge and heavy and useless.

'And Moses stretched out his hand over the sea; and the Lord caused the sea to go back by a strong east wind all that night, and made the sea dry land, and the waters were divided!' Johann cried from the back of the crowd. There were screams of joy, and children crying with fear, as he walked through them all to stand on the

363

brink of the quayside and look down into the harbour, where crabs were scuttling across the silt of the harbour floor and fish were slapping their tails in trapped pools of water. 'And Moses stretched out his hand over the sea; and the Lord caused the sea to go back by a strong east wind all that night, and made the sea dry land, and the waters were divided!' he said again. 'See – God has made the sea into dry land – just for us. This is the way to Jerusalem!'

Isolde's cold hand crept into Luca's. 'I'm afraid.'

Luca was breathless with excitement. 'I've never seen anything like it. I didn't dream it could happen! He said it would happen but I couldn't believe it.'

Ishraq exchanged one frightened glance with Isolde. 'Is this a miracle of your God?' she demanded. 'Is He doing it? Right now?'

On board the grounded ship, the tethered horses and the donkey were rearing against their ropes. Freize walked among them, trying to calm them down as they pulled their heads away from their halters, their hooves clattering against the wooden stalls. The wooden gang-plank had sunk down at one end with the ship. Now it splintered and broke, falling down into the silt of the harbour.

'Hush, my lovelies, be calm! Be calm!' Freize called to the horses. 'We're all settled here now. High and dry, nothing to fear, I am sure. Be calm and in a moment I'll have you out of here.'

'Follow me! Follow me!' Johann cried, and started down the stone steps of the quay. 'This is the way, this is the way to Jerusalem! This is the way made straight!'

The children followed him at once, filled with excitement at the adventure. At the back someone started to sing the Canticle of Simeon: 'Lord, now lettest thou thy servant depart in peace, according to thy word: For mine eyes have seen thy salvation, Which thou has prepared before the face of all people . . .'

'God shows us the way!' Johann cried out. 'God leads us to the Promised Land. He makes the wet places dry and we shall walk to the Holy Land!'

'Should we go with him?' Isolde asked Luca, trembling with hope and fear. 'Is this truly a miracle?'

Luca's face was alight. 'I can't believe it! But it must be. Johann said that there would be dry land to Jerusalem, and here is the sea pouring away from the land!'

The children were singing like a thousand-strong choir, spilling down the steps of the harbour, some of them jumping off the wet steps and laughing as they went ankle deep into the silt, picking their way through the thick wet weeds where the shells of big black mussels crunched under their feet, walking hand in hand, scores of them, hundreds of them, side by side, winding their way around the grounded ships and old wrecks, to the mouth of the harbour where the sea still retreated before them, further and further out towards the horizon, far quicker than they could walk, as it built a bridge of land for them, just for them, all the way to Palestine.

'I think we should go,' Luca decided, his heart racing. 'Go with them now. I think it's a true miracle.'

Luca went to the head of the harbour steps, Brother Peter beside him. 'D'you think this is true?' Luca shouted, his brown eyes bright with excitement.

'A miracle,' the older man confirmed. 'A miracle, and that I should see it! Praise be to God!'

'What are you doing?' Ishraq demanded, alarmed. 'What d'you think you're doing?'

'I have to see,' Luca spoke over his shoulder, his eyes fixed on the disappearing sea. 'I have to see the new land. Johann is leading the children to Jerusalem. I have to see this.'

Freize, on the grounded boat, trying to steady the horses, suddenly let out a sharp yelp of pain. The pocket of his jacket was jumping and squirming. His fingers were bloody from where he had reached inside. He tried again and pulled out the small ginger kitten. She was a little ball of spitting terror, her fur on end, her eyes madly green. She struggled wildly in his grip, he let her drop to the deck and she bounded away, agile as a monkey, up the straining mooring rope to the quayside, racing for the inn. But she didn't go in the open door, she swarmed up the vine that grew by the door and scrambled onto the tiled roof. She did not stop there but went higher, up to the very smoke vent, and balanced on top of the highest point on the quayside, her claws scrabbling on the terracotta tiles, as she clung to the roof, yowling with terror.

'No!' Freize suddenly shouted, his voice loud and frightened over the singing of the children. He vaulted over the side of the boat, dropping heavily into the sludge of the harbour floor. He struggled round the grounded boat to the lowest of the wet harbour steps, slipping on the seaweed and grabbing a mooring ring in the wall to stop himself from falling. He crawled, his feet slipping and sliding, to the top of the steps where Luca, almost in a trance, was starting to walk down, his face radiant. Freize barrelled into him, grabbed him round the waist pushing him back to the quayside, and thrust him bodily towards the inn.

'I want to see ...' Luca struggled against him. 'Freize – let me go! I'm going! I'm walking!'

'It's not safe! It's not safe!' Freize babbled. 'The kitten knows. The horses know. God help us all. Something terrible is going to happen. Get into the inn, get into the attic, get onto the roof if you can. Like the kitten! See the kitten! The sea is going to turn on us.'

'It's parting,' Brother Peter argued, standing his ground. 'You can see. Johann said that it would part for him and he would walk to Jerusalem. He's going, the children are going; we're going with him.'

'No, you're not!' Freize pushed Luca roughly towards the inn, slapping him on his shoulders in frustration. 'Take Isolde!' he shouted into Luca's bright face, shaking his shoulders. 'Take Ishraq! Or they'll drown before your eyes. You don't want that, do you? You don't want to see the waters come back and sweep Isolde away?'

Luca woke as if from a dream. 'What? You think the sea will come back?'

'I'm sure of it!' Freize shouted. 'Get them to safety. Get them out of here! Save the girls! Look at the kitten!'

Luca shot one horrified look at the kitten which was still clinging to the topmost point of the roof, spitting with fear, and then grabbed Isolde's hand and Ishraq's arm and hurried them both into the inn. Isolde would have held back but Ishraq was as frightened as Freize, and dragged her onwards. 'Come on!' she said. 'If it's a miracle, then the sea will stay dry. We can follow later. Let's get inside, let's get up to our bedroom. We can look from the window. Come on, Isolde!'

Freize saw they were on their way to safety and turned back and ran down the stone steps to the damp floor of the harbour, his boots churning in the deep mud. 'Come back!' he shouted to the children. 'Come back. The sea will turn! That's not the way!'

They were singing so loudly, in such happy triumph, that they did not even hear him. 'Come back!' Freize yelled. He started to run after them, slipping on the silt and the weeds, splashing doggedly through the puddles of seawater in his big boots. The slowest children at the back turned when they heard him and paused when they saw him coming, waving his arms and shouting.

'Go back!' Freize commanded them. 'Go back to the village!'

They hesitated, uncertain what they should do.

'Go back, go back,' Freize said urgently. 'The sea will turn, it will wash into the harbour again.'

Their blank faces showed that they could not understand him, their whole conviction, their whole crusade, was pressing them onwards. Johann had promised them this miracle and they believed that it was happening then and there. All their friends, all their fellow pilgrims were convinced, they were singing as they walked, further and further towards the harbour mouth where the receding sea shone white as it rushed away southwards. They all wanted to go together. They could see their road unfolding before them.

'Sweetmeats,' Freize said desperately. 'Go to the inn, they are giving away free sweets.'

Half a dozen children turned, and started to go back to the quayside.

'Hurry!' Freize shouted. 'Hurry or they'll be all gone. Run as fast as you can!'

He caught another half-dozen children and told them the same thing. They turned to go back and so did their friends who were a little before them.

Freize battled his way, pushing through the children to the front of the crowd. 'Johann!' he shouted. 'You are mistaken!'

The boy's face was bright with conviction, his eyes fixed on the sea that still receded steadily, invitingly, before him. The harbour mouth was dry, and yet still the sea drained away and the tawny mud unrolled before them like a Berber rug, like a dry smooth road all the way to his destination. 'God has made the way dry for me,' he said simply. 'You can walk with me. Tomorrow morning we will walk into Palestine and dine on milk and honey. I see it, though you do not see it yet. I am walking dry-shod, as I said we would.'

'Please,' Freize shouted. 'Walk tomorrow. When it has had time to dry out properly. Don't go now. I'm afraid the waters will come . . .'

'You are afraid,' Johann said gently. 'You doubted from the beginning, and now you are afraid, as you will always be afraid. You go back. I shall go on.'

Freize looked back to the quayside. A scuffle caught

his eye. The girl that he had first met with the bleeding feet was trying to get back to the quayside. Two boys had hold of her and were dragging her onward, trying to catch up with Johann. 'You let her go!' Freize called to them.

They held her tightly, pulling her onwards. Freize turned and ran back for her, burst through the two of them, pulled her away. 'I want to go back to shore!' she gasped. 'I'm frightened of the sea.'

'I'll take you,' he said.

Mutely, she lifted up her arms to him. Freize bent down and swung her up onto his shoulders, and turned to run clumsily back to the quayside, ploughing through the mud which sucked wetly at his feet, calling to the children to follow him as he ran.

He could hear the church bell of Piccolo starting to toll loudly, as the villagers poured out of their homes down to the quayside, the fishermen aghast at the state of the harbour and the loss of their ships. People were staring in wonderment at the anchors and chains lying alongside the beached craft, at the lobsters, dry in their pots, at the sudden extraordinary revelation of the floor of the harbour which was usually sixty feet under water.

Freize flung the little girl up the green steps and shouted at the people gathered there, starting to come down the steps to see the floor of the sea. 'Go back! Go to your homes! Go to the hills! Get as high as you can. The waters will come back! There's going to be a flood!'

Freize ploughed his way across the harbour mud to the grounded ship where the horses were rearing and kicking in the stalls on the boat. 'Be still my dears!' he called breathlessly. 'I'm coming for you!'

A few people, remembering stories of inexplicable great waves in fairy tales and folk stories, felt the chill of old fears at their backs, and turned and started to run. Their panic was infectious, and in moments the quayside was empty, people banging into their houses and bolting the doors, climbing to the upper windows to look out towards the sea, other people running past them, up the steep streets to the highest point of the village, to the walls around the landward side of the town, some taking shelter in the church and climbing up the stone steps of the bell tower to look out to sea. A few women ran against the terrified crowd, down to the quayside, shading their eyes against the dazzle of bright sunshine on wet mud, calling their children's names, begging them to come away from the crusade, to come home.

What they saw made them moan with horror. On the dry bed of the harbour, advancing in a ragged half-circle, as if going to dance hand-in-hand, were the children, singing as they went, certain of salvation. And, beyond them, far away towards the horizon, but coming closer with incredible speed, was the white crest of a great wave, higher than a tree, higher than a house, as high as the church tower itself, as fast as a galloping horse. The children, looking to Johann, or with their eyes on heaven, did not see it, did not see anything. They only understood their danger when they started to feel it. The water which had been sucking away from under their feet so they were triumphantly dry-shod on the sea bed, started to gurgle and flow forwards again. The smaller children were knee deep in moments; they looked down, and cried out, but their voices were drowned in the singing.

They pulled on the hands of the bigger children beside them, trying to get their attention, but the children swung hands gladly, and went on. Then they all heard it. Over the sound of their own canticle they heard the deep terrible roar of the sea.

When they looked up, they saw the wave coming towards them, heard its full-throated rage, and knew that the water that had flowed away so quickly, emptying the harbour in mere moments, had turned on them and was coming back as one wave, as one great surge. At once, some of them cried out and spun around, broke the line and tried to run, thigh deep in water, as if they dreamed that they could outrun the sea. But most of them stood stock still, holding each other's little hands and watching, open-mouthed, as the wall of the wave powered up to them and then fell down upon them and buried them in full fathoms in a second.

Moments later it hit the town. Boats that had been beached on the floor of the harbour were now thrown roof-high, tossed up and dropped down again. The first wave hit the quayside wall and crashed upwards like an eruption, and then, terrifyingly, beyond reason, flowed on, out of its bounds, rushing past houses, up alleyways, towards the market square where no sea had ever been. The quayside disappeared at once underwater, the panes of the windows of the inn smashing in a fusilade, as the waves breached the walls and poured inside the inn, into all the quayside houses. In Ishraq and Isolde's bedroom the two girls flinched back as the windows splintered like ice in a flood and the water poured in; they were waist deep in seconds and yet the wave still came on, the water still rose.

'This way,' Luca yelled beside them. He kicked out the frame of the window. Wood and the remaining horn panes of the window whirled away as the sea thrust him backwards. Soon the water in the room was up to their shoulders, Ishraq and Isolde off their feet, and flailing in the icy seawater as they gripped each other's hands, bobbing in the turbulence as the waves crashed into the little room and washed out again. Isolde dropped the broadsword, it fell like a lance in the murky water.

Luca swam towards Isolde, the current pushing them deeper into the room and away from the torrent surging in the open window. 'Take a breath!' he shouted, and with his arm around her shoulders, he dragged her under the water as if he would drown her. She slipped from his grip and went like an eel through the broken aperture to the raging water outside. He bobbed up and saw Brother Peter supporting Ishraq, both of them, faces raised to the ceiling of the room, mouths upturned, snatching at the last inches of air.

'We have to get out of the window!' he shouted. He gulped air, grabbed at Ishraq and thrust her deep down into the water of the room. He felt her struggle and then turn towards him and he pushed her clumsily towards the open window and swam behind her, forcing her on. A hand on his foot told him that Peter was following them.

Luca had his eyes open underwater, though all he could see was a swirl of grey and all he could hear was the ravenous roar of the wave as it reclaimed the land. But then he saw that the faint square of the window was blocked, and he realised that Ishraq was not through, she was caught.

Her gown had snagged on one of the broken spars of the window; she was trapped inside the broken window frame deep below the water. Luca shot up for the ceiling of the room again, snatched a breath and dived down. He could see air pouring from her mouth in a stream of silver, as her hands struggled with the gown. Luca swam towards her, grabbed hold of her shoulders, and when she turned her face to him, pressed his mouth to hers, desperately giving her air from his mouth to hers. For a moment they were locked together, gripping like lovers as he breathed into her lungs and then he kicked up to the ceiling again, snatched at a breath, his lips against the roof beams, then he dived down again. He was afraid she was still caught. Then he saw her shrug, like a snake sloughing a skin, like a beautiful mermaid, and she was out of her gown and her chemise was a flash of white and she escaped through the hole of the window and was outside, leaving her gown waving in the flood like a drowned ghost.

Ishraq, Luca, and Brother Peter burst, choking and desperately heaving for air, into a terrifying open sea, an ocean where the village had been, with nothing around them but little islands of roofs and chimneys, the current snatching them at once and dragging them inland.

'Take my cloak!' came a scream from above.

Ishraq looked up, choking, fighting against the rush of water which was peeling her away from the roof of the inn and rushing her inland, and saw Isolde, clinging to the chimney of the inn with one hand and reaching down with the other. She was holding out her cloak twisted like a rope towards them. Ishraq grabbed it and pulled herself towards the roof, fighting the current that threatened to tear her away. She could feel the overlapping tiles like slippery steps under her scrabbling feet and hands. Clinging like a monkey, Ishraq gripped the twisted cape and swarmed up the steep slope of the roof, buffeted by the waves, crawling through the rough water, getting higher and higher until she made it into the dry on the very apex of the roof, followed by Brother Peter, and then Luca. All four of them sat astride the roof, as if they were riding it, while the crash of the water below made the building sway, and the terrifying swiftness of the surge flung loose ships at the height of chimneys towards them. They clung together in the boil and terrible noise of the flood and prayed to their own gods.

'If the building goes ...' Brother Peter shouted in Luca's ear.

'We should rope together,' Luca said. He took their capes and knotted them into a line. The girls wrapped their arms around the middle section. They all knew that they were preparing for little more than drowning together.

'See if we can catch some driftwood,' Luca shouted at Brother Peter.

Brother Peter said no more. They watched in horror as lumber and wreckage, uprooted trees and an overturned market stall thudded into the wall of the inn, and the roof below them. They heard the roof shed its tiles into the water and felt the roof beams shift. An old wooden chest bobbed up from out of the attic below them and Luca reached out and grabbed hold of it, struggling to hold it against the current. 'If you fall in the water, you must hang on to this!' he shouted at the two girls, who were clinging to each other as they realised that if the building collapsed the old chest would not save them, they would go down, tumbled among roof beams and tiles, certain to drown.

Isolde leaned down and put her face against the ridge tiles of the inn, closing her eyes against the terror of the boiling flood around her, whispering her prayers over and over by rote, the words of her childhood, though she was too frightened to think. Ishraq stared wide-eyed as the sea boiled around them, watched the waters thrust and break on the roof, as they rose steadily higher. She looked at Luca and at Brother Peter, watched Luca struggling to hold the wooden chest balanced on the roof and saw that it might support her and Isolde but that the men would be lost. She gritted her teeth, and watched the rising water, trying to measure its height, as the waves broke against the roof, each time coming a little closer to them. A sudden eddy would make a high wave break over her feet and she could see Isolde flinch as the cold water snatched at her foot, but then the dip between the waves would make it seem as if it was ebbing. Ishraq held her foot very still and counted the unsteady roof tiles between her foot and the water. She glanced over at Luca and saw that he was doing the same thing. Both of them were desperately hoping that the wave was at its full height, that the flood had run inland and was now steadying, both of them trying to calculate the rise of the waters to know how long before they would be hopelessly engulfed.

Luca met her eyes. 'It's still rising,' he said flatly.

She nodded in agreement and pointed. 'It's two tiles below me now, and before it was three.'

'It will be over the roof in an hour,' Luca calculated. 'We'll have to be ready to swim.'

She nodded, knowing that it was a death sentence, and crept a little closer to Isolde. And then, slowly, after what felt like long, long hours, the waters started to become still. The sea coiling and recoiling like a wild river around the town flowed through ancient streets, spat out of hearths, swirled through windows, gurgled in chimneys; but the incoming roar of the wave fell silent, the groan of the earth was finished, and the water steadied, one tile below Ishraq's bare foot.

Somewhere, all alone, a bird started to sing, calling for its lost mate.

'Where's Freize?' Luca suddenly asked.

The group's slowly dawning relief at their own escape suddenly turned into nauseous fear. Luca, still clenching his knees on the sides of the roof, raised himself up and shaded his eyes against the bright sunshine. He looked out to sea, and then down to the quayside. 'I saw him running out towards the children,' he said.

'He turned some of them back. They got into the inn yard,' Isolde replied in a small voice. 'I saw that.'

'He turned around,' Brother Peter said. 'He was coming back in, carrying a little girl.'

Isolde let out a shuddering sob. 'What happened?' she asked. 'What just happened?'

Nobody answered her. Nobody knew. Luca tied his cloak to the chimney, and using it to steady himself like a rope, climbed down the steeply sloping roof, kicking his booted feet between the displaced tiles. He looked down. The water level was falling now, as the sea flowed away. It was below the window of the girls' room. He held on to the end of the cloak and got his feet onto the sill of their smashed window.

'Climb down to me,' he said. 'I'll help you in.'

Brother Peter gripped Isolde's hands and lowered her down the rope of capes towards Luca, who held tight to her legs, her waist and her shoulders as she scrabbled over him and dropped into the room, knee deep in flood water. Ishraq followed, naked but for her linen chemise. Brother Peter came last.

The girls' bedroom was draining fast, the water sluicing through the gaps in the floorboards to the room below, as the water level all over the village dropped and the sea drained out of houses, down the higher streets and gurgled in drains and watercourses.

'You'd better stay here,' Luca said to Ishraq and Isolde. 'It may be bad downstairs.'

'We'll come,' Isolde decided. 'I don't want to be trapped in here again.'

Ishraq shuddered at the wet chaos that had been their room. 'This is unbearable.'

They had to force the door; Luca kicked it open. It was

crooked in its frame as the whole house had shifted under the impact of the wave. They went down the stairs that were awash with dirt and weed and debris, and slippery underfoot. The whole house which had smelled so comfortingly of cooking and woodsmoke and old wine only a few hours ago, was dank and wet, and filled with the noise of water rushing away, and of loud dripping, as if it were an underwater cave and not an inn at all. Ishraq shuddered and reached for Isolde. 'Can you hear it? Is it coming again? Let's get outside.'

Downstairs was even worse, the ground floor chest deep in water. They held hands to wade through the kitchen and out into the yard. Isolde had a sudden horror that she would step on a drowned man, or that a dead hand would clasp round her foot. She shuddered and Luca looked around at her. 'Are you sure that you wouldn't rather wait upstairs?'

'I want to be outside,' she said. 'I can't bear the smell.'

Outside in the stable yard was the terrible sight of drowned horses in their stalls, their heads lolling over the stable doors where they had scrabbled and reared, gasping for air; but the innkeeper was there, miraculously alive. 'I was on the top of the haystack,' he said, almost crying with relief. 'On the very top, chucking down some hay, when the sea came over my yard wall, higher than my house, and just dropped down on me like an avalanche. Knocked me flat but knocked me down on the hay. I breathed in hay while it battered down on me and then it tore me to the stable roof, and when I stopped swimming and put down my feet, I was on an island! God be praised, I saw fishing ships sail over my stable yard, and I am here to say it.'

'We were on the roof,' Ishraq volunteered. 'The sea came rushing in.'

'God help us all! And the little children?'

'They were walking out to sea,' Isolde said quietly. 'God bless and keep them.'

He did not understand. 'Walking on the quayside?'

'Walking on the harbour floor. They thought the sea had dried up for them. They walked out towards the wave as it came in.'

'The sea went out as Johann said it would?'

'And then came in again,' Luca said grimly.

They were all silent for a moment with the horror of it.

'They swam?'

'I don't think so,' Luca said.

'Some of them came back,' Ishraq said. 'Freize sent some of them back. Did you see them?'

The innkeeper was stunned. 'I thought they were playing a game, they ran through the yard. I shouted at them for disturbing the horses, they were kicking and rearing in their stalls. I didn't know. Dear God, I didn't know. I didn't understand what they were shouting, or why the horses were so upset.'

'Nobody knew,' Isolde said. 'How could we?'

'Did Freize come in with the children?' Luca demanded.

'Not that I saw. Have you seen my wife?' the man asked.

They shook their heads.

'Everyone will be at the church,' the innkeeper said. 'People will be looking for each other there. Let's go up the hill to the church. Pray God that it has been spared and we find our loved ones there.'

They came out of the yard of the inn and paused at the quayside. The harbour was ruined. Every house that stood on the quayside was battered as if it had been bombarded, with windows torn away, doors flung open and some roofs missing, water draining from their gaping windows and doors. The ships which had been anchored in the port had been flung up and down on the wave, some washed out to sea, some thrown inland to cause more damage. The iron ring on the quay where their ship had been tied was empty, its ropes dangling down into the murky water. The gangplank had been washed far away, and their ship and the horses and Freize were gone. Where it had grounded on the harbour floor was now an angry swirl of deep water – it was unbelievable that this had ever been dry, even for a moment.

'Freize!' Luca cupped his hands to his mouth and yelled despairingly into the harbour, towards the town, and back over the sea again.

There was no answering shout, only the terrible agitated slapping of the sea, washing too high, against the harbour wall, like a familiar dog which has risen up and savaged terribly and now settles back down again.

The church was a scene of families greeting each other, others crying and calling over the heads of the crowd for missing children. Some of the fishing ships had been at sea when the wave had risen and some people thought that they might have been able to ride out the storm; the older men, who had heard of stories of a monster wave, shook their heads and said that such a wall of water was too steep for a little boat to climb. Many people were sitting silently on the benches which ran all round the side of the church, their heads bowed over their hands in fervent prayer while their clothes streamed water onto the stone floor.

When the wave had hit the town some people had got to the higher ground in time – the church was safe, the water had rushed through it at knee height, and anything west and north of the market square was untouched by the flood. Many people had clung to something and had the wave wash over them, half-drown them but rush on, leaving them choking and terrified but safe. Some had been torn away by the force of the water, turning over and over in the flood that took them as if they were twigs in a river in spate, and their families put wet candles in the drenched candle stands for them. Nobody could light candles. The candle which had burned on the altar to show the presence of God had blown out in the blast of air that came before the wave. The church felt desolate and cold without it, godforsaken. The priest, Father Benito, was missing.

Luca, desperate for something to do to help restore the village to normal life, went to the priest's house and took a flint and, finding some dry stuff in a high cupboard, lit a fire in the kitchen grate so that people could come and take a candle flame or taper and spread the warmth throughout the drowned village. He took a burning taper into the church and went behind the rood screen to the altar to light the candle.

'Send Freize back to me,' he whispered as the little flame flickered into life. 'Spare all Your children. Show mercy to us all. Forgive us for our sins and let the waters go back to the deep. But save Freize. Send my beloved Freize back to me.'

Brother Peter seated himself in the church before the damp church register and started a list of missing persons, to post on the church door. Every now and then a bedraggled child would come to the door and his mother would fall on him and snatch him up and bless him and scold him in the same breath. But the list of missing persons grew and grew in Brother Peter's careful script, and no-one even knew the names of the children on their crusade. No-one knew how many of them had walked dry-shod in the harbour, no-one knew how many had turned back, nor how many of them were missing, nor even where their homes had been.

Ishraq borrowed a gown and a cape from the priest's housekeeper and then the five of them – Isolde and Ishraq, Luca, Brother Peter and the innkeeper – went back to the inn, looking out to sea as if Freize might be swimming home. 'I can't believe it,' Luca said. 'I can't believe he didn't come with us.'

'He went out in the harbour to try to get the children to come back to land,' Ishraq said. 'It was the bravest thing I'll ever see in my life. He pushed us towards the inn and then he turned back. He went out towards the sea.'

'But he always comes with me. He's always just behind me.'

'He made sure we were safe,' Isolde said. 'As soon as we

were running for the inn he went back for the children in the harbour.'

'I can't think how I let him go. I can't think what I was doing. I really thought that the sea was going out, and I would walk with them, and then everything happened so fast. But why would he not come with me? He always comes with me.'

'God forgive me that I did not value him,' Brother Peter said quietly to himself. 'He did the work of a great man today.'

'Don't talk of him as if he's drowned!' Isolde said sharply. 'He could have climbed up high like we did. He could be on his way back to us right now.'

Luca put his hand over his eyes. 'I can't believe it,' he said. 'He's always with me. I can't get rid of him! – that's what I always said. And he did a courageous thing, while I ran. But I thought he was with me. He's always with me.'

They stood for a moment on the quayside, looking at the empty sea. 'You go on,' Luca said. 'I'll come in a moment.'

At the inn they found the innkeeper's wife in the kitchen, furiously throwing buckets of muddy water from the stone-flagged kitchen into the wet stable yard outside.

'Where the hell have you been?' the innkeeper demanded of her, instantly angry.

'In my laundry room,' she shouted back. 'Where else would I be? Where else do I ever go when there is trouble? Why didn't you look for me? The door was jammed and I was locked in. I'd still be in there if I hadn't broken it down. And anyway, I come out here and the yard is empty and the kitchen filled with water! Where have you been? Jaunting off when I could have been drowned?'

Her husband shouted with laughter and clasped her round her broad waist. 'Her laundry room!' he exclaimed to the girls. 'I should have looked there first. It's a room without windows, backs onto the chimney breast – whenever there is trouble or a quarrel she goes there and tidies the sheets. But what woman would go to a laundry room when the greatest wave that has ever been seen in the world is rushing towards her house?'

'A woman who wants to die with her sheets tidy,' his wife answered him crossly. 'If it was the last thing in the world, I'd want to be sure that my sheets were tidy. I heard the most terrible groaning noise and I thought straight away that the best place I could be was in my laundry room. I was tucked in there, heart beating pit-a-pat, when I heard the water banging into the house. I sorted my linen and I felt the cold water seeping under the door like an enemy. But I just kept arranging the linen, and sang a little song while the water got to my knees. Is it very bad in the village?'

'As bad as a plague year, but come all at once,' the inn-keeper said. 'Your friend Isabella is missing and her little girl. Like a plague year, a terrible year, but all the deaths done in an afternoon, in a moment, in a cruel wave.'

The woman glanced out into the yard where the horses were drowned in their stalls, and the dog limp and wet like a black rag at the end of his chain, and then she turned her face from the window as if she did not want to see.

'Hard times,' she said. 'Terrible times. What do they think it means, the sea rushing onto the land like this? Did Father Benito say anything?'

Everyone turned to Brother Peter. He shook his head.

'He is missing too, and I don't know what it means,' he said. 'I thought I was witnessing a miracle, the parting of the waters – now I think I saw the work of Satan. Satan in his terrible power, standing like a wall of water between the children of God and Jerusalem.'

'Perhaps,' Luca said coming in the kitchen door. 'Or perhaps it was neither good nor evil. Perhaps it was just another thing that we don't understand. It feels like our destiny is to live in a world that is filled with things that we don't understand, and ruled by an unseen God. I know nothing. I can't answer you. I am a fool in the middle of a disaster, and I have lost my dearest friend in the world.'

Quietly, Isolde reached out and took his hand. 'I'm sure everything will be all right,' she said helplessly.

'But how could a loving God ever take Freize?' he asked her. 'How could such a thing happen? And in only a moment? When he saved us and was going to help others? And how shall I live without him?'

~

As darkness fell they got the fire lit in the kitchen and they took off some of their wet clothes to be dried before it. Most of their goods, their clothes, the precious manuscripts and the writing desk had gone down with the ship. They found the crusader sword in the rubble of the bedroom and the innkeeper's wife found an old gown for Isolde and belted it around her narrow waist with a rope.

'I have your mother's jewels safely sewn into my chemise,' Ishraq whispered to Isolde.

She shook her head. 'Rich in a flood is not rich at all. But thank you for keeping them safe.'

Ishraq shrugged. 'You're right. We can't hire another Freize, not if I had the jewels of Solomon.'

People from the village who had been flooded out of their homes came to the inn and ate their dinners at the kitchen table. There was a cheese that someone had been storing in a high loft, and some sea-washed ham from the chimney. Someone had brought some bread from the only baker in the village whose shop stood higher up the hill, beyond the market square and whose oven was still lit. They drank some wine from bottles which were bobbing around the cellar, and then the villagers went back to their comfortless homes and Brother Peter, Luca, Isolde and Ishraq wrapped themselves up in their damp clothes and slept on the kitchen floor, with the innkeeper and his wife, while the rest of the house dripped mournfully all around them. Luca listened to the water falling from the timbers to the puddles on the stone floor all night, and woke at dawn to go out and look for Freize in the calm waters of the grey sea.

All morning Luca waited on the quayside, continually starting up when a keg or a bit of driftwood bobbed on the water and made him think it was Freize's wet head, swimming towards home. Now and then someone asked him for a hand with heaving some lumber, or pushing open a locked door, but mostly people left him alone and Luca realised that there were others alongside him, walking up and down the quayside, looking out to sea as if they too hoped that a friend or a husband or a lover might miraculously come home, even now, swimming through the sea that now lapped so quietly at the harbour steps that it was impossible to believe that it had ever raged through the town.

Brother Peter came down to see him at noon as the

church bells rang for Sext, the midday prayers, carrying some paper in his hand. 'I have written my report, but I can't explain the cause of the wave,' he said. 'I don't know if you want to add anything. I have said that Johann was following his calling, that the sea had parted as he said it would, when he was swallowed up by a flood. I don't attempt to explain what it means. I don't even comment on whether it was the work of God to try us, or the work of the Devil to defeat Johann.'

Luca shook his head. 'Me neither. I don't know. I don't know anything.'

'Would you want to add anything?'

Again, wearily, Luca shook his head. 'It might just be something of Nature,' he suggested. 'Like rain.'

The older man looked towards the sea where the great wave had come from nowhere and then lain flat again. 'Like rain?' he repeated incredulously.

'There are many, many things that happen in this world and we really don't know how,' Luca said wearily. 'We don't even understand why it rains somewhere and not elsewhere. We don't understand where clouds come from. You and I are scratching about like hens in the dirt trying to understand the nature of grit. Not seeing the mountains that overhang us, not knowing the wind that ruffles our stupid feathers. We don't understand the wave, we don't understand a rainbow. We don't know why the winds blow, nor why the tides rise. We know nothing.'

'We can't blame ourselves for not understanding the wave. Nobody has seen anything like this in their lifetime!'

'But they have! It has happened before,' Luca exclaimed. 'Last night the fishermen around the fire had all heard of great waves. Someone said they thought that the pestilence – the great plague – was first started by a wave a hundred years ago. What I am saying is that it might be caused by something other than the will of God; something which works in a way we don't yet understand but which we might come to know. If we had known more, we might have known that it would happen. When the water went out we would have known it was gathering itself to return. We could have guarded the children. And Freize ... and Freize ...' he broke off.

The older man nodded, seeing that Luca was close to breaking down. 'I'll send this off as it is,' he said. 'And we'll go on looking for him.'

'You think it's hopeless,' Luca said flatly.

Brother Peter crossed himself. 'I'll pray for him,' he said. 'Nothing is hopeless if God will hear our prayers.'

'He didn't hear the children singing hymns,' Luca said flatly, and turned and stared out to sea. 'Why should He hear us?'

At dinner time, Isolde went down to the quayside to find Luca, wrapped in his cloak, looking at the darkening horizon. 'Will you come in for dinner?' she asked. 'They have dried out the dining room and stewed a chicken.'

He looked at her without seeing her heart-shaped face and grave eyes. 'I'll come in a moment,' he said, indifferently. 'Start without me.'

She put a hand on his arm. 'Come now, Luca,' she whispered.

'In a moment.'

She took a few steps back and waited for him to turn

around. He did not move. She hesitated. 'Luca, come with me to dinner,' she commanded sweetly. 'You can't stay here, you do no good mourning alone. Come and have something to eat and we'll come out together, afterwards.'

He did not even hear her. She waited for a little longer and then understood that he was deaf to her and could hardly see her. He was looking for his friend, and could see nothing else. She went back to the inn alone.

~

The darkness of early autumn found Luca still seated on the quayside, still looking out at the darkening sea. A few of the mothers whose children had been lost on the crusade had come down and thrown a flower or a cross made from tied twigs into the gently washing water of the harbour, but they too were gone by nightfall. Only Luca stood waiting, looking out to the paler line of the horizon, as if the act of staring would make Freize visible, as if he gazed for long enough he would be bound to see the wet head of Freize, and his indomitable beaming smile, swimming for home.

The church clock chimed for Matins: it was midnight.

'You fear you have lost him, as you lost your mother and father,' a cool voice said behind him, making him swing around. Ishraq was standing in the shadows, her head uncovered, her dark hair in a plait down her back. 'You believe that you failed them, that you failed even to look for them. So you are looking for Freize, hoping that you will not fail him.'

'I was not even there when they were taken,' he said bitterly. 'I was in the monastery. I heard the bell started to

392

toll, the warning tocsin that rang in the village when they saw the galleys of the slaving ships approaching. We hid the holy things in the monastery and we locked ourselves into our cells and prayed. We spent the night in prayer. When we were allowed to go out, the abbot called me from the chapel and told me that he was afraid that the village had been attacked. I ran down to the village and across the fields to our farmhouse, which was a little way out towards the river. But I could see from a long way off that the front door was banging open, the house was empty, all the things of value were gone, and my mother and father disappeared.'

'They came like a wave from the sea,' Ishraq observed. 'And you did not see them take your parents nor do you know where they are now.'

'Everyone says they are dead,' Luca said blankly. 'Just as everyone thinks Freize is dead. Everyone I love is taken from me, I have no one. And I never do anything to save them. I lock myself into safety or I run like a coward, I save myself, I save my own life, and then I realise that my life is nothing without them.'

Ishraq raised a finger, to silence him. 'Don't pity yourself,' she said. 'You will lose all your courage if you wallow in sympathy for yourself.'

He flushed. 'I am an orphan,' he said bitterly. 'I had no friend in the world but Freize. He was the only person in my life who loved me, and now I have lost him to the sea.'

'And what do you think he would say?' she demanded. 'If he saw you here like this?'

Luca's mask of sorrow suddenly melted and he found he was smiling at the thought of his lost friend. Colour rushed into his cheeks and his voice choked. 'He would say,

"There's a good inn and a good dinner, let's go and eat. Time enough for all this in the morning.'"

Ishraq stood waiting, knowing that Luca's heart was racing with grief.

A cry broke from him and he turned to her and she opened her arms to him. He stepped towards her and she held him tightly, her arms wrapped around him as he wept with great heaving sobs, on her shoulder. She said nothing at all but just held him, her arms wrapped around him in a hug as strong as a man's, rocking him gently as he wept broken-hearted for the loss of his friend.

'I never told him,' he finally gasped, as the truth was wrenched out of him. 'I never told him that I loved him as if he were my own brother.'

'Oh he knew,' she assured him, quietly and steadily in his ear. 'His love for you was one of his greatest joys. His pride in you, his admiration for you, his pleasure in your company was well known to him and to us all. You did not need to speak of it. You both knew. We all knew. He loved you and he knew you loved him.'

The storm of his weeping subsided and he pulled back from her, wiped his face roughly on his damp cloak. 'You will think me a fool,' he said. 'As soft as a girl.'

She let him go at once, and stepped back to perch on one of the capstans, the mooring posts where they tied up the ships, as if she were settling down to talk all night. She shook her head. 'No, I don't think you a fool to mourn for one you love.'

'You think me a weakling?'

'Only when you were writing your life into a ballad of self-pity. On the contrary, I thought that you were too strong in your grief. You can't bring him back to life by your determination. Alas, if he is lost to us then you cannot bring him back again by wishing. You have to know that there are things you cannot do. You have to let him go. Perhaps you will have to let your parents go too.'

'I can't bear to think that I will never see any of them again!'

'Perhaps the task of your life is to think the unthinkable,' she suggested. 'Certainly, your mission is to look at the unknown and try to understand it. Perhaps you are called to understand things that most people never consider. Perhaps you have to find the courage to think terrible things. The disappearance of your parents, like the loss of Freize, is a mystery. Perhaps you have to let yourself know that the very worst thing that could have happened, has indeed taken place. Your task is to start to think about it, to ask why such things happen? Perhaps this is why you are an Inquirer.'

'You think my grief prepares me for my work?'

She nodded. 'I am certain of it. You will have to look at the worst things in the world. How can you do that if you have not faced them in your own life, already?'

He was quiet, turning over her words in his mind. 'You're a very wise woman,' he said as if seeing her for the first time. 'It was good of you to come down here for me.'

'Of course I would come for you,' she replied. 'I would go anywhere for you.'

He was thinking of something else. 'Did Isolde come earlier?'

'Yes. She came to fetch you for dinner. But you were deaf and blind to her.'

'That was some time ago?'

'Hours.'

'It's very late now, isn't it?'

'Past midnight,' she said. She rose and came close to him as if she would touch him again. 'Luca,' she said his name very quietly.

'Did Isolde ask you to come for me?' he asked. 'Did she send you to me?'

A rueful smile flickered across her face and she took a careful step back from him. 'Is that what you would wish?'

He made a little gesture. 'I dare not hope that she is thinking of me. And today she has seen me act like a fool and yesterday like a coward. If she thought of me at all before now, she will not think of me again.'

'But she is thinking of you, and of Freize,' Ishraq claimed. 'She and Brother Peter are at church now, praying for him and for you.' She considered him. 'You know that you will serve your love of him best if you come back to the inn now and take your grief like a man, and live your life in such a way that he might be proud of you?'

She could see him square his shoulders and knew she had brought him to himself.

'Yes,' he said. 'You are right. I should be worthy of him.'

Together they turned for the inn. At the doorway, where a torch burned, set in the wall beside the door, its yellow flickering light reflected in the wet cobbles beneath their feet, he stopped and turned to her. He took her face in both his hands and looked into her dark eyes. Without fear or coquetry she stood still and let him hold her, slowly closing her eyes as she turned her face up to him. She felt a sense of belonging to him, as if it were natural to stand, face to face, all-but embracing.

Luca breathed in the scent of her hair and her skin and put a kiss between her eyebrows, where a child would be signed with the sign of the cross at baptism. Ishraq felt his kiss where her mother used to kiss her – on the third eye, where a woman sees the unseen world – and she opened her dark eyes and smiled at him as if they understood each other; then they went quietly into the inn together.

The next day was a Sunday but nobody thought that they should rest for the Sabbath. The lower half of the town was a mess of wreckage and filth. Luca helped in clearing up the village, his teeth gritted as he shifted piles of wood and rubble and found, among the roof beams and broken spars the bodies of some of the drowned children.

Reverently, Luca and the other men used an old door as a stretcher and carried the little corpses two at a time up to the church and laid them down in a side chapel. The light was burning on the altar as the midwives of the village washed the bodies and prepared small shrouds. Luca prayed over the lost children and then went up to the cliff just outside the village walls where they were making a new graveyard for the drowned, as there was not enough space for them to be laid all together in the old churchyard.

Luca helped the men digging the graves in the hard soil, swinging a pick, and felt a sense of relief when he stripped off his shirt and worked in his breeches, sweating with the hard labour against the unyielding earth under the bright unforgiving sun.

Ishraq brought him some ale and some bread at midday and saw the grimness of his face and the tension in his broad shoulders. 'Here,' she said shortly. 'Rest for a moment. Eat, drink.'

He ate and drank without seeing the food. 'How could I be so stupid as to let him go?' he demanded. 'Why didn't I make sure that he was behind us? I just assumed he was there, I didn't think twice.'

Just then a girl limped up to the makeshift wall that they had built around the little graveyard. 'Where's the other man?' she demanded.

The two of them started as if they had seen a ghost. It was Rosa, the girl with the bleeding feet that they had seen on the very first day. The little girl that Freize had carried back, through the mud of the harbour, just before the wave had struck.

'He told me to run back to the inn for sweetmeats,' she said accusingly. 'I'm here to tell him he's a liar. There were no sweets. The kitchen was empty, and there was a terrible noise. It frightened me so much that I ran up the hill and when I looked behind the sea was chasing me. I ran and ran. Where is he? And where's Johann the Good and the other children?'

'I don't know where the man is right now,' Luca said, his voice a little shaky. 'We haven't seen him. He went out in the harbour to try to get all you children back to high ground, away from the sea. That's why he lied to you about sweets. He wanted you to get to safety. Then the great wave came … but he can swim. Perhaps he is swimming now. Perhaps your companions and Johann have been washed in somewhere, and are walking back right now. We're all hoping for them all.'

Her face trembled. 'They're both gone?' she asked. 'They're all gone? The sea took them? What am I to do now?'

Luca and Ishraq were silent for a moment. Neither of them had any idea what this little girl should do.

'Well anyway, come with me to the inn and we'll get you some food and something to wear and some shoes,' Ishraq said. 'Then we'll think what would be the best for you.'

'He saved you,' Luca said, looking at her white face trembling on the edge of tears. 'We'll care for you for his sake, as well as for your own.'

'He lied to me,' she complained. 'He said there were sweets and there was a great wave and I could have drowned!'

Luca nodded. 'He did it to save you,' he repeated. 'And I am afraid that it is he who is drowned.'

She nodded, hardly understanding, and then took Ishraq's proffered hand and walked down the hill to the village with her.

~

Luca's day had started at dawn on the quayside looking out to sea, and dusk found him there too. But when it grew dark he came in and ate his dinner as a man who has set himself a dreary task to do. After dinner he prayed with Brother

Peter and the little party listened as Brother Peter read the story of Noah, of men and women and the animals saved from a Flood. The little girl Rosa, who had never heard the story before went to bed with her head full of the rainbow at the end of the story.

The rooms had been dried out and the landlady had borrowed dry bedding. She offered Rosa a truckle bed in the warm kitchen. The four travellers, so conscious that they were missing one, that they should be five, went to their beds early. The inn was filled with people who had come in from villages to the north of Piccolo who had lost their children to the crusade, but hoped that they had been saved from the wave. The murmur of their quiet talking, and some of the mothers crying, went on all night. Brother Peter and Luca took a share in the big bed of the men's room but Luca spent the night gazing blankly at the ceiling, not sleeping at all.

Isolde and Ishraq went to their bedroom and plaited each other's hair in unhappy silence.

'I keep thinking about him,' Isolde started, 'and how sweet and funny he was.'

'I know.'

They had no night gowns, so they hung their robes on the post of the bed and prepared to sleep in their linen shifts. Isolde knelt in prayer and mentioned Freize by name. When she rose up, Ishraq saw that her eyes were red.

'He ran back for the horses,' Ishraq said. 'When he heard them crying and neighing. He knew that something bad was happening. He wouldn't leave them on board. He called the children to shore, he saw that we were safe, and then he went to the horses.'

Isolde climbed into the bed. 'I've never met a man more steady,' she said. 'He was always cheerful and he was always brave.'

'I was unkind to him,' Ishraq confessed. 'He asked me for a kiss and I threw him down in the stable yard at Vittorito. I regret it now, I regret it so much.'

'I know he said that he was offended at the time, but I think he found it funny,' Isolde volunteered. 'I think he liked you for your pride. He spoke of it and laughed, as if he were offended and admiring, both at once.'

'Right now, I wish I had given him a kiss,' she said. 'I liked him more than I told him. Now I wish I had been kinder.'

'Of course you could not kiss him,' Isolde said sorrowfully. 'But it was so like him to ask! I wish we had all been kinder to him. We never tell people that we love them for we think, like fools, that they are going to be with us forever. We all act as if we are going to live forever, but we should act as if we would die tomorrow, and tell each other the best things.'

Ishraq nodded, she got into bed beside her friend. 'I love you,' she said sadly. 'And at least we have always said goodnight like sisters.'

'I love you too,' Isolde replied. 'D'you think you can sleep?'

'I just keep thinking of the wave, that terrible wave. I keep thinking of him out in the water, under the water. I just keep thinking that if he is drowned – what difference does it matter if I sleep or not? If he is drowned, what would it have mattered if I had kissed him or not?'

They lay in silence until Isolde's quiet breathing told

Ishraq that she had fallen asleep. She turned in the bed and closed her eyes, willing herself to sleep too. But then her dark eyes suddenly snapped open and she said aloud: 'The kitten!'

'What?' Isolde murmured sleepily but Ishraq was already out of bed pulling her cape over her shift, stepping into her slippers.

'I have to get the kitten.'

'Go to sleep,' Isolde said. 'It's probably tucked up warm in the hay loft. You can get it in the morning.'

'It's not in the hay loft. I'm going now.'

'Why?' Isolde asked, sitting up in bed. 'You can't go now, it's dark.'

'There's a ladder in the men's room,' she said. 'They were mending the roof beams today. There's a ladder from their room that goes through the beams and up to the roof.'

'Why?'

'Because the kitten's still up there.'

'It's almost certainly gone. It'll have got itself down when the roofer was up there.'

'What if it hasn't?' Ishraq rounded on her friend. 'Almost the last thing I saw Freize do was lift that kitten out of his pocket, and it was when it ran for the roof that he knew of the danger. It warned us. We should make sure it's safe.'

'It didn't know what it was doing.'

'But Freize did. He was kind to it, just as he was kind to everyone, to every animal. I'm going to get the kitten down. He wouldn't leave it there till morning.'

'Ishraq!' Isolde cried out, but the girl was already pulling on her cape, opening the ill-fitting bedroom door, crossing the little landing, and opening the door of the men's room.

Ishraq heard the snoring of several men, and grimaced at her own embarrassment. 'I am sorry,' she said clearly into the darkened room. 'But I am going to walk through this room and go up that ladder.'

'Is that a lass?' came a hopeful, sleepy inquiry. 'Wanting some company? Want a little kiss and a cuddle, bonnie lass? Want a little company?'

'If anyone touches me,' Ishraq went on in the same courteous tone, closing the door behind her and stepping carefully into the dark room. 'I will break his hand. If two of you try it together, I will kill you both. Just so you know.'

'Ishraq?' said Luca, still wide awake. 'What the hell are you doing?' He rose up out of the darkness, naked but for his breeches, and they met at the foot of the ladder.

'Fetching the kitten,' she said. 'Leave me alone.'

'Are you mad? What kitten?'

'Freize's kitten,' she said. 'The one he had in his pocket.'

'It'll have got itself down.'

'I'm going to see.'

'In the middle of the night?'

'I only just remembered it,' she confessed.

'Oh for God's sake!' Luca was suddenly furious with her, worrying about a kitten in a town filled with parents who had lost their children. 'What does a kitten matter? In the middle of all this? In the middle of the night when half these people have cried themselves to sleep and everyone is missing someone?'

Ishraq did not answer him but turned and put her foot on the first rung of the ladder. 'It's pitch black,' Luca cautioned. 'You'll fall and break your neck.'

He made a gesture to stop her, but she angrily slapped

his hand away and went up the little ladder to the roof. A ridged plank, a scrambling board, stretched up to the apex of the roof and she went up it like a cat herself, on her hands and bare feet. She could see nothing but the darkness of the roof against the greyer skyline. She got to the very top and sat astride, gripped the tiles with her knees, feeling them sharp through the thin linen of her shift. She heard her harsh breathing and knew that she was afraid. She raised her head and looked at the chimney. Of course, there was no kitten there. She bit her lip as she realised that now she would have to make her way down again, that she had taken a grave risk and for nothing.

'Kitten?' she said to the empty roofs of Piccolo, seeing the streets below them torn by the sea and cluttered with driftwood, the doors banging empty on wet rooms. 'Kitten?'

A tiny little yowl came from the base of the chimney, where the tiles were warmed by the escaping smoke. Tentatively, the little animal rose up and stalked towards her, along the narrow apex of the roof.

'Kitten?' Ishraq said again, utterly amazed.

It came towards her outstretched hand and she picked it up, as a mother cat would, by the scruff of its skinny little neck, and she tucked it under her arm, holding it tightly against her. A muffled mew told her that it was uncomfortable but safe, as she crouched low on the roofer's board and went down again till her questing feet found the ladder, and then went one rung after another, through the hole in the roof into the darkened room until she felt Luca's hands on her waist and he lifted her down and she was safe inside the room with his arms around her.

'I've got it,' she said.

For the first time in long days she heard a warmth in his voice. 'You're mad,' he said. 'That was the most ridiculous thing to do, the stupidest thing I have ever seen.'

But he did not let her go and for a moment she leaned against his naked chest. 'I was terribly afraid,' she admitted.

She felt his cheek against her hair, and the warmth of his body against her own, and she paused. For a moment she thought that anything might happen, and she did not draw back. It was Luca who steadied her on her feet, then stepped away, releasing her and saying, 'Are you going to let it go?'

'I'll take it to the kitchen and get it some milk,' she said. 'I'll keep it for tonight. If we had not seen it run we would not have known we were in danger. We owe our lives to it.'

He took her hand and guided her through the room full of sleeping men, and closed the door behind them.

'It's an odd thing,' he said. 'Odd that it knew to get up high.' Together, they went down to the kitchen.

The kitten struggled in Ishraq's grip and she put it gently down on the floor. The tiny creature shook its head, as if complaining at being held so tight, and sat on its fluffy rump and washed its back feet, and then found a warm corner in the log basket by the fire, and settled down for sleep.

'There's a writer,' Ishraq said, trying to remember her studies. 'Oh! I can't remember his name! Aelianus or something like that. He says that frogs and snakes know when there is going to be an earthquake – they get out of their holes in time.'

'How do they know?' Luca demanded. 'What do they know?'

'He doesn't say,' she said. 'I read him in the Arab library in Spain. I can't remember more than that.'

They walked up the stairs together to the doorway of her room.

'Why was it so important to you that you should save it?' he asked her in a whisper, conscious of the many sleepers in the quiet house – Isolde just the other side of the door. 'Why did the kitten matter, when so much else has been lost? You're not sentimental about animals. You're not sentimental about anything, usually. Yet you risked your life.'

'I suppose, for that very reason: that so much has been lost,' she said. 'We failed to save the children, we failed to save half the town, we came with all our learning and your mission to understand and yet we knew nothing and when something so terrible happened we could do nothing. We were useless. We did not even save ourselves. We lost Freize. He was the most ignorant of us all and yet he was the only one who knew what was happening. But I could at least save Freize's kitten.'

He took her hand and held it for a moment. 'Goodnight,' he said quietly. 'God bless you for that. God bless you for thinking of him.' And then he turned and brought her hand, palm up, to his mouth, and gently put a kiss in the middle, then closed her fingers over it.

Ishraq closed her eyes at the touch of his mouth on her hand. 'Goodnight,' she whispered, and held her fingers tight where his lips had touched her palm.

In the morning, the four of them, with Rosa trailing behind Isolde at a faithful trot, went to the church where they helped the harassed priest and clerk to write out descriptions of children who were missing, to post on the gate of the little church. The pieces of paper fluttered in the wind, naming children who might never see their homes again, calling on parents who would never come to find them. Father Benito had survived the flood clinging to the bell tower and now took his seat at the confessional. A queue of people waited to confess to him, and the sense of death was heavy in the little church – it lay over the harbour like a low cloud. More and more people were coming slowly in the gate to the north of the town, seeking the children who had gone with Johann, hoping that they had escaped the flood. They looked at the slurry of filth and water and the broken timbers in the market square as if they still could not believe that an evil tide had flowed high into the very heart of Piccolo and receded, leaving nothing but devastation.

In the lady chapel alongside the church the little bodies were being prepared for burial. Grim-faced, Luca and Brother Peter noted the clothes, the hair colour, the age, any little oddness of appearance, or brightness of hair, so that the children might be identified if their parents ever came seeking them. When they had looked into every blue, blanched face, and noted every missing tooth and freckled nose, they waved the two wise women forward who sewed the bodies into the newly-made shrouds, and laid them, two to a roughly-made stretcher, ready to be carried to the new cemetery beyond the walls of the town, for burial.

The wise women, who served as folk healers, as midwives and layers-out in the little village, did their work with a steady reverence for the little bodies, but they looked askance at Brother Peter and Luca; and when Isolde, Ishraq and Rosa came into the church they turned away their heads and did not greet them at all.

'What's the matter with them?' Ishraq muttered to Isolde, sensing the hostility but not understanding it.

'They'll be grieving,' Isolde suggested.

The new cemetery had been made beyond the church, just outside the walls of Piccolo, on newly-consecrated ground beyond the north gate. It was overlooking the sea, and here the gravediggers stood around, leaning on their spades, beside a great hole, dug deep and wide for all the children to be laid together, just as they had rolled up together in sleep when they were following Johann and believed themselves to be blessed. Isolde took one look as the men laid the little shrouded bodies gently in the bottom of the wide trench, and then led Rosa to stand behind the priest, where his robes, billowing in the wind from the sea, hid the view of the grave and the little bodies bundled together.

Father Benito read the service for burial, his voice clear over the constant crying of the seagulls, and the more distant noise of people sweeping their houses, cleaning their wet rooms, and repairing roofs and windows all over the town. Half a dozen people attended the little service, and as they walked away from the gravediggers, filling in the great hole with the dusty soil of the region, the priest promised that he would commission a stone monument to name the children as the pilgrims who walked into the sea. 'If you ever come back here, you will see that we have not forgotten them,' he said to Brother Peter. 'Nor our own losses.'

'D'you know yet how many of the townspeople are missing?' Luca asked quietly.

The priest crossed himself. 'About twenty people,' he said. 'And half a dozen of our own children. It is a terrible blow but this is a community of people who experience terrible blows, very often. In a bad plague year we would lose that number. If there is a storm which catches the fishermen at sea we might lose a ship or even two, five or six fathers lost at sea and five or six families thrown into grief and want. When the Black Death came through here a century ago, the village was emptied – half of them dead in a month, the fields barren of crops because there was no one to plant, the fish spawned in the sea without fishermen!

God sends these things to try us; but this week He has sent us a trial indeed.'

'A curse on them not a blessing!' they heard a woman pantingly scream, running up the stone steps, out of the little town gate, and then ploughing breathlessly up the hill towards them, her gown bunched up in her fist, her hair wildly loose, her face ugly with grief. 'Let Satan drag them down to hell! You should have thrown their bodies over the cliff, not given them a grave in sacred ground. Curse them all!'

'What's this?' the priest spread his arms wide and intercepted her as if she were a runaway horse, halfway up the hill. 'What's this, Mistress Ricci? What are you doing running around like this? For shame, Mrs Ricci! Calm yourself!'

She glared wildly around, it was obvious that she hardly saw him. 'They should be flung in the sea not buried with rites!' she cried. 'Beware. They are the storm-bringers! You are honouring our murderers! Demons! Every one of them!'

Half a dozen people, some coming down the hill from the simple funeral, others attracted from inside the village by the noise at the gate, started to gather around. 'Storm-bringers?' somebody repeated, a note of fear in their voice. 'Storm-bringers?'

'Devils,' she said flatly. 'These false children, saying that they were on a crusade! Weren't they storm-bringers all along? Pretending to a holy quest, just to trick us? Were they mortals at all, that they appeared here without so much as a father or mother between them? Led by a boy as beautiful as an angel but with strange sea-blue eyes?

And we gave them bread, and meat and cheese and they unleashed this horror on us? And now my son is missing at sea and my husband too, and the storm-bringers have destroyed our peace. And you dare to bless them? And bury them like Christians? Giving them our ground just as we gave them our own kin?'

The priest exchanged one anxious glance with Luca.

'What is she talking about?' Luca asked quickly.

'This is a fishing town, dependent on the sea for their livelihood, dependent on good weather for their safety,' Father Benito answered him. 'They cling to the belief that there are storm-bringers who can make spells and call up bad weather.'

'They believe this as a truth?' Luca whispered. 'A literal truth? They think that people can whistle up a wind, bring down a storm?'

'They have seen such things.' Father Benito spread his hands. 'Inquirer, I can tell you on oath. I have seen such things. I saw a woman call up a storm onto the mast of the ship of a man she hated. I saw it with my own eyes: the woman swore a curse on him as his ship sailed from port, and the one deckhand who swam to safety spoke of cold terrible lights dancing around the mast until the ship went down.'

'We have had a crusade of storm-bringers, God help us,' the woman cried out. 'And then you bury them in holy ground?'

The priest turned to her. 'Mistress Ricci, the children were drowned as innocents. They were on a holy crusade. They were singing hymns as they walked out to sea.'

She shot a pointing finger at Rosa. 'All of them?' she

413

demanded, her face twisted with cunning. 'Were they all drowned? Or did some of them cause the wave but then escape scot-free? Is there not, right here, a little girl who was one of the first into town and begging for bread, and yet she ran through the town ahead of the wave, silent – not warning anyone – and now here she is at the funeral of the others? Rejoicing in her work? Taunting us? Who is she? And what's she going to do next? Bring down thunder? A plague? Are snakes going to come out of her hair? Frogs from her mouth?'

'Now, that's enough,' Isolde commanded quietly, stepping forwards to shield the little girl. 'She's just a child. I am sorry for your grief, Mrs Ricci, but we have all lost someone we love. We must comfort each other ...'

'But who are they?' Mrs Ricci looked from Isolde's sympathetic face to Luca. 'And how can you be so sure that they are mortal children? All very well for you to say that she is a child, that they were mortal children, but they didn't act like mortal children. They came without parents, from who knows where! Did they not call up the great wave and ride away on it? Like the storm people they are?'

The priest shook his head sorrowfully, raised his hand in blessing and turned away from the angry woman, refusing to answer her questions. He made his way through the little gate into the town, but nothing would discourage Mrs Ricci, and now the wise women were beside her, staring at Rosa and clenching their hands in the gesture against witchcraft.

'This is ridiculous,' Isolde drew Rosa to her side, then went to follow the priest. At once the three women darted forward and started to close the gate against her. Ishraq stepped quickly forwards and took the weight of the wooden door, pushing back against the angry women, her dark gaze on Mrs Ricci. 'Don't,' she advised briefly. The three women, cowed by Ishraq's gaze and the strong push at the gate, gave way and Isolde and Rosa walked through it into the town, Ishraq closely behind them as if on guard.

'No, wait,' a man said, putting a hand out to delay Father Benito as he headed for the church. 'Not so fast, Father. Answer the women. What they say is true. There were children who ran back into town ahead of the flood. How did they know to run? Some of them got clear away?'

'Did they warn the others?' another man asked. 'Did they warn us? No! They didn't!'

Another woman nodded. 'They ran in silence,' she said. 'One went past me and never said one word of what was coming.'

Rosa's cold hand crept into Isolde's palm. 'We were just running away,' she whispered.

Ishraq stepped up beside Isolde, putting the child between them as if to protect the little girl from the increasingly angry crowd that was now blocking the lane from the church, their voices echoing loudly in the narrow street. Father Benito went on through them, and climbed the steps to the church turning to see more people joining the crowd from the market square, people coming out of their houses, still dirty from their work of salvage and repair, their faces suspicious and fearful.

'Did they not tempt our children into the harbour with their promises? Did they not bear false witness and lure us on? And then the wave came. What about their leader, Johann? Have we seen his body? Or did he go sailing back into the clouds having called up the wave to drown us all?'

'That's right!' someone said from the back of the crowd. 'We don't know who they were, and they came just before the wave.'

'They called up the wave!' someone shouted. 'You're right, Mistress Ricci! They brought the wave down on us!'

'I will have vengeance!' Mrs Ricci raised her voice above the growing murmur of the crowd. 'I swear I will have vengeance for my son and for my husband! I will see the bringers of storms burned as witches and their ashes scattered into their own storm winds.'

Isolde flinched at the words and tightened her grip on Rosa, who crept as close as she could get, as if she would hide under Isolde's rough cape. Luca and Brother Peter went up the steps of the church to Father Benito, readying themselves to face the crowd, to try to calm them. Luca glanced across to see Ishraq rise gently to her toes, as if preparing for a fight.

'Now let's all be calm,' Luca said firmly, pitching his voice so that it could be heard over the crowd and the mad crying of the seagulls. 'I am an Inquirer, appointed by the Pope himself. I have been sent out into Christendom to make a map of fears, and if your good Father Benito agrees that we should hold an inquiry into this strange and frightening flood then I will do so here.'

The crowd rounded on their priest. 'Call an inquiry!' someone shouted. 'Name the wicked ones!'

Father Benito paused. 'You want me to ask an Inquirer of the Holy Father's own order to ask why the sea should surge into Piccolo?' he asked sceptically. 'Why don't I ask him what makes rain? Or why thunder is so loud?'

'You laugh at her grief?' one of the wise women accused him, pointing to Mrs Ricci. 'You won't answer her? You won't even hear us?'

The angry murmur of the crowd rose into a roar of outrage. Father Benito saw that there was no reasoning with them like this. He glanced at Luca and surrendered. 'Very well. As you wish. Brother Luca Vero – would you hold an inquiry? We should hear what these good women have to say. It will be better for us all if all the fears are spoken aloud and you can tell us if there was anything that we could have done to prevent the flood.'

'There!' Another of the wise women was triumphant. 'We will name the guilty ones!'

'I will inquire into the cause of this wave, and I will tell the Pope what I decide.' Luca ruled. 'If anyone has caused it, I will see that they are charged with causing such a disaster, and I will see that they are punished.'

'Burned,' Mrs Ricci insisted. 'And the ashes blown away on the storm wind that they called up.'

'I will see that justice is done,' he promised, but his level tones only angered her more. She dived towards him and snatched at his hands, shouting furiously into his young face. 'You know there are witches who call up storms? You know this?'

Luca had to force himself not to flinch away from her. 'I know that many people believe this. I haven't found anyone guilty of such a thing myself. But I have read of it.'

'Read of it!' someone said scornfully. 'You've just seen it happen! What book can tell you what has just happened to us? What book was ever written that speaks of a wave that destroys a town, on a sunny day? For no reason?'

Luca looked around; the little crowd around them was steadily growing in number, as more and more people came up from the market square, and stepped out of the doorways of their houses. They were no longer pale with grief, shocked into silence; they were angry and becoming dangerous, looking for someone to blame for their tragedy.

'I think there may be books which tell of this,' he said carefully. 'I have not read them myself, it is the wisdom of the ancients which the Arabs have in their libraries. This is something that we should understand, so as to make ourselves safe. I will consider carefully what you, and everyone else has to say. I will start my inquiry this afternoon, at the inn.'

'You should start there indeed,' one of the midwives from the church said pointedly. 'That's the very place to start. You could start in the inn, in the upper room, in the attic bedroom.'

'What?' Luca asked baffled at the sudden rise of hostility in her voice, at the meaning of her accusation.

She raised a pointing finger. The crowd was silent, watching as she slowly turned around until she was facing Ishraq and Isolde, the little girl Rosa between them. At once there was a ripple of approval.

'Name them!' someone said.

'Go on!'

'Name the storm-bringers!'

'The upper room,' she said. 'The safe room. Safe for them, up there, calling up a storm; calling up a terrible wave and then sailing up to perch on the roof like seagulls while the flood drowned us mere mortals beneath them.'

'They didn't fly up to the roof!?'

'Didn't they wait out the storm safe and high above the town?'

'I can vouch for these two ladies,' Luca interrupted. 'I was on the roof myself.'

'You said yourself that the Arabs knew how the waves were caused . . .'

'I said they had the books, they are books from the ancients . . .'

'She's an Arab! Isn't she? Does she know Arab learning? Does she know how to call up a wave?'

Ishraq stepped forward to defend herself, her dark eyes blazing, as Luca put up his hand to command silence. 'This young woman is well-known to me,' he said. 'She is in the household of the Lord of Lucretili, a Crusader Lord, a Christian Lord. There is no question that she could have done anything wrong. I can promise you . . .'

There was a sudden swirl of seagulls, disturbed from feeding on the flooded rubbish of the town, and they spiraled upwards into the sky, screaming their wild calls, right above the heads of the crowd.

'The souls of the drowned!' someone exclaimed.

Several women crossed themselves.

'Calling for justice!'

'I can promise . . .' Luca went on.

'You can't,' one of the wise women cut disdainfully through his speech. 'For you don't know the half of it. You were talking to Johann the Pilgrim, blind as a fool, when the two young women were outside the walls of the town calling up a storm in the green lake.'

There was a murmur of real consternation. A woman

drew back from Ishraq and spat on the ground before her. Half the women of the crowd crossed their fingers, putting their thumb between the second and third finger to make the old sign against witchcraft, making their hands into fists.

'The green lake?' someone demanded. 'What were they doing there?'

'What is this?' Brother Peter asked stepping forward.

The old woman did not retreat, but her friend joined her and they both stood beside Mrs Ricci, their faces contorted with hate. 'We saw them,' she said so loudly that the newcomers at the very back of the crowd could hear every word of her damning accusation. 'We saw the two young women, dressed so dainty and looking so innocent. Slipping out of town as night fell and coming back all wet in darkness. They went to the green lake and summoned a storm at twilight. And the next day the wave came. The young women called the wave up that night, and next day the bad children led our children into its path.'

'Of course we did not!' Isolde burst out, looking round at the pinched angry faces. 'You must be mad to think such a thing!'

'Mad?' someone shouted. 'It is you that are mad to bring such a thing down on us!'

'Calling up a storm in the green lake, leading our children out to drown. "Thou shalt not suffer a witch to live!"'

'Yes!' a man shouted from the back of the crowd. 'The Bible itself says: "Thou shalt not suffer a witch to live!"'

The mass of people pressed closer to the two young women and the little girl between them. Rosa dived beneath

Isolde's cloak and clung around her waist, crying for fear. Isolde was as white as the kerchief over her hair. Ishraq stepped in front of her, spread her hands, balanced on the balls of her feet, ready to fight.

Luca spread his arms, raised his voice. 'These are my friends,' he declared. 'And we have lost our own friend to the sea, just as you have lost your dear ones. You cannot think that these young women would call up a wave that would drown our friend.'

'I do think it,' Mrs Ricci hurled the words at him. 'We all think it. It is you who are misled. How will you hold an inquiry if you will not ask the most important questions? What were they doing in the lake?'

Baffled, Luca turned to Isolde. 'What were you doing in the lake?'

She flushed red with anger that he should interrogate her before this crowd. 'How dare you ask me?'

His temper flared with his fear of the crowd. 'Of course I ask you! Don't be such a fool! Answer me at once! What were you doing?'

'We were washing,' she said, disdainful of him, of the crowd. 'We went for a wash.'

'Washing!' the women scoffed. 'In the green lake? As night fell? They are storm-bringers, you can see it in their faces.'

There was a dangerous roar of agreement from the crowd and it encouraged the wise women on the attack.

'You will name the storm-bringers?' the woman pressed Luca. 'These women who came with you, and the child who came later, their little accomplice? You will try all three of them?'

421

'It was the children and the two women who called up the wave. That child would know. You must question her,' a man commanded from the back of the crowd, his jacket dirty with sludge from baling out his house. 'And we will burn all three of them together.'

'Yes!' a new woman agreed with him. 'If they are guilty we will drown all three of them in our own harbour.'

Rosa's little hand clenched onto Isolde's steady grip. 'What are they saying?' she whispered. 'What do they think we have done?'

'I assure you these women are innocent,' Luca began. 'And the child also.'

'Then try them!' someone shouted.

'You say that you are an Inquirer – hold an inquiry!'

'Right now!'

'I will hold an inquiry,' Luca tried to seize control of the angry crowd. 'I will hold an inquiry this afternoon. A proper inquiry . . .'

'Not this afternoon – now!' the man with the dirty jacket shouted him down.

'I'll hold an inquiry,' Luca insisted through gritted teeth. 'A proper inquiry at the time that I appoint, and Brother Peter will write a report to the lord of our order and to the Holy Father. And you shall give evidence on oath of what you have seen –' he glared at the angry women – 'what you have really seen – not what you imagine. And if there has been any witchcraft or magic I will find it out and punish it.'

'Even if she has seduced you with her witch skills?' Mrs Ricci asked, her voice clear and accusing. 'She, who crept into the men's room in the night?'

Isolde's cheeks burned red for shame, but it was Ishraq who stepped forward and spat out her reply. 'There is no witch, and there is no seduction. There are friends and fellow travellers, Christians and pilgrims and a terrible, terrible tragedy which you make worse by your slurs and scandals. Let the Inquirer hold his inquiry without fear or favour and we will all abide by his judgement.'

'Right now, then,' Mrs Ricci insisted.

'Right now,' said another voice, the commander of the guard of the sea walls. 'I would know what made the sea turn on us.'

'Right now,' Brother Peter conceded, frightened by the hostility and the numbers of the crowd. 'We'll go to the inn and meet in the dining room. I'll get some paper and ink from Father Benito. We will hold an inquiry, as we are bound to do, and you shall have your say.'

The man in the dirty jacket suddenly lunged forwards, grabbed Luca by the jacket, thrust his big face forwards. 'Right now!' he shouted. 'We said right now, we mean right now! Not down at the inn! Not when you have fetched paper! Not when you have whispered together and made up a story. Now! Justice for the drowned!'

Luca pushed him away but he was a strong, angry man, and he did not release his grip. Ishraq flexed her fingers and looked around as if to measure how many people might try to drag them down. Isolde saw from her face that she thought they would not escape a beating, perhaps worse. The two young women stood a little closer, knowing that they were hopelessly outnumbered.

'Justice for the drowned!' someone else shouted from the back and then there were more people, running up the narrow streets, shouting and catcalling. 'Justice for the drowned!'

'Right now,' Luca offered. Gently he pushed the big man away, sensing that the whole crowd was on the edge of a riot. 'Where? In the church?'

'In the church,' the big man agreed, and he released Luca and led the way to the church with half the village following, and the other half running through the streets to join them. He looked back at Brother Peter. 'And you write it down, like you should,' he insisted. 'There's ink and paper in the church. And if they are guilty you write down that they are to be given to us, the people of Piccolo, for us to do as we please.'

'If they are guilty,' Father Benito specified.

Ishraq took a look around, thinking that she and Isolde and Rosa might be able to break away. Isolde took a firm grip of Rosa's hand, lifted the hem of her own long gown ready to run.

'Not so fast,' Mrs Ricci said with an evil smile. 'You're coming too. Don't think you'll get away again to bathe in the water and call down a wave from hell on us poor Christians, you vile heretic and you vile witch and you vile child.'

Ishraq looked at her, the fury in her dark gaze veiled by her dark lashes, and the three of them submitted to being hustled into the church.

The people filed into the church, ranged around the stone walls and stood in a murmuring hush, waiting for what was to happen next. Luca took a seat in the choir stalls, Brother Peter on one side of him, Father Benito on the other, the witnesses, as they came up to make their statements took the front row of the opposing choir stalls, the light on the altar behind the rood screen shining warmly on them all. The commander of the sea walls waited at the door. The hushed holiness of the place silenced the crowd but they were still determined to see justice done, and one after another, the villagers stepped up to the choir stalls and spoke of their experiences with the crusade and then with the flood.

They reported seeing the children begging and praying. They all agreed that Johann had preached of the end of days and had promised that they would be able to walk dry-shod to Jerusalem. They all reported that he had tempted them, by promising them sight of a beloved lost kinsman. People wept again as they said that Johann had spoken to them personally, described events that he could not possible have known unless he had been guided by the Devil himself, that they had been sure of him as an angel, now they knew he was accursed.

Brother Peter made notes, Luca listened intently, fearing more and more that some terrible wrong had happened in this town and that he had missed it. Remorsefully, he remembered coming into the town at dusk, after riding all day with Isolde, quite entranced by her, noticing nothing about the gateway, the harbour or the inn. He remembered saying goodnight to her on the stairs of the inn, thinking of nothing but the closeness of her and that if she had leaned a little nearer they could have kissed. He thought of the arrival of the children on the quayside and how he had looked up to see the two beautiful girls at their window as they had called down that hundreds of children were on the road; he had heard what they had said, but what he had seen was the two exquisite young women. He remembered warning Ishraq that she should not wear her Arab dress and how he had told her that her skin was the colour of heather honey. He knew now that he had been instantly and completely persuaded by Johann, that he had been determined to join the crusade to Jerusalem, hoping selfishly that he would see his parents again. Distracted, filled with sinful desire, obsessed with his own hopes and fears, Luca blamed himself for being quite blind to the events unfolding before his very eyes, and letting this town be swept through by the flood.

He should have been a Noah, he thought – he should have known that the flood was coming and prepared a safe haven. If he had been a true Inquirer, and not a lovesick boy, he would not have been distracted and perhaps he would have seen something: a movement of the sea, the largeness of the moon – something that could have warned him of the disaster that was coming. Luca sat very still, listening intently, filled with shame at his own failure.

'What about the young ladies?' one of the midwives called from the body of the church. 'You are asking about things that we know, that we all know. What about the young ladies and what they were doing?'

At once there was a murmur of suspicion and anxiety in the echoing chancel. 'Call them. And have them answer to you.'

Wearily Luca rose to his feet and looked into the shadowy body of the church. 'Lady Isolde, Mistress Ishraq!' he called. He could see the girls coming slowly from where they had been kneeling at the back of the church and then the quiet patter of their leather slippers as they came up the stone-flagged aisle and hesitated. Solemnly, he waved them into the choir stalls opposite his seat, so that they should take their place like the other witnesses. He looked at them, and he knew he was looking at them as if they were strangers to him: strangers filled with the incomprehensible powers of women.

'And the child,' someone insisted. 'The child who escaped the wave.'

Isolde bowed her head to hide her resentment, and went back down the aisle and returned with Rosa holding her hand.

The two of them sat opposite him, in silence, Rosa between them, their eyes on the floor. Luca remembered that when he first met Isolde she was accused of witchcraft and now she sat before him accused of the worst of crimes, once again. He could not help but feel a superstitious shiver that so much trouble seemed to swirl around her, though she always looked, as now, so shiningly innocent. He couldn't help but think that a woman who was truly good would not have one slander against her name, let alone two. This woman seemed to attract trouble as iron bars sown in a field will attract a thunderstorm.

His anxiety about her strengthened his resolve to hold a proper inquiry. He dismissed his feelings for Isolde and stared at her critically, without affection, and tried to see her, as these people saw her: a strange, exotic and danger-ously independent woman.

'You have been accused of working as a storm-bringer,' he said, his voice firm and level. 'Both of you have been so accused, by people who say that you went out of the town

427

as night was falling, to a place called the green lake and that there you called up a storm by splashing and making waves in the lake.'

The two young women looked at him in utter silence. Luca flushed as he imagined that he saw contempt in their level gaze.

'What do you say?' he asked them. 'To these charges? I am bound to put them to you, you are bound to answer.'

'They are unworthy of an educated man,' Ishraq said icily. 'They are the fears of fools.'

There was a buzz, like an angry swarm of bees, at the arrogance of her tone. One of the wise women looked around triumphantly. 'Hear how she calls us fools!'

'Answer,' said the commander of the sea walls.

'Even so,' Luca said, irritated, 'you will answer. And be advised not to abuse these good people. What were you doing at the lake?'

'We went out of the town in the afternoon,' Isolde spoke for them both, her voice very clear and steady. 'We wanted to wash and the landlady didn't have hot water for us, nor a bath that we could carry up to our room.'

'Why would they want to wash? In November?' one of the women said from the centre of the crowd standing before the chancel steps. People murmured in agreement. Ishraq looked around at them scornfully.

'The stable lad had told us of a place where boys went swimming . . .' Isolde went on.

'So what young lady would go there?' someone demanded. 'What young lady would go where the boys go? These must be girls of bad repute, little whores.'

Isolde gasped at the word, and looked at Luca,

expecting him to silence the shouts. He said nothing to defend her.

'And the gatekeeper says they went out at night.'

'It was afternoon,' Isolde insisted.

Luca raised his hand on the groan from the crowd and the single shout: 'Liar. Dirty liar!'

There was a scuffle at the doorway, as the door banged, and the porter from the west gate came into the church.

'You tell him,' they pushed him forward till he arrived before Luca, Father Benito, and Brother Peter,

'You are?' Brother Peter dipped his pen in the ink.

'Porter. Gatekeeper Paolo. I saw the women, and I warned them to be back inside the gates before dusk,' he said.

'Was the sun setting as they left?' Luca asked.

'It must have been, for I warned them of the curfew.'

'What did they say?'

'They said they were going for a walk.'

'Why should they lie?' someone shouted. 'If they were going for a wash? Why not say that?'

'And they went out as night fell! Why would they do that?'

'They went out as night was coming, so that no one could see them calling up a storm in the green lake!'

Luca looked at Isolde and saw defiance in her dark blue eyes. She looked as she did when he first met her, a woman against the world, despite her own desire to live at peace in her home. A woman driven to defiance. A woman with no trust in him, nor in any man: a woman at bay.

'Tell these people,' he said. Suddenly he broke into Latin, confident that she would understand him but few other

429

people in the church would. 'Please, please my dearest, trust us with the truth. Tell them that you would not call up a storm. Tell them that you are not a storm-bringer. Ishraq too. Just tell them. For God's sake, Isolde, we are all in trouble here. I can only ask you questions – you have to save yourself. Tell them what you were doing.'

For a moment he thought she would defy him; defy them all from her pride. But then, slowly, Isolde rose to her feet and stepped down from the choir stalls to face the crowded church 'I am no storm-bringer,' she said, speaking simply and loudly so that her words echoed off the stone walls. 'I am no witch. I am a woman of good repute and good behaviour. I am a woman who does not obey a father, since my father is dead, nor do I obey a husband, since I have no fortune and no man will take me without a dowry. I don't obey my brother, since he is false and faithless. So you see me as I am – a woman without a man to represent her, a woman alone in the world. But none of this – none of this makes me a bad woman. It makes me an unlucky one. I am a woman who would not knowingly do a wicked act. I cannot prove this to you, you have to trust me, as you trust your mothers and your wives and your sisters. I have to call on you to think of me with generosity, as a good woman of high repute, raised to be a lady in a castle. And my friend here, Ishraq, was raised beside me almost as my sister, she is the same.'

Ishraq slowly rose to her feet, and stood beside Isolde as if she were answering to a tribunal on oath. 'I am a heretic and a stranger,' she said. 'It is possible, you know, to be a stranger and yet not an enemy. I have done nothing to harm anyone. I did not call up the wave. I don't believe that any mortal has the power to call up a wave like this. I would never have called up a wave to hurt the children, nor you, and I would never have done anything to put our travelling companion, my friend Freize, in danger.'

Luca, who had been looking down at his papers, praying that the village people would hear the raw sincerity in Isolde's explanation, suddenly flicked his gaze up to see Ishraq's dark eyes were filling with tears. 'He was a true friend, and a loyal heart,' Ishraq's voice was low, choked with tears. 'I think he wanted to be my sweetheart and I was such a vain fool that I refused him a kiss.'

There was a murmur of sympathy in the room from some of the younger women. 'Ah, God bless you,' one of them said. 'And now you've lost him. Before you could tell him.'

'I've lost him,' Ishraq agreed. 'And now I'll never be able to tell him that I loved how he laughed at things, and I loved how kind he was to everything, even a kitten, and how he understood things without learning. He was no scholar but he was wiser than I will ever be. He taught me that you can be wise without being clever. The last thing he did – almost the very last thing on earth that he did – was to send me and Isolde and his friend Luca to safety. That's how we got back to the inn, that's how we knew to get high, up to our room and then to the roof. There was no mystery about it. It was Freize who had the sense to notice that his kitten was crying for fear, and he saw the kitten climbing up to the roof. He guessed from that the water would flow back. He had no schooling but he noticed things. He was not too proud to see things. He could learn – even from a kitten. He was a fine young man; and I am grieving for him now.'

'I have lost the dearest sweetheart that a woman might have. I lost him through my own pride and my own folly and I only knew that he was a fine young man when he sent me to safety and went back himself to save the horses. You have to know that I would never ever have done anything that would endanger him. You can call me a heretic. You can call me a stranger. But you can't think that I would have put Freize in the way of a great wave – I would never have hurt him.'

'Let me through!' a voice from the doorway interrupted and the crowd parted as the stable boy came in, propelled by the innkeeper, red-faced and furious.

'What's this? Brother Peter asked, alarmed by the sudden noise, and then, as he recognised the innkeeper with the landlady behind him, he said: 'Dear Lord, who is this now?'

'He's got something to say,' the landlord said. 'Dirty little tyke.'

The boy, his face as scarlet as his twisted ear, ducked his head before Luca's gaze.

'Do you have something to tell us?' Luca asked. 'You can speak without fear.' To the innkeeper he said: 'Do let him go, that can't be good for him.'

'I followed them,' the boy confessed, rubbing his ear. 'Out of town, and down to the lake.'

There was a whisper of excitement from the packed church.

'What did you see?'

The lad shook his head, his colour deepening. 'They went naked,' he confessed. 'I watched them.'

Oddly, Luca's colour rose too, burning red in his cheeks, in his ears. 'They undressed to swim?'

'They swam and they washed each other with soap. The water was cold. They squealed like little piglets. They washed their hair, they plaited it. Then they got out of the water.'

'Did they do anything,' Luca paused and cleared his throat. 'Did they do anything like making waves in the water, pouring water from a jug, did they say words over the water, did they do anything that was not washing and swimming?'

'They played about,' the boy said. He looked at Luca as if he hoped he would understand. 'They swam and splashed and kicked. They were ... very ...'

'Very?'

'Very bonny.' His chin dropped to his chest, his whole body slumped with his shame. 'I watched them. I couldn't look away. She ...' he made a shrugging gesture with his shoulder towards Isolde, as if he did not dare to point a finger. 'She wore a shift. But t'other one went naked.' He looked up and saw Luca's flushed face. 'Stark naked and she had skin like burned sugar all over. It was the most beautiful thing I have ever seen. And her ...'

'You will have to confess,' the priest interrupted quickly, before the boy could continue his description of Ishraq glowing like a peach, naked in the lake. 'You have had unclean thoughts.'

The boy went an even deeper red. He looked imploringly at Luca. 'So bonny,' he said. 'Anybody would have watched. Anybody would have unclean thoughts. You couldn't look away.'

Luca dropped his eyes to his papers, conscious of his own guilty desire. 'Yes, very well,' he said shortly. 'I think

433

we understand that. But at any rate you saw nothing that made you think they were calling up the wave?'

'They weren't doing that,' the boy said flatly. 'They were just playing about and washing like girls. And anyway, it was the middle of the afternoon.'

'The porter warned them of the curfew?'

'He always warns everyone,' the boy said to a murmur of agreement. 'He always closes the gate early and he always opens it late. He never keeps time. He always does just what he wants and then tells all of us that we are too late or too early.'

Luca looked around the room, testing his sense that the people were satisfied, that he could declare the inquiry over. He saw the angry spiteful faces of Mrs Ricci and the two wise women, but he also saw the exhaustion in the other people, who were grieving for the children and the loves they had lost, and now felt that they had wasted their time, accusing girls who had done nothing more than walk out of town in the after-noon for a swim.

'I am satisfied that neither the children of the pilgrimage nor these lady travellers did anything to summon the wave,' he said. His words were greeted in silence, and then a sigh of agreement. 'I shall so report,' he said.

'I agree,' said the commander of the sea guard.

'We agree,' Father Benito said, rising to his feet and look-ing around his flock. 'This is a sorrow which came upon us for no reason that we can yet understand. God forgive us and help us in the future.'

'And the little girl?' the landlady asked. She looked to where Isolde was holding Rosa's hand. 'She is cleared too?'

'How can they all three be cleared?' one of the midwives said irritably.

'Because they are all three innocent,' Luca said sternly. 'There is no evidence against them.'

'Rosa is innocent of everything,' Isolde confirmed to the landlady. 'Can we find a home for her? She is far from her village and all alone in the world.'

The villagers nodded and slowly filed from the church, some of them stopping to light a candle for loved ones who were still missing. Luca nodded to Brother Peter. 'Perhaps give them all a glass of grappa down at the inn?' he asked. 'For good will?'

Brother Peter nodded and whispered the order to the innkeeper who bustled off with his wife. Brother Peter started to collect up his papers. There was a space and a silence for Luca and the two young women.

'You're cleared,' Luca said to them both. 'Again.'

They smiled a little ruefully. 'We don't seek trouble,' Isolde said.

'It seems to follow you.'

Ishraq heard the criticism in his voice. 'If any woman steps outside the common way then she will find trouble,' she said simply. 'It does follow us. We have to fight it.'

'You are thinking about the wave?' Isolde asked Luca as he watched Brother Peter reading through his notes.

'This is no report,' Luca said, frustrated, flicking at the papers with his fingertips. 'This is nothing. This is a village scandal, a few old women frightening themselves. But the question that they ask is the right one. What caused such a thing? What could make such a great wave happen? I can say that it was not you two – washing in a lake – but I can't tell them what it was. And most importantly, I can't tell them if it could happen again. Could it happen again? Tonight, even?'

Isolde crossed herself at once at the thought of such a terror, and Luca lowered his voice so the people leaving the church would not hear.

'I have been thinking of this too, and I think it may have been an earthquake, the fall of a mountain or a mighty cliff, perhaps far far away,' Ishraq said, surprisingly. 'Perhaps it caused a wave, just one great wave, as a bowl of water will make waves and spill over, if you were to throw a stone into it.'

Brother Peter rose to his feet and smiled at the prosaic image, typical of a woman who cannot imagine the earth as void and empty, and darkness upon the face of the deep; and the spirit of God moving over the waters, as the Bible itself describes. 'The ocean is not a bowl of water,' he corrected her gently. 'It does not move with waves because someone throws a stone. It is not rocked in a basin for you to wash dishes in.'

'I am not saying that it is. But small things sometimes work the same way as larger. The wave may have been caused by an earthquake, a great falling of rock. Just as you can make a wave in a bowl of water if you throw in a pebble.'

'That's true,' Luca said. 'But what made you think of this?'

'Plato describes the drowning of the country of Atlantis in just such a way,' she said. 'He says that a great earthquake caused a great wave which drowned the island.'

'Plato?' Brother Peter repeated sceptically. 'How has a

girl such as you read Plato? I've heard of him, but I've read nothing that he wrote. There are no copies of anything he wrote.'

'No, not that you could read, not translated into Italian; but we Arabs have his books. A few of them have been translated from the Greek into Arabic. I read a little part of them in Arabic when I was in Spain, with Isolde and her father, and I was allowed to attend the university. Plato is a philosopher who talks about great mysteries such as the wave, and has strange understandings.'

'You were privileged,' Brother Peter said irritably, scooping up the papers and stoppering the bottle of ink. 'A heretic and a woman to read such a thinker. You must take care that it does not strain your nature, putting too much pressure on you. Women cannot think of abstractions.'

She gave a small shrug. 'My brain is well enough so far, though I thank you for your concern. At any rate, Plato says that the drowning of Atlantis might have followed a great movement of the earth. It made me think that this might be a natural occurrence, not an act of God, nor of the Devil, nor of storm-bringers – if there are such people. Perhaps it occurs naturally, from the world of nature. Though why God would make a world where such a thing could happen, is another question.'

Brother Peter knew himself to be on firmer ground. 'Ah, you ask an important question. It is because the perfect world that God first made was destroyed by sin in the garden of Eden, when the woman ate the apple.'

Isolde exchanged a quick smiling glance with Luca. They both knew that Ishraq and Brother Peter would be quarrelling within a moment.

437

Ishraq looked at him quite blankly. 'What is wrong with eating an apple?'

'Because it does not mean an apple. The apple signifies knowledge.'

Luca winked at Isolde.

'The woman wanted knowledge?'

'Yes,' Peter said, adopting his teacher's voice. 'But it was God's will that the woman and her husband should be innocent of knowledge.'

Ishraq looked as if she did not need his instruction. 'I would have thought an all-seeing God could have foreseen that a woman would want knowledge,' she said. 'Why should she not? Why should I not? Would any woman want to live in ignorance? Would any man? And what does it benefit God to have people so ignorant that they are like these poor peasants – believing that people call up storms and the Devil takes the time and the trouble to make them unhappy?'

Brother Peter was almost too irritated to speak. He picked up his papers, bowed to the altar and turned away. 'There is no point trying to explain such things to you,' he said. 'You are a heretic and a girl.' It would have been impossible to say which he thought was worse.

'The Lord Lucretili believed that a girl could study, without straining her nature,' Ishraq insisted. 'Women like Hypatia of Alexandria taught Plato to her students without illness. So when Lord Lucretili was in Spain he sent me to study at the university of Granada. Education is important to us heretics. There are many Arab women who are educated. We Moors believe that a woman can study as well as a man. We do not think that it is godly for a woman to be an ignorant fool.'

'But he did not send his daughter, Isolde, to learn heretic knowledge? He took care to protect her,' Brother Peter said pointedly.

'I wish he had!' Isolde interrupted.

'The lessons were in Arabic or Spanish,' Ishraq said. 'Lady Isolde speaks neither. And besides, she was raised to be a Christian lady ruling her lands.'

'But how would we ever find out?' Luca asked, almost to himself, going down the aisle to the open doorway, and looking downhill to the harbour to the quietly moving sea with its ugly burden of wreckage. 'How would we discover if the earth had moved and caused the wave? If it happened far out at sea, or even under the sea? If no one was there to see it happen? How could we ever discover the cause?'

Father Benito walked beside him. 'You know, the people of the village tell a story of a great earthquake that threw down the harbour walls – all this was about a hundred years ago – and it was followed by a great wave that washed all the boats out to sea and destroyed all the houses two lanes back from the harbour. The bell tower of my own church was thrown down when the ground shook. It was rebuilt; we have the stonemason's costs still in the church records. That's how I know it to be true.'

Ishraq nodded towards Luca. 'An earthquake followed by a wave,' she remarked.

'A hundred years ago?' Luca pressed Father Benito. 'Exactly a hundred?'

'More,' he said quietly. 'The earthquake was in 1348. And after the wave the Black Death came to the village. First the ground shook, then the wave came, then the plague. God forbid that this wave brings the pestilence also.'

'The Black Death?' Brother Peter queried.

The priest nodded. 'The quake was worst in Friuli, but they felt it as far away as Rome. It shook this village. I have the accounts of the church rebuilding, which is how I know the dates. It was almost impossible to get the stone masons to repair the tower, for within months of the wave, they were all dead of the Black Death.'

'I shall write this in my report,' Luca said. 'Perhaps we should see it as a warning. Do you think you should store grain, and food? In case a pestilence follows this wave, as it did a hundred years ago?'

Father Benito crossed himself. 'God forbid,' he said. 'For last time they had to dig great plague pits in the graveyard to take all the bodies. I wouldn't want to have to open them again. They buried half the village, more than a hundred people, old and young. And the priest himself died. God spare me.'

'God help us all,' Luca said solemnly. 'Perhaps this is, as they say, the end of days.' No one answered him, and he turned and went down the hill to the quayside alone.

Brother Peter and the two young women watched him go. Father Benito murmured a blessing, closed the church doors, and went quietly away to his damp house.

Brother Peter sighed and led the way down the hill to the inn on the quayside. 'I suppose we had better get a ship and move on,' he said. 'There's nothing we can do here any-more. We'll sail across to Split as we planned.'

'Sail?' Ishraq repeated 'Go by sea?'

'Are we giving up on Freize?' Isolde asked bleakly. 'Are we not looking for him any more, not waiting for him?'

'We could leave a message for him, as to where to find us,

if he were ever to return. But I can't believe that he survived the flood,' Brother Peter replied. 'What would be the point of us waiting here?'

'For fidelity!' Isolde exclaimed. 'Because we can't just go on!'

Ishraq shook her head. 'No. We may as well leave. It does Luca no good to wait and watch here. We'll have to find a boat and go on with our journey. Can you find someone to take us, Brother Peter? Would you like me to go and ask?'

'A few ships came into port this morning, which seem to have escaped damage. I'll find someone. Shall we set a time and go tomorrow?'

'In the morning,' Ishraq said. 'I suppose you'll all want to attend Mass before we sail. We can go after Prime.'

Brother Peter looked curiously at her as they went together down the cobbled steps. 'Don't you want to confess your soul and attend the service now that you have seen God work in such a mysterious way? Should you not turn to our God, now that you have been in such danger? I could explain our beliefs to you. I could convert you.'

Ishraq smiled at him, indifferent to his concern. 'Ah, Brother Peter, I know you are a good man and would like to save my soul. I don't know what caused the wave. I don't know how I am going to find the courage to set out to sea; but it doesn't inspire me to pray to your God.'

~

Isolde agreed that they should leave the following day but she could not bring herself to tell Luca. 'Will you tell him?' she asked Brother Peter. 'I can't bear to do it.'

He waited until the hour before dinner while they were all four sitting in the dining room before a smoky fire of damp wood, and then he said quietly, 'Brother Luca, I think we can do nothing more in this town and I will send my report tomorrow. I will write that we can find no certain explanation for the wave, though some wild thoughts from pagan and heretical writers have been mentioned.'

Luca barely raised his head.

'And I have found a master who will take us on his ship tomorrow. We can go after Prime.'

'We stay,' Luca said instantly. 'At least for a few more days.'

'We have a mission; and there is nothing more to be done here,' Brother Peter repeated steadily. 'We will send your report tomorrow, we can warn Milord and His Holiness that we have seen a powerful sign of the end of days. We can warn them that a previous earthquake was followed by a wave that was followed by the pestilence called the Black Death. But we serve no one by waiting here – and anyway, if a plague is coming we should leave.'

Isolde reached out and put her cool hand over Luca's clenched fist as it lay on the table. 'Luca,' she said quietly.

He turned to her as if she might have answers to his agonising questions. 'I can't go,' he said passionately. 'I can't just sail away from here as if nothing is wrong. I can't just continue on. Freize came with me, he was following me on this quest. He would never have been here but for love of me. I don't see how to do it without him. If I had been washed out to sea, he would not have left me. He would not have run for his safety and left me behind.'

'He would want you to complete your mission,' Isolde

said, trying to comfort him. 'He was so proud of you. He was so proud that you had been called to this work and that he could serve you.'

At the thought of Freize's joyful boasting, Luca nearly smiled, but then he shook his head. 'You must see, I have to stay here until . . .'

'We will leave instructions and money that his body is to be buried if it is washed ashore,' Ishraq said, surprising them all with the brisk clarity of her tone. 'If you are thinking of that; we can provide for him, as you would wish. But I was speaking to one of the fishermen and he says there is a strong current a little further beyond the harbour and perhaps Freize and all the children have been washed far away. Their bodies may never be found. Perhaps we should think of them all as buried at sea. Brother Peter could bless the waves as we sail to Split.'

Luca rounded on her in anger. 'You speak of his burial? The burial of my friend Freize? Blessing the waves? You have given him up for dead?'

She gazed at him steadily. 'Yes, of course. Weren't you thinking the very same thing, yourself? Isn't it the very thing you have been afraid to think for days?'

He flung himself from the table and wrenched open the door. 'You're heartless!' he flung at her.

She shook her head. 'You know I am not.'

He paused. 'How can you talk about blessing the sea?'

'I thought you would want to say goodbye,' she said.

'How dare you say that I must think of this?'

'It is your life's work to think of difficult things.'

Isolde gasped and would have intervened but she saw the

443

steady way that Ishraq held Luca's angry glare, and she fell silent. Luca's temper burned out as quickly as it had come. He breathed out a shuddering sigh, came back into the room and closed the door behind him and leaned back against it as if sorrow had weakened him.

'You're right of course,' he said. 'You're right. I just don't want it to be true. I'll leave instructions with Father Benito in the morning and – Brother Peter, perhaps you will write to our monastery and tell them what has happened and ask them to tell his mother? I will write myself later . . .'

Isolde rose and put her hand in his; she laid her cheek against his shoulder. Brother Peter watched them without comment, though his expression was completely disapproving.

'And we'll take ship tomorrow,' Ishraq pursued.

'Ishraq!' Isolde exclaimed. 'Be at peace! Leave him alone!'

Stubbornly, Ishraq shook her head. 'Luca is not at peace,' she said, nodding to him. 'And you crying over him doesn't help him at all. Better that we do something, rather than sit here mourning. In my religion Freize would have been buried by sunset on the day that he died. We'll always remember him whether we take a ship to Split now or the day after. But,' she nodded at Luca, 'this is not a young man who should be left to mourn for a long time. He has had too many losses already. Grief must not become a habit for him.'

Isolde looked up into Luca's strained face. 'This is a hard counsel,' she said.

'She's right,' he said bitterly. 'I can do nothing here but weep for him, like a girl. We'll go tomorrow, after Prime.'

They went to their rooms to pack their things, but they had almost nothing to pack. Everything but the clothes they were wearing had gone down with the ship. They had bought new rough cloaks from the tailor in the little town but new boots or hats, or a writing box for Brother Peter, would have to wait till they got to a bigger town. The manuscripts which Brother Peter and Luca carried to advise them on legends, folklore and previous investigations were irreplaceable. They would have to buy new horses when they got to Split, and a new donkey to carry their goods.

'How far do you think it is from Split to Buda-Pest?' Isolde asked idly, looking out of the window of their bedroom. 'I am so tired of travelling. I am so tired of everything. I wish we could just go home to my own home and live on my own lands, where I belong. I wish that none of this had happened.'

'You can't wish to be back in the nunnery,' Ishraq objected. 'You can't wish to be under the command of your brother.'

Isolde turned her face away and shook her head. 'I wish I were a girl in my father's care again,' she said. 'I wish I could be home.'

'Well, Freize said that we would be about a week on the road,' Ishraq replied, trying to cheer her friend. 'And the only way to get your own home back is to get your godfather's son to support you. It's a long journey, but with luck it leads us home at last.'

Isolde turned into the room. 'I don't know how we'll

445

manage without him. I can't imagine setting out on a journey without him.'

'Without him complaining?' Ishraq suggested with a faint smile. 'Without him endlessly complaining about the road, and about the mission, and about Brother Peter's secret orders?'

Isolde smiled. 'We'll miss all that,' she said. 'We'll miss him.'

~

It was a quiet group that assembled for dinner. Much of the company had left the inn since the burial of the bodies of the children, and travellers on the coastal roads had heard of the disaster that had hit all the fishing villages along the coast and were skirting the blighted areas and travelling inland. Nobody had much appetite and there seemed to be nothing much to say.

'Where is Rosa?' Isolde asked the landlady. 'Is she in the kitchen with you?'

'She's worked like a little cook, and now she's eating her dinner as good as gold,' the landlady said, pleased. 'That was a good thought of yours, my lady. That was kind Christian work.'

'What did Lady Isolde do?' Luca raised his head in momentary interest.

'She took me to one side and she prayed with me and Rosa together. She showed Rosa my linen room and the child saw the beauty in it. She'll make a good kitchen maid and a good housemaid. I was spared from the terror of the flood, locked safe in my linen room; I can't help but warm to a girl who admires it. She can stay here with us. Lady

Isolde has offered to pay for her keep for her first month and then she'll earn her wages. I'll look after her.'

'That was well done,' Luca said quietly.

Isolde smiled at him. 'It wasn't hard to see that they might help each other. And Rosa will have a good home here and learn a trade.'

'That's good,' Luca said, losing interest.

'The town of Split tomorrow,' Brother Peter said, trying to be cheerful. 'We'll probably get in about dawn if we leave early.'

Isolde directed her words to Luca. 'And then Zagreb.'

There was a clatter of noise in the stable yard and a cheerful 'Halloo!' from outside. It was an incongruous yell in a town gripped with mourning. The innkeeper opened the kitchen door and said, 'Hush, don't you know what has passed here? Keep the noise down. What do you want?'

'Some service!' came the joyous shout. 'Some stabling for the bravest horses ever to swim for shore! Some dinner for a great survivor! Some wine to toast my health in! And news of my friends. The two beautiful lasses and the brilliant young man? And the sour-faced priest that travels with us? Are they here? Have they gone on? Swear to me that they are safe as I have been praying?'

Luca went white, as if he thought he was hearing a ghost and then he exclaimed, 'Freize!' and leapt up from the table, overturning his chair, and dashed down to the kitchen, and out through the back door to the stable yard.

There, standing at the head of his horse and holding the reins of four others, with the tired donkey behind them, was Freize: sea-stained and dirty, but alive. As he saw Luca

447

outlined in the light from the kitchen, he dropped the reins and spread his arms. 'Little Sparrow, thank God you're safe! I have been riding for miles fretting about you.'

'I! Safe! What about you?' Luca yelled and catapulted himself into the arms of his boyhood friend. They clung to each other like long-lost brothers, slapping each other's backs, Luca patting Freize all over as if to assure himself that he was alive. Freize caught Luca's face in his hands, and kissed him roundly on both cheeks and then wrapped his arms around him again.

Luca thumped his shoulders, shook him, stepped back and looked at him and then hugged him again. 'How ever did you—? How did—? I didn't know where you were – why didn't you run for the inn with us? I swear I thought you were right behind me – I'd never have left you on your own!'

'Did you get up on the chimney like the kitten?' Freize replied to the torrent of questions. 'Are you all safe? The girls? Both girls?'

As the two young men spoke at once, Ishraq and Isolde came running out of the inn door and threw themselves on Freize, hugging and crying and saying his name. Even Brother Peter came out into the yard and thumped him on the back. 'My prayers!' he cried. 'Answered! God be praised He has brought Freize back to us. It is a miracle like the return of Jonah onto dry land from the belly of the fish!'

Ishraq, tucked under Freize's arm with Isolde clinging to his other side, glanced up. 'Jonah?' she asked. 'Jonah swallowed by a great fish?'

'As the Bible tells us,' Brother Peter said.

She laughed. 'The Koran also,' she said. 'We call him

Jonah or Yunus. He preached for God.' She thought for a moment and then recited:

'Then the big Fish did swallow him, and he had done acts worthy of blame.

Had it not been that he (repented and) glorified Allah,

He would certainly have remained inside the Fish till the Day of Resurrection.'

Brother Peter's delight faded slightly. 'It's not possible,' he said. 'He was a prophet for God, our God.'

'For our God too,' Ishraq said, pleased. 'Perhaps, after all, they are one and the same?'

~

The innkeeper paddled around the waters in his cellar for a special bottle of wine, two special bottles, three, as more and more people came to hear the extraordinary story and drink Freize's health. Even those who had lost brothers or sons at sea were glad that at least one life had been spared. And his survival gave hope to those who were still waiting. The landlady brought some cheese and chicken to the table, some bread fresh-baked in the re-heated oven, and half the village piled in to watch the restored Jonah eat his dinner and hear how he had been saved from the terrible destruction.

'I saw the wave and I was running for the inn after you when I heard the horses kicking down their stalls on the ship, so I ran back to them . . .' Freize started.

'Why didn't you come with us?' Isolde scolded him.

'Because I knew that the little lord would care for you two, but there was no one to care for the horses,' he explained. 'I saw you set off at a run and I splashed across the harbour to where the boat was stranded. I got on board – Lord! the boat was sitting on the harbour floor – and I thought that I would set them free, let them run away, and catch them later. But as I was trying to get close enough to cut the ropes, talking to them and telling them all would be well, the world made me a liar indeed for I looked over the shoulder of the horse on the seaward side, and I saw the great wall of water, as high as a house, racing towards us and already in the mouth of the harbour. I had seen it shining like a white wall, a long way off, but it came faster than I had dreamed.'

There was a little groan from the people who had lost their children, at the thought of the great wave. 'I did nothing,' Freize admitted. 'God knows, I was no hero. Worse than that. I ducked down between one horse and another and I fairly buried my face in Rufino's mane. I was so afraid I didn't want to see what was coming. I thought it was my death coming for me, I don't mind admitting. I could hear a great roar, like a beast coming for me. I closed my eyes and clung to a horse and cried like a baby.

'I could hear it – dear God, a noise that I hope I never hear again – a grinding sliding screaming noise of the water storming towards me and eating up everything in its path. It hit the little ship like a hammer blow on a wooden box and threw us up in the air like we were a splinter. I had my arms around Rufino's neck like a child crying on its mother's lap. I'm not ashamed to say I was weeping in terror, as we went up and up and up. I could feel the moorings tear away, and I could feel the back of the boat stave in and next thing we were roaring away, boat and horses and me, with the wave rushing us inland like little ducks on a flood.'

'What could you see? Did you see the children?'

'God bless and keep them, I saw nothing but the sky and the land ahead of us and then the boiling water like a pan of grey soup, and I heard nothing but the roar of the waters and my own frightened cries. The horses wept in fear too, and the little donkey; we were seven sorry beasts, as we stormed over dry land, the world buckling and folding underneath us, and I thought the world had ended and it was another great flood and I, a failed Noah, with none of my kind on board, and no preparation done.'

He paused and nodded at Luca. 'I really did think it the end of the world and hoped that somewhere you were safe and taking note.'

Luca laughed and shook his head, as Freize went on. 'Then, and this was a bad moment, the wave sort of took a breath, like it was a living devil and thinking what would be the worst thing that it could do, and I felt the tide turn beneath what was left of the boat and we started to run back out to sea again, back the way we had come, but bumping and grinding against things that I could not even see, and crashing against things in the dark. That was a terrible moment; that was as bad as before, worse. I thought I would be halfway to Africa and on only half of a boat. Then the keel caught: I could feel it spin against something, and then it grounded and I was fool enough to hope that I would step out on dry land, when a rush of water hit us again and the boat tipped over, throwing us into the sea and into darkness and everything was rushing around me, and great trees were turning over and over crashing around my frightened head and I was never knowing whether I was upwards or downwards or simply drowned.

'I kept tight hold of Rufino and I felt that he kept tight hold of me and that we were better when we shared our fears together. When the boat tipped over I was flung towards his back and gripped on like a child, legs around his belly, arms around his neck, and whispered to him that he had better get us out of danger for I was no use to man nor beast, being a great coward.

'When the boat had crashed it had smashed itself and so he was freed, all the horses' tethers were free, and I could feel Rufino take great leaps as he swam in the flood. And glory to God and to the horse in particular that he bobbed and swam and struggled, and neighed out loud as if he was saying his prayers. I clung to him and sometimes he was washed from under me, and I was clinging to him and swimming beside him, but then I got my legs around him again, and then I felt him struggling in mud, not in water, and then I heard his hooves ring on stone, and though I had no idea where we were, at least I knew we were on land.'

'Praise be!' someone said.

'Amen,' Isolde replied fervently.

'Indeed,' Freize said. 'And bless the horse. For I would not have lived through that, but for the strength and wisdom of a dumb beast. So you tell me who is the wiser?'

Ishraq could see Brother Peter biting his tongue to stop himself replying that the horse, any horse, was undoubtedly wiser than Freize.

'And then when we were sure we were on land again, and hoping that the sea was never coming back, I looked around me and found that they had all stayed together, like the sensible beasts they are; even the little donkey who likes to play the fool had stayed with us. I gathered up their halters

452

and I climbed back on Rufino, without saddle or bridle, and, though we were all so weary, I rode a little way uphill, for though I could see the water was seeping away, I was still very afraid of it. As soon as I thought we were high enough and dry enough I told my five horses and the little donkey that we would spend the night and rest, and try for Piccolo in the morning.

'Well, we were further away than I knew, for we have been walking all this long while back to you and I've seen many sad sights all along the way. Good houses ruined, good fields destroyed by salt, and more drowned animals and good people than I could bear to see. All the villages I passed by are filled with sad people seeking their own, and burying their dead. Everywhere I walked they asked me had I seen this child, or that woman, and I was sick to my heart that I had to say that I was alone in my ship like a poor ill-prepared Noah, and saw no one and nothing from the moment that the great wave came.

'And I didn't stop, except to sleep at nights, which I did once in a farmer's damp barn, and once in a wrecked little inn, for I was so anxious to come back here and find you. All the way I have tormented myself that the wave was too fast for you and that I had saved five horses and a little donkey, God bless them; but lost the most precious man in the world to me.' He looked at Luca. 'Little sparrow. Did you perch all night on the roof?'

Luca laughed shakily. 'I have been sick with grief for you. I thought you were dead for sure.'

Freize wiped his mouth with the back of his hand. 'I was a Noah,' he said grandly. 'A Noah of six beasts, and all of them geldings, so of no use to anyone. But I did ride my ark in a great flood. If I had not been so weak with fear I would have been impressed by the adventure. It was the strangest thing. And when I have stopped being so afraid of the memory it will make a very good story and I shall tell it at length. And when I have forgotten that I cried like a coward I shall give myself many good speeches and be the hero of my story. You have it now as it was – before improvements. You have it as a true history and not a poem. I am not yet a troubadour, I am a mere historian.' He turned to Isolde. 'And you, my lady? I have been fretting about you, without your squire at your side to guard you. You were not hurt?'

She gave him her hand and he kissed it. 'I'm just so very pleased to have you with us again,' she said simply. 'We have all been praying for you. We had special prayers said for your deliverance, and every day we have been looking and looking out to sea.'

He flushed with pleasure at the thought of it. 'And the horses are well,' he assured her. 'Shaken, of course, and tired – oh they are weary – poor beasts. I doubt they'll go very willingly on board a ship again, but they are fit to travel.' He turned to Ishraq. 'And you were safe? You got quickly to the inn. I trusted you to see the danger and run. I knew you would understand.'

She nodded gravely at him. 'Safe,' she said.

'And Brother Peter. I am glad to see you,' Freize volunteered.

'And I you.' The clerk extended his hand and shook Freize's hand with unmistakable warmth. 'I have been afraid for you, on the flood. And I have missed you these last days. I have regretted some hard words that I said to you. I am more glad than I can tell you, to see you safe and back with us. I prayed for you constantly.'

Freize flushed with pleasure. 'And the children of the crusade? Were they all lost? God bless them and take them into His keeping.'

'Some were saved,' Isolde said. 'Saved by you. The ones that you warned and sent back to the village got as far as the church and were safe. They're travelling home, while the little girl Rosa, with the hurt feet, who you sent back, is here and will serve as a kitchen maid at the inn. But many of them, most of them, were taken by the sea.'

'It's been a terrible disaster,' Luca said quietly. 'We buried some of them this afternoon. We were going to leave tomorrow. We would have left you messages, where to come. But now we'll wait here a few more days, and you can rest.'

'No, we can go. I can sleep on the ship,' Freize said, 'if someone can promise me that such a wave will never happen again. If you promise me that the sea will stay where it ought to be, I'll get on board and sail tomorrow. I think God has sent me a sign that I will not die by drowning.'

Brother Peter shook his head. 'Nobody knows what it means, or what caused it,' he said, not looking at Ishraq. 'So nobody can say if it will ever come again. But it has not happened in this generation, not even for a hundred years. We can only pray that it never happens again.'

'Is there no way of knowing?' Freize asked Luca. 'I admit that I'd cast anchor more happily if there was any way of knowing for sure.'

Luca frowned. 'It's the very thing I have been puzzling about,' he said. 'The horses seemed to know.'

'They did know,' Freize said certainly. 'And the kitten knew too.'

'And there was a terrible noise, and the sea went out, drained away, before it came in.'

'The wave itself didn't rear up out of nothing,' Freize was thinking out loud. 'It was rolling in, as if it might have come from some distance, as if it might even have swelled and grown out at sea. If anyone had been far out at sea they might have seen it beginning.'

Luca nodded, and a few people crowded around Freize to ask more questions and he answered, pausing only to drink wine, happy to be in the middle of the crowd and the centre of attention. He did not speak again to Ishraq, nor she to him, until almost everyone had gone. Brother Peter was putting his cape around his shoulders to go up the hill to the church for the night service, and Luca, Isolde, and Freize were following him. Ishraq saw them out of the front door of the inn and was closing the door on the cold night air, as Freize turned back to speak to her.

'You were safe?' he asked. 'I knew that you would get Isolde out of danger.'

'I'm safe,' she said. 'But I was very afraid for you.'

He beamed. 'Afraid for me? Well, we agree on that. I was afraid for myself.'

'It was a brave thing to do – to go back to free the horses.'

He shook his head. 'To tell you the truth, I don't think I'd have done it if I'd known the wave was coming so quick. I'm no hero, though I am sorry to say it. Very sorry to have to confess it to you.'

'I have something for you,' she said smiling. 'Hero or not.'

He waited.

From the inner pocket of her cape she produced the sleepy little kitten. Freize cupped his big hands and she put it gently into them. He took the kitten up to his face and inhaled the scent of warm fur, as the little thing stretched for a moment, and then wound its golden tail over its white nose and snuggled down clasped in his big hands.

'You saved it for me?'

'I woke in the night, last night, thinking of you and remembering it, and I got out of bed and went up the ladder to the roof in the darkness, and fetched it down from the chimney pot.'

'You went up and down the roof in darkness?'

'I should have remembered it before.'

'Was it not dangerous?'

'Nothing like you in the flood.'

'You were thinking of me?'

'Yes,' she said frankly.

'Worrying about me?' he suggested.

'Yes.'

'Perhaps crying for me? A little? When nobody was looking?'

She smiled a little, but she did not look away or pretend to shyness. She made a small nod of assent. 'I cried for you and I told the whole village that I was sorry I had been unkind to you.'

'Perhaps you were wishing that you had kissed an honest man when he asked you kindly, and not thrown him down in the mud, that time in Vittorito?'

Again, the tiny nod told him that she had thought very kindly of him and regretted the missed kiss.

'You could always kiss me now,' Freize suggested.

To his surprise, she did not refuse him, though he had expected her to box his ears for asking. Instead she stepped towards him and put one hand over the soft kitten in his cupped hands, as if to caress them both. She put her other hand on the nape of his warm neck, and drew his head down to her, and she kissed him, tenderly and fully on the lips so that he inhaled her breath, and tasted the soft dampness of the tender skin of her mouth.

~

Ishraq waited in their shared room for Isolde to come back from church and took her cape as she entered, and stood behind her as she sat on the wooden three-legged stool. Ishraq untied the ribbon in Isolde's blonde hair and ran her fingers through the plaits, pulling them loose. Slowly, luxuriously, she combed the beautiful golden ringlets till they lay heavy and smooth over Isolde's shoulders, and then plaited them back up for the night. The girls changed places and Isolde combed and then plaited her friend's thick dark hair, twisting the locks around her fingers.

'Isn't it a blessing that he is safe?' she said quietly, 'I had lit half a dozen candles for him in the church and then I was able to give thanks.'

Ishraq bowed her head under the gentle caress. 'Oh, yes.'

'He came running after us up the hill to church and he looked filled with joy.'

'Yes, I expect he did.'

'Did you give him his kitten?'

Ishraq nodded.

'Was he very pleased?'

'Yes.'

Something in Ishraq's reserve warned Isolde, who gave the fat dark plait a little admonitory tug. 'What are you not telling me?'

Ishraq turned to face her friend. 'How do you know that there is something that I am not telling you?'

'Because his face was alight with joy. Because you are saying nothing – but you look the same as he did. So what passed between the two of you?'

Ishraq hesitated. 'You won't like it,' she guessed.

'Of course I won't mind. Whatever it is. Why would I mind? Did he promise you his service for life, like he did to me?'

'Oh no. He doesn't think of me as a grand lady. He doesn't want to be my squire. He asked me if I was sorry for throwing him down in the mud at Vittorito. And I said I was sorry.'

'You apologised?' Ishraq was amazed. 'You never apologise!'

'Well, I said sorry to him.'

'Is that all?'

'I said I wished that I had kissed him that time and not tripped him up.'

'Ishraq!' Isolde was playfully shocked. 'What a thing to say to him! What can he have thought?'

'Oh that was nothing. He asked me could he kiss me now?'

'Well, he was bound to. And I hope you refused him kindly?'

'Oh,' Ishraq said nonchalantly. 'I wanted to. So I kissed him.'

Isolde was genuinely shocked. She dropped the comb and stared at Ishraq's reflection in the little mirror. 'You kissed him?'

The girl nodded. 'Yes. Yes, I did.'

'How could you allow him? I know you were happy that he came back safely – we all are – but how could you forget yourself so? How could you permit him? A servant?'

'I didn't really allow him. I didn't "permit him", as you say.'

'He never forced you?' Isolde was horrified.

'No! No! It was I who kissed him.'

This was even worse. 'But Ishraq, your honour!'

The girl met her friend's stunned gaze. 'Oh! Honour!'

'What do you mean?'

'I suddenly felt, I suddenly thought, that nothing mattered more to me than that I had thought him dead, and that I was so happy that he was alive. I had thought he was lost and here he was – just as he had always been. And I was so glad of that – nothing else seemed to matter.'

Isolde shook her head. 'If you were so happy for him, you could have given him a favour or a gift. You could have let him kiss your hand. But to lower yourself to kiss him! What about your honour as a lady?'

'I am sick of all of this,' Ishraq said impatiently. 'Like in the church today – people doubting our reputation just because we were going to wash where the boys swim. As if all that matters is how a lady behaves around boys! I want my honour to be about me as a person, not me as an object with boundaries and gateways, as if I were a field, as if

I were a property with hedges. One man can touch my hand, one can see my face, but another can't even speak to me. If my honour is a real thing then it can't depend on whether a man sees my face, or touches my hand, or kisses my lips. If I am an honourable woman then I am an honourable woman like a man is an honourable man – whatever I wear, however I appear. It is about my respect for myself – not how the world sees me, not what events happen. I know that I am an honourable woman, I don't stoop to sin, I don't embarrass myself, I don't do things that I know to be wrong. I know I am a good woman whether I wear a veil or keep my hair plaited out of sight. I felt that I could, in honour, give him the kiss that he once asked for, and that I wanted to do so. And I did so.'

'A lady should be untouchable until marriage,' Isolde stated the absolute rule that they had both been taught from childhood. 'Her husband should know that she has known no other man, that no other man has been closer to her than to kiss her hand. He must know that she has felt no desire, permitted no touch.'

'It's not true,' Ishraq said roundly. 'You are a lady, a great lady, and you will make a great marriage with some high lord. But you will have known love and you will have felt desire.'

'I won't!' Isolde insisted. 'I would never admit to it.'

'But there is more to life than trying to fit inside men's idea of an honourable woman!' Ishraq exclaimed. 'We didn't come away from the castle and then run away from the nunnery to live as if we were still enclosed.'

Isolde was scandalised. 'We should live as we were brought up to live! Not like loose women on the road, not as if we had no hopes of ourselves, no standards, no self-respect!'

'Not me,' Ishraq declared boldly. 'I am out of the castle, I am out of the nunnery. I'm not going to wear a hood any more, I'm not going to wear a veil. I am going to dress as I please and do what I think right and I am going to kiss who I want to, and even lie with someone if I want to. My honour and my pride are in my heart, not in my dress, and not in what the world says.'

Isolde was genuinely distressed. 'You can't throw away your reputation, Ishraq. You can't become a loose woman, a shamed woman.'

'Nobody shames me,' Ishraq said proudly. 'But I will choose my own path and who I love and who loves me.'

'When we were in church, before Luca, accused of being storm-bringers, we told everyone that we were women of good reputation!' Isolde cried out. 'It was one of the things that saved us. Everyone could see that we wouldn't have gone running after boys to the green lake; everyone knew that we said that we were ladies of high regard, of good name. You risk everything if you behave lightly. It's a terrible thing to do.'

'We were saved in the church because the stable lad said that we had done nothing but swim,' Ishraq argued. 'All that about being the Lady of Lucretili might impress a few peasants but it means nothing. If the boy had not proved that we left the town gate in daylight and gone for a swim they would have burned us as storm-bringers whether we were virgins or not. We have to fight for our way in the world; nobody is going to give us safe conduct because we try to be ladylike.'

'You won't be a fit companion for me, and Luca would be horrified,' Isolde stormed. 'Luca does not want to travel with a girl who has lost her honourable name. He would not tolerate you in his presence, if he thought you were dishonoured. He would send you away if he knew you had kissed his servant.'

'No he wouldn't, for he knows what it is to want someone to hold you, to want the comfort of love. When he was in his sorrow on the quayside I held him in my arms.'

'What?' Isolde nearly screamed.

'I held him for pity when he was weeping, and I was not shamed. He did not think I was dishonoured. I was not shamed when he kissed me.'

Isolde gasped. 'He kissed you?'

'Yes. He was not horrified. He didn't think me dishonoured.'

'He kissed your lips?' Isolde's voice was shrill.

'No! Not like that! How can you think such a thing? He kissed me tenderly, gently, on my forehead.'

'How do you mean?'

Ishraq was irritated. 'What do you think I mean? He held my face in his two hands and he kissed me on my forehead, practically on my hood. I hardly felt it. It was almost on my hood.'

'It can't have been on your hood if you felt it! If it had been on your hood you would not have known he had done it. So was it on your forehead or your hood?'

'What difference does it make? What difference does it make to you?'

'Was it on your forehead?'

'Why would it matter? He's obviously in love with you.

463

I held him in my arms like a sister, I held him while he wept for his friend, and then, when he came into the inn, he gave me a kiss of tenderness: we were both grieving for Freize.'

'You were hardly grieving very much, if you were kissing another man.'

Ishraq looked incredulously at her friend, and then crossly got to her feet, kicking the stool out of the way under the bed. 'What on earth is the matter with you about all this?' she said rudely. 'You are screaming like a stuck pig.'

'I am so shocked by you!' Isolde's voice quavered as if she were about to cry.

'Shocked by what? By my holding a young man in my arms who was grieving for his friend? Or by my kissing a young man when he had just come back from the dead?'

'And him! How could he? How can we travel with them – how can we travel at all – if you are going to be like this? How can we face them tomorrow knowing that you have kissed not just one but both of them!'

Ishraq almost laughed and then looked again at Isolde's distressed face, saw even in the flickering candlelight the shine of tears on her pale cheeks. 'Why you're crying! Isolde, this is ridiculous. What's the matter with you? Why are you so upset?'

'I can't bear that he should kiss you!' burst out the girl. 'I hate it. I hate you for allowing it! I hate you!'

There was a stunned silence.

'This is about Luca. Not about me or Freize, not about my honour. It is about Luca,' Ishraq said.

Isolde dropped on the bed and put her face in her hands. 'No, it isn't.'

'So you are in love with him,' Ishraq observed coldly. 'This is serious.'

'No! Of course not! How can it possibly be?'

'You are jealous that I held him in my arms, and that he took my face in his hands and kissed me on the forehead.'

'Shut up!' Isolde rounded on her friend in a fury. 'I don't want to hear about it, I don't want to think about it. I don't want to have to imagine it, I wish you had not done it, and if you do it again – if you even think of doing it again – then we will have to part. I can't stay with you if you are going to become some sort of . . .'

'Some sort of what?' Ishraq demanded icily.

'Some sort of whore!' Isolde spat out in her rage.

Ishraq was shocked into silence, then she got into bed, pulled up the covers of the bed as far as they would go, up to her chin, and turned over as if ready for sleep. 'If you were a man I would have thrown you down for saying such a name to me,' she said to the limewashed wall. 'But as it is, I see that you are a stupid jealous girl who fears that the man she loves is being taken from her.'

Isolde gasped, but could not deny it.

'A jealous girl, a stupid girl,' Ishraq went on bitterly, still with her back turned. 'A girl truly dishonoured by thinking such things of her friend and saying such a word to her friend. That is dishonour, that is to be poor in heart. And you are wrong, so wrong. I would not take the man you loved away from you, even supposing that he would be willing. I would not do such a thing to you, for I never forget that we love each other like sisters, and

465

that our love should matter more than what we might feel for a man. A passing man,' she said driving the point home, into the silence of the darkened bedroom. 'A man that you met just a month ago. A man who is promised to a monastery and to an order and is not free to kiss anyone, anyway. A young man who probably cares for neither of us.

'But you have put your stupid girlish feelings for him above your love for me. And then you accuse me of being dishonoured! And then you call me a foul name! You're no sister to me, Isolde, though I have lived my life thinking of you as dearly as a sister. But at the first sight of a handsome young man you become a rival. A stupid rivalrous girl. You're not fit to be my sister, you don't deserve my love.'

She heard a sob behind her, but she refused to turn around.

'And it is you who are dishonoured,' she said fiercely. 'For you are in love with a man who is not free, and who has not spoken to your family to ask for your hand in marriage. So you are a fool.'

She was answered by a little shaky gasp.

'Goodnight,' Ishraq said frostily, and closed her eyes and fell, almost at once, asleep, as Isolde got on her knees at the foot of the bed and prayed to God for forgiveness for the sin of jealousy, for speaking cruelly and wrongly to her dearest friend; and then – reluctantly – owning the truth to herself: she prayed for forgiveness for the terrible sin of desire.

In the morning the two girls were pointedly polite to each other, but hardly spoke at all. Luca and Freize, in the joy of being reunited, completely failed to notice the icy atmosphere. Brother Peter regarded the young women critically, and thought to himself that they were – like all women – as changeable as the weather, and as inexplicable. He would have thought they would be overjoyed to have the favourite Freize back with them again – but here they were sour-faced and silent. Why would God make such beings but for the trouble and puzzlement of men? Who could ever doubt that they were a lesser being to the men that God had made in His image and set over them for their guidance? What could he do but thank God for preserving him from their company by keeping him safe in a religion governed by men in an order exclusively male?

As Freize went down to the harbour to confirm the arrangements for them to sail, Luca, Brother Peter and Isolde went up the hill to the church for Terce, the third service of prayer in the day. Isolde made her confession to the priest and then kneeled in prayer, her face buried in her hands throughout the Mass. When it was over, and the men had said farewell to Father Benito, she was still kneeling. They left her to follow them and walked back to the inn.

Freize greeted them on the threshold of the inn, his face grave. 'We can't take a ship to Split,' he said. 'I found a man who has just come from there. He'll be the first of many. The town is all but destroyed, the country for miles around laden with broken boats and upturned trees, wrecked houses and drowned barns. The place was hit by a greater wave than we were; it is far worse than here. There's no house standing for miles around, and nothing to eat that has not been spoiled with salt water. We can't go to that coast at all.'

Luca shook his head at himself. 'I should have thought of that! What a fool I am! Of course we won't be the only town that had the wave. If the sea moved, then every town on the coast would have been affected.' For a moment they could see him furiously thinking, then he turned to Brother Peter. 'If we knew which town was worst affected then we would know which town was closest to the source of the wave,' he said. 'If Ishraq is right, and it was like a pebble in a bowl, then the wave is deepest nearest to where it starts and gets more and more shallow as it rolls away. If we knew where the wave was greatest we might at least discover where it came from.'

468

'That's true,' Brother Peter said. 'But . . .'

Suddenly, shockingly, the warning bell of the lookout on the harbour wall started to sound, a single jangling bell, an urgent clangour, terrible for the whole village, terrifying for those on the quayside.

'Not again!' Brother Peter exclaimed. 'God save us from another wave.'

'Where's Isolde?' Freize demanded urgently. 'Where did you leave her?'

'At the church,' Luca shouted. 'Get up there, get to higher ground! Where is Ishraq?'

Everyone tumbled out of the inn, the innkeeper and Ishraq among them.

'Why are they ringing the tocsin?' Luca demanded of him. 'Is it another wave?'

'No!' the innkeeper said. 'Look, see they're raising the signal.' He yelled above the pealing bell, so the people clamouring in the yard could hear. 'God bless us, it's not a wave, it's a slave galley. That's the bell for the warning. That's the bell that warns of a slave galley. The guard has raised the signal on the harbour fort. Don't run for high ground. It's not the sea, it's a raid! Take your places! Guardsmen! Take your places in the fort!'

Luca's face grew dark with anger. 'A slave galley? Raiding now? When the people have just lost their children to the sea?'

At once the men of the village started to run to the squat little fort that guarded the harbour, shouting to each other that it was not a wave but the warning bell for a slave galley. The women raced for their homes calling for their children. They could hear doors slamming from all over the village

469

as frightened families bolted themselves inside. Isolde came running down from the church. 'Father Benito says there is a slave galley coming into port!' she said breathlessly. 'He saw it from the tower.'

They crowded into the inn where the innkeeper was lifting a formidable handgun out of a cupboard, with a box of gunpowder. Freize stepped back from the dangerous-looking instrument. 'Won't that be too wet to fire?'

'Couldn't I dry it quickly on the fire?' he asked.

'No!' Freize said hastily. 'No! Much better not.'

Luca turned to the two young women. 'You'd better go to your room and lock yourselves in. We'll go down to the harbour fort and do what we can to stop them landing.'

'The laundry room,' the landlord advised. 'Go with my wife and the little maid Rosa. You can mend laundry while you wait. Nobody will ever find you there.'

When the two girls were about to argue Luca raised his hand. 'You can't come with us. What if they were to take you? Go and lock yourselves in as this good man says.'

Jealously, Isolde saw that he turned to Ishraq, trusting her to cope in this new emergency. 'Take a weapon in with you, in case they come,' he said to her quietly. 'Knives from the kitchen, an axe from the yard. And don't open the door till you know it's safe.'

'Of course,' she said quickly, and led the way upstairs.

'Go,' he said quietly to Isolde. 'I can do nothing, unless I know you are safe.'

'And Ishraq,' she said, testing him. 'You trust her to defend us.'

'Of course,' he said, and was then puzzled when she turned on her heel, without another word to him, and ran upstairs without even wishing him good luck.

Luca, Freize and Brother Peter followed the innkeeper down to the harbour.

'We too should get into safety,' Brother Peter said anxiously. 'We're not equipped to fight.'

'I'd use my bare hands against them,' swore Luca. 'I'd go after them with a hammer, with the broadsword!'

Freize exchanged one fearful look with Brother Peter and hurried after his master.

The innkeeper had paused on the quayside and was shading his eyes, looking out to sea. Men pushed past him, hurrying to the little round fort that guarded the entrance to the harbour, where they were handing out pikes. Half a dozen men were heaving on a wooden capstan. With a great groaning creak it yielded and slowly as it turned it hauled a sunken chain out of the water to stretch across the harbour mouth, and bar the entrance.

'It's not like a raiding ship,' the innkeeper said, puzzled. 'I've never seen them approach so slowly before. And it's coming in under a white flag. Perhaps they were damaged out at sea. It's coming in too slowly and there are no cannon on deck, and there's a white flag at the spur. It's not an attack.'

'Could be a trick,' Luca said suspiciously, squinting to see the distant outline of the ship that was coming slowly, cautiously, closer. 'They would stoop to anything.'

They hurried on to the little fort. An older man was there, shouting orders. 'Is it a raid?' the innkeeper asked him. 'Captain Gascon, is it a raid?'

'I'm ready for one,' was all he grimly replied. 'Tell me what they're doing.'

Luca stepped to the edge of the quay, and got his first clear sight of the ship that had sailed through his nightmares ever since he had learned that his mother and his father had been captured. It was a narrow ship, lying very low in the water with oars stretching out either side, scores of them, in two banks, one above the other, rowing slowly now, but moving absolutely as one. Over the noise of men running to get weapons and taking their places in the tower behind him he could hear the steady beat-beat-beat of the drum keeping the rowers to a slow tempo. A wicked spike extended from the prow as if it would tear the very land itself, a white scarf billowing from the killer blade in a temporary gesture of peace.

The first sail was down, tightly lashed, but he could see at once that the second sail, in the middle of the ship, had been torn down and had brought the mast down with it. They had cut it away, but the ropes were still trailing over the side; and the broken stem of the mast was jagged and raw. At the stern of the ship, on a raised platform, the master of the galley himself held out a broad white sheet in his upraised arm, so that the signal for parley fluttered like a flag at front and back. They came slowly towards the chain, as if they feared nothing, and then, as the rhythm of the drum changed they did an extraordinary manoeuvre, feathering the oars all together, so that the ship moved neither forwards nor back, despite the swift inward current, but stayed, rocking in the churned water of the harbour, waiting before the chain, as if they could dream that any town in Christendom would ever willingly admit them.

'What are they doing?' shouted the captain, frantically loading the only weapon, an old culverin, inside the fort.

'Holding still before the chain,' Luca replied. 'As if they think that we would ever lift it to them.' He felt his heart thudding fast at his first sight of one of the many ships that were such a terror to every port and riverside village in Europe.

Every year the Ottoman slave galleys or the Barbary corsairs took thousands of people into captivity; whole towns had been abandoned because of the raids, villages destroyed. The slaving raids were a curse and blight on every coast in Europe. They raided all the way from Africa to Iceland, creeping up quiet rivers and inlets at night, falling on isolated farmhouses and stealing people away. Now and then they would sail into a town, steal all the treasures and burn all the wooden houses to the ground. Families, like Luca's own, had been torn apart by the brutal kidnaps. For Luca, safe in the monastery, the news that his father and his mother had been enslaved was worse than if he had been told that they had died. For the rest of his life he feared that perhaps his mother was working as a house slave in a Muslim household, perhaps – or far worse – slaving to death in the fields, or brutalised by her owner. His father was probably serving in a galley like this one, chained to the oars and rowing every day all day, never raising up from his seat but sitting in his own dirt with the heat of the sun on his back, trained like an obedient mule to pull and pull when commanded, till his strong heart gave out under the strain and he died still rowing, and they unchained his hands from his oar and threw his wasted body over the side.

'Luca,' Brother Peter said, shaking his shoulder. 'Luca!'

473

Luca realised he had been staring blindly, filled with hatred, at the galley. 'It's just that – for all I know – my father is slaving on one of these,' he said. 'I'm going to get a pike.'

The captain came out from the fort, the ancient culverin in his hand, a slow burning fuse in another. 'Hold this,' he said, thrusting the handgun into Brother Peter's unwilling hands.

'I really can't . . .'

'What do you want?' the captain shouted over the water, cupping his hands around his mouth. 'What do you want? I have cannon trained on your ship.'

'Do you?' asked Freize, surprised.

'No,' the captain said. 'A town like this can't afford a cannon. But I'm hoping he doesn't know that.'

'Anyway, they can sail after they have been holed,' Luca said bitterly. 'You could have a cannon and fire it and hit him and still he would come on. They can stay afloat when they are filled with water. They are all but unsinkable.'

'Can I give this back to you?' Brother Peter asked faintly, proferring the weapon and the smoking fuse. 'Really, I have no skills . . .'

Silently Freize took the weapon from the clerk.

'I need a mast and a new sail,' the shout came back across the water in perfect Italian. 'I will pay a fair price for it.'

The captain looked at Luca. 'You can see they need a mast.'

'Could still be a trick,' Luca said. 'Don't let them in.'

'How did your mast break?' the captain bellowed.

There was a little silence. 'A terrible wave,' came the reply. 'You will have had it here, *Inshallah*. We have seen

474

its path all along this coast. You and I, we are all equally powerless against the greatness of the sea. We are all sailors. We all need help sometimes. Let us in to your harbour to repair our ship. And I will remember that you have been a brother of the sea to me.'

Brother Peter crossed himself at the Muslim blessing.

'Did you see any children in the water? Any children swimming?' shouted Captain Gascon, the commander of the fort.

'Allah – praise be His holy name – help them, yes, we saw them; but we were running before the wind and our sail came down. We could reach only two of them. We pulled them on board and have them safe. You can have them if you will give us a mast and a sail.'

'Show them,' prompted Luca.

'Show them to us,' the captain of the fort shouted.

The master of the ship bent down and spoke to someone in the waist of the ship. He lifted and half pushed two children to stand in the prow. They clung to each other and turned white, frightened faces towards the shore.

The captain exchanged one look with Luca.

'We've got to get the children back,' Luca said.

'Why should we help you?' Captain Gascon shouted. 'You are our enemy.'

The master of the ship made a little gesture with his hands, commanding the slaves to keep feathering the oars, holding the galley just clear of the chain, as the drum beat still thudded. 'Because we are all men who have to face the sea,' he said simply. 'Because we wish to put our enmity aside, since the greater enmity of the sea has been shown to

475

us. If you sell us a mast and a sail we will pay you well for them. And we will return these children for free.'

'Would you agree to never come here in war again?' the captain asked. 'No raids.'

The man shrugged his shoulders. 'You are not to know, but I'm not a slave taker. I am on a journey, not raiding. I don't raid anyway.'

'Can you command that the slaving galleys don't raid our village?'

'I can request it of them.'

'Then swear to me that you will urge the slaving galleys never to come here again.'

'Not for a year,' the man bargained.

'Ten years,' the captain of the fort demanded.

'Two.'

'Five.'

'*Heras*. All right,' he said in agreement. 'Five.'

'And instead of payment for the mast, make him release all the slaves from the galley,' Luca suggested.

The captain hesitated.

'You don't need money,' Luca said. 'We don't need paying for a mast and a sail. This is a great opportunity. Let some of those poor devils get home to their families.'

'Do you have any Christians at the oars?' The captain yelled.

'Of course.'

'Any Italian men?'

A brief shout for help came clearly across the water and then they could hear the sound of a quick blow.

'We may have some,' the man at the stern of the galley said cautiously. 'Why?'

476

'You must release them all to us, and we will give you mast and sails for free.'

'I cannot release them all, or we cannot row home,' he said reasonably.

'You can sail!' Luca shouted, interrupting the negotiations as his anger overcame him. 'You can sail with the mast and sails that we will give you! Those men must be freed.' He found he was shaking with rage and that he had stepped out of the shelter of the fort. 'I'm sorry,' he said to the captain, stepping back. 'I should not have interrupted.'

Luca rejoined Freize. 'I can't bear it,' he said in an undertone. 'My own father might be on that damned ship. That might have been his voice that called out that he was Italian. That might have been him who was struck.'

'God help him,' Freize said quietly. To the captain he said, 'Probably best to make them wait outside the harbour and we bring the mast and sails down the spit, so they don't come inside the chain. Probably safer not to let them in too close to the town. They may carry the plague, as well as being a people who are not well known for their reliability, in the friendship line of things. Not that I wish to be unpleasant.'

'You will row back down there,' the captain shouted, pointing to the seaward side of the fort. 'You can tie alongside at the very end there. You must stay where we can see you and all your men must stay on board the ship. We will bring you the mast and sail and you will release all the Italians you have on board. Agreed?'

There was a low groan from the captives of other kingdoms.

'Listen to them!' Luca said fiercely. 'Hear them!'

477

'I will release ten Italian men,' the master of the galley said. Still the drum sounded, regular as a heartbeat. The sea raised the galley up and down and the master of the ship swayed easily standing on the prow deck, as graceful as a dancer as the rowers kept the ship exactly where he had commanded it to be: still on a moving sea.

'No, all of them,' the captain said steadily. 'You stole these men from us, now you need our help. You must restore all the Italians to us.'

There was a brief silence.

'Or go,' Luca shouted. 'Though the wave is going to rise again, and this time you will not survive it. It will wash you to hell.'

At once they could hear the master of the ship laugh. 'What do you know of the wave?' he demanded.

'We have great scholars here,' the captain of the fort said with dignity. 'This is an Inquirer, from Rome. He understands all about the ways of the sea, of land and of the heavens.'

'Has he read Plato?' the commander of the slave ship taunted. 'Has he read Pliny?'

Hopefully the captain of the fort looked at Luca. He gritted his teeth and shook his head.

'Do they agree to the price for the mast or not?' Freize prompted.

'Do you want our help?' the captain demanded. 'For we have named our price.'

The master of the galley said something quietly to himself. Then aloud, he said, 'I agree.' He gave an order and at once the oars dipped and rowed on only one side of the ship while the other side of rowers held it steady. It was an extraordinary

478

piece of seamanship; Luca acknowledged the masterful control of the galley, even as he stared at them with hatred. The ship turned almost on itself, and glided to where the captain of the fort had directed them. The oars that were beside the quay folded themselves in, like a monstrous skeletal wing, so that the craft could come close to shore, and two men leapt on shore and took up the ropes, prow and stern.

'Go to the sailmaker,' the captain ordered his men inside the fort. 'Get a lateen sail off him. Tell him we'll all settle up later. And you, run to the shipyard and get them to bring a mast down here. As fast as you can. Tell them to hurry. Tell them why. I want those scoundrels back out at sea and away from here as soon as possible.' To Luca and Brother Peter he said, 'Will you come and see that the rowers are freed?'

'I'll come,' Luca said.

'I go with him,' Freize added.

Brother Peter hesitated. 'We are travelling with a young woman who is under our protection,' he said. 'She is not obedient to the orders of the Church nor to our command; but she does know languages. I believe she has read – er – Plato. She may speak their language. It might be useful to have her with us, in case they try to cheat.'

'A Muslim woman?' the captain was scandalised. 'You men of the Church are travelling with a heretic?'

'She's slave to the lady that we are escorting to her godfather's son,' Luca said quickly.

'Oh, a slave,' the captain said. 'That's all right then. Can you fetch her?'

'It brings her into danger,' Luca said quietly to Brother Peter. 'What if they try to take her?'

'She's enslaved already,' the captain said reasonably. 'Why would you care? And your friend is right, she can listen to their talk, and warn us if this is a double-cross.'

'I'll fetch her,' Freize offered, handing the smoking culverin to the captain, and setting off to the inn at a trot, coming back with Ishraq.

She was almost unrecognisable. She had been dressed by the landlady in the clothes of the stable lad. Her long hair was caught up under his floppy hat, and she was wearing his dirty trousers, baggy shirt, and jerkin. The hat was pulled so low over her face that there was no way of seeing that she was a beautiful girl. Only her slim ankles showing above the clumsy heavy shoes betrayed her, to anyone who was looking closely. She stood behind Freize as if she were a frightened youth.

'This?' the captain said, his idea of a beautiful girl in Luca's private harem disappearing quickly.

'This,' Luca said. To Ishraq he said, 'Keep right out of the way and if it goes wrong at all, then run back to the hiding place in the inn. Get yourself to safety and we will follow. Save yourself before anything else. But listen to what they say. You speak Arabic, don't you?'

'Of course,' she said quietly.

'Warn us if they are pretending to agree with us, but planning something among themselves. The moment you hear them plotting something, just touch my sleeve, I'll be watching for a sign from you. They say that they need our help but these are devils. Devils.'

From the shadow of the hat her dark eyes regarded him. 'These are my people,' she said quietly. 'These that you are calling devils.'

'These are nothing to do with you. They are devils,' he said flatly. 'They took my father and my mother from their own safe fields and I don't know where they are now, or even if they are alive.'

She started to put out her hand to him, and then she remembered Isolde's jealous rage and tucked both her hands firmly in the jacket pockets. 'I'm ready,' she said.

Freize stood one side of her and Luca the other. From the sailmaker's loft came four men, carrying a heavy rolled sail on their shoulders. Further down the quayside a dozen men carrying ropes slung under a long mast were walking in slow step towards the fort.

The captain of the fort came forwards to meet them. 'Are you all carrying knives?' he asked. They nodded in silence. 'Keep them hidden until I give the word,' he said. 'If they keep the peace then we will too. If anything goes wrong fall back on the fort.' To Ishraq he said, 'Warn us at once if you suspect anything.'

She nodded. 'I understand.'

He glanced at Luca. 'Are you ready, Inquirer?'

Luca nodded, and they led the way past the fort to where the quayside sloped down to the sea and the galley was held to the harbour wall by two waiting men. One of them was a tall broad man from the coast of Benin, his black face completely impassive, his dark eyes scanning each one of them as they walked towards him. The other was a tall white man, blond-haired and blue-eyed. The master of the galley stood in the stern of his ship, the drummer beside him.

The master was a young man, little more than eighteen, richly dressed in a pair of wide navy brocade pantaloons with beautiful red leather short boots. He had a richly embroidered white linen shirt, the sleeves billowing, and a surcoat over the top, encrusted with precious stones. At his side he wore a belt with a long curved sword and on his head – strangest of all for Luca – was a tight small white turban with a stone and the white floating plume of egrets' feathers at the front. His skin was tanned golden, his eyes dark, squinting now against the bright sky as he looked up at the quay as the Christians arrived, followed by the men carrying the sail and the long mast. He stood like a young man filled with joy in his own strength and confidence, accustomed to command. He was, as even Luca could see at once, dazzlingly handsome.

Luca, the captain of the fort, Freize and Ishraq came to the brink of the quay so that they could look down into the slaving galley; it was a pitiful sight. Every oar had two men chained to it, and there were forty, perhaps fifty oars. That was only the first deck. Below the enslaved rowers was another deck with another set of men chained to their oars, dressed in rags, burned brown as dried nuts from the constant blaze of the sun, sitting in their own filth, dully awaiting the order of the pounding drum. Luca gave a horrified exclamation and stepped back, cupping his palm over his nose and mouth against the stench, trying not to retch.

'Will you help us to fit the mast?' the master asked.

Ishraq listened carefully to his accent, looked from the one man onshore to the other, strained to get a sense of their purpose, to see if there was double-dealing planned here. Unnoticed, she eased her feet out of the ill-fitting shoes. If she was going to have to run or fight, she was not going to stumble.

'First, you will release the Italians,' Luca said, his anger in every clipped word.

'Are you in command here?' the young man asked politely, bowing his head a little. The great ruby in his turban winked in the sunlight. 'Are you the one that he said was an Inquirer? From Rome?'

'I am visiting the town. The commander of the defence is this captain,' Luca explained.

'You are a traveller?'

Luca nodded.

'Appointed by the Pope?'

'I am a papal Inquirer,' Luca said. 'But it is no business of yours. What are you doing here?'

He laughed as if something had amused him. 'Oh, I have been inquiring too – I take an interest in coastal defences.'

Ishraq eased towards Luca. 'He's a very senior commander,' she muttered. 'See the ruby in his turban and the jewels in his coat.'

'Where are you going to?' Luca asked.

'Homeward bound,' he showed them a taunting smile. 'We call it home now. You called it Constantinople, but we call it Istanbul. Do you know why?'

At the new name that the conquering infidels had given to the Christian city of Constantinople, Brother Peter hissed in horror and crossed himself. The commander laughed at the gesture. 'We named it from the Greek.'

Luca, who had not been taught Greek, gritted his teeth on his own ignorance.

'The Greek *istimbolin* means "in the city". We are in the city now and we will never lose it. So we have called it In-the-city.'

'What's your name?' Luca asked.

'Radu Bey,' he replied. 'Yours?'

'Luca Vero.'

'Priest?'

'Novice.'

'Ah, I know who you are,' he said with sudden under-standing. 'You're one of those commanded to make inquiry for the secret order. You will be a servant of the Order of Darkness.'

Luca exchanged a quick shocked glance with Brother Peter. 'What do you know of the Order of Darkness?' he demanded.

'More than you would think. A lot more than you would think. Am I right?'

'I don't discuss it with you.'

'Do you know your commander? Milord, does he call himself? Do you know any other Inquirers?'

Luca kept his face impassive.

'I think not,' the commander said in Arabic, quietly, almost to himself. 'It's just how I would do it.'

'He said "I think not ... it's just how I would do it,"' Ishraq translated in Luca's ear.

'First, the children,' Luca said, as the Piccolo men, sweat-ing, dumped the long heavy mast beside the folded sail.

'Will you take them, whether they want to come with you or no?' Radu asked. 'Will you take them against their will?'

'No, of course not. But why would they choose to go into slavery with you?'

'Because they are not going to be enslaved. They're going to be janissaries. The greatest soldiers in the world.

They might rise through my army, they could become commanders.' He smiled at Luca, inviting him to see the joke. 'When we conquer Italy, they could be the ones riding at the head of the invading army, the triumphant army. Either one of them could rise to be governor, and come back to his home as a lord. He could march into his own village, he could live in the castle in the place of the Christian lord. They may prefer this future to coming back to plough the fields and muck out stables for you.'

Luca ignored him and called directly to the children. 'Do you want to come ashore? I will see that you get back to your homes. You have been saved from the flood by a miracle. Do you want to come home now and go back to your father and mother and serve God?'

'They are brothers,' Radu remarked, watching them. 'And their father beat them every day, and their mother starved them. That's why they ran away in the first place. I don't think they'll want to go back home.'

'I can put you into a monastery,' Luca offered. 'You can live and work in the Church. That's how I was raised, and Freize my friend here. It was all right. We ate well, we were educated.'

'But you didn't learn Greek,' the slave galley commander taunted him.

'That hardly matters,' Luca said, irritated.

Clearly the boys did not know what to do.

'My brother and I were both taken by the Ottomans,' Radu remarked to the boys. 'We might be an example to you. We chose different routes. He went home to the Christians and is now a great commander; one of the greatest, a man of high ambition, advisor to the Pope himself. You could take his path and rise as well as he did. You could go with these men; I am sure they would put you in a safe place.

'But consider me! I stayed in the Empire and I am as great a commander as my brother. I eat better than him, I am certain that I am better dressed, and I am on the winning side. The Ottoman Empire is over-running the world, our frontiers expand every year. We award merit not accident of birth. If you are clever and hard-working you will rise. Now you two can choose. By luck – by the breaking of a mast and the loss of a sail you are free to choose. Not many boys get such a choice. It is a moment of destiny – fate – funny that it should come to two such little boys as you.'

'We'll go with you,' the eldest boy said. He looked up at the handsome face. 'You promise that we can stay together and that we will not be made slaves?'

'You will live with a family of Turks in the country, and they will feed you and educate you. You will have to work hard but you will be trained as soldiers. You will be forbidden to marry or take up any trade but soldiering. When you are big and strong enough, you will join the army and serve the Sultan Mehmet II, as I do. His command runs from Wallachia to Armenia and there's no doubt that you will march into Christendom, to the very gates of Vienna and beyond, to Paris, to Rome, to Madrid, to London. Every year we advance. Every year the Christians are defeated and fall back before us. You will be on the winning side under my command. The Christians say themselves that the end of days is coming for them. They predict that the world will end: we know that it will be us who ends it for them.'

486

'We will never be defeated,' Luca said fiercely. 'You lie to the boys. We will never be defeated and you will never ride into Vienna, for we are under the hand of God.'

'*Inshallah*, we are all under the hand of God,' the Muslim said quietly. 'But clearly, even you must see, that us both believing this makes no difference to who wins the battles. At the moment, as you must see, we are winning.'

'We will never renounce our faith!'

'We don't ask you to. You can believe what you like. You can even pray as you like. But we will rule all of Christendom.'

'Come home!' Luca exclaimed, holding out both hands to the boys as if he would have them jump on shore.

The eldest boy shook his head. 'Thank you very much,' he said with careful politeness, 'but this man saved us from the flood and will teach us to be soldiers like him. We'll stay with him.'

'Don't you want to see your home again? Your mother and your father?'

'Not at all,' the boy said clearly. 'They treated us worse than their hounds. We will make a new home.'

Luca stepped back, looked at Brother Peter. 'I have no words,' he said wretchedly. 'I have failed these children twice over. Once when I could not foresee the wave, and now I cannot stop them selling their souls to the Devil.'

Radu smiled. 'Cheer up, Inquirer! The galley slaves won't choose to stay with me. They are all yours, poor wretches. Now, I'll have to unchain them. I will have to take my men and go down among them.'

The commander of the fort, Captain Gascon, glanced at Luca, who was still silent, looking at the children. 'You can go down slowly and unchain them,' Gascon ordered, tightening his grip on the gun. 'No tricks.'

Radu Bey nodded to the man with the drum who unsheathed a massive blade, and stepped down behind him, on guard. He barked an order in Arabic. Luca glanced at Ishraq who nodded and whispered, 'He said: "Who is Italian?"'

Several men raised their heads and called out: '*Eccomi!*'

One man responded a little after the others.

'*Dove sei nato, pretendente?*' snapped Radu Bey.

The rower stumbled to understand the simple Italian sentence. '*Napoli,*' he stammered, naming an Italian town, but speaking unconvincingly late with a Spanish accent.

'I don't think so,' Radu Bey said simply, and the man dropped his head to his oar and gave himself up to despair.

'We have to release them all,' Luca exclaimed, watching this doomed exchange. 'All the slaves. We have to attack the galley and get them free.'

'We can't,' the captain of the fort shook his head. 'There are too many of them.' He nodded to the ship; seated among the slaves were free men, the janissaries of the Ottoman army, ready to row or fight as the captain ordered. All down the centre of the ship were their comrades, armed with great scimitars and cutlasses, handguns stuck casually in their belts. 'They'll have cannon mounted in the prow,' he said. 'Rolled back out of sight for now, but it will be armed and ready to fire. They've lost a mast but they can still take this ship out to sea at fighting speed. I'll be happy if he just keeps to his word and we get the Italians off without trouble.'

'My father may be enslaved on one of these hellholes!' Luca said, anguished.

'Let's do what we can here today,' Freize advised quietly. 'See if we can get some men freed, then think about the rest.'

Radu Bey had been moving steadily and quietly among the ranks of the oarsmen, turning one key and then another. The freed men rose carefully to their feet, wary of the armed men around them, and put their hands on their heads, turning around as they were bid and walking through their fellows without looking to either left or right. Seven men from the upper deck went unsteadily up a narrow gangplank to the quayside, and then three came up from the lower. As they touched the stone of the quayside some of them fell to their knees to thank God. One man's legs buckled from being seated at his oar for so long that he sank to the ground, and he could not rise up again.

'Get them away,' the captain of the fort said to the men who had brought the sail. 'Poor devils! Take them to the hovel where they put the lepers, and get them washed and fed and kept there.'

'That's my side of the bargain,' Radu Bey said, indifferent both to the men crying with relief on the quay and those groaning in the galley. 'Will you help fit the mast?'

'We won't set foot on your ship,' Gascon replied. 'We'll leave the sail and the mast here and you can fit it yourself. If you're not gone by sunset I will turn the cannon on you, as you wait here.'

'We'll be gone,' Radu assured him. 'And we won't come back, as I promised. Will you sell us some food?'

'I'll send some down to you, and fresh water. Give water to these poor devils.'

'I should like to go onto the ship,' Brother Peter suddenly

said, surprising everyone. 'I should like to go among the rowers with the priest and hear confessions of the men, and bless them.'

Radu laughed abruptly. 'What for? Do you think you will raise them from the dead? For these men think they are dead and gone to hell. Don't come down, priest. We'll eat you instead of bread.'

Brother Peter hesitated. 'I should bless them,' he insisted.

The commander of the galley did not even bother to reply. The fair man who was holding the rope on the shore laughed. 'Half of them are converted to the Muslim faith anyway,' he volunteered, speaking Italian with a strong English accent.

'Are you English?' Luca exclaimed.

'Captain Marcus, English privateer, advising General Radu Bey.'

'Are you enslaved?'

'Oh no. I am paid. I am going to command my own galley next year. I am a free man, a commander, serving the Empire. I'm a volunteer, a mercenary.'

'How can you do this to your fellow Christians?' Brother Peter demanded, trembling.

'It's a hard world,' the man said cheerfully. 'I used to ship slaves from Ireland for the French. Then I was on an English privateer preying on the Spanish. I don't mind the nationality, I do mind being on the winning side. Right now, I am on the winning side. The Ottoman Empire is unstoppable, take my word for it.'

'I shall send my men on shore for the mast,' Radu interrupted, snapping his fingers to half a dozen men who came forwards and waited for their orders. 'Can I come onshore to dine?' Radu spoke directly to Luca. 'Will you ask me to dinner?'

'You are the enemy of my country, and my church, and my family,' Luca replied.

'So think of me as on parole,' Radu Bey suggested. 'Why not bring some food and set a table here, and we can dine and talk while they are repairing the ship.'

'You'll have to disarm,' Luca said, looking at the wicked curved sword.

'Of course. And you have to swear not to kidnap me. We have to dine as friends and then part as enemies.'

Luca hesitated.

'I know Plato,' Radu Bey said temptingly. 'Pliny too. I have a manuscript with me that I take everywhere I go. It talks about this coast, it tells of a wave. The ancients knew about this. It's in Arabic, but I'll read it to you over dinner.'

'It tells of a wave?' Luca repeated.

'And it has a map.'

'I'll get the table set,' Luca ruled, tempted beyond bearing at the thought of the ancient learning.

'Take care,' Gascon whispered to him.

'If they know how to tell that a wave is coming, we have to learn the secret.'

~

While the servants came out from the inn under Freize's watchful supervision, and set up the trestles and board midway along the quayside, Ishraq went back and released Isolde from the hidden laundry room and told her that Luca was dining with an infidel.

'How could he?' Isolde demanded. She peered out of the

doorway of the inn to where Luca was standing at the end of the quay, watching Radu strip himself of a small arsenal of weapons and lay them down on the cobblestones.

Ishraq hesitated. She could not describe the power and charm of Radu, glittering in his beautiful clothes on the boat that could move so swiftly and powerfully in the water, hold still like a bird of prey, hanging in the water like a peregrine falcon hangs in the air, or fold its oars like wings to come close to the harbour wall, docile as a collar dove.

'Luca wants to talk to him,' she said. 'He wants to know all about Arab learning.'

'He's walking very close to sin,' Brother Peter said, coming upon the girls. 'And danger.'

They watched Radu unsheath the curved blade of his sword, and from his belt produce two daggers. From a pocket inside his surcoat came the assassin's weapon, a stiletto, and from a holster tied inside his pantaloons a beautiful miniature handgun. He laid it all on the cobbles at Luca's feet with an air of quiet pride at the armoury he carried.

'Will you dine with him?' Isolde asked Peter.

'Not I! My conscience would not allow it.'

'Freize will serve,' Ishraq reassured her. 'And he is carrying a knife, and he will be watching all the time.'

'Why would Luca not just send him away?' Isolde fretted. 'An infidel! A slaver!'

'Because Radu said he had a manuscript,' Ishraq answered. 'He taunted Luca that he had not read the philosophers. Luca wants to know what caused the wave. Radu says that he knows.'

'He's prepared to risk his life for this knowledge?' Isolde asked incredulously.

'Oh yes,' Ishraq said as if she too thought that knowledge was worth almost any risk.

Freize came quickly down the quayside and saw them at the door, peering out. 'I was looking for you,' he said to Brother Peter. 'The little lord wants you to come and write down all that the infidel lord says. He wants a note of the manuscripts.'

Brother Peter hesitated. 'I won't break bread with such a man.'

'Nobody is asking you to dine,' Freize said, irritably. 'He is asking you to be his clerk. To write things down. And since you came with us to be a clerk, since we were forced to travel with you and have you every step of the way because they told him he had to have a clerk, it seems only reasonable that you should be a clerk now. On account of the fact that I can serve dinner and save him from being beheaded by the foreign lord or poisoned by the foreign lord or dragged into that damn boat by the foreign lord; but I can't write, so I can't write down the endless lies that the foreign lord says. But you can. And so you should. And so you will.'

Brother Peter stared stubbornly into Freize's angry face. 'I shall not. I will not be dictated to by an infidel.'

'You're a clerk!' Freize bellowed. 'You are supposed to be dictated to.'

'I will not sit at his table.'

'Do it standing!'

'I'll go,' Ishraq volunteered. 'I can do it.'

She dived into the inn and came out with paper, a quill pen and an ink pot.

'You can't go,' Isolde said at once.

'I have to.'

493

'It's dangerous.'

'Luca needs me.'

'And what do I do?' demanded Isolde, irritated beyond bearing. 'What am I supposed to do, while you are there with Luca? Suddenly, you are the only one that can be of any use? When is he going to need me?'

'Go to your bedroom window and keep watch for us,' Freize advised. 'Watch the sea in case another galley happens to come along. And if you see anything, scream like a banshee. I don't trust them any more than you do.'

He turned to Brother Peter. 'Does your precious conscience allow you to keep watch for us? While we are half a step from danger and you are yards away, down the quayside?'

'Yes, of course.'

'Then you stand half way between the inn and the fort, and if you hear her scream, raise the alarm and turn the men out of the fort to help us.'

Isolde hesitated, longing to be at the table with Ishraq.

'Go on,' Freize said. 'Ishraq has to come because she speaks the language and she can write. But he'd want to keep you out of the way.'

'Oh, I know she is quite indispensable,' Isolde turned abruptly, without a word to Ishraq, and went up the stairs.

~

Freize and Ishraq followed the servants carrying baskets of bread and bottles of oil and wine and water. Luca glanced around and saw them coming, then turned his attention to the galley.

Radu, now completely unarmed, brought a box covered in

oiled pony skin from his ship. He held it before him so that Luca could see there was no trick, and walked towards the table that the servants were setting up. 'Two manuscripts,' he said quietly. 'Only two. I chose to bring these with me because they are about this coast. I have been sailing along it and comparing what I see to what they saw more than a thousand years ago. These are copies of ancient writings held in our libraries. We have the greatest libraries in the world, and translators and philosophers working all day, every day.'

Luca had a sudden pang of envy that he had no teacher and no books to guide him in boyhood and that the greatest library he had ever seen had been at his monastery where they had three manuscripts and a Bible chained to a desk. But first he had to ask Radu something else.

'I want to find a man and a woman. I believe they were taken on a slaving raid.'

Radu started to unwrap the waterproof cover. 'Really? Taken recently?'

Luca gulped. 'Years ago, four years ago. My parents.'

'Do you know what ship was raiding? The name of the commander?'

'I don't even know if he took them or killed them.'

'It's hard to trace people after a long time,' Radu said indifferently. 'But sometimes it can be done. There are thousands of slaves taken every year, but it can be done. You will want to ransom them, I suppose? You need to speak with Father Pietro, in Venice. He buys slaves from us when their families raise the money; he's accustomed to finding people. Every year he buys a few thousand unnamed slaves with money given from your church and returns them to their homes.'

495

'He does?' Luca blinked. 'I've never even heard of him.'

'Of course. Someone has to trade between us. We are two mighty trading empires, and there are all sorts of people coming and going all the time. There are many middle agents, but he's the best that I know. You are always kidnapping our people and we yours. He deals in the sales of holy relics too. We can't make them fast enough for you. You have an unending appetite for human bones, it seems.' He laughed. 'We could almost think you gnaw on them like dogs. Fortunately, we have an unending supply from our endless victories. What name is it?'

'Vero,' Luca said ignoring the insult to holy relics. 'My mother and father. Where would I find Father Pietro?'

Radu smiled. 'On the Rialto of course. Slaves are a trade like any other. I should think you can buy anything there.' He shouted towards his boat. 'Anyone heard of a man named Vero?'

'Gwilliam Vero,' Luca prompted.

'Gwilliam Vero. Taken about four years ago. Rowers, you can speak!'

One head went up. 'On Bayeed's ship,' he said. 'Two years ago.'

'There you are,' Radu said indifferently. 'Father Pietro may be able to trace him for you, if he's not dead already.'

'Who is Bayeed?' Luca asked urgently. 'Where is his ship?'

Radu shrugged. 'I don't know Bayeed. He'll be a slave raider, and where his ship is right now, no one knows – could be anywhere, working the Italian coast, perhaps Spain, or France. They raid and then take their stock back home for sale. You'll have to ask Father Pietro.'

'Is the man sure? The slave who knows my father. Can I ask him?'

'He's sure. No one speaks to me unless they are sure. You can't ask him.'

Luca exclaimed with frustration but Radu Bey was untroubled. He pulled out a chair from the table and sat himself down, looking around him as if he was pleased with this unexpected dinner on land.

The soldiers were coming off the galley now, one by one up the gangplank to take the measurement of the rough-cut mast. They brought with them woodworking tools. They would pare down the mast to fit it exactly to the place on the deck. Below them on the ship, other men were cutting away the broken spars and throwing them into the water.

'Alive,' Luca said. He was shaking with emotion. 'My father is alive.'

Radu looked at him without sympathy. 'I suppose it's hard to lose a parent if you love him,' he said indifferently. 'My father gave me and my brother as hostages, to Sultan Murad. I never saw him nor my mother again. I've never been home. My father traded me and my brother for his throne. I don't forgive him for that. I might have done the same in his position; but I'll never forgive him for giving the two of us away. His own sons.'

'I've spent years praying that my parents were still alive and that I might see them again.'

'Yes, I suppose you will have done,' Radu said without concern.

'My father!' Luca was choked with emotion. He shaded his eyes with his hand. 'Excuse me, I had thought that I would never see him again. You have given me hope.'

The servants from the inn put food on the table, some meats, some bread, cheeses, smoked fish, fresh stewed fish, a bottle of wine. Radu held out his hands and one of the servants poured water into his palms for him to wash, and gave him a towel of linen to dry them. He served himself liberally and then passed his plate to Luca. 'Forgive me. I will eat with a better appetite, if you would taste everything they have brought for me. I don't wish to be an impolite guest but equally, I want to survive this dinner.'

'Very well,' Luca said.

Radu waited patiently while Luca took a spoonful of everything.

'The wine, if you will forgive my suspicious nature,' Radu gestured to the bottle. Ishraq stepped forward and poured a small amount into a glass and handed it to Luca.

He took a sip. 'Don't you refuse wine? I thought you could not drink alcohol?'

'Not when I am at sea, or on campaign.' Radu watched Luca for signs of poison, but all he could see was a young man struggling to take in extraordinary news.

'If I could get him back, if I could find her, then I would be an orphan no longer.'

'Stranger things have happened,' Radu said cheerfully, and seeing that Luca showed no signs of illness, he started to eat with relish, watching the work on his ship and now and then glancing back at the quayside to see that he was safe from a landside attack. Ishraq stood behind Freize and watched the Ottoman with a steady, unwavering gaze.

'I am sorry. You have quite unmanned me,' Luca said

recovering himself. 'I can hardly believe that my father lives. My father, that I thought was lost to me, still lives. Praise be to God.'

Radu, chewing on a chicken leg, nodded. 'You understand that life on the galleys is hard? Few men live beyond a few years. He might have died since this man saw him, he might be dead now, might die before you get him ransomed.'

Luca nodded. 'But I have been without hope, and you have given me hope.'

Radu laughed shortly at the thought of being the bearer of good tidings to a sentimental Christian, and reached for some stewed fish. 'I am glad to be – what do you call it? – a herald angel. And your mother?'

'Will I be able to find her?'

'Perhaps more easily than him. If she is working for a master he will know her name, he might even have taken pity on her and offered her to be ransomed back. Unless she is in a harem and her master has taken a fancy to her. Was she pretty? Fertile? You might have half a dozen brown-skinned brothers and sisters.'

Luca's fists clenched on the table. 'She is my mother,' he said warningly. 'I won't hear a word . . .'

Behind him Freize tensed, readying himself for a fight but Ishraq stepped swiftly forwards, her hat pulled low over her eyes. 'More wine, Sires?' she lifted the bottle and deliberately clunked it against the back of Luca's head in passing. 'Sorry, Sir.'

'Clumsy fool,' Luca gasped, recovering himself. He took a breath and turned to Radu. 'We won't speak of my parents. You will not speak of my mother. Now, to business.

The manuscript. You don't object that my clerk's lad makes a note of what we say?'

Radu shook his head. 'Not at all.' He looked at Ishraq who pulled out a stool to sit down, and dipped the quill in the ink. For a moment their eyes met: dark into dark. 'Interesting boy,' he said. 'An Arab?' He said a few rapid words in Arabic. Ishraq did not allow herself even a flicker of response, though he had said to her, 'Are you an Arab boy? Do you want me to free you?'

'Half-caste,' Luca said indifferently. 'The child of a slave.'

'Does he understand Latin?'

'No,' Luca said. 'Only enough to write what I say, that's all he's good for.'

'You should teach him,' Radu advised. 'It's amazing what a bright boy can learn.'

'Were you a bright boy?'

Radu smiled. 'My brother and I were more than bright, we were brilliant boys. Our father gave us to the Sultan as hostages for his alliance and though he did not intend it, he sent us to perhaps the only court in the world where we would be educated by the best in the world. We were raised with Sultan Murad's son Mehmet, we were taught with him – five languages, mathematics, geography, philosophy – in short: the meaning of the world and how to describe it.'

'And now?'

The smallest shadow crossed Radu Bey's face – Ishraq saw it, but nobody else did. 'My brother went home. He inherited my father's throne and agreed to hold our home-lands for the Ottoman Empire, but he was faithless and turned against us. He's overthrown now – in exile, but he'll be gathering an army I don't doubt, and hoping to recapture his little kingdom again. He is dead to me. I doubt I'll ever see him again. He chose the wrong side. He is my enemy. Our fates have led us in opposite directions: he is a great Christian commander, and I am one of the greatest commanders that my friend the Sultan Mehmet can put in the field.'

'And you carry manuscripts with you everywhere that you go? You study?'

'I read, all the time, and then I read some more. This is the way to understanding. I believe that one day we will understand everything.' He smiled. 'Shall I read what Plato says about earthquakes? It's translated from the Greek into Arabic. I'll translate it as I read for you, as best I can.'

Carefully, he unwrapped the manuscripts that were written in beautiful Arabic letters on scrolls of vellum. Meticulously he spread them out, and with a glance at Ishraq, started to read. 'Now, this is the bit you will find interesting: Here ... he talks about a great island in the Atlantic, a huge country, bigger than Libya and Asia put together ... and he says, hmm ... "*There occurred violent earthquakes and floods; and in a single day and night of misfortune all your warlike men in a body sank into the earth, and the island of Atlantis in like manner disappeared in the depths of the sea. For which reason the sea in those parts is impassable and impenetrable, because there is a shoal of mud in the way; and this was caused by the subsidence of the island.*"'

'Earthquake and the land sinking?' Luca confirmed. 'An army of men sinking down into the earth? A great island sinking down into the sea and then nothing but a shoal of mud where it had been?'

'It sounds as if there was an earthquake so great that it swallowed up an army. An earthquake which caused the sea to drown a huge country.' Radu read on. 'Plato is telling of this because Socrates has been talking about an account of a city with earthquakes and floods.' Radu's smooth voice paused. 'That's about it.'

'Earthquakes and floods? As if they come together?'

Radu nodded. 'Also, one of our own Arabic thinkers suggests that the earthquake moves the land under the sea. If you can imagine it, the land beneath the sea rises up, and the water is forced to flow away from it.'

Luca made sure he did not look at Ishraq, who kept her head bowed over the paper, rapidly writing.

'What else does he write about, Plato? What else does he say?' Luca was transfixed.

'He writes about everything, really.' Radu saw Luca's entranced face. 'Ah, you must get hold of a manuscript and have a Greek translate it for you.'

'I could learn Greek,' Luca said eagerly. 'If I were to have a manuscript in Greek I could understand it. I can learn languages quickly.'

'Can you?' Radu Bey smiled. 'Then you should come to our library in Istanbul. There is so much there, I can't begin to tell you. Plato, for instance, talks about all of the real world that can be observed. He is very interesting about things that he has seen and heard about.'

'Like what?'

'He talks about the real world that sits behind the things that you cannot observe. That there is another reality we do not touch. A world that we can't eat like food, a world that doesn't trip us up, like rocks. There is a reality which is more real, that sits behind all this.'

'So how would we ever see it?'

'That's the very thing. This is the unseen world behind the real one. We wouldn't see it, we would only know it. We would understand it with our minds, not with grabbing hold of it and looking at it.'

'The things that we can see and taste are of no help to understanding?'

'They are shadows on the wall. Like a child making shapes in candlelight. The real thing is the candle, not the shadow. But all the child observes is the shadow.'

Luca looked at Radu as if he would lay hold of him and shake information out of him. 'I want to understand!'

Radu wiped his mouth and then started to roll up the manuscript again. 'Come to Istanbul,' he offered. 'Come with me now. There are students there who can speak in your language; they will take you into the library. You can read the documents we have, you can study. Are you a mathematician?'

'No!' broke from Luca in frustration. 'Not as you would mean!'

Radu smiled. 'Plato studied with his tutor Socrates, and in turn he taught Aristotle. You are not a mathematician yet because you have to try to understand things alone. This is not a single thing that you can learn. It is about a body of knowledge – one man builds on another man's learning. You need to understand those who have gone before you – only then can you ask questions and learn yourself.'

Luca rose to his feet, his hands shook a little and he

tucked them into his robe so that the sharp-eyed Ottoman soldier could not see that he was deeply tempted at the thought of a library of mathematical manuscripts. 'This has been an interesting meeting for me; but I have to remember that you are the enemy of my faith, of my country, and of my family.'

'It is so. But you could change your faith, and your country, and your family is anyway lost to you.'

'I could not change my faith,' Luca said shortly.

'Perhaps all faiths are shadows on the wall,' Radu Bey said, crinkling his dark eyes as he looked up at Luca. 'Perhaps there is a God like a burning torch, but all we can see is the shadows that we cast ourselves when we walk in front of the flame. Then we see great leaping shadows and think that this is God, but really it is only our own image.'

Luca's eyes widened slightly. 'I will pray for your soul,' he said. 'For that is terrible heresy.'

'As you like,' Radu Bey said with his handsome lazy smile. 'Did you write it all down, boy?'

Ishraq kept her head down. 'I did, milord.'

'Heresy and all?'

Ishraq stopped herself from looking up and smiling into his warm dark face. 'Yes, sir.'

'Well, leave your papers here and carry these to the ship for me,' he said carelessly. He passed her the wrapped box of manuscripts and to Luca he extended his hand. They gripped each other, hand to elbow, and felt the power in each other's arms.

'You are too good to chase around a failing country asking ignorant people what is going wrong in their poor lives,' Radu said quietly to Luca. 'You are too intelligent to be employed studying the night-terrors of old ladies. I know your commander – he has pledged his life to the wrong side and he will find the price is too high. He will sell his soul, thinking that he is doing the work of God, but he will find the world changes and he is left far behind. Come on board with me now and we will sail for Istanbul, for the libraries and for the study you can do.'

Luca released him. 'I keep faith,' he said, a little breathlessly. 'Whatever the temptation.'

'Oh, as you wish,' Radu Bey said gently, then turned and walked towards the ship.

Ishraq shot a quick glance at Luca, and at his nod, followed Radu Bey down the quayside carrying the box of manuscripts. Quietly, over his shoulder, the Ottoman threw a sentence to her in Arabic, 'If you are a slave I will free you. Come down to the quayside at sunset and jump into the ship and we will take you away. If you are a girl, as I think, you will be safe. I give you my word. If you are a scholar, no – I know you are a scholar, girl or boy – you should come with me to Istanbul where you can study.'

Carefully, she said nothing.

'Your master is a fool to choose ignorance over learning,' he said. 'He chooses to stay with the side which is losing. He chooses to stay with a God who can foresee only the end of days. Will you remember me, when you see me again?'

Startled, she blurted out in Arabic: 'Yes!'

He turned and smiled at her, his heart-stopping good looks quite dazzling in the midday sunshine. 'Remember me well,' he said. 'And when you see a man who reminds you of me – and I think you will see a man that you would take for my very twin brother – then remember that you are in the most terrible danger, and that you should come to me.'

'I cannot come to you,' she said, recovering herself and speaking in Italian. 'Ever. Never.'

He spread his hands and made her a little smiling bow. 'I think there will come a day when you pray to come to me,' he said, and took the parcel from her hands and stepped down to the prow of his galley. 'Sister mine, these Christians are not half as kindly as they seem. I know this for I was born and bred by them, and abandoned by them, just as you have been.'

'I'm not abandoned,' she said, suddenly urgent that he should hear her. 'Nobody abandoned me.'

'They must have done,' he said. 'Your father must have abandoned you, or your mother. For here you are, with skin like honey and eyes like dates and yet you are in service to a *Franj,* and you don't acknowledge your people, nor come home with us when we invite you.'

'I'm with my people,' she said stubbornly.

'No, you're not, they're *Franj* – foreign to us.'

There was a little silence.

'You are skilled,' he said. 'You've been well-taught; you walk like a fighter and you write like a scholar.'

She said nothing.

'You are working for people who think that you are going to hell,' he pointed out.

She handed the box to him and stepped off the raised deck to the quay.

'When the day comes that you see a man who looks like me, you should turn your back on him and come to me,' he repeated his warning. 'Otherwise you will see terrible

things, you will do terrible things, you will look into the
abyss itself. You will start to believe that you are in the hell
that these Christians have invented.'

She pulled her cap over her eyes, she turned her collar
up, as if against rain, and she turned and walked away from
him – though she would rather have been walking to him.

~

The village watched the Ottoman galley all day through
the shuttered windows of the quayside houses, and from
the arrow-slits of the fort, as the men planed the mast
to fit, set it in the boat, rigged the stays and the sail, and
then, finally, as they had promised, cast off at sunset and
started to row out past the little fort and the dripping
obstacle of the chain.

'Stop that ship!' The shout echoed in the narrow streets
over the clatter of hooves as a horse and rider scrabbled
down the cobbled steps towards the port. Luca whirled
around, on guard against fresh danger.

'Stop that ship! In the name of the Holy Father, stop it!'

After one moment of hesitation, Luca ran to the fort,
waving his arms. 'Stop the ship! Someone is coming!'

The horse burst from the shadow of the buildings, the
rider bent low over his neck as the sparks flew from the
horse's hooves skidding on the stone cobbles. He flung himself to the ground and shouted, 'I command you to stop it!'

The men spilled out from the fort, demanding to know
what the matter was now.

The stranger threw himself at Luca. 'Stop it! That ship is
commanded by the greatest enemy to Christendom!'

'How could we stop it?' Captain Gascon demanded

irritably. 'It's under sail and they are rowing? We have no way to stop it.'

The stranger stamped his feet in his rage. 'That ship is commanded by a devil!'

'The ship is gone,' Luca exclaimed. 'And, anyway they have no cannon here. We can't bombard it. And it was under a flag of truce. Why d'you want it held? What is your authority?'

Then he saw the dark blue robe, the piercing black eyes inside the shadow of the hood, and realised they were terribly familiar. Brother Peter, beside him, dropped to one knee. 'Milord,' he said simply.

Luca hesitated. 'Is it really you, my lord?'

The man looked past them both to the slave galley as the wind filled the sails and the rowers lifted their oars, and then shipped them. As if he were mocking them, the tall figure standing at the raised stern of the ship released a standard in gorgeous irridescent blues and greens with great golden eyes, a long ribbon of precious cloth of gold meticulously embroidered to look as if it were overlaid with peacock tails, the symbol of nobility in the Ottoman empire, the standard of a great man of a conquering country.

'Was that Radu cel Frumos?' the lord demanded. 'Answer me! Damn you! Was that Radu cel Frumos?'

'He called himself Radu Bey,' Luca said carefully. A quick glance at Brother Peter, who was still on one knee, his hand on his heart, assured him that the furious hooded man, glaring after the vanishing ship, was the lord who had recruited him to the Order of Darkness. Luca knelt beside Peter and put his hand on his heart.

'Greetings, lord.'

'Get up,' he spat, not even looking down at them.

'I'm sorry that we didn't know you wanted him detained,' Brother Peter said quietly. 'He was here with his ship after an accident with the mast. If we had known … But they were heavily armed, and we had no cannon or anything more than the local guard.'

'You will know in future. If ever you meet him,' Milord snatched his breath, and fought for patience. 'If you ever meet him again, you are to entrap him if you can and send for me. If you cannot capture him then kill him outright. He is my greatest enemy. I will never forgive him for opposing me – at every turn he is my antithesis. He is second in command to Sultan Mehmet II. He breached the walls at Constantinople. He is head of their army. He is the worst enemy of Christendom that I can name. There is no one I would rather see captured than him. There is no one I would rather see dead at my feet. He is an agent of Satan. He alone is a sign of the end of days.'

Luca and Brother Peter exchanged one uncomfortable glance and rose to stand before him.

Out at sea the gorgeous flag dipped in ironic salute and was taken in. The three men watched the ship grow smaller and smaller as it went swiftly away on the darkening sea, and then the early evening twilight enveloped it.

'So, he is gone laughing at us,' the lord said. 'He treats us like land-bound fools shouting after a ship sailing away. But you will remember this. And next time – for there will be a next time – you will not let him treat you so.'

'Never,' Brother Peter assured him.

The lord took a moment to recover his temper. 'I have read your report on the children's crusade, and on the great wave,' he said to Luca. 'My path crossed with your messenger as I was riding here to see the crusade for myself. You can tell me more after dinner.'

'It's a poor inn,' Luca warned him. 'They are still repairing and drying out.'

'No matter. Were you on your way to Split?'

Luca shook his head. 'No, Milord. That side of the sea was even worse hit by the great wave than this has been. It's destroyed. We can't go that way; there are people fleeing from there to come here, poor as it is. We were going to write to you for new orders.'

The lord paused, thinking. 'You can go overland, north towards Venice. There's something I want you to look at there.'

He passed the reins of his horse to Freize without another word and turned and went into the inn.

'Venice is it now?' Freize asked the horse dourly. 'Rides in here like one of the horsemen of the apocalypse and the other three are coming along behind in their own time, and tells us we're going to Venice. Well and good. Well and good, and you and I are nothing but dumb animals as you know, and I should remember.' He stroked the animal's neck and the big head turned to gently sniff at him. 'So do you know what he's planning?' Freize asked conspiratorially.

He waited as if he really thought that the horse might speak to him. 'Confidential?' he said. 'That's understandable, I suppose. But never tell me that he doesn't confide in you?' When the horse was silent, Freize patted its side and undid the tight girth. 'Ah well. A man who keeps a secret from his horse is a secretive man, indeed.'

In the inn, Ishraq and Isolde, who had been watching from the taproom window as the ship set sail, melted away up to their room as the strange lord called for the innkeeper. He ordered a glass of wine and a fire lit in the dining room, commanded the best bedroom available for himself, refused completely to share with other travellers, agreed a price for his exclusive use, and then, finally, sat down in the great chair and pulled off his riding boots and said that he would dine alone, but that Luca and Brother Peter should come to him after dinner.

'Who is he?' Isolde took Brother Peter by the arm as he bowed his way out of the dining room, and closed the door on the stranger with an air of relief.

'He is the lord commander of our Order.'

'What's his name?'

'I cannot tell you that.'

'What is his authority, then?'

Brother Peter looked almost afraid. 'He is high in the counsels of the Holy Father,' he said. 'He is trusted with discovering the end of days. The Order walks on the frontier of this world and the next, patrolling the frontier of the Christian and the infidel worlds. There is no man in greater danger. There is no man more fearless.'

'Is he wealthy?'

'Of course.'

'How many men does he command?'

'Nobody but him knows. And only he knows.'

'How long have you worked for him?'

Brother Peter thought. 'Many years,' he said.

'What is the name of the Order?'

'Some people call it the Order of Darkness,' he said cautiously.

'Is that the name he calls it?'

He smiled. 'I don't know what he calls it.'

'So it has another name?'

'Probably many.'

'Is Luca sworn to it?' she asked. 'Sworn as a celibate soldier, or Inquirer, or whatever it is?'

'Not yet,' he paused. 'You have to serve, you have to prove your worth, and then you are sworn to it,' he said. Unaware of what he was doing, he touched his hand to his upper arm.

'They mark you?' she guessed acutely.

His hesitation told her that she was right.

'Show me,' she said instantly.

He hesitated.

'Why would you not show me? Are you ashamed of your loyalty?'

'Of course not!' he said, stung. Carefully, he rolled up his sleeve and on his upper arm, inscribed into his flesh in a tattoo, he showed her the sign of the Order.

She was silent as she looked at it, the dragon eating its tail, the symbol of eternity and the suggestion of circularity – a fear that feeds on itself. 'Is Luca marked like this? Has the lord had him scarred too?'

'No. Not yet.'

'Will he have to swear himself to the Order and then be marked?' she asked, knowing the ways that men bind themselves to each other.

His silence told her that she had guessed correctly.

'Brother Peter. I am asking you this in very truth, not as an inquisitive girl; but as a soul in waiting for the Holy Kingdom. Luca is one of the special children of God: do you not think that he should be free in the world? Don't you think that he should be free to travel and study and call no man master? Don't you think that he is a special young man with a purity of vision and a wisdom that should not be bound to any other man? Don't you think that he is gifted and that he should be free?'

He shook his head. 'You might think that. You might think that he should be free to study and learn, hone his skills, but these are not ordinary times. If these were ordinary times I might agree with you but these are the end of days. The Order may save us from the end of days or it may guide us through to whatever happens beyond the end. The Order needs men like Luca. He understands things at first sight. He can calculate with numbers as quickly as most men can form words. He may have the gift of tongues and be able to speak any language. Don't you distract him or try to lead him away. He is vital to the work of the Order. I have seen many Inquirers and never one who understands as quickly and compassionately as Luca Vero.

'You have asked me many questions and I have answered you so that I can tell you this: the work of the Order is the saving of the world itself. It could not be more important. The only thing you should do is to help Luca in his work for the Order. Anything else is the work of Satan. Remember it.'

She bowed her head. He had a moment's fierce joy that she listened to his instruction. 'I know there is nothing more important than his work,' she said humbly. 'And besides, I don't have any influence over him.'

Brother Peter nodded, and went upstairs to find Luca.

$\sim$

Luca and Brother Peter spruced themselves up in the attic bedroom as well as they could, given that all the clothes they had were those they were wearing during the flood or had since bought from the limited stores of the tailor of Piccolo.

Luca took his boots down to the kitchen to beg for some oil to polish them. 'I'll meet you in the dining room,' Brother Peter promised. 'It will look better if we arrive after each other, than if we go in together. Will you tell our lord that you spoke with the infidel?'

'Why not?'

The clerk shrugged. 'Clearly, my lord is no friend to him. The moment that he saw him he called for us to arrest him.'

'The infidel knew the history of the wave. I had to ask him about it. I had to be able to report what might have caused it.'

'Will you tell Milord that I would not come with you to write down what the infidel said?'

'If he asks me directly. But I thought you were obeying your conscience? I would have thought you would have been proud to tell him that you refused to speak with his enemy?'

Again Brother Peter shrugged. There was no way of telling whether he would be commended for his discretion in avoiding the infidel, or condemned for failing to do his duty as Luca's clerk.

'This is nothing!' Luca asserted. 'Whether we spoke to him or we avoided him is nothing to the rest of it! We nearly died. We saw the crusade. We were on our way to Jerusalem, walking on the bed of the sea. We were driven back by a wave as big as a church steeple that drowned everything in its path. Extraordinary things are happening all around us nearly every day.'

Brother Peter heaved up a pair of ill-fitting breeches and fastened the rope from his gown around them to hold them up around his thin hips. 'I've never known him come out from Rome to an inquiry before,' he confessed. 'It makes me nervous.'

Luca hesitated. 'He has never come out to meet an Inquirer at his work before?'

'Never.'

'Why would he come for me?'

'That's what I am asking myself.'

~

Freize was to serve the dinner and was in the kitchen, helping the flustered landlady spoon up a meat stew onto trenchers of dark bread. Ishraq and Isolde were to dine in their room. 'I'll carry up the food for the ladies,' Freize offered.

'I've come down for it,' Ishraq said from the doorway. 'And I'll bring the things down again. I knew you would be busy in the kitchen.'

'Lord love you and bless you,' the landlady said. 'And him a gentleman from Rome and everything damp still.'

'It's fine,' Ishraq assured her. She took their two bowls of stew and some rough bread and started for the stairs. Freize held the door open for her.

'What did he say to you?' he asked her quietly as she went past him.

Her head came up. 'What did who say?'

'The infidel nobleman. He spoke to you in his foreign language. He took you aside to the boat, when you were carrying his package for him. I saw you go with him, but I have no skill in languages. But I saw him speak quietly. I didn't know what he said to you – nor what you said to him?'

'I didn't understand him,' she said quickly. 'He spoke too fast.'

'So what did you reply?'

'That I couldn't understand him.'

There was a second, a split second when Freize saw her dark eyes slide away from him, and he knew that she was lying. 'Seems to be an important man,' he said easily.

'Very learned, from what he was saying to Luca,' she said indifferently, and went from the room and started to climb the stairs.

'Are you serving dinner, or flirting with the young lady?' the landlady demanded from her place by the blazing fire where she was spooning fat over a roasting duck on the spit.

'Flirting,' Freize replied instantly. 'Firstly with the young lady and now – thank the lord she has gone – I can start on my greater quarry: yourself. Shall we go to your laundry room? Shall we say to hell with the duck and will you lock me in and ravish me among the sheets?'

~

The lord from Rome ate better than he could have hoped in a village recovering from a disaster, and pushed back his chair and bit into a fresh apple. Luca, and Brother Peter arrived with the fruits and sweetmeats to stand before the dining room table and report as best they could about the Crusade, about the wave, about the slaving galley, and waited for his opinion.

He sat at his ease, in a robe of beautiful dark blue cloth but with the hood over his head so that his face was in shadow. 'I've heard of this Plato you speak of,' he said. 'And I've read him. But only in Greek. We have a manuscript in Rome but it's an imperfect copy. They had a better one in our library in Constantinople, but that's now in Muslim hands with the rest of the wealth of Christendom, all our great library now owned by the infidel. Brother Peter, you can give me a copy of what the infidel said.'

Brother Peter nodded his head. He did not explain that the copy had been made by Ishraq.

'You are still travelling with two ladies?' the lord said. 'They arrived with you, and they are still here?'

'I have tried over and over again to send them with another party,' Peter exclaimed. 'Circumstances have prevented them leaving us.'

'The ones from the nunnery?' Milord asked Luca.

'Yes. They escaped from the nunnery, as you know, and we met with them on the road. They were in some danger as they were travelling alone. They travel with us for safety, only until they can find another party to join. They were very helpful at Vittorito, as I reported, and again here. The Lady Isolde spoke so well that she all but averted a riot by some ignorant people who were making accusations of storm-bringers. And Ishraq is unusually learned. She was very helpful with the infidel ship; she speaks Arabic.'

The lord shrugged as if he did not much care about the ladies, but since the light did not penetrate his hood to illuminate his face, Luca could not tell if he approved or not.

'That's all right,' he said indifferently. 'You wrote to me already that the slave is skilled?'

'She's not a slave but a free woman,' Luca explained. 'Half Arab but raised at the Castle of Lucretili. She speaks languages and she studied in Spain. The former Lord of Lucretili seems to have planned to train her up as a scholar. He let her read medicine, and study Arab documents. She is very skilled in many things as you will have seen from my report.'

'What's her faith?' the lord asked, going to the main, the only, question.

'She seems to have none,' Brother Peter said heavily. 'She does not attend church but I have never seen her pray as a Muslim. She speaks of God with indifference. She may be an infidel, a Muslim or even some sort of pagan. But she's not Christian. At least, I don't think so.' He hesitated and then said the words that would protect her from an inquisition and a charge of heresy. 'We consider her as a Moor. She obeys Christian laws. She does not bring herself into scandal. She behaves modestly, like a maid. I can find no fault in her.'

Luca looked at his newly polished boots and said nothing about Ishraq coming into the mens' room in her nightgown and cape and going up the ladder for the kitten, and coming down again into his arms.

'And where are they going? Didn't you write that they were going to Buda-Pest?'

'Lady Isolde is the god-daughter of the late Count Wladislaw of Wallachia. She wants to ask his son to help her gain her inheritance from her brother. The new count is at the court of Hungary – his kingdom has been captured by a pretender.'

'Does she know him?' he asked with sudden intensity. 'Count Wladislaw? The son or the father? Has she ever seen him?'

'No, I don't think so.'

The lord laughed shortly as if this were amusing news. 'How things come about!' he said. 'Well, they can travel with you if they wish, and if you have no objection. For I want you to go to Venice. That lies on their way since they can't go to Croatia in the wake of the wave. You can start tomorrow. If anything occurs, or you hear of anything on your way, you must stop and investigate; but when you get to Venice there is work for you to do. There are stories of much gold on the market.'

'Gold?'

'In coins, gold coins. It is of interest to me because some-one, somewhere has obviously found gold, a lot of gold, mined it, and is pouring it into the Venice markets. Or perhaps someone has a store of gold that they have found or thieved, or released. Either way, this is of interest. Also, the gold appears in Venice in coins, not in bars – which is unusual. So there is a forger there, somewhere, tucked away in the Venice ghetto, making very good quality English nobles, of all things, from a new source of gold. Beautiful English nobles with their old King Edward on a ship on one side and the rose of England on another – but they're perfect.'

'Perfect?'

He reached inside his robe and brought out a coin. Luca took the heavy gold weight in his hand and turned it over looking at the beautiful engraving, the handsome rose and the lettering around the edge.

'Notice anything?'

'Shiny,' Luca said. 'Beautiful.'

'Exactly, it's too heavy and unworn. Nobody's clipped them, nobody's shaved them. They've not been passed around and half a dozen petty crooks tried to scrape a paring off them. They're all full weight.' In the darkness of the hood Luca could glimpse a small smile. 'They're too good for this world,' he said. 'And that's the very thing of interest to us: something which is too good for this world.'

'You want me to investigate?' Luca asked. 'You want me to look for a forger or a coiner?'

'I have reason,' the lord said, without explaining it to

him. 'Get there, mingle with people, buy and sell things, handle the coins, change money, gamble if you have to . . .'

Brother Peter raised his head and repeated, 'Gamble?'

'Yes, go and see the money changers, do whatever you have to do to get hold of a lot of these coins and look at the quality. If there is a forger doing extraordinarily good work, then I want to know. Identify him, and write to me at once. Pass yourself off as a young merchant with money to spend on trade. Talk about taking a share in a ship: buy things, spread money around, handle a lot of money, let people know that you are wealthy. Hire a couple of manservants, take this pair of women with you, if they will go. If they will agree to it, pass yourself off as a family, buying a house in Venice. Brother Peter and you can seem as brothers, one of the women, the Lady Isolde, can appear as your sister, her servant can travel with her. Make up a story, but put yourself in the society of wealthy people, in the market for gold coins.'

'You want us to lie?' Brother Peter confirmed, quite horrified at these instructions. 'Perform a masquerade? Receive forged coins and gamble with them?'

'Trade?' Luca asked. 'Game?'

'For the greater good,' Milord said without a flicker of discomfort.

'Let me make sure that I understand,' Luca specified. 'You want us to set ourselves up, lie about who we are, pretend to be people that we are not, so that we attract these gold, probably counterfeit, coins. We become a false thing to attract a false thing.'

'Inquirer, you know as well as I that two false things

probably create a real thing. Go and pretend your way to a truth. See what you see when you are behind a mask.'

Luca and Brother Peter exchanged a look at these extraordinary instructions. But then Luca spoke of his own interest: 'The infidel lord said that there was a man on the Rialto who might be able to trace my father,' he said hesitantly. 'When we go to Venice, I must find him. I will do it at the same time as I look for this gold. I promise I won't neglect my work for you, but I have to speak with him.'

'I thought your father was dead?' Milord asked casually.

'Disappeared,' Luca corrected him, as he always corrected everyone. 'But the infidel lord had a galley slave who said that he had seen my father on a ship commanded by a man named Bayeed.'

'Probably lying.'

'Perhaps. But I have to know.'

'Well, maybe you can buy him back with this mysterious gold,' the lord said, a smile beneath his hood. 'Perhaps you can do the work of the Lord at a profit to the Church.'

'We will need funds,' Brother Peter remarked. 'It will be expensive, a masque like this.'

'I have funds for you. The Holy Father himself is pleased with your work. He commanded me to make sure that you have funds for this next inquiry. I will see you both again, after Prime, tomorrow morning. I leave then. Now I would talk with Brother Vero.' He paused. 'Alone.'

Peter bowed and went out.

Peter opened the dining room door abruptly on Ishraq and Freize who were outside in the hall. Ishraq, with the empty dinner dishes in her hands, was openly eavesdropping though pretending to be on her way to the kitchen. Freize was apparently on guard.

'Can I help you?' Brother Peter asked with weighty sarcasm. 'Either of you?'

'Thank you,' said Ishraq promptly, not at all embarrassed at being caught listening at the door. 'You're very kind.' She handed him the heavy board with the dishes.

'And we were hoping to know – where next?' Freize asked.

'You know where next,' Brother Peter said irritably, taking the burden of the board and heading towards the kitchen. 'Since you have been listening at the door, I assume you know where next: Venice. And Milord says that the ladies may come with us and pretend to be of our party. We are to appear as a merchant family, you two are to appear as servants.' He paused and looked disapprovingly at the two of them. 'In order to pass as our servants, you will have to work. You will have to carry dishes perhaps. I do hope it's not an inconvenience to you.'

He dumped the plates on the kitchen table, ignored the flustered thanks of the innkeeper's wife, and went up the stairs to the attic bedroom room he shared with Luca and the other travellers. Ishraq and Freize were left alone.

'A breath of air?' Freize suggested, gesturing to the front door and the greying sky and sea beyond.

She went out before him and he offered her his arm to walk along the quayside in a quaint careful gesture. She smiled and walked beside him, arm in arm, like a young betrothed couple. She noticed that she liked his touch, his closeness, the warmth of his arm, the gentle support as they walked across the cobbles. She felt comfortable with him, she trusted him to walk beside her.

'The thing is,' Freize confided, 'the thing is, that I heard you with the infidel lord, on the quayside earlier today, and it's somewhat disturbing, to know that he spoke to you kindly and that you responded. I know that he spoke to you in a strange language – perhaps Arabic. And I know that you answered. Then, when I asked you, you told me that he said something you couldn't understand. Now, I don't want to call a young lady a liar; but you can see that I would have some concerns.'

She was silent for a moment.

'What I want to know is what he said and what you replied. And also: why you told me that he spoke too fast for you to understand?'

They took half a dozen steps before she replied to him. 'You don't trust me?'

He shook his head. 'I'm not saying that. All I'm saying is that I heard him speak to you in a foreign language, and I heard you reply in the same language. But when I asked you, you denied it.' He hesitated. 'It would make anyone wonder. We don't need to talk about trust. Let's talk about wonder.'

She paused, releasing his arm. 'You brought me out here to question me?' she accused him.

'Sweetheart mine, I have to know. Don't get all agitated with me. I have to know. Because he is the enemy of Luca's Milord. You heard him. He said he was the worst enemy in the world. So I have to take an interest. I am sworn in love and loyalty to the little lord, and he is sworn to the rather quiet lord in the blue hood, and so I am bound to want to know what you are saying to his most deadly enemy.'

'You don't trust me,' she said flatly. 'After all that we have been through.'

'Sweeting,' he said apologetically. 'Usually I am the most trusting man in the world, ask anyone! I am a great lummock of trust. But here, in these circumstances, I am filled with doubts. I have been thrown about on a great wave, I have been nearly drowned, and now I am troubled by our new acquaintances.' He spread his big hand to show her his reasons for concern, counting on his fingers. 'I don't trust the infidel lord. That's one. I thought him a most dominant and glamorous character and I have a craven aversion to dominant and glamorous men, being myself humble and ordinary except for moments (I remind you) of great heroism. Two: I don't trust Luca's lord, whose face I have never yet seen, but who seems to frighten Brother Peter out of his wits. He has the ear of the Pope – and that makes him rather important, and I have an aversion to important men, being myself very humble, except (I remind you) for my moments of greatness. He turns up without warning, and he has the best linen and the best boots I have ever seen. That troubles me, since I don't expect to see a man of the Church in the linen of a lord. Three: I don't always trust your lady given that she is flighty and easily disturbed, and a woman and so naturally prone to error and misjudgement, and today she has been like a caged wolf. I don't know if you have noticed but she is not even speaking to you? And four: I barely trust myself, what with floods and handsome infidel and miracles, moody girls and well-dressed priests, and so many things that I comprehend as well as the horse – well not as well as him, actually. So don't, I beg you, take offence that I don't trust you. You are just one of many things that I can't trust. You're number five on my list of fears and worries. Dearest, I mistrust and fear a whole handful of things. Believe me, I doubt everything else long before I would ever doubt you.'

She was not diverted by his list, as he hoped she would be, but turned frosty-faced, without saying a word, and stalked back towards the inn. Freize, watching her, thought that he had never before seen a woman who could walk like an irritated cat.

He saw that he had offended her, and very deeply, and went after her with two long strides and caught her at the door. 'Don't be angry with me,' he said softly into her ear. 'Not when you were so sweet to me when I came back to you through the flood. Not when you can be so kind to a little thing like the kitten, and so loving and tender to a big thing, a big foolish thing like me.'

She was not to be persuaded. 'Well, it doesn't matter anyway, since you are going to Venice,' she said coldly. 'Perhaps my lady won't want to come with you to Venice.

Perhaps we'll go at once to Buda-Pest and leave you, then you can doubt someone else.'

'Ah no,' he said quickly, putting his hand in hers to swing her gently round. 'Of course it would matter. Wherever we were going. But you must come with us to Venice. You can get to Buda-Pest from Venice as easily as from here. And besides, the lord in the hood is giving us money to set up a house in Venice. You would like to do that. We shall set out our stall as a prosperous family. Your lady can live as she should, as a lady in a beautiful palace with lovely clothes for a little while. We can all get a bath in hot water – think of that! You can buy some lovely clothes. Perhaps we shall make a fortune. Perhaps you will like Venice.'

'It hardly matters what I like,' she said irritably. 'It's only ever what she likes.'

'I know. But you'll make friends again,' he counselled gently.

'What do you mean?'

'You'll make up your quarrel.'

'We haven't quarrelled. What do you think we are? We're not stupid girls to have a quarrel over nothing. We have never quarrelled in all our lives. You don't begin to understand us. You don't have any idea about me.'

'He's a handsome young man,' Freize said gently, showing no sign of his amusement at her indignation. 'He's bound to cause a bit of a yowling in the cat basket. Bound to set the little kittens scratching at each other.'

He nearly laughed out loud to see her chin come up and her temper flare in her dark eyes. But then he admired how she caught herself, and acknowledged the truth of what he was saying.

527

'Well, we've never quarrelled before,' she explained.

'The two of you were never on your own with a handsome young man before,' he returned. 'There was no real cause.'

She giggled. 'You make us sound rather ... ordinary.'

'Little cross hens in a hen house,' he said comfortably. 'Very, very ordinary. But at least you have me to fall back on.'

'When would I fall back on you?'

'When he prefers her to you. When he makes his choice; if it's not you. When you are down to the bottom of the barrel. And have to scrape.'

Again he saw her colour rise. But she managed to laugh. 'Ah, but you swore loyalty to her already. I'm not such a fool that I don't know that everyone always prefers her to me. Everyone always will.'

'Don't you believe it,' he said tucking her hand in his arm again. 'I worship her from afar. I have promised her that she can call on me as her squire. I have offered her my fealty, of course. But you ...'

She was ready to be offended. 'Me? Don't you worship me from afar?'

'Oh no. You, I would bundle up behind the hayrick, lift up your skirts, and see how far I could get!'

He was ducking before she even swung at him and he laughed and let her go as she turned in the inn door.

And she was laughing too, as she went up the stairs to the bedroom that she shared with Isolde to tell her that they were all to go to Venice, and that they could stay with the two young men for a little while longer, whoever was in love, whoever was preferred, whatever might happen.

528

The evening grew steadily darker. Luca and his lord spoke quietly of the cause of the wave, of the learning of the ancients, and of the signs of the end of days, and then Luca left the lord to pray alone, and go to his solitary bedroom.

In the kitchen the fire was banked down, Freize dozing before it, seated in a wooden chair with his booted feet cocked on the chimney breast. He started up when he heard the dining room door close. 'I waited up to see you to bed,' he said, rubbing his eyes and yawning.

'I think I can get up the stairs safely,' Luca remarked. 'You don't need to tuck me in.'

'I know,' Freize said. 'But it's so good to be together once more. I wanted to say goodnight.'

'Where are you sleeping?' Luca asked. 'Our bedroom is packed tight with guests. And Milord won't share.'

'She said I could bed down here,' Freize said, gesturing to the pallet bed of straw in the corner of the kitchen where the kitten was already fast asleep. 'I'll be warmer than all of you.'

'Good night,' Luca opened his arms and the two young men hugged. 'Dear God, Freize, it's good to have you back again.'

'I can't tell you what it means to be safe on dry land and know that you and the girls are safe,' Freize said. 'I was even glad to see that miserable monk.'

Luca turned and went quietly up the stairs, and the door creaked and then there was silence. Freize shucked off his boots and loosened his belt, gently moved the kitten to one side, and stretched himself out on the pallet bed. He put his hands behind his fair head and readied himself for sleep.

Half dozing, he heard Milord go quietly up to his bedroom and the click as he dropped the latch on his door. The kitten settled itself on Freize's throat and Freize fell deeply asleep.

He was drifting in and out of pleasant dreams when the tiniest noise jolted him into wakefulness. It was a hiss, like the sound of a sleeping snake, a whisper of cloth. He opened his eyes but some apprehension of danger warned him to lie completely still. Through the open kitchen door he could see the darker hallway of the inn, and beyond that, the open front door. Even then, he did not move but lay watching and saw two dark silhouettes against the starlit sky. One was a woman; he could see her slight shoulders and her bare feet, the gleam of silver on one toe. The other was a man completely robed and hooded in black. Freize recognised at once Luca's lord who Brother Peter had called Milord and who had insisted on sleeping alone.

It was Ishraq who stood with him, and it was her whisper and the susurration of her chemise under her cape that had woken Freize. She paused in the doorway, her hand on the lord's arm, and Freize saw the lord turn his hooded face towards her, but could not hear his reply.

Whatever he said, whatever he murmured so quietly that Freize's straining ears could make out no words, it satisfied the girl, for she released his arm and let him go. He stepped out onto the quayside; Freize noted that he walked like a dancer, his boots made no sound, he was as quiet as a cat, and he disappeared into the darkness in the next second. The girl stood for a moment longer, looking after him, but as he went from shadow to shadow in the darkness he disappeared as if by magic.

Carefully, she closed the door, holding her finger under the latch so that it did not make the slightest noise. She turned towards the kitchen. Freize snapped his eyelids shut so that she could not see the gleam of his eyes by the ebbing firelight, and sighed a little, as a man deeply asleep. He felt her watching him. By her complete silence he knew that she was standing still and studying him, and he felt, despite his attraction to her, despite his affection for her, a chill at the thought of those dark eyes looking at him from the darkness, as her companion, her accomplice, went quietly down the quayside, on who knew what mission?

Then he heard the first stair creak, just a tiny noise, no more than the settling of an old house, drying out after a flood, and knew that she had slipped up the stairs, and a little draught of air told him that she had opened and closed her bedroom door.

Freize waited for moments, listening to the silence, knowing that the two of them, the young woman and the dark lord, could move as quietly as ghosts. What the hooded lord was doing, speaking to Ishraq whom he had declared a complete stranger to himself, and then creeping out to the dark quay, he could not begin to imagine. What Ishraq was doing, silently closing the door behind him, acting as his porteress, he could not think. He lay still, turning over treacheries and uncertainties in his mind, and then he sat up in his pallet bed, pulled on his boots in case of an emergency, and spent the rest of the night dozing in the chair by the fireside, on guard – but against what, he did not know. At some time, just before dawn, he thought he was on guard against fear itself, and that he could hear it, quietly breathing at the keyhole.

The inn was stirring at dawn, the lad who slept in the stable yard bringing in wood for the kitchen fire, the innkeeper's wife coming down yawning to bake the bread which had been rising in a pungent yeasty mound all night long, and the innkeeper running up and down stairs with jugs of hot water for the guests to wash before they walked up the hill to attend Prime at the church. The church bell was starting to toll when Freize started at the sound of a shout from the top of the stairs.

He was out of the kitchen and racing up the stairs, two at a time, to the door of the lord as Luca came tumbling downstairs from the attic room. The door stood open and the lord was there, his hand held out, shaking slightly. As Luca and Freize came towards him he turned his face away from them, pulled the hood over his head to hide his face, and then showed them what he had in his hand.

533

'Radu Bey,' Luca said at once recognising the standard in the lord's hand. It was a perfectly circular beautiful piece of fabric, richly embroidered in gold and turquoise, green and indigo, to look like the eye of a peacock's feather, the symbol of nobility in the Ottoman empire, the colour of the standard that Radu Bey had laughingly unfurled from his galley while Luca's lord had shouted impotently for his arrest.

'How?' Luca stammered. 'What does it mean? Where did it come from?'

'I found it this morning, pinned on my heart. On my heart! It was fastened to my robe with a gold pin. He sent a killer to pin this on me, as I slept. He pinned it over my heart. This is his warning. This is a message from Radu Bey telling me that he has put his mark on me; he could have put his dagger through my heart just as easily.'

The lord thrust the perfectly circular, beautiful badge into Luca's hand. 'Take it!' he swore. 'I can't bear to touch it. It is as if he put a target on my heart.'

'Why would he do such a thing?'

'To warn me. To boast that he could have killed me. It's how they work. It's what they do. They warn you, and the next time they come, they kill you.'

'Who?' Freize asked. 'Who came?'

'The Assassins,' the lord said shortly. 'He has set an Assassin on me.'

'An Assassin?' Brother Peter asked, coming down the stairs. 'An Assassin has been in the inn?'

Isolde and Ishraq, disturbed by the noise, came out of their attic bedroom, and stood at the doorway, their capes thrown over their night gowns. 'What's happening?' Isolde demanded, coming down the stairs.

Luca turned to her. 'Someone got into the inn last night, and left Milord a message. A threat.'

Freize was watching Ishraq, on the steps above them all. She was quite still, her face impassive; she was looking at the lord.

'How did he get in?' Isolde asked.

Slowly, as if she felt his gaze upon her, Ishraq turned her eyes to Freize, and looked at him, her dark eyes revealing nothing.

'They can climb walls like cats, they can run along rooftops,' Milord said, shaken. 'They study for years how to enter a room in silence, how to kill without warning and leave again. They are trained killers, they take a target and hunt him down until he is dead,' he broke off. 'This is a warning for me.'

'Did he come in the window?' Luca strode across the room and swung open the shutters and one side squeaked loudly. 'No, you would have heard that.'

'The front door is never locked,' Freize volunteered. 'He could just have let himself in.' Ishraq's gaze was steady on his face. 'And out again.'

She raised her eyebrows slightly and turned a little away.

'What does it mean?' Luca asked the lord. 'Why would he do this?'

'It means that I am under sentence of death,' he said. He exhaled and gave a shaky little laugh. 'I am a dead man walking,' he said. Beneath his hood they could see his faint bitter smile. 'If the Assassins have a command to kill me, they will send one of their number, and then another, and then another, until I am dead, or until they are countermanded.'

'What are the Assassins?' Isolde asked, coming down the last steps, Ishraq following her. 'Who are they?'

'They are an order,' Brother Peter replied. 'More like a guild. They take talented youths very young, they teach them all the arts of warfare, all the arts of spying, all the dark arts of deception and weaponry. And then you can hire them: you give them a target and pay them, and they send one Assassin after another until they have fulfilled their mission and their victim is dead.'

'Why did he not kill you then?' Ishraq asked bluntly.

'They did this to Saladin,' Brother Peter explained. 'They put a target on his heart while he slept, fully guarded in his tent, to warn him that if he went on he was a dead man.'

'What did he do?'

'Retreated,' Brother Peter said shortly.

'They are infidels; but they threatened Saladin?' Luca asked, puzzled. 'They threatened their own kind?'

'They honour their order before anything,' Milord replied. 'They will accept any target, of any faith, of any nation. They serve themselves, not religion or race.'

'But why would this galley slaver want to kill you?' Isolde asked, puzzled.

He spoke to her directly for the first time, inclining his head in a small gesture of respect. 'He's no galley slaver,' he said. 'He is one of the greatest men of the Ottoman Empire, he is commander of all the armies, he is head of the janissary soldiers, the elite fighting force. He's the right-hand man of the Sultan Mehmet, who has just triumphed at Constantinople; they are sworn to each other for life. He stands for everything that I fight against – the victory of the Ottoman Empire over Christianity, the invasion of the

Arabs across Europe, the rise of terror, the end of the world. We are enemies, sworn enemies for life. That was the man you had here, and you let him go. Now he warns me that I will not be as lucky if I fall into his hands. He taunts me. This is a game to him. A game to the death. He will know I have commanded you to kill him. This is his way of telling me that he has ordered my death too.'

There was a horrified silence.

'What will you do, Milord?' Luca asked quietly.

The man shrugged, recovering himself. 'I'll go to Prime,' he said. 'Breakfast. Talk with you and Brother Peter, and go on my way. Continue my struggle. Fight for Christ.'

'Will you defend yourself?'

'If I can, for as long as I can. But this tells me that I will die. I won't stop my work. I have sworn an oath to lead the Order of Darkness to guard against fear itself, and I will never give up.'

Luca hesitated. 'Should we not come with you? Should we not defend you against this threat? You should have someone with you all the time.'

His voice was bleak. 'It is a fight to the death,' he said. 'My death or his. And neither my death nor his death is as important as your mission. When I die, a new lord will take my place, you will still have work to do. For now, you go to Venice and trace the signs of the end of days. And I will keep myself as safe as I can.'

He looked at the peacock badge in Luca's hand. 'Get rid of that,' he said. 'I can't bear to see it.'

Silently, Ishraq put out her hand and took it from him. Freize watched her as she tucked it into the pocket of her cape.

The three men and Isolde went up the hill to the church. Freize saw them go from the inn doorway, as Ishraq started up the stairs to pack their few things ready to leave.

'You didn't hear anything, in the night, I suppose?' Freize asked her neutrally.

She turned on the stair, looked him straight in the face, and lied to him. 'No. I slept through it all.'

'Because he must have come up the stairs and stood on the landing floor just below your bedroom, and gone into the room beneath yours.'

'Yes. But he went past the kitchen door too. Did you hear nothing?'

'No. If he had killed the lord, it would have been most terrible. He is my lord's commander. I am bound to defend him. Luca is bound to guard him.'

'But whoever it was didn't kill him,' she pointed out. 'He never intended to kill him. He took him a message, he left the message, and went away again. It is Milord who speaks of death and threatens death. All I saw was a badge from a standard.'

'A message from our enemy,' Freize prompted her. 'And not any old message. A death threat from our enemy.'

'From *your* enemy,' she said. 'To the lord of your lord. But I don't know that I like Luca's commander very much. I don't know that he is my friend. I don't know if I am on his side. I don't know that he is my lord. I don't know if his enemy is my enemy. I don't even know if he's a very good lord to Luca. Perhaps you should think of that, before you ask me how I sleep?'

The four walked back from Prime and the travellers took
breakfast in the inn kitchen while Milord ate alone in the
dining room. When they had finished eating, the two
young women went up to their attic bedroom to prepare for
the journey.

'What will you do with that?' Isolde asked, seeing Ishraq
put the gloriously embroidered peacock eye standard in the
bottom of her little bag.

'Keep it, I don't know,' she said.

'Luca's commander was very afraid,' Isolde observed.
'He wanted it out of his sight.'

'I know.'

'Perhaps you should burn it.'

'Perhaps I will.' Ishraq hesitated. 'But I don't understand
why Luca's lord was so troubled. He was unhurt, after all.'

'If it was an Assassin who pinned it on his chest for a
warning . . .'

'It was no Assassin,' she said. 'It was Radu Bey himself. I
saw him come out. I let him out of the front door.'

'Why didn't you say?' Isolde asked.

'Because I didn't know if Radu Bey had crept in, as silent
as an Assassin, or if Milord had admitted him. I didn't
know what it meant. Now I doubt Luca's lord.'

'He is appointed by the Pope,' Isolde pointed out.

'That doesn't make him a good man,' Ishraq reminded
her. 'There are many appointed by the Pope who persecute
and destroy. And there is more between him and Radu Bey
than we know. And, as he left, Radu Bey warned me.'

'Of what?'

'He asked me had I ever looked in Milord's face, and I said that he is always hooded and in shadow. And he laughed and said that a man of God does not work in darkness. He said that when I see his face I will understand more. He said . . .' she broke off.

'What?' Isolde asked, lowering her voice as if she feared that Milord might be listening to them.

'He said never to let him come too close.'

'Why?'

Ishraq shook her head. 'He didn't say. He said not to let Milord touch me. Not to let him . . .' she hesitated. 'Not to let him kiss me.'

'He's sworn to a monastic order!' Isolde objected.

'I know. But it wasn't because it would be a sin,' Ishraq tried to explain. 'He said it as if . . . as if it would be danger-ous. As if his touch might be . . . dangerous.'

There was a frightened silence. Then Isolde shook her head. 'We can trust no one,' she said.

'We can trust Luca, and Freize,' Ishraq said. 'We're safe with them. And I know that Brother Peter is a good man. But I don't trust Luca's lord nor his Order.'

'We can trust each other,' Isolde suggested, tentatively. She stretched out her hand to her friend and Ishraq stepped into her embrace. For a moment they stood together, then Ishraq stepped back. 'We can trust each other,' Ishraq ruled. 'And we have to. For I think we are in a very danger-ous world.'

~

After his breakfast, Milord came down to the inn kitchen and gave Brother Peter a set of sealed orders, and a heavy

540

bag of cash. 'And a note to the Jewish moneylenders in Venice,' he said. 'You will want for nothing while you search for the forgers.' Brother Peter tucked the sealed orders into his jerkin; Freize rolled his eyes to heaven.

'Will you guard the money for me, Freize?' Brother Peter asked.

'I'll carry the orders too if you like,' Freize grinned at him.

'No. I don't think that giving them to you would be to put them in safekeeping. I'll keep the orders myself, and open them when I am commanded and not before. But I'd be glad to know that you were guarding the purse.'

Freize nodded, secretly pleased at being trusted. As Brother Peter handed over the heavy purse of gold, the lord turned to Luca. 'I'll talk with you privately before I leave,' he said, and led the way into the dining room.

The stable lad was laying the fire. As the two men came in, he ducked his head in a bow and scuttled out. Luca closed the door behind him as the lord seated himself before the table, his back to the light, and gestured to the opposite chair. 'You can sit,' the lord said.

Luca obeyed and waited.

'You have seen a lot,' the man said to him. 'You have completed four inquiries and seen some of the horror and the strangeness of the world in these dangerous times. And you have looked without flinching.'

'I flinched when I saw the wave,' Luca confessed. 'I was very afraid.'

'Fear is not a problem. Fear before something that is truly fearful is what will keep you alive. I was afraid when I found Radu Bey's badge on my heart pinned by an

Assassin. There are fearful things in this world, objects of terror. What I cannot tolerate among the men of my Order is fear of things before they happen, fear of things because they might happen, fear of things that probably won't happen. You don't suffer from fears like that?'

'I'm not afraid of shadows on the wall,' Luca said.

The dark eyes looked at him acutely. 'What do you know of shadows on the wall?'

'Radu Bey, the infidel lord said . . .'

'Oh, he is well read indeed,' the lord said crushingly. 'I am sure we could all learn from him. He has had great teachers. He has given up his own soul, his immortal life so that he should know of this world. Look at his allies! He works with the Order of Assassins: what does that make him if not an Assassin himself?'

Luca was immediately silent, as the lord recovered his temper.

'No matter. He is not important to us now. I am watching you, Luca Vero, and I am encouraged by what I see.'

Luca bowed his head, feeling absurdly pleased at the praise.

'You are in obedience with my commands? You acknowledge the rule of the Order?'

'I do.'

'You understand the work that we are sworn to do, and you continue to do it?'

Luca nodded.

The lord drew his rosewood box towards him. 'If you bare your arm, I will mark you with the first sign of the Order. As you progress I will complete the marks until the seal is completed, and then you will be a full member and may know

542

me, know me by name, you will see my face, and you will know and work alongside other knights of the Order.'

Luca hesitated; he had a strange reluctance to take the mark on his arm.

'You don't want to? You hesitate before this honour?'

'Is this like priestly vows? For I am not sure that I am prepared.'

The lord smiled. 'No. Not really. Is that why you delay?' He laughed to himself. 'You are a young man indeed! No, in our Order you are not sworn to poverty – I am sending you to Venice as wealthy as a lord. You are not sworn to chastity – your private life is your own concern, between you and your confessor. I don't concern myself with any sin or vice unless it affects your work for the Order.'

Luca blinked.

'Remember that you did not complete your novitiate. You are not bound by the vows of a priest; you can choose to take your vows later.'

'I was not sure ...'

'My Order only requires obedience. You must be obedient to me and to my commands and to our mission, which is to guard the frontier of Christendom from the Devil, the pagan and the heretic. You will be an Inquirer and a servant of the Order. How you obey the commandments is between you and your confessor and God. Do you submit to the Order?'

'Yes, my lord,' Luca bowed his head.

There was a small gleam of a smile, and then the hooded figure moved to the newly-lit fire and took a taper from the flame. One by one he lit all the candles in the room and carried each one of them to the table, so that they were shining on Luca as he sat in broad daylight. In the rosewood box the lord had a set of bronze instruments like a set of embroidery needles, and a small pot of what looked like black ink.

'Bare your arm,' he said quietly.

Luca rolled back the sleeve of his robe, and stretched out his arm.

The lord took up a needle, sharp as a stiletto blade. 'Whether you find your father or not, you have a family in this Order,' he said quietly. 'Whether you speak with the Muslim lord or not, you have no lord but me. Whether you travel with the woman or not, your heart is given to your work and to the mapping of fears and the tracing of the end of days. Whatever else you see on your journey, my command is that you look into the very jaws of hell itself and tell me their measurements. Will you do this?'

He pressed the point of the needle to Luca's skin, inside the forearm, halfway between the crook of the elbow and the wrist, and Luca recoiled as he saw the blood well up and felt the sharp scratch.

'I will,' he gasped. He clenched his fist against the pain and watched as again and again the little blade cut and then scratched, opening up the skin, marking him lightly with a tickling sharp pain, making a shape, an unmistakable shape on the pale skin.

The pain deepened, as the cuts took a form. It was the tail of the dragon, exquisitely drawn by a knife on soft flesh. That was all: the first marks of the Order, the scaly tail outlined in the scarlet of Luca's blood.

Luca looked at the drawing in blood, the detail in crimson, then the lord dropped his hooded head to Luca's wound. Luca gasped as the lord's soft mouth came down on his flesh. He felt the prickle of the stubble on his lord's chin and upper lip, erotic as a kiss against his sensitive flesh. He felt the man's teeth nibble the inside of his arm, felt the touch of his warm tongue on his raw skin. Luca felt the blood well into the lord's mouth, as he sucked the flowing blood from the little wounds, then he felt the cool wetness of the man's saliva as the lord raised his head and pulled his hood forwards over his face so that Luca only glimpsed for a moment his mouth, stained red, and the gleam of his black eyes.

Without comment, the lord lifted his head and took a tiny brush, dipped it in the pot of ink, and painted, with meticulous accuracy, over the lines he had cut, the wounds he had sucked. Then, he took a linen napkin from inside the box and pressed it against the red marks, now darkened with black ink. He raised his head and looked into Luca's face. The younger man was pale and his brown eyes were darkened, his breath quick and shallow. The two of them stood in silence, as if something very strange and powerful had taken place.

'There,' said the lord, quietly. 'I have marked you with my symbol. I have tasted your blood. You begin to belong to the Order. You begin to be mine.'

Read on for the next exciting adventure . . .

FOOLS' GOLD

IL VIAGGIO
DI LUCA

VENICE

RAVENNA

ADRIATIC SEA

N
NW NE
W E

RAVENNA, SPRING 1461

The four horse riders halted before the mighty closed gates of the city of Ravenna, the snow swirling around their hunched shoulders, while the manservant Freize rode up to the wooden doors and, using his cudgel, hammered loudly and shouted: 'Open up!'

'You won't forget what to say,' Luca reminded him quickly.

Inside, they could hear the bolts being slowly slid open.

'I should hope I can – though naturally truthful – tell a lie or two when required,' Freize said with quiet pride, while Brother Peter shook his head that he should be so reduced as to depend on Freize's ready dishonesty.

The gateway pierced the great wall that encircled the ancient city. The defences were newly rebuilt; the city's conquerors, the Venetians, were spreading their unique form of government – a republic – through all the neighbouring cities, fuelled by gold, driven by trade. Slowly the little sally-port door opened and a guard in the bright livery of the victors presented arms and waited for the travellers to request admission.

Freize launched himself into a mouthful of lies with ill- concealed relish. 'My lord,' he said, gesturing to Luca, 'a young and wealthy nobleman from the west of Italy. His brother: a priest.' He pointed to Brother Peter who was indeed a priest, but was serving as Luca's clerk and had never met him before they were partnered on this mission. 'His sister is the fair young lady.' Freize gestured to the beautiful girl who was Lady Isolde of Lucretili, no relation at all to the handsome young man but travelling with him for safety. 'And her companion the dark young lady is riding with her.' Freize was nearest to the truth with this, for Ishraq had been Isolde's friend and companion from childhood – now they were exiled together from their home, looking for a way to return. 'While I am . . .'

'Servant?' the guard interrupted.

'Factotum,' Freize said, rolling the word around his mouth with quiet pride. 'I am their general factotum.'

'Going where?' the guard demanded, putting out his hand for a letter which would describe them. Unblushingly, Freize produced the document sealed by Milord, the commander of their secret papal Order, which confirmed the lie that they were a wealthy young family going to Venice.

'To Venice,' Freize said. 'And home again. God willing,' he added piously.

'Purpose of visit?'

'Trade. My young master is interested in shipping and gold.'

The guard raised his eyebrows and shouted a command to the men inside the town. The great gate swung open as he stood deferentially to one side, bowing low as the party rode grandly inwards.

'Why do we tell lies here?' Ishraq asked Freize very quietly, bringing up the rear as servants should. 'Why not wait till we get to Venice?'

'Too late there,' he said. 'If Luca is going to pass for a wealthy young merchant in Venice someone might ask after his journey. Someone may see us here at the inn. We can say we came from Ravenna. If they bother to enquire, they can confirm here that we are a wealthy family and hope that they won't trouble to look beyond, all the way back to Pescara.'

'But if they do trace us back, beyond Pescara, to the village of Piccolo then they'll learn that Luca is an Inquirer, working for the Pope himself, and you are his friend, and Brother Peter his clerk, and Isolde and I are no relation at all but just young women travelling with you for safety on our way to Isolde's kinsman.'

Freize scowled. 'If we had known that Luca's master would have wanted him to travel disguised we could have started this whole journey with new clothes, spending money like lords. But since he only condescended to inform us at Piccolo, we have to take the risk. I will buy us some rich elegant capes and hats here in Ravenna and we'll have to get the rest of our clothes in Venice.'

The guard pointed the way they should go, towards the best inn of the town, and they found it easily, a big building against the wall of the great castle, on the little hill above the market square. Freize jumped down from his horse and left it standing, as he opened the door and bellowed for service for his master, then he came back out and held the horses while Luca, Lady Isolde and Brother Peter swept into the inn and ordered two private bedrooms and a private dining room, as befitted their great rank. Freize helped Ishraq down from her horse and she went quickly after her mistress as Freize led all the horses and the pack donkey round to the stable yard.

As they settled into their rooms they could hear the bells of the churches chiming for Vespers all over the city, the air loud with their clamour, birds whirling into the sky from the many towers. Isolde went to the window, rubbed the frost away from the panes, and watched Brother Peter and Luca leave the inn and head towards the church through the occasional swirls of light snow.

'Aren't you going to church?' Ishraq asked, surprised, as Isolde was usually very devout.

'Tomorrow morning,' Isolde said. 'I couldn't concentrate tonight.'

Ishraq did not need to ask her friend why she was so distracted; she only watched her gaze follow the young man as he strode down the cobbled street.

~

When the men came back from Mass they all dined together in the private room, Freize bringing up food from the kitchen. When he had spread all the plates, the pie, the pitadine – a sort of pancake with rich savoury toppings – the venison haunch, the roast ham, the braised chicken and the sweetbreads, on the table, he stood by the door, the very picture of a deferential servant.

'Freize: eat with us,' Luca commanded.

'I'm supposed to be your general factotum,' Freize repeated the grand word. 'Or servant.'

'No one can see,' Isolde pointed out. 'And it feels odd when you don't sit down. I like you to eat with us, Freize.'

There was no need for her to repeat the invitation. Freize pulled up a chair, took a plate and started to serve himself generously.

'Besides, this way you'll get two dinners,' Ishraq pointed out to him with a little smile. 'One now, and one in the kitchen later.'

'A working man needs to keep up his strength,' Freize said cheerfully, buttering a thick slice of bread and sinking his white teeth into it. 'What's Ravenna like?'

'Old,' Luca remarked. 'The little that I have seen of it so far. A great city, wonderful churches, as beautiful as Rome in some parts. But before we leave tomorrow I want to go to the tomb of Galla Placidia.'

'Who's that?' Isolde asked him.

'She was a very great lady in ancient times, and she prepared herself a great tomb that the priest at church told me to go and see. He says it is very beautiful inside, with mosaics from floor to ceiling.'

'I should like to see that!' Ishraq remarked and then flushed, anxious that Isolde would think that she was trying to get into Luca's company.

As soon as Isolde saw her friend's embarrassment she blushed too and said quickly: 'Oh but you must go! Go with Luca while I pack our bags for the journey. Why don't the two of you go in the morning?'

Brother Peter looked from one red-cheeked girl to

another as if they were troubling beings from another world altogether. 'What on earth is the matter with you now?' he asked wearily.

'If you are to pass as my sister and Ishraq as your servant then you had both better come and see the tomb,' Luca said, quite blind to the girls' embarassment. 'And surely Ishraq should always accompany you, Isolde, when you are walking around a strange city. You should always have a lady-in-waiting.'

'And in any case, we can't go halfway across Christendom with you two carrying on like this,' Freize said gently.

'Why, what's the matter?' Luca looked from one to another, noticing their confusion for the first time. 'What's going on?'

There was an awkward silence. 'We had a disagreement,' Isolde said awkwardly. 'Before we left Piccolo. Actually, I was in the wrong.'

'You two quarrel?' Luca exclaimed. 'But I've never known you quarrel. What's it all about?'

Freize, who knew that they had quarrelled over Luca, stepped into the silence. 'Lasses,' he said generally to the table. 'Often upset about one thing or another. Highly strung. Like the little donkey. Think they know their own mind even when it's not quite right.'

'Oh don't be ridiculous!' Ishraq said crossly. She turned to Isolde. 'I should want everything to be as it was between us, and anything else will work itself out.'

Isolde, her eyes on the table, nodded her fair head. 'I am sorry,' she said, her voice low. 'I was utterly wrong.'

'That's all right then,' Freize said with the air of a man having brought about a diplomatic compromise in a difficult situation. 'Glad I settled it. No need to thank me.'

'You had better pray for patience,' Brother Peter said crossly to the two girls. 'God knows, I have to.' He rose from the table and went solemnly out of the room. As the door closed behind him the four young people exchanged rueful smiles.

'But what was the matter?' Luca persisted.

Freize shook his head at him, indicating he should be silent. 'Best left alone,' he advised. 'Like the little donkey when it has finally settled itself down.'

'Anyway, it's over,' Isolde ruled, 'and we should go to bed as well.'

As soon as she rose to her feet Luca held open the door for her and followed her out into the hall. 'You're not upset with me, about anything?' he asked her quietly.

She shook her head. 'I was quite at fault with Ishraq. She told me that she had held you in her arms for comfort, when you were grieving, and I was angry with her.'

'Why would you be angry?' he asked, though his heart was hammering in his chest, hoping that he had guessed her answer.

She raised her face and looked at him honestly, her dark blue eyes meeting his hazel ones. 'Alas, I was jealous,' she said simply. He saw her little, rueful, smile. 'Jealous like a fool,' she confessed.

'You were jealous that she held me in her arms?' he said very low.

'Yes.'

'Because you and I have never held each other close?'

'Well, we cannot,' she reasoned. 'You are promised to the priesthood and I was born a lady. I can't go around kissing people. Not like Ishraq. She's free to behave as she wants.'

'But you do want me to hold you?' He stepped closer and whispered the question against her blonde hair, so that she could feel the warmth of his breath.

She could not say the word, she merely leaned her head towards him.

Very gently, very softly, as if he was afraid of startling her, Luca put one arm around her slim waist and the other round her shoulders and drew her close. Isolde rested her head on his shoulder and closed her eyes to savour the intense pleasure that rushed through her as she felt the length of his lithe body against her, and the strength in his arms as they tightened around her.

'Did she tell you I kissed her forehead?' Luca whispered in her ear, delighting in the touch and the rose-water scent of this young woman that he had desired since the moment that he had first seen her.

She raised her head. 'She did.'

'Were you jealous of that too?'

There was a gleam of mischief in his eyes, and she saw it at once and smiled back at him, 'Unfortunately, I was.'

'Shall I kiss you as I kissed her? Would that make it fair?'

In answer she closed her eyes and raised her face to him. Luca longed to kiss her warm mouth but instead, obedient to his offer, he gently kissed her forehead, and had the satisfaction of feeling her sway, just slightly, in his arms, as if she too wanted for more.

In a moment she opened her dark blue eyes.

'Shall I kiss you on the lips?' Luca asked her.

It was a step too far. He sensed her flinch and she leaned back so she could see his warmly smiling face.

'I think you should not,' she said, but, in contradiction, her arms were still around his waist and she did not let him go. His arms held her close and she did not step back.

Slowly, he leaned forwards, slowly her eyes closed, and she raised her mouth to his. Behind them the door opened and Freize came out with the dishes from dinner. He checked himself when he saw the two of them, enwrapped in the darkened hall. ''Scuse me,' he said cheerfully, and went past them to the kitchen.

Luca rapidly released Isolde who put her hands to her hot cheeks. 'I should go to bed,' she said quietly. 'Forgive me.'

'But you're not angry with Ishraq, nor upset with your-self any more?' he confirmed.

She went to the stairs but he could see that she was laughing. 'I scolded Ishraq like a fishwife!' she confessed. 'I accused her of loose behaviour for allowing your kiss. And now here am I!'

'She'll forgive you,' he said. 'And you will be happy again.'

She went up the stairs and turned back and smiled at him. He caught his breath at the luminous loveliness of her face. 'I am happy now,' she said. 'I think I have never been as happy in my life as I am now.'

~

In the morning, as Freize went out to buy new and beautiful capes and hats for their sea voyage to Venice, Brother Peter and Luca – holding to their pretence of being merchant brothers – and Isolde and Ishraq – as their sister and her companion – went to walk in the town of Ravenna.

It was a small city, tightly enclosed within the

encircling walls, the great castle dominating the jumble of shabby roofs around the castle hill. The morning was bright and sunny, the early frost melting from the red tiled roofs. Rising to the blue sky, at every street corner, were the tall bell towers of great churches. A shallow canal flowed into the very centre of the town, where a market sold everything on the stone-built quay. The city had been the capital of the ancient kingdom, and the great stone roads running north and south, and east and west, across the whole of Italy crossed at the very heart of the old city.

The two girls hesitated beside the great church that towered over the area, admiring the rose-coloured brick. 'The church is what takes your eye, but the tomb I want to see is just here,' Luca said, and led the way to a modest little building set to one side.

'This little place?' Isolde ducked under the low opening, Ishraq followed her, Brother Peter behind her. The building was in the shape of a cross and they entered by the north door. For a moment they paused at the entrance of the tiny building and then as Isolde crossed herself, and bent her knee, Luca exclaimed at the explosion of colour.

Every part of the arched interior was glistening, almost as if it had been freshly painted. The walls, the floor, even the curved ceilings were rich with bright mosaics. Isolde gazed around her in amazed delight, Ishraq could not take her eyes from the roof above their heads, which was deep sea blue, studded with hundreds of golden stars. It was like a silk scarf sweeping over their heads and down into the arches on all four sides.

'It's beautiful!' Ishraq exclaimed, thinking how similar

it was to the rich designs of the Arab world. 'What is it? A private chapel?'

'It's not a church at all, it's a mausoleum,' Brother Peter told her. 'Built by a great Christian lady hundreds of years ago for her own burial.'

'Look,' Isolde said, turning back to the door where they had entered. A spacious mosaic over the doorway showed a warmly coloured scene of the Good Shepherd, leaning on his crook, crowned with a golden halo and surrounded by his sheep. 'How could they do this hundreds of years ago? The tenderness of the picture? See how he touches the sheep?'

'And that is the story of a Christian risking his life for the gospels,' Brother Peter said piously, pointing to the opposite wall where a man was depicted running past the flames of an open fire, with a cross over his shoulder and an open book in his hand. 'See the gospels in the library?'

'I see,' Ishraq said demurely. In this exquisite and holy place she did not want to tease Brother Peter about his devotion, or to express her own scepticism. She had been raised in the Christian household of Isolde's father, the Lord of Lucretili, but her mother had taught her to read the Koran. Her later education encouraged her to examine everything, and she would always be a young woman of questions rather than of faith. She looked around the glittering interior and then found her attention caught by a wash of colour on some white mosaic tiles. Someone had glazed the open windows of the mausoleum and one of the pieces of glass had been broken. The morning sunlight, shining over the chipped surface, threw coloured rays on the white tiles and even on Ishraq's white headscarf.

'Look,' Ishraq nudged Isolde. 'Even the sunlight is coloured in here.'

Her words caught Luca's attention and he turned and saw the brilliant spread of colours. He was dazzled by the rainbow shining around Ishraq's head. 'Give me your scarf,' he said suddenly.

Without a word, her eyes on his face, she unwrapped it, and her dark thick hair tumbled down around her shoulders. Luca handed one end to her and kept the other. They spread it out to catch the light from the window. At once the white silk glowed with the colours of the rainbow. Together, as if doing a strange dance, they walked away from the window and saw the colours become more diffuse and blurred as the stripes grew wider, and then they walked back and saw that the brightly coloured beam narrowed and became more distinct.

'The broken glass seems to be turning the sunlight into many colours,' Luca said, wonderingly. He turned back to the mosaic that he had been examining. 'And look,' he said to her. 'The mosaic is a rainbow too.'

Above his head was a soaring wall going up to the vault above them, decorated exquisitely in all the colours of the rainbow, and overlaid with a pattern. Luca, his hands holding out Ishraq's scarf, nodded from the rainbow mosaic to the rainbow on the scarf. 'It's the same colours,' he said. 'A thousand years ago, they made a rainbow in these very colours, appearing in this order.'

'What are you doing?' Isolde asked, looking at the two of them. 'What are you looking at?'

'It makes you think that a rainbow must always form the same colours,' Ishraq answered her when Luca was silent,

562

looking from the scarf to the mosaic wall. 'Does it? Is it always the colours as they have shown here? In this mosaic? Don't look at the pattern, look at the colours!'

'Yes!' Luca exclaimed. 'How strange that they should have noticed this, so many hundreds of years ago! How wonderful that they should have recorded the colours.' He paused in thought. 'So, is every rainbow the same? Has it been the same for hundreds of years? And if the chip of glass can make a rainbow in here, what makes a rainbow in the sky? What makes the sky suddenly shine with colours?'

Nobody answered him, nobody had an answer. Nobody but Luca would ask such a question; he had been expelled from his monastery for asking questions which verged on heresy, and even now, though he was employed by the Order of Darkness to inquire into all questions of this world and the next, he had to stay within the tight confines of the Church.

'Why would it matter?' Isolde asked, looking at the rapt expressions of her two friends. 'Why would such a thing matter to you?'

Luca shrugged his shoulders as if he was returning to the real world. 'Oh, just curiosity, I suppose,' he said. 'Just as we didn't know the cause of the great wave in Piccolo, we don't know what makes thunder, we don't know what makes rainbows. There is so much that we don't know. And while we don't know the answer, people think that these strange tricks of nature are carried out by witchcraft or devils or spirits. They frighten themselves into accusing their neighbours, and then it is my job to discover the truth of it. But I can't give them a simple explanation, for I don't have a simple explanation. But here – since whoever made these mosaics knew the colours of the rainbow – maybe they knew what caused them too.'

'But why are you interested?' Isolde pursued. 'Does it matter what colour the sunset was last night?'

'Yes,' Ishraq said unexpectedly. 'It does matter. For the world is filled with mysteries, and only if we ask and study and go on discovering will we ever understand anything.'

'There is nothing to understand, for it has already been explained,' Brother Peter ruled, speaking with all the authority of the Church. 'God set a rainbow in the sky as his promise to Man after the Flood. *I will set my bow in the clouds, and it shall be the sign of a covenant between me, and between the earth. And when I shall cover the sky with clouds, my bow shall appear in the clouds.*' He looked gravely at the young women. 'That is all you need to know.'

He turned his hard stare to Luca. 'You are an Inquirer of a holy Order,' he reminded the younger man. 'It is your duty and your task to inquire. But beware that you do not ask about things outside your mission. You are commanded by our lord and by the Holy Father to discover if the end of days is coming. You are not commanded to ask about everything. Some questions are heretical. Some things are not to be explored.'

There was a silence as Luca absorbed the reproof from the older man.

'I can't stop myself thinking,' Luca replied quietly. 'Perhaps God has given me curiosity.'

'Nobody wants to stop you thinking,' Brother Peter said as he opened the low door to the mausoleum. 'But Milord will have made it clear when he hired you, that you are to think only inside the limits of the Church. Some things are not known – like the change of a man into werewolf, like the cause of the terrible flood – and it is right that you hold an inquiry into them. But God has told us the meaning of the rainbow in His Holy Word, we don't need your thoughts on it.'

Luca bowed his head but could not stop himself glancing sideways at Ishraq.

'Well I shall go on thinking, whether your Church needs it or not,' she declared. 'And the Arab scholars will go on thinking, and the ancient people were clearly thinking too, and the Arab scholars will translate their books.'

'But we are obedient sons of the Church,' Brother Peter ruled. 'And actually, what you think – as a young woman and an infidel – does not matter to anyone.'

He turned and led the way out and they obediently followed him, Isolde lingered in the doorway. 'It's so beautiful,' she said. 'As if it were a freshly painted fresco, the colours so rich.'

There was a little pause before Luca came out, and she saw he was putting something in the pocket of his breeches, under the fold of his cape.

'What d'you have there?' Isolde whispered to him, as Brother Peter led the way back to the inn.

'The chipped piece of glass,' he said. 'I want to see if we can make a rainbow with it, anywhere.'

Gravely, she looked at him. 'But isn't it God's work to make a rainbow? As Brother Peter just said?'

'It's our work,' Ishraq corrected her. 'For we are in this world to understand it. And like Luca, I want to see if we can make a rainbow. And if he is not allowed to do it, then I will try. For my God, unlike yours, has no objection to me asking questions.'

~

Freize was waiting for them back at the inn and they mounted up and rode the little way out of Ravenna alongside the silted-up canal to the old port of Classe. The ferry boat was waiting for them at the stone harbour wall.

'But do you have the courage to get on board?' Ishraq teased Freize, who had not been on board a ship since he had been swept away by a terrible storm.

'If Rufino my horse can do it, then I can do it,' Freize answered. 'And he is a horse of rare courage and knowingness.'

Ishraq looked doubtfully at the big skewbald cob, who looked more doltish than knowing. 'He is?'

'You need to look beyond ordinary appearances,' Freize counselled her. 'You look at the horse and you see a big clumsy lump of a thing, but I know that he has courage and fine feelings.'

'Fine feelings?' Ishraq was smiling. 'Has he really?'

'Just as you look at me and you see a handsome down-to-earth straightforward sort of ordinary man. But I have hidden depths and surprising skills.'

'You do?'

'I do,' Freize confirmed. 'And one of those skills is getting horses on board a boat. You may sit on the quayside and admire me.'

'Thank you,' Ishraq said, and sat on one of the stone seats let into the harbour wall, as he led all five horses and the little donkey to the wooden gangway which stretched from boat to quay.

The horses were nervous and pulled away and jibbed, but Freize was soothing and calm with them. Ishraq would not feed his joyous vanity by applauding; but she thought there was something very touching about the way that the square-shouldered young man and the big horses exchanged glances, caresses and little noises, almost as if they were talking to each other, until the animals were reassured and followed him up the gangway to their stalls on the boat. Freize loaded their saddlebags and the crusader broadsword that had belonged to the Lord of Lucretili – Isolde's father. All their other things: Brother Peter's writing desk, the rolled manuscripts, had been lost in the flood.

There were no other travellers taking the ship that day, and so when the horses were safely loaded, they all took hunks of bread and pots of small ale for breakfast, and followed Freize on board as the master of the ship cast off and set sail.

It took all day and all night to sail to Venice going before a bitterly cold wind. The girls slept for some of the time in the little cabin below the deck but in the early hours of the morning they came out and went to the front of the ship where the men were standing, wrapped against the cold, waiting for the sky to lighten. Ishraq's attention was taken by a small sleek craft coming towards them on a collision course, moving fast in the dark water, a black silhouette against the dark waves.

'Hi! Boatman!' she called over her shoulder to the captain of the boat who was at the rudder in the stern of the boat. 'D'you see that galley? It's heading straight for us!'

'Drop the sail!' the man bellowed at his son, who scurried forward and slackened the ropes and dropped the mainsail.

'Here! I'll help,' Freize said going back to haul the sail down. 'What's he doing, coming at us so fast?'

The two girls, Brother Peter and Luca watched, as the galley, speeding towards them, powered by rowers hauling on their oars to the beat of a drum, came closer and closer.

'A galley should give way to a vessel with sails,' Brother Peter remarked uneasily. 'What are they doing? They look as if they want to ram us!'

'It's an attack!' Luca suddenly decided. 'They are coming straight for us! Who are they?'

Brother Peter, squinting into the half-darkness, exclaimed: 'I can't see the standard. They're showing no light. Whose boat is it?'

'Freize!' Luca shouted, turning to the deck and grabbing a boathook as the only weapon to hand. 'Beware boarders!'

'Get the sail back up!' Brother Peter shouted.

'We can't outsail them,' Ishraq warned.

A galley with a well-trained rowing crew could travel much faster than the lumbering ship. Ishraq looked around for a weapon, for somewhere that they could hide. But it was a little boat with only the stalls for the horses on deck, and a small cabin below.

Freize joined them, his club in his hand. He pulled a knife out of his boot and handed it to Ishraq for her defence. His face was grim.

'Would this be the Ottoman lord come back for us?' he asked Luca.

'It's not an Ottoman pirate,' Luca said, staring at the oars biting into the waves as the galley came swiftly closer. 'It's too small a craft.'

'Then someone else is very eager to speak with us,' Freize said miserably. 'And it looks like we can't avoid the pleasure.'

Slowly, as their little caravel came to a halt and wallowed in the water, the galley changed course and drew up alongside them. Two of the rowers got to their feet and threw grappling hooks upward at once, gripping the rail of the boat. Isolde resisted the temptation to throw them off, as the rowers in the mysterious galley hauled on the ropes and drew in close.

Summoning their courage, Luca and Isolde looked down into the galley at the rowers, who were free, not chained; and at the man who stood in the stern.

'Who are you? And what do you want with us?' Luca demanded.

The commander at the back of the boat had drawn his cutlass. The cold light glinted on the hammered blade. He looked up at them both, businesslike. 'I am commanded by the Lord of Lucretili to take that woman into my keeping,' he said, pointing at Isolde. 'She is the runaway sister to the great lord and he has commanded her to come home.'

'Your brother!' Ishraq exclaimed under her breath.

'I'm not her,' Isolde said at once in the strong accent of a woman from the south. 'I don't know who you are talking about.'

The man narrowed his eyes. 'We have followed your trail, my lady,' he said. 'From the convent where the lord your brother entrusted you to the good sisters, to when you fell in with these men of God, to the fishing village, to here. You were charged with witchcraft . . .'

'She was cleared!' Luca interrupted. 'I am an Inquirer for the Church, commanded by the Pope himself to discover the reasons for strange happenings in this world, and to see the signs for the end of days. I examined her, and I sent my report to the lord of my Order. I have cleared her of any wrongdoing. She's not wanted by the law of the land nor of the Church.'

The man shrugged. 'She can be innocent of everything but she's still the Lord of Lucretili's sister,' he said flatly. 'She's still his possession. If he wants her back then no one can deny his rights to her.'

'What does he want her for?' Ishraq asked, joining the two of them on the rail of the little ship. 'For he was quick enough to get her out of the house when her father died, and quick enough to make an accusation which would have seen her burned to death. Why does he want her back now?'

'You too,' the man said shortly. 'The slave, Ishraq. I am commanded to take you back too.' He turned to Luca. 'You have to give that one to me because she is a runaway slave and the lord is her master. And the lady has to be given to me because she is the Lord of Lucretili's sister and as much a part of his property as his chair or his horse.'

'I am a free woman,' Ishraq spat. 'And so is she.'

He shrugged as if the words were meaningless. 'You're an infidel and she is his sister. She was at the disposal of her father and then, on his death, her brother. He inherited her like the cows in his fields. She's his property just like a heifer.'

He turned his attention to Brother Peter. 'If you prevent her coming with me then you have stolen Lord Lucretili's property: his slave and his sister, and I will have you charged as a thief. If you keep her you are guilty of kidnap.'

Freize sighed. 'Difficult,' he remarked into the silence. 'Because legally, you know, he's right. A woman does belong to her father or brother or husband.'

'I don't belong to my brother any more,' Isolde suddenly asserted. She slipped her hand in Luca's arm and gripped his elbow. 'We are married. This man is my keeper. I am his.'

He looked from her determined face to Luca's set jaw. 'Really? Is this so, Inquirer?'

'Yes,' Luca said shortly.

'But you are a man of the Church? Tasked to inquire into the end of days and report to your Order?'

'I have broken my vows to the Church and taken this woman as my wife.'

Brother Peter choked but said nothing.

'Wedded and bedded?'

'Yes,' Luca said gripping Isolde's hand.

There was a moment, and then the man shook his head. He smiled disbelievingly, looking up at them both. 'What? You bedded her? Took her with lust, had her beneath you, made her cry out in joy? You two kissed with tongues and you caressed her breasts? You held her waist in your hands, and she gladly took you into her body?'

Isolde's face was blazing red with shame. Ishraq looked furious.

'Yes,' Luca said unblinking. 'We did all that.'

'Kiss her.'

'You can't ...' Isolde began, but Luca turned to her and put a finger beneath her chin to raise her face and then he kissed her slowly and deeply, as if he could not bear to move his mouth away from hers. Despite her embarrassment Isolde could not stop herself, her head tipped back, her arms came around his shoulders, they held each other, her hand on the nape of his neck, her fingers reaching into his hair.

Luca raised his head. 'There,' he said, a little breathlessly, when he finally let her go. 'As you see. I do not hesitate to kiss my bride. We are husband and wife, she is my chattel now. Her brother has lost all his rights over her. She belongs to me.'

Freize nodded sagely. 'A wife must go with her husband. His rights come first.'

Brother Peter's face was frozen with horror at the lies spilling out of Luca's mouth but he said nothing.

The Lucretili man turned to him. 'Am I supposed to believe this? What about you, Priest? Are you going to tell me you are married to the other one? Are you going to kiss her to prove it?'

'No,' Brother Peter said shortly. 'I live inside my vows.'

'But these two are truly husband and wife? In the sight of God?'

Brother Peter opened his mouth. A little swell rocked the boat and he put his hand on the rail to steady himself.

'You are their witness before God,' the man reminded him. 'I conjure you, in His name, to tell me the truth.'

Brother Peter gulped.

'On your oath as a priest,' the man reminded him. 'The truth, in the sight of God.'

Brother Peter turned to Isolde as she stood, her arm still around Luca's waist. 'I am sorry,' he said, his voice very low. 'Very sorry. But I can't lie on God's name. I cannot do it.'

She nodded. 'I understand,' she said quietly and moved away from Luca as he let her go.

'He doesn't have to say anything,' Ishraq spoke up. 'I will bear witness.'

The man shrugged. 'Your word means nothing. You are an infidel, and a slave and a woman. Your words are like birdsong in the morning. Too loud, and completely meaningless. Now,' he turned his attention briskly to Luca. 'Send both of the women over the side of the ship or I will order my men to board your craft and we will take them by force.'

Luca looked down; there were about a dozen men in the galley, fully armed. He glanced at Freize, who stoically hefted his cudgel. Clearly, they could fight; but the odds were heavily against them. They were certain to lose.

The commander turned to the boatman, who was grimly listening in the stern of the boat. 'You are carrying stolen goods: these two women belong to the Lord of Lucretili. If I have to, I will board your ship to take them, and there may be damage to your ship or danger to you. Or you can give them up to me and there will be no trouble.'

'I took them in good faith as passengers,' the boatman shouted back. 'If they are yours, they can go with you. I'm not responsible for them.'

'There's no point fighting,' Isolde said very low to Luca. 'It's hopeless. Don't try anything. I'll give myself up.'

Before he could protest, she called down to the man in the galley below: 'Do you give your word that you will take us safely to my brother?'

He nodded. 'I am commanded not to harm you in any way.'

She made up her mind. 'Get our things but leave the sword,' she said over her shoulder to Ishraq, who quickly went to the cabin and came out with their two saddlebags, tucking Freize's knife out of sight, into the rope at her belt.

'And what is to happen to me?' Isolde demanded. She beckoned Ishraq to go with her as she went to the prow of the boat. The commander gestured to Luca and Freize that they should haul his boat alongside, so that the young women could climb down over the rail and into the waiting galley.

'Your brother believes that you are trying to get to the Count of Wallachia for his help. He thinks you will try to get an army to come against him and claim your home. So he's going to marry you to a French count who will take you away and keep you in his castle.'

'And what about me?' Ishraq asked, as Luca, Freize and Peter each took a grappling iron and, pulling on the ropes, walked the galley to the prow of the boat.

'You, I have to sell to the Ottomans as a slave, in Venice,' the man said. 'I am sorry. Those are my orders.'

Luca, whose father and mother had been captured by an Ottoman slaving galley when he was just a boy, went white and gripped the rail for support. 'We can't allow this,' he said to Freize. 'I can't allow it. We can't let this happen.'

But Freize was watching Isolde, who had suddenly halted at the news that Ishraq would not be with her. 'No. She comes with me,' she said. 'We are never separated.'

The man shook his head. 'My orders are clear. She is to be sold to the Ottomans.'

'Be ready,' Freize whispered to Luca. 'I don't think she'll stand for that.'

574

Isolde had reached the front of the ship. Stowed at her feet was an axe kept for emergencies – if a sail came down in a storm or if fishing nets had to be cut free. She did not even glance at it as she stepped up on the tightly knotted anchor rope, so that she could look down over the rail at the man who had come for her. 'Sir, I have money,' she pleaded. 'Whatever my brother is paying you I will match, if you will just go back to him and say that you could not find us. Your men too can have a fee if you will just go away.'

He spread his hands. 'My lady, I am your brother's loyal servant. I have promised to take you back to him and sell her into slavery. Come down, or I will come and get you both, and your friends will suffer.'

She bit her lip. 'Please. Take me, and leave my friend. You can tell the lord my brother that you could not find her.'

Wordlessly, he shook his head. 'Come,' he said bluntly. 'Both of you. At once.'

'I don't want any fighting,' she said desperately. 'I don't want anyone hurt for me.'

'Then come now,' he said simply. 'For we will take you one way or another. I am ordered to take you dead or alive.'

Freize saw her shoulders set with her resolve, but all she said was: 'Very well. I'll throw my things down first.'

The commander nodded and put a hand on the grappling iron rope and drew his galley closer to their gently bobbing ship. Isolde leaned over the rail, holding the heavy saddlebag. 'Come closer,' she said. 'I don't want to lose my things.'

He laughed at the acquisitive nature of all women – that Isolde should be such a fool as to be still thinking of dresses while being kidnapped! – and hauled the galley in even closer. The moment that it was directly under the prow of the ship Isolde dropped the saddlebag down to him. He caught it in his arms, and staggered back slightly at the weight of it, and at the same time she snatched up the hatchet and, with three or four quick, frenzied blows, hacked through the rope which held the heavy ship's anchor against the side of the boat.

Solid hammered iron, monstrously heavy, it plunged downwards and crashed straight through the galley's light wood deck, and straight through the bottom of the galley, smashing an enormous hole and breaking the sides of the craft so the water rushed in from the bottom and from the sides.

In a second Ishraq had jumped to be at her side, and had thrown her knife straight into the man's face. He took the blade in his mouth and screamed as blood gushed out. Luca, Freize, and Brother Peter took the grappling irons and flung them onto the heads of the rowers below them, as water poured into the galley and the waves engulfed the ship.

'Hoist the sail!' Luca yelled, but already the boatman and his lad were hauling on the ropes and the sail bellied, flapped and then filled with the light wind and the ship started to move away from the sinking galley. Some of the rowers were in the water already, thrashing about and shouting for help.

'Go back!' Isolde shouted. 'We can't leave them to drown.'

'We can,' Ishraq said fiercely. 'They would have killed us.'

There were some wooden battens at the front of the boat. Isolde ran to them and started to haul on them. Freize went

576

to help her, lifted them to the rail and pushed them into the water to serve as life rafts. 'Someone will pick them up,' he assured her. 'There are ships up and down this coast all the time and it will soon be light.'

Her eyes were filled with tears, she was white with distress. 'That man! The knife in his face!'

'He would have sold me into slavery!' Ishraq shouted at her angrily. 'He was taking you back to your brother! What did you want to happen?'

'You could have killed him!'

'Why should I not kill him? You're a fool to worry about him.'

Isolde turned, shaking, to Brother Peter. 'It is a sin, isn't it, to kill a man, whatever the circumstances?'

'It is,' he allowed. 'But Ishraq was defending herself ...'

'I don't care!' Ishraq claimed. 'I think you are mad to even think about him. He was your enemy. He was going to take you back to your brother. He was going to sell me into slavery. He would have killed us both. Of course I would defend myself. But if I had wanted to kill him, I would have put the knife through his eye and he would be dead now, instead of just missing his teeth.'

Isolde looked back. Some of the crew had clambered back aboard the wreckage of their boat. The commander, his face still red with blood, was hanging on to the battens that she and Freize had thrown into the water.

'The main thing is that you saved yourself and Ishraq,' Luca said to her. 'And they'll have to report back to your brother, so you should be safe for a while. Ishraq was wonderful, and so were you. Don't regret being brave, Isolde. You saved all of us.'

577

She laughed shakily. 'I don't know how I thought of it!'

Ishraq hugged her tightly. 'You were brilliant,' she said warmly. 'I had no idea what you were doing. It was perfect.'

'It just came to me. When they said they would take you.'

'You would have gone with them rather than fight?'

Isolde nodded. 'But I couldn't let you be taken. Not into slavery.'

'It was the right thing to do,' Luca ruled, glancing at Brother Peter, who nodded in agreement.

'A just cause,' he said thoughtfully.

'And your knife throw!' Luca turned to Ishraq. 'Where did you ever learn to throw like that?'

'My mother was determined I should know how to defend myself,' Ishraq smiled. 'She taught me how to throw a knife, and Isolde's father the Lord of Lucretili sent me to the masters in Spain to learn fighting skills. I learned it at the same time as my archery – and other things.'

'We should give thanks for our escape,' Brother Peter said, holding the crucifix that he always wore on a girdle at his waist. 'You two did very well. You were very quick, and very brave.' He turned to Isolde. 'I am sorry I could not lie for you.'

She nodded. 'I understand, of course.'

'And you will need to confess, Brother Luca,' Peter said gently to the younger man. 'As soon as we get to Venice. You denied your oath to the Church, you told a string of untruths and—' he broke off, 'you kissed her.'

'It was just to make the lie convincing,' Isolde defended Luca.

'He was tremendously convincing,' Freize said

admiringly, with a wink at Ishraq. 'You would almost have thought that he wanted to kiss her. I almost thought that he enjoyed kissing her. Thought that she kissed him back. Completely fooled me.'

'Well, I shall give thanks for our safety,' the older man said and went a little way from them and got down on his knees to pray. Freize went down the ship to speak to the boatman at the rudder. Ishraq turned away.

'It was not just to make the lie convincing,' Luca admitted very quietly to Isolde. 'I felt . . .' he broke off. He did not have words for how he had felt when she had been pressed against him and his mouth had been on hers.

She said nothing, she just looked at him. He was fascinated by the ribbon which tied her cape at her throat. He could see it fluttering slightly with the rapid pulse at her neck.

'It can never happen again,' Luca said. 'I am going to complete my novitiate and make my vows as a priest, and you are a lady of great wealth and position. If you can raise your army and win back your castle and your lands you will marry a great lord, perhaps a prince.'

She nodded, her eyes never leaving his face.

'For a moment back then, I wished it was true, and that we had married,' Luca confessed with a shy laugh. 'Wedded and bedded, as the man said. But I know that's impossible.'

'It is impossible,' she agreed. 'It is quite impossible.'

Some hours after, the sky slowly grew bright and the five travellers got up from where they had been sitting at the back of the boat and went to the prow to look east where the rising sun was turning the wispy clouds pink and gold with the dawn light. From the back of the boat the boatman called to them that they were entering the Lagoon of Venice, God be praised that they were safe at last after such a night, and at once they felt the movement of the ship quieten as the waves stilled. This inland sea, sheltered by the ring of outer islands, was as calm as a gently moving lake, so shallow in some parts that they could see the nets of fishermen pinned just beneath the surface of the water, but deep channels wound around the islands, sometimes marked by a single rough post thrust into the lagoon bed.

Ishraq and Isolde gripped each other's hands as their little ship found its way through a dozen, a hundred little islands, some no bigger than a single house and a garden, with a wherry or a small sailing boat bobbing at the quay. Some of the smaller islands were little forests and mudflats, occupied only by wading birds, some looked like solitary farms with one farmhouse and outbuildings with roofs thatched with reeds, the whole island subdivided into little fields. The bigger islands were bustling with people, ships loading and unloading at the stone quays, the chimneys of low houses bursting with dark smoke, and they could glimpse the red shine of furnaces inside the sheds.

'Glassworks,' the boatman explained. 'They're not allowed to make glass in the city because of the danger of fire. They're terrified of fire, the Venetians. They have nowhere to run.'

As they drew closer to the city, the islands became more built-up, bordered by stone quays, some with stone steps down to the water, the bigger ones with paved streets and some with little bridges linking them, one to another. Every house was surrounded by a garden, sometimes an orchard. Every big house stood behind high stone walls, so that the travellers could just see the tops of the leafless wintry trees and hear the birdsong from the gardens.

'This is the Grand Canal now,' the boatman said as the boat went slowly up the wide, sinuous stretch of water. 'Like the main road, like the biggest high street of the city. The biggest high street in the world.'

Now the bigger houses were built directly onto the canal, some of them with great front doors that opened straight onto the water, some of them had a gate at the front of the house to allow a boat to float directly into the house as if the river were a welcome guest.

As Isolde watched, one of these water doors opened and a gondola came out, sleek as a black fish, with the brightly dressed gondolier standing in the stern and rowing with his single oar as the gentleman sat in the middle of the boat, a black cape around his shoulders and an embroidered hat on his head, his face hidden by a beautifully decorated mask which revealed only his smiling mouth.

'Oh! Look!' she exclaimed. 'What a beautiful little boat, and see how it came out of the house?'

'Called a gondola,' the boatman explained. 'The Venetians have them like land dwellers have a litter or a cart to get about. Every big house has a watergate so that their gondola can come and go.'

Isolde could not take her eyes from the beautiful craft, and the gentleman nodded his head and raised a gloved hand to her as he swept by.

'Carnival,' Brother Peter said quietly as he saw the magnificently coloured waistcoat under the gentleman's dark cape and the brilliantly coloured mask that covered his face. 'We could not have come to the city at a worse time.'

'What's so bad about the carnival?' Ishraq asked curiously, looking after the black gondola and the handsome masked man.

'It is twenty days of indulgence and sin before Lent,' Brother Peter replied. '*Carnevale* as they call it, is a byword for the worst behaviour. If we were enquiring into sin we would have nothing to do but to point at every passer-by. The city is famous for vice. We will have to stay indoors as much as possible, and avoid the endless drinking and promenading and dancing. And worse.'

'But what a grand house!' Isolde exclaimed. 'Like

a palace! Did you see inside? The stone stairs coming down to his own private quay? And the torches inside the building?'

'Look!' Ishraq pointed ahead of them. There were more houses directly on the water's edge, most of them standing on little islands completely surrounded by water, the islands connected with thin, arching wooden bridges. On the left side the travellers could see the spires of churches beyond the waterfront houses, and at every second or third house they could see a narrow dark canal winding its way deeper into the heart of the city, and smaller canals branching from it, each one crowded with gondolas and working boats, every quay busy with people, half of them dressed in fantastic costumes, the women tottering on impossibly high shoes, some of them so tall that they had a maidservant to walk beside them for support.

'What are they wearing on their feet? They're like stilts!' Ishraq exclaimed.

'They are called chopines,' Brother Peter said. 'They keep the ladies' gowns and feet clear of the water when the streets are flooded.' He looked consideringly at the women, who could not stand unsupported but looked magnificent, tall as giantesses, in their beautiful billowing long gowns. 'The Holy Church approves of them,' he said.

'I would have thought you would have called them a ridiculous vanity?' Ishraq asked curiously.

'Since they prevent dancing, and women cannot walk about on their own while wearing them, they are a great discouragement to sin,' Brother Peter replied. 'That's a great advantage.'

'It is as everyone said, the city is built on the water,' Isolde said wonderingly. 'The houses stand side by side like boats moored closely in a port.'

'I've never seen anything like it. How will the horses get about?' Freize asked.

'The boatman will take them a little out of the city, after he has set us down,' Brother Peter told him. 'When we need them, we'll take a boat to get to them. There are no horses in Venice, everyone goes everywhere by boat.'

'The goods for market?' Freize asked.

'Come in by boat and are loaded and unloaded at the quayside.'

'The inns?'

'Take travellers who leave and arrive by boat. They have no stable yards.'

'The priests who attend the churches?'

'Come and go by boat. Every church has its own stone quayside.'

'Aha, and so how do they get the stone for building?' Freize demanded, as if he was finally about to catch Brother Peter in a travellers' tale.

'They have great barges that bring in the stone,' Brother Peter replied. 'Everything comes by boat, I tell you. They even have great barges that bring in the drinking water.'

This was too much for Freize. 'Now I know you are deceiving me,' he said. 'The one thing this city does not lack is water! They must be born with webbed feet, these Venetians.'

'They are a strange and unique people,' Brother Peter conceded. 'They govern themselves without a king, they have no roads, no highways, they are the wealthiest city in Christendom, they live on the sea and by the sea. They are expanding constantly, and their only god is trade; but they have built the most beautiful churches on every canal and decorated them with the most inspiring holy pictures. Every church is a treasure house of sacred art. Yet they act as if they are as far from God as they are from the mainland and there is no way to get to Him but a voyage.'

Now they were approaching the heart of the city. The broad canal was walled on either side with white Istrian stone to make a continuous quay, occasionally pierced by a tributary canal winding deeper inside the city. Many of the smaller inner canals were crossed by little wooden bridges, a few were crossed by steeply stepped bridges of white stone. The ferry was losing the cold breeze and so the boatman took down the sails and set to row; he took an oar on one side, and his lad heaved on the other. They wound their way through the constant river traffic of gondolas going swiftly through the water with loud warning cries from the gondoliers in the sterns of 'Gondola! Gondola! Gondola!'

The canal was crowded with fishing ships, the flat-bottomed barges for carrying heavy goods, the ferry boats heaving with poorer people, and criss-crossing through the traffic going from one side to the other were public gondolas for hire. To the two young women who had been raised in a small country castle, it was impossibly busy and glamorous, they looked from right to left and could not believe what they were seeing. Every gondola carried passengers, heavily cloaked with their faces hidden by carnival masks. The women wore masks adorned with dyed plumes of feathers, the eyeholes slit like the eyes of a cat, a brightly coloured hood covering their hair, a bejewelled fan hiding their smiling lips. Even more intriguing were the gondolas where the little cabin in the middle of the slim ship had the doors resolutely shut on hidden lovers, and the gondolier was rowing slowly, impassive in the stern. Sometimes a second gondola followed the first with musicians playing lingering love songs, for the entertainment of the secret couple.

'Sin, everywhere,' Brother Peter said, averting his gaze.

'There's only one bridge across the Grand Canal,' the boatman told them. 'Everywhere else you have to take a boat to cross. It's a good city to be a ferryman. And this is it, the only bridge: the Rialto.'

It was a high wooden bridge, many feet above the canal, arching up so steeply that even masted ships could pass easily beneath it, rising up from both sides of the canal almost like a pinnacle, crowded with people, laden with little stalls and shops. There was a constant stream of pedestrians walking up the stairs on one side and down the other, pausing to shop, stopping to buy, leaning on the high parapet to watch the ships go underneath, arguing the prices, changing their money. The whole bridge was a shimmer of colour and noise.

The square of San Giacomo, just beside the bridge, was just as busy, lined with the tall houses of the merchants. All the nations of Christendom, and many of the infidel, were shown by their own flag and the national costume of the men doing business at the windows and doorway. Next to them stood the great houses of the Venetian banking families, the front doors standing open for business, absurdly costumed people coming and going, trading and buying in all seriousness, though dressed as if they were strolling players, with great plumed hats on their heads and bright jewelled masks on their faces.

In the square itself the bankers and gold merchants had their tables laid out all around the colonnade, one to every arch, and were trading in coin, promises and precious metals. When money was changing hands the masks were laid aside, as each client wanted to look his banker in the eye. Among them were Ottoman traders, their brightly coloured turbans and gorgeous robes as beautiful as any costume. Venice had all but captured the trade of the Ottoman Empire and the wealth of the East flowed into Europe across the Venice traders' tables. There was no other route to the East, there was no easy navigable way to Russia. Venice was at the very centre of world trade and the riches of east and west, north and south poured into it from every side.

'The Rialto,' Luca reminded Freize. 'This is where that infidel, Radu Bey, said that there was a priest, Father Pietro, who ransoms Christian slaves from the galleys of the Ottomans. This is it, this is the bridge, this is where he said. Perhaps Father Pietro is here now, perhaps I will be able to ransom my father and mother.'

'We'll come out as soon as we are settled in our house,' Freize promised him. 'But Sparrow, you will remember that the Ottoman gentleman, Radu Bey, seems to be the sworn enemy of the lord who commands your Order, and neither he nor t'other inspire me with trust.'

Luca laughed. 'I know. You do right to warn me. But Freize, you know I would take advice from the Devil him-self if I thought I could get my father and mother back home. Just to see them again! Just to know they were alive.'

Freize put his hand on his friend's shoulder. 'I know,' he said. 'And they will have missed you too – they have missed your growing up and they loved you so dearly. If we can find them and buy them out of slavery it will be a great thing. I am just saying – don't get your hopes up too high. They were captured by the Ottoman slavers and it was an Ottoman general who told us that we might buy them back. Just because he was well-read and spoke fair to you does not make him a friend.'

'Ishraq liked him too, and she's a good judge of character,' Luca objected.

A shadow crossed Freize's honest face. 'Ishraq liked him better than she liked the lord of your Order,' he told Luca. 'I wouldn't trust her judgement with the foreign lord myself. I don't know what game he was playing with her when he spoke to her in Arabic that only she could understand. Come to that, I don't know what game she was playing when she swore to me that he said nothing.'

'And here is your palazzo,' the boatman remarked. 'Ca' de Longhi, just west of the Piazza San Marco, very nice.'

'A palace?' Isolde exclaimed. 'We have hired a palace?'

'All the grand houses on the canal are palaces, though they are all called Casa – only the Doge's house is called a palace,' the boatman explained. 'And the reason for that, is that they are each and every one of them, the most beautiful palaces ever built in the world.'

'And do princes live here?' Ishraq asked. 'In all these palaces?'

'Better than princes,' he smiled at her. 'Richer than princes, and greater than kings. The merchants of Venice live here and you will find no greater power in this city or in all of Italy!'

He steered towards the little quayside at the side of the

house, leaned hard on the rudder and brought the boat alongside with a gentle bump. He looked up at the beautiful frescoes on either side of the great water door, and all around the house, and then at Luca with a new level of respect. 'You are welcome, Your Grace,' he said, suddenly adjusting his view of the handsome young merchant who must surely command the fortune of a prince if he could afford such a palace to rent.

Freize saw the calculating look and nudged the boatman gently. 'We'll pay double for the trouble and danger,' he said shortly. 'And you'll oblige us by keeping the story of the galley to yourself.'

'Of course, sir,' the boatman said, accepting a heavy purse of coins. He jumped nimbly onto the broad steps, tied the boat fore and aft and put out his hand to help the ladies on shore.

Glancing at each other, very conscious that they were playing a part, Ishraq and Isolde, Luca and Brother Peter stepped onto the stone pavement before their house. The door for pedestrians was at the side of the house, overlooking the smaller tributary canal. It stood open and the housekeeper bobbed a curtsey and led the way into the cool shaded hall.

First, as always, before they did anything else, Brother Peter, Luca and Isolde had to go to church and give thanks for their safe arrival. Ishraq and Freize, as an infidel and a servant, were excused.

'Go to the Rialto,' Luca ordered Freize. 'See if they have heard of Father Pietro. I will come myself to speak with him later.'

Luca, Brother Peter and Isolde, with her hood pulled modestly forward, left the house by the little door onto the paved way beside the narrow canal and turned to their right to walk through the narrow alley to the Piazza San Marco where the great church bells echoed out, ringing for Terce, sending the pigeons soaring up into the cold blue sky, and the gorgeously costumed Venetians posed and paraded up to the very doors of the church itself.

Ishraq and Freize closed the side door on their companions and stood for a moment in the quiet hall.

'May I show you the rooms?' the housekeeper asked them, and led them up the wide flight of marble stairs to the first floor of the building where a large reception room overlooked the canal with huge double-height windows leading to a little balcony. The grand room was warm, a small fire burned in the grate and the sunshine poured in through the window. Leading off were three smaller rooms.

The housekeeper led them up again to the same layout of rooms on the upper floor. 'We'll take the top floor,' Ishraq said. 'You can have the first.'

'And above you are the kitchens and the servants' rooms,' the housekeeper said, gesturing to the smaller stairs that went on up.

'Kitchens in the attic?' Freize asked.

'To keep the house safe in case of fire,' she said. 'We Venetians are so afraid of fire, and we have no space to put the kitchens at a distance from the house on the ground floor. All the space on the ground floor is the courtyard and the garden, and at the front of the house the quay and the watergate.'

'And are you the cook?' Freize asked, thinking that he would be glad of a good lunch when the others came back from church.

She nodded.

'We'll go and run our errands and perhaps return to a large lunch?' Freize hinted. 'For we had a long cold night with nothing but some bread and a few eggs, and I, for one, would be glad to try the Venice specialities and your cooking.'

She smiled. 'I shall have it ready for you. Will you take the gondola?'

Freize and Ishraq exchanged a delighted grin. 'Can we?' Ishraq asked.

'Of course,' she replied. 'It's the only way to get around this city.' She led the way down the marble stairs to the ground floor, to the waterside front of the house, and their own private quay, where their gondola rocked at its moorings. The housekeeper waved them down the final flight of stairs and indicated the manservant who came out of a doorway, wiping his mouth and pulling on his bright feathered cap.

'Giuseppe,' she said by way of introduction. 'He will take you wherever you want to go, and wait and bring you home.'

The man pulled the boat close to the quay, and held out his hand to help Ishraq aboard. Freize stepped heavily after her and Ishraq cried out and then laughed as the boat rocked.

'This is going to take some getting used to,' Freize said. 'I am missing Rufino already; how ever will he manage without me?' He turned to the gondolier, Giuseppe. 'Can you take us to the Rialto?'

'Of course,' the boatman said and loosened the tasselled tie that held the gondola prow against the wall of the house. He stepped onto the platform in the stern and with one skilful push of the single oar thrust them out of the house and into the teeming water traffic of the Grand Canal.

Freize and Ishraq sat in the middle of the boat and looked around, as their boat nosed through the crowded canal. Hucksters and merchants were on little ships, coming close to every craft and offering their wares, wherries and rowing boats for hire were threading their way through the traffic, great barges carrying beams and stone took the centre of the canal and rowed to the beat of the drum. Freize and Ishraq, the fair, square-faced young man and the brown-skinned, dark-haired girl in their expensive private gondola, drew glances as the gondolier drew up at the Rialto Bridge with a flourish, leaped ashore, and offered his hand to Ishraq.

She drew her hood over her head and her veil across her face as she stepped on the shore. She noticed that there were serving women, and working women, beggars and store keepers, and women in gaudy yellow with heavily painted faces, tottering along on absurdly tall shoes; but there were no gentlewomen or noblewomen on the wide stone square before the bridge, and at all the windows of the trading houses there were severe-looking men in dark suits who seemed to disapprove of a young woman in the square among the businessmen.

'Where d'you think Father Pietro might be?' Freize asked, staring around him.

The square was so filled with people, so noisy and so bustling, that Ishraq could only shake her head in wonderment. Someone was charming a snake for a handful of onlookers, the basket rocking from one side to another as he played his pipe, the straw lid starting to lift, only a dark eye showing, and a questing forked tongue. A row of merchants had their table under the shelter of the broad colonnade, and were changing money from one foreign currency to another, the beads on the abacus rattling like castanets as the men calculated the value. Beside the river, a belated fisherman was landing his catch and selling it fresh to a couple of servants. The huge fish market had opened at dawn and sold out a few hours later. There was a constant swirl of men coming and going from the great trading houses which surrounded the square on all sides. Errand boys with baskets on their heads and on their arms dashed about their business, shoppers crowded the little stores on either side of the high Rialto Bridge, traders shouted their wares from the rocking boats at the quayside; every nationality was there, buying, selling, arguing, making money, from the dark-suited German bankers to the gloriously robed traders from the Ottoman Empire, and even beyond.

'We'll have to ask someone,' Ishraq said, quite dazzled by this, the busiest trading centre in the world. 'He could be next to us, and we wouldn't know it. He could be two steps away and we would hardly spot him. I've never been in such a crowd, I've never seen so many people all at once. Not even in Spain!'

'Like hell,' Freize said matter-of-fact. 'Bound to be crowded.'

Ishraq laughed and turned away from the river to look for someone, a priest or a monk or a friar that she could ask, then she saw the gambler.

The girl had laid out her game on the stone floor of the square, covering one of the white marble slabs with sand, to make a little area where the play could take place. The crowd had gathered around her, three deep. It was the ancient game of cups and ball: Ishraq had seen it played in Spain, and had been told it came from ancient Egypt; she had even seen it at Lucretili Castle when she was a little girl and a troubadour had taken her pocket money off her with the simple trick.

It was three downturned cups with a little ball hidden underneath one of them. The game player moved the cups at dazzling speed, then sat back and invited the onlookers to put down their coins before the cup where they had last seen the ball.

It was the simplest game in the world since everyone knew where the ball was, everyone had watched as the cup was moved. Then the player lifted the cups and *voila*! The ball was not under the one that the crowd had picked. The player lifted another cup and it was under the second one. The player picked up the pennies of the bet, showed the empty cups, showed the little ball – but in this case it was a most beautiful translucent glass marble – put the ball under the cup again, bade the onlookers to watch carefully, and moved the cups around, two or three times, at first very slowly, and then a dozen moves, very fast.

What attracted Ishraq to this game was the game player. She was a girl of about eighteen years old, dressed in a brown gown with a modest hood; her pale intent face was downturned to her work but when she looked up she had dark eyes and a bright smile. She sat back on her heels when she had moved the cups and looked up at the crowd around her with an air of absolute trustworthiness. 'My lords, ladies, gentlemen ...' she said sweetly. 'Will you bet?'

Nobody looking at her could think for one moment that she had managed some sleight of hand. Not while they were all watching, not in broad daylight. The ball must be where she put it first: under the cup on the right which she had slid to the left, swirled to the centre, back to the right, then there had been some moving of the other cups as a rather obvious diversion, before she had finally moved it again to the centre.

'It's in the middle,' Freize whispered in Ishraq's ear.

'I'll bet you that it isn't,' Ishraq said. 'I was following it, but I lost it.'

'I watched it all the while! It's plumb in the middle!' Freize fumbled with coins and put down a piccoli – a silver penny.

The girl waited for a moment until everyone had put down their bets, most of them, like Freize, favouring the central cup. Then she upturned the cup and showed it: empty. She scooped up all the coins that the gamblers had put down on the stone before the empty cup, and put them in the pocket of her apron, and then showed them the empty cup on the left, and then finally the glass marble beneath the right-hand cup. Nobody had guessed correctly. With a merry smile which encouraged them to try their luck again, she smoothed the sand with her hand, placed the marble under the left-hand cup and swirled the cups around once more.

Ishraq was not watching the cups this time, but observing an older man who was moving among the crowd, standing close to the group of gamblers. He looked like a betting man himself, his gaze was bright and avid, his hat pulled low over his face, his smile pleasant. But he was watching the crowd, not the fast-moving hands of the girl.

'That's the shill,' Ishraq said to Freize.

'The what?'

'The shill – her partner. He might distract the crowd at the exact moment that she makes the switch, so that

597

they don't see where the cup has gone. But I think she's too good for that. She doesn't need anyone to distract the gamblers, so all he has to do is watch the crowd and prepare for trouble. Certainly he'll take the money when she has finished and walk her home.'

Freize hardly glanced up, he was so fixed on the game. 'This time, I'm certain, I know where the marble is.'

Ishraq laughed and cuffed his bent head. 'You will lose your money,' she predicted. 'This girl is very good. She has very quick hands and excellent poise. She looks at her calmest when her hands are going fastest. And she smiles like an honest child.'

Freize pushed Ishraq's hand away, confident of his own skill. He put down a second piccoli before the cup on the left and was rewarded with a little gleam from the girl in the brown gown. She lifted the cups. The marble was under the right-hand cup.

'Well I—' Freize exclaimed.

Ishraq's dark eyes smiled at him over her veil. 'How much money do you have?' she asked. 'For they will happily take it all day, if you are fool enough to put it down.'

'I saw it, I am sure!' Freize exclaimed. 'I was completely sure! It was like magic!'

The girl in brown glanced up and winked at him.

'It's a clever game, and you are a clever player,' Freize said to her. 'Do you ever lose?'

'Of course,' she replied with a slight Parisian accent. 'But mostly, I win. It's a simple game, good for amusement and for a few pence.'

'More than a few pence,' Ishraq observed to herself, looking at the pile of small silver coins that the girl scooped up.

'Will you try your luck again?' the girl invited Freize.

'I will!' Freize declared. 'But I cannot bet my lucky penny.'

With great care he took a penny from the breast pocket of his jacket, kissed it, and put it back. The girl laughed at him, her brown eyes twinkling.

'I hope it works for you this time,' she said. 'For it has not done much for you so far.'

'It will,' he promised her. 'And this time, I shan't take my eyes off you!'

She smiled and showed him the three empty cups. Freize squatted down so that he was opposite her and nodded as she put the marble on the ground and then the central cup on top of it. Watching carefully, he saw she slid it to the right, and then round to the extreme left, she hopped another cup around it and then she took it back out to the left again. There was a dizzying swirl of cups as she slid one and then another and then she was still.

'Which one?' she challenged him.

Freize tipped all the small coins from his purse into his hand and put them down before the cup on the left. All the men around him, who had been watching, put their coins down too.

With a little laugh the young woman lifted the left-hand cup. It was empty. She lifted the middle cup, and there was the shining marble stone.

Freize laughed and shook his head. 'It's a good game and you outwitted me completely,' he admitted.

'It's a cheat!' someone said in a hard voice behind him. 'I have put down the best part of a silver lira and watched for half an hour and I can't see how it's done.'

'That's what makes it a good game,' Freize said to him smiling. 'If you could see how it was done it would be a trick for children. But she's a bonny lass with the quickest hands I've ever seen. I couldn't see how it was done and I practically had my nose in the cups.'

'It's a cheat, and she should be thrown out of the city as a trickster,' the man said harshly. He looked like a sulky fool in his masquing costume of bright blue, with a dancing cap on his head and a dangling bell which tinkled as he thrust his face forwards. 'And you're probably part of the gang.'

'The gang?' Freize repeated slowly. 'What gang would this be?'

'The gang who are using her to cheat good citizens out of their hard-earned money!'

Freize looked past the angry man to his friends. 'Best get him home?' he suggested mildly. 'Nobody likes a bad loser.'

'I should report her to the Doge!' the man insisted, getting louder, his bell jingling as he nodded his head. 'I have friends in the palace – I know several of the Council of Forty. I can write a denouncement and put it in the box as easily as the next good citizen. The city depends on honest traders! We don't like cheats in Venice!'

Freize rose to his feet and let the man see his height, his broad shoulders and his honest friendly face. Ishraq noticed the girl gather her money into a purse and tuck it under her robe, and the swift glance that passed between her and her accomplice in the crowd. Quietly, her partner moved so that he was between her and the disgruntled gambler. For a girl working as a gambler in the streets she looked surprisingly apprehensive at this minor trouble. Ishraq would have expected her to be accustomed to brawls.

'It's really nothing to do with us,' Ishraq suggested quietly, putting a hand on the back of Freize's jacket. 'And we don't want to draw attention to ourselves. Why don't we just go now?'

'I want my money back!' the man said loudly, tossing the hem of his cape over his shoulder and stripping off his blue gauntlets as if he were readying himself for a fight. 'I want it now.'

The shill stepped forwards so that he was beside the girl, who bent down to smooth the sand out and kept her head low, almost crouching down, as Freize spoke to the angry man in blue.

'Now you wait a moment,' Freize said, completely ignoring Ishraq's warning. 'Did you bet that the pretty stone was under the cup?'

'Yes!' the man said. 'Over and over.'

'And were you wrong?'

'Yes! Over and over!'

'And did you put your money down?'

'Six times!'

'Six times,' Freize marvelled. 'Then I have good advice for a man as clever as you. Don't waste your time here: go to the university!'

Completely distracted, the man hesitated and then asked: 'Why? What d'you mean?'

Everyone waited for Freize's answer, the shill standing protectively over the girl as she looked curiously upwards.

'At the university, at Padua, they take students who study for years. And here, in one morning, you have taken six tries to discover that her hands are quicker than your eyes. See how slow you are to observe the obvious! Think how long you could study at Padua! It could be the occupation of a lifetime. You could become a philosopher.'

There was a roar of laughter from the man's friends, and they slapped him on the back and called him 'Philosopher!' and jostled him away. Ishraq watched them go and turned back to see the young woman was laying out the game again. The little quarrel had attracted more attention and this time there were more bets, on all three cups, so that she was forced to pay out to some players. She took some silver and handed over two quarter gold nobles and then packed up her cups and her ball and swept the white sand into the crevices of the paving stones to indicate that play was ended for the day.

'Thank you,' she said briefly to Freize and she fastened her little satchel.

'Thank you for the game,' Freize said. 'I am new in town and it is a pleasure to see a pretty girl at her work. What's your name, sweetheart?'

'Jacinta,' she said. 'This is my father, Drago Nacari.'

'A pleasure to meet you both,' Freize said, pulling off his hat and smiling down at her as she rose to her feet and handed the heavy purse of money to her father.

'Have you heard of a priest called Father Pietro?' Ishraq asked her, recalling Freize to their task.

She nodded. 'Everyone knows him. He sits over there, at the corner of the bridge; he has a little desk and a great list of many, many names of people enslaved, poor souls. He comes after Sext. You will find him here after the clock has struck one.' She gave them a little bow and walked away from them. Her father tipped his hat to them both and walked with her. Freize looked after her.

'I think I am in love,' he said.

'I think you are hopelessly fickle,' Ishraq said. 'You swore a lifetime of service to Isolde, you insisted on a kiss from me, you flirted with the innkeeper's wife in Piccolo, and now you are chasing after a girl who has done nothing but take money off you.'

'But her hands!' Freize exclaimed. 'So fast! So light! Think, if you married her, of the cakes she would make! She must make fantastic pastries with hands as quick and light as that.'

Ishraq giggled at the thought of Freize lusting after a young woman because he thought she would make a good pastry cook. 'Shall we wait for Father Pietro?'

Freize nodded, looking round. 'While we're waiting, we could change some coins. I have a handful of coins that I took from Milord's funds. Luca has to study the gold coins here, the lord of his Order commanded him to look at the gold nobles. Shall we try that man, see if he has any English nobles?'

They walked over to a long trestle table. Behind it, on a row of stools, sat the money changers. Each man had a small chalkboard beside him, and constantly wrote and rewrote the exchange rate of the coins he had to offer. One man was busier than all the others, he had a queue of men waiting to do business with him. As they watched, he altered his sign to read:

Two Venetian Ducats for One Gold Noble of England.

Ishraq nudged Freize. 'He has them,' she said quietly. 'That moneylender. He has English gold nobles, and at a better rate than all the others.'

Freize stepped up to the man, who was dressed all in black, except for a bright round yellow badge that he wore on his chest, his dark hair plaited away from his clean-shaven face, a small black cap, the *kippah,* on the back of his head, his fingers busy with a small worn abacus, two locked boxes on the table before him, a young man standing for protection behind him.

'I'd like to change some money,' Freize said politely.

'Good day,' the man replied. 'Today, I am only offering English gold, English gold nobles. Their value at the moment is of two Venice ducats.'

'Good day to you,' Freize replied. 'Is that good value? I am a stranger in the city.'

'I am Israel, the Jew. I can promise that you will find no better price.'

Freize took out his purse and emptied it onto the desk, then he went through all his pockets, of his breeches and his jacket, and even the band of his hat, producing coins from the most unexpected places, much like a conjuror.

'What are you doing?' Ishraq asked, amused.

'Can't be too careful,' Freize said. 'You steal my purse from me but – *ecce!* – half my fortune is in my hat.'

The trader started to sort the copper from the silver, the bronze and the chips of metal, and weigh them.

'Do you have much English gold?' Freize said casually.

'I buy only gold of the best quality,' the man replied. 'And last year these English nobles started to become available in great numbers. They are excellent quality, the best gold that can be got. They are as good as gold: the coin is pure gold, there is nothing added and nothing taken away.'

He started to weigh the coins against tiny weights, the smallest the size of a grain of wheat, in a precisely balanced scale. 'I see you are a traveller,' the man remarked. 'For here are coins from Rome and from Ravenna, and from the west of Italy too.'

'I'm in the service of a lord from the west of Italy.' Freize told the lie that they had agreed. It was coming more and more easily to him. 'A young lord who wants to visit this city and try his hand at trade here. He has a share in a cargo in a ship which is coming in any day now.'

'He could come to nowhere more prosperous. I wish him good fortune,' the man said quietly. 'Tell him to come to me for fair dealing in gold. Now,' he paused and looked doubtfully at the scales. 'I am sorry to have to tell you that some of your coins are not very good. Some of them have been clipped to make them into smaller coins, and some of them have been shaved and the value stolen from them.'

Freize shrugged. 'It's the luck of the road. I trust you to deal fairly with me. Oh!' he exclaimed. 'I had forgotten.' He leaned over the table and picked out one copper penny coin. 'I should not have put this among the others,' he said. 'It's my lucky penny. I don't want to change it. I keep it for good fortune.'

'Since when did you have a lucky penny?' Ishraq asked him. 'I thought you were just telling that girl a story. What's so lucky about it?'

'I had it in my pocket when I was snatched by the sea, and when everything else was washed from my pocket I still had this one penny,' Freize said. 'And do you see? It was minted by the Pope himself, in the Vatican, in the year of my birth. It's practically an amulet. What could be luckier than that?'

The merchant bowed slightly and put the rest of the copper coins in his set of scales, balanced a weight against them and showed Freize the result. 'That's your copper.'

'No worse than I expected,' Freize said cheerfully. 'Try the silver.'

'I can give you a half noble for it all,' the trader said, weighing the handfuls of coins and chips of metal in his scales.

'I'll take it,' Freize replied.

The man tipped the copper coins into a little sack, and the silver into one of the boxes at his side. He opened the other box and, before Ishraq could glimpse more than the gleam of gold, took out an English half noble and handed it over to Freize.

'You don't weigh it?' Ishraq asked him. 'You trust the weight of the English noble?'

He made a little bow to her. 'This is why everyone wants the English noble coins. They are all, always, full weight.'

Confidently, he tossed it into the scales and showed her the weight. 'Fifty-four grains,' he said. 'A full noble is 108. They all are. Always. They are perfect coins.'

'It looks like new!' Freize exclaimed. 'As if it were fresh from the mint.'

The man nodded. 'As I said, they're very fine coins,' he confirmed.

'But how can it be so shiny and fine?' Ishraq asked him. 'Since it must have come all the way from England, from the royal mint in England?'

The man shrugged. 'Actually, it came from the English royal mint in Calais,' he said shortly. 'You can tell by the signs on the coin if you look closely.'

'They hardly look like coins at all,' Freize said, accustomed to the worn and jagged currency that he usually carried, coins that had been snipped and clipped by people wanting to break them down into smaller currency, or worn smooth by years of use.

'Put it away before someone with less discernment takes it off you,' the merchant recommended. 'And before you make people think that there is something wrong with it.' He glanced down the row of tables. Some of the traders were watching them. 'We all exchange money here, the town depends on trade, like it depends on water. Nobody wants anyone looking at a coin and wondering about its value. A good piccoli buys you a loaf of bread and a fish for your dinner. Tell people that a piccoli is not really worth a penny, but only half a penny, and you'll only get a loaf and no fish. Faith in the currency is what makes trade in this town. We don't like people questioning our coins. Our coins are good, these nobles are exceptionally good, everyone else is trading them for more than two ducats. I shall put up my price again tomorrow. You are lucky that I have these at this price today. Take it or leave it.'

'Indeed I wasn't questioning it,' Freize said pleasantly. 'I was admiring it, I was so impressed by the quality. Thank you for your patience.'

He bowed politely to the money changer and then the two of them turned away and strolled towards the Rialto Bridge. 'Let me see it,' Ishraq said curiously. 'What's the coin like?'

607

In answer, Freize handed it to her. It was as bright as newly minted, newly polished gold. There was a picture of a king in the prow of his ship on one side, and an eight-petalled heraldic rose on the other side. In English currency it was worth three shillings and four pence, a sixth of a pound; in Venice it could be exchanged today for a gold ducat, tomorrow it might be more or less.

'It looks like new,' Freize remarked. 'Whatever he says.'

'But who would be minting fake English nobles in Venice?' Ishraq wondered aloud.

'And that's the very question that Milord has set Luca to answer,' Freize agreed. 'But I can't help but wonder why Milord is so interested. It's hardly a sign of the end of days. It's hardly a holy inquiry. Since Luca is appointed to the Order of Darkness to travel throughout Christendom and find the signs for the end of the world, why would he be ordered to discover the source of gold coins in Venice? I would have thought it was rather a worldly question for an Order that was established by the Pope to discover the date of the end of the world. What do they care about the value of English nobles?'

He saw, in her downturned face, the same scepticism about Milord that he felt. 'Ah, you don't like him any more than I do,' he said flatly.

'I don't know him,' she said. 'Who does know him? He has never let any of us see his face. He didn't tell us anything, beyond ordering us to come to Venice in disguise to find out about the coins. He commands Luca and Brother Peter as the commander of their Order but he gives us no reason to trust him. He hates the Ottomans as if they were poison – well, I understand that – they have conquered Constantinople, and he thinks that if they reach Rome then the world will end. But I don't see how to trust a man who lives his life as if he were always on the very edge of world disaster. His whole work, his whole life is waiting for the end of the world. He's an angry man and a fearful man, I really don't like him.'

'And so you let his enemy into our house,' Freize said gently.

'I let him *out* of the house,' she corrected him. 'I heard the Ottoman Radu Bey on the stairs, I don't know how he got in. He said he had just visited Milord and I let him out of the house. I didn't know that he had threatened Milord. I don't know that I even care if he did.'

'Milord said that the intruder was an Assassin. That he could have been stabbed as he slept.'

'Milord says a lot of things,' she replied. 'But it was Radu Bey for sure who got into his room and pinned his own badge over Milord's heart as he slept. He could have killed him, but he did not. I can see that he and the Ottoman lord are enemies – they're on either side of the greatest war there is: the Jihad to one, the Crusade to the other – but that doesn't tell me which is the right side, which is the better man.'

She had shocked him. 'We're Christians!' he exclaimed.

'We serve Luca who serves the Church. The Crusade is a holy war against the infidel!'

'You are,' she pointed out. 'You four are. But I'm not. I want to make up my own mind. And I simply don't know enough about Luca's lord – or about the Ottoman lord either.'

'We have to follow Luca's lord, we can't desert Luca,' Freize pointed out. 'I love him as a brother and your lady won't leave him unless she has to. And you?' He gave her a quick sideways smile. 'You're head over heels in love with him, aren't you?'

She laughed. 'I'm not head over heels for anyone,' she said. 'I keep my two feet on the ground. He makes my heart beat a little faster, I grant you that. But nothing in this world would send me head over heels, I like to be right side up.'

'One day,' Freize warned her solemnly. 'One day you will find that you are head over heels in love with me. I pray that you don't leave it too late.'

She laughed. 'What a mistake that would be! Look at how you run after other women!'

'And on that day,' Freize predicted without paying any attention to her laughter, 'on that day, I will be kind to you. I will take you in my arms, I will allow you to adore me.'

'I'll remember that!' she said.

'Remember this too,' Freize said more seriously. 'Luca is sworn to obey the lord of his Order. I have promised to follow and serve Luca. You are travelling with us. You can't support our enemies.'

'And what of your friends?' she challenged him. 'And Luca's mysterious errands for his Lord? A servant of the Church coming to Venice in carnival time, ordered to speculate in gold and trade in a cargo? Is this holy work in your Church?'

The bell of San Giacomo started to ring over their heads and flocks of pigeons fluttered from their roosts in the church tower, interrupting them. 'One o'clock,' said Ishraq. 'And here, I think, is Father Pietro.'

The two of them watched as an elderly grey-haired man wearing the undyed wool robes of the Benedictine order came from the church, still crossing himself, his forehead damp with holy water, and walked across the crowded square. Traders, merchants and passers-by greeted him by name, as he threaded his way through the crowd, making the sign of the cross over a child who ducked for the blessing, until he arrived at the foot of the Rialto Bridge where a small stone pillar – usually used for hitching boats – served as his seat.

He took his place, and the servant who had followed him through the crowd set up a small table for writing, unfurled a long, rolled manuscript and presented the priest with a pen. Father Pietro looked around him, bowed his head briefly in prayer and then dipped his pen in the inkwell and waited, pen poised. Clearly, he was open for business, but before Ishraq or Freize could speak to him a little crowd had gathered around him, shouting out the names of missing relatives, or asking for information.

As Ishraq and Freize watched, the friar looked through his list, noted down new names, reported on ones he could find, and advised the supplicants. For one young man he had great news: his cousin had been located in the occupied lands in Greece, and the master was ready to sell.

Much of Greece had been invaded by the Ottoman

Empire and the Greeks had to serve the Ottoman lords and pay an annual tribute. This man was labouring as a slave on a farm of one of the Ottoman conquerors. The lord had named his price and Father Pietro thought it was a fair one, though it was a *lira di grosso* – ten ducats, a year's pay for a labouring man.

'Where am I to get that sort of money?' the man demanded.

'Your church should make a collection for your kinsman,' the friar advised. 'And His Holiness the Pope makes a donation every year for the freeing of Christians. If you can raise some of the money I can ask for the rest. Come back when you have at least half and we will convert it into the English gold. The slave owners only want to be paid in English gold nobles this year. Even the tribute from the occupied lands has to be in English nobles this year. But I will get you a fair rate from the money changers.'

'God bless you! God bless you!' the young man said and darted away into the crowd.

A few other people drew near and had a muttered consultation, and then Freize and Ishraq were before the friar's little table.

'Father Pietro?' Freize inquired.

'That is my name.'

'I am glad to find you. I will bring my master to you – he is anxiously seeking his parents who were taken into slavery.'

'I am sorry for him, and for them. I pray that God will guide them home,' the man said gently.

'Can I bring him here to you, tomorrow?' Freize asked.

'Yes, my son. I am always here. It is my life's work to seek out the poor lambs stolen from the flock. What is the name of his father and mother?'

'Their family name was Vero and he has had news of his father. His father was Gwilliam Vero, said to be a galley slave on a ship owned by . . .' Freize slapped his hand on his broad forehead.

'Bayeed,' Ishraq prompted. 'But we were told that was some years ago. We are not certain where he is now.'

Father Pietro inclined his head. 'I know of this Bayeed. I will look through the lists I keep at home, and ask some newly released slaves tonight,' he said. 'Bayeed sold one of his slaves to me a little while ago. Perhaps that man will know of Gwilliam Vero. I hope I will have some sort of answer for you tomorrow.'

'Bayeed himself sold a galley slave to you?' Ishraq queried.

'He is a merchant,' Father Pietro said calmly, as if nothing in the world could surprise him. 'He trades in slaves like the merchants from England trade in cloth. Christian souls are a form of merchandise to him, like any other, God forgive him. He sold a slave to me for ten ducats – though he insisted on being paid in English gold – so we sent him eight English nobles – they were worth less then than they are now.'

'Why don't they take their ransom in ducats?' Ishraq asked. 'That's the currency of Venice, surely?'

'They always want either solid gold or a currency that they can trust. This year they want the English nobles because there are always 108 grains of gold in each coin. They know what they are getting when they get English gold. Some coins of other countries are made with very impure metal. You will find the piccoli here contain hardly any silver at all. They are almost all tin. Beware of forgeries.' The priest turned his gentle gaze on Ishraq. 'And you, child? What are you doing so far from home? Are you enslaved or free?'

'I'm free.' Ishraq blushed behind her veil. 'My mother came to this country of her own free will and I was brought here with her.'

'Your father is a Christian?'

'I don't know my father,' she said, her voice muffled with embarrassment. 'My mother never told me his name. But she said they were married. My father was a Christian and my mother was free.'

'And what is your faith?'

'My mother taught me the Koran, and the Christian lord who brought us to his home read me the Bible. But now they are both dead. I practise no religion, I am afraid that I have no faith.'

He gave a little gasp of dismay at her lack of godliness, and shook his head. 'My child, I shall pray for you, and hope that you can find your way to the true faith. Would you come to me for instruction?'

'If you insist,' Ishraq said awkwardly. 'But I am sorry to say Father that I am not a good student of religion.'

He smiled at her, as if her boldness amused him. 'Because you are such a good scholar for other studies? What do you read, my learned daughter?'

She nodded, ignoring the gentle sarcasm. 'I really am a student, Father. I am interested in the new scholarship,' she said. 'The learning of the Greeks that the Arab scholars are starting to translate, so that we can all learn from them.'

'God bless you, my child,' he said earnestly. 'I will pray that God moves your heart to come to Him, and that you become content to learn through revelation, not through study. But don't you want to go to your home again?'

She hesitated for a moment, struck that this was the second time a stranger had asked her of the home she could barely remember. 'I don't really know where I would call home now. The house where I was raised – the castle of Lucretili – has been claimed by a thief – my friend's brother – and I am sworn to help her get it back. I'd be glad to fight for it and see it returned to her. But even if we win, even if she goes home to live there – I won't be able to say that it is truly my home.' She looked at him with her direct dark gaze. 'Father, sometimes I fear that I don't belong anywhere. I have neither father nor mother nor home.'

'Or perhaps you are free,' he said quietly.

It was so novel a thought that she said nothing in reply.

He smiled. 'To belong somewhere is always to owe something: a debt of loyalty, your work or your time, your love or your taxes. You are an unusual young woman if you do not belong to a man nor to a place. You are not commanded by a master or a father or a husband. That means you are free to choose where you live. That makes you free to choose how you live. The service of the Lord is perfect freedom.'

'I am ...' Ishraq stammered. 'It is true. I am free.'

He raised a finger. 'So make sure you choose rightly, my daughter. Make sure that you walk in the way of God. You are free to live freely inside His holy laws.'

He turned to Freize with a gentle smile. 'And you, my son in Christ?'

'Oh, I'm of no interest to anyone,' Freize said cheerfully.

'First a kitchen boy in a monastery, now a servant to a young master, never enough money, always hungry, always happy. Don't you worry about me.'

'You attend church?' the father prompted.

'Yes, of course, Father,' Freize agreed, feeling a tinge of guilt that though he regularly attended, he seldom listened.

'Then walk in God's holy ways,' the Father urged him. 'And make sure that you give to the poor, not to gamblers.'

Ishraq raised her eyebrows, surprised that the priest had seen them gambling with the cups and ball game. 'Are they always there?' she asked.

'Every day, and God knows how many piccoli they collect from the foolish and the spendthrift,' he said. 'They are a trap for the unwary and every day they leave here with a purse full of silver coins. Don't you waste your money on them again.' He smiled and raised his hand over them both in a blessing. 'And tell your master, I will see him tomorrow.'

~

The gondola arrived back at the grand house, to find Isolde, Brother Peter and Luca waiting for Ishraq and Freize. Isolde had unpacked the new clothes that had survived the journey from Ravenna, and had looked all around their new grand quarters. She took Ishraq upstairs to their floor, as Freize, in the men's quarters, told Luca that they had found Father Pietro.

'It's the most beautiful house I have ever seen,' she confided in Ishraq. 'Lucretili was grand, but this is beautiful. Every corner is like a painting. There is an inner courtyard, on the side of the house, with a roofed walkway on all the four sides which leads to a pretty walled garden. When the weather is warmer we can walk round the courtyard and sit in the garden.'

'Surely we'll walk on the quays and the piazza? And we'll take the gondola out?' asked Ishraq.

Isolde made a little face. 'Apparently, the ladies of Venice don't go out much. Maria, the housekeeper, said so. We'll have to stay indoors. We can go out to church once a day, or perhaps to visit friends in their houses. But mostly ladies stay at home. Or visit other ladies in their homes.'

'I can't be cooped up!' Ishraq protested.

'That's how they do things in Venice. If we want to pass as the sister and companion of a prosperous young merchant, we'll have to behave that way. It won't be for long – just till Luca finds the source of the gold coins and sends a report to Milord.'

'But that could be weeks, it could be months,' Ishraq said aghast.

'We can probably go out on the water in our own gondola,' Isolde suggested. 'As long as we are veiled, or sit in the cabin.'

Ishraq looked blankly at her. 'We are in one of the richest, most exciting cities in Christendom and you're telling me that we're not allowed to walk around it on our own two feet?'

Isolde looked uncomfortable. 'You can probably go out to the market with Freize or a chaperone,' she said. 'But I can't. I wasn't even allowed to listen to the lecture, even though it was held in the chapel beside the church.'

'What lecture?' Ishraq was immediately interested.

'At the church there is a priest who studies all things. He is part of the university of Venice, and sometimes he goes to Padua to study there. He was giving a lecture after Sext and Luca waited to hear him. Luca talked to him about the rainbow mosaic in the tomb of Galla Placidia.'

'And what did you do?'

'Brother Peter brought me home. Brother Peter does not believe in women studying.'

Ishraq made a little irritated gesture. 'But was Luca impressed with the lecture?'

'Oh yes, he wants to go again. He wants to learn things while he is here. There is a great library inside the Doge's Palace, and a tradition of scholarship. They have manuscripts from all over the world and a printing workshop which is making books. Not hand-painting them and copying them with a pen and ink, but printing hundreds at a time with some sort of machine.'

'A machine to make books?'

'Yes. It can print a page in a moment.'

'But I suppose neither you nor I can listen to the lectures? Or go to see the books made? All this study is just for men? Though in the Arab world there are women scholars and women teachers?'

Isolde nodded her head. 'Brother Peter says that women's heads do not have the strength for study.'

'*Testa di cazzo*,' Ishraq said under her breath, and led the way downstairs.

They found Luca and Brother Peter in the dining room overlooking the Grand Canal. Luca had the shutter on the tall windows closed and had opened one of the laths a tiny crack so that a beam of light was shining onto the piece of glass he had taken from the chapel at Ravenna. He looked up as they came in: 'I spoke to one of the scholars at San Marco,' he remarked to Ishraq. 'He says that before we even think about the rainbow we have to consider how things are seen.'

Ishraq waited.

'He said that the Arab philosopher Al Kindi believed that we see things because rays are sent out from our eyes and then bounce off things and come back to the eye.'

'Al Kindi?' she repeated.

'Have you heard of him?'

'During my studies in Spain,' she explained. 'He translated Plato into Arabic.'

'Could I read his work?' Luca rose up from the table and put down the piece of glass.

She nodded. 'He's been translated into Latin, for certain.'

'You would have to be sure it was not heretical writing,' Brother Peter pointed out. 'Coming as it does from the ancient Greeks who knew nothing of Christ, and through an infidel thinker.'

'But everything has been translated from the Greek to the Arabic!' Luca exclaimed impatiently. 'Not into Italian, or French or English! And only now is it being translated into Latin.'

Ishraq showed him a small smug smile. 'It's just that the Arabs were studying the world and thinking about mathematics and philosophy when the Italians were—' She broke off. 'I don't even know what they were doing,' she said. 'Was there even an Italy?'

'When?' Isolde asked, pulling out her chair and sitting at the table.

'About 900 AD,' Ishraq answered her.

'There was the Byzantine empire and the Muslim occupation, there wasn't really an Italy, I don't think.'

Freize helped to carry the dishes down from the kitchen but once the dining room door was shut, he dropped the pretence, and sat down to table with them. Isolde, looking around the table, thought that they could very well pass as a loving happy family. The affection between the four young people was very clear, and Brother Peter was like a stern, slightly disapproving, older brother.

'They invented Gorgonzola cheese,' Freize announced, carving a large ham and passing out slices.

'What?' Luca choked on a laugh, genuinely surprised.

'They invented Gorgonzola cheese, in the Po Valley,' Freize said again. 'I don't think the Italians were studying the meaning of the rainbow in the year 960. They were making cheese.' He turned to Luca. 'Don't you remember Giorgio in the monastery? Came from the Po Valley? Very proud of their history. Told us about Gorgonzola cheese. Said they'd been making it for five hundred years. Good thing too. Probably more use than rainbows.' He served himself with two great slices of ham and sat down and buttered some bread.

'You are a source of endless surprises,' Luca told him.

'Glad to help,' Freize said smugly. 'And I have more. You'll be interested in this.' Freize put down the bread, wiped his fingers on his breeches and brought the gold half noble coin out of his pocket. 'I exchanged some of my smaller coins for this. A gold half noble from England. Isn't this one of the coins that Milord wanted you to investigate?'

Luca held out his hand and looked at the bright coin. 'Yes – an English half noble. It's perfect,' he said. 'Not a mark on it.'

He passed it to Brother Peter who studied it and then

handed it on to Isolde. 'Why is Milord so interested in these coins?' she asked.

Ishraq and Freize exchanged a hidden look as Isolde named the very question that was troubling them.

'He believes that someone may have opened a gold mine and is minting them in secret,' Brother Peter said. 'Such a man would be avoiding tax, and avoiding the fines he should pay to the Church. Milord would want to see that the Church reclaimed those taxes. It would amount to a fortune. Or some criminal may be forging them.'

'So do you think the coins are forged? Made to look like English nobles but made from lesser metal?' Luca asked.

'The money changer said they were from the English mint in Calais,' Freize explained. 'But he was very stern with us when I asked him about them – he warned me not to ask questions. He didn't want anyone saying anything which might spoil the value of the coins.'

'Is the value good?'

'They might be overvalued, if anything,' Freize volunteered. 'They were rising in price as we stood there. He said he would put up his exchange rate tomorrow. Apparently everyone wants to trade in them – there were men queuing behind us. Everyone says they are solid gold, without any alloy. That's very unusual. Most coins are a mixture of precious metal and something lighter. Or good ones are shaved and clipped. But these seem to be perfect.'

'There's only one way to be sure. We'll have to test them to see how much real gold is in each coin,' said Luca.

'How shall we test it?' Isolde asked. 'We can't ask the goldsmiths – as Freize said, they won't welcome questions about the quality of their coins.'

Brother Peter looked slightly uncomfortable. He put his hand to the inner pocket of his jacket.

'You've got orders!' Freize said accusingly, eyeing the small scroll.

'Milord honoured me . . .'

'More secret orders!' Freize exclaimed. 'Where do we have to go now? Just when we are settled and have discovered *fegato alla veneziana*? When Luca is studying at the university, and is going to see Father Pietro? Just when he might find his father? Don't say we have to leave! We haven't completed our mission, we've not even started! The girls haven't even bought their carnival clothes!'

'Peace! Peace! We don't have to move yet,' Brother Peter said. 'And if it was an order from Milord, then the fact that you have discovered a Venetian culinary speciality of liver and onions, and that the girls want new dresses, would not prevent us. This is vanity, Freize. And greed. No, Milord simply gave me instructions for our time in Venice. How we are to go to the Rialto when our ship comes in and claim our share of the cargo. How we are to sell it at a profit, a manifest of the cargo it is carrying. And here, a list of the tests we were to make on the gold coins, when we had them.'

He looked at Ishraq. 'The instructions are in Arabic,' he said awkwardly. 'This is infidel learning. I thought you might read them to Brother Luca, and he would test the gold.'

Ishraq beamed at him in gleeful triumph. 'You need my learning, Brother Peter?'

The older man gritted his teeth. 'I do.'

'You don't think that translating a recipe for testing gold

will strain my poor woman's intelligence to breaking point?'

'I hope that you will survive it.'

'You don't think that such knowledge should be kept to men, only to men?'

'Not on this occasion.'

She turned to Luca. 'Do you want me to translate the recipes for you? Will you test the gold?'

'Of course,' Luca said. 'We can use the spare room next to mine. We will have our own goldsmith's assay room!'

Only Freize caught the shadow that crossed Isolde's face at the thought of the two of them working all day together in the small room.

'And tomorrow, I will go out and exchange some more coins for gold,' Brother Peter said. 'We will have to test a number of coins to be sure.'

'And the lasses can buy new gowns,' Freize said happily. 'And masks, and hats. And I shall look through my boxes and see if I can't find some more coins to turn into English gold nobles. A man could make a small fortune in this town by doing nothing but buying at the right time.'

Immediately after breakfast, the following morning, Ishraq and Luca were side by side at a table in the spare room off the dining room, quiet with concentration. Luca was staring at half a dozen beautiful golden coins purchased by Brother Peter from the money changers. Ishraq had a scroll of manuscript before her. Carefully she unrolled it, weighted the top and bottom so that it could not roll up, and started to translate from the Arabic into Italian. 'It says first you have to look, to see if it has been stamped or marked by the goldsmith or mint.'

Luca squinted at the coins, one after another. 'Yes,' he said. 'They're all marked as English nobles, minted by the English at Calais. They're all marked in exactly the same way. Identical.'

He made a note on a piece of paper beside him, and then carefully put the paper over the coin and gently rubbed a coloured stick of sealing wax over it. The image on the coin showed through. 'Now what?'

Ishraq tucked a lock of dark black hair behind her ear. 'Check for discolouration, especially wear,' she read. 'If another metal is showing through the gold, then this is gold plate, a gold veneer laid over a cheaper metal.'

Obediently, Luca turned over every coin and looked at the beautifully bevelled edges of the whole coins. 'They're perfect. All of them. Same colour all the way round.'

'Bite it,' she said.

'What?'

She giggled, and he glanced at her and smiled too. 'It's what it says here. Gold is soft, bite it, hold it in your mouth for the count of one hundred, and then look at it. If it is gold, your teeth should mark it.'

'You bite it,' Luca replied.

'I'm the translator,' she said modestly. 'You're the assayer. I am a mere woman. In your faith I think it is Eve that tells you to bite the apple. Clearly, the woman gives the instruction and the man bites. Besides, I'm not cracking my teeth on it. You're the one that wants to know: you bite it.'

'God Himself tells us your sex bit the apple first,' Luca pointed out. 'So we'll both bite one,' he decided, and handed her a half noble and kept a whole coin for himself. Solemnly, they both put the coins at the side of their mouths, bit down, held the coins, counted to one hundred and then looked at the result.

'I'm amazed!' she said.

'I can see my teeth marks!' he agreed.

'Gold then.'

'Write it down,' Luca instructed her. 'What's the next test?'

'We have to scratch it with an earthenware plate.'

Luca went to the door, opened it and yelled down the stairs. 'Freize! Bring me a bowl from the kitchen!'

'Hush!' Freize said, labouring up the stairs. 'Lady Isolde has half of Venice in her room above us, fitting her with gowns, creating headdresses for her and Ishraq.'

'I need a bowl from the kitchen!'

'Pewter?' Freize asked, preparing to go on, up the narrow stairs to the attic.

'No! No! Earthenware!'

'Earthenware he says,' Freize complained to himself. They could hear his footsteps going the long way up to the kitchen and then coming back down. 'Earthenware, as you asked,' he said, peering curiously into the room.

'And now go away,' Luca said hard-heartedly, though it was clear that Freize was aching to join in. To Ishraq he said: 'Now what?'

'You have to break it. We need a smashed piece of earthenware.'

Luca slammed the bowl against the edge of the table, and it shattered into a hundred pieces.

'Oh fine, just break it!' came Freize's voice from behind the closed door. 'Don't worry about it, for a moment. Shall I fetch another for your lordship?'

'And take a piece and scratch the gold with it,' Ishraq translated. 'A black scratch means the gold is not real but a gold scratch shows the metal is true.'

Luca drew the earthenware shard across the face of the gold noble. 'It's good,' he said tersely. He pressed down hard and then looked again. 'Definitely good.'

'Now we have to saw it in half.'

He raised his eyebrows at the thought of damaging the coin. 'I'll saw one of the quarter nobles,' he said. 'I won't touch the full noble.'

She shook her head. 'Oh for heaven's sake! Saw one of each: a noble and a half noble and a quarter noble. Go on, Luca. It's not as if it's your money. Milord is paying for all of this.'

'You have expensive ideas,' he complained. 'If you had been brought up as a farmer's son like me you would not willingly be sawing coins in half.'

She laughed at him, and he did as she requested and soon the coins lay halved on the bench before them.

'Are they the same colour all the way through?'

Luca picked up a magnifying glass and scrutinised the coins. 'Yes,' he said. 'There's no skin on any of them, nor any trace of a different colour inside. They're yellow all the way through, like pure gold.'

'So now, it's the last test: we have to weigh the coins,' she said. 'Weigh them very accurately.'

Luca paused. 'All right. What weight should they be?'

'A full noble is 108 grains,' Ishraq said scowling at the manuscript, trying to understand the symbols. 'It says that density is equal to mass divided by volume.'

'Hang on a minute,' Luca said. 'Say that again.'

'Density is equal to mass divided by volume,' she repeated. 'The test is to weigh pure gold and then weigh the test gold to find the mass. Then the second test is to put it in water and see how much the water level rises. That gives the volume.'

'Mass,' Luca repeated. 'Volume.'

Ishraq thought that he looked for a moment like a troubadour when he sings a particularly beautiful song. The words, which made no sense to her, were like poetry to him. 'Density.'

'It says here that we are to take a piece of pure gold and then put it in a measured jug of water and see how much the water rises. Then we do the same with the same weight of our test gold. Gold which has been mixed with other lighter metals will move more water. Gold that is pure is more dense – it will displace less water.' She broke off. 'You know, I'm reading the words but I feel like a fool. I don't understand what we are to do. Do you understand what is meant?'

Luca looked transported. 'Density is equal to mass divided by volume,' he said quietly. 'I do see. I do see.'

He did not bother to shout for Freize but ran up to the kitchen himself and came back down with a clear glass of water. 'We'll have to go out to a goldsmith and buy some pure gold,' he muttered.

'What for?'

'So that I know how dense pure gold is. So that I know how much the water rises. So that I can compare it with the coins.'

'Oh! I see,' Ishraq exclaimed, suddenly understanding. 'I have a gold ring, that I know is pure gold.'

'It's hollow, it's in the shape of a ring,' Luca said, thinking furiously aloud. 'Doesn't matter. The central hole has no weight. We are weighing the gold of the ring not measuring the area. Get it.'

'It's Isolde's mother's ring,' Ishraq explained. 'I have carried it and her family jewels for her ever since we left home.'

'Are you sure it is pure gold?'

She nodded. 'The Lord of Lucretili would have given his lady nothing less,' she said.

He did not even hear her, he was looking from the gold nobles to the water in the glass. Ishraq ran from the room up the stairs to the girls' rooms and lifted her gown, to rip at the hem of her linen shift.

'What on earth are you doing?' Isolde asked. She was standing on a wooden chair, a dressmaker kneeling before her, hemming a gown. On one side a tirewoman was making a magnificent headdress and there were carnival masks all around the room, silks, satins and velvets thrown everywhere in a jumble of richness and colour.

'Getting your mother's gold ring,' Ishraq said tersely, tearing at the strong hem stitches. 'For Luca to weigh against the gold nobles.'

'Still?' Isolde said irritably. 'You've been locked in all morning. And I heard you drop a plate.'

'Smashed it,' Ishraq said cheerfully, retrieving the ring and pulling down her dress again.

'Make sure he doesn't damage it,' Isolde said disagreeably. 'That ring is valuable.'

Ishraq said nothing but raced back to Luca. He was pacing up and down, scowling in thought, he hardly noticed her come in until she put the ring into his hand.

At once he turned and put it on the delicate spice scales that Freize had brought them from the kitchen. He added the tiny weights – the smallest was half a grain of wheat. Isolde's mother's ring was just over 121 grains.

'Write it down,' Luca ordered Ishraq. 'The ring is pure gold, 121 and a half grains. Now. How much water does it move?'

Luca lifted it from the scale and put it into the water glass. At once the water rose within the glass. With a sharp

630

piece of chalk Luca marked where the water level rose, and then hooked the ring out with a fork and held it over the water so that every drop fell back into the glass and the water level was the same as before.

'You are certain this is pure gold?' he asked quietly.

Ishraq was impressed with his concentration. 'Certain,' she whispered.

'Well, the noble should be 108 grains,' Luca said. 'And the noble plus half of one of the quarter nobles should be exactly 121 and a half grains. So the mass is the same. If it is less dense, then it has been mixed with tin or something lighter than gold, and the water will rise higher.' Gently, without making a splash, he dropped the full coin into the glass of water, and then dropped the sawn half of the quarter noble on top of it.

They both held their breath as the water level rose, sticking to the side of the glass, but definitely rising up and up until it reached the mark set by the ring.

'The coins are pure gold,' Luca said in quiet triumph. 'Someone, somewhere is either stealing pure gold English nobles fresh from the mint in Calais, or else they are mining the purest gold, and forging their own.'

～

The five of them were elated, as if they had found the gold mine itself.

'So what next?' Isolde asked. 'How will we find the mint? How will we find the forgers?'

'Could we buy so much gold that the money changer cannot serve us from his own store?' Luca suggested. 'Then we'll ask him where we can go to collect it. If he won't say, we'll have to watch him, see where he goes to get a chest of gold.'

'We can take it in turns to watch ...' Ishraq started.

Luca shook his head. 'No, not you,' he said. He glanced at Isolde and saw her nod in agreement. 'I am sorry, Ishraq, but you can't. If we want to pass as a wealthy family then you two have to behave like ladies. You can't come to the Rialto and spy on the gold merchants.'

'Really, we can't,' Isolde told her.

'I could go dressed as a common girl. Or dressed as a boy! Isolde has bought a room-full of costumes and masks! It is carnival time, almost everyone is disguised.'

'It's not worth the risk,' Brother Peter ruled. 'And besides, you should not be wandering the streets exposed to danger. It happens that we are here in the only time of year that women are allowed out of their homes at all. All the women in Venice will dress up in disguise, wear masks, and go out on the streets for the twenty days before Lent, the city is never more unruly than now. They are a most extreme people. This is an exception, a time of utter licence, the rest of the year ladies only go out to visit privately in each other's houses or to church.'

'But as it's carnival, surely we can go out masked and disguised?' Ishraq insisted. 'Even if it is only for these weeks?'

'Only if you want to be mistaken for the whores of the city,' Brother Peter said crossly. 'You would be advised not to go out at all. It is a time of great sin and debauchery. I would advise you to stay indoors. Indeed, I have to request that you stay indoors.' He glanced at Luca for his agreement. 'Since you are travelling with us and have agreed to enact the pretence that we are your guardians, I think it is right that you should give us the power to decide your comings and goings.'

'Nobody has that power over me,' Ishraq said quickly. 'I don't give it to you, I don't give it to anyone. I didn't leave home and then run away from the nunnery to be ordered about by you and Luca.'

Luca flushed. 'Nobody is ordering you,' he said. 'But if we are to keep up the pretence that we are here as a noble family you will have to behave like the companion of a noblewoman. That's simply what you agreed to do, Ishraq.'

'I'll go out masked,' she promised herself.

'As long as someone goes with you,' Luca compromised. 'Apparently the whole city goes quite mad for the days of carnival. But if Freize goes with you, or the housekeeper, you should be all right.'

'So can I come with you to the Rialto this afternoon?' she asked. 'To see Father Pietro? If I am masked?'

Luca shook his head. 'This is my quest,' he said. 'I go alone.

Freize beamed. 'I go alone too,' he said. 'I'll go alone with you.'

~

The two young men left the house together; Ishraq and Isolde, at the upper-floor window, watched the black gondola nose into the middle of the Grand Canal and swiftly cut through the busy waterway.

'I'm going out,' Ishraq said. 'I'm going to get us boys' clothes so that we can walk around as we please.'

Isolde brightened. 'Do we dare?'

'Yes,' Ishraq said firmly. 'Of course we dare. We've come all the way across Italy. We're hardly going to be stuck indoors now because a couple of priests think that Venice is too sinful for us to see.'

'I've ordered us both gowns from the sempstress.'

'Yes, but I don't want gowns, I want costumes. I want disguises. I want boys' clothes so that we can go where we like. So no one knows who we are.'

'Go then,' Isolde said excitedly. She put her hand into the pocket of her modest grey gown and pulled out a purse. 'Here. Brother Peter gave me this, for alms for the poor and for candles at church, and for other things – who knows what – that he thought we might need: trinkets that ladies of a noble family might have. Go and get us breeches and capes and big masks!'

Ishraq laughed, pocketed the money and went from the room.

'And get me a big hat.' Isolde slipped from the room and leaned over the marble staircase to call to her friend. 'One that will hide my hair.'

'And I'll trade with some of your mother's jewels!' Ishraq called softly up the stairs.

Isolde hesitated. 'My mother's jewels? Which ones?'

'The rubies,' Ishraq insisted. 'This is our chance to make a fortune. We'll trade in the jewels and buy English gold nobles and watch them rise in price. When they've doubled in value we'll buy the rubies back and you'll still have them plus a fortune to hire your army to march on your brother.'

'We could make so much money just by trading in the nobles?' Isolde asked, tempted at the thought.

'We might,' Ishraq said. 'Shall I do it? Shall I go to the money changer and buy gold nobles with your rubies?'

'Yes,' Isolde said, taking a chance, tempted by the

thought of a fortune easily made which might win her back her inheritance. 'Not the broadsword, I can't let that out of my keeping. But take the rubies. Yes, take them.'

~

At the Rialto the two young men found Father Pietro in his usual place, the bustle of the crowd all around him, someone juggling with daggers nearby, and a performing dog circling slowly and mournfully, a small ball balanced on his nose, his clown-faced owner passing the hat. They did not notice Ishraq, dressed as a boy, hat pulled low over her pinned-up hair, a black mask over her eyes, arrive to do business with Israel, the money changer.

'This is my master,' Freize introduced him, elbowing his way through the crowd to get to the priest. 'This is Luca Vero.'

'You are seeking your father,' the Friar said gently. 'And I am glad to tell you that I have news of him.' He looked at Luca's sudden pallor. 'Ah, my son. Are you ready to hear it?'

Luca bent his head and said a swift prayer. 'Yes,' he said. 'Tell me at once.'

'A slave that I ransomed from Bayeed last year told me that Gwilliam Vero was serving on his ship then,' Father Pietro said quietly. 'He was alive and strong then, only last year. It may be that he is still slaving on the ship now.'

'He might be alive?' Luca repeated as if he could not believe the news. 'Now? This very day?'

'He might. I can send a message to Bayeed, and ask if your father is alive and if Bayeed would accept a ransom for him.'

Luca shook his head, to clear his whirling thoughts. 'I can't think! I can't believe it!'

Freize put a gentle hand on his back. 'Steady now,' he said as if he were soothing a horse. 'Steady.'

'Yes. Of course,' Luca said to the priest. 'Please. Do it at once. When would we hear back?'

'If Bayeed were at Constantinople—' The priest corrected himself. 'Istanbul as they call it now, God forgive them for taking our city, the Rome of the East, the home of God – well, if Bayeed was there it would take about two weeks to get a message to him. But you might be lucky. I heard he had come into Trieste. If that's true, then we might get a message to him within a few days. He may even be coming to Venice.'

'Days?' Luca repeated. 'He might be coming here?'

The priest put his hand gently over Luca's clenched fist. 'Yes, my son. You might have an answer in days. If he is in port at Trieste, and my messenger can find him, and get a ship back to us with the price.'

Luca and Freize exchanged one amazed glance.

'Days,' Luca repeated. 'I might see my father within the week?'

'Usually Bayeed will reply at once. But it won't be cheap. He will ask around a *lira di grosso* for a working slave – that's ten ducats.' He paused. 'That's about five nobles.'

Luca nodded. He had mentally converted the currency in a moment, even while Father Pietro was speaking. He could not help but think of the fortune that he was carrying on this mission, but did not own: the wealth that Milord had entrusted to him, to pretend to be a trader in Venice, the gold coins that he had tested, the suspect coins made with real gold that he was ordered to buy, the share of the cargo of the ship which was even now, sails spread, coming across the seas from the east to bring a small fortune to him, the

636

money he had been given to lay around to make the illusion of wealth. 'I have that,' he said quietly. 'I have a fortune. I can pay. For the freedom of my father, I would pay that willingly.'

Freize leaned towards his ear. 'It's not really yours,' he reminded his friend. 'How will it be when Milord wants you to account for it?'

'I have to use it!' Luca said fiercely. 'For my father's freedom, I would steal it outright! But this is just borrowing. I will explain to Milord. I will make it up to him with the profit I will make trading in the English nobles.'

The priest nodded. 'I will write tonight then, and send Bayeed an offer to pay. I expect that they will want it in English gold nobles. That is the currency they prefer, both for ransom and tribute this year. It will be five English nobles, they may settle for four and a half, the value of the English noble is rising. It would be better for us to fix the price at once. Everyone seems to think that the value of the noble is going to reach the sky.'

'I can get the coins,' Luca assured him. 'I can pay him in English nobles.'

'And I have some other news for you as well.'

Luca waited.

'The man who had served with your father said that your father had learned where his wife had been taken. He knew that your mother was enslaved as a house servant, to a family that served the emperor. Your father had seen them buy her at the auction before Bayeed bought him. It may be that she lives, that she is working for them still. If they have moved with the court then they will be in Istanbul now, God forgive them for stealing our city.'

Luca almost staggered under the news. Freize took his

arm. 'Steady,' he said. 'Steady now.' Carefully, he put Luca on his feet, patted his back. 'You all right, Sparrow?'

Luca brushed his hand away. 'My mother?'

'This is old news,' the friar cautioned. 'Your father said that he saw her sold to a man who looked like he might be a good master, years ago; but of course she might not still be with them now.'

'But you said that she was sold to a family who were connected to the sultan's court?'

'Yes. And that is a good service, easy work. I could write to one of the court officials and inquire for her,' the priest said quietly. He lifted his pen. 'What is her name?'

'Clara,' Luca said. 'Clara Vero. I can hardly believe this. I cannot believe this. I was told they were dead when I was no more than a boy of fourteen. They were taken from our farm, just a little place. Nobody even witnessed the kidnap. I had given up all hope of ever seeing them again. I have grieved for them ever since. I have feared that I was an orphan without parents.'

'God is merciful,' the old priest said gently. 'Praise Him.'

'It's quite a miracle,' Freize confirmed. 'Amen. Bear up, Sparrow.'

Luca bowed his head and whispered a prayer. 'When shall I come to you again, Father?' he asked.

'I will send to you as soon as I have news, any news at all,' the priest said gently. 'It will be a few days before we know of your father, months before we can trace your mother. You will have to learn patience. Your servant tells me you are living in the palazzo of the de Longhi family?'

'Yes,' Luca nodded. 'Yes. Send to me there.'

'You have come a long way from a little village, from

your farm,' the priest remarked. 'Clearly, you have enjoyed much worldly success.'

Luca, shaken by the news of his parents, was quite at a loss. He could not find a ready lie.

'My master has been lucky in trade,' Freize interrupted swiftly. 'We have come to Venice to trade in gold, for it is his speciality. And we have a share in a cargo which is coming in from Russia. But he was determined to see you and ask you if you could find his father. He's a most devoted son.'

The priest smiled. 'Perhaps you will give some of your wealth to the Church,' he said to Luca. 'There are many Christians who could be ransomed back to their family, just like your father and mother, if we only had the money for their ransom.'

'I will,' Luca promised, shaken with emotion. Freize saw that he hardly knew what he was saying. 'I will. I would want to be generous. I would want others to come home too. God knows, if I had my way, there would be no men and women in slavery and no fatherless children waiting for them.'

'God be with you then, my son.' The priest drew the sign of the cross in the air. 'And may He guide your way as you trade in gold and sell your cargo. For that is a very worldly business and you will need to guard yourself against criminals.'

'And no need to tell all of Venice our business,' Freize said quietly. 'The little farm then – the great fortune now: my master doesn't like it talked about.'

'I don't gossip,' the priest said gently. 'My trade is in information about poor lambs lost from the flock. My work depends upon my discretion.'

'Fair enough,' Freize nodded and turned to follow

Luca. 'Much gold around here, is there?' Freize asked nonchalantly.

'I have never seen so many English gold nobles in my life before,' the priest said. 'Truly God is good. For the Ottomans are demanding to be paid in gold nobles and many people have given me gold nobles for my work, and their price rises every day so I can buy more souls with the lucky coins. I have traded all my savings into the gold nobles so that I can do my work, praise Him.'

~

Back at the house Ishraq dashed in the side door to the street just as the gondola carrying Freize and Luca nosed into the watergate that opened into the front of the house. She ran up the stairs, taking them two at a time, to the girls' floor as the men were walking together up from the water level to the main floor. She bundled capes and breeches and sturdy shoes under her bed, and showed Isolde the purse of gold coins.

'How much did you get for the rubies?' Isolde asked quickly in a whisper.

'Ten and a half gold nobles,' Ishraq replied. 'It was the best I could do.'

Isolde gulped at the thought of speculating with her mother's jewels. 'I hope they gain value,' she said nervously. 'The rubies were my mother's greatest treasure. We will be able to get them back?'

'We'll have them and their price in gold,' Ishraq declared. 'Everyone says that the nobles will be worth more, even tomorrow. People are gambling on good prices tomorrow even now, as the market is closing. We could sell them at a profit tomorrow, and get the rubies back.'

Isolde crossed her fingers and tapped them against Ishraq's forehead in an old silly game from their childhood.

'Lucky luck,' Ishraq replied. 'You go on down to him, I'll put this purse under the mattress.'

~

As Isolde entered the room Luca's face lit up and he took her hands, as he told her that he thought he might be able to ransom his parents. 'This is wonderful news,' she said. 'This is the greatest thing that could happen for you.'

For a moment they stood hand-clasped, and he realised that he had been hurrying home just so that he could tell her this news, that as soon as he had heard it, he had wanted her to know too.

'You understand,' he said wonderingly. 'You understand what this means to me.'

'Because I lost my father too,' she said gently. 'Only mine has gone from me forever, into death. So I do understand how you can long for him, how his absence has been a grief for all of your life. But if your father can return to you, if your mother can come home, what a miracle that would be!'

'I would leave the Church,' Luca said almost to himself. 'If they were to come home I would leave the Church to live with them at our farm once again. I would be so proud to be their son and work in their fields. I would want nothing more.'

'But your work – the Order of Darkness? They say that you have a great talent for understanding, that you must go throughout the world and read the signs for the end of days. Brother Peter says it is your gift and your calling. He says you are the greatest Inquirer he has ever seen at work, and he has travelled and advised many Inquirers.'

He smiled at the praise. 'Really? Did he say that?'

'Yes!' she smiled ruefully. 'When he was scolding me. He told me that I must not distract you from doing God's work. That you have a calling, a vocation. He says you are exceptional.'

'Even so, I would go back to my father and mother if they were to be free and come home. Of course, I would complete my mission here, I would not leave anything undone. But if my parents were to come home I would never want to be parted from them again. I wouldn't want to be exceptional, I would want to be an ordinary son.'

She nodded. Of all of them, Isolde understood homesickness. On the death of her father, her brother had cheated her out of her lands and the castle that was to have been hers. She lost her inheritance, her father and her faith in her brother all at once. 'But you know, we can never really go back,' she said gently to him. 'Even if I raise an army from my godfather's son and defeat my brother and get my lands returned to me, even if I ride into my own castle gate and call it mine once more, it will never be the same. Nothing can ever be as it was. My father will still be dead. My brother will still have betrayed me. I will still be alone in the world but for Ishraq. I will still have known grief in the loss of my father and anger in the betrayal of my brother. My heart will still be hardened. I will never be the same, even if the castle were still standing.'

'I know,' he said. 'You're right. But if my parents could return home, or if you could live where you belong, then, in our own ways, in our own places, we could make new lives for ourselves. New lives in the old places. New lives where we truly belong. We could start again, from where we began.'

She understood at once that their lives would take them in very different directions. 'Oh Luca, if I were to win Lucretili back, I would live very far from your farm.'

'And I would be such a small farmer, I could never even speak to such a grand person as the Lady of Lucretili. You would ride past my farmhouse and not even look at me. I would be a dirty farmer's boy behind an ox and a plough and you would be on a great horse, riding by.'

Without exchanging another word they both thought – yes, whatever is ahead of us, whatever new life we make, it can never be together – and quietly, they released their clasped hands.

'We can't neglect our mission.' Brother Peter came into the room and saw them turning away from each other. 'That's the main thing. That's the only thing. I am glad that you have traced your father, Luca. But we must remember that we have work to do. We have a calling. Nothing matters more than tracing the signs of the end of the world.'

'No, I won't forget what I have come here to do,' Luca promised. 'But since Milord commanded us to trade and even gamble, this is a chance for me. I need to earn some gold on my own account. I will need a small fortune to ransom both my parents.'

'You might get it by trading,' Ishraq remarked, coming into the room. Isolde shot one guilty look at her. 'If you were to buy English nobles now, everyone says they will be worth twice what you pay for them, by only next month. This is a way to make money which is like magic. You buy now, and you sell in a month's time and someone gives you twice what you paid.'

'But how?' Isolde asked nervously, directing the question to Luca. 'I see that it happens, I see that half of Venice is counting on it happening – every day a little profit is added. But how does it happen?'

'Because everyone wants the English nobles, and they think that there are more buyers than coins to be bought,' Luca said. 'It is like a dream. Everyone buys expecting to make a profit and so the value goes up and up. It could be anything that they are running after. It could be nobles or shells, or diamonds or even houses. Anything that can be exchanged for money – so that its value can be seen to increase. If more people want it, they outbid each other, and the price rises.'

'But one day it will burst like an over-blown bladder,' Ishraq predicted. 'The trick is to make sure that you have sold before that day arrives.'

'And how do you know when that day comes?' Luca asked her, and was surprised to see the anxious look that passed between the two young women.

'Why, I was hoping you would know,' Isolde confessed. 'We have bought some nobles.'

'You have?' Luca laughed. 'You are speculators?'

The girls nodded, wide-eyed as if they had frightened themselves.

'How much?' Luca asked, sobering as he saw how serious they were.

'Ten and a half nobles,' Isolde confessed.

He made a soundless whistle. 'How did you afford them?'

'I sold my mother's rubies,' Isolde confessed. 'Now of course I am afraid that I will never be able to buy them back.'

'Will you tell us when you think we should sell?' Ishraq asked him.

He nodded. 'Of course, I'll do my best. And we'll be in the market every day, watching the prices. You can see for yourself.'

'And they are gold, solid gold – we tested them,' Ishraq reminded him. 'Whatever happens they can't fall below the value of gold.'

'Perhaps Luca will win his fortune?' Brother Peter said, turning to them with a letter in his hand, deaf to their conversation. 'Luca, you have been invited – actually, we have all been invited – to an evening's gambling, in a neighbouring palace, the day after tomorrow. A letter of invitation came while you were out. Our name seems to have got about already, and the lies we have told to pass as a wealthy family. There was an invitation to a banquet also.'

The two girls looked up.

'Shall we go?' Luca asked.

'I think we have to,' Brother Peter said heavily. 'We have to mix with people who have these gold nobles to discover where they come from and how much English gold is circulating. Milord himself said that we would have to gamble to maintain the appearance of being a wealthy worldly family. I shall pray before we go out and when we come back. I shall pray that the Lord will keep me from temptation.'

'For any woman is certain to fling herself at him,' whispered Ishraq to Isolde, prompting a smile.

'And shall we come?' Isolde asked. 'Since I am to play the part of your sister?'

'You are invited to visit with the ladies of the house.' Brother Peter handed over a letter addressed to Signorina Vero.

'They think I have your name!' Isolde exclaimed to Luca and then suddenly flushed.

'Of course they do,' Brother Peter said wearily. 'We are all using Luca's name. They think I am called Peter Vero, his older brother.'

'It just sounds so odd! As if we were married,' Isolde said, red to her ears.

'It sounds as if you are his sister,' Brother Peter said coldly. 'As we agreed that you should pretend to be. Will you visit the ladies while we go gambling? Ishraq should accompany you as your servant and companion.'

'Yes,' Isolde said. 'Though gambling and a banquet sound like much more fun than visiting with ladies.'

'We are not going to have fun,' Brother Peter said severely. 'We are going to trace false gold and to do this we will have to enter into the very heart of sin.'

'Yes indeed,' Isolde agreed but did not dare look at Ishraq whose shoulders were shaking with suppressed laughter. 'And we will do our part. We can listen for any news of gold while we are talking to the ladies, we can ask them what their husbands are paying for the gold nobles on the Rialto and where they think they are coming from.'

The next morning, Freize, Luca and Brother Peter went again to the Rialto Bridge to see the money changers. 'How will we know how much gold they keep by them?' Brother Peter asked anxiously, as the gondola wove its way through the many ships. 'We need to demand enough to make them go to their suppliers, so that we can see where they go. But how shall we know how much to ask for?'

'I saw only one chest behind the Jewish money changer, when we went before, I don't think he carries many coins into the square. But I don't know what he might keep at home,' Freize said.

'Brother Peter has shown me the manifest for the cargo that Milord has given us,' Luca volunteered. 'It's due to come in from Russia next week. We'll get a quarter of the cargo of a full-sized ship. We are talking about a fortune.'

Freize whistled. 'Milord has this to give away? What's the ship carrying?'

'Amber, furs, ivory.'

'How is Milord so wealthy?' Freize asked. 'Is he not sworn to poverty like the brothers in our abbey?'

Brother Peter frowned. 'His business is his own concern, Freize; nothing to do with you. But of course, he has the wealth of the Holy Church behind him.'

'As you say.' Luca adjusted his view of his mysterious master yet again. 'I knew he had great power. I didn't know he could command great wealth too.'

'They are one and the same,' Brother Peter said dolefully. 'Both the doorway to sin.'

'Indeed,' Freize said cheerfully. 'And clearly, none of my business, dealing as I do with petty power and small change.'

'We'll say that we want to trade the cargo for gold, as soon as the ship comes in,' Luca decided. 'We'll ask them if they keep enough gold in store. I'll show them the manifest if I need to. We'll have to match our words to what seems most likely and make it up as we go along.'

Brother Peter shook his head. 'I am lying every time I draw breath in this city,' he said unhappily.

'Me too,' Freize said without any sign of discomfort. 'Terrible.'

The gondolier drew the craft up to the water steps and held the boat alongside the quay. 'Shall I wait?'

'Yes,' Luca said as he stepped ashore.

'The ladies will not need the gondola?'

'The ladies will not go out,' Brother Peter ruled. 'They could only go to church in our absence, and they can walk to San Marco.'

The gondolier bowed in obedience, as the men went up the quay steps to the busy square. Freize looked around at once for the pretty girl who gambled with the cups and ball. She was kneeling before the game, a square of pavement sprinkled with white sand, the three cups tipped upside down before her. Her taciturn father was standing nearby, as always.

'I'll just be a moment,' Freize excused himself to Luca and Brother Peter, and went over to her. 'Good morning, Jacinta,' he said and was rewarded by a bright smile. 'Good morning, Drago Nacari,' he said to her father. 'Are you busy today?'

'Busy as always,' she said, smoothing the sand and setting out the cups. Freize watched as she put the cloudy marble under one cup and then swopped them round and round, swirling them quickly until they came to rest. He watched for a few times and then he could resist temptation no longer.

'That one,' Freize said with certainty. 'That one, I would put my life on it.'

'Just put your pennies on it,' she said with a quick upwards flash of her brown eyes. 'I don't want your life.'

'It's the right-hand one,' Luca said quietly beside him. 'I was watching. I am certain.'

'Whatever you think,' the girl said. 'Why don't you both bet?'

Luca put down a handful of small coins on the right-hand cup but Freize put down all the contents of his purse on the centre cup.

She laughed as if a customer's winning gave her real pleasure, and she said to Freize: 'Your friend has quicker eyes than you! He is right.' She scooped up all the money before the central cup that Freize, and most of the crowd, had chosen, and to Luca she counted up his piccoli and handed him a quarter English noble. 'Your winnings,' she said. 'You get your stake back three times over.'

'It's a good game to win,' he said, taken aback to have one of the English coins passed into his hand as if it were ordinary currency.

She misunderstood his hesitation. 'That's a quarter English noble. It's as good as a half ducat,' she said. 'It's a good coin.'

'I hope you're not questioning the gold coins?' someone asked from the crowd.

'Not at all. I'm just surprised by my good fortune,' Luca said.

'It's a rare game to win,' Freize grumbled. 'But a clever game, and a pleasure to watch you, Jacinta.'

'Have you come to see Father Pietro again?' she asked. 'For he doesn't come till the afternoon.'

'No, my master here is a trader. He is arranging to sell a great cargo that will come in any day now,' Freize said glibly. 'Silks. Wouldn't you love a silk dress, Jacinta? Or ribbons for your shiny brown hair?'

She smiled. 'Oh very much! Shall you gamble them on my cups and ball? A dress for me if you lose three times over?'

Freize grinned at her. 'No I shall not! You would get a wardrobe full of dresses, I am sure, a ship full!'

She laughed. 'It's just luck.'

'It's a very great skill,' Luca told her. He lowered his voice: 'But I will tell you a secret.'

She leaned forwards to listen.

'I did not see that the marble was under the right-hand cup – your hands move too swiftly for me to see. I should think you are too quick for almost anyone. But I guessed that it would be the right-hand cup.'

Her eyes narrowed, she looked at him. 'A lucky guess?

'No. A guess based on what I could see.'

'And what did you see?'

'You're right-handed,' he told her. 'And the strongest move is to push away, not pull towards. When you move the cups around, you favour the cup with the hidden marble, and you favour the movement to your right. Three times out of the seven that I watched, you sent the cup with the marble to your right. And at the end of the day, when you're a little tired, I should imagine that you favour your right even more often.'

She sat back on her heels. 'You counted where the cup ended up? And remembered?'

Luca frowned. 'I didn't set out to count,' he explained. 'But I couldn't help but notice. I notice things like patterns and numbers.'

She smiled. 'Do you play cards?'

Luca laughed. 'You think I could count cards?'

'I'm sure you could,' she said. 'If you can count cards and remember them you would win at Karnöffel. You could play here, on the square. There is a fortune to be won – everyone here has money in their pockets, everyone believes that they might be lucky.'

Luca glanced back to Brother Peter, who was waiting for them with an air of wearied patience. 'I don't gamble, my brother would not like it. But it is true that I would be able to remember the hands.'

651

'If you learned a set of numbers, how many would you be able to remember?' she asked.

He closed his eyes and imagined that he was a boy running down a portico with colonnades of numbers flicking past him. 'I don't know, I've never tried. Thousands, I think.'

'Sir, do you see numbers in colours?'

It was such an extraordinary question that he hesitated and laughed. 'Yes, I do,' he confessed. 'But I think it is a rare illusion. An odd trick of the eye, or perhaps of the mind. Who knows? Of no use, as far as I know. Do you see numbers as colours?'

She shook her head. 'Not I. But I know that some people who can understand numbers see them in colours or as pictures. Can you understand languages at first hearing?'

He hesitated, shy of boasting, remembering the bullying he suffered when he was a child for being a boy of exceptional abilities. 'Yes,' he said shortly. 'But I don't regard it.'

She turned and summoned her father to come closer with a toss of her head. Drago Nacari came over and shook Luca's hand in greeting. 'This is my father,' Jacinta introduced him. To her father she spoke in rapid French: 'This young man has a gift for numbers and for languages. And he is a stranger new-come to Venice, and he came to us today.'

Drago's grip on Luca's hand suddenly tightened. 'What chance! I have been hoping and praying that such a man like you might come along,' he said.

'Last night I had a dream,' the girl said quietly to Luca. 'I dreamed that a deer with eyes as brown and bright as yours came into the San Giacomo Square, stepping so that

652

its hard little hooves echoed on the Rialto Bridge, and the square was a meadow and it was all green.'

'He's a wealthy trader,' Freize interrupted. 'Just playing the game for fun. Not a gambler. Not likely to be any help to you in your line of work. Not like a deer, not like a deer at all.'

'Do you understand me?' Drago asked Luca in Latin.

'I speak and read Latin,' Luca confirmed. 'I learned it when I was in my monastery.'

'Do you understand me?' Drago asked him in Arabic.

Luca frowned. 'I think that is the same question,' he said tentatively. 'But I don't speak Arabic. I'm just guessing.'

'Well, you won't understand this,' Drago said in Romany, the language of the travelling Egyptians. 'Not one word of what I say!'

Luca laughed. 'Now this is just lucky, but some gypsies came to my village when I was a child,' he said. 'I heard them speak and understood at once.'

'Do you know the language of birds?' Drago asked him very quietly, in Italian.

Luca shook his head. 'No. I've never heard of it. What is that?'

'I am studying some manuscripts which puzzle me,' Drago Nacari remarked without answering the question. 'There are numbers and strange words and something that looks like code. I said – only last night – that I must pray that God sends me someone who can understand numbers and languages, for without some help I will never make head nor tail of them. And then my daughter dreamed of a deer, walking over the Rialto Bridge. And today you come to us.'

'Except, he's not a deer,' Freize remarked. 'And roasted venison is not on the menu.'

'Why would the dream mean me?' Luca asked.

Jacinta smiled at him. 'Because you are as handsome as a young buck,' she said boldly. 'And the deer walked like you do, proudly and gracefully with his head up, looking round.'

Freize leaned forwards. 'Perhaps it was me that you dreamed of? A handsome buck, or at least a horse? Or a handsome ox. Steady, and well-made. When he was a boy I nicknamed him Sparrow because he was so slight, long-legged and half-starved.'

'You do indeed resemble a handsome horse,' she said with a sweet smile. 'And I liked you the moment we met.'

'What sort of manuscripts?' Luca could not hide his interest.

'This is like a book with pictures and writing. But the pictures are of no plant or person that I have ever seen, and I cannot understand the language of the writing around them.'

'Have you taken them to the university here, or in Padua?'

The man spread his hands. 'I am afraid to do so,' he admitted. 'If these manuscripts contain secrets and are profitable, then I should like to be the one who profits from them. If they are heretical then I don't want to be the one to bring them to the Church and be punished for it. They will ask me where I got them, they will ask me what they mean. They may accuse me of forbidden knowledge, when I know nothing. You see my dilemma?'

'Are these on the list of banned books?' Freize asked cautiously. 'My master can't read anything that might be heresy.'

The man shrugged. 'As I can't even translate their titles, I don't know what they are.'

'Why would you trust me?' Luca asked.

Drago smiled. 'If you translate them you will be translating a few pages of a very long book. They would make little sense to you. You'd have to be a philosopher to begin to understand them. You say you're a trader. It's a quicker way to a fortune than studying the wisdom of the ancients. But I would promise you a share in anything I discovered through your scholarship.'

'I would certainly be most interested to see them,' Luca said eagerly. 'And we are travelling with a lady ...'

'His sister's companion,' Freize added, trying to maintain the fiction of their identity. He leaned his shoulder heavily against Luca. 'And see, your brother is waiting for us, and getting impatient.'

Luca glanced over his shoulder to Brother Peter, who was looking frankly alarmed at the time they were spending with street gamblers. 'Yes, just a moment. The lady that I mean is my sister's companion. She is half Arab, and could help us with the Arabic. She studied in Spain at the Moorish universities and is very well-read. She was educated as a true scholar.'

'An educated woman?' Jacinta asked eagerly.

'Shall I bring the manuscript to your house?' Drago Nacari asked him.

'Come,' Luca invited him. 'Come this afternoon, Ca' de Longhi on the Grand Canal. I should be most interested to see it.'

'We will come as soon as we have finished here,' Drago promised. 'After Sext.'

'Agreed,' Luca said.

The man bowed and Jacinta knelt once more and brushed the sand over the square of the paving stone. Freize dropped down to his knee to say a quiet goodbye to her. 'So shall I see you this afternoon? Will you come with your father?'

'If he asks me to come,' she replied.

'Then I shall see you again, at our house the Ca' de Longhi.'

She smiled. 'Either there, or I am always here in the morning. Perhaps tomorrow you will come and place a bet and you will be lucky.'

'I am very lucky,' Freize assured her. 'I was snatched by a terrible flood and I came home safe. I was in a nunnery where everyone was half mad and I came out unscathed, and before all of that I was apprenticed as a kitchen-lad in a country monastery and the only boy that I liked in the whole world was summoned to Rome and turned into a lord and he took me with him. That's when I got my lucky penny.'

'Show it to me again,' she demanded, smiling.

He produced it from a pocket in his shirt. 'I keep it apart from my other money now, so I don't spend it by accident. See? It is a penny minted by the Pope himself in the year of my birth. It survived a flood with me and I didn't spend it as I found my way home. Lucky through and through.'

'Will you not bet with it?' she asked. 'If it's so lucky?'

'No, for if it were to fail just once and I were to lose it, it would break my heart,' Freize said. 'And all my luck would be gone. But I would give it to you ... for something in exchange.'

'Lend it to me,' she said smiling. 'Lend it to me and I promise I will give it back to you. As good as before but a little better.'

'A keepsake?' he asked. 'A sweetheart's keepsake?'

'I won't keep it for very long,' she said. 'You'll have it back, I promise.'

At once he handed it over. 'I shall want it returned with a kiss,' he stipulated.

Shyly, she kissed her fingertips and put them against his cheek.

'See how lucky I am already!' Freize beamed, and was rewarded by a flash of her eyes from under her dark eyelashes, as he jumped up and followed Luca.

~

Luca led Brother Peter and Freize across the busy square to the line of money changers whose long trestle table was set back under the portico, each trader seated, with a young man with a stout cudgel or a menacing knife in his belt standing behind him.

'That's the one, on the left,' Freize prompted him. Luca went towards the man whose little hat and yellow round badge showed him to be a Jewish money changer. He sat alone, at the end of the row, separated from the Christian moneymen by a little space, as if to indicate his inferior status.

'I would talk business with you,' Luca said pleasantly.

The man gestured that Luca might sit, as his boy brought a second stool. Luca sat, and Brother Peter and Freize stood behind him.

'I am an honest man of business,' the money changer

said a little nervously. 'Your servant will confirm that I gave him a fair exchange for his coins when he came the day before yesterday. And actually, the value has risen already. I would buy the English nobles back from him and give him a profit.'

Freize nodded, and smiled his open-faced beam. 'I have no complaint,' he said cheerfully. 'I'm hanging on to them and hoping they will rise in value again.'

'I have a share in a ship coming in from the East, carrying Russian goods,' Luca said, leaning towards the money changer so that no-one else could hear. 'I want to prepare for the sale of the cargo, as soon as it comes into port.'

'You have borrowed against it?' the money changer asked acutely.

'No!' Brother Peter exclaimed.

'Yes,' Luca said speaking simultaneously.

They exchanged an embarrassed look. 'My brother denies it, for he hates debt,' Luca explained quickly. 'But yes, I have borrowed against it and that is why I want to sell the cargo quickly, as soon as it enters port, and for gold nobles.'

'Of course,' the man said. 'I would be interested in buying a share but I don't carry that many nobles to hand. I keep my fortune in different values. You would accept a payment in silver? In rubies?'

'No, I only want gold,' Luca said. 'My preference would be gold coins. These English nobles, for instance?'

'Oh, everyone wants English nobles, they are driving up the price! It's ridiculous.'

'Perhaps. But that makes them better for me. I want to get them while they are rising in price. The value of my cargo would be perhaps a thousand English nobles?'

The merchant lowered his eyes to the table before him. 'A very great sum, Milord!'

'It is easily worth that.' Luca lowered his voice. 'Almost all furs.'

'Indeed.'

'Squirrel, fox, and beaver. I told my agent to only buy the very best. And some silks, and amber, and ivory.' Luca spread the cargo manifest on the trader's table, letting him see the goods that had been ordered.

The trader nodded. 'So. If your cargo is as good as you describe . . .'

'But I will only sell for the English nobles.'

'It would take me a few days to get that sum together,' the money changer said.

'You could get the full amount?'

'I could. When would your ship come in?'

'It's due next week,' Luca said. 'But of course, it could be delayed.'

'If it is very late you will find the gold nobles have risen in value and I will only be able to pay for the cargo at the current value of the nobles. But I will offer you a fair price for the furs, and I am very interested in the amber. I will pay you a deposit now if you would let me have first look at the goods, and first offer?'

'You perhaps want a pound of flesh as well?' Brother Peter demanded irritably.

The merchant bent his head, ignoring the insult. 'I will offer in English nobles.'

'But where will you get so many coins?' Brother Peter asked. 'From these other money changers?'

The trader looked along the row of little tables. 'They don't like to work with me except for an extreme profit,' he said. 'And it is not always good for a man of my religion to do business with Christians.'

'Why not?' Brother Peter asked, bristling.

The Jewish money changer gave him a rueful smile. 'Because, alas, if they decide to deny a debt I cannot get justice.'

'Even in Venice?' Luca asked, shocked. He knew that all of Christendom was against the Jews, who only survived the regular riots against them because they lived in their own areas under the protection of the local lord; but he had thought that in Venice the only god was profit, and the laws protecting trade were rigidly enforced by the ruler of Venice, the Doge.

'It is better for people of my faith in Venice than elsewhere,' the merchant conceded. 'We are protected by the laws and by the Doge himself. But here, like everywhere, we prefer to work only with men that we can trust. And anyway, I can get all the gold nobles I need without going to the Christian money changers.'

'You will go to the Arab bankers?' Brother Peter was suspicious. 'You will go to gold merchants? We don't want the whole of Venice knowing our business.'

'I will say nothing. And it does not matter to you where I get the nobles as long as they are good. I go to my own merchant. Only one. And he is discreet.'

'And the English nobles are the best currency, aren't they?' Luca confirmed. 'Though it is surprising that there are so many of them on the market at once.'

The man shrugged. 'The English are losing the war

against France,' he said. 'They have been pouring gold into France to pay for their army in Bordeaux. When they lost Bordeaux last summer, the city was sacked and the campaign funds disappeared. As it happens, the money chests all came here. These things happen in wartime. That's their sorrow and our gain, for the coins are good. I have tested them myself, and I can get them at a good price.'

'And who is your supplier?' Brother Peter asked bluntly.

The merchant smiled. 'He would prefer all of Venice not to know *his* business,' he said. 'You will find me discreet, just as you asked me to be.'

'When will you get them?' Luca asked.

No one but Luca would have noticed the swift, almost invisible glance that went from the money changer towards the street-gambling girl's father, who was helping her pack up her game, apparently quite unaware of the money changers. But Luca was watching the Jew as closely as he had watched Jacinta playing the cups and ball game.

'By tomorrow,' the man said. 'Or the next day.'

'Very good,' Luca said pleasantly. 'I'll come again tomorrow. Perhaps I'll have news of my ship then.'

'I hope so.' The merchant rose from his stool and bowed to the three men. 'And please, do not speak of your ship with others till we have concluded our business.'

They crossed the square together and got into the gondola, Freize throwing a casual smile and salute to Jacinta as they went by. The gondolier steered out into the middle of the canal, as Freize said quietly: 'Put me down on the far side. I'll stick to the merchant like glue and come home to report later.'

'Take care you're not seen,' Luca cautioned him.

'Carnival!' Freize said. 'I'll buy a mask and a cape.'

'Just follow him,' Luca said. 'Don't try to be a hero. Just follow and watch and then come home. I don't expect us to solve the mystery in one step. Things might not be as they appear.'

'This is Venice,' Brother Peter said miserably. 'Nothing is as it appears.'

~

As the two men set off for home in the gondola, Freize strolled back to the Rialto Bridge, pausing only to buy a handsome dark red cloak, a matching elaborate mask and a gloriously big red hat in one of the many stalls that lined the bridge. He put them on at once and went down the steep steps of the bridge into the Campo San Giacomo. Jacinta and her father had already finished for the day, and gone away. As Freize looked around he saw the money changer picking up his papers, locking them in his box and gesturing to his young guard to carry box and table away. He himself carried the two little stools.

With the enormous red hat bobbing gently on his head, and the mask completely obscuring his face, Freize was confident that he would not be recognised, but realised that he was rather noticeable even among the flamboyant carnival costumes, as he watched the money changer weave quietly through the crowds around the Rialto Bridge and make his way inland.

'Now then,' Freize admonished himself, pulling the hat off his head and crushing the bobbing peak down into the brim and snapping off three overarching plumes, to make an altogether smaller and more modest confection. 'I think

I made the mistaking of buying a hat out of vanity and not from discretion. But if I fold it like so ...' He paused to admire the reduced shape. 'That's better, that's surely better now.'

Freize followed the money changer and his lad at a safe distance, ready to step into a doorway if the man looked round, but the old man went steadily onward and his page boy led the way, never looking back. They went down one dark street after another, twisting and turning around little alleyways to find the way to little wooden bridges, some of which had to be lowered by the young man for the merchant to cross, and then raised up again so that the water traffic was not blocked. At the larger canals the pair had to wait at the steps leading down to the water for a flat-bottomed boat to ferry them across for the price of a piccoli. Freize stood behind them, shrinking into the shadows, waiting for them to cross and go on their way, before he whistled the boat back to ferry him over. He had to fall back and was afraid then that he had lost them, but he heard their footsteps echoing on the stone quayside as they went under a bridge, following the canal, and he could hurry after them, guided by the sound. It was a long and rather eerie walk, through the quiet dark back streets of the city with every path running alongside a dark silent canal, and the constant sound of the splash of water against weedy stone steps.

Freize was glad to arrive at a corner, just in time to see them knocking on the side door to a house on the very edge of the Venice foundry district, where the air was smoky and dark and the canals were cloudy with the soil of the tanneries and stained with dye from cloth. All the dirty work of the city was done in this area, and the Jews of the city mostly lived here, keeping to their own ways, beside their synagogue shielded by a high wall and a bolted gate. Freize peered around a corner and saw the door of the house open, and in the candlelight that spilled out he saw the pretty young woman, Jacinta, admit the two men into the house.

'The gambling girl,' Freize remarked to himself. 'Now that's a little odd. There's no great fortune to be made taking small coins from playing cups and ball, and yet – that's a pretty big house. And the money changer has come here as his first call when he wants a lot of gold nobles.'

He pulled his big hat down over his mask and waited, leaning back in a darkened doorway. After nearly an hour the Jewish money changer came out, followed by his lad, and the two of them went through the narrow gate into the Jewish quarter. Freize did not dare to follow, knowing that he would be conspicuous among all the dark-suited men who wore the compulsory round yellow badge. But he waited outside the gate and watched as the money changer and his boy turned sharply right, into a tall thin house that overlooked the dark canal. Over the doorway swung the three balls, the ancient insignia of the money changer and lender.

'Hi, lad, tell me, who lives in there?' Freize asked a passing errand boy, who was clattering along the street with some newly forged metal rings for barrels, slung like hoops over his shoulder.

Freize pointed at the house behind the gate, and the boy glanced back over his shoulder. 'Israel the moneylender,' he said shortly. 'He has a stall in the Campo San Giacomo, every day, or you can tap on the door and borrow money any time, night or day. They say he never sleeps. And if he ever did, you cannot rob him for his wealth is guarded by a golem.'

'A golem? What's that?'

'A monster made from dust, obedient to his every word. That's why nobody ever burgles his house. The golem is waiting for them. It has the strength of ten men, and he controls it by the word on its forehead. If he changes a letter of the word the golem crumbles to dust. But if the golem attacks you it goes on and on forever, until you are dead.'

'Inconvenient,' Freize commented, believing none of this. He fell into step beside the young man as they crossed the wider square. 'And do you know who lives in that house?' He pointed to Jacinta's house, where the moneylender had visited for an hour.

The boy broke into a trot. 'I can't stop, I have to get these to the cooper by this afternoon.'

'But who lives there?'

'The alchemist!' the boy called back. 'Nacari, the alchemist, and the pretty girl that he says is his daughter.'

'Are they guarded by a golem?' Freize shouted after him in jest.

'Who knows?' the boy called back. 'Who knows what goes on in there? Only God, and He is far, far away from here!'

'And you are certain that they didn't see you?' Luca demanded. Freize was proudly reporting on his work as the group ate dinner together, the doors closed against eavesdroppers. Freize's plate was piled high: his reward to himself for good work well done.

'They did not, for I didn't go near the Nacari house. And I am certain that the money changer did not see me, nor his page boy.'

Luca looked at Brother Peter. 'And the boy on the street called Nacari an alchemist?'

Brother Peter shrugged. 'Why not? He's a street gambler, we know that for sure. He could equally be a magician or a trickster? A bloodletter, an unqualified physician, perhaps a dentist? A trader in old manuscripts and in love potions? Who knows what he does? Certainly nothing known and certified with a proper licence from the Church.'

There was a silence. It was Isolde who said what everyone was thinking. 'And perhaps Drago Nacari is a coiner as well as everything else. Perhaps he's a forger.'

'We tested the coins ourselves,' Luca reminded her.

'That only proves that some of them are good.'

'But why would they make English gold nobles?' Ishraq asked. 'Wouldn't he do better to make gold bars?'

'Not necessarily,' Brother Peter said. 'If you forged gold bars then most of your customers would buy them to have them worked at once, into gold goods or jewellery. That's when you'd be in danger of them discovering the base metal inside the bar. But if you forge perfect-looking coins, especially some with a persuasive story behind them – English nobles made in the Calais mint to pay the English soldiers – it all makes sense, and you can release the coins onto the market. We know that they are traded against Venetian ducats at two to one. And the money changer said they were rising in price.'

'But we tested them,' Luca reminded him. 'Others must test them and find them good.'

'Perhaps they are very good forgeries,' Brother Peter said suspiciously. 'At any rate, no one says anything against them.'

'They're still rising in price,' Ishraq confirmed. 'I looked today. They're up again.'

Isolde shot her a quick smile. 'You are a trader,' she whispered.

'But what would such a man buy instead?' Luca wondered aloud. 'Once you have sold your forged gold coins? What do you buy with the profit? How do you take the profit?'

'Jewels,' Isolde guessed. 'Small things that you can easily take away if you get caught.'

'Books,' Ishraq volunteered. 'Alchemy books so that you can practice your art. Old manuscripts, as we know he has. Precious ingredients for your craft.'

'Horses,' Freize said. 'So you can get away.'

Luca exchanged an affectionate glance with his friend. 'And because you'd always buy horses.'

Freize nodded. 'What would you buy?' he asked Brother Peter curiously.

'I'd buy Masses for my soul,' Brother Peter answered. 'What matters more?'

There was a brief respectful silence. 'Well, they don't look like wealthy people,' Freize said. 'There's the daughter working every morning in the street for handfuls of silver, and she's not wearing gold bracelets. She said she would gamble with me for a silk dress. She answered the door as if they didn't have a maid. But they have that big house. It doesn't add up.'

'How can we find out more?' Luca puzzled aloud. 'How can we find out what they're doing?'

'We could break in,' Ishraq volunteered. 'We know that they are out every morning, gambling at the Rialto. The father is always there with her, isn't he? And Freize thinks they have no maid.'

'They've been there every morning that we've seen so far,' Freize said cautiously. 'And he is coming here this afternoon. They have a manuscript to show Luca.'

'They asked me if I would look at it. I said you might be able to read it, if it is in Arabic,' Luca said to Ishraq.

'Is it about alchemy?'

'He said it was a mystery to him. But obviously it is something strange. He does not want to take it to the university nor to the Church.'

'Well, I can try to read it with you this afternoon. And tomorrow morning why don't you go to the square and gamble with them, keep them there, while I go to the house and break in?'

'You can't go alone,' Isolde said. 'I'll come with you.'

'No, that would be to walk straight into danger.' Luca was instantly against the idea.

'And immodest to go wandering round the streets of Venice in carnival time,' Brother Peter said crossly. 'We have already agreed that it shouldn't be done. The young women must stay indoors like Venetian ladies.'

'Carnival time is the very thing that makes it possible,' Ishraq replied. 'We can go disguised. I can dress as a young man and Freize can come with me as my servant. You and Brother Peter go and gamble, and since they have never seen Isolde, she can go separately from both of us and act as lookout. If they pack up early or start to come home, she can get ahead of them, run ahead of them, and bring us warning at their house so we can get out and away.'

'You'll just go in, have a look round, and come away again,' Luca ruled.

She nodded. 'I'll get in through a window and open the door for Freize.'

Luca hesitated. 'Can you do that? Can you climb up a house wall and get in through a window?'

Isolde smiled. 'She's climbs like a cat,' she said. 'She was always getting in and out of the castle without the sentries knowing.'

Luca glanced uncertainly at Brother Peter, whose face was dark with disapproval.

'We are to go gambling in the square while a woman in our care is breaking into a house?' Brother Peter demanded. 'And no doubt thieving? While a young lady, a noblewoman, the Lady Isolde of Lucretili, acts as a lookout? Like some kind of gang of thieves?'

'So that we can write Milord's report,' Luca reminded him. 'He told us we were to find out where the English gold nobles were coming from. We're on the way to discovering the source.'

Brother Peter shook his head sadly. 'It's hard for me to countenance sin,' he said. 'Even for a great cause. Milord is our commander and the Order of Darkness is pledged to understand the rise of heresy, the signs of darkness, and the coming of the end of the world. Often, in this work I have had to study terrible sin. But never before have I had to be a party to it.'

'It's hardly terrible sin, you're only gambling for piccoli,' Freize said cheerfully. 'We might have to do far worse. And anyway – look on the bright side – you might win.'

~

The five of them waited in their grand palace for the arrival of the alchemist and his daughter. Isolde was confined upstairs and so she peered down the great marble staircase, hoping to glimpse the stranger when he came up the steps from the watergate. Ishraq was waiting on the first floor in the dining room, which they had equipped as a study, with paper and pens laid out on the dining table. Freize, dressed in a dark jacket and looking like a servant, was ready to greet the alchemist as his boat came into the private quay, and to usher him upstairs. Brother Peter had shut himself in his room to write the report to Milord, and Luca was holding his chip of glass up to the light, and idly measuring and drawing half arcs of rainbows while gazing out over the Grand Canal.

'I think that's him,' he said to Ishraq as a small gondola detached itself from the seething traffic of the Grand Canal and turned towards the watergate of the palazzo. Luca crossed to the door with three swift steps. 'Freize!'

'Ready!' came the shout from the lowest level of the house. Luca turned and looked upwards to the upper floor and caught a glimpse of Isolde's smile before she stepped back, out of sight. It was as if she had sent him a message of encouragement, or blown him a kiss; the smile was for him alone, as if she was saying that she had faith in him.

He heard Freize greet the man and, looking down, saw him leading the dark-robed figure up the stairs to the first floor. Luca went forward to greet him with his hand held out.

'I am Luca Vero,' he said. 'Thank you for coming.'

'Drago Nacari,' the man replied formally. 'Thank you for inviting me to your home.'

They entered the room and Ishraq rose up from her seat behind the table. She was wearing Moorish dress: tunic and pantaloons, her scarf covering her hair and half veiling her face. She bowed to Drago Nacari and he took off his hat and swept a bow to her.

'This is my sister's companion, Mistress Ishraq,' Luca introduced her. 'I thought she might be able to help us with your manuscript. She speaks Arabic and Spanish and she is a scholar.'

'Of course,' the man said. 'I am honoured to meet you.'

'Did you not bring your daughter with you?' Ishraq asked.

'No,' he said. 'She is studying at home.'

The three of them sat at the great table, Drago at the head, and Luca and Ishraq on either side of him. He was carrying a satchel and he put it on the table, unfastened the ties and slid out a sheet of parchment painted with beautiful symbols and plants, and closely written with a clerk's well-wrought handwriting.

'Where did you study?' he asked Ishraq politely. 'Do you recognise any of this?'

'I was in the service of the Lord of Lucretili,' she said. 'He was a great crusader lord and he took an interest in the people and the learning of the Moors. He took me to Spain to study with the philosophers at the universities. I was allowed to study geography and astronomy, some medicine and languages. It was a great privilege.'

He bowed his head. 'I have studied in Egypt,' he said. 'I read Arabic but I cannot understand this. It is definitely an alchemy text. I know that much for certain. So we may expect certain things.'

'What things?' Luca said.

'A mixture of symbols and numbers and words,' the man answered. 'Alchemists have symbols, special signs for many elements, and for many processes.' He pointed to one symbol. 'That means to heat gently, for instance, any alchemist would recognise it.'

'Do you think this is a recipe?' Luca asked. 'An alchemy recipe?'

Drago spread his hands. A small gold ring on his finger caught the light. 'That, I don't know,' he said. 'I hope so, of course. I hope it is a recipe for the one thing, the greatest thing, the thing we all seek.'

'And what is that?' Luca asked. He was scanning the first page of the manuscript trying to see what words stood out. Nothing was recognisable, he could not even see a pattern.

'Of course, we all seek the stone,' the man said quietly. 'The philosophers' stone.'

'What is that?' Luca asked.

Drago glanced at Ishraq to see how much she knew of the stone.

'It is the stone which changes base material to gold,' she said quietly. 'And water thrown on the stone when it is hot becomes the elixir of life, it can prolong life perhaps forever, it can make the old young, it can make the sick well. It is the one thing that all alchemists hope to make. It would solve all the troubles of the world.'

'And you trust me to translate this with you?' Luca asked Drago Nacari. 'If we could understand it, this document might mean the end to death and the beginning of limitless wealth for any one of us, for all of us.' For a moment he thought what he would do if he had the stone and could command a fortune, an unstoppable fortune. He thought he would buy the freedom of his parents, of all slaves. Then he would buy the castle of Lucretili and give it to Isolde. Then he would ask her to marry him, he would be a man so rich that he could propose marriage to her. He broke off from his dream with a short laugh. 'Already I am dreaming

674

what I would do if I had the stone, and could make gold,' he said. 'Why would you trust us strangers with this?'

'This is only one page of many,' Drago said. 'And it's not a recipe for stewing oysters, it's not easy. Even if you were to read every word you still would be far from making the stone. To make the stone you would need to study for years. You need to purify yourself and everything you touch. I have been working for decades and only now am I starting to be ready. You may be very clever – Jacinta says that you have quick eyes and a good ear, and, of course, she dreamed of you – but you have not studied for years, as I have done.'

Ishraq smiled. 'And also there is the question of desire,' she said.

'Desire?' Luca repeated the single inviting word.

Drago Nacari nodded. 'You *are* learned then,' he confirmed to Ishraq.

'If you desire wealth, if you are bound to the world by greed, then you cannot find the stone for you are not pure in heart,' Ishraq explained. 'The only man or woman who can find such a thing would be he or she who wanted it for others. Someone who did not want it for themselves. It is the purest thing in the world, it cannot be discovered by someone with dirty hands, it cannot be snatched in a greedy grasp.'

Luca nodded. 'I think I understand. So let's have a look at it.'

'It's not Arabic,' Ishraq said. 'Though some of the symbols are like Arabic symbols.' She pointed to one sign. 'This one, and perhaps these.'

'It's no language that I recognise,' Luca said. 'Have

you shown it to a Russian? Or to someone from the East?'

Drago shook his head. 'Not yet. I hoped to be able to understand it on my own, but I have studied it for months now, and I see that I need help.'

'I don't recognise these plants,' Ishraq said. 'I've never even seen them, not in the garden, not in a herbal. Do you know them?'

Luca did not answer her. He was looking at the writing and scribbling something down. Ishraq immediately fell silent, and looked from Luca's notes to the manuscript.

'It might be a cipher,' he said. 'A code.'

'Based on what?' Drago Nacari whispered, as if he feared being overheard.

'Based on old numbers,' Luca said. 'Latin numbers. I, II, III and so on. Look here,' he pointed to a string of words. 'These words recur: "or, or, or, oro". These could be code for numbers. How old is this manuscript?'

Drago shook his head. 'Not more than fifty years old, I believe.'

'And who was the author?'

'I don't know. I only have a few pages of it. I believe it was written in Italy, but I had it from a scholar who had a library in Paris.'

'A Frenchman?'

Drago hesitated. 'No. I had it from an English lord. He was a great philosopher, but he was not the author. He was ... He was with the English court in Paris.' He broke off and saw that Ishraq was scrutinising him with a narrowed dark gaze.

'What was his name?' she asked bluntly.

'I cannot tell you.'

'Was he a wise man?' she asked. 'Did he know the language of birds?'

He smiled at her. 'Yes, yes he did.'

'What is the language of birds?' Luca asked curiously.

Drago answered him. 'It is the coded speech of alchemists.'

'So this book was owned by an alchemist, and it is not likely to be written in either English or French. More likely to be based on Italian or perhaps Latin?'

'And it is not a chimera?' Ishraq asked the alchemist directly. 'You spend your mornings helping your daughter deceive people. This is not another deceit? Not simply a pretence? We cannot waste our time on a sleight of hand. And we are not fools to be robbed.'

'My daughter earns her keep,' he said defensively. 'And no one is cheated. It's a fair game.'

'I don't criticise her,' Ishraq said. 'But it's an odd occupation for a young woman whose father is hoping to find the secret to make gold from dust, who has studied – as you say you have done – for decades. In the afternoon you pursue the wisdom of ages and in the morning you play with fools.'

'We did not always live as we do now, we did not always have a patron,' Drago explained. 'We did not always live here. We did not always have this manuscript, and the other pages – the recipe for deep transformation.'

'You gambled for your living before you found your patron?'

'Yes.'

'And you gamble still?'

'By way of explaining our presence here.'

'Did the patron give you the house and the manuscript

together?' Ishraq asked casually. 'And tell you to pass as street gamblers?'

'He did. Two years ago,' Drago said.

'And what does he expect for his generosity?'

'A share, of course,' Drago said. 'When we have the answer that he seeks. Most alchemists have a patron, how else could we afford the ingredients? How else could we undertake years of study?'

'He must be a generous man, for sure a patient man,' Ishraq said and was surprised to see no answering smile from the alchemist.

He was grave. 'I don't know him at all,' he said quietly. 'He is my patron. He is my lord. He gives me sealed orders often through a third person. I have only met him twice. He is not a friend.'

'You don't like him?' she asked acutely.

His face was closed. 'I don't know him,' he said.

'What's this?' Luca asked suddenly.

He was pointing to a small pen-and-ink drawing at the foot of one page. Ishraq bent close and saw that it was a dragon, tail in its own mouth, the symbol of Luca's own Order. His lord had tattooed the first part of the symbol on Luca's forearm, as he completed the first part of his apprentice-ship. The lord had promised that he would add the rest of the dragon and the detail of its scales until Luca, like Brother Peter, like Milord himself, carried the entire symbol on his own flesh: a different version from this little sketch, but clearly the same symbol.

'That is the sign of ouroboros,' Drago said. 'That is an alchemical sign. It means eternal life, a life that is forever renewed. The dragon feeds on itself, it eats its own tail, it drinks its own blood, it goes on forever. All is in one. One is in all.'

Luca was a little pale. 'I know this sign,' he said. 'It is an emblem for an Order.'

'The Order of the Dragon?' the man confirmed. 'The Order of my patron.'

'The Order that I am thinking of is known as the Order of Darkness,' Luca corrected him.

'Darkness,' the man repeated softly. 'The darkness of the first matter, of Al Khem which gives its name to alchemy, the primary material which changes into one thing, and then another, into two and then three, and finally into the stone, into gold. Everything comes from darkness. This Order is well named if it makes the journey from darkness to gold.'

'They hope to go from ignorance to understanding,' Ishraq murmured.

Luca shook his head as if to clear his thoughts. 'What does this mean?' he asked. 'You speak as if everything is connected with everything else.'

Drago Nacari smiled. 'Without a doubt it is,' he said.

'Luca here knows of an Order which is called the Order of Darkness,' Ishraq said slowly. 'The Order is commanded by his lord. We don't see his face. It exists to discover the end of days, the end of the world, the end of all things, of life on earth. Now you show us its symbol: the dragon eating its own tail, a sign of eternity, of life itself. You speak of the Order of the Dragon, and you too are commanded by a lord who you don't know.'

'Many great men work in secret,' Nacari volunteered. 'In my business, everyone works in secret.' He rose to his feet. 'Shall I leave this page with you for you to study?'

'If you will,' Luca said.

'But show it to no one else,' he said. 'We don't want it to fall into the hands of those who might use it against the world. Since we don't know what it says, it could be something that does not transmute to purity and good, but something which goes the other way.'

'The other way?' Ishraq repeated. 'What other way?'

'Into the shadow of darkness, into death, into decay,' he said. 'Into our destruction and the end of man. Into what you call the end of days. The dark is as real as light. The other world is just a fingertip away. Sometimes I can almost see it.'

'Do you see any signs of the end of days?' Luca asked him. 'I have a mission to know. Do you think the world is going to end? The infidel is in Constantinople, his armies have entered Christendom – is Christ going to come again and judge us all? Will the world end, and will He harrow hell? Have you seen signs of it in your work? In the world which you say is just a fingertip away?'

The man nodded as he turned towards the door. 'I think the time is now,' he said. 'I see it in everything that I do. And every day I have to conquer ...'

'Conquer what?' Ishraq asked him when he broke off.

'My own fears,' he said simply. He looked at her directly, and she was sure that he was speaking the truth. 'These are dark times,' he said frankly. 'And I fear that I serve a dark master.'

~

Next morning the little group divided. Ishraq, dressed in the costume of a young man about town, with a dark black cape around her shoulders, her long hair pinned up under a broad black velvet hat, and a black and silver mask hiding her face, set out with Freize in attendance as her squire, taking a passing gondola to the quay near to the Nacari house at the edge of the Jewish quarter. Luca and Brother Peter took the house gondola to the Rialto Bridge, and Isolde, dressed as modestly as a nun, with her face hidden beneath a great winged hood, walked down the alleyways and over the little bridges to the San Giacomo church on the square beside the Rialto Bridge. She took up a position under the portico of the church and watched as Brother Peter and Luca strolled into the square, and went to watch the cups and ball game.

'Have you come to try your luck, my masters?' Jacinta asked, as pleasantly as always. She smiled at Luca. 'My hands are quick today. I think I shall outwit you.'

Luca chinked silver piccoli in his hand. 'I think I am certain to win,' he said.

She laughed. 'Watch carefully then,' she invited him, and as a small crowd gathered round she put the gleaming marble ball under an upturned cup and moved the cups slowly, and then at dazzling speed, until they came to rest and she sat back, smiled and said: 'Which cup?'

~

Isolde glanced out of the square, down the maze of streets and waterways so that she should be certain which way she would have to go if she had to run before the Nacaris to warn Ishraq and Freize, and then bowed her head as if saying her prayers. She found she was truly praying for them all. She prayed for her own safety: that her brother's men had gone back to Lucretili and her brother would give up his pursuit. She prayed for Luca's quest to find his parents, and for her own mission to get back to her home. 'Please,' she whispered, 'please let us all be safe and not exposed to danger nor be a danger to others.' She tried to concentrate, but she found her mind strayed. She fixed her gaze on the image of the crucified Christ but all she could think of was Luca, his face, his smile, the way that she could not help but be near him, lean towards him, hope for his touch.

Guiltily, she shook her head and pinched her clasped hands. She closed her eyes and bowed her head again to pray for the safety of Ishraq and Freize as they went, disguised, to the Nacari house.

~

Ishraq and Freize were far from needing prayers, gleefully excited by their mission as they approached the tall crowded houses just outside the Jewish quarter. Ishraq loitered behind as Freize went boldly up to the side door which stood on the quayside and hammered on the knocker. There was silence from inside.

'Anybody in?' Freize shouted.

A woman from the far side of the narrow canal threw

open her shutters and called down. 'They're at the Rialto, they're there every morning.'

'Can their maid not let me in? Don't they have a page boy?'

'They have no maid. They have no servants. You'll have to go to the Rialto if you want them.'

'I'll go there then and find them,' Freize called back cheerily. 'I'll go now. Thank you for your help.'

'Pipe down,' the woman advised rudely and slammed her shutters.

Freize exchanged one wordless glance with Ishraq and set off, apparently in the direction of the Rialto Bridge. As quiet as a cat, Ishraq tried the handle of the door in the garden wall. She felt it yield, but the door would not open. Clearly, the Nacaris had locked it behind them when they left the house. Ishraq dropped back, took a short run at the garden wall and leaped up, her feet scrabbling to find a purchase on the smooth wall, until she got her knee on a branch of ivy and heaved up to the top of the wall and dropped down on the far side.

She was on her feet in a moment, looking alertly all around the garden in case anyone had heard her. Already she had spotted a tree that she would climb if a guard dog came rushing towards her, or a watchman, but there was silence in the sunlit garden, and a bird started to sing. On tiptoe, Ishraq went towards the house and tried the door that led from the garden to the storeroom. It was locked and the shutters were closed on the inside. She turned to her right and tried the shutters on the windows. They too were firmly bolted from the inside. She looked up. Overlooking the garden was a pretty balcony with a spiral stone staircase that led down to the lawn and the peach tree.

Quiet as a ghost, Ishraq slipped up the stairs and found the window to the bedroom had been left latched open. She put her slim hand into the gap beneath the window and flicked the catch. As the window swung open, Ishraq went head first through the opening and landed as quietly as she could in a heap on the floor.

At once she was on her feet, listening, sensing that the house was empty. She tiptoed from the room to the landing, head cocked, looking down the well of the stair. Nothing moved, there was no sound. Lightly, she ran down the stairs and unbolted the door just as Freize was walking briskly – a man with business to attend to – past the house. One swift sideways step and he was inside, and the door was closed behind him.

They beamed at each other. Ishraq slid the bolts across the door, locking it against the street. 'In case they come back unexpectedly,' she said. 'Come on.'

They went first into the big room at the front of the house that overlooked the canal and found a table piled with rolls of manuscripts and some hand-copied bound books. Ishraq looked at them without touching. 'Philosophy,' she said. 'Astronomy, and here – alchemy. These are a lot of books. It seems that he was telling the truth when he said he had been studying for decades.'

'They both have,' Freize corrected her. He pointed to a writing table beside the bigger table. There was a brown scarf over the back of the chair, and on the table a page of paper with a carefully copied drawing, and a page of notes. He looked from the book to the paper. 'She's translating something,' he said. 'She's studying too.'

Ishraq came and looked over his shoulder. 'Alchemists

often work in pairs, a man and a woman working together for the energy that they bring,' she said. 'Alchemy is about the transmutation from one form into another, liquids to solids, base to pure. It needs a man and a woman to make it work, it needs the spirit of a woman as well as that of a man.'

'How d'you know all this?' Freize asked curiously.

Ishraq shrugged. 'When I was studying in Spain, the Arab philosophers often studied alchemy texts,' she said. 'One of the universities even changed from studying the philosophy of Plato to that of Hermes the Alchemist. They said that there was more to learn from alchemy than from the Greeks – that gives you an idea of how important the work is, how much there is to understand. But this material is far beyond me.'

Freize picked up a curiously shaped paperweight, a long pyramid of sparklingly clear glass, and then found a brass stamp beneath the paper. 'What's this?' Freize asked. 'Their seal?'

Ishraq picked up the little gold stamp and looked at the base. It was an engraved gold picture, for stamping the hot wax of a letter or a parcel to mark the insignia.

'This looks like a royal crest, or a ducal crest. Why would the Nacaris have it to seal their letters?'

'Get a copy of it, we should show it to Luca,' Freize advised. 'I'll look round upstairs,' he said.

She heard him going quietly upstairs and the creak of the door as he put his head into the two bedrooms, then the slight noise as he went upwards to the empty attic bedrooms for the servants. She was so intent on her work of heating the sealing wax at the embers of the fire, and dripping the melted wax onto a spare sheet of paper, that she hardly noticed as he came down the stairs again and went to the back room, the storeroom. She pressed the seal into the wax and saw the clear image. But then she heard him say urgently: 'Ishraq! Come and see.'

Replacing the stick of wax just as it had been, putting the seal back into its velvet-lined case and waving the paper page to dry the cooling wax, she went to the store room at the back of the house and froze as Freize heaved open the heavy door.

The room was no longer the homely store of a small Venice house, it was an alchemist's workplace. The place stank of decay and rotting food, and a subterranean smell of mould and vomit. Ishraq put a hand over her nose and mouth trying to block the stench. Next to the doorway, a great round tank with a wooden lid bubbled and gave off a nauseating stink of death.

'My God,' Ishraq said, gagging. 'It's unbearable.'

Freize shot one horrified look at her. 'It smells like a midden,' he says. 'Worse than a midden, a plague ground. What are they cooking?'

Under the window, before the locked shutters, was a stone bench. Into the flat surface had been carved four small circular depressions, each one filled with charcoal ready for burning, each one ready with a tripod and a pan, or a small cauldron. On the shelves were strange-shaped metal baths, and some expensive glass containers, with spouts and tubes for pouring and distilling liquids. Standing on the floor in massive coils, and towering as tall as Ishraq, was a great glass distillation tube with its dripping foot oozing a yellow slime into a porcelain bowl. On a big table in the centre of the room there were trays of candle wax, some with flowers or herbs face down into the wax as their essences drained away.

Freize looked around, his square face pale, his eyes darkening with superstitious fear. 'What is this? What in God's name are they doing here?'

Under an airtight bell jar, which stood in a shallow bath of water, there was a small brown mouse on a platform, sitting up and cleaning its whiskers, beside a burning candle.

'Are they roasting it?' Freize whispered. 'Torturing it, the poor little creature?'

Ishraq shook her head, as shaken as her friend. 'I don't know. I've never seen anything like this before.'

The stone hearth beneath the chimney had been raised to waist-height – as high as a fire in a forge – and great bellows beside the chimney and cracks in the stone fire-back showed that it had been heated beyond bearing. Now it had burned down to red embers, but they could see that in the grey ashes there were hundreds, perhaps thousands, of the piccoli silver coins, glowing like a thousand little eyes, pooling as they cooled into strange ominous shapes.

'What are they doing to the money?' Freize demanded.

Ishraq shook her head in bewilderment.

A range of shelves held the dried bodies of small animals: trapped mice, rats bought from the rat catcher and missing their tails, birds with their heads flopped to one side, a desiccated nest with four dried-out nestlings, and jar after jar of dead insects of all sorts. Freize made a face of disgust. 'What do they do with these? Is this for alchemy? Is it magic? Are they killing things here for sport, for devilment?'

Once more, Ishraq shook her head. 'I don't know.' She turned her eyes from the little limp bodies and could not suppress a shiver.

Against one wall was an empty chair, as tall as a throne, draped in purple velvet, with a purple velvet cape and robe beside it. Turned to the wall was a hammered silver mirror.

'What's that for?' whispered Freize. 'Who is that for?'

'It might be for scrying,' Ishraq replied. 'Foreseeing the future. If one of them has the gift of Sight.'

'What would they do then?' Freize asked in fascinated horror.

'Look in the mirror, see visions,' Ishraq answered briefly.

Draped around the mirror was a tent-like structure with curtains that could be let down for privacy, and before it was a small table like an altar. Above it was pinned an illuminated manuscript in green ink.

'The Emerald Tablet.' Ishraq read the Arabic symbols. She turned to Freize. 'These are the rules of alchemy,' she whispered. 'It says: These are the commandments that guide all seekers of this truth.'

'What does it say?' Freize asked. 'Does it tell you what to do? Does it say how to make gold?'

Ishraq shook her head, her eyes dark with fear. 'I can translate it for you, but I can't explain it,' she warned him.

'So tell me!' he said.

'Rule one,' she read. *''Tis true without lying, certain and most true: that which is below is like that which is above, and that which is above is like that which is below, to do the miracles of one only thing. And as all things have been, and arose from one by the mediation of one: so all things have their birth from this one thing by adaptation.'*

Freize looked back, over his shoulder at the dead animals on the shelves. 'What does it mean?' he asked unhappily. 'For I can understand nothing but cruelty here.'

'These are mysteries,' Ishraq told him. 'I did say that I can't explain it.'

'You did,' Freize confirmed. 'And you spoke fairly then. Can we go now, d'you think?'

Ishraq looked round. 'We should search for the gold nobles,' she reminded him.

'God knows what we will find if we open these boxes,' Freize said anxiously. 'Dead grandmothers, if not worse. The lad said there was a golem to guard the Jewish banker. I thought he was joking.'

'A what?' Ishraq asked suddenly intent.

'A golem. A sort of guardsman, a monster with a word of command on his forehead.'

Despite herself Ishraq shivered.

'Let's go,' Freize urged her.

'Wait,' she said. 'We've got to see . . .'

On the table were two tablets of wax with strange insignia drawn on their surface, and under the table, covered in a velvet cloth, was a chest. Ishraq bent down and tried to slide the bolts. They did not move. It was somehow locked.

'Don't,' Freize said bluntly. 'Don't force it open. What if there is . . .' He broke off, he realised he could not imagine what the alchemists might have in a small locked chest.

On the furthest wall a great glass vessel suddenly released a gush of foul-smelling liquid into a tray. They both jumped nervously at the splashing sound. Then they saw that below the big table was another closed box, broader than the one beneath the altar. This one was unlocked. Ishraq tried it, and Freize stepped forward to help her lift the heavy lid. She glanced at him and saw his face screwed up in a grimace of fear at what they might find. The lid opened. Freize still had his eyes closed.

'Look,' she whispered, quite entranced.

Freize opened his eyes. 'Now, will you look at this?' he whispered, as if it were his own discovery, and he was showing it to her. 'Will you look at this?'

Inside the box was a metal tray with a dozen indentations, almost like a sweetmeat maker would use to make little bonbons. But each indentation was beautifully wrought. They were moulds. Freize squinted to be sure what he was seeing. 'Moulds for coins,' he said. 'Moulds for English nobles. See the shape of them? See the picture on the moulds? The king in the boat and the rose?'

'So they really are coiners,' Ishraq whispered. 'Alchemists, as we have seen; but they are coiners as well. Practising magic and crime side by side. They really are.' She looked around. 'I wouldn't have thought it. But they really are coining gold nobles. So they make them here, at this forge. But where do they keep the coins? Where's the gold?'

'Hadn't we better get out of here?' Freize suggested. 'If they come back and catch us, God knows what they might do. These are not simple magic-makers, these are a couple of criminals turning over a fortune.'

'Let's be quick,' Ishraq agreed. Freize closed the lid on the box of moulds, looked around the room and saw for the first time, set low on the floor, the arched entrance to the cellar.

'See that?' he pointed it out to her.

'Can we open it?' Ishraq was there in a moment. The half-door was locked. Ishraq looked around for the key as Freize bent down, put the sharp blade of his knife in the

690

keyhole, and turned carefully. There was a series of clicks and the door swung open. Ishraq raised her eyebrows at Freize's convenient range of skills.

'You didn't learn that in the monastery.'

'I did actually,' he said. 'Kitchen stores. I was always hungry. And Sparrow would have faded away if I hadn't fed him up.'

Ishraq bent down to swing the door outwards and peer through. The door was so low that she had to go down on her hands and knees and then lie on her belly and squirm forwards.

'What can you see?' Freize whispered behind her.

'Nothing, it's too dark,' she replied, coming back out again.

He turned to the chimney and lifted down a rushlight, lit it at the fire, and handed it to her. Ishraq thrust it into the dark opening, wriggled her shoulders through and looked down. Freize held her feet.

'Don't fall,' he warned her. 'And don't for pity's sake leave me here.'

Fitfully, the flame flickered, illuminating the dark moving water at the end of the stone quay, immediately below her, and on the stones a glint here, a blaze of reflected light there, and then finally a cold draught of air blew the light out altogether and left her in damp blackness with nothing but the eerie slap of the dark waters to warn her of the edge of the quay.

'What can you see?' Freize's voice whispered from the room behind her. 'Come back! What can you see?'

'Gold,' Ishraq said, her voice quiet with awe. 'An absolute fortune in sacks and sacks of gold nobles.'

~

Brother Peter and Luca watched the gamblers at their place and then went into San Giacomo Church. As they had expected, Father Pietro was kneeling at a side chapel before the flickering flame of a candle placed at the feet of an exquisite statue of the Madonna and Child. Both men bent their knee and crossed themselves. Luca went to kneel in silence beside the priest.

'You do not disturb me, because I was praying for you,' Father Pietro said quietly, hardly opening his eyes.

'I suppose that it's too soon for any news?'

'Perhaps tomorrow, or the next day. You can come to me on the Rialto or I can send you a message.'

'I'll come to you,' Luca promised. 'I hardly dare to pray for the safety of my father. I hardly dare to think that he might come home to me.'

The priest turned and made the sign of a cross over Luca's bowed head. 'God is merciful,' he said quietly. 'He is always merciful. Perhaps He will be merciful to you and your father and your mother.'

'Amen,' Luca whispered.

Father Pietro looked up at the serene face of the Madonna. He smiled at her, as a man who knows that his work is blessed. Luca thought that a more superstitious man would have thought that the beautiful statue smiled back.

'Thank you, Father Pietro,' he said. 'I thank you from the bottom of my heart.'

'Thank me when your father holds you in his arms, my son,' the priest replied.

Luca and Brother Peter completed their prayers and

went to the back of the church and quietly opened the great wooden door and slipped out together.

Luca squinted at the brightness of the sunlight on the square, looked in one direction, and then another, and then quietly said: 'Oh no.'

The place where Jacinta had laid out her game earlier was empty. Drago and his daughter were missing.

And Isolde, their lookout, had vanished into thin air.

~

Isolde, her long skirt bunched into her hand, was running as fast as she could, through the narrow alleyway, her feet pounding on the damp cobblestones of the poorer streets, speeding up as she crossed a square paved with flagstones. She had watched Jacinta play for a crowd of people and Nacari stand over her and then suddenly, without a word of warning, far ahead of their usual time, they had packed up the game, stepped to the quayside and hailed a passing gondola.

Isolde, her breath coming short, hammered over the little wooden bridges, hailed the ferry boats in a panting shout, and then raced down the road from the bridge to where the Nacari's tall house stood, trying to beat them by running the short cut which Freize had described to her, while the gondola went round the long way on the little canals.

She recognised the house at once from Ishraq's drawing and hammered on the door. 'Freize! Ishraq!' she shouted.'Come away!'

In the quiet house, the hammering on the door was shockingly loud. In the storeroom, Ishraq and Freize, locking up the hatch, both jumped in fear at the explosion of noise. Freize's first terrified thought was that the mysterious golem had come for them, as Ishraq started for the hall. 'It's Isolde,' she said.

'Open the door, quick,' Freize said. 'She'll turn out the watch in a moment.'

Ishraq raced along the narrow hall and slid the bolts to throw open the door.

'They've left the square, they could be coming here!' Isolde gasped. 'I don't know where they're going, they took a gondola. I ran as fast as I could.' Her nun's hood had fallen from her head, and her blonde hair was tumbling down around her shoulders. She was panting from her run.

Ishraq at once put her arm around her friend's shoulders as if to leave at once. 'Come on,' she said to Freize. 'Let's go.'

'Not out of the front door, they left it bolted from the inside,' Freize reminded her.

As she hesitated, Isolde glanced down the narrow canal and saw the frightening silhouette of the shadow of the prow of a gondola on the canal wall, just as it was about to turn the corner and see them, on the doorstep of the house. They heard the gondolier cry a warning: 'Gondola! Gondola! Gondola!'

'Too late!' Isolde whispered. 'We'll have to go inside.'

They slipped back into the hall, closing the front door behind them.

'Out through the garden,' Ishraq hissed. 'Quickly, or they'll see us as they come in.'

She drew Isolde through the house as Freize bolted the door to the street.

'My God, what is that smell?' Isolde hesitated and put her

hand over her mouth as they went past the open door to the storeroom. 'It's like death.'

'Quick,' Ishraq said, closing the door and leading the two of them through the living quarters and out through the door into the little courtyard garden.

'You go,' she said. 'I'll lock up behind you and come out through the bedroom window.'

'I'll go!' Freize volunteered. 'You get out.'

He was too late. Ishraq was already racing up the stairs to the upper room. Freize turned to Isolde. 'We'll have to get over the wall,' he whispered. 'The garden door is locked and they have the key.' He cupped his hand for Isolde's shoe. 'Come on,' he said. 'Like getting up on a horse!' Isolde stepped up and he threw her upwards so that she caught the branch of the tree and heaved herself up to the top of the wall. Arduously, Freize hauled himself up beside her, and then paused. They both clung to the top of the wall, and watched, horrified, as below them the Nacaris, father and daughter, walked to the garden door, produced a key and let themselves in. They opened the door to the house, and went inside.

'What can we do?' Isolde whispered. 'We have to get her out!'

'Wait,' Freize advised.

Ishraq, in the house, went swift-footed silently up the stairs. She heard the garden door open and the Nacaris come in. She heard Jacinta remark on the coldness of the day and then she heard, frighteningly clear, Drago say: 'What's that noise?'

Silently, Ishraq slid across the treacherous floorboards to the bedroom window and eased herself out. She flung

695

herself down the spiral stone staircase to the garden and saw her two friends, poised on the top of the wall.

'Get down!' she hissed. 'They're in the house. They'll see us if they look out of the window!'

Freize jumped down into the street and reached up for Isolde, who dropped down into his arms as Ishraq stretched for a low bending bough, and swarmed her way upwards. As soon as she was at the top of the wall she too lowered herself down and then jumped clear.

They were facing a small tributary canal and further down the water was a little swing wooden bridge.

'This way,' Isolde said, pulling up the hood of her robe over her blonde hair, and leading the way at a brisk walk. She wiped her face with her sleeve. 'I haven't run so fast since we left Lucretili,' she remarked to Ishraq.

'You always were fast,' her friend said. 'Faster than me. Now I should teach you to fight.'

Isolde shook her head in a smiling denial.

'She doesn't like the thought of hurting people,' Ishraq explained to Freize.

The three of them crossed the bridge and started along the quay on the far side.

'I don't think I will ever have the stomach for fighting,' Isolde remarked. 'I can't bear it. Even that scramble has left me trembling. And now, I'd better walk home on my own.'

'Will you be all right?' Freize asked, torn between his desire to escort her to safety and maintaining the deception of being Ishraq's servant.

'Oh yes,' she said. 'I tremble very easily, but I'm not a coward.'

'I should go with you,' he hesitated.

Ishraq laughed. 'If there's any trouble she can run,' she said. 'She can certainly run faster than you.'

Isolde smiled. 'I'll go on ahead and see you at home.'

~

Freize and Ishraq strolled home together, along the Grand Canal, Ishraq careful to swagger ahead of Freize like a young prince, right until the moment when they came to the quay which ran to the side door of their house. Then she glanced to left and right, checked that there was no one at the windows and no one on the canal, and slipped down the street and scurried into the side door.

Isolde leaped up from where she had been sitting at the door and hugged her friend. 'Good! I was waiting for you. The others are home too.' She called across the stone hall. 'They're back!' as Freize came through the side door and Luca and Brother Peter opened the door to their rooms.

'Come in,' Luca said. 'How did you get on?'

Brother Peter recoiled in horror from Ishraq's young prince costume. 'She should change her clothes,' he said, covering his eyes. 'It's heresy for a woman to dress as a man.'

'I'll be one moment,' Ishraq promised.

She raced up the stairs, taking them two at a time, just like a boy, and they could hear her hurling her clothes into a chest and scrabbling into a gown. She came running downstairs with her dark hair tumbling down, and only at Brother Peter's scandalised glare did she twist it into a casual knot and pin it at the nape of her neck. Luca smiled at her. Anyone but the old clerk would have been struck by her agile grace in boys' clothes and her careless beauty when she was dressed once again as a girl in a conventional gown. 'I like you in costume,' he said.

'It's against God's will and the teaching of the Church,' Brother Peter said. 'And certainly a doorway to sin.'

'Well, it was useful,' Ishraq defended herself. 'So tell me about the square, was everything all right?'

'Everything,' Luca said shortly. 'We gambled, she won as usual, took a small purse of silver coins for the morning's work and gave them to her father. We spoke to the money changer and he said he would have enough nobles for us when the ship comes in. He says he has made an arrangement and has about a thousand gold nobles to hand. We saw Father Pietro in church. He's had no reply yet. Then it was dreadful when we came out of church and saw that they had left early. And then Isolde was gone too! But I see you're safe. How did you get on? Did you have to break into the house?'

'I got in through an open window,' Ishraq said. 'And then I let Freize in. They may have suspicions, they might have thought that they heard something; but they can't be sure that anyone was ever inside.'

'They don't have a servant – well, they can't have one. They daren't have one. The storeroom is completely devoted to alchemy. It reeks of magic and decay. Any servant would report them at once. In the main room, where they study, there were more pages like the one they brought to us. There were about ten pages that I could see, I couldn't read any of them. Plants that are unknown, language that you can't even spell out. And I copied this,' she put the piece of paper in front of Luca. 'I thought it was odd that they should have such a seal.'

He scrutinised it. 'I wouldn't know whose seal it is,' he said.

They both turned to Isolde, whose family had their own crest. She recognised it at once. 'Oh! That's the seal of one of my godparents,' she exclaimed.

'Count Wladislaw? Of Wallachia?' Brother Peter asked respectfully.

'No,' she said. 'Another one. My godmother.'

'How many do you have?' asked Freize. 'How many does a girl need?'

She shrugged with a smile. 'My father was very very well connected. This godmother was very grand indeed. She was the wife of John, Duke of Bedford, Regent of France. She was Jacquetta, the Dowager Duchess.'

'Who?' Freize asked.

'Her husband was brother to the great king of England, Henry V, who conquered France for England. John the duke was regent in France when the little prince of England came to the throne,' she said. 'When the French rose up under their king Charles VII, he fought them, and he captured their leader, Joan of Arc.'

'Yes,' Luca said, recognising a part of the story that he knew. 'I know who you mean, I've heard of him. He burned Joan of Arc as a witch.'

'The Church judged that she was guilty of witchcraft and heresy,' Isolde remarked. 'But I never met the duke, he died when I was still a baby. They say that he ruled France like an emperor. He maintained a huge army, he had magnificent palaces in Paris and Rouen, he made the laws, he issued coins. After he died, his widow, my godmother, remarried. She lives in England now, at the court of Henry VI.'

'But why would these street gamblers have the duke's seal?' Brother Peter asked. 'They have forged it, presumably, but why would they want it?'

'Would it be to seal the chests of gold?' Isolde asked. 'That they say is English gold? Chests from the English mint would have the regent's seal on them, wouldn't they?'

Everyone was silent, and then Luca reached across to her and grasped both her hands. Ishraq rescued the paper with the copied seal as it slipped from Isolde's grip.

'Brilliant,' he said. 'That's so brilliant. They seal it with his crest so that it gives credence to the forged gold being genuine English nobles. Because the duke would have been in charge of the mint at Calais. He would have commanded them to make gold, he would have shipped the gold out to the soldiers. If a chest or even a hundred chests went astray, they would all have had his seal on them. Then, years later, if someone forges gold and wants to pretend that it came from the mint, they mark each coin with the mark of the mint at Calais, and they sell it in boxes sealed with the regent's seal.'

Isolde glowed as he held her hands, the two of them standing, quite still, as if they had forgotten the others in the room.

'But are they really making gold?' Brother Peter asked drily. 'Before we get so excited about these imaginary chests? Sealed so cleverly with this imaginary seal? And this brilliant guess as to why they have the seal. Is there any gold there?'

'Oh yes,' Freize said smugly. 'Don't you worry about

that. There's sackfuls of the stuff. Sackfuls of it. And Ishraq found it.'

'You did?' Luca turned to her.

'We went to the storeroom. The whole place is used for alchemy,' Ishraq said. 'The fireplace is like a forge. We saw silver still in the fire. It had been heated so hot that the chimney was cracked.'

'Why would they do that?' Isolde asked. Nobody could answer.

'And we found moulds for English nobles,' Freize said. 'It looks like they pour liquid gold into the moulds.'

'And then we found a cellar doorway and the sacks of gold,' Ishraq said, lowering her voice. 'The door is a little hatch from the storeroom, like you'd find leading to a cellar. But instead of a cellar the half-door leads down to the quay. The sacks of gold are on a quay. Beyond is the canal, and a water-door. I should think that they drop the sacks from the storeroom, through the hatch, onto the quayside and then a boatman comes and loads the gold onto a boat.'

'How much gold?' Brother Peter asked. 'How much did you see?'

'I saw two sacks that were open and perhaps four behind them that had been sewn up. A fortune,' Ishraq said.

Luca dropped into a seat at the window. 'Great work,' he said to Ishraq and Freize. 'Great work.'

He turned to Brother Peter. 'So is our mission complete?' he asked doubtfully. 'We were told to find the source of the gold and answer whether it was a theft or gold mined from a new source. We can tell Milord it is a forger, and that we have found the forge.'

'But we don't know how they actually make the nobles,'

Freize pointed out. 'We saw the moulds. But we didn't see any gold ore.'

'D'you think that it's possible that they have found a way to refine it from silver?' Isolde asked. 'From the silver they had in the forge? She wins a lot of silver every day. Every day they go home with pursefulls of little silver coins.'

'The coins in the fire!' Ishraq nodded at Freize.

'We must write our report,' Brother Peter decided. 'And we will have to turn them in to the authorities. Milord was clear to me that we must inform the Doge's officials as soon as we had identified the forger.'

Awkwardly, he turned to Ishraq. 'I was ungracious about your disguise,' he said. 'You have done great work for the Order, you were brave and enterprising.' He hesitated. 'And you make a very neat young man,' he conceded. 'You don't look heretical at all.'

'Bonny,' Freize said admiringly. 'She looks good enough to eat.' He was rewarded by Ishraq's surprised giggle. 'And she climbs like a clever little monkey,' he said. 'If you wanted a burglar for a wife she would be the very one.'

'But it does not mean that you can dress up and go out every day,' Brother Peter continued. 'This was an exception. And tonight, in any case, the two of you will go out as modest and elegant young ladies. Our reputation as a wealthy young family all depends on your behaviour.'

'Oh the party!' Isolde exclaimed. 'With all this, I had completely forgotten about it.'

'Keep your ears open for any mention of gold,' Brother Peter ordered. 'And remember that you are young ladies of good family, kept very strictly at home.' He looked at Isolde as if he had more confidence in her playing the part of a well-behaved young lady than Ishraq. 'I am looking to you, Lady Isolde, to set an example,' he said.

Isolde curtseyed modestly and shot a hidden laughing glance at Luca. 'Of course,' she said.

The five of them set out in the gondola. Freize would accompany them and wait with the other servants in the servants' room. The gondola would moor at the quay beside the house, bring back Ishraq and Isolde from their visit, and then go out again for Luca and Brother Peter. The men thought they would be out till late, perhaps past midnight.

The men were wearing the hoods of their capes over their heads, and dark plain masks over their eyes. Isolde could see only Luca's smiling lips as he looked at her strange beauty. She had a dark blue cape with a dark blue hood pulled over her fair hair. She wore a mask which covered her forehead, eyes and nose, so that her dark blue eyes gleamed at him through the slits of the mask. Blue feathers sprouted from the side of the mask and curled like a high question mark around her head. She looked exotic and strange and lovely. Beside her, Ishraq in black was like a beautiful sleek shadow, only her mouth showing below a black mask which was shaped like a dark moon and starred with silver.

Luca leaned towards Isolde and whispered to her, his mouth against her ear. 'I have never in my life seen anyone as beautiful as you,' he said.

Isolde, quite entranced, turned and smiled at him, her dark eyes gleamed through the slits in the mask.

'Meet me,' Luca whispered to her. 'Meet me tonight. As soon as we can get away from this party.'

He felt, rather than heard her swift gasp of shock and knew he had gone too far, stepped too close. He waited for her refusal, for a moment he was afraid that she would be offended. But then she leaned her head a little towards him and breathed, rather than whispered her reply.

'I will.'

The city was in carnival mood, every window over-looking the Grand Canal bright with candlelight and every dark canal and quayside busy with bobbing gondolas. Sometimes they glimpsed a couple entwined in the double seat of a gondola, their hoods drawn forward to hide their kisses, their hidden hands seeking to touch. In some, a pair of lovers had gone into the cabin of the gondola and closed the doorway, leaving the gondolier to idle in the stern, keeping the ship steady in the water as the clandestine candlelight shone through the slats of the door and windows. Brother Peter turned his head away and crossed himself to prevent the infection of sin.

On the quayside, as their gondola approached the palace, they could see a huge crowd, beautifully dressed in the extraordinary costumes. Men dressed as monsters and angels, women in silks of every colour towering high as they stood on the chopines that were the mark of a fashionable lady. Some of them were dressed so brightly, and stood so proudly, that it was clear, even to the young travellers, that the women were showing themselves off for sale. They were the famous Venetian courtesans, and it would cost a man a small fortune to spend a night with any one of them, traded like everything else in this merchants' city.

Everywhere people were mingling, talking, flirting behind their masks, sometimes pushing their masks on top of their heads to expose their lips for a stolen kiss, sometimes turning away into a quiet garden or a darkened doorway. Isolde glimpsed the smiling face of a woman as a man took her hand and led her into the shadows. At the quayside she saw a man lightly step from one rocking boat into another, laughing like a child on stepping stones, invited by the wave of a silver glove.

It was irresistibly exciting. Every gondola burned a torch at the stern, or carried a swinging lantern at the prow, and the young women could see that men and women were making assignations on the water, and then their gondolas would slip away together to the darker side canals, where they would drift side by side so that the women could flirt behind their painted fans, and the men make extravagant promises.

On the white stone quayside the wooden chopines clattered like castanets as if they were inviting men to come and dance. Bursts of music came from one doorway and another and they could hear the bright laughter of men and women. Isolde exchanged one longing glance with Luca as if she wished that the two of them could go somewhere alone together at once, and dance and laugh and kiss.

'Isolde,' Ishraq whispered a warning to her. 'Your mask

doesn't hide what you are thinking. You look as if you are ready to sin like a Venetian.'

A ready flush rose from Isolde's neck to her cheeks. 'Ishraq,' she said quietly. 'I have to kiss him again. I think I will die if I don't kiss him.'

Ishraq could not restrain a shocked giggle. 'Really? But you said . . .'

The great watergate to the palace stood open, the bright torches reflected in the glassy waters of the canal as the gondolas queued to enter the palace and leave the guests on the red carpet which stretched extravagantly, to the brink of the lapping dark water.

'It is like a strange other world,' Isolde marvelled. 'So much wealth and so much beauty.'

'So much sin!' Brother Peter mourned quietly.

At last it was their turn and their gondola slid through the archway and drew up to the palace steps. Brightly costumed servants stepped forwards to steady the craft, but before they could get out, Isolde glanced back to the canal and saw a gondola with four beautiful women hesitate at the water entrance behind them, the women exquisitely painted and rouged, and wearing high headdresses and exotic masks. One of them waved a lazy hand to Luca and called out the name of her house. 'On the Grand Canal,' she said. 'Come at midnight when you leave here!'

'Sin all around us,' Brother Peter said, shaking his head in horror.

'I know what I said about never kissing a man before marriage!' Isolde whispered fervently to Ishraq, as she rose to her feet and pulled her hood forwards. 'But that was weeks ago, it was before we pretended to be married. And

708

then he kissed me, so I know what it's like now, and besides it's carnival, and everyone, everywhere we go is courting and making love.

'Don't you see it?' she urged her friend. 'Don't you feel it? It's as if the very air is caressing the skin of my neck, is touching my lips. Don't you feel it? I can hardly breathe for desire.'

Isolde stepped out of the gondola and stood at the water's edge. Ishraq was helped on shore and took her hand and held it tightly as they waited for the two men to disembark. 'Isolde, what are you going to do?'

Isolde's dark blue eyes glittered like sapphires through the dark blue of her mask. 'Will you help me?'

'Of course! Always! But not to a disaster. Shouldn't I be holding you back?'

'No,' Isolde said. 'Not any more.'

'We'll follow you as you go in,' Brother Peter said, getting out of the gondola and gesturing that the two young women should lead the way up the stairs to the inside of the palace. Isolde, as if recalled to the proper behaviour for a young woman of a noble family, tightened the tie on her mask and went up the marble steps into the brightly lit house.

~

They were expected, and at once a lady-in-waiting took the two young women up the sweeping stairs to the upper floor where the lady of the house was entertaining her friends. Menservants greeted Luca and Brother Peter and took their capes and hats, leaving them in their dark masks, and showed them up to the first floor. Freize, always at his happiest when he was heading towards dinner, stepped into the servants' hall at the canal side.

As she climbed the stairs, Isolde looked back and saw Luca swallowed up by the crowd of young men, and heard the rattle of dice and a cheer as someone won a small fortune at cards, and a ripple of laughter from the courtesans who would entertain the men, while the ladies had to go up to the next floor.

'Greetings, how pleasant to meet you.' The lady of the house, Lady Carintha, came forward and took their hands. She was an elegant woman, dressed in dark blue, almost the match of Isolde's gown, except that hers plunged low at the front and almost slid off her broad shoulders in an open invitation. Her shining gold hair was piled up on the top of her head, in a swirl of blue silk, except for three ringlets which fell over her creamy naked shoulders. Her eyes, a calculating blue, scanned the two young women and her rouged mouth smiled without warmth.

'You can take your masks off now we are indoors and among friends.' She exclaimed at their beauty. 'Oh my dears! How you are going to break hearts in this wicked city of ours! One of you so very fair and one so very dark, no man could resist the two of you. Most of them will want both of you together!'

She drew them forwards and introduced them to other ladies, who were drinking wine from brightly coloured glasses and eating small sweet pastries. 'Some wine?' She pressed a couple of glasses on them. 'But I daresay I should not praise your looks, for you will have heard it all before. You will have dozens of lovers already, you must tell me all about them.'

'Not at all,' Isolde said, flushing.

The lady laughed and patted her cheek. 'Only a matter of time for both of you, only a matter of moments, I swear it. Indeed! Why not tonight? I can't believe how beautiful you are, and you match so well together. You must always go around together, you are each a perfect foil for the other.' She turned to Ishraq. 'You must have a lover, I am sure! Someone who prefers brunettes?'

Ishraq shook her head, not at all flattered by the woman's cloying warmth. 'No. We have been brought up very carefully. I have no husband.'

'Someone else's husband then?' someone suggested, prompting laughter from all the ladies.

'My lady's brother is very strict,' Ishraq said, hiding her irritation behind a polite smile. 'We go out very little.'

'The older brother, yes! You can see it clearly. No one would invite him for an affair of the heart. But the other brother, the younger one, Luca Vero, now he cannot be so very virtuous? Surely? Don't disappoint me! He is truly a man that turns heads! No one as tempting as that could be monkish.'

Someone else laughed and agreed. 'Turns heads! I'd turn down the sheets!'

'We were looking out of the window at him! We are so jealous of Carintha having him for a neighbour,' one of the ladies told Ishraq, squeezing her elbow. 'We've all laid bets on her taking her own gondola and serenading him! She would, you know. She's quite shameless! If she sets her heart on him, she'll have him!'

They laughed, again, as Ishraq silently detached herself from the stranger's hold.

'You'd open your front door for me, wouldn't you?' Lady Carintha asked, putting her hand on Isolde's arm. 'Open the door and let me run up the stairs to your brother's room?'

Isolde gave a little shiver, but did not shake off the unwelcome caress. 'I am sorry. I would not be allowed,' she said shortly.

'Then he'll have to give me a key himself!' Her ladyship smiled and turned to take a glass of wine. Ishraq saw Isolde grit her teeth, and tweaked her sleeve to remind her to be polite to her hostess.

'Make sure you tell him that I shall visit,' Lady Carintha turned back and whispered to both girls. 'I am absolutely serious. I had one look at him and I knew who would be my lover for this *Carnevale*. Good Lord, I might not be able to give him up for Lent!'

Isolde made a little exclamation and tore herself away from Lady Carintha's touch. Her ladyship hardly noticed.

'I've never failed,' she went on to one of her friends, ignoring Isolde's half-turned back. 'I've never failed to capture a young man once I've set my heart on him. Do you think he is a virgin? That would be too delicious! I shall be as innocent as him! You know I think I could tremble. D'you know, I think I could gasp?'

'Surely he can't be!'

'Not with looks like that!'

'Someone must have beaten you to it, Carintha!'

'This is unbearable!' Isolde exclaimed in an undertone to Ishraq.

'Be patient,' she replied. 'We only have to stay for an hour. And have you seen her earrings?'

'What about them?' Isolde said crossly.

'Half English nobles,' Ishraq pointed out. 'Drilled for the clasp.'

There was gambling for the ladies in this salon too,

and conversation, though there was little to talk about but fashion and love affairs. Isolde drew Ishraq away from the spiteful women and towards the gambling tables. There were musicians playing in one corner and half a dozen women dancing listlessly together.

'I am afraid that I have no money,' Ishraq confessed to Carintha, who followed them, sipping greedily from her wine glass. 'I didn't think to bring any. Though I changed some money only a few days ago. I bought English gold nobles, I changed all that I had into English nobles. Do you think that was wise?'

'Oh! aren't they divine? They're all I use now,' Carintha replied. 'As clean as if someone had washed them for me. Have you seen my earrings?'

'She just remarked on them,' Isolde said.

'Aren't they lovely?' Lady Carintha turned her head one way and another so that they could see. In her ears, dangling from gold pins, were two half noble coins. 'I'm having a necklace made of them too. I shall start a fashion. Everyone will want them.'

'They are such pretty coins. Are they minted in Venice?' Ishraq wondered aloud, watching the play at the table and not looking at Carintha at all.

'Certainly not,' she said. 'They are English, through and through. My husband trades in them. They come from the English treasure house at Bordeaux. When they lost Bordeaux last year the French captured their treasury, all the wealth of John of Bedford, the Regent of France. And now they need nobles so badly in England that they are buying them back again. They have no gold at all, poor things. My husband works with all the English merchants and they are buying up nobles by the thousand and sending them home to England.' She laughed. 'And every day, the poor dears have to pay more gold for their own coins because now everyone wants them!'

A woman went past her and flicked Carintha's earring, making it dance. 'Delightful,' she said. 'Amusing.'

'And where does your husband get the English nobles from?' Isolde asked lightly. 'Since the English themselves don't have enough?'

'Oh, the most amusing Jewish banker,' Lady Carintha volunteered. 'You would not think, to look at him, that he had a penny to rub, one against the other. But he supplies my husband with English nobles, and so I get my pretty earrings!'

'Convenient,' Ishraq remarked.

'But as for you two lovely girls,' Lady Carintha went on to Ishraq, 'it doesn't matter that you have no money with you. You can borrow from me and repay me next week. I shall be your banker. I should think that your credit is good enough! We all hear that the handsome young man has a ship coming in from Russia any day now! And your young lady is a great heiress, is she not?'

'Unimaginably so,' Ishraq said, honest at last. 'You could not imagine her fortune. Not even I can truly describe it.'

~

The party for the ladies broke up at about ten o'clock, and they left by the outer staircase while the party for the gentlemen was still, noisily, in full swing on the first floor. Clearly – as the women rouged their lips and tied masks on their faces and slipped away in their gondolas – many of them were going on to other parties or to assignations.

Lady Carintha was going to join the men who were still gambling. She winked at her friend and Isolde heard her whisper Luca's name.

'But we have to go home,' Ishraq remarked resentfully as Freize helped her into the gondola. 'When all the world is free to walk around and do as they please.'

'Let's get the gondola to drop us on the quay and walk about,' Isolde suggested quietly. 'Nobody will know who we are, since we have our masks and our capes, and Brother Peter is not at home to know what time we get in.'

'Oh yes!' Ishraq exclaimed, and turned and told the gondolier to let them get out at the steps in the side canal, they would enter through the side door. The gondolier's smile and Freize's silent nod told them at once that neither man believed for a moment that the women were going straight into the house; but it was carnival time and anything was allowed, even for wealthy young ladies. The gondolier set them down where they asked, and then pushed off with Freize still aboard, to go back to wait for Brother Peter and Luca to emerge from the gambling party.

Arm in arm, the girls sauntered around the streets revelling in their sense of freedom, in walking along the shadowy quays with the silk of their gowns swishing around their ankles, their masks hiding their faces, knowing that they looked strange and exotic and beautiful in this strange and beautiful city.

Almost every doorway stood open and there were lights and parties inside. Every so often someone called to them and invited them to come in and take some wine, come in and dance. Laughingly, Isolde refused and they walked on, loving the sense of excitement and adventure.

'What a horrible woman Lady Carintha is,' Isolde remarked as they turned their steps homeward again.

'Because she said that she wanted Luca, and asked you to let her into his room?' Ishraq teased. 'She thinks you're his sister, she was not to know that you . . .'

'That I – what?' Isolde asked, coming to a standstill.

Ishraq was not at all intimidated. 'That you would be so offended at the thought of taking her to him.'

'I was offended. Anyone would be offended. She's old enough to be his mother. Ugh, with those ridiculous coins in her ears!'

'It's not because of her age or her appearance. Besides, she's not more than thirty. You were upset that she wants to take him as her lover because you want him for yourself!'

For a moment she thought that her friend would take offence, for Isolde had stopped still, and then she suddenly admitted: 'It's true! I can't pretend to you or to myself any longer! I want him so much it's like a fever! I can think of nothing else but what it would be like if he were to hold me, if he were to touch me, if he were to kiss me. I know I am mad to think like this. But I can't think of anything else. He asked me to meet him, and I didn't answer, but I was longing to say "yes".'

'It's *Carnevale*,' Ishraq said comfortingly. 'It's Venice. As you said, the whole city seems to think like this. The whole city has gone mad for pleasure. And he is the most handsome young man that either of us has ever seen.'

'Do you . . . desire him too?' Isolde asked, hesitating almost as if she were frightened of the very word. 'Seriously? Like I do? Are you in love with him, Ishraq?'

Ishraq laughed quietly. 'Oh yes,' she conceded. 'A little.

He's very attractive, I don't mind admitting it. But I don't think of him as you do. It's not as hard for me as it is for you. I can just look at him and think him absolutely desirable and utterly handsome, and then I can look away. Because he's not for me. I know that. He doesn't see me in that way, and there is no possibility of any sort of honourable love between us. And actually, very little chance of dishonourable love either! He is sworn to the Church and I am an infidel. He is in the Order to stamp out heresy and I am born to question. We could not be more different. But you . . .' she paused.

'What?' Isolde urged her on. 'Me, what?'

'He's in love with you,' Ishraq said quietly. 'He can't take his eyes off you. I think if you said the word, he would give up the Church for you and marry you in San Marco tomorrow.'

'I can't.' Isolde gave a little moan. 'I can't. I have to get my lands back, my castle back. And anyway he can't. He is a novice at his monastery, and Brother Peter told me that I must do nothing that would distract him from the Order of Darkness. He's one of the few men appointed to trace the signs of the end of the world and warn the Pope himself. If the world is going to end this year it is vital that Luca does his work and reports to his lord in Rome. His Order is our only defence against the rise of heresy and magic and the end of the world. I should not think of him in any way except as a soldier of the Church, a crusader, like my father was. I should honour him for his work. I shouldn't be thinking of him like this at all.'

Ishraq shrugged. 'But you are. And so is he.'

'I can't stop myself thinking!' Isolde exclaimed. 'And I

dream! I dream of him almost every night. But I can never do anything. I would be ruined completely if I did more than kiss him. If I ever get back to my castle I would never be able to marry any man of honour or position if it was known I had been in love with Luca. There's no point in all the danger we are risking to win back my inheritance, if I have lost my honour. I could never go home to be Lady of Lucretili if I was dishonoured.'

'If no one ever knew . . .' Ishraq suggested.

'I would know!' Isolde exclaimed. 'I would never be able to offer my love to another man, I would never be able to marry. I would know always that I was dishonoured, that I was not fit to be a great man's wife. I have to be able to promise my future husband an untouched heart in an untouched body.'

'But can you go on like this?'

'What shall I do?' Isolde demanded with a wail. 'What shall I do? When I heard her speak of coming to our house I thought I would kill her. I can't bear to let her near him. I can't bear to think of her touching . . .' Isolde clapped her hand over her mouth to prevent herself speaking. But nothing could stop her thoughts; she closed her eyes as if she could not bear to imagine Luca and Lady Carintha together.

'If no one ever knew . . .' Ishraq repeated slowly. 'If you could love him, kiss him, even lie with him, and no-one ever know?'

'How could no one ever know? I would know! He would know! You would know!'

'If it only happened once? Just once. And we were all three sworn to secrecy?'

There was a long silence between the two girls. Isolde took her hand down from her mouth and whispered: 'What?'

'If it only happened once. And nobody knew about it? If you and I never ever spoke of it? If you could do it, and yet let it be like an unspoken dream? Would you be satisfied if you were his lover, his first ever lover, and he yours; but he never saw your face, he never said your name, and you never admitted what you had done? Not even to me? It was a secret of the night, of *Carnevale*, and nobody remembered it after Lent?'

Isolde put a trembling hand on her friend's arm. 'If we never spoke of it. If it only happened once. If it was like a dream, for I am dreaming of him every night ...'

Before Ishraq could answer she saw the house gondola turn from the main traffic of the canal. She dragged her friend back into the shadow of the side of the house.

'There's our gondola!' she whispered. 'And Luca and Freize and Brother Peter coming home.'

They watched the gondola as it pulled up once again in the side canal, at the side steps. 'I want to walk,' Luca explained, his voice slightly slurred from wine. 'I want to walk around.'

'You had much better come home and say your prayers and go to bed,' Brother Peter said.

'In an hour or so,' Luca insisted. 'You go in.'

'I'll come with you,' Freize offered.

'No,' Luca insisted. 'I want to walk alone and clear my head.'

Freize took his arm. 'Are you meeting Lady Carintha?' he whispered. 'Because I can tell you now, that's nothing but trouble ...'

Luca pulled himself free, refusing to admit to any assignation, though his heart pounded at the thought of a dark blue dress and mask. 'I'll just walk around,' he said, and stepped unsteadily ashore.

With a shrug, Brother Peter ordered the gondolier to take him and Freize round by boat to the watergate and left Luca climbing the steps to the quayside.

Isolde and Ishraq shrank back against the wall as Luca got to the top of the steps and turned and looked back over the Grand Canal, a big yellow moon high above, the bright stars shining in the darkness of the sky. He stood for some time, listening to the sounds of distant music and laughter.

'And all in a moment I know that I love her,' he said simply, speaking to himself but hearing the words fall into the quietness of the night and mingle with the lapping of the canal on the steps. 'It's extraordinary, but I know it. I love her.'

He gave a quiet laugh. 'I'm a fool,' he said. 'Half-promised as a priest, fully committed to the Order of Darkness, on a quest, and she is a lady of such high birth that I would not even have seen her if I had stayed as a novice in my monastery.'

He fell silent. 'But I have seen her,' he said steadily. 'And she has seen me. And tonight I understand for the first time what people mean by … this …' he broke off and smiled again. 'Love,' he said. 'What a fool I am! I love her. I have fallen in love. *Coup de foudre*. In love, in a moment.'

He opened the door to the walled garden and let himself in. The girls heard his footsteps crunch the gravel and then silence as he threw himself onto the bench beneath the tree.

On the shadowy quayside the girls stood in horrified silence.

'Was he speaking of her?' Ishraq said wonderingly. 'Of Lady Carintha? Has she done what she said she would do? Seduced him, already, and in only one meeting?'

Isolde turned, and Ishraq could see the shine of tears on her pale cheek beneath the dark blue mask. 'He said that he fell in love tonight,' she said, her voice low with misery. 'Fell in love, *coup de foudre*, all in a moment, tonight. With a lady he would never have seen if he had stayed in the monastery. He's in love with that woman. That painted—' Isolde bit off her words as another gondola edged to the quayside stairs and Lady Carintha, in a cape and hood of deep blue, with an exquisite mask of navy feathers, snapped her fingers for the gondolier to help her step onto the stairs and up to the quayside.

'She's meeting him!' Isolde exclaimed in an anguished whisper as she and Ishraq shrank deeper into the shadows. 'She's meeting him in our garden!'

The two young women stood, pressed against the wall, hidden in the shadows while the big spring moon lit the quayside as brightly as day. Lady Carintha, with her back to them, took a tiny looking glass from the gold chain at her waist and scrutinised her dark blue mask, her smiling painted lips, her blue silk hood and cape. Her gaze went past her own reflection and she saw, in the mirror, the two girls, pressed back against the wall, and broke into a quiet laugh.

'The pretty virgins!' she said. 'Walking the streets. How quaint! And I am meeting a third pretty virgin! What a night for a debauch! Will you come with me?'

Even Ishraq, usually so bold, was stunned into silence at the woman's bawdiness. It was Isolde, with tears hidden by her mask, who stepped forward and said: 'You shall not meet him. I forbid it.'

'And who are you to forbid or allow a grown man what he shall do?' Lady Carintha asked, her voice filled with careless scorn. 'He wants me. He's waiting for me. And nothing will stop me going to him.'

'No, he's not!' Isolde said wildly. 'He asked me to come to the garden. You can't come in.'

'His sister?' Lady Carintha asked. 'My! You are a stranger family than I thought.'

'She means me,' Ishraq intervened. 'He asked her to bring me to him.'

Lady Carintha put her hands on her hips and looked at the two younger women. 'Well, what are we to do? For I won't share him. And we can't all go in together and let him choose. That would be to spoil him, and besides, I don't take gambles like that. I'm not lining up against you two little lovelies.'

'But you like to gamble,' Ishraq pointed out. 'Why don't we gamble for him?'

Lady Carintha gave a delighted laugh. 'My dear, you are wilder than you appear. But I have no dice.'

'We have nobles,' Ishraq pointed out. 'We could toss for him.'

'How very appropriate,' she said drily. 'Who wins?'

'We each toss a noble until there is an odd one out. That woman wins. She goes into the garden. She has time with Luca – whatever she does nobody ever knows – and we never speak of it,' Ishraq ruled. 'Do you agree?'

'I agree,' Isolde whispered.

'Amen,' Lady Carintha said blasphemously. 'Why not?'

Ishraq took the borrowed nobles from her pocket and gave Isolde one, and took another for herself. Lady Carintha already had hers in her hand.

'Good luck!' Lady Carintha said, smiling. 'One, two three!'

The three golden coins flicked into the air all together, turned and shone in the moonlight, then each woman caught her own as it fell, and slapped it on the back of her hand. They stretched out their hands each holding a hidden coin under the palm of the other hand. Slowly, one at a time, one after the other, they uncovered them.

'Ship,' said one, showing the engraved portrait of the king in his ship on one side of the coin.

'Ship,' said another, uncovering her coin.

The two of them turned to the third as she raised her fingers and showed them the shining face of her coin.

'Rose,' she said, and without another word, turned to the door in the high wall, turned the heavy ring of the latch, and went quietly in.

~

The light of the moon suddenly dimmed as a cloud crossed its broad yellow face. In the garden, Luca rose to his feet as very, very quietly, the garden gate opened and a masked figure stood underneath the arch. Luca stared, as if she were a vision, summoned up by his own whispered desire. 'Is that you?' he asked. 'Is it really you?'

Silently, she stretched out her hand to him. Silently, he stepped towards her. Luca drew her into the shade of the tree, pushing the door shut behind them. Gently he put his hand around her waist and held her to him, she turned up her face to him in the darkness, and he kissed her on the lips.

She made no protest as he led her under the roof of the portico and they sat on the bench in the alcove. Willingly, she sat on his knee and wound her arms around his neck, rested her head on his shoulder and inhaled the warm male scent. Luca drew her closer, heard his own heart beating faster as he unlaced the back of her gown and found her skin, as smooth as a peach beneath the dark coloured silk. Only once did she resist him, when he went to untie her mask and put back the hood of her robe, and then she captured his hand to prevent him from unmasking her, and put it to her lips, which made him kiss her again, on her mouth, on her throat, on the warm hollow of her collar bones until he had spent the whole night in kissing her, the whole night in loving her, in learning every curve of her body, until the first light of dawn made the canal as dark as pewter, and the garden as pale as silver, and the birds started to sing and she rose up, gathered her shadowy cloak around her, pulled the hood to hide her hair, shading her face when he would have kept her and kissed her again, stepped silently out of the garden gate and disappeared into the Venice dawn.

～

Next morning the five of them met for a late breakfast. Luca jumped to his feet to pull out a chair for Isolde and she thanked him with a small smile. He passed her the warm rolls, straight from the kitchen, and she took the bread basket with quiet thanks. Luca was like a man who had been staring at the sun, utterly dazzled, hardly knowing himself. Isolde was very quiet, Ishraq said nothing.

Freize raised his eyebrows to Ishraq as if to ask her what was going on, but serenely she ignored him, her eyes turned down to her plate, smiling as if she had a secret joy. Finally, he could contain himself no longer. 'So how was your party, last night?' he asked cheerfully. 'Did it go merrily?'

Isolde answered smoothly. 'We went upstairs to meet Lady Carintha, and we borrowed some gold nobles from her to gamble. I suppose we'll have to return them. The women were a vain, vapid lot. They spoke of nothing but clothes and lovers. Brother Peter is quite right, it is a city empty of anything but sin. We came home, as you know, about ten o'clock and strolled about for a few minutes and then went to bed.'

Luca was staring at his plate, but he looked up just once, as she spoke. He stared at her, as if he could not understand the simple words. She did not glance at him, as he pushed back his chair from the table and went to the window.

'So what are we to do today?' Freize asked.

'As soon as Luca and Ishraq have completed work on the manuscript and returned it to the alchemist and his daughter then we must report them to the authorities,' Brother Peter said firmly. 'If you could return it today, we could report them today. I would prefer that. I don't want them coming to our house again. They are criminals and perhaps dabbling in dark arts. They should not visit us. We should not be known as their friends.'

'How do we report them?' Ishraq asked. 'Who do we tell?'

'We'll denounce them,' Brother Peter said. 'All around

the city and in the walls of the palace of the Doge there are big stone letter boxes with gaping mouths. They call them the *Bocca di Leone,* the mouth of the lion. Venice is the city of the lion: that's the symbol of the apostle, St Mark. Anyone can write anything about anybody and post it into the *Bocca.* All Luca has to do is to name the pair of them as alchemists, Freize and I will sign as witnesses, and they will be arrested as soon as the Council reads the letter.'

DENONTIE SECRETE
CONTRO CHI OCCVLTERÁ
GRATIE ET OFFICII
O COLLVDERÃ PER
NASCONDER LA VERA
RENDITA D ESSI

Isolde blinked at the Venetian way of justice. 'When will the Council read the letters of denunciation?'

'The very same day,' Brother Peter said grimly. 'The boxes are constantly checked and the Council of Ten reads all the letters at once. This is the safest city in Christendom. Every man denounces his neighbour at the first sign of ill-doing.'

'But what will happen to Drago and Jacinta?' Freize asked. 'When this council reads your accusation?'

Brother Peter looked uncomfortable. 'They will be arrested, I suppose,' he said. 'Then tried, then punished. That's up to the authorities. They'll get a fair trial. This is a city of lawyers.'

'But surely alchemy isn't illegal?' Isolde objected. 'There are dozens of alchemists working in the university here, and even more at Padua. People admire their scholarship, how else will anything ever be understood?'

'Alchemy isn't illegal if you have a licence, but some applications of alchemy are illegal. And forgery is a most serious crime, of course,' Brother Peter explained. 'Anyone making gold English noble coins anywhere outside an official mint is a forger, and that is a crime, that is very heavily punished.'

'Punished how?' Freize interrupted, thinking of the pretty girl and her bright smile.

'The Council will hear the evidence, make a judgement and then decide the punishment,' Brother Peter said awkwardly. 'But for coining, it would usually be death. They take their currency very seriously, here.'

Freize was shocked. 'But the lass – the bonny lass—'

'I don't think the Doge of Venice makes much exception for how pretty a criminal is,' Brother Peter said heavily. 'Since the city is filled with beautiful sinners, I doubt that it makes much difference to him at all.'

Freize glanced at Luca, who was still gazing out of the window. 'Seems too harsh,' he said. 'Seems wrong. I know they're forgers, but it seems too great a punishment for the crime. I wouldn't want to turn them in to their deaths.'

Luca, hardly listening, glanced up from his silent survey of the canal. 'They would be aware of the punishment before they did the crime,' he said. 'And they will have made a fortune. Didn't Ishraq say they had six sacks of gold on the quayside? And didn't you see the moulds for making the gold yourself, and their furnace?'

'I don't say they're innocent, I just think they shouldn't die for it,' Freize persisted.

Luca shook his head as if it were a puzzle too great for him. 'It's not for us to decide,' he ruled. 'I just inquire. It's my job to find signs for the end of days, and if I find sin or wrongdoing I report it to the Church if it is sin, or to the authorities if it is a crime. This, clearly, is a crime. Clearly it has to be reported. However pretty the girl. And these are Milord's orders.'

'They're not just forgers,' Freize pressed on. 'They're Inquirers, like you. They study things. They're scholars. They know things.'

He reached into the deep pocket of his coat and brought out a little piece of glass. 'Look,' he said. 'They're interested in light, just like you are. I stole this for you. Off Jacinta's writing table.'

'Stole!' Brother Peter exclaimed.

'Stole from a forger! Stole from a thief!' Freize retorted. 'So hardly stealing at all. But isn't it the sort of thing you're interested in? And she's studying it too. She's an Inquirer like you, she's not a common criminal. She might know things you want to know. She shouldn't be arrested.'

He put it on the table and uncurled his fingers slowly so that they could see the little miracle that he had brought from the forger's house. It was a long, triangular-shaped piece of perfectly clear glass. And as Freize put it on the breakfast table between Isolde and Ishraq, the sun, shining through the slats of the shutters, struck its sharp spine and surrounded the piece of glass in a perfect fan of rainbow colours, springing from the point of the glass.

Luca sighed in intense pleasure, like a man seeing a

miracle. 'The glass turns the sunlight into a rainbow,' he said. 'Just like in the mausoleum. How does it do that?'

He reached into his pocket and brought out the chipped piece of glass from Ravenna. Both of them, side by side, spread a fan of rainbow colours over the table. Ishraq reached forward and put her finger into the rainbow light. At once they could see the shadow of her finger, and the rainbow on her hand. She turned her hand over so that the colours spread from her fingers to her palm. 'I am holding a rainbow,' she said, her voice hushed with wonder. 'I am holding a rainbow.'

'How can such a thing be?' Luca demanded, coming close and taking the glass piece to the window, looking through it to see it was quite clear. 'How can a piece of glass turn sunshine into a rainbow arc? And why do the colours bend from the glass? Why don't they come out straight?'

'Why don't you ask them?' Freize suggested.

'What?'

'Why don't you ask them to show you their work, or tell you about rainbows?' Freize repeated. 'He's known as an alchemist, he'll be used to people coming to him with questions. Why don't you ask him about the rainbow in the tomb of Galla Placidia? See what we can learn from them before we report them? Surely we should know more about them. Surely you want to know why she has a glass that makes a rainbow?'

'You're sweet on the girl,' Ishraq accused bluntly. 'And you're playing for time for them.'

Freize turned to her with his comical dignity. 'Actually, I have a great interest in the origin of rainbows,' he said. 'I don't even know what girl you mean.'

Isolde laughed and even Brother Peter raised his head at

the clear joy in her voice. 'Ah Freize, admit it! You have fallen in love in this city, where everyone seems to be in love.'

'Everyone?' Luca asked her pointedly, but she turned her head away from him with a little colour in her cheeks, and did not reply.

Freize put his hand over his heart. 'I tell no secrets,' he said gallantly. 'Perhaps she admires me? Perhaps not. I would not say a word to anyone, either way. But I still think you should talk to her and to her father before you hand them over to the Doge and his men. We need to know more of what they were doing in that strange secret room of theirs. And why can't we warn them that the game is up and they should pack up their business and go away?'

'They can hardly pack up and go on their way, and nothing more be said!' Brother Peter exclaimed irritably. 'They have swindled the merchants of the city of a fortune: making a market, profiteering in the gold nobles. They have cheated the nation of England of thousands of gold coins, perhaps hundreds of thousands, receiving the gold nobles stolen from them. We ourselves have bought gold nobles, giving good money in exchange for bad. This is a serious crime. They must be stopped. And anyway, Milord's orders are clear: we must report them.'

'But they're not bad coins,' Ishraq pointed out. 'They're growing in value every day. Everyone is making money. They have made no one poorer. Actually, everyone is getting richer. Us too. The Venetians themselves don't want the coins questioned. We tested the nobles, ourselves, as Milord said that we should. The coins are good, as good as gold. And now they're being exchanged for more than gold. The coins are better than gold.'

'I'll visit them,' Luca decided. 'I need to see their work. And we'll ask them about it. And we'll agree what to do.'

'Milord has given orders,' Brother Peter warned him. 'He commanded us to find them and then report them. He didn't say that we should understand why they are doing it, or their other work. His instructions were plain and simple: go to Venice, find the coins, find the suppliers, report them.'

'He must be obeyed,' Luca agreed. 'And I don't question our orders. We will report them as he commands. But not immediately. First, I will go and see them. I'll take Freize and –' he turned to Ishraq – 'will you come too? And bring the manuscript page.' He hesitated for a moment, clearly wondering if he could ask Isolde to come.

'If Ishraq is to come she'll have to be masked and hooded and travel from door to door by gondola,' Brother Peter ruled. 'And, in her absence, Lady Isolde will have to stay at home, or go to church.'

'I'll stay at home,' Isolde said rapidly, almost as if she wanted to avoid the confessional at church. Almost, as if she wanted to avoid Luca. 'I'll wait for you to return.'

'You'll wait for me?' Luca said, so quietly that only she could hear him.

The glance she directed at him was very cool. 'I only meant I would wait for Ishraq to come back with the gondola,' she said with a sweet smile that told him nothing.

~

'In the name of all the saints, what have I done? Have I offended her?' Luca demanded of Ishraq as they sat side by side in the gondola double seat, Freize with his back to the prow was in the seat before them.

'No, why?' Ishraq asked blandly.

'Because I thought . . . last night . . . she was so beautiful.'

'At the party?' Ishraq prompted him.

'On our way there, yes. I thought that she was so light-hearted and so warm, she smiled at me and wished me good luck as we were in the gondola – and her eyes were shining through her blue mask and I thought that perhaps after the party we might meet . . . And then after the party, in the garden, I thought . . . and then today she hardly speaks to me.'

'Lasses.' Freize leaned forwards to make his own contribution to the low-voiced conversation. 'Like the little donkey. Easily set on one course, hard to disturb once they have chosen their own wilful path.'

'Oh nonsense!' Luca said. To Ishraq he said more pressingly: 'Has she said nothing about me? Did she say nothing to you about last night?'

'About the party?' Ishraq said again.

'After the party?' Luca hinted tentatively. 'After . . . ?'

Ishraq shook her head, her face utterly blank. 'She has said nothing, for there is nothing to say. It was an ordinary party and we came home early. We walked for a few minutes and then we went to bed. We had nothing to say.' She paused, lowered her voice and looked directly at Luca. 'And you had better say nothing too.'

He looked at her, searching for her meaning. 'I should say nothing?'

She looked at him and nodded her head. 'Nothing.'

~

Left in the quiet house, Brother Peter had the breakfast things cleared and put his writing desk on the table to start

732

the long task of preparing the coded report to the Lord of the Order, to tell him that the forgers had been discovered, that they would be reported to the authorities at once, and asking for instructions for their next mission. Their work would go on: the Lord would command them to go to another town, another city, to discover more signs of the unknown world, of the end of days.

They would go on, Brother Peter thought, a little wearied, on and on until the Second Coming, when they would at last understand all things, instead of as now – glimpsing uncertain truths. The world was going to end, that at least was certain, and it would happen soon: perhaps in this year, perhaps in this very month. A man in Holy Orders must keep watch, be ready, and his companions, his funny endearing travel companions, must be gathered in, supported, taken with him as they went together on their journey from now to death, from here to the end of everything.

Isolde went up the stairs to the girls' floor and watched the house gondola with Luca, Ishraq and Freize pull out of the palace watergate and join the traffic on the Grand Canal. She put her hands to her lips and sent a kiss after the boat. But she made sure she was far back from the window so that even if Luca looked up, he would not see her.

Her attention was taken by another gondola that seemed to be coming directly to their house, and she went to the head of the stairs to listen. She could hear the housekeeper send the maid down to the watergate to greet the visitor, and then, looking down the well of the stairs, she saw a slim heavily ringed hand on the bannister coming up the stairs. 'Lady Carintha,' Isolde said with distaste.

For a moment she wondered if she could say that she was not at home, but the impossibility of getting Brother Peter to condone such a lie, or the housekeeper to make her excuses, convinced her that she would have to face her ladyship. She glanced around their room, straightened a chair, closed the doors to their bedrooms and seated herself, with as much dignity as she could manage, on the window seat.

The door opened. 'Lady Carintha!' the housekeeper exclaimed.

Isolde rose to her feet and curtseyed. 'Your ladyship!'

'My dear!' the woman replied.

'Please do sit.' Isolde indicated the hard chair by the fireside, where a little blaze warmed the room, but Lady Carintha took the window seat, with the bright light behind her, and smiled, showing her sharp white teeth.

'A glass of wine?' Isolde offered, moving towards the sideboard. 'Some cakes?'

Her ladyship nodded, and the half nobles in her ears winked and danced. Isolde noticed that now she had a necklace of big fat nobles wound around her white neck, the gold very bright against her pale skin, the weighty coins hanging heavily on the gold chain. Isolde poured the wine and handed Lady Carintha a plate of little cakes.

'I must repay you for our gambling debts,' Isolde said pleasantly. 'You were so kind to lend us the money.' She went into her bedroom and came out with a purse of gold coins. 'I am grateful to you. And thank you so much for inviting us to your lovely party.'

'Nobles?' Lady Carintha asked, weighing the purse in her hand.

Isolde was glad that Ishraq had converted the rubies into

nobles, and that she had these to repay Lady Carintha so that there was nothing owed between them. 'Of course,' she said quietly.

'Aha, then I will have made money!' Lady Carintha said gleefully. 'For they are worth more this morning than they were last night. I have stolen from you by just lending them to you for a night. You are repaying me with the same coins but they are of greater value. Isn't it like magic?'

'You're very welcome to your profit,' Isolde said through her gritted teeth. 'Clearly, you are as skilled as any Venetian banker.'

'Actually, you have another treasure that I want,' Lady Carintha said sweetly.

Isolde's expression was beautifully blank. 'Surely, I can have nothing that your ladyship desires! Surely, you have only to ask your husband for anything that takes your fancy.'

Her ladyship laughed, throwing her head back and showing her long white throat and the twists of the laden gold chain. 'My husband allows me some of my treats, but he can't provide them all,' she said meaningfully. 'I am sure that you understand me?'

Isolde shook her head. 'Alas, your ladyship. I have been brought up in the country. I am not accustomed to your city ways. I can't imagine what agreement you have with your husband, except to honour and obey him.'

Her ladyship laughed shortly. 'Then you are more of a novelty than I even thought!' she said. 'I will be plain with you then, country girl. If you want to walk about Venice as you were walking last night, or meet someone, or be absent from your house for a night, I will help you. You can say

735

that you are visiting me, you can borrow my gondola, you can borrow my cape and my mask, even my gowns. If you concoct a story, you can rely on me to support it. You can say that you spent the night with me, and I will tell everyone that we sat up and played cards. You can lie your pretty head off and I will back you up, no questions asked. Whatever it is that you want to do, however . . . unusual. Do you see?'

'I think I see,' Isolde said. 'You will cover up lies for me.'

'Exactly!' Lady Carintha smiled.

'And if I wanted to lie, and go out of the house in secret, then this would be very useful to me,' Isolde said crushingly. 'But since I don't, it is largely irrelevant.'

'I know what I know,' Lady Carintha remarked.

'That would be the very nature and essence of knowledge,' Isolde replied smartly. 'Everyone knows what they know.'

'I know what I saw,' her ladyship persisted.

'You saw me, or perhaps Ishraq, go into our garden. Or perhaps we saw you go into our garden. Perhaps we would swear to it. Our agreement was that nothing would be said about last night. What of it? Your ladyship, this is meaningless. You had better be plain. What do you want of me?'

'I will tell you simply then, country girl. Tonight you will open your watergate to my gondola, you will lead me up the stairs to your brother's room, you will let me out again at dawn. And you will say nothing of this to anyone, and even deny it, if you are ever asked.' She put a hand on Isolde's knee. 'No one will ever ask,' she promised. 'I am always beautifully discreet.'

'But what if my brother does not want you brought to his room?' Isolde was a little breathless, she could feel her temper rising beyond her control. 'What if he thinks you too old, or too well-worn? What if he does not desire you, and wishes you far away?'

Lady Carintha laughed and smoothed her blue gown over her hips, as if she were remembering Luca's caress from last night. 'He won't be the first young man who has woken up to find me in his bed. He won't be the first young man to be glad of it.'

'He is not an ordinary young man,' Isolde warned her. 'He is not like any other young men that you have met before.'

'I agree, he is quite extraordinarily handsome,' Lady Carintha said. 'And I have a quite extraordinary desire for him. I think I am going to have a quite extraordinary love affair.'

Isolde jumped to her feet, as if she could not sit still for a moment longer. 'On my honour: you will not!' she swore.

'Why should you mind? If I help you in turn? Or if you don't want an alibi for your own love affair, shall I help you meet young men? Or shall I just give you gifts?' Her ladyship put her hand to the dancing coins in her ears. 'D'you want these? You can have them! But be very sure that I am going to have your brother. I shall take him as if he were my toy, and I shall leave him besotted with me. That's how it is. I shall leave him like an addict for a drug. He will spend the rest of his life longing for me. I shall teach him everything he needs to know about women, and he will never find a better lover than me. He will spend the rest of his life searching. I will have spoiled him for any ordinary woman.'

'No,' Isolde said flatly. 'He will not long for you. And don't offer me your disgusting money or your repellent cast-offs, for I don't want them. I must ask you to leave. You won't come back.'

'Indeed I will come back,' the woman swore. 'In secret, with or without your help. You can wake in the night and know that he is with me, in the room just below yours. Or he will come to me. D'you think he doesn't want me? D'you think I would be here without his explicit invitation? Last night he asked me to come home with him. Last night after the party. He wanted to meet me in the garden. He is in love with me, there's nothing you can do to stop it.'

'He is not!' Isolde's voice quavered as she realised that Lady Carintha was probably speaking the truth and that Luca might well have arranged to meet her. He might have been waiting for her in the garden when the gate opened. 'He is not, and I would never let you into his room. Even if I did not—' she broke off remembering the lie that they must tell. 'Even if he were not my brother I would not condone it. You are an evil disgusting woman. Never mind Luca, I would not take you to Freize's bedroom, for he is too good for you!'

'Your servant!' the woman half screamed.

'General factotum!' Isolde shouted at her. 'He is a general factotum! And worth ten of you! For he is a great general factotum and you are an old whore!'

Lady Carintha launched herself at Isolde, slapped her face and pulled her hair. Isolde, furious, clenched her fist as she had seen Ishraq do when readying for a fight and punched the older woman – smack – on the jaw. Carintha reeled back at the blow, fell against the table, recovered and then came forward again, her hands outstretched, her fingernails like claws, aiming for Isolde's eyes. She raked Isolde's cheek with her right hand before Isolde grabbed her arm and twisted it behind her. With Carintha screaming with pain and trying to kick backwards with her high-heeled shoes, Isolde pushed her, slowly gaining ground, through the open doorway to the top of the stairs just as Brother Peter, at his most hospitable and dignified, was mounting the steps and saying: 'I was told that Lady Carintha had honoured our house with a visit . . . Good God! What is this?"

'She's leaving!' Isolde panted, her cheeks scarlet from rage, her face streaked with blood. 'The old whore is on her way out.'

Recklessly, she pushed Lady Carintha towards the stairs, and the woman almost fell into Brother Peter's arms, grabbed him to steady herself and then thrust him away and tore down the steps. 'A plague on you!' the scream rang up the stairwell. 'A plague on you, you prissy girl, and your pretty-boy brother. You will be sorry for insulting me.'

Her ladyship paused at the bottom of the well of the stair and looked back up at them – Isolde with her blonde hair tumbling down where her ladyship had pulled it, her right cheek scratched and bleeding, Brother Peter utterly stunned.

'And who are you, anyway?' Carintha demanded, suddenly swinging from rage to cunning. 'For you are like no family that I have ever met before. And why do you keep your brother as closely guarded as a priest? What sister gambles for time with her brother? What game are you playing? Who knows you? What business do you have? Where does your money come from? You'll have to answer to me!'

'Oh! No game! I assure you, your ladyship ...' Brother Peter started down the stairs after her but she turned and was gone, and then they heard her shouting for her gondolier, and the sound of the canal door opening as her gondola went quickly away.

In the sudden silence, Brother Peter turned and looked at Isolde. 'What on earth is this all about?' he asked. 'What were you doing fighting with her like a street urchin? Lady Isolde! Look at you! What were you thinking of?'

Isolde, tried for one sentence, tried for another, and then could say nothing but: 'I hate her! And I hate Luca too!' and ran into her room and slammed the door.

~

Luca, Freize and Ishraq waited at the quayside outside the alchemist's house until the bell for Nones rang and they saw Drago Nacari and Jacinta coming towards them from the direction of the Rialto Bridge.

Freize went forwards to greet the girl and to bow to her father, and then they came towards the front door, Jacinta producing a giant key from the purse under her outer robe.

'This is a surprise and a pleasure,' the alchemist said warily.

Luca nodded. 'I wanted to return to you the page of manuscript. I can't see how to make any progress with it. I was hoping that there would be a code that I could understand, but whatever I try, it doesn't come out.'

The man nodded. 'Would you discover more if you had the entire book?'

'I might,' Luca said cautiously. 'But I couldn't be sure of

740

it. The more words you had to compare, the more likely to discover their meaning. And some might recur which would tell you they were commonly used words, but I couldn't promise it. I've made no headway, I don't have enough skill—' He broke off as the alchemist opened the door and ushered them inside.

'Come into my study.' The alchemist showed them into the large room where the table was heaped with papers. Quickly, Jacinta closed the big double doors to the store-room, but the guests could smell the strange sweet smell of rotting vegetation, and, beneath the smell of decay, some-thing more foul like excrement.

'That's the smell of dark matter,' the alchemist said, matter-of-factly. 'We get used to it; but for strangers it's a disturbing scent.'

'You refine dark matter?' Luca asked.

The man nodded. 'I have the recipe for refining ...' He paused. 'To the ultimate point. I am guessing that is why you have really come today? You could have sent the page back by a messenger. I am assuming that really, you wanted to see our work.'

The girl stood with her back to the storeroom door as if she would bar them from entering, she looked at her father as if she would stop him speaking. The alchemist glanced at her and smiled, returning his attention to Luca. 'Jacinta is anxious for me, for our safety,' he said. 'But I too have had a dream about you, and it prompts me to trust you. Shall I tell you what it was?'

Luca nodded. 'Tell me.'

'I dreamed that you were a babe in arms. You were some-how shining. Your mother brought you to me, and told me that she had found you. You were not a child born of man,' he said quietly. 'Does that make any sense to you?'

Ishraq drew a quick breath and glanced at Freize. Luca's unhappy childhood, when his whole village had called him a changeling, was known only to Freize, and the travelling companions, but they would never speak of it outside the group.

'I have spent my life denying that I was a changeling,' Luca said with quiet honesty. 'My mother told me that it was only ignorant frightened people who would say such a thing, and that I should deny it. I have always denied it. I will always deny it, for her sake, for her honour as well as my own.'

'Your mother would have her reasons,' Drago Nacari said gently. 'But in my dream you were faerie-born, and to be faerie-born is a great privilege.'

Jacinta stepped forwards from the door and put her hand on Luca's arm. 'I knew that you could see the cups move,' she said gently. 'Then you told me that you could calculate where they would stop. No ordinary man can see them move, it's too fast. And nobody could calculate the odds of them stopping in one place or another. You are gifted. Perhaps you are gifted in a way that is not of this world. Dr Nacari too is a gifted seer. He is speaking a truth from his dream. Perhaps even a truth that cannot be understood in this world.'

'Doctor?' Ishraq asked.

Jacinta turned to her. 'This is not my real father,' she said. 'We are partners in this venture. He is a great alchemist, I am his equal. In the world we pass as father and daughter because the world likes to place women in the care of a man, and the world likes a woman to have an owner. But in the real world, the world beyond this one, we are equal seekers after truth, and we have come together to work together.'

'Not his daughter?' Freize said bluntly, grasping the one fact he could be certain of, in this talk of one world and another.

She smiled at him. 'And not a young woman either,' she said. 'I am sorry to have deceived you. Dr Nacari and I have worked together for many many years, and we have discovered many things together. Among them, an elixir which prolongs life itself. I am an old, old soul in a young body. You, Freize, make this heart beat faster; but it's only fair that I should tell you, that it is a very old heart. I'm an old woman behind this young face.'

Freize glanced at Luca and raised his shoulders. 'This is beyond me, Sparrow,' he said. 'Someone is mad here, it might be me or them.'

But it was Ishraq who spoke next. 'It's about the gold,' she said frankly. 'We have come about the gold. We have come to warn you.'

The alchemist smiled. 'Was it you that broke into our house, Daughter?'

Freize shook his head in instant denial, but Ishraq met the older man's eyes fearlessly, and nodded. 'I am sorry. We are commanded to find the source of the gold nobles. Our master demanded that we pretend to be a wealthy young family and investigate. We followed Israel the money changer and he came to your door. So we knew you had a store of gold nobles.'

'We knew as soon as we came home, that someone had been into the inner room. And the things ... the dark

743

matter, the mouse in the jar, the coins in the fire, they were all disturbed, just a little, by your presence. Things are not the same when they are watched. Something changes when it has been seen.'

'You knew we had been in the room?' Freize asked sceptically.

Luca stirred at the suggestion that an object might sense an observer; but Ishraq simply answered: 'Yes, I thought you might know. And we took a print of the Duke of Bedford's seal and a piece of glass from the writing table.'

'The rainbow glass,' Luca said. 'The glass that makes a rainbow when the light falls on it. I have been interested in rainbows since I saw the mosaic at Ravenna. Do you know how they are made in the sky? How does the glass do it on the earth?'

'The glass splits the light into its true colours,' the alchemist told Luca, understanding his longing for knowledge. 'Everyone thinks that light is the colour of sunshine. But it is not. It is made of many colours. You can see this when it goes through the glass.'

'Is it always the same colours?' Luca asked him. 'I saw a mosaic of a rainbow, an ancient mosaic, centuries old, and it was the same colours that we see today. The ancients must have somehow known that light made a rainbow.'

'Always the same colours,' Jacinta confirmed. 'And always following the same order. Light appears as clear brightness when all the colours flow together, but if you allow a beam of light to fall on a piece of glass, cut in the right way, it will split the light into its colours and you can see them. Put another piece of glass on the rainbow and you can make them meld together again and become invisible once more. One piece of glass can split the light, and then another makes it whole again.'

'So what makes a rainbow in the sky?' Ishraq asked.

Jacinta turned to her. 'I believe that the drops of water of the rain split the light, just like the glass splits it. You often see the rainbow against rain clouds, or against mist.'

Luca nodded. 'That's true, you do.'

'But the interesting question to me ...' Jacinta went on. 'The interesting question is: why is it curved?'

'Curved?' Freize asked, utterly baffled, but wanting to join in.

The alchemist smiled at him. 'Why would the bow of the rainbow be curved?' he asked. 'Why would it not run straight across the sky?'

Freize shook his head, even Luca was blank.

'Because it follows the line of the earth. It proves that the earth is not flat but shaped like a ball. And the great length of the rainbow proves that the ball is far greater than philosophers think, and round, not humped. It tells us that the earth is round but bigger than we thought. Much bigger than we thought.'

Freize put his hands down and held on to the table, as if to steady himself. 'Why would you think such a thing?' he said, complaining of their imaginations which made the ground heave beneath his feet. 'Why would you repeat such a disturbing thing? And obviously untrue. Why would you say such a thing, even if you are mad enough to think it? It makes my head spin.'

Jacinta put her small hand over his as he gripped the table. 'Because we consider all possibilities,' she answered.

'And it is true about the world being round. But of course, people don't like to think about it.' She looked up and smiled at Luca. 'Keep the glass piece,' she said. 'And see what light shines through it. Who knows what you will discover?'

'And what about you?' Ishraq asked. 'You know, you can't stay here, counterfeiting coins. This has to stop.'

'You call us counterfeiters?' The alchemist drew himself up to his full height. 'You think I am a common criminal?'

For the first time Ishraq felt uneasy. She looked from Jacinta to the man who had passed as her father and remembered that she, Luca and Freize were three, against the two of them. But there was something about these two that made her wonder if they were safe, even with those odds. 'I didn't mean to offend you, Doctor Nacari; but what else am I to think?' she said carefully.

'We saw the silver piccoli in the hearth,' Freize said bluntly. 'We saw the sacks of gold at your watergate. We know that you supply Israel, the money changer, with his gold coins. We assume that you supply others. You've got the seal of the Duke of Bedford, we know it's his seal. Altogether, it looks very bad.' He turned to Jacinta. 'It looks as if you are counterfeiting gold. You may be as old as my great-grandmother and the world may be round – though I have to tell you that I doubt it – but I would not have any harm come to a lass with a smile like yours.'

At once she beamed, as radiant as a girl. 'Ah Freize,' she said intimately. 'You have a true heart. I can see that as clearly as I can see anything.'

The alchemist sighed. 'Come in here,' he said. He opened the door to what had once been the storeroom in the house and the warm rotting smell intensified. He led the way into the inner room and Luca looked around in amazement from the vat of rotting garbage, to the bubbling, dripping glass vessels.

'I won't deny that we have started to make gold,' the alchemist said to Freize. 'There are the moulds for pouring the gold. Here . . .' He pointed to a great round crock sealed and thrust into the deep heat of the fire. 'Do you know what they call that?'

Freize dumbly shook his head.

'The philosophers' egg,' he said and smiled. 'It absorbs an unbearable heat and inside it the metals, pure and impure, melt and blend. When we pour the molten mix into the moulds we make gold nobles.'

'Pure gold?' Luca confirmed, hardly able to believe it. 'Because we tested some coins when we first arrived in Venice.'

'Those would have been the first we ever had, from our patron. We didn't make them. Those were real gold nobles, from the Calais mint. We sowed the market with them. At first we just sold the coins he provided, creating an interest in the market, watching the price rise, and then we started to make our own. We have only just started making our own, from mixed metals. They pass as gold, they are just one step away from being pure gold, they are close, very close to perfect. I need only a little time to make them pure. I have to work on them some more. One last stage of refinement.'

'We can't do it here, any more,' Jacinta reminded him. 'They are good to warn us. We'll have to move on.'

'Yes, I see we must be on our travels again. We will have to tell our patron that we have to find a new home.'

747

Ishraq saw the young woman turn from the alchemist with regret, saw her glance at a bell jar on the table. Where the little brown mouse had been on their last visit, there was now another creature, a little like a lizard. Ishraq could not see more than the hairless back and the little outspread legs as the creature slept on its tiny belly at the bottom of the jar.

'Who is your patron?' Luca asked.

The alchemist smiled at him. 'He works in secret,' he said. 'He works in darkness. But we have done what he wanted us to do. He commanded us to come here and put the coins that he gave us into the market place, and then make our own, and now we are only one step from pure gold, only one step from eternal life.'

'Wait a moment, you brought gold coins here?' Freize asked. 'You didn't make them all here?'

'Our first task was only to trade gold coins.' Jacinta moved to the table and tossed a cloth over the bell jar. The little thing inside moved as the cloth fell down, hiding it from sight, and then lay still. 'We found a trader we could trust – Israel, the man that you know – and then we put the gold nobles out into the market. We watched the traders bid for them and drive up the price. Everyone wanted them. We created a fashion for them, and we supplied them in thousands from our store. Our second task, once people were calling out for the coins, was to take enough silver to make our own gold. To refine it and work on it according to the recipe. You saw us collecting silver in the market square, with the cups and ball game. You saw the coins heating up in the forge. Then, when we had converted it into gold we sold our alchemical gold into the market we had created for the real gold nobles. But you have seen all this. You know how we do it?'

Freize shook his head. 'We were in a hurry,' he said, looking slightly embarrassed. 'We visited, as it were, like burglars.'

The alchemist turned to Luca. 'If I could have gone on here with my work I would have changed this vat of dirt into gold itself. Imagine it. The purest metal from the basest filth. But as it is, we have made a start, transforming the piccoli. We collected purses of silver and copper. Jacinta won it for us every day. Israel gave us more.'

'But where did those first gold coins come from?' Freize asked, clinging to the few facts that he thought he might be able to understand. 'Your master's gold that he gave you? The first gold that you didn't make, but only sold on. Where did your master get it?'

Jacinta lifted some of the glass jars off the table and put them up high, on the shelves. Ishraq glimpsed the desiccated bodies of a couple of mice, and one splayed specimen, pinned on a board, which looked like a dead cat. The young woman tidied them out of sight, and then turned to answer Freize.

'They were true gold nobles,' she said. 'We cannot be accused of forging them, they were the real thing. Gold nobles created and stored by John, Duke of Bedford. A great alchemist. A great adept. They came in his caskets for us to use, under his own seal.'

'From the mint at Calais? He had them made from real gold and stored to pay the English troops? When he was regent?' Luca asked.

749

She laughed and wagged a finger at him as if it was a great joke. 'Ah, don't ask me!' she said. 'He commanded the mint, so they may be English gold. They might be the real thing. But he also owned the manuscript book that we showed you, he was translating it when he died. His is the recipe that we are using to turn dark matter into gold. He spent his life and his fortune trying to make the philosophers' stone. Who knows whether the gold came from mines or from his alchemical forge? Who knows? Who cares? As long as it is good coin?'

'Because if it's alchemy gold, then he had found the secret of life, and you have it, even if you can't read it yet!' Ishraq exclaimed. 'You are working towards it. In the pages of the manuscript, in your forge here, in your still, you have the secret of how to make gold from nothing, how to make eternal life!'

Jacinta smiled. 'Of course we do. But if we had stolen the gold and all that we have made is a clever forgery, then we are counterfeiters and we will confess it to no one,' Jacinta replied steadily. 'So don't ask me which it is. Because I won't say.'

Freize sat down heavily on one of the stools. 'It's beyond me,' he said. 'But I know one thing ...'

There was silence in the room but for the gurgle in the vat of first matter, and the drip of a distilling pipe.

'No, I know two things,' Freize said, thinking furiously. 'The world is flat, of course, for if not how could hell be below and heaven above? And that I was taught in the monastery and they even had a picture of it on the wall of the church that I saw several times a day and many times on Sunday so I am sure of that at least: hell below, earth in the middle and heaven above.

'And the other thing is something that I know, but you do not. Something that you should know, and be warned. Our master, that is to say Luca's master, Milord, has ordered that we find the counterfeiters and report them. Our travelling companion, Brother Peter, will obey him, whether we agree or not. If you want to save your skins, you had better pack and go. It doesn't matter if you confess to alchemy or confess to counterfeiting, or deny them both, for Brother Peter will report you; and I, for one, would rather not see the Doge's men come here and take you off to boil you in oil.'

'They boil forgers?' the girl asked with a horrified shudder.

'God knows what they do to them,' Freize said to her. 'But sweetheart, you don't want to find out.'

Solemnly the alchemist nodded. 'You are right to remind us that we are in danger. We will take the most precious things and leave tomorrow, at dawn.'

'Better go tonight,' Freize prompted him.

'I am sorry for it,' Luca said. 'I see that you have been doing great work here. I should have loved to work with you. I should have been honoured to see the transformation from first matter to gold.'

The man shrugged. 'We will have to start again. But this time we start with a proven recipe. Making gold is for the greedy criminals of this world. We wanted to make life itself. That is the point of alchemy, translation from the lesser to the greater till the purest point of all. Gold is nothing, life is the great secret.'

Luca shook his head at the waste of them packing their treasures and leaving when they were on the brink of discovery. 'I wish to God you could tell me all that you know,' he said.

'Then we are equal, for I wish to God that you could tell me what you know, for I think you have it in you to be a great adept,' the alchemist said gently. 'Mortal born or changeling boy, you have the third eye.'

'What?' Freize asked. 'What do you say he has got?'

Drago Nacari put his forefinger to the centre of his own forehead, between his eyebrows, and then pointed to Luca's forehead. Luca flinched as if at a touch. 'The third eye,' Drago said. 'The gaze that can see the unseen things. I think you are indeed of faerie blood – you are a changeling.'

'We've got to go,' Freize decided, disturbed by this talk about his friend. He got to his feet and took Jacinta's hand and kissed it. 'We'll do what we can to prevent Brother Peter reporting you at once. But don't you wait upon your going – pack up at once, for your own safety.'

She took his hand and put it to her cheek in a brief, warm gesture. 'Thank you,' she said. 'I will remember you as the sweetest thing in this extraordinary city. Truer than true gold itself, a finer thing than we could refine.'

He flushed like a boy, and turned to the alchemist and gave him an awkward nod. 'Sorry,' he said. 'About the breaking and entering. Work, you understand.'

Drago Nacari nodded in return. 'Sorry about the false coins,' he said. 'Work, you understand.'

Luca went to the doorway and bowed to them both. 'I wish you the very best,' he said. 'And we will not report you till tomorrow, after dawn, at the earliest. You will have till then to get away.'

The young woman came after them, and slipped her slim hand into Freize's pocket.

'What's this?' he asked, pausing.

'Your penny,' she said softly. 'I promised I would return it to you. It is as true as you.' She raised her face to his and Freize bent down and kissed her warm lips. 'Good luck follow you,' she said. 'Blessings be.' She went back to stand beside Drago Nacari, beside their bench, in the noisome laboratory among the bubbling stills.

Freize looked back, to get a last sight of her, and thought that they were like a lost couple heroically going down on a little boat, sunk by their own determination, then he caught up with Ishraq and Luca as they went quietly out of the front door and closed it behind them.

~

The waves lapped at the stone quays as their gondola went down the small canals. 'Drop me here,' Luca said suddenly. 'I want to see if Father Pietro is still at the Rialto Bridge.'

'We'll wait for you,' Ishraq decided. The gondola took Luca to a set of stairs in the quayside and he ran lightly up and then crossed the square to where Father Pietro was seated, in his usual place, with his little table before him and his tragic roll of names unfurled.

'Father Pietro, do you have news?'

The priest leaped to his feet and came to Luca with his hands held out. 'Praise God!' he said. 'Praise God, I have news. My messenger saw Bayeed and was able to take a passage on a fast ship back to me with the greatest of news.'

'My father? Gwilliam Vero?'

'He is found. He is found, my son!'

A great darkness clouded Luca's vision, he felt his head swirl. Out of the mist he felt the priest grab his arm, tap his cheek. 'Luca? Luca Vero?'

'I'm all right,' Luca gasped. 'I could not hear. I cannot believe what I heard! My father is alive? And can we ransom him?'

The priest beamed at him. 'I didn't know you had friends in high places. You should have told me that you had a great friend.'

'I don't,' Luca stammered. 'I have no great friend. I am all but friendless. Until this moment I was all but an orphan. I don't know what you mean.'

'A very great man had already sent a message to Bayeed, asking him if he had a Gwilliam Vero on board, telling him that he must release him to his son Luca, if requested. You know who did that?'

Luca started to shake his head. 'I know no one except . . . the man who told me of you, he went by the name of Radu Bey.'

Father Pietro laughed delightedly. 'Because that is his name. And a great name among the infidel. If you have his friendship then you are favoured by one of the greatest men in the Empire.'

'I had no idea . . . I met him only once. I asked about my father and one of his slaves said he was with Bayeed. I had no idea he would think of me again. He showed no interest in me or my father, he didn't seem to care at all. And he is the mortal enemy of my lord.'

'Well, he's no enemy of yours. He took an interest, and to great effect. Bayeed was ready for your request, he regarded it as a request from the sultan, Mehmet II himself, and he sends me this reply.' The priest showed Luca a small piece of paper with a scrawl of black ink and a roughly stamped seal.

Gwilliam Vero, galley slave   *Five English nobles*

Father Pietro frowned a little. 'He's kept his price at five English nobles, though their value has risen, and is still rising. That'll cost you twelve ducats now. Last week it would have been ten.'

'It's all right,' Luca said, still breathless with the news. 'I have funds, I have nobles.' He shook his head again. 'I am stunned. I am dazzled.' He drew a breath. 'What do we do now? Do I go to fetch him?'

Father Pietro shook his head. 'No, certainly not. You give me the money and I send it by my emissary to Bayeed. My man will leave tonight, pay over the money and receive the slave, your father. He'll take him to an inn and get him a wash and some food, and some clean clothes. I find that all the men want to take a moment to return to life.' He smiled. 'It's a shock you know, the rolling back of the rock from the tomb. A man needs to take a moment to come back to life. He has to learn what has happened during the passing of the years, he has to prepare himself for the world he left so long ago. It is different, you see. Sometimes a man will have losses to mourn. How long has your father been gone?'

'Four years,' Luca said. 'That's why I want to fetch him myself, at once.'

'You only have to wait a little longer, my son. My messenger will bring your father to you.'

'How long?' Luca demanded impatiently.

'If you give me the money, my agent can sail for Trieste at once. He'll be there by tomorrow evening or at worst the next day, a day to ransom him, and get him fed and clothed, then two days' journey home.' The priest had been counting on his rosary beads, as an abacus. 'Say five days in all. You will see him within the week.'

'I'll get the money,' Luca swore, all thought of the alchemists driven from his mind. 'I've got my gondola here. I'll get the money to you.'

'Before sundown. I will be here until dusk.'

'At once! At once!'

Father Pietro nodded. 'One moment, my son,' he said gently. 'I would bless you.'

Luca curbed his impatience and dropped to his knees.

With great gentleness, the priest put his hand on the young man's bowed head. '*In nomine Patris et Filii et Spiritus Sancti.*'

'*Amen,*' Luca replied fervently.

The priest kept his hand on Luca's warm head, he imagined that he could almost feel the whirling thoughts swirling beneath his fingers. 'Prepare yourself,' he said gently. 'You will find him much changed.'

Luca rose to his feet. 'I will love him, and honour him, however he is,' he promised.

The priest nodded. 'He will have led a life of brutal cruelty, he will be scarred by it, outwardly on the skin of his back, in the brand on his face, and perhaps inwardly too. You must expect him to be different.'

'But I am changed too,' Luca explained. 'He last saw me as a boy, a novice hoping to be a priest. Now I am a man. I have loved a woman, I have kept my love for her as a secret,

I have seen some terrible things and looked at them and made a judgement. I am in the world and I am worldly. We will both see a great difference in each other. But I have never stopped loving him, and I know he would never have stopped loving me.'

The priest nodded. 'So be it,' he said gently. 'And I shall pray that the love of a father for his son and the love of God helps you both in your reunion.'

'Where shall I meet him?' Luca demanded.

'Meet me here again, at the Rialto, at Sext, in four days' time, for news, and then you can come every day till he arrives,' Father Pietro said.

'I'll be here,' Luca promised. 'Four days from now.'

Dazed, he walked away from the busy bridge and found his way to the waiting gondola. He shook his head to the questions of Ishraq and Freize. 'My father is found,' is all he said. 'I am to send the money. He is to come home to me.'

Back at the house Brother Peter was waiting for them at the watergate stairs.

'I have no idea what is going on,' he complained. 'That woman came, and she and Isolde had some kind of quarrel, a terrible fight, and now Isolde is locked in her room and won't come out, nor speak to me, and she says she will never ever speak to Luca as long as she lives.' He turned to Luca. 'What have you done?'

The rush of crimson which rose from his white collar to his black hat betrayed him. 'Nothing,' he said, glancing guiltily at Ishraq. 'I've done nothing.'

Ishraq stepped out of the gondola and went up the stone stairs, past the men's floor to the upper floor, into the big room where the reflection of the water made rippled light on the ceiling, and tapped on the door to Isolde's bed-room. She turned to see that Luca had followed her, his hat twisted in his hands, his young face wretched.

'Isolde?' she called. 'Are you there?'

'Yes,' came the muffled monosyllable from inside.

'What's the matter?'

'That woman was here and I punched her and she scratched my face, she pulled my hair and I pulled hers and we were like fishwives in the Rialto. I was not better than her. I was like a jealous ... *puttana*. I demeaned myself!'

'Why?' Ishraq was finding it hard not to laugh.

'Because she said ... she said ...' Isolde choked on a sob.

'Ah.' Ishraq was moved at once. 'Don't cry. It doesn't matter what she said.'

'It does matter. She says that Luca made an assignation with her and that was why she came to the house last night, that he was going to lie with her in the garden. They had agreed to meet. He wanted her. And she ordered me to let her into the house tonight. She says that he wants her. She says that she will make him desire her. She says that she can drive him mad for her, that he will be her toy.'

'I never!' Luca exclaimed unconvincingly. He stepped towards the door, and rested his forehead lightly against the panel, as if he would feel Isolde's cool hands on his face. 'I never invited her,' he said. 'Not at all! Or at any rate, not exactly.'

'Are you there too?' Isolde exclaimed, from the other side of the door, her voice muffled by the wood as if she were leaning her lips to the panel, to be as close to him as she could.

758

'I'm here. I'm here.'

'Why? Why are you there?'

'Because I cannot bear the thought of you being unhappy. And never because of me. Because I would do anything in the world to make you happy. I would give everything I own to prevent your distress. There is only one woman for me. There has only ever been one woman for me. There only ever will be one woman that I love.'

'She said you were ready to fall in love with her.'

'She lied.'

'She said that she can make you fall in love with her.'

'She cannot, I swear that she cannot.'

'She said that you had agreed to lie with her after the party, that you had agreed to meet.'

He stammered. 'I did agree. I was a fool, and she said… it doesn't matter. But then in the garden I thought it was not her, but another. . . . Isolde . . . I don't know what happened. I thought . . . I hoped . . . I was certain it was . . .'

'Luca, I think she is a bad woman, a vile woman.'

'Isolde, I am a man, I felt desire, I touched, I kissed . . . but it was dark, I didn't know . . . all along I thought it was . . . I didn't know it was her. I was half-drunk, I was thinking of . . .'

'Don't say. Don't think. Don't say what you thought. You can never say what you thought. You can never say who you thought you were with.'

'I'll say nothing,' he swore, his hands flat against the door, his forehead pressed to the wood, his lips whispering so that only she could hear him.

'No one will ever say who went into the garden last night,' Ishraq said to him quietly. Luca turned to her and saw her dark gaze on him. He gasped as a thought struck him as powerful as a bolt of desire. 'Ishraq? Was it you?'

'We won't even think about it,' she said.

Silently, she gave him a little smile, turned away and crept down the stairs.

'Ishraq?' Isolde whispered.

'She's gone. She said nothing,' Luca replied. 'But I must know! Beloved . . .'

'What? What did you call me?'

'I called you beloved, for that is what you are to me. If you insist then I shall never speak of the night in the garden and the stranger who came to me. If you tell me it was a terrible mistake, then it was a terrible mistake. If you tell me it was a moment of love, out of time and out of place, never to be mentioned again, then I will believe that. If you tell me that it was a gift from another girl that I love almost as much as I love you, then I will keep that secret too. But if you tell me it was a dream, the most wonderful dream that I could have, then I will believe that. I am yours to command. It is a secret, even if I don't know it. But I know that I love only you. Only you.'

There was a long silence from the other side of the door and then he heard the key turn in the lock and Isolde stood there, her hair tumbled down, her eyes red from crying.

'Can you keep the secret and never even ask? Never know for sure? Can you never ask and live not knowing?'

'I don't know,' Luca said honestly. 'I dreamed I was with you, I longed to be with you, I had taken too much wine, I am so much in love with you that I thought I was with you. Can you tell me? Was I mistaken? Terribly mistaken? Or was I the happiest man in all of Venice?'

Slowly she shook her head. 'I can never tell you,' she said. 'You will have to live with never knowing for sure.'

Strangely, he did not press her for an answer, it was as if he understood. Simply, he opened his arms to her and she stepped towards him and laid her head on his shoulder and her hot face against his shirt.

'I will never ask,' he said. 'It was like a dream. A most wonderful dream of something that I did not dare to dream. It can stay as a dream. If you order it: I just had a most wonderful dream.'

~

Brother Peter and the two young women were waiting for Luca and Freize to come home in the gondola from the Rialto Bridge. Luca had dashed out of the house with a purse of gold nobles, a hurried kiss on Isolde's hand, desperate to get the money to Father Pietro at once.

'It is the money that Milord gave us to support our lie that we are traders,' Brother Peter said anxiously, standing at the window and looking down at the busy canal. 'It's not for Luca to use to ransom his father.'

'Milord must have known that Luca would use the money to save his father. And Luca might be lucky and earn it back with trades and gambling. Aren't the nobles worth more today than when we first bought them?'

'Usury,' Brother Peter said depressingly. 'He should not be making money by trading in a currency.'

'He's supposed to!' Ishraq said impatiently. 'Milord commanded it. He's supposed to trade. And if he makes a profit on his cargo he can surely spend it as he likes!'

Brother Peter shook his head. 'A good and careful servant

would make the profit for the glory of God,' he said. 'And then give it all back to Milord. That is good stewardship. Think of the parable of the talents.'

'But when Luca's father comes home, that will be to the glory of God,' Isolde remarked. 'And the greatest joy that Luca could have. Surely, we must be glad for him?'

'I cannot help but fear what he is becoming, when he rides around in a gondola like a young merchant prince.' He glanced down at her. 'I can't help but fear for you too. Fighting with that woman like a fishwife. Your father did not raise you to behave like this, Lady Isolde.'

She nodded. 'I'm ashamed of how I behaved,' she said. 'I am ashamed of more than you know, Brother Peter.'

'Have you confessed?' he asked her very quietly. Ishraq tactfully stepped to the back of the room and left Isolde to answer.

She shook her head. 'I am too ashamed to confess.'

'You were born and bred to be a lady,' Brother Peter reminded her. 'A lady with duties and obligations. It is your part in life to show self-control, good manners, self-discipline. You cannot be ruled by your heart in love, or by your temper and start fighting. You are meant to be better than this. Your father raised you for a great place in the world, not to be a silly girl with love affairs and fights. You carry his broadsword to remind you he was a crusader.'

She looked up at him. 'I know this,' she said. 'But I am not in a world where I can behave well and people around me behave well. I am in a world of temptation and anger. I want to be able to fight for myself. I want to be able to feel desire and act. I want to be able to defend myself against attack. I want to use the broadsword in my defence, not just carry it.'

'A lady will find her defenders. The men around you will speak for you if needs be,' Brother Peter assured her, not realising that he was recommending a view of women which had kept them powerless for centuries, and would lead them to be victims of male anger and male power forever.

She bowed her head. 'I will try,' she said, for she did not know this either.

At the back of the room, Ishraq, who disagreed with everything that Brother Peter had said, shook her head and could not stop herself making a little 'tut' noise of annoyance.

'There they are now,' Brother Peter remarked, seeing the boat swerve through the busy traffic on the canal.

They heard Giuseppe call: 'Gondola! Gondola! Gondola!' in his bubbling cry as he turned the gondola across the bows of the other boats and steered it neatly into the house, and then they heard Luca and Freize, talking quietly as they came up the stairs and entered the dining room.

'Is everything all right?' Isolde asked Luca, going straight to his side as she saw his slight frown.

He nodded. 'We sent seven nobles in case he asked for more. It ought to be all right. It's just that the nobles are soaring in value against every other sort of coin. The slaver will not know what their value is in Venice when he sells my father in Trieste. It's going up so fast you have to be at the money changer's table to see it change. It's even going up against gold.'

'How can a coin be more valuable than its ingredient?' Ishraq asked. 'How can a gold coin be more valuable than gold itself?'

'Because people trust the gold noble even more than gold,' Freize answered her. 'There was a long queue before Israel, the money changer. People were changing solid gold into nobles because it is worth more than its own weight. People are taking their gold jewellery, their wives' necklaces, and exchanging them by weight for a gold noble, and then adding more to buy the coin. Buy a gold bar and it could be lead with a gold skin. You don't know, you have to get it tested. Buy a gold necklace and you don't know what you're getting. But all the gold nobles are always good, and they're all worth more today than they were yesterday.'

The travellers exchanged an uncomfortable glance.

'This is getting more and more serious,' Brother Peter said. 'People are speculating in gold nobles but only we know where they came from. Only we know that some of them are not pure gold and have been made by alchemy!'

He crossed the room and checked that no one was listening at the door and then gestured that they should all sit around the table. 'We have to decide what to do. This situation is getting worse and worse. I know you feel tenderness towards the alchemist and his daughter but we are bound to report them at once.'

Luca paused for a moment, almost as if he was reminding himself that he was on a mission, and that he was the Inquirer. Slowly, he took the chair at the head of the table. For the first time it was as if he was consulting Brother Peter as his clerk – not as his mentor. 'Wait. We have to think this through,' he ruled. 'Some things are clear. We can report to Milord, that we have completed our inquiries and we know what has happened here. The alchemist pair came with gold that they had obtained from their patron to trade on the market of Venice. They admit that they released many gold English nobles, but will not say whether this was alchemical gold that they had made or alchemical gold from the great master John, Duke or Bedford, or whether it was true gold, earthly gold, from the mint that he controlled at Calais.'

'Agreed,' Brother Peter said. 'And I have prepared the report in code, saying just this. It is ready to go once you have signed it.'

'They also said that the world was round,' Freize pointed out. 'And the pretty girl said that she was an old lady. So it might be that they are just mad, poor things.'

'Peace!' Luca commanded him. 'Most scholars believe that the world is round.'

'They do?' Freize was scandalised. 'What about the other side?'

'What other side?'

'The underneath. If the world is round, are we balanced on top? And what about the underneath? The underneath of the ball? What's it sitting on? That's the question. Never mind rainbows! And what happens when you go round the middle? If you travelled to the underneath you would fall off.' He put both hands to his head and gently pulled his own ears. 'You would be upside down! It makes me dizzy just thinking about it.'

'Never mind all that. They were talking about something else entirely different.'

'Why were they talking about the world being round at all?' Isolde asked, distracted from the most important issue by Freize's confusion. She leaned forwards and gently took his hands from his ears. 'Hush, Freize. Be calm. It's no worse than thinking that if the world were flat, you could travel to the edge and fall off it.'

'Fall off it?' he repeated, horrified. 'There is an edge?'

'We were talking about rainbows,' Luca explained briefly to Isolde.

'Actually, that's no comfort,' Freize said quietly to Isolde. 'Actually, it's worse. Falling off the edge? Saints save us!'

'But, to our business with them,' Luca said, interrupting the digression. 'They say that after some weeks of trading the Bedford gold they started to make gold nobles of their own, with the Duke of Bedford's own recipe. And then they released these gold nobles on the market with the others. So we can be sure that there is already a mixture of good English gold nobles and alchemy gold nobles coming onto the market together.'

'Can you tell one from another?' Brother Peter asked. 'Or are they all equally good?"

'They seemed to suggest that their own gold, made from silver and base metal, needed another stage of refining. They said they needed more time,' Ishraq replied, worried.

'Lady Carintha had new gold nobles in a necklace,' Isolde offered. 'They looked as good as the others. If they were alchemy gold, you couldn't tell by looking.'

'But their main work, their greatest work, was not the gold, they said, but life,' Freize said. 'They said that. Didn't they?'

'They did,' Luca confirmed. 'They were very clear that the making of gold was a lesser art, one for greedy men. Their principal ambition was to make, not the philosophers' stone that can turn everything into gold, but the philosophers' elixir – to make life itself.'

'They have a powerful number of dead animals,' Freize pointed out. 'In all those jars. And for people making life they have a terrible stink of death in their storeroom.'

'The young woman said that she was an old woman,' Ishraq told Brother Peter. 'She said she was not as she seemed. She said that she was an old woman in a young woman's body, and that she and the man she calls her father had worked together for many many years.'

There was a little silence.

'But they said many things that cannot be true,' Freize reminded them. 'I don't even want to think about it.'

'We have to report them,' Brother Peter said heavily. 'I see that they are philosophers, and their work is perhaps valuable, but Milord was clear that we had to find the counterfeiters, and this pair have admitted to making coins. He said that we must report them – and we have to do so.'

'Give them the rest of today to pack up and go and we will report them after dawn tomorrow,' Luca ruled.

'Milord said . . .'

'Milord wanted Radu Bey dead,' Ishraq cut in scornfully. 'He accused him of being an assassin but Radu Bey only put his badge on Milord's heart. Milord told Luca that it was possible to buy his father's freedom months after he first met him. He said nothing before Luca knew it already. He could have told Luca how to free his father when they first met, but he did not bother to do so. Milord gives orders but they are not always to our good. Milord can wait a day.'

There was a sharp indrawn breath from Brother Peter. 'You are disrespectful,' he reproved her. 'Milord never ceases in the work of the Order. Night and day he serves God and the Holy Father. He fights the powers of darkness

767

and the infidel in this world and the other. I am sworn to the Order and so is Luca Vero. Milord is the commander of our Order and we have to obey him. We are sworn to him. We bear his badge.'

'But I am not!' Ishraq insisted. 'Don't look so shocked, I am not suggesting that we disobey him. I don't oppose him. Brother Peter, I don't oppose your mission, I don't even argue with you and I have served you well over the last few days. All I say is that we should do as Luca thinks and report the alchemists tomorrow at dawn. It's what we promised them.'

'I think so too,' Isolde agreed, exchanging a quick hidden glance with Luca, as if they had made a promise and would always be a partnership. 'Tomorrow, as Luca says.'

'Tomorrow,' Freize said. 'That's fair enough.'

Brother Peter looked from one determined young face to another. 'Very well,' he said with a sigh. 'So be it. But tomorrow at dawn.'

He rose from the table and walked to the door, stiffly dignified, when there was a sudden tolling of the bell in the watergate and a sound of men, a whole brigade of men, running up the marble stairs, their boots hammering on the stone. The door banged open, was held open by the fore-runners of the Doge's guard, who poured into the room followed by an officer, beautifully dressed, holding a silver handgun, cocked and ready to fire. 'You're under arrest,' he said abruptly.

Luca's chair crashed to the floor, as he pushed it back and jumped before Isolde to shield her. 'What charge?'

'We've done nothing!' Brother Peter exclaimed, falling back from the door as the man rushed into the room.

Behind the men, the ashen face of the housekeeper peered in, and behind her, gleaming with triumph, came Lady Carintha, dressed in scarlet, her mask tipped to the top of her head like a false face, with her husband in tow.

'This is a private matter,' Luca said as soon as he saw her. He turned to the officer. 'Commander, there is nothing to investigate, no crime here. There has been a misunderstanding between myself and the lady, an unfortunate quarrel between neighbours.' He crossed the room at once, and bowed low and took her hand. 'I am sorry if I offended you,' he said. 'I meant no insult.' He bowed to her husband. 'An honour to meet you again, Sir.'

'He's no trader,' she said bluntly to the Doge's officer, completely ignoring Luca. 'And I doubt that they are brothers. She is certainly not his sister, and God knows who the Arab slave is. Is she their dancing girl? Is she in his harem? Is she their household witch?'

Amazingly, Ishraq did not fire up to defend herself against the insults, but meekly bowed her head and went quietly to the door. 'Excuse me,' she said.

'Where's she going?' Lady Carintha snapped.

'To my room,' Ishraq said, her eyes modestly turned down. 'I am kept in seclusion. I cannot be in this roomful of men.'

'Oh, of course.' The officer waved her away, as she drew the veil of her headdress across her face and the soldiers stepped back to let her go past.

'That's a lie!' Lady Carintha exclaimed. 'She's not in seclusion, at all. She's a bold-faced slut. If you let her go, she'll be running away!'

'No one to leave the house!' the officer ordered Ishraq. 'You may only go to your room.'

Ishraq bowed very humbly, and went up the stairs to her room.

'Put a man on her door,' the officer ordered and one of the soldiers followed her at a respectful distance.

'My dear,' Lady Carintha's husband said quietly. 'We can leave the officer to make his inquiry. Now that you have done such good work of denouncing them.'

'They're forgers,' Lady Carintha said to the officer. 'Look what she gave me.'

She threw onto the table the purse that Isolde had given her to repay the gambling debts. 'False gold,' Lady Carintha accused. 'Counterfeit coins. Counterfeit English nobles as well, which is worse. Arrest them.'

Isolde was ready to brazen it out. 'There's nothing wrong with the gold,' she claimed. 'And if there is, I had it in good faith. I bought these nobles in Venice thinking they were good. I would not have paid someone like you in a false coin. I would not have done anything that might cause you to return here!'

'I don't come for pleasure, be sure of that!' the woman snapped. She turned to her husband. 'See how she speaks to me! Who would ever be fooled into thinking she was raised as a young lady? She's as false as the coins in the purse.'

'Lady Carintha . . .' Luca said quietly. 'Let us discuss this as friends. There is no need for ill feeling.'

'We are honest merchants, a family of honest merchants.' Brother Peter repeated the lie with so little conviction that it was as bad as confession.

'Arrest them!' Lady Carintha demanded.

'Shall I fetch our travelling papers?' Freize asked the

officer. 'Our letters of introduction? You will see we have a sponsor, a very important man.'

The guardsman nodded. Freize went to the door.

'Look at the coins!' Lady Carintha shouted. 'Never mind his letters. He can forge letters as well as coins, I daresay.' She thrust her hand into the purse, and they saw her beautiful face change, the anger was suddenly wiped from her features as she froze, and then her face contorted with a sort of horror.

She pulled her hand out of the purse and they saw her fingers were sticky with some red liquid, almost like blood. 'My God,' she exclaimed in disgust. 'Look at my hand! The coins are bleeding. They are so false they are bleeding like the wounds of murdered men.'

She turned to show her hand to her husband and he recoiled from her – repulsed by her fingers reddened as if she had dipped them in an open wound. Every man in the room flinched from her as if she were oozing blood like a murdered corpse.

She felt a strange sensation on her neck, like a crawling insect, and put her clean hand to her ear. The gold noble earrings were dripping blood onto her neck. The gold noble necklace was making a trail of red at her throat as if someone had taken a knife and sliced into her.

'Clean me!' she said, her voice shaking. 'Get it off me.'

Nobody could bear to step towards her, nobody could bring themselves to touch her. They could only watch in terrified fascination as the gold noble earrings drip-dripped blood down her white neck and stained the low-cut lace at the top of her gown.

'Get it off me!' she screamed, her fingers slipping at the

intricate clasp of the necklace, unable to grip for the red liquid. 'It's burning me! It's scalding my skin! Get it off me!'

Her husband forced himself to step forwards to help, gritting his teeth against his distaste. The officer drew his dagger and put the blade of his stiletto under the clasp of the necklace, careful not to touch the oozing coins.

'Cut it off!' Lady Carintha screamed. 'It doesn't matter that it's gold. Get it off me! It's bleeding on me! It's burning! It's burning my skin!'

Her husband held the necklace away from the nape of her neck as the young officer pulled upwards and away with his knife. His knife was as red as if he had stabbed her in the heart, and the necklace pulled against her neck and made her shriek before it clattered to the ground, smearing scarlet on the marble floors as if a murder had been done in the horrified room.

There was a sudden black flash of something going past the window, but only Luca, facing in that direction, saw that it was Ishraq, pointed like a spear in a long fearless dive, from her high bedroom window into the canal.

'What the hell was that?' demanded the officer of the guard, pushing past Lady Carintha to look out of the window. 'I saw something go by ...'

'Nothing,' Luca said, going to the window. 'A cormorant perhaps.' In the canal he could see a circle of bubbles but nothing else.

'A murdered body bleeds when the murderer comes near!' Lady Carintha declaimed, pushing herself forward, scrubbing with a cloth at her reddened neck. 'These coins are bleeding because they are in the house of the counterfeiters!'

'I'm going to have to search your property,' the officer said, turning from the window to Brother Peter.

Luca was still looking out at the Grand Canal. After what felt like a long, long time he saw Ishraq's dark head, wet as a seal, emerging from the water. Someone pulled her on board a rowing boat and she crouched in the prow, but they did not return to the house. The boatman leaned over his oars and rowed as hard as he could down the canal, before anyone from the palazzo could raise the alarm or come after them. They were out of sight in a moment. Luca guessed Freize was at the oars and Ishraq was urging him on to warn the alchemists.

'So what was that?' The officer returned to look out with Luca. 'Looked like something was thrown from an upper window.'

'I'll go and see,' Isolde volunteered. 'My servant may have dropped something.'

'You'd better not have thrown away any evidence,' the officer warned. 'We can drag the canal, you know.'

'Of course not!' Isolde said.

Before anyone could stop her, she pushed past Lady Carintha and ran up the stairs to her room. They heard her slam the door and turn the key in the lock as Lady Carintha poked the bleeding necklace with the toe of her satin shoes and said, her voice shaking: 'False coins, false hearts. Bleeding coins are a sign of guilt. These are wicked people. You must arrest them all. Especially the young women. They must be put to the question.

They must be taken to the Doge's Palace, and held in his prisons.'

'Where did you get this purse from?' The officer spilled the bloodstained coins onto the dinner table, they smeared their sticky redness in a pool.

Brother Peter exchanged one brief look with Luca.

'I can find out,' the officer said. 'I only have to ask in the Rialto and someone will tell me. But it would be better for you if you were to answer me now.'

Luca nodded. Clearly, they would have to tell the truth. 'We got our nobles from the money changer Israel,' he said. 'But I am certain that he thought that they were good. We certainly thought they were good. It was a simple transaction between two honest parties.'

The officer turned his head and spoke briefly to one of his men. At once he left the room and they could hear him running down the stairs.

'I am arresting you on suspicion,' the officer said.

'Of what?' Luca said. 'We may have received forged nobles, but so has Lady Carintha. Where did she get her necklace from? It was not from us! We are buyers of coins, not counterfeiters. You can search the house.'

'We know Lady Carintha, she is a Venetian born and bred, and her husband is a great trader in this city, his name is in the Gold Book. He is on the Council. You, on the other hand, have just arrived and everything about you is strange. Lady Carintha says you are not what you seem, you have been arranging to buy a fortune in gold from one money changer, you speak of a ship that has yet to come in, you are often seen with Father Pietro and you seem to be favoured by one of the greatest enemies of Christendom.'

Luca raised his eyebrows at the extent of the officer's knowledge. 'You have been watching me?'

'Of course. We watch all strangers. Venice is filled with spies. There is a *Bocca di Leone* for denouncing the guilty in every square. And you have great wealth and dubious friends. You have been under suspicion from the moment you arrived.'

'He is not a dubious friend. Radu Bey was a chance meeting. He chose to help me trace my father who was captured as a slave of the Ottomans. The city of Venice itself trades with the Ottoman Empire. The Doge himself trades with Radu Bey.'

'But the Doge does not use counterfeit coins,' the man returned.

'He does,' Lady Carintha said spitefully, pulling her earrings out of her ears and throwing them down on the table with a shudder. They sat in a little pool of redness, oozing wetly. 'He almost certainly does. His hands will be bloody too.'

'What?'

'Since this family arrived, everyone in Venice has gone mad for the English gold. Ask my husband. The price has soared. No doubt the Doge has bought them, no doubt he has sold them on. Perhaps his hands are dirty too. Perhaps we are all going to be ruined.' She rubbed her stained hands against the skirts of her gown and shuddered. 'What *is* this?'

'It looks like a sort of rust,' Luca said. 'Perhaps the metals are breaking down, and rusting away.'

She looked at him and her beautiful face was twisted with jealousy and spite. 'Rusting gold?' she said. 'Against the laws of nature. You and that sister of yours? Unnatural too.

As unnatural as forgery. As false as counterfeit coin.'

'What are you suggesting?' the officer asked her. 'Are you saying they are sinners as well as criminals?'

'God knows what they are guilty of,' Lady Carintha swore. 'You should take them in at once. He is false as the most beautiful gold coin, and she passes for a lady but fights like a cat. Who knows what they have done together?'

'My dear . . .' her husband interpolated.

'I want to go home.' Lady Carintha suddenly became soft and tearful. She turned to her husband. 'We have done our duty here. I can't bear it here with these bloodstained coins in this house of wicked strangers.'

Solemnly, he nodded. 'Do your duty for the Doge and the Republic,' he said pompously to the officer. 'The survival of the greatest city in the world depends on our wealth and our trustworthiness. This family – if they are truly a family and not a counterfeiting ring in disguise – have challenged both. They must be destroyed before they destroy us! Arrest them at once and take them before the Council of Ten!'

The two of them were too powerful to be denied. The officer looked from Luca to the stained gold nobles scattered over the table. 'I am arresting you on suspicion of counterfeiting coins, trading in false gold with a Jew, and incestuous relations with your sister,' he said. 'You will have to come with me. In fact, I am arresting you all.'

Brother Peter put his hand over his eyes and made a little noise like a low sigh, but at that moment, the door opened and Isolde came into the room. She was transformed. She was wearing her blonde hair piled high on her head and a tall scarlet pointed headdress on top of it that made her look six feet tall. She was wearing one of her most beautiful Venetian-made gowns in a deep crimson, the slashed sleeves showing white silk underneath. She stood very tall and very proudly. Beside her Lady Carintha looked old and tawdry with her dirty neck and her bloodstained ears.

'This has gone far enough,' Isolde ruled. 'It must stop now.' At her tone of command the officer hesitated, and Lady Carintha's husband made a half bow, halted by a sharp hidden pinch from his wife.

'I am Lady Isolde of Lucretili,' Isolde said directly to the officer. 'This is my mother's signet ring. You can see our family crest. I am travelling with my servant and companion Ishraq, and with this escort: my tutor Brother Peter, a man of unquestioned probity, his scholar Luca Vero and our manservant and general factotum. We decided to pass as a noble family interested in trade in order to travel without being known and for my personal safety.'

'Why would you do that?' the officer queried. Lady Carintha stood dumb, clearly overwhelmed by Isolde's grandeur.

Isolde answered the officer, completely ignoring the woman. 'My brother has usurped my place at the castle,' she said. 'He is passing himself off as the new Lord of Lucretili. I don't want him to know that I am going to seek help against him from my godfather's son. That is why we are travelling through Venice. That is why we assumed different names.'

'And who is your godfather's son, Milady?' the officer asked deferentially.

'He is Count Vlad Tepes the Third, of Wallachia,' Isolde said proudly.

The officer and all the guards pulled off their hats at the mention of one of the greatest commanders on the frontiers of Christendom, a man who had defended his country of Wallachia from the unstoppable Ottoman army, been driven out, and would, without a doubt, conquer it again. 'You are the great count's god-daughter?' the officer confirmed.

'I am,' Isolde said. 'Actually, I am carrying his crusader sword. He and my father exchanged swords. So you see, I am a woman of some importance.' She took another step into the centre of the room and looked Lady Carintha up and down with an expression of utter contempt. 'This woman is a bawd,' she said simply. 'She keeps a disorderly house with gambling and prostitutes. She boasts of her own immorality and she quarrelled with me only when I refused to join in her lascivious ways.'

Slowly, Lady Carintha's husband detached himself from her gripping hand and turned to look at her.

'I imagine it is well known to everyone but you, Sir,' Isolde said gently to him. 'Your wife is little more than a common whore. She has quarrelled with me because I would not let her into this house at night and lead her to the room of this young man of my household, whose spiritual well-being is my responsibility. She wanted to lie with him, she offered to buy time with him by giving me jewellery or an alibi for my own absences, or introduce me to a lover. She said she would make him into her toy, she would have him for *Carnevale* and then give him up for Lent.'

Brother Peter crossed himself at the description of sin. Luca could not take his eyes off Isolde, proud as a queen, fighting for their safety.

'She's lying,' Lady Carintha spat.

'When I treated these offers with contempt, this woman attacked me,' Isolde said steadily.

Lady Carintha crossed the room and stood, her hands on her hips, glaring at Isolde. 'I will slap your face again,' she said. 'Shut up. Or you will be sorry.'

'I am sorry that I have to speak like this at all,' Isolde said glacially, one glance at Brother Peter as if she was remembering his claim that a lady should not fight for herself. 'A lady does not tell such shameful secrets, a lady does not soil her mouth with such words. But sometimes, a lady has to defend herself, and her reputation. I will not be bullied by this old streetwalker. I will not be scratched and pinched by such a she-wolf.' She smoothed back the veil which flowed from her headdress and showed the officer the scratch marks on her pale cheek. 'This is what she did to me this very afternoon for refusing her disgusting offers. I will not be assaulted in my own home. And you should not work at her bidding. Any denunciation from such as her means nothing.'

'Absolutely not!' he said, quite convinced. 'My lord?' He turned to Lady Carintha's husband. 'Will you take the woman home? We cannot accept her denunciation of this family when she clearly has a private quarrel with them. And this lady,' he bowed towards Isolde, who stood like a queen, 'this lady is above question.'

'And she receives forged coins,' Isolde added quietly. 'And gambles with them.'

'We'll go,' Lady Carintha's husband decided. To Isolde he bowed very low. 'I am very sorry that such a mis-understanding should have come about,' he said. 'Just a misunderstanding. No need to take it further? I would not want our name mentioned to the count, your kinsman. I would not have such a great man thinking badly of me. I am so sorry that we have offended, inadvertently offended . . .'

Isolde inclined her head very grandly. 'You may go.'

The officer turned to Brother Peter and Luca. 'I apolo-gise,' he said. 'Of course, no arrest. You are free to come and go as you please.'

He bowed very low to Isolde, who stood very still while he ordered the men from the room, and they waited until they heard the clatter of their boots on the stairs and then the bang of the outer door.

There was a sudden total silence. Isolde turned and looked at Brother Peter as if she expected him to criticise her for being too bold. Brother Peter was silent, amazed at this newly powerful version of the girl he had seen before as a victim of her circumstances: clinging to a roof in a flood, bullied in a nunnery, weeping for the loss of her father.

'I will defend myself,' she said flatly. 'Against her, or against anyone. From now on, I am going to fight for myself.'

~

Freize rowed in determined silence, heaving the little boat through the water, until Ishraq, hunched in the prow, shivering a little in her dripping gown, looked behind and said: 'Nobody's following.'

He paused then, and stripped off his thick fustian jacket. 'Here,' he said. 'Put this round your shoulders.'

Almost she refused, but then she took it and hugged it to her.

'You look like a drowned rat,' Freize said with a smile, and set to the oars again.

She made no reply.

'A sodden vole,' Freize offered.

She turned her head away.

'It was a hell of a dive,' he said honestly. 'Brave.'

Ishraq, like a champion of the games receiving the laurel crown, bent her head, just a little. 'I'm cold,' she admitted, 'and I hit the water with a terrible blow. I knocked the air out of myself.'

'You hurt?' he asked.

He saw her indomitable smile. 'Not too bad.'

They found their way through the network of little

canals towards the industrial quarter of the city, and rowed slowly along the outside of the steep wall, until Ishraq said: 'That must be it. That must be their watergate. It's on the corner.'

The alchemists had no gondola, and their gate was closed, the two halves of wrought metal bolted together. Ishraq was about to pull the bell chain which hung beside the gates when Freize raised his hand for her to wait, and said: 'Listen!'

They could hear the noise of someone pounding on the outer door to the street, they could hear someone shout: 'Open in the name of the law! In the name of the Doge: open this door!'

'We're too late,' Freize said shortly. 'They must have got to the money changer, and he must have told them that he got the nobles here.'

Ishraq listened to the loud hammering. 'The guard isn't in yet,' she said. 'We might be able to get them away . . .'

Without another word, Freize rowed the boat towards the gate and Ishraq leaned over the prow and struggled to push the heavy bolt upwards. But whenever she pushed against the gate, the boat bobbed away. Finally, in frustration she stepped out of the boat altogether and, clinging to the wrought iron of the gate, her bare feet flexed on the trellis work, she used all her strength to push the bolt upwards. Stretching between the stationary gate, and the one which was opening, she kicked off from the anchored gate and swung, slowly inwards, dangling over the cold waters.

Freize brought the boat up against the opening gate and Ishraq stepped down into the prow and then turned as he took the little boat against the internal quay. She jumped ashore and took the rope, tying it to the ring in the wall.

Now they could hear the noise more clearly, the hammering on the door echoing through the stone storeroom and through the wooden hatch to where they stood on the quay.

'Sounds like a raid,' Freize said.

Cautiously, he tried the hatch which led from the quay to the storeroom. It opened a crack and Freize looked in.

'They've bolted the door to the street,' he said. 'But I can hear the Doge's men are breaking it down now. You wait here.' Freize pulled the hatch from its housing and jumped upwards, getting his chest and belly over the ledge, and wriggled through the low gap. There was a crash from inside the house as he got to his feet, and Freize whirled around to see Jacinta running through the door, her arms filled with rolls of manuscript, a chest of papers in her hand.

She recoiled for a moment, as she saw Freize's broad frame and the open hatch and then she recognised him. 'Thank God it's you!' she exclaimed. She thrust the papers at him. 'They can't have these,' she said. 'No one can see these. They're secret.'

'Get in the boat,' Freize said shortly, throwing the papers through the hatch. 'We've got one in your watergate, waiting.'

'I have to fetch . . .'

They could hear a steady violent thud at the front door as the men took a ram to it and started to break it in. Drago was gathering up small glass jars in his haste, passing them through the hatch to Ishraq, who stacked them pell mell into the bottom of the boat.

'Come!' Freize shouted at the pretty girl, who was piling small spice boxes one on top of another to carry away. 'That door won't hold! Come now or you will lose everything!'

She raced towards the hatch and handed the boxes to Ishraq on the waterside. Drago was through the hatch already and at the oars of the boat. 'Come!' he commanded her.

'The baby!' she shouted.

'Baby?' Freize repeated, horrified.

There was a crash as the outer door to the street yielded to the battering ram and then shouts as the guard came up against the locked storeroom door. Jacinta dragged a stool across the stone floor and jumped up on it so that she could reach the highest shelf. She stretched out her hands for the bell jar where Freize and Ishraq had first seen a little brown mouse beside a flickering candle, and then, on their later visit, seen the naked lizard-like thing.

'This ...' she said, as the kitchen door burst open and a band of the Doge's guards hurled themselves into the storeroom. One man threw himself at her, grabbing her around the knees and bringing her down.

The bell jar flew from her hands and smashed on the floor. The young woman screamed, struggled in the man's grip, writhing like a serpent as her cap fell off and her rich russet hair tumbled down around her shoulders. Freize took hold of the guardsman in a strong grip from behind, pulling him off her, so he was facing Jacinta as she wormed out of the man's grip. Freize saw her, saw her transformed: her long straggling locks of completely white hair, her face gnarled and old, her merry brown eyes pouched under drooping eyelids and her wrinkled lips stretched over tooth-less gums as she gave a croaky scream.

For one second they were all frozen still with horror, and then the guardsman released her with a bellow of shock, pushed her away from him, thrusting her away like a man in terror. In that moment she was out of his arms, and through the hatch, wriggling like a white-headed snake through the gap, down to the quay, and into the boat, and Drago and Jacinta were gone.

'Good God!' the man said. 'Did you see? Did you see that?'

Freize did not reply, so shocked that he could not catch his breath. Then he saw the contents of the bell jar that Jacinta had tried so hard to save. Amid the broken shards of the glass bell jar there was a little creature. At first he thought it was a lizard, only pale and pink. Then he thought it was a kitten that they had obscenely skinned and left to bleed. Then he saw the thing more clearly. The little being rose up on its hind legs and held up its arms to him, and he heard a tiny piping voice say: 'Help me! Help me!'

The other guardsmen were pouring into the storeroom and kicking in the wooden frame of the hatch that led to the quay. Among the turmoil of the broken glass and the stamping of leather boots the little thing scuttled in fear and called again to Freize: 'Help me!'

Compassion overcame his disgust and with a horrified shudder Freize bent down towards the tiny animal which stood no taller than six inches, like a perfectly formed naked man, but with a grimace of fear on its miniature bare face, and a word written in silver across its forehead: *EMET.*

Freize could not bring himself to touch it, but he pulled the cap from his head and laid it down. The little thing took a bold leap and landed in the cap like a fish in a net. Freize shook his head in horror and bafflement. 'What am I to do with you?' he whispered.

He heard the breath of a whispered reply: 'The canal.'

~

The guardsmen had kicked out the old wooden hatch that closed off the quay and now they saw Ishraq's pale frightened face in the opening.

'There's a girl here!' someone shouted. 'Get her!'

One man bent down and tried to climb through the opening as Freize made a mighty dive, hands first, getting in before him, blocking the gap with his shoulders. 'Ishraq!' he yelled, and thrust the cap towards her.

She caught the cap in her hands. 'What?' she recoiled at the little being, curled up inside. 'What's this? My God Freize! What is it?'

The soldiers fell on Freize's legs and dragged him backwards from the hatch. 'Get it in the river!' Freize shouted to her. 'Get it in the water.' Someone trod on his outstretched hands in their haste to get through the hatch to capture Ishraq. 'Let it go!' Freize yelled. 'Set it free! And get away yourself!'

He saw her duck away from the hatch towards the canal, but then someone kicked him in the head and something fell beside him with a loud clatter, and then everything was dark.

~

Wet and dripping, Ishraq approached the garden gate of the palazzo on the Grand Canal, and tried the latch. It yielded and she stepped into the garden. It was dusk, and the waning spring moon was rising over the shadow of the wall. She was still wet, and her hair was in rats' tails down her back, her expensive costume torn into strips and tied out of the way. She stepped warily into the enclosed space and looked up at the house.

Everything seemed quiet. Ishraq tiptoed barefoot to one of the windows and listened. There was silence; she cupped her hand over her eyes and peered in. The room was empty. Carefully, Ishraq went under the shade of the portico to the garden door and pushed it open. There was a slight creak but in a moment she was in the stone-flagged back hall, and then, picking up her damp skirts, she crossed the hall and mounted the stairs, past the main room and up to the floor that she shared with Isolde.

The door to their rooms was locked. Ishraq tapped the rhythm that they had used from childhood

♩ ♩ ♫

and at once the door opened and Isolde pulled her in.

'I have been waiting and waiting for you. You're freezing! Are you safe? You're soaked! Did you get to them in time?'

Isolde ran to her room and fetched a linen sheet and started to towel Ishraq's hair, while the girl pulled off her wet torn clothes.

'I got to them before the Doge's men came, and they got away. Their equipment was broken and I think they captured Freize.'

'No! We must tell Luca!'

Ishraq took a blanket and wrapped it around her bare shoulders. 'Has the guard all gone?'

'They left only one man behind, at the watergate. That's why I stayed locked in, up here, though they have gone. They didn't see you go, so they think you're locked in here with me. Change your clothes and nobody will ever know you were out of the house. There's nothing to connect us with the alchemists. Hurry – we have to tell Luca and Brother Peter about Freize.'

Ishraq rubbed her hair dry, pulled on a dress and tied her hair back in a knot. 'Let's go,' she said.

The two young women hurried down the stairs and into the main room. Brother Peter and Luca were at the window, looking down to the darkening canal, as the door behind them opened and they turned around and saw Ishraq.

'Thank God you're safe!' Luca exclaimed. 'What a dive you made! Ishraq, what a risk you took!' He crossed the room and hugged her to him. 'You're still wet!' he said.

Brother Peter was shaking his head. 'I suppose you went to warn them,' he said. 'Were you seen?'

'Worse,' Ishraq said briefly. 'I am sorry, Brother Peter. They saw me, but I got away; and they caught Freize.'

'Freize!'

'We rowed there together. We went in by their watergate. We could hear the Doge's men at the front door. The alchemist and Jacinta were trying to get their things, the books and the manuscripts and some herbs and things from their work room. They got into our boat . . .' Ishraq broke off at the memory of the horror of the young woman with the old, old face and straggling white hair who had rushed

788

past her to get into the boat. 'Anyway. They got away in our boat. But the men charged in; and they got Freize. I swam for it.'

She stopped again. Somewhere in the water, not far from her as she had dived off the quay, had been the little thing, something like a baby, something like a lizard, something like a frog. She had held the cap towards the water's edge and seen it jump into the water, seen it dive, the soft skin of its back gleaming palely as it went deep down into the canal.

'What happened?' Isolde asked, seeing the expression of blank horror on her friend's face.

Ishraq shook her head. 'I don't know what they were doing there,' she said. 'I don't know what they had done. I don't know what they had made, in that bell jar of theirs. I don't know what sort of thing it was.'

'What sort of thing?' Luca repeated, taking her hand.

She met his honest brown eyes with a deep sense of relief, as if Luca was the only person that she would be able to tell.

'Luca,' she whispered. 'I want to tell you.' She hesitated. 'But I am afraid to even speak. It was horrific – and pitiful. I want to tell you. I can't.'

Without thinking, he put his arm around her shoulders and walked her away from the other two. When their heads were close together and his arm was tight around her waist, he felt her lean towards him and relax against him, as if he were warm, as if he were safety for her.

'You can tell me,' he said. 'Whatever it was.'

She turned her face to his neck and then raised her mouth to whisper in his ear. She could smell the light clean scent of his hair; he smelled of the real world, of normality, of a young man. She felt desire as if it were the only real thing in a dangerous world filled with mysteries. It was as if the only thing that was real, the only thing that she could trust, was Luca. 'I think they had made a homunculus,' she breathed.

He froze at the word and turned to face her. 'Would that be what they meant by saying they were making life?'

Her eyes dark with fear, she nodded. 'Perhaps. I don't know.'

'What was it like?'

'Like a tiny man, like a horrible tiny man. I thought it was a lizard but it was a person, a tiny, tiny person. It was in the bell jar. I think they had made it in the jar. Jacinta was trying to get it away, but when the bell jar broke, Freize took it up and passed it through the hatch to me.'

'Why? Why did Freize save it?'

A ghost of a smile touched her lips. 'Because that's what he's like; because he's Freize,' she said. 'If it called out to him, he would have to answer. It wanted to be in the canal. Freize had put it in his cap. I held the cap to the edge of the canal and it jumped out.' She shivered. 'I didn't throw it in,' she said quickly. 'I wasn't trying to drown it. He told me to set it free. It jumped in and then it dived down, like a fish, and then it was gone.' She gave a deep shudder.

'What?' Luca asked.

'Luca, it wasn't like a fish, it was just like a child. I saw its face as it bobbed in the canal. It took a breath and then dived down. I saw its rump and the soles of its little feet as it went down. Like a child but tiny, as small as a rat, but swimming like a man. Horrible.' She gave a shuddering sob. 'It was horrible.'

He held her closer as she trembled. 'And then?'

790

She raised her head and spoke so that the others could hear her. 'I dived into the water and I swam round to the side canal beside the Nacari house. I waited in the water. I kept down low. I saw the Doge's guards bring Freize out in manacles. He was walking all right, he was not hurt; but he looked dazed. They put him into their galley, the guards' galley with a wooden prison at the back, and I ducked down below the water to let them go past me into the Grand Canal, then I swam out too. I swam for a long time until a fisherman picked me up and brought me back here.'

She turned her face to Luca's shoulder. 'It was terrible,' she said with a little moan of fear. 'It was really terrible, Luca, being in the water and knowing that the little thing was in the water too. I was afraid it would come on the fishing boat with me. I was watching the oars in case it climbed on board. I was afraid it would follow me home.'

She gave a shaky sob. 'I kept waiting for the touch of its little hand in my hair,' she whispered. 'I thought it would hold on to me and make me bring it home.'

He tightened his grip on her. He held her close, her face against his neck, so that she could not see the horror on his own face, the fear of the unknown, the ancient fear of the creature which is not of earth or air, which is not beast, fish or fowl.

'What if it's a golem?' she breathed.

He composed himself and faced her. 'There is no such thing,' he said staunchly. 'It's not like you to frighten yourself with imaginary fears, Ishraq! It was a lizard, or a plucked bird, or something like that. It won't come after you. It can't have swum. It will have drowned in the canal. It's nothing. You're safe.'

He turned from her, as if the matter was closed, and to Brother Peter he said: 'We'll have to go and get Freize out. We'll probably have to say who we are to clear our names. We'll have to take our papers from Milord. Will you come with me?'

Brother Peter nodded, appalled at the whole situation. 'I'll get my cape. The young ladies should go to their rooms, and stay there.' He looked severely at them both. 'If anyone comes at all don't admit them. Don't say anything, and don't show yourselves. The Doge's guard will stay at the watergate but don't speak to him.' He scowled at Ishraq. 'Don't you go diving out of the window,' he said crossly. 'Just wait here till we get back, and try not to cause more trouble.'

~

The guard at the watergate had been reinforced by a second man and they had clearly been ordered to allow anyone from the household to go to the city magistrates.

'Do you think they were waiting for us to confess?' Luca asked Brother Peter quietly, as the two guardsmen took their seats in the gondola at prow and stern.

'Yes,' Brother Peter replied shortly.

'They were waiting for us to ask to go to the palace?'

'They would perhaps have ordered us to attend later, after midnight. They mostly work at night. They usually arrest people at night.'

Luca nodded, hiding his growing fear. 'Do you think that they didn't believe Isolde is the Lady of Lucretili?'

'They believed her. But they would still want to question us if they know you have been working with the forgers.'

'They can't know that,' Luca argued, denying his own doubt.

'They probably do,' Brother Peter said dourly.

There was no sound for a moment but the slap of water against the gondola's single oar, and another boatman crying: "Gondola gondola gondola!" as he made a blind turn into a small tributary canal.

'They will release Freize to us, won't they?' Luca confirmed.

'It depends on three things,' Brother Peter said drily. 'It depends on what he has done. It depends on what they think he has done. It depends on what they think that we have done.'

Giuseppe rowed the gondola just a little way up the Grand Canal and then drew up between the forest of black mooring poles in the canal at the imposing white carved front of the Doge's Palace.

'What's that?' Giuseppe suddenly demanded, startled, looking down at the glassy waters of the canal.

'What?' Brother Peter asked irritably.

He shook his head. 'I thought I saw something,' he said. 'Something like a white frog, swimming beside us. Odd.'

'Help me out,' Brother Peter said crossly. 'I have no time for this.'

Flanked by the guardsmen, Luca and Brother Peter went up the shallow steps to the quay, where the waves were slapping like a gabble of denunciations, and then the two men and the guards waited before the great palace doors, where a row of burning torches showed their pale faces to the sentries.

'I need to consult the Council of Ten,' Luca said with

793

more confidence than he felt. 'We are on business for the Pope.'

Boyishly, he feared that the man would simply ignore him, but the sentry saluted and pushed open a low door cut inside the great ceremonial gate, and Luca and Brother Peter ducked their heads and went through.

At once they caught their breaths. They were in a massive courtyard, big enough to house an army, as broad and wide as a square of the city: the heart of the Doge's Palace. On their left was a great wall of red brick pierced by white windows, new-built and all but completed. Ahead of them was a white stone façade and behind that the towering bulk of the Doge's own chapel, the massive church of San Marco. On their right was a wall as high as a white cliff, studded with windows. It was the Doge's Palace, the heart of government, and all the offices. Most of the windows showed a light – the Republic never slept, business was always pressing; and spying and justice were done best at night. The whole courtyard was ringed by a square colonnade studded with huge white towers. Above the colonnade rose a series of narrow windows, placed one set on top of the other in the three tall storeys. It was as if all four walls of the palace were staring down at them with blank accusing eyes.

Two guards came towards them and guided them to the building on their right, and led the way up the stone staircase. Luca found he was growing more and more apprehensive with every step he took. At the top of the stairs, the guard tapped on the huge wooden door, and a smaller door swung open. A man dressed in the black robes of a clerk, seated on a small plain chair at a wooden desk, beckoned them in.

'I am Brother Peter, I serve the Order of Darkness under the command of the Holy Father. We are ordered to inquire into the end of days and all heresies and signs of the end of the world. This is Luca Vero, one of the Inquirers.' Brother Peter was breathless by the end of his introduction, it made him sound nervous and guilty.

'I know who you are,' the clerk said shortly. To the guards before and behind them, he said simply: 'Take them to the magistrates. They're expected.'

One guard led the way through the narrow passage, the other followed behind. Luca was certain that they were being observed, that the lattice work in the wood panelling in the walls served as a window for another room and that an inquisitor was watching them walk by, and judging their anxious faces. Luca tried to smile and stride confidently, but then thought he must appear as if he were playing a part, as if he had something to hide.

The corridor twisted round and round; clearly they were threading between secret rooms, their footsteps muffled on the uneven wooden floors. As they walked, dozens of half wild cats scattered before them, as if these tunnels were their home. They stopped before a great door, where a silent sentry stood. The man nodded and stood aside, opened the door only to reveal a second closed door behind. He tapped, it swung open, and Luca and Brother Peter went into the room where three magistrates, wearing dark robes, were seated behind a great polished table. To the side, four clerks were seated around a smaller table. There was a fire in the fireplace for the comfort of the magistrates but it did not heat the room, which was miserably cold.

The double doors swung shut, first the inner one with a sharp bang, then the outer door with a dull thud, making the room soundproof, almost airtight. Luca and Brother Peter stood before the table in complete silence.

At last, the magistrate in the central seat looked up at them. 'Can I help you, my lords?' he asked politely. 'You want to give evidence to us?'

Luca swallowed. 'I am Luca Vero, an Inquirer for the Order of Darkness, sanctioned by the Holy Father himself to investigate the rise of heresy, the danger of the infidel, and the threats to Christendom. This is my clerk and advisor, Brother Peter.'

Blandly, the three regarded Luca. Moving as one, they turned their heads to look at Brother Peter, and then back again.

'My servant was in the course of making an inquiry for me at the house of an alchemist, Drago Nacari,' Luca went on. 'He was arrested by the Venice guard. He has done nothing wrong. I have come to request his release.'

The magistrate glanced at his two colleagues. 'We were expecting you,' he said ominously. 'We have been watching you for some days.'

Luca and Brother Peter exchanged one aghast look, but said nothing.

'Your papers? To prove your identity?' One of the clerks rose up from the table and held out his hand.

Brother Peter produced the papers from his satchel and the clerk glanced at them. 'All in order,' he said briefly to the silent men at the table. He offered to pass them over the table but they waved them away. Clearly, they were too important to bother with letters of authority.

'Authorised by the Holy Father himself,' Brother Peter repeated.

The clerk nodded, unimpressed by the status of the Church. Uniquely in all of Christendom, all the administrators of Venice were laymen. They had not been recruited and trained by the Church; they served the Republic before they served Rome. Luca and Brother Peter had the misfortune of being in the only city in Europe where their papers would not command immediate respect and help.

'So you are not, as you claimed, servants in the household of the Lady Isolde of Lucretili,' the clerk observed.

'No,' Luca said shortly.

The clerk made a small note as if to record Isolde's lie.

'And what was your business with Drago Nacari, the counterfeiter?' the magistrate seated in the centre of the table asked quietly.

'We didn't know that he was a counterfeiter at first,' Luca said honestly. 'As you see from our instructions, we were on a mission to find the source of the gold nobles. The lord of our Order had told us to come here, to pass as merchant traders, to find whether the nobles were good or fake, and if they were fake, where they had come from.'

'Did you not think to inform us?' was the question from the magistrate on the left.

'We were going to inform you,' Luca replied carefully. 'As you see from our orders, we were commanded to inform you as soon as we had evidence to give to you. Indeed, we were on our way to inform you when our own palazzo was raided, and we were put under house arrest. Then we agreed that we should come and talk with you at dawn. But when our own servant was arrested by you this night, we had to come and disturb you – even though it was so late.'

'Considerate,' the third man said shortly. 'Did you not think to inform us before you began your inquiry? When you arrived in our city looking for counterfeit gold? When you started questioning our merchants and deceiving our bankers? When you started buying counterfeit gold, trading in it, and profiting from the deception? Withholding information which would have affected the price?'

'Of course not,' Brother Peter said smoothly. 'We were obeying the orders of the lord of our Order. We did not know what we might find. If we had found nothing, we would have been very wrong to disturb the confidence of your traders.'

'They are disturbed now,' the magistrate observed.

'Unfortunately, yes.'

'And what was your relationship with Drago Nacari the alchemist?' the second magistrate asked 'For we know he was an alchemist as well as a coiner.'

'He consulted me about a manuscript that he had,' Luca admitted. 'He brought it to my house for me to read, and I returned it to him.'

'And what did it say?'

'I was not able to translate it. Not at all.'

'And what was your impression of his work? When you went to his house?'

'I did not see enough to be sure,' Luca said. 'He certainly had a lot of equipment, he had a number of pieces of work in progress. He had a forge and a vat of rotting matter. He said that it was his life's work and he spoke of the philosophers' stone. But I saw nothing of such importance that I would report to my lord or to you.'

'Everyone speaks of the philosophers' stone,' the Council leader said dismissively.

Another nodded. 'It is irrelevant. He had no licence to practise here so he was a criminal on that count alone.' He paused. 'Was he trying to create a living thing?'

Luca stifled a gasp with a little choke.

Brother Peter stepped into the awkward silence. 'How could he? Only God can give life.'

Luca nodded. 'Excuse me. No. I saw nothing but some dead and dried animals and insects.'

The clerk took a meticulous note.

'So to the most important accusation: that he was coining,' the first magistrate moved on. 'Did you see any evidence of his coining?'

Luca nodded. 'He, himself, showed me the moulds for the coins. He told me that the first coins had come from John, Duke of Bedford, that he had known him long ago in Paris. First he had the duke's true coins and then here in Venice he made a batch of coins according to the duke's recipe, and planned to pass them off as good, using the duke's seal.'

'And yet still, you did not report this to us?' one of the men queried, his voice like ice. 'Counterfeiting is a crime that strikes against the very heart of the Republic. Do you know what a run on a currency can do to traders in Venice?'

Luca shook his head, thinking it wiser to stay silent.

'Ruin them. Ruin us. Ruin the greatest city in the world. And you did not think to report it at once? This criminal confessed to you and you stood in his house and saw the evidence and you did not tell us?'

'We were on our way,' Luca said. 'We were coming to you tomorrow morning. At dawn.'

There was a terrible silence. Finally, the man at the centre of the three spoke. 'Did he tell you how many chests of good coins he had released?'

Luca said: 'No.'

'Did he tell you how many forged coins? The bleeding coins, the weeping coins? They are going bad all over the city tonight. People will be hammering on the shutters of the bankers' houses, demanding their money back as soon as it is light. Nobody wants bloodstained coins. Nobody wants forgeries. How many are out there?'

Brother Peter cleared his throat. 'We were coming to you with the evidence against the forgers at dawn tomorrow. Of course we were going to report all that we knew as soon as we had evidence. We were prevented by the charges laid by Lady Carintha. But we don't know how many coins.'

'But you were able to send your servant out of the house though you were under arrest?' one of the men said silkily. 'In that gravest moment, you did not send him to us to warn us that the coins were melting and bleeding. In that crucial moment you sent him to them – to the alchemists. Why did you do that?'

Luca opened his mouth to speak, four⁻ʲ he had nothing to say, and closed it again.

'Your own officer saw the coins bleed,' Brother Peter said feebly. 'He must have reported to you? He must have sent men to arrest the money changer and the counterfeiter?'

The door to the right of them opened and Freize stood in the opening. His clothes were torn, and he had a black eye and a bruise on his forehead. Someone pushed him from behind, and he took a stumbling step into the room. Luca exclaimed and would have gone forwards, but Brother Peter put a firm hand on Luca's shoulder and held him back.

'Freize!' Luca exclaimed.

'I'm all right,' he said. 'Took a bit of a kicking, that's all.'

'He resisted arrest,' the clerk said to the gentlemen at the table. 'He's nothing more than bruised. He has been held in the inquiry room since his arrest. He hasn't been harmed.'

'Did you send him, this servant of yours, to warn the forger? So that they could get away before our men arrested them?' the head of the Council asked Luca directly, and at once all the clerks paused, their pens poised, ready to write the incriminating confession.

'No! Of course not!' Luca said quickly. He tried to smile reassuringly at Freize but found his mouth was too strained.

'What did you send him for then? Why did he go?'

'I went,' Freize said suddenly. 'I went of my own accord, to see the pretty lass.'

All three heads of the magistrates turned to Freize. 'You went to warn her?' one of them asked him.

Luca could see the trap that Freize was walking towards. 'No!' he said anxiously. 'No he didn't!'

'I went to see her,' Freize said. 'My lord didn't send me. I went of my own accord. I didn't know they were going to be arrested, I didn't know they had done anything wrong. I didn't know anything about them at all really, all I knew was that I had taken a fancy to her. I thought I'd make a visit.' Freize scrunched his battered face into an ingratiating grin.

One of the clerks raised his head and remarked quietly to the leader of the magistrates, 'He escaped from the palace after the guards had gone in. He must have known the alchemists would be arrested next. He took a rowing boat and went straight to them.'

'They got away in the boat that you rowed to them,' the second Council man said. 'You helped them escape, even if you did not go to warn them.'

'Oh for heaven's sake! I asked him to go,' Brother Peter said suddenly, very clearly and as if he were wearied beyond bearing. 'He went at my request to collect some potion for me. I wanted the medicine before they were arrested. Nobody knew about it but me and the alchemist and then this ... this dolt. If he had any sense, when he had seen your guards at the door he would have come away, but he pressed on, to get me my ... er ... potion. And so got himself arrested, injured, and exposed us to this difficulty and me to this terrible embarrassment.'

Everyone looked from Brother Peter's scarlet face to Freize, who kept his eyes on the floor and said nothing.

'And now he's lying to try to protect me from my embarrassment,' Brother Peter said, torn between fury and shame. 'Of course, it only makes it worse. Fool that he is. The alchemist had promised me a – er – a potion. For my – er – affliction.'

'I didn't know you were ill?' Luca exclaimed.

'I didn't want anybody to know anything!' Brother Peter exclaimed, a man at the end of his patience. 'I must have been mad to trust Freize with such a delicate mission. It was a matter of urgency for me . . . I should have gone myself . . . and now . . . Now I wish I had never consulted the alchemist at all.'

'What potion?' one of the magistrates asked.

'I would rather not say,' Brother Peter replied, his gaze on the floor, his ears burning red.

'This is an inquiry into a counterfeiting forge which has had more impact on the safety of the Republic than anything else in a decade!' The magistrate at the end of the table slammed his hand down and swore. 'I think you had better say at once!'

The colour drained from Brother Peter's face. 'I am ashamed to say,' he said in little more than a whisper. 'It reflects so badly on me, on my vows, and on my Order.'

His misery was completely convincing. The leader of the three leaned forward and said to the clerks: 'You will not record this.' To Brother Peter he said: 'You may speak in confidence. If I decide, nothing will go beyond these walls. But you must tell us everything. What potion did you order from the alchemist?'

Brother Peter turned his face from Freize and Luca.

'Shall I order them from the room?'

'They can stay. I am shamed. This is my punishment. They will think me a fool, an old fool.'

'Tell us what you ordered, then.'

'A love potion,' Brother Peter said, his voice very low.

'A love potion?' the man repeated, astounded.

'Yes.'

'A man in your position? In holy orders? On a papal mission? Advising an Inquirer of the Holy Father?'

'Yes. I had fallen into sin and folly. This is why I am so ashamed. This is why this fool is trying to hide his mission. To save me from this shame.'

'Why did you want a love potion?'

Brother Peter's head was bowed so low that his chin was almost on his chest. The bald spot of his tonsure shone in the candlelight. He was completely wretched. 'I was very attracted by Lady Carintha,' he said quietly. 'But I have no . . .' he broke off and struggled to find the words. 'I have no . . . manly abilities. I have no . . . vigour.'

The three magistrates were leaning forward, the clerks frozen, their pens held above the paper.

'I thought Drago Nacari could make me a potion so that she would be drawn to me, despite herself. And if she were disposed to be kind to me – she is such a high-spirited lady – I would want to be man enough for her.' He glanced briefly at the table of gentlemen. 'You can ask her if I was not attracted by her, dazzled by her. She knew it. She knows well enough what she can do to a man. My fear was that I would be unable to respond.'

Two of the magistrates nodded as if they had experienced Lady Carintha's high spirits for themselves, and sympathised with Brother Peter's fears.

'I have little experience with women,' Brother Peter said, his voice a thread, his eyes on the floor. 'Almost none. But I imagined she would want a man who could . . . who would … I feared that if she were to look kindly on me I would not be man enough for her.'

One of the magistrates cleared his throat. 'Understandable,' he said shortly.

'I was a fool,' Brother Peter admitted. 'And a sinful fool. But God spared me the worst of it, for the foolish servant I sent to get the love potion was caught while he was carrying out my sinful errand. And besides, Lady Carintha has turned against all of us. She'll never look at me again.'

'But you knew they were coiners?' one man persisted.

Brother Peter dropped to one knee and rested his forehead against the table. 'That's the worst of it. That's why I sent Freize then. I knew they were the coiners of the false coins, and that once you had found the money changer Israel you would find them. I wanted my love potion before they were arrested. That's why I ordered Freize to go at once, although I knew it was dangerous for him to be found with them. I put him at risk for my own selfish … lust.'

The gentleman rounded on Freize. 'Is that what you were doing there?'

Freize gulped. 'Yes, just as my lord says.'

'Why didn't you tell us at once?'

'Discreet,' Freize said. 'Lamentably discreet. Against my own interests sometimes.'

The three magistrates put their heads together in a swift exchange of words. 'Release him,' the leader of the Council said. 'No charge.'

He rose to his feet. 'If we catch Drago Nacari and his accomplice the young woman then they will be charged as coiners and counterfeiters and you will have to give evidence against them,' he ruled.

'We will,' Brother Peter promised, rising to his feet, his face still downturned.

'In the meantime, we have serious work to do. We are going to have to release reserves of gold to the banks. Everyone is selling gold nobles and everyone wants pure gold instead. The price of nobles is falling to that of piccoli. Our citizens and our traders will lose fortunes in the first hour that they open for business. And now the Ottoman Empire is refusing to take any English coins at all – good as well as bad. We are having to make good what those wicked coiners have done. It will cost us a fortune.'

'I am very sorry that we did not catch them earlier,' Luca said. 'It was our intention, it was our mission.'

The Council nodded. 'Then you have miserably failed in your mission,' the leader said icily. 'You can tell the lord of your Order that you are incompetent and a danger to yourselves and others. And you,' he turned to Brother Peter, 'you failed in your vows. You will no doubt confess and serve a hard penance. You seem to be shamed and you should be ashamed. We are very displeased with all three of you; but there are no legal charges as yet. It seems that you are fools but not criminals. You are incompetent idiots but not wicked.'

'Thank you,' Luca muttered. Brother Peter was too crushed to speak.

'Go then,' the Council leader said, and Luca, Brother Peter and Freize bowed in the contemptuous silence and turned and filed from the room.

~

Not a word passed between them as they crossed the broad

quay from the front door of the ducal palace and got into the rocking gondola. Freize gripped Luca's hand as Luca helped him into the boat, but the two young men said nothing.

Brother Peter drew up the hood of his robe and sat hunched, in the prow of the boat, his back to the other men as they paddled swiftly down the canal and turned in the palazzo watergate and Giuseppe brought the gondola to the quayside.

The guard had already gone from the watergate and there was no soldier on the street door. Luca called up to the girls' level: 'Isolde! Ishraq! We're back!' and heard the girls cross the floor above and come down the stairs as they went into the dining room.

The two girls came in and looked at the three silent men, at Freize's bruised face and Brother Peter's dark expression. Isolde closed the door behind them. 'What has happened?' she asked fearfully.

Luca shook his head. 'I swear that I don't know,' he said. He glanced uncertainly at Brother Peter. 'Perhaps we should never speak of it,' he said carefully.

Brother Peter rounded on him, exploding with rage. 'Fool!' he said. 'Call yourself an Inquirer? And you could not see a lie as wide as that damned canal and twice as deep?'

Isolde recoiled in shock at Brother Peter's rage but Freize went towards him and bowed, with his hand on his heart. 'I thank you,' he said. 'It was the last thing that I expected you to say. I could do nothing but stare like a dolt.'

'Indeed, I was certain that you would play the part of a dolt very well,' Brother Peter said nastily.

Isolde took Freize's hand and turned him towards the candlelight to look at his damaged face. 'They hurt you?'

she said quietly. Gently she touched his cheek. 'Oh Freize! Did they beat you?'

'Not much,' Freize said. 'But Brother Peter here saved me from hanging.'

'Saved you?' Luca asked, still shaken by Brother Peter's abuse.

'Of course,' Brother Peter said roundly. 'Did you really think that I was in the least attracted to that well-hung limb of Satan? Did you really think that I would send an idiot like Freize to a crook like Drago Nacari for a love potion? Do you think that I am a fool like Freize? Like you? To lose my head for a pretty face? And that one not so pretty anyway?'

Luca shook his head, slowly understanding. 'I believed you when you spoke before the Council,' he said. 'Call me a fool, but I believed every word that you said.'

'Then you had better learn the skill to look into men's hearts even when they are lying,' Brother Peter said. 'For you cannot be an Inquirer if you can be fooled by a charade like that.'

'You lied to save Freize?' Isolde asked, grasping the main essential. 'You pretended that you had sent him to the Nacaris for a love potion?' Her voice quavered on a laugh and she tried to keep her face straight, but failed. 'You confessed to lust, Brother Peter? And to needing a love potion?'

Brother Peter would not speak while Ishraq collapsed into giggles. Isolde started to laugh too and Luca gritted his teeth to stop himself from joining them. But Brother Peter and Freize were still grave.

'You laid down your reputation for my safety,' Freize said to him. 'I thank you. I owe you my life.'

Brother Peter nodded.

'You made a great sacrifice for Freize,' Isolde said, recovering from her laughter as she understood the importance of what Brother Peter had done. 'You made yourself look like a fool for him. That's a great thing for you, Brother Peter. That is a great gift you have given for Freize.'

'And you told a lie,' Ishraq wondered.

'I was not on oath, they did not ask me in the name of God,' Brother Peter specified. 'And they were quick to believe that a thin old clerk would dabble in such rubbish for lust of a well-used Venetian matron. I would have hoped that Luca might have thought better of me – but apparently not.'

'I am sorry,' Luca apologised awkwardly. 'I should have guessed at once, but I was overwhelmed . . . and I couldn't think.'

Brother Peter sighed as if they were all of them, equally unbearable. 'We'll say no more about it,' he said stiffly, and left the room.

'He is remarkable,' Isolde said as the door closed on him.

'Saints witness it – he was impressive,' Luca agreed with her. 'He was completely convincing.'

'He admires me,' Freize said confidentially to Ishraq. 'He finds it hard to admit, being a man who thinks very highly of himself – but he thinks very highly of me. This is the proof of it.' He paused. 'And I think very well of him,' he said with the air of a man giving credit where it was due.

~

Venice was seized with panic the next day as soon as the banks opened their doors and the traders set up their stalls.

Ishraq and Isolde hurried to San Marco, with their purse of gold nobles, hoping that they might find someone who would change it into ducats, even into silver, but found all the money changers closed. The church itself was crowded with people on their knees praying for their fortunes, terrified of poverty, terrified that they would be stuck with the worthless gold nobles. The gold coins were sticky with a red rust like blood in every other purse.

Luca, Freize and Brother Peter went to the Rialto by gondola and found the shops were closed and shuttered and all the money changers were absent from their stalls. Nobody wanted anything but true tested gold, and there was no gold to be had.

The great banking houses on San Giacomo Square had only one shutter open at each entrance and they were changing gold for limited numbers of coins, so much for each customer, refusing anything which was stained or wet, desperately afraid that their own reserves would run out.

'I have gold, I have plenty of gold,' Luca heard one of the clerks say at the window. 'There is no need to fear. My lord has gone to fetch more from his country estate. He will be back tomorrow. The bank is good. You need not change all your nobles now. You can change them tomorrow. There is no need to press, there is no need to panic.'

'Tomorrow the value of the English nobles will be as nothing!' the man shouted back at him, and the crowd behind him elbowed each other out of the way and shouted for their turn. 'Even worse than now!'

'I will pay tomorrow,' the clerk insisted. 'You don't have to change them today.'

'Now!' the people shouted. 'Now! Take the English nobles! You were quick enough to sell them! Now buy them back.'

A band of the Doge's guards came swiftly in a galley, trumpet blowing, and marched up the steps into the square. The officer unfurled a proclamation.

'Citizens! You are to disperse!' he shouted. 'The Doge himself promises that there is enough gold. He himself will lend gold to the bankers. Your coins will be exchanged for gold. We will bring the gold from the Doge's treasure stores this afternoon. Disperse now, and go back to your homes. This unrest is bad for everyone.'

'The rate!' someone yelled at him. 'It's no good to me that the banks have gold tomorrow if they won't buy the nobles at today's rate. What's the rate?'

The officer swallowed. 'The rate has been set,' he said. 'The rate has been set.'

'At what?' someone shouted.

He showed them the sealed proclamation, holding it high above his head so that it fluttered in the light spring wind. 'The Doge himself has set the rate that he will pay to all Venetian citizens. He will pay a third of a ducat for every English noble, and so will all the Venetian banks,' he said.

The crowd was suddenly silent, as if at news of a death. Then there was a long slow groan as if everyone was suddenly sick to the belly. It was a moan as everyone in the crowd realised that the fortune they had made in speculating in the English nobles was gone, had gone overnight. Each English noble was now valued at a third of a ducat, though it had been three ducats only yesterday. The merchants who had bought hundreds of English nobles, selling their gold, other currencies and even goods, were staring at ruin.

'The Doge has gold enough to do this?' Luca asked.

'They have to buy back the English nobles one way or another, they have to set a rate or nobody will trade at all. The people will bring down the banks with their demands for gold. This crowd isn't far from riot.'

'This is terrible,' Luca said.

Brother Peter looked at him. 'This is the value of reputation,' he said. 'You saw Lady Isolde defend her reputation. You saw me devalue my reputation yesterday.' He looked at the crowd which was dwindling as the merchants went into their houses, slamming the doors, and the smaller traders walked to stand beside the canal, stunned with shock, trying to face their own ruin in the sparkling surface of the bright waters. 'This is how the market works,' he said. 'Great gains always mean great losses later, and then probably gains again. This is usury. This is why a good man does not play the market. It always brings wealth to a few but poverty to many.'

He grabbed Luca's shoulder and turned him to face the deserted square and a man sobbing with his mouth open wide, drooling with grief and horror. 'Look and understand. This is not what happens when the market goes wrong: this is what happens when the market works. Sudden profit followed by sudden ruin: this is what is supposed to happen. This is the real world. The days when a noble doubled in price overnight were the chimera. The profit is the fantastic dream. The loss is the reality.'

Luca nodded, then his face suddenly clouded. 'The ransom!' he gasped. He turned on his heel and hurried to the Rialto Bridge where Father Pietro usually set up his stall. The low post that he used as a stool was empty, half the stalls on the Rialto Bridge were closed. It was as if everyone was afraid to spend money in any currency.

'Have you seen Father Pietro today?' Luca asked a woman as she was passing by.

Silently, she shook her head and went on.

'Have you seen Father Pietro?' Luca asked a merchant.

He ducked away from the question as if an answer would be too costly.

'We'll come back later,' Brother Peter ruled. 'See if he is here later.'

'It's the ransom for my father,' Luca said, trying to escape the feeling of growing dread. 'They wanted to be paid in English nobles. We sent the money in English nobles as they asked.'

'When did the messenger leave?' Brother Peter asked.

'Yesterday,' Luca said blankly. 'Before dusk.'

'Then perhaps he has kept ahead of the news, and is even now paying the slave owner and your father is safe in his keeping. The messenger is ahead of it. The news has to get from Venice. They might have done the trade already and your father might be safe right now.'

'I should send pure gold, in case the nobles bleed.' Luca took a step forwards to the bank and then fell back, realising that he could not even obtain gold, the banks did not have it; and that he had nothing to buy gold but the dishonoured English nobles.

His young face was gaunt with shock. 'Brother Peter, we put all of Milord's fortune into the nobles. We are ruined with everyone else. We have lost all of Milord's money and I cannot buy gold to free my father!'

Brother Peter's face was sternly grave. 'We gambled, and we have lost,' he said. 'We pretended we were wealthy and now we are poor.'

'I'll have to wait,' Luca said aloud to himself. 'I'll have to wait. I can't see what else to do. I swore I would free my father and now ... I'll have to wait. Perhaps ... but I'll have to wait. There's nothing else to do.'

'Pray,' Brother Peter advised him.

~

They got home to find Freize and the girls sitting before a simple meal of soup and bread. 'The market is almost closed,' Isolde said. 'The stallholders will only accept silver and the price of everything is sky-high.'

Ishraq looked ill with shock. 'They won't take English nobles, not even if you weigh them against gold in front of them, on the spice scales,' she said. 'Even if they can see that the nobles are solid gold they won't trade with them. You can't even buy vegetables with them. They say that nobody knows what they are worth, and now they are saying they are unlucky coins. Nobody can tell a coin that bleeds from one that is good. Nobody wants anything. I sold Isolde's mother's rubies for dross. I ruined her.'

Isolde put her hand on Ishraq's shoulder. 'Don't blame yourself,' she said quietly. 'We're no worse off than everyone else in Venice.'

'Everyone else who was greedy enough to try to trade in coins,' Ishraq said bitterly. 'I kept those jewels safe through a flood, through a robbery and through the criminals of the nunnery. And then I robbed you myself.'

'Enough,' Brother Peter said quietly. 'You have done no

worse than the great men of business. We'll see what gold you can get for the coins tomorrow, when the Doge releases his treasure. You can go out early. Freize can take you to the money changers at dawn.'

Ishraq nodded, her face still downcast. 'We know what we'll get,' she said miserably. 'One ducat to three nobles. And I sold the rubies when it was almost the other way round.'

'We have work to do,' Brother Peter said to Luca.

'What?' Luca said. He found he was exhausted, sick with worry about the ransom for his father. He could not even bring himself to remind Ishraq that he shared her failure. Actually, he had been more foolish than her, trading in Milord's fortune for English nobles, trying to buy his father's freedom in forged currency, ruining himself and betraying his father.

'We have to write to Milord,' Brother Peter ruled. 'We'll have to tell him what has happened here. And I will have to put it into code before you sign it. We should get the report sent today. Better that he hears from us than from someone else in Venice.'

'Who reports to him from Venice?' Freize asked, looking up from his bowl of soup.

'I don't know,' Brother Peter replied. 'But someone will.'

Luca sat at the table and drew the ink and pen and paper close. 'I hardly know where to begin,' he said.

'From the end of the last report. We had told him that we had located the forgers and were going to report them,' Brother Peter reminded him.'He is bound to be very displeased that we did not report them.'

'We found the counterfeiters but we let them go.' Luca

listed their mistakes. 'We put all of Milord's fortune into English nobles and they are now worth only a tiny part of their former price. We have lost him a fortune.'

'And by letting the counterfeiters go and the currency fail we have ruined many good men and destroyed confidence in Venice,' Brother Peter added. 'I have never been involved in such a disastrous inquiry before.'

'What will he do?' Luca asked nervously.

Brother Peter shrugged. 'I don't know. I've never failed so badly. I've never been with an Inquirer who failed to report a crime, who associated with the criminals and who disobeyed orders.'

There was a terrible silence. 'I am sorry,' Luca said awkwardly. 'I am sorry for failing the Order, and him, and you.'

To his surprise, Brother Peter raised his head and gave Luca one of his rare smiles. 'You need not apologise to me,' he said. 'You pursued the truth as you always do – steadily and persistently, with flashes of quite remarkable insight. But the truth is that speculation and profiteering and trade is a rotten business, and it falls in on itself like a rotten apple, eaten out by maggots. Milord knows this as well as you and I. He sent us into a city of vanities and we have seen its ugly side. We have done nothing wrong ourselves, but we have followed his orders in a sinful world. If we had reported the coiners earlier they still might have got away. It was Ishraq and Freize who helped them escape – not us who belong to the Order. And even if we could have stopped them earlier, we would have been too late – they had already released the bad coins into the market by the time we knew. They had released the coins before we even got here. We were too late to prevent it.'

'I thank you,' Luca said awkwardly. 'You are generous to overlook my mistakes. You wanted to report the forgers earlier, and you were right. We should have done that. And I thank you for saving Freize.'

Brother Peter turned his head away. 'We won't talk of that,' he said. 'We won't put that in the report.'

~

Next day Isolde was waiting for Luca in the dining room when he came down to breakfast. 'I couldn't sleep for thinking about your father,' she said. 'I have been praying that they ransomed him before they had the news about the nobles.'

Luca's handsome young face was drawn. 'I couldn't sleep either,' he said. 'And we will have to wait until Sext to see Father Pietro, if he comes today. He may not come at all.'

'Let's go to church and pray,' she said. 'And then we could walk to the Rialto. May I come with you?'

Luca shrugged. 'Since nobody cares who we are any more, I don't see why you shouldn't come with me.'

'I want to come with you,' she said.

'We'll all go,' he said, his mind on his father.

Tentatively, she reached out to him, but he had already turned away to call up the stairs for Freize. His back was turned to her, he did not even feel her touch when she gently kissed the fingers of her hand and pressed the kiss to the cuff of his sleeve.

~

The moment that the five of them stepped out of the house it was apparent that some fresh disaster had hit the city.

People were gathered on street corners, their faces grave. Everyone was whispering as if there had been a death in the city. The gondoliers were not singing; the boats were busy on the canal, but there were no cries of people selling their goods. Everyone had laid aside their bright costumes, there was no spirit of carnival in the ruined city: Lent had come early to Venice this spring, early and cold.

'What now?' Luca demanded anxiously.

All five of them walked quickly to the Piazza San Marco and found that many of the merchants were assembled in the square already, and many of the foreign traders, their costumes bright, their slaves around them, were waiting on the quayside before the Doge's Palace. The balcony before the Doge's window was draped with flags and standards. 'Looks like he is going to speak to the people,' Brother Peter said. 'We'd better wait and hear what he is going to say.'

Freize and Luca put the two young women between them, anxious about the push and sway of the growing crowd. 'What d'you think is happening?' Isolde said quietly to Luca.

He shook his head.

'Will it be about the gold nobles?'

'Surely not. Since the Doge has already set the price, what more is there to say?'

There was the bright shout of a trumpet fanfare and the Doge stepped out from the windows onto the balcony and raised his hand to acknowledge the crowd. Slowly, he took off his distinctive hat and bowed.

'He is a citizen of Venice just as they all are,' Brother Peter explained. 'It's a most extraordinary system. He's not a king or a lord, he is one of the citizens, they choose him for the post. So he shows that he is in their service. He goes bareheaded to them.'

In reply, the crowd took off their hats. Isolde and Ishraq made a little curtsey and stood still.

'I am sorry that I have bad news for us all,' the Doge said, his voice so loud and steady that even the men at the furthest edge of the crowd could hear him.

'As you know, the gold nobles which were being made in this city, without our knowledge or consent, have failed us. The bleeding nobles can be exchanged for three gold nobles to a ducat. At no more than thirty nobles per man a day.'

There was a little whisper that ran through the crowd, but most people had heard the proclamation yesterday, this was old bad news.

'I have today had a public complaint from the ambassador of the Ottoman Empire,' the Doge went on. At once a complete silence fell on the square, someone at the back moaned and was still. The Ottoman Empire was the greatest power in the world. The uneasy peace between the Ottoman Empire and Venice was essential if the city were to survive. The Ottomans commanded the Mediterranean Sea and the Black Sea. Their armies had occupied the lands to the east of Venice. If the Ottoman ambassador was unhappy then the city was on the brink of terrible danger.

'It seems that the Christian countries that pay tribute to the Ottoman Empire have this year all paid their debt in gold nobles,' the Doge said. 'Alas ...' he paused. 'Alas,' he said again. There was a low groan from the crowd.

'Alas for us. The Ottomans believe that we have

knowingly given them worthless dross. So they say that we have failed to pay them the proper tribute as agreed. They say that we agreed to pay in gold nobles but we have sent them rust.'

There was a low gasp from every man in the crowd. Failure to pay tribute to the Ottomans would call down an immediate and powerful punishment on all the tribute states. It could cause a renewed war and thousands would die before the unstoppable Ottoman armies.

'Therefore the Council and I have decided that we will redeem the failed English nobles from the Ottomans also, and that we will pay them the same as we pay to you: a third of a ducat for each noble. They will only get a small portion of tribute this year, and we hope that they will understand that this is all we can do.'

There was a moan like a breeze blowing through Piazza San Marco. Someone started crying in fear, and a man walked blankly away from the rear of the crowd, knowing that his homeland would be ruined, and that there was nothing he could do to prevent it.

'We are therefore raising a tax on every house in Venice, to help us meet these great debts,' the Doge said steadily. 'I, and every member of the Council, will pay, and will loan the city more gold from our own fortunes. I urge you all to pay in full, pay in gold, for the sake of our city and great republic. If you have to use your wife's jewellery then do so, if you have to take the gold leaf from your furniture then do so, if you have to cut off the handles from your gold gates then do so. I shall take my wife's jewellery, my mother's jewellery. I shall take the gold leaf from my throne. I shall take the gold handles from my doors and sell the masterpieces from my walls. We must all surrender our most beloved treasures. This is our time of need; you must answer. God bless you and God save Venice.'

'Amen,' the crowd said with one low voice, and the Doge turned on his heel and went, bareheaded, back inside the palace.

Isolde turned to Luca, and saw that he was white with shock.

'Come,' Brother Peter said shortly, and led the way back to the palazzo.

'I must go to the Rialto and see Father Pietro . . .' Luca protested.

'No! We have to do something first.'

'Brother Peter?'

'Come!'

'What?' Ishraq trotted beside him, trying to keep up with his long strides. 'What's so important?'

'Milord gave me some orders that I was to open the moment that I learned that the territories were going to default on their tribute.'

'He knew this was going to happen?' Ishraq suddenly stopped. 'Milord knew that the territories would use bad coin?'

'He can't have known that,' Brother Peter strode on, unhesitating. 'How could anyone know that? But he was prepared for it. He was prepared for anything on this mission. In the event of there being a default he gave me some orders to open. We have to open them now.'

Isolde and Luca were half running to keep up with Brother Peter's great strides. Luca caught at Isolde's hand,

and kept pace with him. Freize came swiftly behind them.

'How does he know such things?' Freize demanded of himself. 'Those sealed orders? How does he write them ahead of time. Just to torment me?'

Brother Peter pushed through the crowd to get to the side entrance and enter the palazzo.

He went without hesitating, upstairs to his bedroom and brought the sealed orders out to the rest of them in the dining room. Luca pulled out chairs for Isolde and Ishraq and then seated himself at the head of the table. Freize dropped onto a stool near to the door. 'The sealed orders,' he said irritably. 'Always. Out they come. Always bad news.'

Brother Peter took no notice of anyone. He broke the seal and spread the paper on the table. He frowned and pushed it over to Luca. 'You read,' he said. 'You can translate the code much quicker than I.'

Luca took the paper, scowled for a moment, and then slowly read aloud.

'*In the event of the territories failing to pay tribute to the Ottoman overlords, you are to take this note to the Hungarian ambassador, show him the seal, and authorise them to buy the false coins with the gold that they have in store. You are to take this note to the Comarino family and authorise them to use their private gold store to buy the false coins. You yourself are to use whatever coins and whatever gold you have to buy the English nobles at the lowest price you can offer for them. You will not sell any English gold nobles that you have. If the ship comes in after you have read these orders, you will use all the cargo to buy the devalued English gold nobles at the lowest price possible.*'

Luca stopped reading and put down the paper. 'Has he gone mad?'

'But everyone else is selling gold nobles, for far less than their value,' Isolde said. 'Everyone is selling: not buying.'

'They have no value,' Ishraq pointed out.

'What do we do?' Luca asked.

'As he orders,' Brother Peter said wearily. He rose up from the table and held out his hand for the letter for the Hungarian ambassador and for the Comarino bank. 'Shall I take these? And you buy the nobles with whatever coins we have left? And go to a bank and promise them that we will take their nobles in exchange for the cargo, when the ship comes in?'

'But why?' Ishraq asked. 'Why would Milord want us to spend good money on bad?'

Brother Peter's face was as dark as when he had confessed his pretended shame. 'I don't know,' he said. 'I don't need to know. I am to obey Milord's commands and do the work of God though it leads me into the deepest sin. I have to trust him. I have to trust his judgement. I have to obey his orders. Look what happened when we disobeyed!' He glanced up. 'Will you come with me, Freize?'

'Of course,' Freize said with his quick sympathy. He glanced at Luca. 'If I may?'

'Go,' Luca said absently. 'I'll go through the treasure chest and take what gold we have left to the money changers. There's not much, but they'll be glad to take it in return for the worthless nobles, I don't doubt.'

'But why?' Ishraq demanded. 'Why would Milord want you to buy the bleeding nobles? When everyone knows they are no good?'

'I don't ask why,' Brother Peter answered her.

'We'll help,' Isolde spoke for her and Ishraq.

'But I do! I ask why!' Ishraq exclaimed.

'I'll send the gondola back for you,' Brother Peter said heavily, and they heard him and Freize go down the stairs together to the watergate and call for Giuseppe.

Luca went into his bedroom and drew a great wooden chest out from beneath his bed. The girls followed him and watched as he opened the lid.

'You have a small fortune here,' Ishraq whispered as she saw the gold nobles in the little purses.

'I had a small fortune,' he corrected her. 'Now it is almost worthless.'

He moved the purses of the gold nobles and found beneath them a single gold bar and three gold rings.

'I'll buy your bleeding nobles from you,' Luca offered. 'If you will take the low price that Venice has set. At least I can take them off your hands.'

'No,' Ishraq said, forestalling Isolde, who was eager to accept. She turned to her friend. 'It was my mistake to try to make money on this market, but if we sell the nobles at this rate then we have lost your mother's rubies forever.

Let's hold on to our nobles, bad as they are, and see what happens. Luca's lord must be planning something. He must have some reason to want to buy nobles.'

'Nothing can happen!' Isolde said irritably. 'You traded my mother's jewels for fools' gold. We have to pay the price.'

'But Milord is doing something else,' Ishraq said cautiously. 'He's buying false coins. He's buying fools' gold.'

'But you don't know what for? You don't know why?'

'I don't,' Ishraq said. 'But I know he's no fool. I'll keep our English nobles until he sells his.'

'When we could have gold instead?' Isolde said regretfully, gesturing to Luca's handful of gold rings.

'If you won't take this then I have to go to the Rialto and buy dross,' Luca said. 'I wish we could write to Milord to make sure it is what he wants. I cannot believe this is what he intended. I wish we knew what he plans. For this is madness: throwing good money after bad.'

~

When the gondola came back for Luca and the two young women, they were ready to go to the Rialto, with their gold and silver coins in their purses and pockets, and the rings on their fingers. The bridge was busy again – the news that the exchange rate for the gold nobles had been fixed by the Doge himself had made people confident enough to open their shops. Only the money changers were still missing, and where Israel had sat there was an obscene scrawl on his board and, in spiky thick letters, the word *Arrestato*.

Luca went at once to the mooring post at the foot of the bridge and started forwards when he saw the priest, bending over his little writing table.'Father Pietro!'

Slowly, the old priest turned to look at the young man and, at the sorrow in his lined face, Luca did not need to ask more.

'The nobles failed,' the priest said quietly. 'Bayeed is not in Trieste; he came to Venice yesterday for repairs to his ship and moored near to the Arsenale. My messenger found him there. So he knew all about the failure of the coins as soon as we did. The nobles bled when he tipped them out of the purse, and then he heard the Doge announce that the whole Ottoman Empire believes that it has been cheated. He thinks that Venice tried to cheat his empire, and that you tried to cheat him. He called me a cheat also. I am sorry, my son.'

'He is here?' Luca could hardly believe that his father was in the same city, just one mile away, in the dockyard where the galleys were built. 'Then I can go to him. I have some gold, I can promise more . . . I can explain!'

Father Pietro nodded. 'We will try again, in a month or so. When Bayeed's anger has abated.'

'But he cannot be angry with us . . . we have all been cheated!'

Father Pietro shook his head, tears filling his eyes, turning his head away from Luca.

'What is it?' asked Ishraq quietly, coming up behind Luca and sensing the older man's distress. 'What is it, Father?'

Blindly, the old man reached out to her and she took his hand on her shoulder, as if to support him 'Wait a moment,' she said to Luca, who was breathlessly impatient. 'Wait, let the Father speak.'

The old man raised his head. 'Forgive me. This has

been a blow. This has been a terrible blow. Last year the Ottoman Empire took tribute from the Christian territories that it had invaded in pure gold and the best of coins. As they always do. Sometimes they take goods, of course, always they take young boys to serve in their armies. This is how it is. This is how the Christian lands suffer for their defeat by the infidel. This is how the Christian rulers pay for peace: they have to pay tribute in gold and in children. This is our suffering, this is our Station of the Cross.' He paused.

'Last year, before tribute time, they let it be known that they would take gold or the English nobles. Then, as the English nobles went up in value, they said they would only take the coins. Everyone works to pay the tribute, the whole country has to pay the tax to give to the Ottoman overlords. This year they only wanted the gold coins. They loved the gold coins, the English nobles.'

'And what happened?' Luca asked, unable to contain himself any longer. 'When did they find out?'

'The coins bled,' the old man said simply. 'Bled like the wounds of Our Lord. Bled into the hands of the murderous infidel. And they swore that they had been cheated. They think they have been cheated by us. They think we gave them false coins on purpose, so that they would take the tribute home and spread it throughout their country, destroying trust in every village market throughout their infidel empire. They think that we planned this to ruin their markets and their traders and empty their treasury. And so they are angry – beyond anger – and they are sending back the bleeding coins and demanding gold. We will have to find gold,' he said. 'We will have to pay a third of a ducat for each false noble. God help us all. People will starve to death to get this tax together. Half of Greece will be ruined. All of the Christian lands conquered by the infidel will be crucified all over again.'

'And my father?' Luca breathed.

Father Pietro rubbed his face with his hands. 'He will remain enslaved,' he said shortly. 'Along with the half a dozen other men who expected their freedom today or tomorrow. Yours was not the only ransom we paid. Bayeed has sent back the false coins and will set sail tonight cursing us for cheats. He accuses us of double dealing, my reputation as an agent for enslaved men is destroyed. My years of service are made worthless. My name is shamed.'

He took a breath, trying to steady himself. 'We will try again, my son, we will try again. We will find our courage, and I will rebuild my reputation and we will try again. But your father will not be free this month, nor the next.'

'But I sent the money.' Luca could hardly speak. 'I sent the money in good faith.'

'And Bayeed would have released your father in good faith. But you sent counterfeit coins, my son. You sent fools' gold, and Bayeed is no fool.'

Luca turned away like a man stunned, as Brother Peter and Freize came up to the little group. 'Give me the purse,' Brother Peter said shortly. 'There is a bank here that will give me the bad nobles for Milord's gold or silver, they will take coppers – whatever we have.'

Wordlessly, Luca held out the purse.

'You are buying the counterfeit coins?' the priest asked in utter amazement. 'The bleeding nobles?'

829

Brother Peter hushed him, and nodded. 'I should not have spoken aloud. I beg you not to repeat it.'

'But why, my son?' Father Pietro said quietly, putting a hand on Brother Peter's arm as he took the purse from Luca and the girls pulled the rings off their fingers. 'Why would you buy false coins?'

'Because I am ordered to do so,' Brother Peter said shortly. 'God knows, I take no pleasure in it and it makes no sense to me.'

Father Pietro turned to Luca but the young man was silent, and stood as if he were dreaming. Ishraq and Isolde stood on either side of him, and when he did not move, took his arms and guided him, like a fever patient, back to the gondola. They helped him down the steps and waited with him in the boat until Brother Peter and Freize joined them.

'They will keep the nobles at the bank for me until we are ready to leave this accursed city,' Brother Peter said. 'We will have sacks and sacks of dross to carry.' He turned to Freize. 'You'll have to buy us another donkey to carry nothing but rust.'

Dully, Luca shook his head. Isolde and Ishraq exchanged a worried glance behind his back. Giuseppe guided the gondola into the centre of the canal. 'Home?' he asked monosyllabically.

Nobody replied until Freize said: 'Home,' and they all thought how cheerless the word seemed today.

'My father will never come home,' Luca said quietly.

'We'll try again,' Isolde assured him. 'We know where he is now, and we know how to get a message to Bayeed. We'll try again. And we know where your mother may be. We can try again, Luca. We can hope. We can save money and make them an offer. We can try again.'

He sighed wearily, as if he were tired of hoping, and then he rested his chin in his hands and stared across the water as if he wished he were somewhere else, and not in the most beautiful city in Christendom.

~

They had a quiet cheerless dinner. Brother Peter said nothing but a few words for grace over the dishes, Luca was completely silent, Freize tried a few remarks and then gave up and concentrated on eating. Isolde and Ishraq watched Luca, ate a little, and said a few words to one another. After dinner, Brother Peter rose up, gave thanks, said a quiet goodnight to them and went into his room and closed the door.

'I will go to him,' Luca said suddenly. 'Bayeed the slaver. I will go and see him.' Suddenly decisive, he rose up from the table. 'They could sail at any moment. I'll go now.'

'What for?' Ishraq asked. 'We have nothing to buy your father's freedom with.'

'I know he won't trade,' Luca said. 'But I want to try to see my father. Just to see him. To tell him that I tried and I will try again.'

'Can I come with you?' Isolde asked quietly.

'No,' Luca said shortly. 'Stay here. I have to go at once. I can't think . . .' He broke off and bent his head and kissed her hand. 'Forgive me. I can't think of you now. I have to go to my father and tell him I will find him again, wherever that monster takes him, and I will free him. If not now, then soon, as soon as I can.'

Freize cleared his throat. 'Better take Ishraq,' he said. 'For the language.' He turned to her. 'Can you wear your Arab clothing?' he asked.

She nodded and ran to change out of her gown.

'And money,' Freize said. 'To bribe the guard, there's bound to be a guard.'

Luca rounded on him. 'I have no money!' he shouted. 'Thanks to your pretty girlfriend and her father I have no money to buy my father's freedom!'

'I'll give you something,' Isolde interrupted. 'Don't blame Freize. It's not his fault. I've got something. A little gold ring.'

'I can't take your mother's jewellery.'

'You can,' she said. 'Please, Luca. I want to help.'

She ran from the room to fetch it and came back with two thin rings in her hand.

'I'll get Giuseppe,' Freize said and went downstairs leaving Luca alone with Isolde. She took his hand and pressed the rings into his palm. 'It's worth it,' she said. 'For you to see your father, to bring him some hope.'

'Thank you,' he said awkwardly. 'I am grateful. I really am.'

'Please let me come with you,' she whispered.

He shook his head, and she thought he had not really heard her, he did not even see her stretch out her hand to him as he went from the room; and then she heard him run swiftly down the stairs to the waiting gondola.

~

Giuseppe, standing tall in the stern of the gondola, worked the single oar, rowing the narrow black boat down the

Grand Canal in silence broken only by the splash of the waves. The light from the lantern in the prow bobbed and danced, reflecting in the dark water; the waning moon traced a silvery path before them. Ishraq sat with her back to the gondolier. The two young men sat facing her, Luca constantly turning to look towards their destination over the glossy darkness of the moving tide.

Even at night, even on the water, even during carnival they could see that the city had been hit by loss. There were far fewer people in costume, there were far fewer assignations. One or two determined lovers were being slowly rowed around, the door of the cabin tightly shut; but Venice was in mourning for money, quietly at home, turning over bleeding gold nobles, trying to settle up the accounts.

Luca was taut with nerves, staring ahead into the darkness as if he would see the towers of the Arsenale looming up before them. They went past the square of San Marco where the lights burning in the high windows of the Doge's Palace showed that surveillance was unsleeping. Freize nudged Luca.

'They held me in a room like a wooden box,' he said. 'And from the little window of the box I could see a rope, two ropes, hanging from the high ceiling, and a set of stairs to climb up to them.'

'Do they hang men indoors?' Luca asked without interest.

'Not by the neck. They hang them by their wrists till they give information,' Freize said. 'I was glad to be most ignorant. Nobody would waste their time hanging me, if they wanted information. You would have to hang me by my heels to shake a thought out of my head.' He had hoped to make Luca smile, but the young man only nodded briefly and carried on staring into the darkness.

There was a cold wind coming across the water and it blew ravelled strips of dark cloud across the stars. There was a waning moon which helped the gondolier to see the bank. It was a long way. Ishraq wrapped her cloak tightly around her and pulled her veil over her mouth for warmth as well as modesty.

'Here,' Giuseppe said finally. 'Here is where the galleys are moored overnight when they wait for repair.'

Luca stood up and the gondola rocked, perilously.

'Sit down,' Giuseppe said. 'What is the name of the captain?'

Ishraq turned to tell him: 'Bayeed.'

'From Istanbul?'

'Yes.'

Giuseppe pointed to a long low building. 'The galley crews sleep in there,' he said. 'The master goes into town. He will come back at dawn, perhaps.'

'In there?' Luca looked with horror at the building, the barred windows, the bolted doors.

'Sentry on the door,' Freize remarked quietly. 'Sword in his belt, probably a handgun too. What d'you want to do?'

'I just want to see him,' Luca said passionately. 'I can't be so near him and not see him!'

'Why don't we try bribing the sentry?' Ishraq suggested. 'Perhaps Signor Vero could come to the window?'

'I'll go,' Freize said.

'I'll go,' Ishraq overruled him. 'He won't draw his sword on a woman. You can watch out for me.'

Luca fumbled in his pocket and found Isolde's two rings. 'Here.'

Ishraq took them, recognised them at once. 'She gave you her mother's rings?'

'Yes, yes.' Distracted, Luca dismissed the importance of the gift. 'Go to him, Ishraq. See what you can do.'

Giuseppe brought the gondola to the quayside. Ishraq went up the steps and walked towards the sentry, careful to keep in the middle of the quay so that he could see her slow progress towards him, spreading her hands so that he could see she was carrying no weapon.

'*Masaa Elkheir*,' she called from a distance, speaking Arabic.

He put his hand to his sword. 'Keep back,' he said. 'You're a long way from home, girl.'

'You too, warrior,' she said deferentially. 'But I would have words with you. My master wants to speak with one of the galley slaves. He will pay you, if you allow such a thing, for your kindness. He is a *faranj*, a foreigner and a Christian, and it is his father who is enslaved. He longs to see the face of his father. It would be a kindness to let them speak together through the window. It would be a good deed. And you would be well rewarded.'

'How well rewarded?' the man asked. 'And I want none of the English nobles. I know they are as precious as sand. Don't try to cheat me.'

In answer she held up a golden ring. 'This to let him come to the window,' she said. 'The same again as we sail away safely.'

'He must come alone,' the man stipulated.

'Whatever you say,' Ishraq said obediently.

'You give me the ring and go back to your gondola and send him. The gondolier and everyone else to stay on board. He can have a few minutes, no more.'

'I agree,' Ishraq said. She made a gesture to show that she would throw the ring and he snapped his fingers to show that he was ready. Carefully she threw it into his catch, and then went back to the gondola.

'You have a few moments, and he has to have the other ring at the end of your talk,' she said. 'But you can go to the window. You can talk for only a few minutes.'

Luca leapt out of the gondola and was up the steps in a moment. He gave a nod to the sentry and went quickly to the window. It was set high in the wall but there was a barrel nearby. Luca rolled it under the grille, and jumped up on it. Dimly he could see a dark room, filled with sleeping men, and he could smell the stench of exhaustion and illness.

'Gwilliam Vero!' he said in a hoarse whisper. 'Gwilliam Vero, are you in there?'

'Who wants him?' came a muffled reply, and Luca recognised, with a gasp, the accent of his home village, his father's beloved voice.

'Father, it's me!' he cried. 'Father! It is me, your son Luca.'

There was a silence and then a scuffling noise, and the sound of a man curse as Gwilliam made his way, stumbling over the sleeping men, to the window. Luca, looking in and downward, could see the pale face of his father looking up from the sunken floor below.

'It's you,' Luca said breathlessly. 'Father!' He tightened his grip on the bars over the window as he felt his knees weaken beneath him at the sight of his father. 'Father! It's me! Luca! Your son!'

The old man, his skin scorched into leather by the burning sun on the slave galley deck, his face scored with deep lines of pain, peered up at the window where Luca peered in.

'I was trying to ransom you,' Luca said breathlessly. 'Bayeed refused the coins. But I will get pure gold. I will buy your freedom. I will come for you.'

'Do you know where your mother is?' His voice was husky, he rarely spoke these days. When they slaved over the oars, obedient to the beat of the pace-drum, they never spoke. In the evening when they were released to eat there was nothing to say. After the first year he had ceased to weep, after the second year he had stopped praying.

'I am looking for her,' Luca promised. 'I swear I will find her and ransom her too.'

There was a silence. Incredulously, Luca realised that he was within speaking distance of his long-lost father and he had so much to say that he could not find words.

'Are you in pain?' he asked.

'Always,' came the grim reply.

'I have missed you and my mother,' Luca said quietly.

The man choked on his sore throat and spat. 'You must think of me as dead to you,' was all he said. 'I believe I am dead and gone to hell.'

'I won't think of you as dead,' Luca exclaimed passionately. 'I will ransom you and return you to our farm. You will live again, as you used to live. We will be happy.'

'I can't think of it,' his father flatly refused. 'I would go mad if I thought of it. Go, son, leave me in hell. I cannot dream of freedom.'

'But I—'

'No,' came the stern reply.

'Father!'

'Don't call me Father,' he said chillingly. 'You have no Father. I am dead to you and you to me. I cannot think of your world and your hopes and your plans. I can only think about today and tonight, and then the next one. The only hope that I have is that I will die tonight and this will end.'

He turned to go back into the darkness of the prison, Luca saw the scars from the whip on his back. 'Father! Don't go! Of course I will call you Father, of course I will ransom you. You can hope! I will never leave you. I will never stop looking for you. I am your son!'

'You're a changeling.' Gwilliam Vero rounded on Luca. 'No son of mine. You said you would ransom me but you have not done so. You say you will come again but I cannot bear to hope. Do you understand that, Stranger? I cannot bear to hope. I don't want to think of my farm and my son and my wife. I will go mad if I think of such things and live like this – in hell. I have no son. You are a stranger. You are a changeling. You have no reason to ransom me. Go away and forget all about me. I am a dead stranger to you, and you are a changeling boy to me.'

Luca shook with emotion. 'Father?' he whispered. 'Don't speak so to me ... you know I am ...'

Gwilliam Vero stepped away from the light of the grille and all Luca could see was darkness.

'Enough!' the sentry said flatly. He gestured to Luca to get down from the barrel and go away. When Luca hesitated he put his right hand on the hilt of his long curved scimitar, and felt for the handgun strapped to his belt with the other.

Ishraq stepped off the gondola and, holding the ring high above her head, came slowly across the quay. 'Come, Luca!' she said gently.

He stumbled down from the barrel, and grabbed hold of it to support himself, as his knees buckled beneath him.

'Come on,' Ishraq beckoned to him. She saw his face was contorted with shock. 'Luca!' she said urgently. 'Pick yourself up, get back to the gondola. We have to leave.'

'He denied me!' he gasped. He levered himself to his feet, using the barrel, but she saw he could not walk.

'Be a man!' she said harshly. 'You are putting Freize and me in danger here. Now we must go. Find your feet! Walk!'

The sentry stepped closer and drew the wicked blade from the scabbard. It shone in the moonlight. Ishraq knew that he could behead Luca with one blow, and would think nothing of it.

'Get up, fool!' she said and the anger in her voice cut through Luca's grief. 'Get up and be a man.'

Slowly, Luca straightened up and hobbled, awkwardly, towards her. As soon as he was within reach she grabbed his arm and put it over her shoulders so that she could take his weight. 'Now walk,' she spat. 'Or I will stab you myself.'

'We thank you,' Ishraq called towards the sentry, her voice sweet and untroubled. She sent the gold ring spinning through the air to him. She put her arm around Luca's waist and helped him, as if he were mortally wounded, walk slowly and painfully to the gondola, step heavily on board and sit in silence as Giuseppe cast off, spun the gondola round, and headed back towards the palazzo.

~

Isolde was waiting up for them but Luca went past her without a word, into his bedroom, and closed the door. She looked to Ishraq for an explanation.

'I don't know it all,' Ishraq said quietly, scowling with worry. 'We couldn't hear what his father said, but Luca went white as if he was sick and his legs went from under him. We only just got him back to the gondola, and since then he has said nothing to either of us.'

'Did his father blame Luca for the ransom failing?'

Ishraq shook her head. 'Luca said nothing, I don't know. His father must have said something terrible; it just felled him.'

'Did you comfort him?' Isolde asked. 'Couldn't you talk to him?'

Ishraq gave her a crooked little smile. 'I was not tender to him,' she said. 'I was hard on him.'

'I'm for my bed,' Freize said. 'I was glad to get away from that quayside.' He nodded at Ishraq. 'You did well to get him walking. Perhaps he'll talk to us in the morning.' He yawned and turned to the door.

'You must be worried for him,' Isolde said, putting her hand on his arm.

Freize looked down at her. 'I am worried for us all,' he said. 'It feels as if we are all bleeding in this city, not just the false nobles. Trying to make money in speculation and not in honest work has cost us all, very dear. I don't think we even know how much.'

~

At dawn there was a sudden hammering on one of the bedroom doors. 'Get up!' they could all hear Luca shouting. 'Get up!'

Ishraq and Isolde lighted their candles from the dying embers of the fire in their room and pattered down the stairs, pulling shawls around their nightgowns. Freize was already on the shadowy stairs, his club in his hand, ready for an attack. Luca was hammering on Brother Peter's bedroom door.

'Let me see that letter! Show me that letter!'

Brother Peter unlocked the door and came out, long-legged as a stork in his nightgown. He gave one reproachful look at the young women, turned his gaze from their bare feet and said: 'What is it? What is this uproar? What's happened now?'

'The orders! The orders! The sealed orders that you opened yesterday! Let me see them.'

'You read them yourself!' Brother Peter protested. 'Why do you need to see them again?'

'Because I have to understand,' Luca said passionately. 'Always! You know what I'm like. I have to understand. And I don't understand this. I was so distressed at the loss of my father that I couldn't think. I lay down to sleep and in the darkness all I could see before my eyes was the letter from Milord: the orders. Show them to me!'

Ishraq's brown eyes were shining. 'I ask why!' she repeated to herself.

Brother Peter sighed and went back into his room. He came out pulling on his robe over his nightshirt, with the letter in his hand. He gave it to Luca and sat down at the dining table with the air of a man tried beyond endurance. The others pulled out their chairs and took their places around the table in silence, while Luca read it, and reread it. Only Ishraq looked intently from his absorbed face to the letter and back again.

'What are we to do, when we have bought up the false nobles with all the gold that Milord provided?' Luca asked, hardly glancing up from the page.

'We are to store it at the bank, and open the orders with our next destination,' Brother Peter said.

'We are not to test the nobles? To separate the bad from the good?'

Brother Peter shook his head.

'So Milord does not care if there are good nobles among the bad,' Luca muttered to himself. 'Why would that be? Can he know already?' To Brother Peter he said: 'And he told you to open the instructions to buy the counterfeit coins as soon as you learned that the Ottomans had accused the occupied countries of trying to cheat?'

'As I did,' Brother Peter said patiently. 'As I told you.'

There was a silence. 'What are you thinking, Luca?' Ishraq said quietly.

Luca looked across the table at her with a hard

intensity. 'What are you thinking?' he countered. 'For you have been suspicious of Milord from the moment that you met him. And yet you did not sell your nobles once you knew he was buying. You refused to sell your bleeding nobles to me for gold. Isolde wanted to – but you refused.'

'I don't trust him,' she confessed. 'I think he did you no favour with the ransoming of your father. First, he didn't tell you about Father Pietro at all – it was Radu Bey, an Ottoman commander and your lord's especial enemy, who did that. Then, if your lord had any reason to believe that the coins would fail he could have told you, to make sure that you paid the ransom in pure gold, or paid early. Then the coins would have failed but you would still have got your father back.'

'Yes,' Luca conceded. His mouth turned in a bitter twist for a young man. 'This I know.'

'Your lord allowed the failure of the ransom,' Ishraq accused. 'He let you try when he knew that the bad coins would be discovered.'

'Milord's doings should not be questioned!' Brother Peter said hotly. 'His calling is to command us, not to answer to us.'

'Yes, but I question everything,' Luca explained. 'Like Ishraq. And what she says is true: he did not think of me, nor of my father, when he planned that we should come here. We have suffered, all of us, and so have many others: the alchemists, Israel the money changer, the people who have been left with worthless coins, the territories who will be punished for failing to pay a tribute, the city itself. There are many who will curse the day that Milord ordered us to trace forged gold nobles. All we did was expose the forgeries and break the market.'

'Surely, all that he planned here was to find the counterfeiters,' Brother Peter reasoned. 'We were told to find them and report them to the authorities. We were told to stop them making false coins. We were here to inquire and then enforce the law. There was nothing wrong in that. There was much good. It was our failure that we did not find them and stop them quickly enough.'

In answer, Luca silently raised the letter that commanded them to buy the false coins.

'No, I don't know why he wanted us to buy,' Brother Peter admitted.

'But I have an idea,' Luca said slowly. 'What if Milord knew all along that there were counterfeit nobles being made by Drago Nacari and Jacinta? What if he knew from the very beginning that they had great chests of gold nobles from the Duke of Bedford, that they were putting onto the market, and that they also had a recipe to make more? What if he sent us here too late on purpose?'

Ishraq nodded. 'But he would have known that sooner or later you would find them. He knew that you would not stop until you found them. So he must have wanted them to be exposed, he wanted them to put the false nobles out into the market place, and only then be arrested.'

'I find them, they escape – but that is by the way – for the main thing is that they are unveiled. My task was to expose the forgery. My task was to be so blunderingly clumsy, so obvious, that all of Venice would know that there were counterfeit coins and a massive forgery had taken place.' Luca's face was white and bitter. 'He knew that I would

845

go after the scent like a stupid hound – showing everyone where I was going, a hue and cry all on my own.'

'The coins bled,' Ishraq pointed out. 'That exposed the Nacaris, not us.'

'We were going to expose them,' Freize said. 'Brother Peter insisted on it. Those were the orders. The coins bled the night before we would have reported them. We had all agreed to obey Milord's orders. They would have been exposed one way or another.'

Luca nodded. 'The bleeding coins made no real difference,' he said. 'They were the flaw in the Nacaris' work. But the Nacaris would have been unveiled by us and reported.'

'And then the price of the nobles collapses.' Ishraq was thinking aloud with Luca. 'As soon as everyone knows they are forged. As soon as the forgers are arrested.'

'And everyone wants to sell, and the Doge sets a tiny price, a price for scrap metal.'

'And everyone sells; but Milord commands us to buy,' Ishraq said. She tapped her hand on the table as she suddenly realised what she was saying. 'Because he knows that some of the nobles are good. Some of them will be old coins from England, they will be good. We tested them, we know that they are good. Perhaps all of the coins that came from the Calais mint were good. And if we buy up all of them, good and bad together, then some of them will be worth far more than the price that we pay for them.'

'And we will have made Milord a small fortune,' Luca breathed.

Brother Peter bowed his head. 'The Church,' he said. 'We will have made a small fortune for the Church. We must be glad of it. It is holy work to make a fortune for the Church. These have been dark days but perhaps we have done the right thing.'

'But the Ottomans . . .' Ishraq said slowly.

Luca switched his gaze to her. 'What about them?'

'They are sending back the bleeding nobles, and they are accepting a reduced tribute. They believe, that they were paid in worthless coins. They have been cheated of their tribute, they have been hugely cheated of the fee they draw from the conquered lands. They are settling for a reduced fee this year.'

'They should not have it, they should not collect it in the first place!' Brother Peter burst out. 'They deserve to be cheated. It is God's work to cheat them!'

Ishraq ignored him, she looked at Luca. 'And they have suffered failure too. All their banks and merchants and traders will be at a loss – like we are. Milord has struck a powerful blow at the very heart of the Ottoman Empire,' she said. 'If this is his crusade he has had a powerful victory thanks to you. They may have won Constantinople; but this year they are much the poorer.'

Luca nodded. 'Bayeed is poorer too,' he said. 'He rejected the ransom but some of the coins must have been good.' He paused. 'And my father suffers for it,' he said. 'My father suffers for this brilliant trick, and so do so many others.' He shook his head. 'So many, many others.'

Freize looked from one to another. 'So what do we do now?' he asked into the silence.

Nobody spoke and then slowly the four young people realised that there would be orders. One by one they looked towards Brother Peter. 'I know that when our work here is successfully concluded we have to ride north,' Brother Peter volunteered. 'I am to open the orders later, but we are to set out northerly.'

'And what's in the orders then?' Freize asked bitterly. 'For I don't think we can bear to succeed again like this. Luca has lost his father, Isolde has lost her fortune, and we have sickened ourselves of Venice and nearly ruined the city.'

Ishraq rose from the table and opened the shutters. A cold morning light came into the room, making the candles look tawdry. Isolde blew them out.

'We have completed our work here?' Luca looked older in the grey light from the windows. 'Another successful mission?' he asked bitterly. 'Our enemies cheated of their money, some people made bankrupt, my father still enslaved, his heart broken, and I am disowned by him. He denied me. He called me a changeling and dishonoured my mother and me. We have accomplished all that Milord wanted? We can leave? Our work is done? We should be happy?'

'Often, it is hard,' Brother Peter said quietly to the younger man. 'You are walking a solitary path in hard country. Often a victory does not feel like victory. There is a great work of which we are only a small part. We cannot tell what part we play. We have to trust that there is a great cause that we serve in our own small way.'

Luca bowed his head over his clasped hands and closed his eyes as if he were praying for courage.

'And I wonder where the alchemists have gone,' Isolde said, speaking for the first time since Luca had called them all into the room. Luca raised his head and looked at her.

'I wonder where they have been ordered to go,' Isolde said. 'For they have their patron, who gives them orders, just as we have Milord.'

There was a silence as Isolde, and then all the others, realised what she had said.

'They have a patron that they don't know,' she went on, wonderingly. 'He commanded them to come here and to make the counterfeit coins, he commanded them to make the alchemy coins. He ordered that they should find the secret of life. He sent them here, and then Milord sent us after them.'

Slowly, Luca rose to his feet and went to the windows. There was a little paler strip of cloud to the east where dawn was beginning to break.

'They said they had a patron that was no friend,' Ishraq supplemented. 'They never saw his face but he sent them orders, and gave them the recipe for the false nobles. He gave them the chests of the good nobles too. He told them to make a market for the coins and then swell it with forgeries.'

'Do you think that it was perhaps Milord who commanded them?' Luca asked, speaking almost idly, not turning back to the room but staring out of the window at the silvery canal and the black cormorants sitting on the water and then suddenly folding their wings and plunging below for fish. 'Do you think that Milord ordered both the counterfeiters and those that were to unveil them? Did he command both the hind and the hounds. Do you think he played both sides at once?'

'Perhaps to him it is a game.' Isolde came and stood beside him and put her hand on his shoulder. 'Like the cups and ball that Jacinta played. Perhaps Milord has quick hands too, nobody can see what he is doing till the end of the game. Perhaps he has cheated us all.'

~

They rode away from Venice heading north, the warm spring sun on their right-hand side. Brother Peter led the way with Luca behind him, Isolde at his side. Behind them came Freize and Ishraq, and the little donkey heavily laden followed Freize's big cob Rufino. Another donkey came behind the first, also carrying sacks of gold nobles. Some of them were rusting away inside the leather purses, but in every rusting coin there was a heart of solid gold. Milord's great gamble would pay off.

Everyone was happy to be leaving the city behind them. Brother Peter was glad to be in his robes again and not living a lie, Ishraq was revelling in the freedom of being on the road and not cooped up as a Venetian lady companion, Isolde was setting off to her godfather's son with renewed determination, and Luca was heading for his next inquiry with a sense that the world was filled with mystery – even his own mission puzzled him.

'Are you glad to leave Venice?' he asked Isolde.

'It is the most beautiful city I have ever seen,' she said. 'But it has a darker side. Do you know I saw the strangest thing as we were going in the ferry to fetch the horses?'

'What did you see?' he asked, eager to be distracted from his own sense of failure and loss.

'I thought I saw a child,' she said seriously. 'Swimming in the water, after our boat. I nearly called out for us to stop. A little child coming after us, but then I saw it was tiny, no bigger than a little fish, but swimming and keeping up with the ship.'

Luca felt himself freeze. 'What d'you think it was?' he asked, trying to sound careless. 'That's odd.'

She looked at him. 'I assumed I had seen a pale-coloured fish and made a mistake. There could be nothing in the lagoon like a tiny person?'

He contained his own shiver of superstition, and leaned towards her to put his hand over hers. 'I won't let anything hurt you,' he promised her. 'Nothing can come after us. And there couldn't be anything like that in the waters.'

Trustingly she let his hand rest on hers, slowly she smiled at him. 'I feel safe with you,' she said. 'And at least Venice taught me to stand up for myself.'

He laughed. 'Will you protect me, Isolde?'

She was radiant. 'I will,' she promised.

'And did you learn to choose the one you love?' he asked her very quietly.

'Did you?' she whispered. 'Do you even know who you chose?'

Luca gasped at her teasing, and laughed aloud, glancing back to see that no one was in earshot.

Behind them, completely deaf to their low-voiced conversation, Freize was wordlessly delighted to be reunited with his horse. Gently, he pulled Rufino's thick mane, and patted his neck, and sometimes leaned forwards to stroke his ears. 'You would not believe it,' he remarked to the horse. 'No roads! No fields! No forage nor meadows, not even a grass verge for you to have a quiet graze. "What sort of a city do you call this?" I asked them.

They could not answer me. For sure, a city that has no room for horses cannot thrive. You must have missed me. Indeed, I missed you.'

The donkey behind him was dawdling. Freize turned in the saddle and gave it a little admonitory whistle.

'The dross of the coins is rusting away,' Ishraq observed, riding alongside him. 'It is dripping from the bags as we go. At this rate we will be left with saddlebags of gold.'

Freize was distracted from his conversation with Rufino. 'He's a clever man, that Milord,' he said. 'What an engine to set in motion! Devious.'

'He's made himself a fortune, but I think his main aim was to cheat the Ottomans,' Ishraq observed. 'And in this round of the battle between him and Radu Bey, I think he has won.'

'Because they were forced to accept only a third of the tribute?'

'Yes,' she said slowly. 'But best of all for him would be – don't you think? – that he made fools of them. He tricked them into sending back good gold. He made them think it was all bad. He tricked us, he tricked Venice, but really he tricked them. That is what will infuriate them worse than the reduced tribute. He destroyed the reputation of the coins and then we bought them up. He made fools of them. It really is fools' gold.'

Freize shook his head at the mendacity of the man. 'He is a cunning man,' he said. 'Deep. But I know that I'd like to ask him one thing,' he said.

'Only one thing? I'd like to ask him lots of things,' she agreed. 'What would you ask?'

'About this world,' Freize said thoughtfully. 'A man like

him with so much knowledge? I'd ask him whether he truly thinks that it might be round, as the pretty girl said.'

She nodded, without a glimmer of a smile, as thoughtful as he was. 'Freize, you do know that the sun stays in the same place all the time, night and day, and the world goes round it, don't you?' she asked.

'What?' he exclaimed so loudly that Rufino threw up his head in alarm, and Freize soothed him with a touch. He looked at her more closely and saw her smile. 'Ah, you are joking,' Freize decided. 'But you don't fool me.' He pointed to the comforting sun, slowly rising up in the sky towards the midday height, and shining down on him, as it had always done. 'East to west, every day of my life,' he said. 'Never failed. Course it goes round me.'

Ahead of them, Brother Peter started to sing a psalm, and the other four joined in, their voices blending in a harmony in the cool air as tuneful as a choir. Freize put his hand in his pocket, seeking his little whistle to play a descant, and suddenly checked.

'I had forgotten! I had quite forgotten!' he exclaimed.

'What?' Ishraq asked, glancing over to him.

In answer he drew a coin from his pocket. 'My lucky penny,' he said. 'The lass, Jacinta, the gambling girl, put it back in my pocket the last time I saw her, and wished me luck with it. I had quite forgotten it. But here it is again. I shall be lucky, don't you think? After all that has passed, to have it returned to me as a gift from her must make it more lucky than ever.'

'Why did she have it?' Ishraq asked. 'Did you give it to her?'

'She took it from me and then returned it as a keepsake,' Freize said. 'Gave me a kiss for it.' Without looking at it closely he passed it over to her. Ishraq took it, and then pulled her horse to a standstill. 'I should think you are very lucky,' she said oddly. 'Very lucky indeed. Look at it.'

Isolde glanced back and, seeing that they had stopped, called to Brother Peter and halted her own horse. The older man rode back and they all gathered round as Freize took his lucky penny from Ishraq and examined it.

'You know, it does look very like gold,' he said quietly. 'But it is the one I gave to her, I swear it. I would know it anywhere. It is my own lucky penny. I recognise the mint and the date, it is mine without a doubt. Just as I gave it to her. But now it looks like gold.'

'Enamelled with gold,' Brother Peter said. 'She put a skin of gold on it for you. Another pretty trick.'

Without a word, Freize handed it to Luca, who took a knife from his belt and made the tiniest of nicks in the side of it. 'No,' he said. 'The same colour all the way through. We can test it properly when we get to an inn; but it looks like gold. It looks like solid gold.'

There was a silence as they each absorbed what this meant.

'You are certain it is your lucky penny and not another gold coin that she gave you?' Isolde asked.

Mutely, Freize passed it to her. 'The penny. My lucky penny. Minted in the Vatican in the year of my birth. She would not have such another. She could not have such another. It must be mine. But now it is as heavy as gold, and soft as gold and golden as gold.'

'Did they do it then?' Ishraq wondered. 'They really did

854

it? They found the philosophers' stone that can change everything to gold, and they turned Freize's penny to gold?' She nodded to Luca. 'D'you remember that they said that they had one more step to take and they would be able to refine any matter to gold? Perhaps they did it, on this one coin, and we were in the room where they did it. They made true gold from dross. They really did.'

'And the Venetians drove them away,' Isolde said. 'Sent them into exile with the secret of how to make gold in their pocket.'

'We gave them the boat!' Freize exclaimed, his voice cracking on a laugh. 'We helped them to run away with the secret of a fortune, the secret that alchemists have never yet found.'

'And not just that. They had the secret of life itself,' Ishraq reminded her. 'The philosophers' stone which makes gold, leads to the philosophers' elixir, the elixir of life that cures death itself.'

'And we lost them,' Luca said, staring at the coin in his friend's hand. 'We were standing by the forge where they had made the secret of life itself, and we let them go, and then we ran away. We have been fools indeed. We have been the greatest fools of all.'

Freize tossed the coin high in the air and they watched it turn and glint in the bright sunshine and fall heavily, as a solid gold coin will fall. He caught it with a slap of his hand, shook his head in wonderment, and put the coin back in his pocket. 'Fools' gold,' he said. 'Fools indeed.'

Ishraq smiled at him. 'Do you still think you're lucky?' she asked. 'Is it still a lucky penny? Since a woman with the secret of eternal life and the secret of how to make gold gave it to you and then she went away forever? With her secrets safely with her?'

'Said I had a true heart, and then turned into my grandmother,' Freize reminded her. 'Gave a little monster into my keeping which frightened me to death. Strangest girl I have ever kissed. But am I lucky? I would say so.'

Luca clapped him on the shoulder with sudden brotherly affection. 'Still lucky,' he said. 'Always lucky. Not hanged for alchemy, not drowned in the flood. The sun going round him, his feet on a flat earth. A golden penny in his pocket. Freize is born lucky. Always lucky!'

'Born to be hanged,' Brother Peter said; but he smiled at Freize. 'No fool.'

Philippa Gregory was an established historian and writer when she discovered her interest in the Tudor period and wrote the internationally bestselling novel *The Other Boleyn Girl.*

Her *Cousins' War* novels, reaching their dramatic conclusion with *The King's Curse*, were the basis of the highly successful BBC series, *The White Queen*.

Philippa's other great interest is the charity that she founded over twenty years ago: Gardens for the Gambia. She has raised funds and paid for over 200 wells in the primary schools of this poor African country.

Philippa is a former student of Sussex University and a PhD and Alumna of the Year 2009 of Edinburgh University. Her love for history and commitment to historical accuracy are the hallmarks of her writing.

Philippa lives with her family on a small farm in Yorkshire and welcomes visitors to her site www.PhilippaGregory.com